timelike
diplomacy

timelike diplomacy

SINGULARITY SKY
IRON SUNRISE

charles stross

SCIENCE
FICTION

SINGULARITY SKY   Copyright © 2003 by Charles Stross
    Publication History: Ace hardcover, August 2003
                            Ace paperback, July 2004
IRON SUNRISE   Copyright © 2004 by Charles Stross
    Publication History: Ace hardcover, July 2004

First SFBC Science Fiction Printing: July 2004

Published by arrangement with:
The Berkley Publishing Group
a division of Penguin Putnam Inc.
375 Hudson Street
New York, NY 10014

Visit The SFBC online at *http://www.sfbc.com*

ISBN# 0-7394-4564-2

Printed in the United States of America.

contents

singularity sky

contents

the day war was declared, a rain of telephones fell clattering to the cobblestones from the skies above Novy Petrograd. Some of them had half melted in the heat of re-entry; others pinged and ticked, cooling rapidly in the postdawn chill. An inquisitive pigeon hopped close, head cocked to one side; it pecked at the shiny case of one such device, then fluttered away in alarm when it beeped. A tinny voice spoke: "Hello? Will you entertain us?"

The Festival had come to Rochard's World.

A skinny street urchin was one of the first victims of the assault on the economic integrity of the New Republic's youngest colony world. Rudi—nobody knew his patronymic, or indeed his father—spotted one of the phones lying in the gutter of a filthy alleyway as he went about his daily work, a malodorous sack wrapped around his skinny shoulders like a soldier's bedroll. The telephone lay on the chipped stones, gleaming like polished gunmetal: he glanced around furtively before picking it up, in case the gentleman who must have dropped it was still nearby. When it chirped he nearly dropped it out of fear: *a machine!* Machines were upper-class and forbidden, guarded by the grim faces and gray uniforms of authority. Nevertheless, if he brought it home to Uncle Schmuel, there might be good eating: better than he could buy with the proceeds of the day's sackful of dog turds for the tannery. He turned it over in his hands, wondering how to shut it up, and a tinny voice spoke: "Hello? Will you entertain us?"

Rudi nearly dropped the phone and ran, but curiosity held him back for a moment: "Why?"

"Entertain us and we will give you anything you want."

Rudi's eyes widened. The metal wafer gleamed with promise between his cupped hands. He remembered the fairy stories his eldest sister used to tell before the coughing sickness took her, tales of magic lamps and magicians and djinn that he was sure Father Borozovski would condemn as infidel nonsense; and his need for escape from the dull brutality of everyday life did battle with his natural pessimism—the pessimism of barely more than a decade of backbreaking labor. Realism won. What he said was not, *I want a magic flying carpet and a purse full of gold roubles* or *I want to be Prince Mikhail in his royal palace,* but, "Can you feed my family?"

"Yes. Entertain us, and we will feed your family."

Rudi racked his brains, having no idea how to go about this exotic task; then he blinked. It was obvious! He held the phone to his mouth, and whispered, "Do you want me to tell you a story?"

By the end of that day, when the manna had begun to fall from orbit and men's dreams were coming to life like strange vines blooming after rain in the desert, Rudi and his family—sick mother, drunken uncle, and seven siblings—were no longer part of the political economy of the New Republic.

War had been declared.

deep in the outer reaches of the star system, the Festival's constructor fleet created structure out of dead mass. The Festival fleet traveled light, packed down into migratory starwisps that disdained the scurrying FTL of merely human clades. When it arrived, fusion pods burned bright as insectile A-life spawned furiously in the frigid depths of the outer system. Once the habitats were complete and moved into orbit around the destination planet, the Festival travelers would emerge from aestivation, ready to trade and listen.

Rochard's World was a backwater colony of the New Republic, itself not exactly the most forward-looking of post-Diaspora human civilizations. With a limited industrial base to attract trade—limited by statute, as well as by ability—few eyes scanned the heavens for the telltale signatures of visiting ships. Only the spaceport, balanced in ground-synchronous orbit, kept a watch, and that was focused on the inner-system ecliptic. The Festival fleet had dismantled a gas giant moon and three comets, begun work on a second moon, and was preparing to rain telephones from orbit before the Imperial Traffic Control Bureau noticed that anything was amiss.

Moreover, there was considerable confusion at first. The New Republic was, if not part of the core worlds, not far out of it; whereas the Festival's origin lay far outside the light cone of the New Republic's origin, more than a thousand light-years from old anarchist Earth. Although they shared a common ancestry, the New Republic and the Festival had diverged for so many centuries that everything—from their communications protocols to their political economies, by way of their genome—was different. So it was that the Festival orbiters noticed (and ignored) the slow, monochromatic witterings of Imperial Traffic Control. More inexplicably, it did not occur to anybody in the Ducal palace to actually pick up one of the half-melted telephones littering their countryside, and ask, "Who are you and what do you want?" But perhaps this was not so surprising; because by midafternoon Novy Petrograd was in a state of barely controlled civil insurrection.

burya rubenstein, the radical journalist, democratic agitator, and sometime political prisoner (living in internal exile on the outskirts of the city, forbidden to return to the father planet— to say nothing of his mistress and sons—for at least another decade) prodded at the silvery artifact on his desk with a finger stained black from the leaky barrel of his pen. "You say these have been falling everywhere?" he stated, ominously quietly.

Marcus Wolff nodded. "All over town. Misha wired me from the back country to say it's happening there, too. The Duke's men are out in force with brooms and sacks, picking them up, but there are too many for them. Other things, too."

"Other things." It wasn't phrased as a question, but Burya's raised eyebrow made his meaning clear.

"Things falling from the skies—and not the usual rain of frogs!" Oleg Timoshevski bounced up and down excitedly, nearly upsetting one of the typecases that sat on the kitchen table beside him, part of the unlicensed printing press that Rubenstein has established on peril of another decade's internal exile. "The things—like a telephone, I think, at least they talk back when you ask them something—all say the same thing; entertain us, educate us, we will give you anything you want in return! And they do! I saw a bicycle fall from the skies with my own eyes! And all because Georgi Pavlovich said he wanted one, and told the machine the story of Roland while he waited."

"I find this hard to believe. Perhaps we should put it to the test?" Burya grinned wolfishly, in a way that reminded Marcus of the old days, when Burya had a fire in his belly, a revolver in his hand, and the ear of ten thousand workers of the Railyard Engineering Union during the abortive October Uprising twelve years earlier. "Certainly if our mysterious benefactors are happy to trade bicycles for old stories, I wonder what they might be willing to exchange for a general theory of postindustrial political economy?"

"Better dine with the devil with a long, long spoon," warned Marcus.

"Oh, never fear; all I want to do is ask some questions." Rubenstein picked up the telephone and turned it over in his hands, curiously. "Where's the—ah. Here. Machine. Can you hear me?"

"Yes." The voice was faint, oddly accentless, and slightly musical.

"Good. Who are you, where are you from, and what do you want?"

"We are Festival." The three dissidents leaned closer, almost bumping heads over the telephone. "We have traveled many two-hundred-and-fifty-sixes of light-years, visiting many sixteens of inhabited planets. We are seekers of information. We trade."

"You trade?" Burya glanced up, a trifle disappointed; interstellar capitalist entrepreneurs were not what he had been hoping for.

"We give you anything. You give us something. Anything we don't already know: art, mathematics, comedy, literature, biography, religion, genes, designs. What do you want to give us?"

"When you say you give us anything, what do you mean? Immortal youth? Freedom?" A faint note of sarcasm hovered on his words, but Festival showed no sign of noticing.

"Abstracts are difficult. Information exchange difficult, too— low bandwidth here, no access. But we can make any structures you want, drop them from orbit. You want new house? Horseless carriage that flies and swims as well? Clothing? We make."

Timoshevski gaped. "You have a *Cornucopia* machine?" he demanded breathlessly. Burya bit his tongue; an interruption it might be, but a perfectly understandable one.

"Yes."

"Will you give us one? Along with instructions for using it and a colony design library?" asked Burya, his pulse pounding.

"Maybe. What will you give us?"

"Mmm. How about a post-Marxist theory of post-technological political economy, and a proof that the dictatorship of the hereditary peerage can only be maintained by the systematic oppression and exploitation of the workers and engineers, and cannot survive once the people acquire the self-replicating means of production?"

There was a pause, and Timoshevski exhaled furiously. Just as he was about to speak, the telephone made an odd bell-like noise: "That will be sufficient. You will deliver the theory to this node. Arrangements to clone a replicator and library are now under way. Query: ability to deliver postulated proof of validity of theory?"

Burya grinned. "Does your replicator contain schemata for replicating itself? And does it contain schemata for producing direct fusion weapons, military aircraft, and guns?"

"Yes and yes to all subqueries. Query: ability to deliver postulated proof of validity of theory?"

Timoshevski was punching the air and bouncing around the office. Even the normally phlegmatic Wolff was grinning like a maniac. "Just give the workers the means of production, and we'll prove the theory," said Rubenstein. "We need to talk in private. Back in an hour, with the texts you requested." He pressed the OFF switch on the telephone. "*Yes!*"

After a minute, Timoshevski calmed down a bit. Rubenstein waited indulgently; truth be told, he felt the same way himself. But it was his duty as leader of the movement—or at least the nearest thing they had to a statesman, serving his involuntary internal exile out on this flea-pit of a backwater—to think ahead. And a lot of thinking needed to be done, because shortly heads would be brought into contact with paving stones in large numbers: the Festival, whoever and whatever it was, seemed unaware that they had offered to trade for a parcel of paper the key to the jail in which tens of millions of serfs had been confined for centuries by their aristocratic owners. All in the name of stability and tradition.

"Friends," he said, voice shaking with emotion, "let us hope that this is not just a cruel hoax. For if it is not, we can at last lay to rest the cruel specter that has haunted the New Republic since its inception. I'd been hoping for assistance along these lines from a—source, but this is far better if it is true. Marcus, fetch as many members of the committee as you can find. Oleg, I'm going to draft a poster; we need to run off five thousand copies immediately and get them distributed tonight before Politovsky thinks to pull his finger out and declare a state of emergency. Today, Rochard's World stands on the brink of liberation. Tomorrow, the New Republic!"

the next morning, at dawn, troops from the Ducal palace guard and the garrison on Skull Hill, overlooking the old town, hanged six peasants and technicians in the market square. The execution was a warning, to accompany the Ducal decree: *Treat with the Festival and you die.* Someone, probably in the Curator's Office, had realized the lethal danger the Festival posed to the regime and decided an example must be made.

They were too late to stop the Democratic Revolutionary Party from plastering posters explaining just what the telephones were all over town, and pointing out that, in the words of the old proverb, "Give a man a fish, feed him for a day—teach him to fish, feed him for life." More radical posters exhorting the workers to demand the means of constructing self-replicating tools rang a powerful chord in the collective psyche, for whatever the regime might have wished, folk memories lived on.

At lunchtime, four bank robbers held up the main post office in Plotsk, eighty kilometers to the north of the capital. The bank robbers carried exotic weapons, and when a police Zeppelin arrived over the scene it was shot to pieces. This was not an isolated incident. All over the planet, the police and state security *apparat* reported incidents of outrageous defiance, in many cases backed up with advanced weapons that had appeared as if from thin air. Meanwhile, strange, dome-like dwellings mushroomed on a thousand peasant farms in the outback, as palatially equipped and comfortable as any Ducal residence.

Pinpricks of light blossomed overhead, and radios gave forth nothing but hissing static for hours afterward. Sometime later, the glowing trails of emergency re-entry capsules skidded across the sky a thousand kilometers south of Novy Petrograd. The Navy announced that evening, with deep regrets, the loss of the destroyer *Sakhalin* in a heroic attack on the enemy battle fleet besieging the colony. It had inflicted serious damage on the aggressors; nevertheless, reinforcements had been requested from the Imperial capital via Causal Channel, and the matter was being treated with the utmost gravity by His Imperial Majesty.

Spontaneous demonstrations by workers and soldiers marred the night, while armored cars were deployed to secure the bridges across the Hava River that separated the Ducal palace and the garrison from the city proper.

And most sinister of all, an impromptu fair began to grow in the open space of the Northern Parade Field—a fair where nobody worked, everything was free, and anything that anybody could possibly want (and a few things that nobody in their right mind would desire) could be obtained free for the asking.

on the third day of the incursion, His Excellency Duke Felix Politovsky, Governor of Rochard's World, entered the Star Chamber to meet with his staff and, by way of an eye-wateringly expensive teleconference, to appeal for help from his Emperor.

Politovsky was a thick-set, white-haired man of some sixty-four years, unpreserved by contraband anti-aging medical treatments. It was said by some that he was lacking in imagination, and he had certainly not been appointed governor of a raw backwater dumping ground for troublemakers and second sons because of his overwhelming political acumen. However, despite his bull-headed disposition and lack of insight, Felix Politovsky was deeply worried.

Men in uniform and the formal dress of his diplomatic staff stood to attention as he entered the richly paneled room and marched to the head of the conference table. "Gentlemen. Please be seated," he grunted, dropping into the armchair that two servants unobtrusively held out for him. "Beck, have there been any developments overnight?"

Gerhard Von Beck, Citizen, head of the local office of the Curator's Office, shook his head gloomily. "More riots on the south bank; they didn't stay to fight when I sent a guard detachment. So far, morale in the barracks seems to be holding up. Molinsk is cut off; there have been no reports from that town for the past day, and a helicopter that was sent to look in on them never reported back. The DR's are raising seven shades of merry hell around town, and so are the Radicals. I tried to have the usual suspects taken into custody, but they've declared an Extropian Soviet and refuse to cooperate. The worst elements are holed up in the Corn Exchange, two miles south of here, holding continuous committee meetings, and issuing proclamations and revolutionary communiqué on the hour, every hour. Encouraging people to traffic with the enemy."

"Why haven't you used troops?" rumbled Politovsky.

"They say they've got atomic weapons. If we move in—" He shrugged.

"Oh." The Governor rubbed his walrus moustache lugubriously and sighed. "Commander Janaczeck. What news of the Navy?"

Janaczeck stood. A tall, worried-looking man in a naval officer's dress uniform, he looked even more nervous than the otherwise controlled Von Beck. "There were two survival capsules from the wreck of the *Sakhalin;* both have now been recovered, and the survivors debriefed. It would appear that the *Sakhalin* approached one of the larger enemy intruders and demanded that they withdraw from low orbit immediately and yield to customs inspection. The intruder made no response, so *Sakhalin* fired across her path. What happened next is confused—none of the survivors were bridge officers, and their reports are contradictory—but it appears that there was an impact with some sort of foreign body, which then ate the destroyer."

"*Ate* it?"

"Yes, sir." Janaczeck gulped. "Forbidden technology."

Politovsky turned pale. "Borman?"

"Yes, sir?" His adjutant sat up attentively.

"Obviously, this situation exceeds our ability to deal with it without extra resources. How much acausal bandwidth does the Post Office have in hand for a televisor conference with the capital?"

"Um, ah, fifty minutes' worth, sir. The next consignment of entangled qubits between here and New Prague is due to arrive by ramscoop in, ah, eighteen months. If I may make so bold, sir—"

"Speak."

"Could we retain a minute of bandwidth in stock, for text-only messages? I realize that this is an emergency, but if we drain the current channel we will be out of touch with the capital until the next shipment is available. And, with all due respect to Commander Janaczeck, I'm not sure the Navy will be able to reliably run dispatch boats past the enemy."

"Do it." Politovsky sat up, stretching his shoulders. "One minute, mind. The rest available for a televisor conference with

His Majesty, at his earliest convenience. You will set up the conference and notify me when it is ready. Oh, and while you're about it, here." He leaned forward and scribbled a hasty signature on a letter from his portfolio. "I enact this state of emergency and by the authority vested in me by God and His Imperial Majesty I decree that this constitutes a state of war with—who the devil *are* we at war with?"

Von Beck cleared his throat. "They seem to call themselves the Festival, sir. Unfortunately, we don't appear to have any more information about them on file, and requests to the Curator's Archives drew a blank."

"Very well." Borman passed Politovsky a note, and the Governor stood. "Gentlemen, please stand for His Imperial Majesty!"

They stood and, as one man, turned expectantly to face the screen on the far wall of the conference room.

"May I ask what I'm charged with?" asked Martin.

The sunshine filtering through the skylight high overhead skewered the stuffy office air with bars of silver: Martin watched dust motes dance like stars behind the Citizen's bullet-shaped head. The only noises in the room were the scratching of his pen on heavy official vellum and the repetitive grinding of gears as his assistant rewound the clockwork drive mechanism on his desktop analytical engine. The room smelled of machine oil and stale fear.

"*Am* I being charged with anything?" Martin persisted.

The Citizen ignored him and bent his head back to his forms. His young assistant, his regular chore complete, began unloading a paper tape from the engine.

Martin stood up. "If I am not being charged with anything, is there any reason why I should stay?"

This time the Citizen Curator glared at him. "Sit," he snapped.

Martin sat.

Outside the skylight, it was a clear, cold April afternoon; the clocks of St Michael had just finished striking fourteen hundred, and in the Square of the Five Corners, the famous Duchess's Simulacrum was jerking through its eternal pantomime. The boredom grated on Martin. He found it difficult to adapt to the pace of events in the New Republic; it was doubly infuriating when he was faced with the eternal bureaucracy. He'd been here for four months now, four stinking months on a job which should have taken ten days. He was beginning to wonder if he would live to see Earth again before he died of old age.

In fact, he was so bored with waiting for his work clearance to materialize that this morning's summons to an office somewhere behind the iron facade of the Basilisk came as a relief, something to break the monotony. It didn't fill him with the stuttering panic that such an appointment would have kindled in the heart of a subject of the New Republic—what, after all, could the Curator's Office do to him, an off-world engineering contractor with a cast-iron Admiralty contract? The summons had come on a plate borne by a uniformed courier, and not as a night-time raid. That fact alone suggested a degree of restraint and, consequently, an approach to adopt, and Martin resolved to play the bemused alien visitor card as hard as he could.

After another minute, the Citizen lowered his pen and looked at Martin. "Please state your name," he said softly.

Martin crossed his arms. "If you don't know it already, why am I here?" he asked.

"Please state your name for the record." The Citizen's voice was low, clipped, and as controlled as a machine. He spoke the local trade-lingua—a derivative of the nearly universal old English tongue—with a somewhat heavy, Germanic accent.

"Martin Springfield."

The Citizen made a note. "Now please state your nationality."

"My what?"

Martin must have looked nonplussed, for the Citizen raised a gray-flecked eyebrow. "Please state your nationality. To what government do you owe allegiance?"

"Government?" Martin rolled his eyes. "I come from *Earth.* For legislation and insurance, I use Pinkertons, with a backup strategic infringement policy from the New Model Air Force. As far as employment goes, I am incorporated under charter as a personal corporation with bilateral contractual obligations to various organizations, including your own Admiralty. For reasons of nostalgia, I am a registered citizen of the People's Republic of West Yorkshire, although I haven't been back there for twenty years. But I wouldn't say I was answerable to any of those, except my contractual partners—and they're equally answerable to me."

"But you are from Earth?" asked the Citizen, his pen poised. "Yes."

"Ah. Then you are a subject of the United Nations." He made a brief note. "Why didn't you admit this?"

"Because it isn't true," said Martin, letting a note of frustration creep into his voice. (But only a note: he had an idea of the Citizen's powers, and had no intention of provoking him to exercise them.)

"Earth. The supreme political entity on that planet is the United Nations Organization. So it follows that you are a subject of it, no?"

"Not at all." Martin leaned forward. "At last count, there were more than fifteen thousand governmental organizations on Earth. Of those, only about the top nine hundred have representatives in Geneva, and only seventy have permanent seats on the Security Council. The UN has no authority over any non-governmental organization or over individual citizens, it's purely an arbitration body. I am a sovereign individual; I'm not owned by any government."

"Ah," said the Citizen. He laid his pen down very carefully beside his blotter and looked directly at Martin. "I see you fail to understand. I am going to do you a great favor and pretend that I did not hear the last thing you said. Vassily?"

His young assistant looked up. "Yah?"

"*Out.*"

The assistant—little more than a boy in uniform—stood and marched over to the door. It thudded shut solidly behind him.

"I will say this once, and once only." The Citizen paused, and Martin realized with a shock that his outward impassivity was a tightly sealed lid holding down a roiling fury: "I do not care what silly ideas the stay-behinds of Earth maintain about their sovereignty. I do not care about being insulted by a young and insolent pup like you. But while you are on this planet you *will* live by our definitions of what is right and proper! Do I make myself clear?"

Martin recoiled. The Citizen waited to see if he would speak, but when he remained silent, continued icily. "You are here in the New Republic at the invitation of the Government of His Majesty, and will at all times comport yourself accordingly. This includes being respectful to Their Imperial Highnesses, behaving decently, legally, and honestly, paying taxes to the Imperial Treasury, and not spreading subversion. You are here to do a job, not to spread hostile alien propaganda or to denigrate our way of life! Am I making myself understood?"

"I don't—" Martin paused, hunted for the correct, diplomatic words. "Let me rephrase, please. I am sorry if I have caused offense, but if that's what I've done, would you mind telling me what I did? So I can avoid doing it again. If you won't tell me what not to do, how can I avoid causing offense by accident?"

"You are unaware?" asked the Citizen. He stood up and paced around Martin, behind his chair, around the desk, and back to his own seat. There he stopped pacing, and glowered furiously. "Two nights ago, in the bar of the Glorious Crown Hotel, you were clearly heard telling someone—a Vaclav Hasek, I believe—about the political system on your home planet. Propaganda and nonsense, but *attractive* propaganda and nonsense to a certain disaffected segment of the lumpenproletariat. Nonsense verging on sedition, I might add, when you dropped several comments about—let me see—'the concept of tax is no different from extortion,' and 'a social contract enforced by compulsion is not a valid contract.' After your fourth beer, you became somewhat merry and began to declaim on the nature of social justice, which is itself something of a problem, insofar as you expressed doubt about the impartiality of a judiciary appointed by His Majesty in trying cases against the Crown."

"That's rubbish! Just a conversation over a pint of beer!"

"If you were a citizen, it would be enough to send you on a one-way trip to one of His Majesty's frontier colonies for the next twenty years," the Citizen said icily. "The only reason we are having this little *tête-à-tête* is because your presence in the Royal Dockyards is considered essential. If you indulge in any more such conversations over pints of beer, perhaps the Admiralty may be persuaded to wash their hands of you. And then where will you be?"

Martin shivered; he hadn't expected the Citizen to be quite so blunt. "Are conversations about politics really that sensitive?" he asked.

"When held in a public place, and engaged in by an offworlder with strange ideas, *yes*. The New Republic is not like the degenerate anarchist mess your fatherworld has sunk into. Let me emphasize that. Because you are a necessary alien, you are granted certain rights by Their Imperial Highnesses. If you go outside those rights, you will be stamped on, and stamped on hard. If you find that difficult to understand, I suggest you spend the remainder of your free time inside your hotel room so that your mouth does not incriminate you accidentally. I ask you for a third time: Do I make myself understood?"

Martin looked chastened. "Y-yes," he said.

"Then get out of my office."

evening.

A man of medium height and unremarkable build, with

brownish hair and a close-cropped beard, lay fully clad on the ornate counterpane of a hotel bed, a padded eyeshade covering his face. Shadows crept across the gloomy carpet as the sun sank below the horizon. The gas jets in the chandelier hissed, casting deep shadows across the room. A fly buzzed around the upper reaches of the room, pursuing a knife-edged search pattern.

Martin was not asleep. His entire inventory of countersurveillance drones were out on patrol, searching his room for bugs in case the Curator's Office was monitoring him. Not that he had many drones to search with: they were strictly illegal in the New Republic, and he'd been forced to smuggle his kit through customs in blocked sebaceous glands and dental caries. Now they were out in force, hunting for listening devices and reporting back to the monitors woven into his eyeshade.

Finally, concluding he was alone in the room, he recalled the fly—its SQUID-sensors untriggered—and put the fleas back into hibernation. He stood up and shuttered the window, then pulled the curtains closed. Short of the Curator's Office having hidden a mechanical drum-recorder in the back of the wardrobe, he was unable to see any way that they could listen in on him.

He reached into the breast pocket of his jacket (rumpled, now, from being lain upon) and pulled out a slim, leather-bound book. "Talk to me."

"Hello, Martin. Startup completed, confidence one hundred percent."

"That's good." He cleared his throat. "Back channel. Execute. I'd like to talk to Herman."

"Paging."

The book fell silent and Martin waited impassively. It looked like a personal assistant, a discreet digital secretary for a modern Terran business consultant. While such devices could be built into any ambient piece of furniture—clothing, even a prosthetic tooth—Martin kept his in the shape of an old-fashioned hardback. However, normal personal assists didn't come with a causal channel plug-in, especially one with a ninety-light-year reach and five petabits of bandwidth. Even though almost two petabits had been used when the agent-in-place passed it to him via a dead letter drop on a park bench, it was outrageously valuable to Martin. In fact, it was worth his life—if the secret police caught him with it.

A slower-than-light freighter had spent nearly a hundred years hauling the quantum black box at the core of the causal channel out from Septagon system; a twin to it had spent eighty years in the hold of a sister ship, *en route* to Earth. Now they provided an instantaneous communications channel from one planet to the other; instantaneous in terms of special relativity, but not capable of violating causality, and with a total capacity limited to the number of qubits they had been created with. Once those 5 billion megabits were gone, they'd be gone for good—or until the next slower-than-light freighter arrived.

(Not that such ships were rare—building and launching a one-kilogram starwisp, capable of carrying a whopping great hundred-gram payload across a dozen light-years, wasn't far above the level of a cottage industry—but the powers that ran things here in the New Republic were notoriously touchy about contact with the ideologically impure outside universe.)

"Hello?" said the PA.

"PA: Is that Herman?" asked Martin.

"PA here. Herman is on the line and all authentication tokens are updated."

"I had an interview with a Citizen from the Curator's Office today," said Martin. "They're extremely sensitive about subversion." Twenty-two words in five seconds: sampled at high fidelity, about half a million bits. Transcribed to text, that would make about one hundred bytes, maybe as few as fifty bytes after non-lossy compression. Which left fifty fewer bytes in the link between Martin's PA and Earth. If Martin went to the Post Office, they would charge him a dollar a word, he'd have to queue for a day, and there would be a postal inspector listening in.

"What happened?" asked Herman.

"Nothing important, but I was warned off, and warned hard. I'll put it in my report. They didn't question my affiliation."

"Any query over your work?"

"No. No suspicion, as far as I can tell."

"Why did they question you?"

"Spies in bars. They want the frighteners on me. I haven't been on board the *Lord Vanek* yet. Dockyard access control is very tight. I think they're upset about something."

"Any confirmation of unusual events? Fleet movements? Workup toward departure?"

"Nothing I know about." Martin bit back his further comment: talking to Herman via the illegal transmitter always made him nervous. "I'm keeping my eyes on the ball. Report ends."

"Bye."

"PA: shut down link now."

"The link is down." Throughout the entire conversation, Martin noted, the only voice he had heard was his; the PA spoke in its owner's tones, the better to be a perfect receptionist, and the CC link was so expensive that sending an audio stream over it would be a foolish extravagance. Talking to himself across a gulf of seventy light-years made Martin feel very lonely. Especially given the very real nature of his fears.

So far, he'd successfully played the gormless foreign engineering contractor with a runaway mouth, held overlong on a two-week assignment to upgrade the engines on board His Majesty's battlecruiser *Lord Vanek*. In fact, he was doing such a good job that he'd gotten to see the inside of the Basilisk, and escaped alive.

But he wasn't likely to do so twice, if they learned who he was working for.

"do you think he is a spy?" asked trainee procurator Vassily Muller.

"Not as far as I know." The Citizen smiled thinly at his assistant, the thin scar above his left eye wrinkling with satanic amusement. "If I had any evidence that he was a spy, he would rapidly become an ex-spy. And an ex–everything else, for that matter. But that is not what I asked you, is it?" He fixed his subordinate with a particular expression he had perfected for dealing with slow students. "Tell me why I let him go."

"Because..." The trainee officer looked nonplussed. He'd been here six months, less than a year out of gymnasium and the custody of the professors, and it showed. He was still a teenager, fair-haired, blue-eyed, and almost painfully unskilled in the social nuances: like so many intelligent men who survived the elite boarding school system, he was also inclined to intellectual rigidity. Privately, the Citizen thought this was a bad thing, at least in a secret policeman—rigidity was a habit that would have to be broken if he was ever to be of much use. On the other hand, he seemed to have inherited his father's intelligence. If he'd inherited his flexibility, too, without the unfortunate rebelliousness, he'd make an excellent operative.

After a minute's silence, the Citizen prodded him. "That is not an acceptable answer, young man. Try again."

"Ah, you let him go because he has a loose mouth, and where he goes, it will be easier to see who listens to him?"

"Better, but not entirely true. What you said earlier intrigues me. Why don't you think he is a spy?"

Vassily did a double take; it was almost painful to watch as he tried to deal with the Citizen's abrupt about-face. "He's too talkative, isn't he, sir? Spies don't call attention to themselves, do they? It's not in their interests. And again, he's an engineer contracted to work for the fleet, but the ship was built by the company he works for, so why would they want to spy on it? And he can't be a professional subversive, either. Professionals would know better than to blab in a hotel bar." He stopped and looked vaguely self-satisfied.

"Good going. Such a shame I don't agree with you."

Vassily gulped. "But I thought you said he wasn't a—" He stopped himself. "You mean he's too obviously *not* a spy. He draws attention to himself in bars, he argues politics, he does things a spy would not do—as if he wants to lay our suspicions at ease?"

"Very good," said the Citizen. "You are learning to think like a Curator! Please note that I never said that Mr. Springfield is not a spy. Neither did I assert that he *is* one. He might well be; equally well, he might not. However, I will be unsatisfied until you have resolved the issue, one way or the other. Do you understand?"

"You want me to prove a negative?" Vassily was almost going cross-eyed with the effort of trying to understand the Citizen's train of thought. "But that's impossible!"

"Exactly!" The Citizen cracked a thin smile as he clapped his subordinate on the shoulder. "So you'll have to find some way of making it a positive that you prove, won't you? And that is your assignment for the foreseeable future, Junior Procurator Muller. You will go forth and try to prove that our irritating visitor of the morning is not a spy—or to gather sufficient evidence to justify his arrest. Come, now! Haven't you been champing at the bit to get out of this gloomy dungeon and see a bit of the capital, as I believe you referred to it only last week? This is your chance. Besides, when you return, think about the story you'll have to tell that piece of skirt you've been chasing ever since you arrived here!"

"Ah—I'm honored," said Vassily. He looked somewhat taken aback. A young officer, still sufficiently fresh from training that the varnish hadn't eroded from his view of the universe, he looked up at the Citizen in awe. "Sir, humbly request permission to ask why? I mean, why now?"

"Because it's about time you learned to do more than take minutes of committee meetings," said the Citizen. His eyes gleamed behind their glasses; his moustache shuddered all the way out to its waxen points. "There comes a time when every officer needs to assume the full burden of his duties. I expect you have picked up at least a clue about how the job is done from the interminable reports you've been summarizing. Now it's time to see if you can do it, no? On a low-risk assignment, I might add; I'm not sending you after the revolutionaries right away, ha-ha. So this afternoon you will go to sublevel two for field ops processing, then tomorrow you will start on the assignment. I expect to see a report on my desk, first thing every morning, starting the day after tomorrow. Show me what you can do!"

the next morning, Martin was awakened by a peremptory rap on the door. "Telegram for Master Springfield!" called a delivery boy.

Martin pulled on a dressing gown and opened the door a crack. The telegram was passed inside; he signed for it quickly, pulled out the contents, and passed back the signed envelope. Blinking and bleary-eyed, he carried the message over to the window and pulled back the shutters to read it. It was a welcome surprise, if somewhat annoying to be woken for it—confirmation that his visa had been approved, his security vetting was complete, and that he was to report at 1800 that evening to the Navy beanstalk in South Austria for transit to the fleet shipyards in geosynchronous orbit.

Telegrams, he reflected, were so much less civilized than e-mail—the latter didn't come with an officious youth who'd get you out of bed to sign for it. Such a shame that e-mail was unavailable in the New Republic and telegrams ubiquitous. But then again, e-mail was decentralized, telegrams anything but. And the New Republic was very keen on centralization.

He dressed, shaved, and made his way downstairs to the morning room to await his breakfast. He wore local garb—a dark jacket, tight breeches, boots, and a shirt with a ruff of lace at the collar—but of a subtly unfashionable cut, somehow betraying a lack of appreciation for the minutiae of fashion. Off-world styles, he found, tended to get in the way when trying to establish a working rapport with the locals: but if you looked just slightly odd, they'd sense your alien-ness without being overwhelmed by it, and make at least some allowances for your behavior. By any yardstick, the New Republic was an insular society, and interacting with it was difficult even for a man as well traveled as Martin, but at least the ordinary people made an effort.

He had become sufficiently accustomed to local customs that, rather than letting them irritate him, he was able to absorb each new affront with quiet resignation. The way the concierge stared down his patrician nose at him, or the stiff-collared chambermaids scurried by with downcast eyes, had become merely individual pieces in the complex jigsaw puzzle of Republican mores. The smell of wax polish and chlorine bleach, coal smoke from the boiler room, and leather seats in the dining room, were all alien, the odors of a society that hadn't adapted to the age of plastic. Not all the local habits chafed. The morning's news-sheet, folded crisply beside his seat at the breakfast table, provided a strangely evocative sense of homecoming—as if he had traveled on a voyage nearly three hundred years into the past of his own home culture, rather than 180 light-years out into the depths of space. Although, in a manner of speaking, the two voyages were exactly equivalent.

He breakfasted on butter mushrooms, sautéed goose eggs, and a particularly fine toasted sourdough rye bread, washed down with copious quantities of lemon tea. Finally, he left the room and made his way to the front desk.

"I would like to arrange transport," he said. The duty clerk looked up, eyes distant and preoccupied. "By air, to the naval beanstalk at Klamovka, as soon as possible. I will be taking hand luggage only, and will not be checking out of my room, although I will be away for some days."

"Ah, I see. Excuse me, sir." The clerk hurried away into the maze of offices and tiny service rooms that hid behind the dark wood paneling of the hotel lobby.

He returned shortly thereafter, with the concierge in tow, a tall, stoop-shouldered man dressed head to foot in black, cadaverous and sunken-cheeked, who bore himself with the solemn dignity of a count or minor noble. "You require transport, sir?" asked the concierge.

"I'm going to the naval base at Klamovka," Martin repeated slowly. "Today. I need transport arranging at short notice. I will be leaving my luggage at the hotel. I do not know how long I will be away, but I am not checking out."

"I see, sir." The concierge nodded at his subordinate, who scurried away and returned bearing three fat volumes—timetables for the various regional rail services. "I am afraid that no Zeppelin flights are scheduled between here and Klamovka until tomorrow. However, I believe you can get there this evening by train—if you leave immediately."

"That will be fine," said Martin. He had a nagging feeling that his immediate departure was the only thing he could do that would gratify the concierge—apart, perhaps, from dropping dead on the spot. "I'll be back down here in five minutes. If your assistant could see to my tickets, please? On the tab."

. The concierge nodded, stony-faced. "On behalf of the hotel, I wish you a fruitful journey," he intoned. "Marcus, see to this gentleman." And off he stalked.

The clerk cracked open the first of the ledgers and glanced at Martin cautiously. "Which class, sir?"

"First." If there was one thing that Martin had learned early, it was that the New Republic had some very strange ideas about class. He made up his mind. "I need to arrive before six o'clock tonight. I will be back here in five minutes. If you would be so good as to have my itinerary ready by then..."

"Yes, sir." He left the clerk sweating over map and gazetteer, and climbed the four flights of stairs to his floor.

When he returned to the front desk, trailed by a footman with a bag in each hand, the clerk ushered him outside. "Your carnet, sir." He pocketed the ornate travel document, itself as intricate as any passport. A steam coach was waiting. He climbed in, acknowledged the clerk's bow with a nod, and the coach huffed away toward the railway station.

It was a damp and foggy morning, and Martin could barely see the ornate stone facade of the ministerial buildings from the windows of his carriage as they rolled past beside him.

The hotel rooms might lack telephones, there might be a political ban on networking and smart matter and a host of other conveniences, and there might be a class system out of the eighteenth century on Earth; but the New Republic had one thing going for it—its trains ran on time. PS1347, the primary around which New Muscovy orbited, was a young third-generation G2 dwarf; it had formed less than two billion years ago (to Sol's five), and consequently, the planetary crust of New Muscovy contained uranium ore active enough to sustain criticality without enrichment.

Martin's coach drew up on the platform alongside the Trans-Peninsular Express. He climbed down from the cabin stiffly and glanced both ways: they'd drawn up a quarter of a kilometer down the marble tongue from the hulking engines, but still the best part of a kilometer away from the dismal tailings of fourth-class accommodation and mail. A majordomo, resplendent in bottle-green frock coat and gold braid, inspected his carnet before ushering him into a private compartment on the upper deck. The room was decorated in blue-dyed leather and old oak, trimmed in brass and gold leaf, and equipped with a marble-topped table and a bell-pull to summon service; it more closely resembled a smoking room back in the hotel than anything Martin associated with public transport.

As soon as the majordomo had left, Martin settled back in one of the deeply padded seats, drew the curtains aside to reveal the arching buttresses and curved roof of the station, and opened his PA in book mode. Shortly thereafter, the train shuddered slightly and began to move: as the train slid out of the station, he glanced out of the window, unable to look away.

The city of New Prague was built just upstream from the tidal estuary of the River Vis; only the Basilisk, brooding atop a plug of eroded volcanic granite, rose much above the level of the plain. Indeed, the train would cruise through the lowlands using just one of its engines. The second reactor would only be brought to criticality when the train reached the foothills of the Apennines, the mountain range that separated the coastal peninsula from the continental interior of New Austria. Then the train would surge in a knife-straight line across nine hundred kilometers of desert before stopping, six hours later, at the foot of the Klamovka beanstalk.

The scene was quite extraordinary. Martin gazed at it in barely controlled awe. Though he didn't like to admit it, he was something of a tourist, permanently searching for a sense of fresh beauty that he could secretly revel in. There wasn't anything like this left on Earth; the wild ride of the twentieth century and the events that had followed the Singularity in the twenty-first had distorted the landscape of every industrialized nation. Even in the wake of the population crash, you couldn't find open countryside, farms, hedges, and neatly planned villages—at least, not without also finding monorails, arcologies, fall-out hot spots, and the weird hillocks of the Final Structure. The lowland landscape through which the Trans-Peninsular Express ran resembled a vision of pre-postindustrial England, a bucolic dreamscape where the trains ran on time and the sun never set on the empire.

But railway journeys pale rapidly, and after half an hour, the train was racing through the valleys in a blur of steel and brass. Martin went back to his book, and was so engrossed in it that he barely noticed the door open and close—until a woman he had never seen before sat down opposite him and cleared her throat.

"Excuse me," he said, looking up. "Are you sure you have the right compartment?"

She nodded. "Quite sure, thank you. I didn't request an individual one. Did you?"

"I thought—" He fumbled in his jacket for his carnet. "Ah. I see." He cursed the concierge silently, thumbed the PA off, then looked at her. "I thought I had a compartment to myself; I see I was wrong. Please accept my apologies."

The woman nodded graciously. She had long black hair coiled in a bun, high cheekbones and brown eyes; her dark blue gown seemed expensively plain by this society's standards. *Probably* a middle-class housewife, he guessed, but his ability to judge social status within the New Republic was still somewhat erratic. He couldn't even make a stab at her age: heavy makeup, and the tight bodice, billowing skirts and puffed sleeves of capital fashion made an effective disguise.

"Are you going far?" she asked brightly.

"All the way to Klamovka, and thence up the naval beanstalk," he said, somewhat surprised at this frank interrogation.

"What a coincidence; that's where I'm going, too. You will excuse me for asking, but am I right in thinking you are not native to this area?"

She looked interested, to a degree that Martin found irritatingly intrusive. He shrugged. "No, I'm not." He reopened his PA and attempted to bury his nose in it, but his unwanted traveling companion had other ideas.

"I take it from your accent that you are not native to this planet, either. And you're going to the Admiralty yards. Would you mind me asking your business there?"

"Yes," he said curtly, and stared pointedly at his PA. He hadn't initially registered how forward she was being, at least for a woman of her social class, but it was beginning to set his nerves on edge, ringing alarms. Something about her didn't feel quite right. *Agent provocateur?* he wondered. He had no intention of giving the secret police any further excuses to haul him in; he wanted them to think he'd learned the error of his ways and determined to reform.

"Hmm. But when I came in you were reading a treatise on relativistic clock-skew correction algorithms as applied to the architecture of modern starship drive compensators. So you're an engineer of some sort, retained by the Admiralty to do maintenance work on fleet vessels." She grinned, and her expression unnerved Martin: white teeth, red lips, and something about her manner that reminded him of home, where women weren't just well-bred ornaments for the family tree. "Am I right?"

"I couldn't possibly comment." Martin shut his PA again and glared at her. "Who are you, and what the hell do you want?" The social programming he'd absorbed on his journey out to the New Republic forbade such crudity in the presence of a lady, but she was obviously no more a lady than he was a Republican yeoman. The social program could go play with itself.

"My name is Rachel Mansour, and I'm on my way to the naval dockyards on business which may well intersect with your own. Unless I'm mistaken, in which case you have my most humble apologies, you are Martin Springfield, personally incorporated and retained by contract to the New Republican Admiralty to perform installation upgrades on the drive control circuitry of the Svejk-class battlecruiser *Lord Vanek*. After Lord Ernst Vanek, founder of the New Republic's Navy. Correct?"

Martin returned the PA to his jacket pocket and glanced out of the window, trying to still a sudden wave of cold fear. "Yes. What business of yours is it?"

"You may be interested to learn that four hours ago, consensus absolute time, the New Model Air Force—whose underwriting service you subscribe to—invoked the Eschaton clause in all strategic guarantees bearing on the Republic. At the same time, someone tipped off the UN Standing Committee on Multilateral Interstellar Disarmament that the New Republic is gearing up for war, in defense of a colony outpost that's under siege. You aren't paying the extra premium for insurance against divine retribution, are you? So right now you're not covered for anything other than medical and theft."

Martin turned back to look at her. "Are you accusing me of

being a spy?" He met her eyes. They were dark, intelligent, and reserved—absolutely unreadable. "Who the hell are you, anyway?"

She shook a card out of her sleeve and opened it toward him. A head—recognizably her own, but with close-cropped hair—floated above it in holographic miniature, wreathed against a familiar backdrop. The sheer unexpectedness of it electrified him: shivers chased up and down his spine as his implants tried to damp down an instinctive panic reaction rising from his adrenal glands. "UN diplomatic intelligence, special operations group. I'm here to find out what the current situation is, and that includes finding out just what last-minute modifications the Admiralty is making to the ships comprising the expeditionary force. You *are* going to cooperate, aren't you?" She smiled again, even more unnervingly, with an expression that reminded Martin of a hungry ferret.

"Um." *What the hell are the CMID doing here? This isn't in the mission plan!* "This is going to be one of those trips, isn't it?" He rubbed his forehead and glanced at her again: she was still waiting for his response. *Shit, improvise, dammit, before she suspects something!* "Look, do you know what they do to spies here?"

She nodded, no longer smiling. "I do. But I've also got my eyes on the bottom line, which is that this is an impending war situation. It's my job to keep track of it—we can't afford to let them run riot this close to Earth. Being garrotted would certainly spoil anyone's day, but starting an interstellar war or attracting the attention of the Eschaton is even worse, at least for the several planets full of mostly innocent bystanders who are likely to be included in the collateral damage. Which is my overriding concern."

She stared at him with frightening intensity, and the card disappeared between two lace-gloved fingers. "We need to get together and talk, Martin. Once you're up at the dockyard and settled in, I'll contact you. I don't care what else you agree to or disagree with, but we are going to have a talk tomorrow. And I'm going to pick your brains, and confirm that you're just a bystander, and tell your insurers you're a safe bet. Do you understand?"

"Uh, yes." He stared at her and tried to look as if he'd just realized that she was, in fact, a devil, and he had signed away his soul. He hoped she'd believe him—naive engineer, sucked in out of his depths, confronted with an agent of Higher Authority—but had a cold sense that if she didn't fall for it, he might be in *real* trouble. Herman and the CMID weren't exactly on speaking terms...

"Excellent." She reached into her purse and pulled out a battered-looking, gunmetal-colored PA. "Speaking. Send: Rabbit green. Ack."

The PA spoke back: "Ack. Message sent." It took Martin a moment or two to recognize the voice as his own.

She slipped the case away and stood to leave the compartment. "You see," she said from the doorway, a quirky smile tugging at her lips, "life here isn't necessarily as dull as you thought! See you later..."

preparations for departure ____

his imperial majesty the Emperor Ivan Hasek III, by grace of God the protector of the people of the New Republic, growled exasperatedly. "Get the Admiral out of bed and make him presentable—I have a cabinet meeting at noon, and I need to talk to him *now.*"

"Yes, sir! I most humbly beg your pardon, and beg leave to be excused to do as Your Majesty commands." The butler virtually bowed and scraped his way off the telephone.

"What's the implied 'or else'?" Duke Michael, the Emperor's brother, inquired drily. "You'd have him clapped in irons?"

"Hardly." The Emperor snorted, showing as much amusement as his dignity permitted. "He's over eighty; I suppose he's entitled to stay in bed once in a while. But if he's so ill he can't even rise for his Emperor in time of war, I'd have to force him to retire. And then there'd be an uproar in the Admiralty. You can't imagine the waves it would make if we started forcing admirals to *retire.*" He sniffed. "We might even have to think about giving them all pensions! That'd go down as well as suggesting to Father that he abdicate."

Duke Michael coughed, delicately. "Perhaps somebody should have. After the second stroke—"

"Yes, yes."

"I still think offering him the fleet is unreasonable."

"If you think that is unreasonable, I don't suppose you'd care to discuss the likely response of their naval lordships if I *didn't* give him first refusal?" The priority telephone rang again before his brother had a chance to answer the pointed question; a liveried servant offered the ivory-and-platinum handset to His Majesty. The Duke picked up a second earpiece, to listen in on the call.

"Sire? My Lord Admiral Kurtz is ready to talk to you. He extends his deepest apologies, and—"

"Enough. Just put him on, there's a good fellow." Ivan tapped his fingers irritably on the arm of his chair, a Gothic wooden monstrosity only one step removed from an instrument of torture. "Ah, Admiral. Just the man! Capital, how splendid to talk to you. And how are we today?"

"Today-ay?" A reedy, quavering voice echoed uncertainly over the copper wires. "Ah-hum, yes, today. Indeed, yes. I'm very well, thank you, milady, I don't suppose you've seen any chameleons?"

"No, Admiral, there are no chameleons in the palace," the Emperor stated with firm, but resigned, persistence. "You know who you are speaking to?"

In the momentary silence he could almost hear the elderly admiral blinking in confusion. "Ah-hum. Your Majesty? Ah, Ivan, lad? Emperor already? How time flies!"

"Yes, Uncle. I'm phoning you because—" A thought struck the Emperor. "Are you up and about?"

"Yes, ahuhuhum. I'm, ah, in my bath chair. It's my old legs, you know. They're awfully fragile. Got to wrap them up in lots of blankets in case they shatter. They don't blow legs the way they used to, when I was a lad. But I'm out of bed now."

"Oh, good. You see, um—" The Emperor's brain went into a wheel-spin as he considered and reconsidered the options. He'd heard, of course, about the Admiral's indisposition, but he hadn't actually encountered it directly until now. A strong case could be made, he supposed, for dismissing the Admiral; the man was patently ill. Charging him with this duty would be unfair, and more importantly, not in the best interests of the state.

But he was still the senior fighting admiral, war hero of the New Republic, defender of the empire, slaughterer of the infidels, conqueror of no less than three bucolic and rather backward colony worlds—and, not to put too much of a point on it, the Emperor's uncle by way of his grandfather's second mistress. Because of the long-standing tradition that admirals never retired, nobody had ever thought to make provisions for pensioning off old warhorses; they usually died long before it became an issue. To dismiss him was unthinkable, but to expect him to lead a naval expedition—Ivan struggled with his conscience, half hoping that the old man would turn it down. No dishonor would accrue—nobody expected an octogenarian in a bath chair to die for the fatherland—and meantime they'd find a hard-headed young whippersnapper to lead the fleet into battle.

Coming to a decision, the Emperor took a deep breath. "We have a problem. Something abominable has happened, and Rochard's World is under siege. I'm going to send the fleet. Are you too ill to lead it?" He winked at his brother the Duke, hoping—

"War!" The old man's bellow nearly deafened Ivan. "Victory to the everlastingly vigilant forces of righteousness waging unceasing struggle on enemies of the New Conservatives! Death to the proponents of change! A thousand tortures to the detractors of the Emperor! Where are the bastards? Let me at them!" The clattering in the background might have been the sound of a walking frame being cast aside.

Duke Michael grimaced unhappily at his brother. "Well I suppose that answers *one* question," he mouthed. "I'm not going to say I told you so, but who are we going to send to push his wheelchair?"

new prague was only a thousand kilometers north of the equator (this planet being notoriously cold for a water-belt terraform) and the train pulled into the Klamovka station shortly after lunchtime. Martin disembarked and hailed a cab to the naval depot at the foot of the beanstalk, pointedly ignoring Rachel—or whatever her real name was. Let her make her own way: she was an unwelcome, potentially disastrous complication in his life right now.

The beanstalk loomed over the military depot like the ultimate flagpole; four tapered cones of diamondoid polymers stretching all the way to geosynchronous orbit and a bit beyond, a radical exception to the New Republic's limitations on technology. Bronzed, bullet-nosed elevator carriages skimmed up and down the elevator cables, taking a whole night to make the journey. Here there was no *fin-de-siècle* ambience: just rugged functionality, sleeping capsules manufactured to a template designed for Kobe's ancient salarymen, and a stringent weight limit. (Gravity modification, although available, was another of the technologies that the New Republic shunned—at least, for non-military purposes.) Martin hurried aboard the first available pod and, to his relief, saw no sign of Rachel.

Upon arrival, he disembarked into the military sector of the space station, presented himself to the warrant officer's checkpoint, and was ushered straight through a crude security scan that probably exceeded his annual allowed dose of X-rays in one go. There was one bad moment when a master sergeant asked him to demonstrate his PA, but the explanation—that it was a personal assist, that it stored all his working notes, and that he'd be unable to cope without it—was accepted. After which he cooled his heels for half an hour in a spartan guardroom painted institutional green.

Eventually a rating came to collect him. "You'd be the engine man?" said the flyer. "We been waiting for you."

Martin sighed unhappily. "And I've been waiting, too." He stood up. "Take me to your CO."

The New Republic had paid Mikoyan-Guerevitch-Kvaerner back on Luna to design them a battlecruiser fit to bear the name of their Navy's founder: one that looked the way a warship ought to look, not like a cubist's vision of a rabies virus crossed with a soft drink can (as most real warships did). Style imposed strictures on functionality: despite which, it was still worthy of a degree of respect—you could be killed by its baroque missile batteries and phased-array lasers just as surely as by a more modern weapon. Besides, it *looked* good, which had enabled MiG to make a killing selling knockoffs to gullible juntas everywhere, demonstrating the importance of being Ernst as the marketing department put it.

In Martin's opinion, the *Lord Vanek* was cut from the same comic-opera fabric as the rest of the New Republic—a comic opera that was far less funny once it had you in its jaws. The ceremonials, flags and Imperial logos splashed across every available surface, the uniformed flunkies, and elaborate pyramid of military etiquette, all suggested to Martin that taking this job had not been a good idea: the gibbeted dissidents hanging from the eaves of the Basilisk had confirmed it. Right now, he'd happily repay his entire fee just to be allowed to go home—were it not for the call of duty.

After a confusing tour of the station's docking facilities and the warship's transit tubes, he fetched up in the doorway of a crowded, red-lit, octagonal space, maintained in zero gee by a local relaxation of the laws of physics. A squat, balding engineering officer was bawling out a frightened-looking teenager in front of an open access panel. "That's the last bloody time you touch anything without asking me or Chief Otcenasek first, you bumbling numb-fingered oaf! See that panel? That's the backup master bus arbitration exchange, there. And *that*"— he pointed at another, closed panel—"is the backup master circuit breaker box, which is what chief told you to check out. That switch you were about to throw—

Martin saw where the officer's finger was pointing and winced. If some idiot conscript did something like that to him, he reflected, he probably wouldn't stop at threatening to strangle him with his own intestines. Although if the idiot had started playing with the MBAX, strangling him would be redundant: it didn't usually have much effect on a charred corpse.

"Engineering Commander Krupkin?" he asked.

"Yes? Who? Oh. You must be the shipyard mechanic?" Krupkin turned toward him, leaving the hapless rating to scramble for cover. "You're late."

"Blame the Curator's Office," snapped Martin. As soon as the words left his mouth, he regretted them. "I'm sorry. I've had a bad week. What can I do for you?"

"Secret state police, hmm? Won't get many of those around here," Krupkin grunted, abruptly conciliatory. "You know something about this toy box, then?"

"MiG sells them. You keep them running. People break them. I fix them. Is that what you wanted to know?"

"That's a good start." Krupkin suddenly grinned. "So let's try another question. What do you know about preferential-frame clock-skew baseline compensators? Specifically, this model K-340, as currently configured. Tell me everything you can see about how it's set up."

Martin spent the next hour telling him all the different ways it was out of alignment. After that, Krupkin showed him a real K-340, not a bodged test article. And then it was time for a working lunch while Krupkin picked his brains, and then a long working afternoon figuring out where everything went and going over change orders to make sure everything was where the paperwork said it was supposed to be. And then back to base for the evening . . .

rachel mansour stood naked in the middle of the hand-woven rug that covered the floor of the hotel room she had rented two hours earlier, in the naval port city of Klamovka: even though it was expensive, it smelled of damp and dry rot, carbolic soap and firewood. She breathed slowly and evenly as she stretched arms and legs in ritual sequence, limbering up. The curtains were drawn, the door locked, and her sensors stationed outside to warn her of intruders: for she was not inclined to explain her state to any hotel staff who might see it.

Rachel was not inclined to explain a lot of things to the people she moved among. The New Republic filled her with a bitter, hopeless anger—one which she recognized, understood to be a poor reflection on her professionalism, but nevertheless couldn't set aside. The sheer waste of human potential that was the New Republic's *raison d'être* offended her sensibilities as badly as a public book-burning, or a massacre of innocents.

The New Republic was 250 years old, 250 light-years from Earth. When the Eschaton had relocated nine-tenths of Earth's population via wormhole—for reasons it hadn't deigned to explain—it had sorted some of them on the basis of ethnic or social or psychological affinity. The New Republic had picked up a mixed bag of East-European technorejectionists and royalists, hankering for the comforting certainties of an earlier century.

The founders of the New Republic had suffered at the hands of impersonal technological change. In the market-oriented democracies of pre-Singularity Earth, they'd seen people cast by their millions on the scrap heap of history. Given a new world to tame, and the tools to do it with, they had immediately established a conservative social order. A generation later, a vicious civil war broke out between those who wanted to continue using the cornucopia machines—self-replicating nano-assembler factories able to manufacture any physical goods—and those who wanted to switch to a simpler way of life where everybody knew their place and there was a place for everyone. The progressives lost: and so the New Republic remained for a century, growing into its natural shape—Europe as it might have been during the twentieth century, had physics and chemistry been finalized in 1890. The patent offices were closed; there were no homes for dreaming relativists here.

Standing naked in the middle of the carpet, she could set it aside for a while. She could ignore the world while her implants ran through their regular self-defense practice sequence. It started with breathing exercises, then the isometric contraction of muscle groups under the direction of her battle management system, then finally a blur of motion as the embedded neural network controllers took over, whirling her body like a marionette through a series of martial arts exercises. A ten-minute cycle performed twice a week kept her as ready for personal defense as an unaugmented adept who spent an hour or more every day.

Whirling and jerking on invisible strings she threw and dismembered intangible demons; it was no great effort to project her frustrations and anger onto them. *This* for the blind beggar she had passed in the street, his affliction curable in a culture that didn't ban most advanced medical practices. *That* for the peasants bound to the soil they tilled by a law that saw them as part of the land, rather than as human beings. *This* for the women condemned to die giving birth to unwanted children. *That* for the priests who pandered to the prejudices of the ruling elite and offered their people the false consolation of the hereafter, when most of the horrors that besieged them had long since been banished from the civilized worlds. And *this* and *this* and *that* for treating her like a third-class citizen. Anger demanded many *kata.*

I do not want this world. I do not like this world. I do not need this world, I do not need to feel sympathetic for this world or its inhabitants. If only they did not need me...

There was a small bathroom next door—an expensive extra in this society. She used it to clean herself as efficiently as possible, sweat and grime washing away like memories. And some of the pessimism went with it. *Things around here are going to get better,* she reminded herself. *That's what I'm here for.*

Once dry, she wandered back into the bedroom and sat down on the edge of the bed. Then she picked up her battered PA. "Get me the UN Consensus Ambassador," she ordered. There was only one UN ambassador in the New Republic; George Cho, permanent representative of the Security Council, to which she was ultimately answerable. (The New Republic persistently refused to recognize any of Earth's more subtle political institutions.)

"Processing. *Beep.* Rachel, I'm sorry, but I'm not available right now. Waiting for information to become available about the incident at Rochard's. If you'd like to leave a message after the tone... *beep.*"

"Hi, George. Rachel here. Calling from Klamovka. Give me a call back; I think I ought to go public, and I want diplomatic backup. Let's talk. Message ends."

She closed the PA and put it down again. Stared moodily at the dresser. Her costume (she found it hard to think of it as regular clothing, even after months of wearing it daily) lay heaped around the dressing table. There were visits to make, forms to be observed, before she could act openly. *Fuck this for a game of soldiers,* she thought. Living by the New Republic's rules had gotten old fast. *I need some civilized company before I go out of my skull.*

Speaking of which, there was that engineering contractor to call. A bit of a cold fish, and not very cooperative, but she be damned if she'd let him throw her off; she could probably dig more out of him in an hour over a restaurant table than she'd be able to get from the Admiralty office in a month of diplomatic cocktail parties and formal memoranda.

She picked up the PA again. "PA, page engineer Springfield's voice mail for me. Speech only. I have a message for him. Message begins..."

george cho, ambassador Plenipotentiary from the United Nations Security Council to the court of His Imperial Majesty, Emperor Ivan Hasek III (by grace of God, et cetera), sweated under his high collar and nodded politely. "Yes, Your Excellency, I quite understand your point. Nevertheless, although the territory in dispute is annexed to the New Republic, I must state again that we believe the situation falls within our remit, if only because it is not a purely domestic affair—unless this Festival is some peculiar tradition of yours that I have not hitherto been apprised of?—and consequently, the ugly matter of Clause Nineteen rears its head again."

His Excellency the Archduke Michael Hasek shook his head. "We cannot accept that," he stated. He stared at Cho from watery but piercing blue eyes. *Bloody foreign busybodies,* he thought. Not that Cho was a bad sort, for a degenerate Terran anarchist technophiliac. He reminded Michael of a bloodhound; baggy-eyed, jowly, perpetually sad-looking, and a mind like a spring-steel trap.

George Cho sighed and leaned back in his chair. He stared past the Archduke, at the portrait of the Duke's father that hung on the wall. Emperor at forty, dead of old age at sixty, Emperor Hasek II: something of a prodigy, a force for progress in an insanely conservative milieu. The man had pulled the New Republic far enough out of its shell to acquire a navy and colonize three or four utterly benighted backwaters. A good student of history. *Dangerous.*

"I notice you looking at my father. He was a very stiff-necked man. It's a trait that runs in the family," Michael observed wryly. "We don't like outsiders sticking their noses into our affairs. Maybe this is short-sighted of us, but—" He shrugged.

"Ah." Cho brought his eyes back to the Duke. "Yes, of course.

However, I am wondering if perhaps the advantages of UN involvement haven't been made clear to you? I believe we have quite a lot to offer; I wouldn't dream of approaching you about this if I didn't think you could benefit from it."

"There are benefits and there are side-effects. Did you have anything specific in mind?" Michael leaned forward.

"As a matter of fact...yes. It comes back to Clause Nineteen; the injunction against use of causality-violation weapons. 'Whosoever shall cause to be deployed a weapon capable of disrupting the et cetera shall be guilty of a crime against humanity and subject to the internationally agreed penalties for that offense.' We know perfectly well that you wouldn't dream of using such weapons against one of your own worlds. But we have insufficient evidence about the intentions of the, ah, aggressor party, this *Festival*. There's a marked shortage of information about them, which is in itself worrying. What I'm suggesting is that it might be advantageous to you to have independent observers from the UN in train with your expedition, to rebut any accusations that the New Republic is committing crimes against humanity and to act as witnesses in the event that your forces are themselves attacked in such a manner."

"Aha." Michael gritted his teeth and smiled at the ambassador. "And what makes you think there's an expedition?"

It was Cho's turn to smile: tiredly, for he had been awake for nearly forty-eight hours at this point, collating intelligence reports, monitoring media, and trying to put together the big picture single-handedly—the New Republic had strictly limited the size of his diplomatic staff. "Come, Your Excellency, are we to believe that the New Republic will allow an insult to its honor, let alone its territorial integrity, to stand without response? Some sort of reaction is inevitable. And given the loss of your Navy's local presence, and the increased state of alert and heavy engineering activity around your bases at Klamovka, Libau, and V-1, a naval expedition seems likely. Or were you planning to get your soldiers there by ordering them to click their heels three times while saying 'there's no place like home'?"

Michael pinched the bridge of his nose, attempting to cover his frown. "I can neither confirm nor deny that we are considering naval action at this time."

Cho nodded. "Of course."

"However. Do you know anything about this Festival? Or what has been going on at Rochard's World?"

"Surprisingly little. You've been keeping a lid on whatever's going on—not very subtly, I'm afraid, the dispatches from the Fourth Guards Division's desperate defense of the colonial capital would be more convincing if the Fourth Guards' relocation from New Prague to Baikal Four hadn't been mentioned in dispatches a month ago. But you're not the only people keeping the lid on it. My people have been unable to unearth any information about this Festival anywhere, which is distinctly worrying. We even broadcast a request for help from the Eschaton, but all that came back was a cryptogram saying, 'P. T. Barnum was right.'" (A cryptogram which had been encoded with a key from a secured UN diplomatic onetime pad, the leakage of which had already caused a major security panic.)

"I wonder who this T. P. Barney was," Duke Michael commented. "No matter. The Festival has had an, ah, catastrophic impact on Rochard's World. The economy is in ruins, there's widespread civil disorder and outright rebellion. In fact—" He stared sharply at the ambassador. "You understand what this means for the guiding principles of our civilization?"

"I'm here strictly as an ambassador to represent the interests of all UN parties in the New Republic," Cho stated neutrally. "I'm not here to pass judgment on you. That would be presumptuous."

"Hmm." Michael glanced down at his blotter.

"It is true that we are considering an expedition," said the Archduke. Cho struggled to conceal his surprise. "But it will be difficult," Michael continued. "The enemy is already well entrenched in the destination system. We don't know where they come from. And if we send a fleet there directly, it may well suffer the same fate as the naval squadron on station. We are therefore considering a rather, ah, desperate stratagem."

Cho leaned forward. "Sir, if you are contemplating a causality violation, I must advise you—"

The Archduke raised a hand. "I assure you, Ambassador, that no global causality violation will take place as a result of actions of the New Republican Navy. We have no intention of violating Clause Nineteen." He grimaced. "However, localized causality violations are sometimes permitted within tactical situations confined to the immediate light cone of an engagement, are they not? I think that... hmm, yes. A UN observer would be able to assure all parties that our own conduct was legal and correct, would he not?"

"A UN observer will scrupulously tell the truth," Cho stated, sweating slightly.

"Good. In that case, I think we may be able to accommodate your request, if a decision is made to prepare a task force. One inspector only, with diplomatic credentials, may accompany the flagship. His remit will be to monitor the use of reality-modification weapons by both sides in the conflict and to assure the civilized worlds that the New Republic does not engage in gratuitous use of time travel as a weapon of mass destruction."

Cho nodded. "I think that would be acceptable. I shall notify Inspector Mansour, who is currently staying in Klamovka."

Michael smiled, fleetingly. "Send my secretary a note. I shall pass it to Admiral Kurtz's staff. I think I can guarantee that he will cooperate to the best of his abilities."

junior procurator vassily Muller, of the Curator's Office, stood in front of the great panoramic window that fronted Observation Bay Four and looked out across a gulf of light-years. Stars wheeled past like jewels scattered on a rotating display table. The spin of the huge station created a comfortably low semblance of gravity, perhaps eighty percent of normal; immediately outside the double wall of synthetic diamond lay the shipyard, where the great cylindrical bulk of a starship hung against a backdrop of cosmic beauty.

Shadows fell across the gray cylinder like the edge of eternity, sharp-edged with the unnatural clarity of vacuum. Inspection plates hung open at various points along the hull of the ship; disturbingly intestinal guts coiled loose, open to the remote manipulator pods that clung to it by many-jointed limbs. It resembled a dead, decaying whale being eaten by a swarm of lime green crabs. But it wasn't dead, Vassily realized: it was undergoing surgery.

The ship was like a marathon runner, being overhauled by surgeons in hope of turning him into some kind of cyborg prodigy to compete in the ultimate winner-take-all sporting event. The analogy with his own, slightly sore head did not escape Vassily: it struck him that the most radical preparation was essential for the struggle ahead. He could already feel the new connections, like a ghost of an undefined limb, firming up somewhere just beyond the edge of his perceptions. Another three days, the medic had assured him in the morning, and he'd find himself able to start training the cranial jack. They'd given him a briefcase full of instructions, a small and highly illegal (not to say horrifically expensive) tool kit, and a priority travel pass to the orbital station on an Air Defense shuttle, bypassing the slow space elevator.

"Procurator Muller, I presume?" He turned. A trim-looking fellow in the pale green uniform of His Majesty's Navy, a lieutenant's rings on his cuffs. He saluted. "At ease. I'm Second Lieutenant Sauer, shipboard security officer for the *Lord Vanek*. Is this your first time up here?"

Vassily nodded, too tongue-tied to articulate a response. Sauer turned to face the window. "Impressive, isn't she?"

"Yes!" The sight of the huge warship brought a great wave of pride to his chest: his people owned and flew such ships. "My stepbrother is on one of them, a sister ship—the *Skvosty*."

"Oh, very good, very good indeed. Has he been there long?"

"Three—three years. He is second fire control officer. A lieutenant, like yourself."

"Ah." Sauer tipped his head on one side and regarded Vassily with a brightly focused gaze. "Excellent. But tell me, how good is this ship, really? How powerful do you think it is?"

Vassily shook his head, still dazzled by his first sight of the warship. "I can't imagine anything grander than a ship like that one! How can anyone build better?"

Sauer looked amused. "You are a detective, and not a cosmonaut," he said. "If you had been to naval college, you would be aware of some of the possibilities. Let us just say, for the moment, that they wouldn't have named it after old Ernst Ironsides if it wasn't the best ship we've got—but not everyone plays by the same rules as we do. I suppose it's only fair, then, for us to play a different game—which is of course precisely why you are here and we are having this conversation. You want to protect that ship, and the Republic, don't you?"

Vassily nodded eagerly. "Yes. Did my CO let you know why I'm here?"

"I have a full briefing. We take anything that might compromise shipboard security extremely seriously; you won't be able to work in restricted areas, but as far as I'm concerned, you're welcome to go anywhere that isn't controlled—and by arrangement, I'm sure we can help you keep an eye on your yard-ape. To tell the truth, it's good for us that you are available for this duty. We have more than enough other problems to keep track of without stalking contractors on the job, and as long as the problem gets wrapped up satisfactorily in the end, who cares whose turf is turned over, eh?"

At this point, Vassily realized that something odd was going on, but being inexperienced, he didn't know quite what could be the matter. Nor did he want to push Sauer, at least not this soon in their acquaintance. "Can you show me where Springfield is working?"

"Unfortunately"—Sauer spread his hands—"Springfield is actually on board at this very minute. You realize that he is working on the interstellar propulsion system itself?"

"Oh." Vassily's mouth made a round "O." "You mean I'll have to go aboard?"

"I mean you *can't* go aboard—not until you've been checked out by medical, received security clearance, gone to three orientation briefings, and been approved by the old man—which won't be until tomorrow at the earliest. So, for the time being, I had better show you to the transient officers' quarters—you have the same privileges as a midshipman while you are on Admiralty turf."

"That would be great," Vassily agreed earnestly. "If you'd lead the way ... ?"

мeanɯhile, the first of the Festival's entourage of Critics was arriving in orbit around Rochard's World.

Once part of a human civilization that had transmigrated into its own computing network, the Festival was a traveling embassy, a nexus for the exchange of cultural information between stars. It was primarily interested in other upload cultures, but anyone would do at a pinch. It had zigged and zagged its way through the sphere of inhabited worlds for a thousand t-years, working its way inward from the periphery, and all the time it had asked only one thing of its willing or unwilling hosts: *Entertain us!*

The Festival was sharply constrained by the density of information that could be crammed into the tiny starwisps that carried it across the interstellar gulf. Unlike a normal upload civilization, the Festival couldn't manufacture its own reality with sufficient verisimilitude to avoid the normal hazards of life in a virtual universe; it was a desert plant, existing as a seed for years at a time between frantic growth spurts when the correct conditions arose.

Like most circus caravans, the Festival accumulated hitch-hikers, hangers-on, and a general fringe of camp followers and parasites. There was room for millions of passengers in the frozen mind-cores of the starwisps, but no room for them to think between stations. Trueminds aestivated during the decade-long hops between planetary civilizations; simple, subsentient supervisors kept the starwisps on course and ran the autonomic systems. On arrival, the servitors built the necessary infrastructure to thaw and load the trueminds. Once contact had been achieved and a course of action decided upon, any residual capacity would be made available to the passengers, including the Critics.

A foam of diamond was growing in orbit around Sputnik, the outer moon of Rochard's World. Strange emulsions stirred within some of the bubbles, a boiling soup of nanomachine-catalyzed chemical reactions. Other bubbles faded to black, soaking up sunlight with near-total efficiency. A steady stream of tanks drifted toward the foam on chaotic orbits, ejecta from the mining plants in the outer system. Within the bubbles, incarnate life congealed, cells assembled by machine rather than the natural cycle of mitosis and differentiation. Thousands of seconds passed, an aeon to the productive assemblers: skeletons appeared, first as lacy outlines and then as baroque coral outcroppings afloat in the central placentory bubbles. Blood, tissues, teeth, and organs began to congeal in place as the nano-assemblers pumped synthetic enzymes, DNA, ribosomes, and other cellular machinery into the lipid vesicles that were due to become living cells.

Presently, the Critics' bodies began to twitch.

the door to the study opened and a liveried footman entered. "Commodore Bauer to see the admiral," he announced.

"Sh-show him in, then!"

Commodore Bauer entered the Admiral's study and saluted. Seated behind an imposing hardwood desk in the center of the huge room (paneled in ferociously expensive imported hardwoods, with raw silk curtains and not a little gold leaf on the cornices), the admiral looked tiny: a wizened turtle sporting a walrus moustache, adrift on a sea of blue-and-silver carpet. Nevertheless, he was in good condition today, wearing his uniform, resplendent with decorations and ribbons, and seated in a real chair.

"Commmmmander. Welcome. Please be seated."

Commodore Bauer walked toward the desk and took the indicated chair.

"And how is your father these days? It's—it's a while since I saw him."

"He's very well sir." *At least as well as he could be, considering he died four years ago.* Bauer looked at his superior sadly. Once the sharpest saber in the New Republic's arsenal, Rear Admiral Kurtz was rusting at a terrifying rate: they must already be planning the funeral. He still had periods of lucidity, sometimes quite extended ones, but forcing him to go on this expedition—and no officer could realistically refuse a royal commission and expect to continue to hold his post—was positively cruel; surely His Majesty must have known about his state? "May I ask why you summoned me, sir?"

"Ah—ah—ah, yes." The Admiral jerked as if someone had

just administered an electric shock to him. Suddenly his expression tightened. "I must apologize, Commodore: I have too many vague moments. I wanted to discuss the flisposition of the—I mean, the disposition—the fleet. Obviously you will be in day-to-day command of the task force, and in overall tactical command once it arrives at Rochard's World. The matter of planning, however, is one to which I feel I can make a contribution." A wan smile flitted across his face. "Do you agree with this?"

"Ah, yes, sir." Bauer nodded, slightly encouraged. The grand old man might be drifting into senility, but he was still razor-sharp during his better moments: if he was willing to sit back and let Bauer do most of the driving, perhaps things might work out. (As long as he remembered who Bauer was, the commodore reminded himself.) They'd worked together before: Bauer had been a junior lieutenant under captain Kurtz during the Invasion of Thermidor, and had a keen respect for his intellect, not to mention his dogged refusal to back down in the face of heavy opposition. "I was led to believe that the General Staff Directorate has some unusual plans for lifting the siege; is this what you have in mind?"

"Yes." Admiral Kurtz pointed at a red leather folder lying on his desk. "Contingency Omega. I had a ha-hand in the first paper, ten years ago, but I fear younger minds will have to refine it into a plan of attack."

"Contingency Omega." Bauer paused. "Wasn't that shelved, because of, ah, legal concerns?"

"Yes." Kurtz nodded. "But only as a plan of att-att-attack. We are not allowed to fly closed timelike paths—use faster-than-light travel to arrive before war breaks out. Leads to all—all—sorts of bother. Neighbors say God doesn't like it. *Blithering nonsense* if you ask me. But we've already been attacked. They came to us. So we can arrive in our own past, but after the attack began: I must confess, I think it is a bit of a pathetic excuse, but there we are. Contingency Omega it is."

"Oh." Bauer reached toward the red folder. "May I?"

"Cer-certainly."

The Commodore began to read.

accelerating to speeds faster than light was, of course, impossible. General relativity had made that clear enough back in the twentieth century. However, since then a number of ways of circumventing the speed limit had turned up; by now, there were at least six different known methods of moving mass or information from A to B without going through *c*.

A couple of these techniques relied on quantum trickery, strange hacks involving Bose-Einstein condensates to flip bits in quantum dots separated by light-years; as with the causal channel, the entangled dots had to be pulled apart at slower-than-light speeds, making them fine for communication but useless for transporting bodies. Some of them—like the Eschaton's wormholes—were inexplicable, relying on principles no human physicist had yet discovered. But two of them were viable propulsion systems for spaceships; the Linde-Alcubierre expansion reciprocal, and the jump drive. The former set up a wave of expansion and contraction in the space behind and in front of the ship: it was peerlessly elegant, and more than somewhat dangerous—a spacecraft trying to navigate through the dense manifold of space-time ran the risk of being blown apart by a stray dust grain.

The jump drive was, to say the least, more reliable, barring a few quirks. A spaceship equipped with it would accelerate out from the nearest star's gravity well. Identifying a point of equipotential flat space-time near the target star, the ship would light up the drive field generator, and the entire spaceship could then tunnel between the two points without ever actually being between them. (Assuming, of course, that the target star was more or less in the same place and the same state that it appeared to be when the starship lit off its drive field—if it wasn't, nobody would ever see that ship again.)

But the jump drive had huge problems for the military. For one thing, it only worked in flat space-time, a very long way out from stars or planets, which meant you had to arrive some way out, which in turn meant that anyone you were attacking could see you coming. For another thing, it didn't have a very long range. The farther you tried to jump, the higher the probability that conditions at your destination point weren't what you were expecting, creating more work for the loss adjusters. Most seriously, it created a tunnel between equipotential points in space-time. Miscalculate a jump and you could find yourself in the absolute past, relative to both your starting point and the destination. You might not know it until you went home, but you'd just violated causality. And the Eschaton had a *serious* problem with people who did *that*.

. This was why Contingency Omega was one of the more sensitive documents in the New Republican Navy's war plan library. Contingency Omega discussed possible ways and means of using causality violation—time travel within the preferred reference frame—for strategic advantage. Rochard's World was a good forty light-years from New Austria; normally that meant five to eight jumps, a fairly serious journey lasting three or four weeks. Now, in time of war, the direct approach zones from New Austria could be presumed to be under guard. Any attack fleet would have to jump around the Queen's Head Nebula, an effectively impassable cloud within which three or four protostellar objects were forming. And to exercise Contingency Omega—delicately balancing their arrival time against the receipt of the first distress signal from Rochard's World, so that no *absolute* causality violation would take place but their arrival would take their enemies by surprise—well, that would add even more jumps, taking them deep into their own future light cone before looping back into the past, just inside the spacelike event horizon.

It was, Bauer realized, going to be the longest-range military operation in the history of the New Republic. And—God help him—it was his job to make sure it worked.

burya rubenstein whacked on the crude log table with a worn-out felt boot. "Silence!" he yelled. Nobody paid any attention; annoyed, he pulled out the compact pistol the trade machine had fabricated for him and fired into the ceiling. It only buzzed quietly, but the resulting fall of plaster dust got everybody's attention. In the midst of all the choking and coughing, he barked, "Committee will come to order!"

"Why should we?" demanded a heckler at the back of the packed beer hall.

"Because if you don't shut up and let me talk, you'll have to answer to Politovsky and his dragoons. The worst *I'll* do to you is shoot you—if the Duke gets his hands on you, you might have to work for a living!" Laughter. "*His* living. What we've got here is an unprecedented opportunity to cast off the shackles of economic slavery that bind us to soil and factory, and bring about an age of enlightened social mobility in which we are free to better ourselves, contribute to the common good, and learn to work smarter and live faster. But, comrades, the forces of reaction are ruthless and vigilant; even now a Navy shuttle is ferrying soldiers to Outer Chelm, which they plan to take and turn into a strongpoint against us."

Oleg Timoshevski stood up with an impressive whining and

clanking. "No worries! We'll smash 'em!" He waved his left arm in the air, and his fist morphed into the unmistakable shape of a gun launcher. Having leapt into the pool of available personal augmentation techniques with the exuberance of the born cyborg, he could pose as a poster for the Transhumanist Front, or even the Space and Freedom Party.

"That's enough, Oleg." Burya glared at him, then turned back to the audience. "We can't afford to win this by *violence*," he stressed. "In the short term, that may be tempting, but it will only serve to discredit us with the masses, and tradition tells us that, without the masses on our side, there can be no revolution. We have to prove that the forces of reaction corrode before our peace-loving forces for enterprise and progress without the need for repression—or ultimately all we will succeed in doing is supplanting those forces, and in so doing become indistinguishable from them. Is *that what you want?*"

"No! Yes! NO!" He winced at the furor that washed across the large room. The delegates were becoming exuberant, inflated with a sense of their own irresistible destiny, and far too much free wheat beer and vodka. (It might be synthetic, but it was indistinguishable from the real thing.)

"Comrades!" A fair-haired man, middle-aged and of sallow complexion, stood inside the main door to the hall. "Your attention please! Reactionary echelons of the imperialist junta are moving to encircle the Northern Parade Field! The free market is in danger!"

"Oh bugger," muttered Marcus Wolff.

"Go see to it, will you?" Burya asked. "Take Oleg, get him out of my hair, and I'll hold the fort here. Try to find something for Jaroslav to do while you're about it—he can juggle or fire his water pistol at the soldiers or something; I can't do with him getting underfoot."

"Will do that, boss. Are you serious about, uh, not breaking heads?"

"Am I serious?" Rubenstein shrugged. "I'd rather we didn't go nuclear, but feel free to do anything necessary to gain the upper hand—as long as we keep the moral high ground. If possible. We don't need a fight now; it's too early. Hold off for a week, and the guards will be deserting like rats leaving a sinking ship. Just try to divert them for now. I've got a communiqué to issue which ought to put the cat among the pigeons with the lackeys of the ruling class."

Wolff stood and walked around to Timoshevski's table. "Oleg, come with me. We have a job to do." Burya barely noticed: he was engrossed, nose down in the manual of a word processor that the horn of plenty had dropped in his lap. After spending his whole life writing longhand or using a laborious manual typewriter, this was altogether too much like black magic, he reflected. If only he could figure out how to get it to count the number of words in a paragraph, he'd be happy: but without being able to cast off, how could he possibly work out how much lead type would be needed to fill a column properly?

The revolutionary congress had been bottled up in the old Corn Exchange for three days now. Bizarre growths like black metal ferns had colonized the roof, turning sunlight and atmospheric pollution into electricity and brightly colored plastic cutlery. Godunov, who was supposed to be in charge of catering, had complained bitterly at the lack of tableware (as if any true revolutionary would bother with such trivia) until Misha, who had gotten much deeper into direct brain interfaces than even Oleg, twitched his nose and instructed the things on the roof to start producing implements. Then Misha went away on some errand, and nobody could turn the spork factory off. Luckily there seemed to be no shortage of food, munitions, or anything else for that matter: it seemed that Burya's bluff had convinced the Duke that the democratic soviet really did have nuclear weapons, and for the time being the dragoons were steering well clear of the yellow brick edifice at the far end of Freedom Square.

"Burya! Come quickly! Trouble at the gates!"

Rubenstein looked up from his draft proclamation. "What is it?" he snapped. "Speak clearly!"

The comrade (Petrov, wasn't that his name?) skidded to a halt in front of his desk. "Soldiers," he gasped.

"Aha." Burya stood. "Are they shooting yet? No? Then I will talk to them." He stretched, trying to ease the stiffness from his aching muscles and blinking away tiredness. "Take me to them."

A small crowd was milling around the gates to the Corn Exchange. Peasant women with head scarves, workers from the ironworks on the far side of town—idle since their entire factory had been replaced by a miraculous, almost organic robot complex that was still extending itself—even a few gaunt, shaven-headed zeks from the corrective labor camp behind the castle: all milling around a small clump of frightened-looking soldiers. "What is going on?" demanded Rubenstein.

"These men, they say—"

"Let them speak for themselves." Burya pointed to the one nearest the gate. "You. You aren't shooting at us, so why are you here, comrade?"

"I, uh," the trooper paused, looking puzzled.

"We's sick of being pushed around by them aristocrats, that's wot," said his neighbor, a beanpole-shaped man with a sallow complexion and a tall fur hat that most certainly wasn't standard-issue uniform. "Them royalist parasite bastids, they's locked up in 'em's castle drinking champagne and 'specting us to die keeping 'em safe. While out here all 'uns enjoying themselves and it's like the end of the regime, like? I mean, wot's going on? Has true libertarianism arrived yet?"

"Welcome, comrades!" Burya opened his arms toward the soldier. "Yes, it is true! With help from our allies of the Festival, the iron hand of the reactionary junta is about to be overthrown for all time! The new economy is being born; the marginal cost of production has been abolished, and from now on, if any item is produced once, it can be replicated infinitely. From each according to his imagination, to each according to his needs! Join us, or better still, bring your fellow soldiers and workers to join us!"

There was a sharp bang from the roof of the Corn Exchange, right at the climax of his impromptu speech; heads turned in alarm. Something had broken inside the spork factory and a stream of rainbow-hued plastic implements fountained toward the sky and clattered to the cobblestones on every side, like a harbinger of the postindustrial society to come. Workers and peasants alike stared in open-mouthed bewilderment at this astounding display of productivity, then bent to scrabble in the muck for the brightly colored sporks of revolution. A volley of shots rang out and Burya Rubenstein raised his hands, grinning wildly, to accept the salute of the soldiers from the Skull Hill garrison.

"the evening news bulletin. And now for today's headlines. The crisis over the invasion of Rochard's World by the so-called Festival continues. Attempts at diplomatic intermediation having been rebuffed, it now appears that military action is inevitable. Word from the occupied territory is hard to obtain, but to the best of our knowledge, the garrison under Duke Politovsky continue to fight valiantly to defend the Imperial standard. Ambassador Al-Haq of Turku said earlier on this program that the government of Turku agreed that the expansionist policies of the so-called Festival represent an intolerable threat to peace.

"The woman who chained herself to the railings of the Imperial residence yesterday morning, demanding votes and property rights for ladies, has been found to have a long history of mental disorders characterized by paranoid hysteria. Leaders of the Mothers' Union today denied any knowledge of her actions and decried them as unfeminine. She is expected to be charged with causing a public disturbance later this week.

"Baseless rumors circulating on Old Earth about the Admiralty's planned rolling series of upgrades to our naval capability caused numerous extraplanetary investment companies to sell stocks short, resulting in a plummeting exchange rate and the withdrawal of several insurance companies from the New Republic market. No announcement has yet been made by the chairman of the Royal Bank, but officials from the chamber of trade are currently drawing up charges against those companies participating in the stampede, accusing them of slander and conspiracy to establish a trade cartel using the current defense alert as a pretext.

"The four anarchists hanged at Krummhopf Prison today were attended by—"

Click.

"I hate this fucking planet," Martin whispered, sinking deeper into the porcelain bathtub. It was the only good feature of the poky little two-room dockside apartment they'd plugged him into. (The bad features, of course, included the likelihood of bugging devices.) He stared at the ceiling, two meters above him, trying to ignore the radio news.

The phone rang.

Cursing, Martin hauled himself out of the bath and, dripping, hopped into the living room. "Yes?" he demanded.

"Had a good day?" A woman's voice; it took him a second to place it.

"Lousy," he said with feeling. *And hearing from you doesn't make it any better,* he thought: the idea of being sucked into some kind of diplomatic scam didn't appeal. But the urge to grumble overrode minor irritation. "Their list of embargoed technology includes cranial interfaces. It's all crappy VR immersion gloves and keyboards: everything I look at now is covered in purple tesseracts, and my fingers ache."

"Well, it sounds like you've had a really good day, compared to mine. Have you had anything to eat yet?"

"Not yet." Suddenly Martin noticed that he was starving, not to mention bored. "Why?"

"You're going to like this," she said lightly. "I know a reasonable restaurant on C deck, two up and three corridors over from security zone gateway five. Can I buy you dinner?"

Martin thought for a moment. Normally he'd have refused, seeking some way to avoid contact with the UN diplomatic spook. But he was hungry; and not just for food. The casual invitation reminded him of home, of a place where people were able to talk freely. The lure of company drew him out, and after dressing, he followed her directions, trying not to think too deeply about it.

The visiting officers' quarters were outside the security zone of the base, but there was still a checkpoint to pass through before he reached the airlock to the civilian sections of the station. Outside the checkpoint, he stepped into a main corridor. It curved gently to the left, following the interior of the station's circumference: more passages opened off it, as did numerous doorways. He walked around a corner and out onto the street—"Martin!" She took his arm. "So pleased to see you!"

She'd changed into a green dress with a tight bodice and long black gloves. Her shoulders and upper arms were bare, but for a ribbon around her throat, which struck him as odd; something in his customs briefing nagged at his memory. "Pretend you're pleased to see me," she hissed. "Pretend for the cameras. You're taking me out to buy me dinner. And call me Ludmilla in public."

"Certainly." He forced a smile. "My dear! How nice to see you!" He took her arm and tried to follow her lead. "Which way?" he muttered.

"You're doing fine for an amateur. Third establishment on the right. There's a table in your name. I'm your companion for the night. Sorry about the cloak-and-dagger bit, but you're being monitored by base security, and if I were officially here as me, they'd start asking you questions. It's much more convenient if I'm a woman of easy virtue."

Martin flushed. "I see," he said. The penny dropped, finally: in this straitlaced culture, a woman who displayed bare skin below her chin was a bit racy, to say the least. Which meant, now he thought about it, that the hotel was full of—

"You haven't used the hotel facilities since you arrived?" she asked, raising an eyebrow.

Martin shook his head. "I don't believe in getting arrested in foreign jurisdictions," he mumbled to cover his discomfort. "And the local customs here are confusing. What do *you* think of them?"

She squeezed his arm. "No comment," she said lightly. "Ladies here aren't supposed to swear." She gathered her skirts in as he opened the door for her. "Still, I doubt this social order will last many more years. They've had to invest a lot of energy to maintain the *status quo* so long."

"You sound like you're looking forward to its collapsing." He held out his card to a liveried waiter, who bowed and scurried off into the restaurant.

"I am. Aren't you?"

Martin sighed quietly. "Now that you come to mention it, I wouldn't shed any tears. All I want to do is get this job over with and go home again."

"I wish my life were that simple. I can't afford to be angry: I'm supposed to help protect this civilization from the consequences of its own stupidity. It's hard to fix social injustices when the people you're trying to help are all dead."

"Your table, sir," said the waiter, reappearing and bowing deeply. Rachel emitted an airheaded giggle; Martin followed the waiter, with Rachel in tow behind him.

She kept up the bubbleheaded pose until they were seated in a private booth and had ordered the menu of the day. As soon as the waiter disappeared, she dropped it. "You want to know what's going on, who I am, and what this is all about," she said quietly. "You also want to know whether you should cooperate, and what's in it for you. Right?"

He nodded, unwilling to open his mouth, wondering how much she knew of his real business.

"Good." She stared at him soberly. "I take it you already decided not to turn me in to base security. That would have been a bad mistake, Martin; if not for you, then for a lot of other people."

He lowered his gaze, staring at the place setting in front of her. Silver cutlery, linen napkin, starched tablecloth overflowing on all sides like a waterfall. And Rachel's breasts. Her dress made it impossible to ignore them, even though he tried not to stare: woman of easy virtue, indeed. He settled for looking her in the face. "There's something I don't understand going on here," he said. "What is it?"

"All will be explained. The first thing I'm going to say is, after you hear my pitch, you can walk away unless you decide to involve yourself. I mean it; I came on heavily earlier, but really, I don't want you around unless you're a willing participant. Right now, they think you're just a loud-mouthed engineer. If they look too closely at me—" She paused. Her lips thinned a little. "I'm female. I'll get precious little mercy if they trip over me by accident, but they don't really think of women as free agents, much less defense intelligence specialists, and by this time tomorrow, I should have my diplomatic credentials sorted out and be able to go public. Anyway: about what's going on here. Are you going to get up and walk out right now, or do you want in?"

Martin thought for a moment. *What should I do?* The solution seemed obvious: "I'll settle for some answers. And dinner. Anything's better than being locked up in that pesthole of a base."

"Okay." She leaned back comfortably. "First." She held up a gloved finger. "What's going on? That's actually a bit tricky to say. The UN has no jurisdiction here, but we've got enough clout to wreck the New Republic's trade treaties with half their neighbors if the New Republic was, for instance, found to be breaking conventions on warfare or application of forbidden technologies."

Martin snorted. "Forbidden tech? Them?"

"Do you really think they'd pass up the chance to steal an edge? The royal family, that is?"

"Hmm." Martin rubbed his chin thoughtfully. "Okay, so they're pragmatic rejectionists, is that what you're saying?"

"In a nutshell." She shrugged. Against his better judgment, Martin found himself staring somewhere below her chin: he forced himself to look up. "Our arms limitation arrangements have no authority here, but things are different closer to home, and a lot of the New Republic's trade flows in that direction. There's some recognition: once I get official accreditation, I've got diplomatic immunity, if they catch me and I live long enough to assert it. Two"—she held up another finger—"the arms limitation controls are to protect people from provoking intervention by the Eschaton. And they work both ways. As long as people stick to boring little things like planet-busting relativistic missiles and nerve gas or whatever, the big E doesn't get involved. But as soon as someone starts poking around the prohibited—for her coming-out party Daddy gave her an emerald *this* big!" She simpered, and Martin stared back, puzzled. Then he smiled fixedly as the waiter deposited a bowl of soup in front of him.

The waiter finished up, poured glasses of wine, and disappeared; Rachel pulled a face. "Huh, where was I? You wouldn't believe how fast the girly-girl routine gets tiresome. Having to act like a retarded ten-year-old all the time...ah yes, the big E. The big E disapproves strongly of people who develop autonomous, self-replicating weapons, or causality-violation devices, or a whole slew of other restricted tools of mass destruction. Bacteria: out. Gray goo: out. Anything that smacks of self-modifying command software: out. Those are all category two forbidden weapons. A planetary civilization starts playing with them, sooner or later the big E comes looking, and then it's an *ex*-planetary civilization."

Martin nodded, trying to look as if all this was new to him; he nipped his tongue to help resist the temptation to correct her last statement. Her engagement with the subject was infectious, and he found it hard to keep from contributing from his own knowledge of the field.

Rachel took a mouthful of soup. "The big E can be extremely brutal. We've got definite confirmation of at least one atypical supernova event about five hundred light-years outside our—the terrestrial—light cone. It makes sense if you're trying to wipe out an exponentially propagating threat, so we figure that's why the Eschaton did it. Anyway, do you agree that it's bad policy to let the neighbor's toddler play with strategic nukes?"

"Yeah." Martin nodded. He took a mouthful of soup. "Something like that could really stop you getting to claim your on-time completion bonus."

She narrowed her eyes, then nodded to him. "Sarcasm, yet. How have you kept out of trouble so far?"

"I haven't." He put his spoon down. "That's why, if you don't mind me saying so, I was worried by your approach. I can do without getting myself slung in prison."

Rachel took a breath. "I'm sorry," she said. "I don't know if that'll go very far with you, but...I mean it. I'd just like to put it in a bigger perspective, though. The New Republic is only 250 light-years from Earth. If the big E decided to pop the primary here, we'd need to evacuate fifty star systems." She looked uncomfortable. "That's what this is about. That's why I had to drag you in."

She looked down and concentrated on her soup bowl with single-minded determination. Martin watched her fixedly; his appetite was gone. She had done a robust job of destroying it by reminding him of why he was here. His parents, he didn't much care for, but he had a sister he was fond of on Mars, and too many friends and memories to want to hear any more about this. It was easier to watch her eat, to admire the flawless blush of the skin on her arms and her *décolletage*—he blinked, picked up his wineglass, and drained it in one. She looked up, caught him watching, grinned widely—theatrically, even—and licked her lips slowly. The effect was too much; he turned away.

"Shit and corruption, man, we're supposed to look as if you're buying me dinner as a prelude to taking me home and fucking me senseless!" she said quietly. "Can't you at least fake some interest?"

"Sorry," he said, taken aback; "I'm not an actor. Is that what we're supposed to look like we're doing?"

She raised her wineglass: it was empty. "Fill me up. Please." She looked at him peculiarly; he twitched upright then reached out, took the wine bottle, and poured some of its contents into her glass. "I didn't want to put you off your appetite. Besides, you're the only civilized company for a couple of thousand miles."

"I'm a drive engineer," he said, wracking his brain for something else to say. *What am I getting myself into?* he wondered desperately. A couple of hours ago he'd been going crazy from boredom and loneliness: now an intelligent and attractive woman—who just happened to be a spy—had dragged him out to dinner. Something was bound to go wrong, wasn't it?

"I like working with machines. I like starships. I—" He cleared his throat. "I'm not so good with people."

"And this is a problem?"

"Yeah." He nodded, then looked at her appraisingly. Her expression was sympathetic. "I keep misreading the locals. *Not* good. So I holed up in my room and tried to stay out of the way."

"And now, let me guess, you're going stir-crazy?"

"After four months of it, that's one way of putting it." He took a mouthful of wine. "How about you?"

She breathed deeply. "Not quite the same, but nearly. I've got a job to do. I'm supposed to avoid getting into trouble. Part of the job is blending in, but it drives you nuts after a bit. Really, doing this face-to-face isn't recommended in the rule book, you know? It'd be safer just to drop an earbug off to relay you a message."

"And you were." He smiled faintly. "Stir-crazy."

"Yes." She grinned. "You too?"

"Anyone waiting for you back home?" he asked. "Sorry. I

mean, is there anyone you're waiting to get back to? Or anyone you can off-load onto? Write letters, or something?"

"Pah." She frowned, then looked at him. "This isn't a profession for someone who's married to anything other than their job, Martin. Any more than yours is. If you *were* married, would you bring your family out to somewhere like the New Republic?"

"No. I didn't mean it like that—"

"I know you didn't." Her frown dissolved into a thoughtful expression. "Just once in a while, though, it's good to be able to talk freely."

Martin toyed with his wineglass. "Agreed," he said with feeling. "I got bitten by that last week." He stopped. She was looking at him oddly, her face stretched into something that might be taken for a smile if he couldn't see her eyes. Which looked worried.

"Smile at me. Yes, that's fine: now hold on to it. Don't stop smiling. We're under surveillance right now. Don't worry about the microphone—that's taken care of—but there's a human operative watching us from the other side of the restaurant. Try to look like you want to take me home and fuck me. Otherwise, he's going to wonder what we're doing here." She simpered at him, smiling broadly. "Do you think I'm pretty?" Her idiot grin was a mask: she inspected him from behind it.

"Yes—" He stared at her, hoping he looked adequately besotted. "I think you're very pretty." In the way that only a good diet and high-end medical care could deliver. He tried to smile wider. "Uh. Actually. Handsome and determined is more like it." Her smile acquired a slightly glassy edge.

Somewhere in the middle of the duel of the smiles, the waiter arrived and removed their bowls, replacing them with a main course.

"Oh, that looks good." She relaxed slightly as she picked up her knife and fork. "Hmm. Don't look around, but our shadow is looking away. You know something? You're too much of a gentleman for your own good. Most of the men in this joint would have tried to grope me by now. It goes with the territory."

"After about fifty or sixty years, most men learn to stop worrying that it'll go away if they don't grab for it with both hands. Trouble is, with no antiaging treatments here—" He looked uncomfortable.

"Yeah, and I appreciate it." She smiled back. "Anyone ever tell you you're cute when you grin? I've spent so long in this dump that I've forgotten what an honest smile looks like, let alone how it feels to be able to talk like a mature adult. Anyway..." he started. Her toe had just stroked the inside of his left leg. "I think I like you," she said quietly.

Martin paused a moment, then nodded soberly. "Consider me charmed."

"Really?" She grinned and slid her toe higher.

His breath caught. "Don't! You'll cause a scandal!" He glanced around in mock horror. "I hope nobody's watching."

"No chance, that's what the tablecloth is meant to cover up." She laughed quietly, and after a moment, he joined her. She continued quietly, "To get the business over with so we can enjoy the meal, tomorrow you're going to go back aboard the *Lord Vanek* and they're probably going to ask you if you want to earn some more money in return for an extension on your contract. If you want to line your pocket and maybe help save several million lives you'll say *yes*. I happen to know that the admiral's staff is going to be using the *Lord Vanek* as flagship, and I'm going to be along too—"

"You're *what?* How are you going to do that?"

"As a diplomatic observer. My job is to make sure the Festival—and I wish I knew a bit more about who they are—don't violate six different treaties. Unofficially, I want to keep an eye on the New Republic, too. There's a bit more going on than anyone's willing to admit; no, make that a lot. But we don't want to let it get in the way of this meal, do we? If you agree, come home with me to a safe house, and I'll fill you in on the rest, while the local Stasi will just think you're making out like any other bachelor engineering contractor. So you're going to go home with a nice fat paycheck, plus a big bonus paid by DefIntelSIG. Everything's going to be *just fine.* Now, how about we forget business and eat our dinner before it gets cold?"

"Sounds okay to me." Martin leaned forward. "About the cover story for the local Stasi."

"Yes." She picked up her fork.

"Does it extend to grabbing a bottle of wine on our way home? And chilling out together afterward?"

"Well I suppose—" She stared at him. He noticed that her pupils were dilated.

"You need someone to talk to," he said slowly.

"Don't I just." She put the fork down. Under the table, out of sight, she rubbed his ankle again. Martin felt his pulse, felt his face flushing. She was focused on him, intent.

"How long has it been for you?" he asked quietly.

"Longer than four months." Suddenly her foot was removed.

"Better eat up," he said. "If you want our cover story to be any good."

"clear channel to Herman, PA."

"Clear channel pending...connected. Hello, Martin. What can I do for you?"

"Got a problem."

"A big one?"

"Female human-sized. Actually she's from Earth, she's gorgeous, and, uh, she does undercover work for the UN defense intelligence SIG. Specializing in causality-violation weapons, disarmament treaty infractions, that sort of thing."

"That is interesting. Say more."

"Name's Rachel Mansour. Has what looks like genuine ID as a UN weapons inspector, and there's no way in hell she's a native or an agent provocateur—not unless they're sending their female agents off planet for education. She says that New Prague is planning some kind of naval expedition to relieve this colony that's under siege, and that she expects they'll try to recruit me tomorrow to do wartime crisis work on the ships. What she wanted me to do—well, basically keep my eyes open for anything fishy or illegal. Strategic weapons violations, I guess. That's an opening position. The question—"

"No forward-leaning analysis, please. Are you aware of any other UN inspectors in the vicinity?"

"Not directly, but she mentioned she has some kind of local backup and diplomatic credentials. She says she'll be along on the expedition. I expect there's a full-scale UN black ops team behind her, probably looking to do some low-key destabilization: it's not as if the New Republic hasn't been asking for it since they began the current naval buildup. I'm pretty sure she was telling me the truth about her mission goals, but only part of it."

"Correct. On what basis did you leave her?"

"I agreed to do what she wanted." Martin paused, unconsciously censoring his testimony, then continued, "If you think it's advisable, I'll accept any offer of wartime work at hazard pay. Then I'll do what she wants: keep my eyes open for illegal activities. Any objection? How bad do you think the situation is?"

"It is much worse than you think."

Martin did a double take. "What?"

"I know of Rachel Mansour. Please wait." His PA fell silent for almost a minute, while he sat in the dark of his rented room and waited anxiously. Herman never fell silent; like a machine running smoothly, his emollient debriefings made Martin feel as if he were talking to himself. Answers there might or might not be, but never silence...

"Martin. Please listen. I have independent confirmation that there is indeed a UN covert mission in the New Republic. Lead special agent is Rachel Mansour, which means they expect serious trouble. She is a heavyweight, and she's been out of sight for almost a year, which implies she's been in the New Republic for most of that time. Meanwhile, the agency representatives on Luna have bought out your personnel files and have been talking to MiG management about contracting you. Furthermore, they are substantially correct in their analysis. The New Republic is preparing to send the entire home fleet to Rochard's World, going the long way around, where they intend to attack the Festival. This is a very bad idea—they obviously do not understand the Festival— but preparations appear to be too advanced to divert at this time.

"It is also quite possible that you will endanger yourself if you appear to be panicking. Given the current level of surveillance you are under, an attempt to cut and run to a civil liner will be seen as treason and punished immediately by the Curator's security apparat; and Mansour is unlikely to be able to protect you even if she wants to. I emphasize, the New Republic is already on a low-key war footing, and attempting to leave now will be difficult."

"Oh shit."

"The situation is not irretrievable. I want you to cooperate fully with Mansour. Do your job and get out quietly. I will attempt to arrange for you to disembark safely once the fleet arrives. Remember, you are in more danger if you run than if you withdraw quietly."

Martin felt a tension he'd barely been conscious of leaving him. "Okay. Do you have any backstop options for me if the UN screws up? Any ideas for how I can get out with my skin intact? Any information about this Festival, whatever it is?"

Herman was silent for a moment. "Be aware that this is now

definitely a direct-action situation." Martin gasped and sat bolt upright. "I want you on hand in case things, to use your own terminology, go pear-shaped. Millions of lives are at stake. Larger-scale political issues are also becoming clear; if the New Republic meets the Festival, it is possible that the resulting instabilities will catalyze a domestic revolution. The UN subscribing bodies, both governmental and quasi-governmental, have a vested interest in this for obvious reasons. I cannot tell you more about the Festival at this point, because you would incriminate yourself if you betrayed any knowledge of it; but it is accurate to say that the Republic is more of a danger to itself than to the Festival. However, in view of the nature of the situation, I am prepared to pay a bonus double the size of that promised by the UN inspectorate if you remain in place after completing their assignment and do as I request."

Martin's throat was dry. "Alright. But if it's that likely to go critical, I want three times the bonus. In event of my death, payable to my next of kin."

Silence. Then: "Accepted. Herman out."

rachel lay in bed, staring at the ceiling, and tried to pick apart her feelings. It was early morning: Martin had left sometime ago. She had a bad feeling about the business, even though it was clearly going well; something gnawed at her below the level of conscious awareness. Presently, she rolled sideways, laid her sleepless head back on the overstuffed pillow beside her, and drew her knees up.

It should have been a simple recruitment meeting: put the arm on a useful contact and brief him for a single task. Nice and objective. Instead, she'd found herself sharing a dinner table with a quiet but fundamentally decent man who hadn't tried to grope her, didn't treat her like a piece of furniture, *listened* with a serious expression, and made interesting conversation: the kind of man who in ordinary circumstances she'd have considered a pleasant date. She'd gone a little bit crazy, walking along a knife edge of irresponsibility: and he'd been stir-crazy too. And now she was worried about him—which wasn't in the plan.

It had come to a head across the kitchen table as they finished discussing business. He had looked up at her with a curious expectancy in his eyes. She crossed her legs, let a foot peep out beneath her skirts. He studied her intently.

"Is that everything?" he asked. "You want me to keep my eyes open for clock-skew rollback instructions, carry the plug-in, notify you if I see anything that looks like a CVD—that's all?"

"Yes," she said, staring at him. "That's essentially everything."

"It's ah—" He looked at her askance, sharply. "I thought there was something more to it."

"Maybe there is." She folded her hands in her lap. "But only if you want."

"Oh, *well*," he said, absorbing the information. "What else is part of the job?"

"Nothing." She tilted her head, meeting his angled gaze, steeling herself. "We've finished with business. Do you remember what I said earlier, back in the restaurant?"

"About—" He nodded. Then looked away.

"What's wrong?" she asked.

"Oh, nothing." He sighed quietly.

"Bullshit." She stood up. "Come on. Let's talk." She reached for his hand and gave him a little tug.

"What?" He shook his head. "I'm just—"

"Come on." She pulled a little harder. "The parlor. Come on."

"Okay." He stood up. He was no taller than she was; and he seemed to be avoiding her eyes. Uncomfortable, really.

"What's wrong?" she asked again.

He chuckled briefly; there was no amusement in it. "You're the first sane person I've met in the past four months," he said quietly. "I was getting used to talking."

She looked at him, steadily. "You don't have to stop," she said.

"I—" He froze up again. *Why is he doing that?* she wondered.

"Say something," she said.

"I—" He paused, and she was afraid he was going to stop. Then he burst out, all at once. "I don't *want* to stop. This place is squeezing me into my own head all the time—it's like being in a vise! The only thing anyone wants of me is my work—"

Rachel leaned against him. "Shut up," she said quietly. He shut up. "That's better." He was, she decided, really good at being leaned on. She put her arms around him; after a moment he hugged her back. "Forget work. Yeah, you heard me. Forget the New Republic. Think you can do that for a few hours?"

"I—" she felt his breath shuddering. "I'll try."

"Good," she said fiercely. And it *did* feel good: here was somebody who she could be sure about. Somebody who seemed to feel the same way about this whole claustrophobic abortion of a culture as she did. He held her steadily, now, and she could feel his hands running up and down her back, exploring how narrow her waist was. "The parlor. Come on, it's the next room."

Martin had stared back at her. "You sure you want this?" he asked. That was part of his charm.

"What's to be unsure about?" She kissed him hard, exploring his lips with her tongue. She felt as if she was about to burst right out of her clothes. He gently pulled her closer and let her dig her chin into the base of his neck; she felt stubble on his cheek. "It's been so fucking *long*," she whispered.

"Same to you too." He took some of her weight in his arms. "Been lonely?"

She barked a hoarse laugh. "You have no idea. I've been here ages; long enough that I feel like some kind of deviant because I talk to strange men and have some role in life besides hatching babies. The way they think here is getting its claws into me."

"What? A big strong government agent like you is letting something like this get to you?" he said, gently mocking.

"You're damn right," she muttered into his shoulder as she felt a tentative hand begin to explore below her waistline.

"Sorry. Just—six months alone in this dump, having to act the part? I'd have gone nuts," he said thoughtfully.

"Been more than six months," she said, looking past the side of his head. *He has nice earlobes,* she noted vaguely as she leaned closer.

"Let's find that wine bottle," he suggested gently. "I think you're going a bit fast."

"I'm sorry," she said, automatically. "I'm sorry." She tensed slightly. "No, you can keep your hands there. Let's walk."

They somehow made it into the parlor—overstuffed armchairs and a display cabinet full of crockery—without letting go of each other.

"At first I thought you were some kind of agent provocateur," he said, "but instead you're the first real human being I've met in this place." He left the statement hanging.

"If all I needed was flesh, there are plenty of sailor boys in this port," she said, and leaned against him again. "That's not where my itch is."

"Are you sure you should be in this job? If you're so—"

"You were going to say vulnerable?"

"Maybe. Not exactly."

She guided him in front of the sofa. "I wanted company. Not just a quick fuck," she explained, trying to justify it to herself.

"You and me both." He held her, gently turned her around so that she was looking into his eyes. "So what do you want this to be?"

"Stop talking." She leaned forward closing her eyes, and found his mouth. Then events ran out of control.

They'd made love with desperate urgency the first time, Rachel lying on the parlor floor with her skirts hiked up around her waist, and Martin with his trousers tangled around his legs. Then they somehow migrated to the bedroom and struggled out of their clothing before making love again, this time gently and slowly. Martin had a thoughtful, considerate manner: talking afterward, he'd mentioned a divorce a few years ago. They'd talked for hours, almost until the artificial dawn, timed to coincide with sunrise on the planet below. And they'd made love until they were both sore and aching.

Now, lying awake in bed after he'd left, her head was spinning. She tried to rationalize it: isolation and nerves are enough to make anyone do something wild once in a while. Still, she felt nervous: Martin wasn't a casual pickup, and this wasn't a quick fuck. Just the thought of seeing him again made her feel an edgy hopeful excitement, tempered by the bitter self-disgust of realizing that mixing business with pleasure this way was a really stupid move.

She rolled over, and blinked: the clock on the inside of her left eyelid said it was just past 0700. In another two hours, it would be time to get confirmation of her diplomatic status, dress, and go kick some New Republican ass. Two hours after that, Martin would be aboard the *Lord Vanek;* it would all be over by 2200. Rachel sighed and tried to catch another hour's shut-eye; but sleep was evading her.

She found herself wandering, seeking out pleasant memories. There was not a lot else to be done, in point of fact: there was a high probability that she would die if her guess about the New Republic's intentions was wrong. And wouldn't that be a grand way to end 150 years? Physically as young as a twentysomething, kept that way by the advanced medical treatments of the mother planet, she rarely felt the weight of her decades; the angst only cut in when she thought about how few of the people she had known or loved were still alive. Now she recalled her daughter, as a child, the smell of her—and what brought *that* back? Not her daughter, the political matriarch and leader of a dynasty. Not the octogenarian's funeral, either, in the wake of the skysail accident. And she couldn't even remember Johan's face, even though they'd been married for fifteen years. Martin, so much more recent, seemed to overlay him in her mind's eye. She blinked, angrily, and sat up.

Stupid girl, she told herself, ironically. *Anyone would think you were still in your first century, falling in love with a tight pair of buttocks.* Still, she found herself looking forward to seeing Martin again tomorrow night. The edgy hopeful excitement was winning over age and cynicism, even though she was old enough to know what it meant. Complications...

the interorbit shuttle unlatched from the naval docking bay and edged outward from the beanstalk, its cold-gas thrusters bumping it clear of the other vehicles that swarmed in the region. Ten minutes after it maneuvered free, the pilot got permission from traffic control to light off his main drive; a bright orange plume of glowing mercury ions speared out from three large rectangular panels hinged around the rear cargo bay doors, and the craft began to accelerate. Ion drives were notoriously slow, but they were also efficient. After a thousand seconds the shuttle was moving out from the station at nearly two hundred kilometers per hour, and it was time to begin decelerating again to meet the ship that now lay at rest almost sixty kilometers from the station.

In orbital terms, sixty kilometers was nothing; the *Lord Vanek* was right on the beanstalk's doorstep. But there was one significant advantage to the position. The ship was ready to move, and move fast. As soon as the dockyard engineer finished his upgrade to the driver kernel's baseline compensators, she'd be ready for action.

Captain Mirsky watched the shuttle nose up to *Lord Vanek*'s forward docking bays on one of the video windows at his workstation. He sat alone in his quarters, plowing relentlessly through the memoranda and directives associated with the current situation; things had become quite chaotic since the orders came down, and he was acutely aware of how much more preparation was required.

Middle-aged, barrel-chested, and sporting a neat salt-and-pepper beard to match his graying hair, Captain Mirsky was the very model of a New Republic Navy captain. Behind the mask of confidence, however, there was a much less certain man: he had seen things building up for a week now, and however he tried to rationalize the situation, he couldn't escape the feeling that something had gone off the rails between the foreign office and the Imperial residence.

He peered morosely at the latest directive to cross his desk. Security was being stepped up, and he was to go onto a wartime footing as soon as the last shipyard workers and engineers were off his deck and the hull was sealed. Meanwhile, full cooperation was required with Procurator Muller of the Curator's Office, on board to pursue positive security monitoring of foreign engineering contractors employed in making running repairs to *Lord Vanek*'s main propulsion system. He glared at the offending memo in irritation, then picked up his annunciator. "Get me Ilya."

"Commander Murametz, sir? Right away, sir."

A muffled knock on the door: Mirsky shouted "open!" and it opened. Commander Murametz, his executive officer, saluted. "Come in, Ilya, come in."

"Thank you, sir. What I can do for you?"

"This—" Mirsky pointed wordlessly at his screen. "Some pompous Citizen Curator wants his minion to run riot over my ship. Know anything about it?"

Murametz bent closer. "Humbly report, sir, I do." His moustache twitched; Mirsky couldn't tell what emotion it signified.

"Hah. Pray explain."

"Some fuss over the engineering contractor from Earth who's installing our Block B drive upgrade. He's irreplaceable, at least without waiting three months, but he's a bit of a loudmouth and somehow caught the attention of one of the professional paranoids in the Basilisk. So they've stuck a secret policeman on us to take care of him. I gave him to Lieutenant Sauer, with orders to keep him out of our hair."

"What does Sauer say about it?"

Murametz snorted. "The cop's as wet behind the ears as one of the new ratings. No problem."

The Captain sighed. "See that there isn't."

"Aye aye, sir. Anything else?"

Mirsky waved at a chair. "Sit down, sit down. Noticed anything out of the ordinary about what's going on?"

Murametz glanced at the doorway. "Rumors are flying like bullets, skipper. I'm doing what I can to sit on them, but until there's an official line—"

"There won't be. Not for another sixteen hours."

"If I may be so bold, what then?"

"Then..." The Captain paused. "I...am informed that I will be told, and that subsequently you, and all the other officers, will learn what's going on. In the meantime, I think it would be sensible to keep everybody busy. So busy that they don't have time to worry and spread rumors, anyway. Oh, and make damned sure the flag cabin's shipshape and we're ready to take on board a full staff team."

"*Ah.*" Murametz nodded. "Very well, sir. Operationally, hmm. Upgrade security, schedule some more inspections, heightened readiness on all stations? That sort of thing? Floggings to improve morale? A few simulation exercises for the tactical teams?"

Captain Mirsky nodded. "By all means. But get the flag cabin ready *first.* Ready for a formal inspection tomorrow. That's all."

"Yes, sir."

"Dismissed."

Murametz left, and Mirsky was alone with his morose thoughts once more. Alone to brood over the orders he was forbidden to reveal to anyone for another sixteen hours.

Alone with the sure, cold knowledge of impending war.

his majesty's battlecruiser *Lord Vanek* lay at rest, sixty kilometers from the Klamovka naval beanstalk. Running lights blinked red and blue along its flanks; the double-headed eagle ensign of the admiral's flag winked in green outline just above the main missile launch platform. Kurtz had been piped aboard two hours earlier; soon the ship would be ready to fly.

Rachel Mansour worked hard at suppressing the treacherous grin of satisfaction that kept threatening to escape. The reaction she'd elicited from the security goons at the entrance to the base almost made up for the preceding three months of isolation and paranoia. They'd barely managed to hold her up before her phone call to the embassy dragged a flustered lieutenant commander out to blush red and stammer in front of her. When he'd half questioned her intent, she'd rammed her credentials down his throat with gusto; he escorted her with her luggage directly to the shuttlecraft for transfer to the battlecruiser, shuddering slightly and glancing over his shoulder all the way. (Evidently self-propelled shipping chests were yet another technology that the New Republic shunned.)

Ludmilla Jindrisek, the cover identity she'd been using for the past month, had dissolved beneath the morning shower; Rachel Mansour, Special Agent, UN Standing Committee on Multilateral Interstellar Disarmament, stepped out of it. Ludmilla Jindrisek simpered, wore fashionable dresses, and deferred to wise male heads; Special Agent Mansour had started her career in bomb disposal (defusing terrorist nukes and disassemblers), graduated to calling in naval strikes on recalcitrant treaty-breakers, and wore a black paramilitary uniform designed specifically to impress militaristic outworlder hicks. It was, she noted, interesting to observe the effect the change of costume had on people, especially as she held her notional rank through equivalence, rather than actual military service. Meanwhile she watched her fellow passengers waiting under the beady eye of Chief Petty Officer Moronici.

The airlock door finally rolled open. "Attention!" barked the CPO. The ratings waiting in the bay stood sharply to attention. An officer ducked through the lock and straightened up: Moronici saluted, and he returned the gesture, ignoring Rachel.

"Very good there," said the officer. "Chief Moronici, get these kids aboard. Don't bother waiting for me, I've got business that'll keep me here until the next run." He glanced at Rachel. "You. What are you doing here?"

Rachel pointed her pass at him. "Diplomatic corps. I'm attached to the Admiral's staff, by special order of Archduke Michael, Lieutenant."

The Lieutenant gaped. "But you're a—"

"—colonel in the United Nations of Earth Security Council combined armed forces. What part of 'by special order of Archduke Michael' don't you understand? Are you going to stand there gaping, or are you going to invite me aboard?"

"Urgh. Um, yes." The Lieutenant disappeared back into the shuttle's flight deck; reappeared a minute later. "Um. Colonel, ah, Mansour? Please come aboard."

Rachel nodded and walked past him. Still carefully expressionless, she seated herself immediately behind the flight deck door, in officer country. And listened.

The CPO was educating the new intake. "At ease, you lads," he growled. "Find yerselves a seat. Front row, facing back, that's right! Now buckle in. All six points, that's right. Check the seat in front of you for a sick bag. Welcome to the vomit comet; this boat's too small to have any gravity emulators and doesn't accelerate faster'n a quadriplegic in a wheelbarrow, so if you get sick in free fall, you're damn well going to throw up into those bags. Anyone who pukes up on the furniture and fittings can spend the next week cleaning 'em. Got that?"

Everyone nodded. Rachel felt cautiously optimistic; it looked as if everyone else on this run, apart from Chief Moronici, was a new assignment to the ship. Which meant her information was probably correct: they were working up to wartime levels, and departure wouldn't be delayed long.

The door to the passenger cabin slid closed; there was a rumble below as automatic pallets rolled in and out of the shuttle's cargo bay. Moronici knocked on the forward door and went through when it opened; he reappeared a minute later. "Launch in two minutes," he announced. "Hang on tight!"

The two minutes passed at a snail's pace. Banging and thumping announced that dockside fuel and support lines were disconnecting; then there was a lurch and a jolt followed by a loud hissing that died away as the airlock seal was broken behind them. "You're all new fish here," Chief Moronici told the flyers. "Not surprising as we're taking on a lot of new crew. Start of a new conscription cycle. Me,"—he pointed a meaty thumb at his chest—"I'm not a conscript. I live on the ship we're going to. And I want to live on it long enough to collect my pension. Which means I don't intend to let you, or anyone else, do anything that endangers me or my home. The first rule of space travel"—they lurched sideways, drunkenly, and there was a disconcertingly loud rattle from underneath—"is that mistakes are fatal. Space isn't friendly; it kills you. And there are no second chances."

As if to emphasize the point, the bottom suddenly dropped out of Rachel's stomach. For a moment, she felt as if a huge, rubbery, invisible gripper was trying to pull her apart—and then she was floating. The ratings all looked as surprised as Chief Moronici looked smug.

"Main engine should come on in about five minutes," Moronici announced. Banging and clicking shuddered through the cramped cabin, as it veered gently to the left: thrusters were busy nudging it out of the dock. "Like I was saying, mistakes here tend to kill people. And I have no intention of letting you kill me. Which is why, while you're on board the *Lord Vanek,* you pukes will do exactly what I, or any other PO, or any officer, tells you to do. And you will do it with a shit-eating grin, or I will ram your head so far up your ass you'll be able to give yourself a tonsillectomy with your teeth. Is that understood?" He continued to ignore Rachel, implicitly acknowledging that she lay outside his reach.

The ratings nodded. One of them, green-faced, gulped, and Moronici swiftly yanked a sick bag from the back of an adjacent seat and held it in front of the man's face. Rachel saw what he was trying to do; the pep talk was as much a distraction from the disorientation of free fall as anything else.

Rachel closed her eyes and breathed deeply—then regretted it: the shuttle stank of stale sweat, with a faint undertone of ozone and the sickly-sweet odor of acetone. It had been a long time since she'd prayed for anything, but right now she was praying with all her might for this ride in a tin can to come to an end. It was the crummiest excuse for a shuttle she'd been on in decades, an old banger like something out of an historical drama. It seemed to go on and on. Until, of course, it stopped with a buffet and clang as they latched on to the *Lord Vanek*'s stabilized docking adapter, then a grinding creak as it pulled them in and spun them up, and a hiss as pressure equalized.

"Erm, Colonel?"

She opened her eyes. It was CPO Moronici. He looked somewhat green, as if unsure how to deal with her. "It's alright, Chief. I've gone aboard foreign naval vessels before." She stood. "Is there anyone waiting for me?"

"Yes'm." He stared straight ahead, as if outrageously embarrassed.

"Fine." She unbuckled, stood, feeling the uneven gravity of the battlecruiser's spin, and adjusted her beret. "Let me at them."

The airlock opened. "Section, pre-sent—arms!"

She stepped forward into the docking bay, feeling the incredulous stares from all sides. A senior officer, a commander if she read his insignia correctly, was waiting for her, face stiffly frozen to conceal the inevitable surprise. "Colonel Mansour, UN Disarmament Inspectorate," she said. "Hello, Commander—"

"Murametz." He blinked, perplexed. "Ah, your papers? Lieutenant Menvik says you're attached to the Admiral's staff. But they didn't tell us to expect you—"

"That's perfectly alright." She pointed him down the corridor that led to the ship's main service core. "They don't know about me yet. At least, not unless Archduke Michael warned them. Just take me to see the Admiral, and everything will be alright."

Her luggage rolled quietly after her, on a myriad of brightly colored ball bearings.

the admiral was having a bad morning: his false pregnancy was causing problems again.

"I feel ill," he mumbled quietly. "Do I have to—to get up?"

"It would help, sir." Robard, his batman, gently slid an arm around his shoulders to help him sit up. "We depart in four hours. Your staff meeting is penciled in for two hours after that, and you have an appointment with Commodore Bauer before then. Ah, there's also a communiqué from His Royal Highness that has a most-urgent seal on it."

"Well bring it—it—it in then," said the Admiral. "Damned morning sickness..."

Just then, the annunciator in the next room chimed softly. "I'll just check that, sir," said Robard. Then: "Someone to see you, sir. Without an appointment. Ah—it's a *what?* A—oh, I see. Alright then. He'll be ready in a minute." Pacing back into the bedroom, he cleared his throat. "Sir, are you ready? Ah, yes. Ahem. You have a visitor, sir. A diplomat who has been seconded to your staff by order of Archduke Michael; some sort of foreign observer."

"Oh." Kurtz frowned. "Didn't have any of them back at Second Lamprey. Just as well, really. Just lots of darkies. Bloody bad sports, those darkies, wouldn't stand still and be shot. Bloody foreigners. Show the man in!"

Robard cast a critical eye over his master. Sitting up in bed with his jacket wrapped around his shoulders, he looked like a convalescent turtle—but marginally presentable. As long as he didn't tell the ambassador all about his ailment, it could probably be passed off as an attack of gout. "Yes, sir."

The door opened and Robard's jaw dropped. Standing there was a stranger in a strange uniform. He had an attaché case clasped under one arm, and a rather bemused-looking commander standing beside him. Something about the man shrieked of strangeness, until Robard worked it out; his mouth twisted with distaste as he muttered, "Invert," to himself.

Then the stranger spoke—in a clear, high voice. "United Nations of Earth, Standing Committee on Multilateral Disarmament. I'm Colonel Mansour, special agent and military attaché to the embassy, attached to this expedition as an observer on behalf of the central powers. My credentials." *That voice! If I didn't know better, I'd swear he was a woman,* thought Robard.

"Thank you. If you'd come this way, please, my lord is indisposed but will receive you in his sleeping quarters." Robard bowed and backed into the Admiral's bedroom, where he was mortified to find the old man lying back on his pillows, mouth agape, snoring quietly.

"Ahem. Sir! Your Lordship!" A bleary eye opened. "May I introduce Colonel, ah—"

"—Rachel Mansour."

"—Rachel Mansour"—he squeaked—"from Earth, military attaché from the embassy! His, er, credentials." The colonel looked on, smiling faintly as the flustered batman proffered the case to the Admiral.

"S'funny name for a c-colonel, Colonel," mumbled the Admiral. "Are ye sure you're not a, a—ah—"

He sneezed, violently, then sat up. "Damn these goose-down pillows," he complained bitterly. "And damn the gout. Wasn't like this at First Lamprey."

"Indeed not," Rachel observed drily. "Lots of sand there, as I recall."

"Very good, that man! Lots of sand, indeed, lots of sand. Sun beating down on your head, ragheads all over the place shooting at you, and not really anything big enough to nuke from orbit. Whose command were you in, eh?"

"As a matter of fact, I was with the war crimes tribunal. Sifting mummified body parts for evidence."

Robard went gray, waiting for the Admiral to detonate, but the old man simply laughed raucously. "Robard! Help me up, there's a good fellow. I say-ay, I never expected to meet a fellow veteran here! To my desk. I must inspect his credentials!"

Somehow they managed to migrate the fifteen feet or so to the Admiral's study without his complaining bitterly about the cost of maternity wear or gingerly inspecting his legs to make sure they hadn't turned to glass overnight—one of his occasional nightmares—and the effeminate colonel discreetly slid himself into one of the visitor's chairs. Robard stared at the man. A woman's name, a high voice, if he didn't know better, he could almost believe that—

"Duke Michael agreed to my presence for two reasons," said Mansour. "Firstly, you should be aware that as an agent of the UN it is my job to report back impartially on any—I emphasize, *any*—violations of treaties to which your government is a party. But more importantly, there is a shortage of information about the entity which has attacked your colony world. I'm also here to bear witness in case they make use of forbidden or criminal weapons. I am also authorized to act as a neutral third party for purposes of arbitration and parley, to arrange exchanges of prisoners and cease-fires, and to ensure that, insofar as any war can be conducted in a civilized manner, this one is."

"Well that's a damn fine thing to know, sir, and you are welcome to join my staff," said the Admiral, sitting upright in his bath chair. "Feel free to approach me whenever you want! You're a good man, and I'm pleased to know there's another vet-eteran of

First Lamprey in the fleet." For a brief moment, he looked alarmed. "Oh dear. It's kicking again."

Mansour looked at him oddly. Robard opened his mouth, but the foreign colonel managed to speak before he could change the subject. "*It?*"

"The baby," Kurtz confided, looking miserable. "It's an elephant. I don't know what to do with it. If its father—" He stopped. His expression of alarm was chilling.

"Ahem. I *think* you'd better withdraw now, sir," said Robard, staring coldly at Rachel. "It's time for His Lordship's medicine. I'm afraid it would be for the best if in future you'd call ahead before visiting; he has these spells, you know."

Rachel shook her head. "I'll remember to do that." She stood. "Good-bye, sir." She turned and departed.

As he was helping the Admiral out of his chair, Robard thought he heard a soprano voice from outside: "—Didn't know you had elephants!" He shook his head hopelessly. Women aboard the Imperial flagship, admirals who thought they were pregnant, and a fleet about to embark on the longest voyage in naval history, against an unknown enemy. Where was it going to end?

the citizen curator was unamused. "So. To summarize, the Navy boys gave you the run-around, but have now allowed you on board their precious battlecruiser. Along the way, you lost contact with your subject for an entire working day. Last night you say he did nothing unusual, but you report patchy coverage. And what else? How did he spend that evening?"

"I don't understand, sir," Vassily said tightly. "What do you mean?"

The Citizen scowled furiously; even at a forty-thousand-kilometer remove, his picture on the screen was enough to make Vassily recoil. "It says in your report," the Citizen said with heavy emphasis, "that the subject left his apartment, was lost for a few minutes, and was next seen dining at a public establishment in the company of an *actress*. At whose apartment he subsequently spent a good few hours before returning to base. And you didn't investigate her?"

Vassily flushed right to the tips of his ears. "I thought—"

"Has he ever done anything like this before? While in New Prague, for example? I think not. According to his file he has led the life of a monk since arriving in the Republic. Not once, not *once* in nearly two months at the Glorious Crown Hotel, did he show any sign of interest in the working girls. Yet as soon as he arrives and starts work, what does he do?"

"I didn't think of that."

"I *know* you didn't." The Citizen Curator fell silent for a moment, but his expression was eloquent; Vassily cringed before it. "I'm not going to do any more of your thinking for you, but perhaps you'd be so good as to tell me what you propose to do next."

"Uh." Vassily blinked. "Run a background check on her? If it's clear, ask her a few questions? Keep a closer eye on him in future...?"

"Very good." The Citizen grinned savagely. "And what have you *learned* from this fiasco?"

"To watch the subject's behavior, and be alert for changes in it," Vassily said woodenly. "Especially the things he doesn't do, as much as those he does." It was a basic message, one drilled into recruits all the way through training, and he could kick himself for forgetting it. How could he have missed something so obvious?

"That's right." The Citizen leaned back, away from the camera on his phone. "A very basic skill, Muller. Yet we all learn best from our mistakes. See that you learn from this one, eh? I don't care if you have to follow your man all the way to Rochard's World and back, as long as you keep your eyes open and spot it when he makes his move. And think about all the other things you've been told to do. I'll tell you this for free: you've forgotten to do something else, and you'll be happier if you notice it before I have to remind you!"

"Yes, sir."

"Good-bye." The videophone link dissolved into random blocks, then went blank. Vassily eased out of his cubicle, trying to work out just what the Citizen's parting admonition meant. The sooner he cleared everything up, proving once and for all that Springfield was or was not a spy, the better—he wasn't cut out for shipboard life. Maybe it would be a good idea to start the new day by interviewing the engineering chief Springfield was working under? Probably that was what the Citizen meant for him to do; he could leave following up on the whore until later. (The idea filled him with an uncomfortable sense of embarrassment.)

No sooner did he poke his nose into the corridor than he was nearly run down by a team of ratings, hustling a trolley laden with heavy equipment at the double. On his second attempt, he took the precaution of looking both ways before venturing out: there were no obstacles. He made his way through the cramped, blue-painted corridor, following the curve of the inner hull. Floating free, the *Lord Vanek* relied on its own curved-space generator to produce a semblance of gravity. Vassily hunted for a radial walkway, then a lift down to the engineering service areas located at the heart of the ship, two-thirds of the way down its length.

There were people everywhere, some in corridors, some in chambers opening off the passageways, and others in rooms to either side. He caught a fair number of odd glances on his way, but nobody stopped him: most people would go out of their way to avoid the attentions of an officer in the Curator's Office. It took him a while to find the engineering spaces, but eventually, he found his way to a dimly lit, wide-open chamber full of strange machines and fast-moving people. Oddly, he felt very light on his feet as he waited in the entrance to the room. No sign of Springfield, but of course, that was hardly surprising; the engineering spaces of a capital ship were large enough to conceal any number of sins. "Is this the main drive engineering deck?" he asked a passing technician.

"What do you think it is? The head?" called the man as he hurried off. Vassily shrugged irritably and stepped forward—and forward—and *forward*—"What are you doing there?" Someone grabbed his elbow. "Hey, *watch out!*" He flailed helplessly, then stopped moving as he realized what was going on. The ceiling was close and the floor was a long way away and he was falling toward the far wall—

"Help," he gasped.

"Hold on tight." The hand on his elbow shifted to his upper arm and yanked, hard. A large rack of equipment, bolted to the floor, came close, and he grabbed and held on to it.

"Thanks. Is this the engineering deck? I'm looking for the chief drive engineer," he said. It took an effort to talk over the frantic butterfly beat of his heart.

"That would be me." Vassily stared at his rescuer. "Couldn't have you bending the clocks now, could I? They curve badly enough as it is. What do you want?"

"It's—" Vassily stopped. "I'm sorry. Could we talk somewhere in private?"

The engineering officer—his overalls bore the name krupkin—frowned mightily. "We might, but I'm very busy. We're moving in half an hour. Is it important?"

"Yah. It won't get your work done any faster, but if you help me now it might take less of your time later."

"Huh. Then we'll see." The officer turned and pointed at the other side of the open space. "See that office cubicle? I'll meet you in there in ten minutes." And he turned abruptly, kicked off, and disappeared into the gloom, chaos and moving bodies that circled the big blue cube at the center of the engineering bay.

"Holy Father!" Vassily took stock of his situation. Marooned, clinging to a box of melting clocks at the far side of a busy freefall compartment from his destination, he could already feel his breakfast rising in protest at the thought of crossing the room.

Grimly determined not to embarrass himself, he inched his way down to floor level. There were toeholds recessed into the floor tiles, and now he looked at them he saw that they were anchored, but obviously designed to be removed frequently. If he pretended that the floor was a wall, then the office door was actually about ten meters above him, and there were plenty of handholds along the way.

He took a deep breath, pulled himself around the clock cabinet, and kicked hard against it where it joined the floor. The results were gratifying; he shot up, toward the office. The wall dropped toward him, and he was able to grab hold of a passing repair drone and angle his course toward the doorway. As he entered it, gravity began to return—he slid along the deck, coming to an undignified halt lying on his back just inside. The office was small, but held a desk, console, and a couple of chairs; a rating was doing something with the console. "You," he said, "out, please."

"Aye aye, sir." The fresh-faced rating hurriedly closed some kind of box that was plugged into the console, then saluted and withdrew into the free-fall zone. Shaken, Vassily sat down in the seat opposite the desk and waited for Engineering Commander Krupkin to arrive. It was already 1100, and what had he achieved today? Nothing, so far as he could tell, except to learn that the Navy's motto seemed to be "Hurry up and wait." The Citizen wouldn't be pleased.

Meanwhile, on the bridge, the battlecruiser *Lord Vanek* was counting down for main drive activation.

As the flagship of the expedition, *Lord Vanek* was at the heart of squadron one, along with three of the earlier Glorious-class battlecruisers, and the two Victory-class battleships *Kamchatka* and *Regina* (now sadly antiquated, relics that had seen better days). Squadron Two, consisting of a mixed force of light cruisers, destroyers, and missile carriers, would launch six hours behind Squadron One; finally, the supply train, with seven bulk cargo freighters and the liner *Sikorsky's Dream* (refitted as a hospital ship) would depart eight hours later.

Lord Vanek was, in interstellar terms, a simple beast: ninety thousand tonnes of warship and a thousand crew held in tight orbit around an electron-sized black hole as massive as a mountain range. The hole—the drive kernel—spun on its axis so rapidly that its event horizon was permeable; the drive used it to tug the ship about by tickling the singularity in a variety of ways. At non-relativistic speeds, *Lord Vanek* maneuvered by dumping mass into the kernel; complex quantum tunneling interactions—jiggery-pokery within the ergosphere—transformed it into raw momentum. At higher speeds, energy pumped into the kernel could be used to generate the a jump field, collapsing the quantum well between the ship and a point some distance away.

The kernel had a few other uses: it was a cheap source of electricity and radioisotopes, and by tweaking the stardrive, it was possible to use it to produce a local curved-space gravity field. As a last resort, it could even be jettisoned and used as a weapon in its own right. But if there was one word that wouldn't describe it, that word must be "maneuevrable." Eight-billion-ton point masses do not make right-angle turns.

Commander Krupkin saluted as a rating held the bridge door open for him. "Engineering Commander reporting on the state of machinery, sir!"

"Very good." Captain Mirsky nodded from his command chair at the rear of the room. "Come in. What do you have for me?"

Krupkin relaxed slightly. "All systems operational and correct, sir," he announced formally. "We're ready to move at any time. Our status is clear on—" He rapidly rattled through the series of watches under his control. Finally: "The drive control modifications you ordered, sir—we've never run anything like this before. They look alright, and the self-test says everything is fine, but I can't say any more than that without unsealing the black boxes."

Mirsky nodded. "They'll work alright." Krupkin wished he could feel as confident as the Captain sounded; the black boxes, shipped aboard only a week ago and wired into the main jump drive control loop, did not fill him with confidence. Indeed, if it hadn't been obvious that the orders to integrate them came from the highest level and applied to every ship in the fleet, he'd have thrown the nearest thing to a tantrum that military protocol permitted. It was his job to keep the drive running, and dammit, he should know everything there was to know about how it worked! There could be anything in those boxes, from advanced (whisper it, *illegal*) high technology to leprechauns—and he'd be held responsible if it didn't work.

A bearded man at the other side of the bridge stood. "Humbly request permission to report, sir."

"You have permission," said Mirsky.

"I have completed downloading navigation elements from system traffic control. I am just now having them punched into the autopilot. We will be ready to spin up for departure in ten minutes."

"Very good, Lieutenant. Ah, Comms, my compliments to the Admiral and the Commodore, and we are preparing for departure in ten minutes. Lieutenant Helsingus, proceed in accordance with the traffic control departure plan. You have the helm."

"Aye, sir, I have the helm. Departure in ten minutes." Helsingus bent over his speaking tube; ratings around him began turning brass handles and moving levers with calm deliberation, sending impulses along the nerves of steel that bound the ship into an almost living organism. (Although nano-electronics might be indispensable in the engine room, the New Republican Admiralty held the opinion that there was no place for suchlike newfangled rubbish on the bridge of a ship crewed by the heroic fighting men of the empire.)

"Well, Commander." Mirsky nodded at the engineer. "How does it feel to be moving at last?"

Krupkin shrugged. "I'll be happier when we're in flat space. There are rumors."

For a moment, the Captain's smile slipped. "Indeed. Which is why we will be going to action stations at departure and staying that way until after our first jump. You can never tell, and the Commodore wants to be sure that no spies or enemy missile buses are lying in wait for us."

"A wise precaution, sir. Permission to return to my station?"

"Granted. Go with God, Commander."

Krupkin saluted, and headed back for his engineering control room as fast as his short legs would carry him. It was, he reflected, going to be a busy time, even with as quietly competent a dockyard consultant engineer as Martin to help him keep the magic smoke in the drive control boxes.

τhe colonι̜ οϝ Critics writhed and tunneled in their diamond nest, incubating a devastating review. A young, energetic species, descended from one of the post-Singularity flowerings that had exploded in the wake of the Diaspora three thousand years in their past, they held precious little of the human genome in their squamous, cold-blooded bodies. Despite their terrestrial descent, only their brains bound them tightly to the *sapiens* clade—for not all the exiles from Earth were human.

As hangers-on, the Critics had no direct access to the Festival's constellation of relay satellites or the huge network of visual and auditory sensors that had been scattered across the surface of the planet. (Most of the Festival's senses were borne on the wings of tiny insectoidal robots, with which they had saturated the biosphere, sending a million for every single telephone that had rained down from orbit.) Instead, the Critics had to make do with their own devices; a clumsy network of spy-eyes in low orbit, winged surveillance drones, and precarious bugs planted on the window ledges and chimney pots of significant structures.

The Critics watched, with their peculiar mixture of bemusement and morbid cynicism, while the soldiers of the First and Fourth Regiments shot their officers and deserted *en masse* to the black flag of Burya Rubenstein's now-overt Traditional Extropian Revolutionary Front. (Many soldiers burned their uniforms and threw away their guns; others adopted new emblems and took up strange silvery arms churned out by the committee's replicator farm.) The Critics looked on as peasants greedily demanded pigs, goats, and in one case, a goose that laid golden eggs from the Festival; their womenfolk quietly pleaded for medicinal cures, metal cutlery, and fabric. In the castle, shots were heard as the servants butchered the Duke's menagerie for food. A rain of gold roubles ordered by some economic saboteur fell widely across the streets of Novy Petrograd, and was equally widely ignored: to that extent, the economic collapse brought about by the Festival's advent was already complete.

"They are truly pathetic," commented She Who Observes the First; she clashed her tusks over a somatic bench that depicted a scene below, some of the few remaining loyal grenadiers dragging a terrified cobbler toward the gates of the castle, followed by his screaming, pleading family. "Unregulated instincts, unable to assimilate reality, bereft of perspective."

"Chew roots; dig deep." Guard Man the Fifth champed lugubriously, demonstrating his usual level of insight (intelligence not being a particularly useful characteristic in tunnel-running warriors). "Tastes of blood and soil."

"Everything tastes of soil to a warrior," She Who Observes snorted. "Eat tubers, brother, while your sisters discuss matters beyond your ken." She rolled sideways, butting up against Sister of Stratagems the Seventh, who nipped at her flank gently. "Sibling-litter-peer. Uncertainty flows?"

"A time of exponentiating changes is upon them." Sister Seventh was much given to making such gnomic pronouncements, perhaps in the naive hope that it would gain her a reputation for vision (and, ultimately, support when she made her bid for queendom). "Perhaps they are disorganized surface-scrabblers, clutching at stems, but there is a certain grandeur to their struggle; a level of sincerity seldom approached by primitives."

"Primitive they are: their internal discourse is crippled by a complete absence of intertextuality. I cringe in astonishment that Festival wastes its attention on them."

"Hardly. They are Festival's antithesis, do you not feel this in your whiskers?" Sister Seventh blinked redly at She Who Observes, pawing for the control tree of the somatic bench. "Here we see a nest-drone." The scene slewed into an enclosed space, following the abducted cobbler into the walls of the castle. "Phenotypic dispersal leads to extended specialization, as ever, with the usual degree of free will found in human civilization. But this one is structured to prevent information surge, do you not see?"

"Information surge? *Prevented?* Life is information!"

Sister Seventh farted smugly. "I have been monitoring the Festival. Not one of the indigines has asked it for information! Artifacts, yes. Food, yes. Machines, up to and including replicators, yes. But philosophy? Art? Mathematics? Ontology? We might be witnessing our first zombie civilization."

Zombies were a topic that fascinated Sister Seventh. An ancient hypothesis of the original pre-Singularity ur-civilization, a zombie was a non-self-conscious entity that acted just like a conscious one: it laughed, cried, talked, ate, and generally behaved just like a real person, and if questioned, would claim to be conscious—but behind its superficial behavior, there was nobody home, no internalized model of the universe it lived in. The philosophers had hypothesized that no such zombies existed, and that everything that claimed personhood was actually a person. Sister Seventh was less convinced. Human beings— those rugose, endothermic anthropoids with their ridiculously small incisors and anarchic social arrangements—didn't seem very real to her. So she was perpetually searching for evidence that, actually, they weren't people at all.

She Who Observes was of the opinion that her littermate was chewing on the happy roots again, but then, unlike Sister Seventh, she wasn't a practical critic: she was an observer.

"I think we really need to settle the zombie question here before we fix their other problems."

"And how do you propose to do *that?*" asked She Who Observes. "It's the subjectivity problem again. I tell you, the only viable analytical mode is the intentional stance. If something claims to be conscious, take it at its own word and treat it as if it has conscious intentions."

"Ah, but I can so easily program a meerkat to chirp 'I think, therefore I am!' No, sister, we need to tunnel nearer the surface to find the roots of sapience. A test is required, one that a zombie will stick in, but an actor will squeeze through."

"Do you have such a test in mind?"

Sister Seventh pawed air and champed her huge, yellow tusks. "Yes, I think I can construct one. The essential characteristic of conscious beings is that they adopt the intentional stance: that is, they model the intentions of other creatures, so that they can anticipate their behavior. When they apply such a model to others, they acquire the ability to respond to their intentions before they become obvious: when they apply it to themselves, they become self-conscious, because they acquire an understanding of their own motivations and the ability to modify them.

"But thus far, I have seen no evidence that their motivations are self-modifying, or indeed anything but hardwired reflexes. I want to test them, by introducing them to a situation where their own self-image is contradicted by their behavior. If they can adapt their self-image to the new circumstances, we will know that we are dealing with fellow sapients. Which will ultimately influence the nature of our review."

"This sounds damaging or difficult, sister. I will have to think on it before submitting to Mother."

Seventh emitted a bubbling laugh and flopped forward onto her belly. "Oh, sibling! What did you think I have in mind?"

"I don't know. But be it anything like your usual—" She Who Observes stopped, seeing the triumphant gleam in her sister's eye.

"I merely propose to Criticize a handful of them a trifle more thoroughly than usual," said Sister Seventh. "And when I'm done, any who live will know they've been *Criticized.* This is my methodology..."

COMMANDER KRUPKIN TOOK nearly two hours to get around to seeing Vassily Muller: it wasn't intentional on his part. Almost as soon as the main drive field was powered up and running, and the ship surfing smoothly away from the Klamovka beanstalk, his pager beeped:

ALL OFFICERS TO BRIEFING ROOM D IMMEDIATELY

"Shit and corruption," he muttered. Passing Pavel Grubor: "The old man wants me right now. Can you take care of the ship-yard technician and find out how long he's going to be in closing out the installation of the baseline compensator? Page me when you've got an answer." He headed off without waiting for a response.

Mikhail Krupkin enjoyed his job, and didn't particularly expect or want any further promotions; he'd been in shipboard systems for the past fourteen years and expected to serve out his career in them before enjoying a long and happy retirement working for some commercial space line. However, messages like this one completely destroyed his peace of mind. It meant that the boss was going to ask him questions about the availability of his systems, and with the strange patch boxes installed in the drive room, the *Lord Vanek* might be mobile, but he couldn't in all honesty swear it was one hundred percent solid.

He didn't know just what was in those boxes, but he was sure there was a reason why the Admiralty was spending several million crowns on a drive upgrade. And in any event, they'd been remarkably cagey about the extra control software for them. Boxes, hooked into the drive, which also hooked into the new, high-bandwidth linkup to the tactical network: something smelled.

All this and more was on his mind as he took the express elevator up to the conference suite in officer country. The door to

Room D was open, waiting for him. Most of the other senior officers were already there. Ilya Murametz, the ship's executive officer, Lieutenant Helsingus from fire control, the usual battle operations team, Vulpis from Relativity… he was probably last, but for the Captain, by reason of having come farthest. "Ilya. What's going on?"

Ilya glanced at him. "The Captain is with the Admiral. When he arrives he will make an announcement," he said. "I don't know anything about it except that it's nothing specific." Krupkin breathed a silent sight of relief; "nothing specific" meant that it wasn't about the running of the ship. Nobody was going to be hauled over the coals today. Not that Captain Mirsky was a martinet by the standards of the New Republican Navy, but he could be merciless if he thought someone was asleep at the switch or not doing his job properly.

Suddenly there was a change of atmosphere in the room. Everyone turned to face the doorway: conversations stopped, and officers came to attention. Captain Mirsky stood for a long moment, surveying his staff. Evidently what he saw gratified him; when he spoke his first words were, "Gentlemen, please be seated." He walked to the head of the table and laid down a thick folder in front of his chair.

"It is now 1130. The door to this room is shut, and will remain shut, barring emergencies, until 1200. I am authorized to inform you that we are now under battle orders. I am not privy to the political discussions behind our orders, but I am informed by Admiral Kurtz's staff that it appears likely that no resolution of the crisis short of war is possible; accordingly, we have been ordered to proceed as part of Task Group One to Rochard's World, by way of Battle Plan Omega Green Horizon." Now he pulled his chair out and sat down. "Are there any questions about the background before I go into our specific orders?" he asked.

Lieutenant Marek raised a hand. "Sir, do we know anything about the aggressor? It seems to me that the censor's office has been more than usually diligent."

Captain Mirsky's cheek twitched. "A good question." Krupkin glanced at the lieutenant; a young hotshot in TacOps, who'd joined the ship less than six months ago. "A good question deserves a good answer. Unfortunately, I can't give you one because nobody has seen fit to tell me. So, Lieutenant. How do you think our armed forces stack up, in a worst-possible-case situation?"

Lieutenant Marek gulped; he hadn't been on board long enough to have figured out the Captain's Socratic style of testing his subordinates' knowledge—a holdover from Mirsky's two tours as a professor in the Naval Staff Academy. "Against whom, sir? If it was just a matter of suppressing a local rebellion, there wouldn't be any problem at all. But Rochard's World had a picket force consisting of a destroyer plus point defenses, and they'd be as good as us at suppression. So they wouldn't be sending us if that was enough to deal with the situation. There must be an active enemy who has already stopped the local picket force intervening."

"An accurate summary." Captain Mirsky smiled humorlessly. "One that holds true whatever we face. Unfortunately, you now know as much as I do, but for one thing: apparently the destroyer *Sakhalin* was *eaten*. I don't know if this is metaphor or literal truth, but it appears that nobody knows who this Festival is, or what they are capable of, or whether the destroyer gave them indigestion. Let us not forget our oath of allegiance to the Emperor and the Republic; whatever they choose to do, we are sworn to be their right arm. If they decide to strike at an enemy, well, let us strike hard. Meanwhile, let us assume the worst. What if the enemy has cornucopia machines?"

Marek looked puzzled. "Couldn't it go either way, sir? On the one hand, they have tools that let them build lots of weapons quickly without getting their hands dirty. But on the other hand, if they're not used to working, isn't there a good chance that they're moral degenerates? The ability to manufacture doesn't confer victory automatically, if the people who have it are weakened and corrupted by their decadent robot-supported lifestyle. How can they possibly have the traditions and *ésprit* of an honorable military force?"

"That remains to be seen," the Captain said cryptically. "For the time being, I prefer to assume the worst. And the worst case is that the enemy has cornucopia machines, and is *not* decadent and cowardly."

Marek shook his head slightly.

"You have a question?" asked Mirsky.

"Uh. I thought—" Marek looked worried. "Is that possible?"

"Anything is possible," the Captain said, heavily. "And if we plan for the worst, with luck all our surprises will be favorable." He glanced away from the naive Lieutenant. "Next."

Krupkin, who as an engineer had his own opinion about the

advisability of banning the use of technologies for social reasons, nodded to himself. While Mirsky wouldn't say so in public, he had a very good idea what the Captain was thinking—*having a decadent robot-supported lifestyle doesn't preclude having military traditions. In fact, it may give them more time to focus on the essentials.* The Captain continued to poll his officers, publicly querying the readiness of their posts.

"—Engineering status. Commander Krupkin?"

Krupkin stifled a grunt of annoyance. "The shipyard contractor is still applying the upgrade patches to our baseline compensators. I am awaiting a precise hand-off estimate, but as of this morning, we expected three more shifts to complete the modifications, and another shift to test them. I have no complaints about his efficiency: he's as good as anyone I've ever worked with, a real virtuoso. Other than that, the secondary compensator set—which is not being upgraded—is fully operational. We are moving at full speed, but will not have full redundancy and the new upgrade modifications ready for another four to five days—at a minimum."

"I see." The Captain made a note on his blotter. He looked back at the engineer: a piercing blue-eyed stare that would have turned a less experienced officer into a nervous wreck. "Can the modifications be expedited? We will be passing into foreign space-time in two days; thereafter, we must anticipate the presence of enemy minelayers and warships along our route."

"Um—probably, sir. Unfortunately, the upgrades aren't straightforward enough for our routine engineering staff. Springfield is a specialist, and he is exerting himself fully. I believe that we might be able to speed things up, but at the risk of errors creeping in because of fatigue. If I can use an analogy, it's like a master surgeon performing an operation. Extra pairs of hands simply get in the way, and you can't prop a surgeon up for days on end and expect his work to remain acceptable. I think we might be able to shave a day or two off the four-to-five-day estimate, but no more."

"I see." Captain Mirsky glanced at Murametz significantly. "But we are still able to move and fight, and the new black-box system is already integrated." He nodded. "Helsingus, how is TacOps?"

"I've been running daily exercises predicated on a standard fleet aggressor profile for the past week, sir, using the standard models Admiralty shipped us. We could do with a bit longer, but I think the boys have generally got the right idea. Barring any major surprises in enemy tactical doctrine, we're ready to deal with them, whoever they are, one-on-one."

"Good." Mirsky sat in thought for a minute. "I have to tell you that I have a meeting this afternoon with Commodore Bauer and a teleconference with the other captains. You should assume that, as of now, this ship is on a war footing. You should be prepared for combat operations in the near future. Meanwhile, I expect daily reports on drive and gunnery readiness.

"That goes for the rest of you, too. I want daily readiness reports. We've wasted a lot of time churning conscripts this month, and I want us up to ninety-five percent operational capability as soon as possible. We will be bunkering a full fuel load and munitions from the supply ship *Aurora* tomorrow, and I expect that, as soon as we spool up for our first jump, we will be going to battle stations. That gives you about thirty-six hours to get ready for action. Are there any questions, gentlemen?"

Helsingus raised a hand.

"Yes?"

"Sir. Minelayers? Where are we going that might be mined?"

Mirsky nodded. "A good point, Commander. Our initial jump is going to be a short-hauler to Wolf Depository Five. I know that's not on a direct course for Rochard's World, but if we go straight there—well, I presume our enemies can plot a straight course, too. What we don't know is how much they know about us. I hope to know more about them this afternoon." He stood up. "If they launch a surprise attack, we'll be ready for them. God is on our side; all the indications are that this Festival is a pagan degeneracy, and all we need to do is be of good heart and man our guns with enthusiasm. Any other questions?" He looked around the room. Nobody raised a hand. "Very good. I am now leaving and will be in closed conference with the Commodore. Dismissed."

The Captain left the room in silence. But as soon as the door closed behind him, there was an uproar.

Martin was in a foul mood. Krupkin had broken the news to him hours earlier: "I'm sorry, but that's the way it is," he'd said. "Double shifts. We're on a war footing. You especially don't get to sleep until the upgrade job is done; orders from the skipper, who is not in a reasonable mood. Once it's done, you can crash out for as long as you want, but we need it before we see combat."

"It's going to be sixteen hours, minimum, *whatever* happens," Martin told him, trying hard to keep his cool. "The patches will be installed and active by the end of this shift, but I can't release the system to you until it's tested out fully. The regression tests are entirely automatic and take twenty thousand seconds to run. Then there's the maneuver testing, which would normally take all week if this was a new hull we were upgrading. Finally, there's drive qualification time which is three months for a new and untested system like the one your Admiralty ordered, and what do *you* think the chances are that you're going to sit still for that?"

"Skip it," Krupkin said briskly. "We're going to be maneuvering on it tomorrow. Can you start the white-box phase today?"

"*Fuck it.*" Martin pulled his goggles and gloves back on. "Talk to me later, okay? I'm *busy*. You'll get your bloody drive mods. Just point me at a bunk this evening." He dived back into the immersive interface, ignoring the commander—who took it surprisingly mildly.

Which was perhaps just as well. Martin was keeping a tight rein on his anger, but beneath the brittle exterior, he was disturbed. The business with Rachel had unsettled him; he was now intensely nervous, and not just because of the volatility of the situation. Her approach had caught him off guard and vulnerable, and the potential consequences ranged from the unpredictable to the catastrophic.

For the rest of the day, he worked furiously, checking the self-extending array of connectors linking the new drive control circuitry into the existing neural networks. He headed off several possible problems in the performance profile of the control feedback sensors, tuned the baseline compensators for extra precision, and added several patches to the inner hard control loops that monitored and pulled the hair on the black hole; but he left the midlife kicker traps alone. And he installed the special circuit that Herman had asked him to add.

He worked on into the evening shift, then started the regression tests going: a series of self-test routines, driven by software, that would exercise and report on every aspect of the drive upgrade. Installing and testing the module was the easy task: tomorrow he'd have to start testing how it interacted with the kernel—an altogether more nerve-wracking experience. So it was that, at 2500, he yawned, stretched, set aside his gloves and feedback sensors, and stood up.

"Aargh." He stretched further. Joints popped with the effort; he felt dizzy, and tired, and slightly sick. He blinked; everything seemed flat and monochromatic after the hours immersed in false-color 3-D controls, and his wrists ached. And why, in this day and age, did warships smell of pickled cabbage, stale sweat, and an occasional undertone of sewage? He stumbled to the door. A passing rating glanced at him curiously. "I need to find a bunk," he explained.

"Please wait here, sir." He waited. A minute or so later, one of Krupkin's minions came into view, hand-over-hand down the wall like a human fly.

"Your berth? Ah, yes, sir. D deck, Compartment 24, there's an officer's room waiting for you. Breakfast call at 0700. Paulus, please show the gentleman here to his room."

"This way, sir." The crewman quietly and efficiently guided Martin through the ship, to a pale green corridor lined with hatches like those of a capsule hotel. "There you are." Martin blinked at the indicated door, then pulled it aside and climbed in.

It was like a room in a capsule hotel or a compartment on a transcontinental train—one with two bunks. The lower one flipped upside down to make a desk when not in use. It was totally sterile, totally clean, with ironed sheets and a thin blanket on the lower bunk, and it smelled of machine oil, starch, and sleepless nights. Someone had laid out a clean overall with no insignia on it. Martin eyed it mistrustfully and decided to stick to his civilian clothes until they were too dirty to tolerate. Surrendering to the New Republic's uniform seemed symbolic; letting them claim him as one of their own would feel like a small treason.

He palmed the light to low, and stripped his shoes and socks off, then lay down on the lower bunk. Presently, the light dimmed and he began to relax. He still felt light-headed, tired and angry, but at least the worst hadn't happened: no tap on the shoulder, no escort to the brig. Nobody knew who he *really* worked for. You could never tell in this business, and Martin had a prickly feeling washing up and down his spine. This whole situation was completely bizarre, and Herman's request that he plonk himself in the middle of it was well out of the usual run of assignments. He shut his eyes and tried to push away the visions of spinning yellow blocks that danced inside his head.

The door opened and closed. "Martin," said a quiet voice beside his pillow, "keep your voice down. How did things go?"

He jackknifed upright and nearly smashed his head on the underside of the bunk overhead. "What!" He paused. "What are you—"

"Doing here?" A quiet, ironic laugh. "I'm doing the same as

you; feeling tired, wondering what the hell I'm doing in this nut-house."

He relaxed a little, relieved. "I wasn't expecting you."

"It's my job to be here; I'm attached to the Admiral's staff as a diplomatic representative. Look, I can't stay long. It would be a *really* bad idea for anyone to find me in your room. At best, they'd assume the worst, and at worst, they might think you were a spy or something—"

"But I *am* a spy," he blurted out in a moment of weakness. "At least, you wanted—"

"Yeah, right, and I've got your secret-agent decoder ring right *here*. Look, I want to talk, but business first. Are the drive upgrades finished?"

His eyes adjusted to the dark; he could see the outline of her face. Short hair and shadows made her look very different, harder and more determined. But something in her expression as she watched him made her look slightly uncertain. *Business first, she said.* "The upgrades are going to take some time," he said. "They're about ready for testing to start tomorrow, but it's a risky proposition. I'm going to be ironing bugs out of the high-precision clocks for the next week." He paused. "Are you sure this is safe? How did you find me?"

"It wasn't hard. Thank MiG for the security system schematics. Life Support and Security think you're alone in here. I thought it was safer to visit in person than to try to page you."

Martin shuffled around and sat up, making room for her, and Rachel sat down next to him. He noticed for the first time that she was wearing a uniform—not a New Republican one. "You're here for the whole voyage?"

She chuckled. "The better to get to know you. Relax. If you want to talk to your local diplomatic representative, that's me. Besides, they need me, or someone like me. Who else is going to negotiate a cease-fire for them?"

"Aah." Martin fell silent for a moment, thinking. He was aware of her next to him, almost painfully so. "You're taking a risk," he said after a while. "They aren't going to thank you—"

"Hush." She leaned closer. He felt her breath on his cheek: "The drive patches you're installing are part of an illegal weapons system, Martin. I'm sure of it. I'm not sure what kind of illegality is being contemplated, but I'm sure it involves causality violation. If they commence training maneuvers shortly, I'll get a chance to see just what they're planning to use the upgrades for. That's why

I need to be here. And why I need your help. I wouldn't normally dump this on you, but I really need your help, active help, in figuring out what's going on. Do you understand?"

"I understand very little," Martin said nervously, priming his autonomic override to keep his pulse steady so as not to betray the lie. He felt unaccountably guilty about withholding the truth from her. Rachel seemed like the least likely person to jeopardize his mission—and he liked her, wanted to be able to relax in her presence freely, without worries. But caution and experience conspired to seal his lips. "I'm just along for the ride," he added. He simply couldn't tell her about Herman. Without knowing how she'd react, the consequences might be disastrous. Might. And it was a risk he dared not take.

"Understand this," she said quietly. "A lot of lives are at stake. Not just mine, or yours, or this ship's, but just about everyone within a thirty-light-year radius of here. That's a lot of people."

"Why do you think this is going to drag the big E into the situation?" he prompted. He was deathly tired and didn't want to have to lie to her. *Can I keep her talking?* he wondered. If she didn't keep speaking, he was afraid he might tell her too much. Which would be a big mistake.

She touched his arm. "The Eschaton will be interested for a simple reason; it is absolutely opposed to causality violation. Please don't pretend you're that naive, Martin. I've seen your résumé. I know where you've been and what you've done. You're not an idiot, and you know what a well-tuned warp drive can do in the hands of an expert. In terms of special relativity, being able to travel faster than light is effectively equivalent to time travel—at least from the perspective of observers in different frames of reference. They see the light from your arrival, which is close to them, a long time before they see the light from your departure, which is a long way away. Because you're outrunning the speed of light, events appear to happen out of sequence. Okay? Same with a causal link, an instantaneous quantum-entanglement communicator. It doesn't mean there's real time travel involved, or that you can create temporal paradoxes, but being able to mess with an observer's view of events at a distance is a boon for strategists.

"The Eschaton doesn't care about such trivial kinds of time travel, but it stamps hard on the real thing; any manifestation of closed timelike paths that could jeopardize its own history. The big E doesn't want anyone doing a knight's move on it, back in time and then forward again, to screw over its origin. Someone tries to build an instantaneous communicator? No problem. They go on to build a logic gate that transmits its output into its own past, where it's wired into the input? That's the basis of acausal logic, and it gives you the first tool you need to build a transcendent artificial intelligence. Poof, the planet is bombarded from orbit with cannibal lemmings or bitten to death by killer asteroids or something.

"Anyway, I don't really care all that much what the New Republic does to the Festival. I mean, maybe I care about individual people in the New Republic, and maybe the Festival folks are really nice, but that's not the point. But I *do* care if they do whatever they're going to do inside Earth's light cone. If it involves large-scale causality violation, the E might decide to take out the entire contaminated zone. And we know it seeded colonies as much as three thousand light-years away—even assuming it still wants humans around, it can afford to wipe out a couple of hundred planets." Martin had to bite his cheek to keep from correcting her. She fell silent. He waited for her to continue, but she didn't; she seemed almost depressed.

"You have a lot of clout. Have you told them what you've deduced? Or told anybody else?"

She chuckled, a peculiarly grim laugh. "If I did that, how long do you think it would be before they chucked me overboard, with or without a vacsuit? They're paranoid enough already; they think there's a spy on board, and they're afraid of minelayers and saboteurs along the way."

"A *spy?*" He sat up, scared. "They know there's a—"

"Be quiet. Yes, a spy. Not one of us; some goon from the Curator's Office who they sent along to keep an eye on you. Be quiet, I said. He's just a kid, some wet-behind-the-ears trainee cop. Try to relax around him. As far as you're concerned, you're allowed to talk to me; I'm the nearest representative of your government."

"When are we going to get off this ship?" he asked tensely.

"Probably when we arrive." She took his hand and squeezed it. "Do your job and keep your head down," she said calmly. "Just don't, whatever you do, act guilty or confess to anything. Trust me, Martin, like I told you before: we're on the same team for the duration."

Martin leaned close to her. She was tense, very tense. "This is quite insane," he said very slowly and carefully as he slid an arm around her shoulders. "This idiotic expedition is probably going to get us both killed."

"Maybe." Her grip tightened on his hand.

"Better not," he said tightly. "I haven't had a chance to get to know you yet."

"Me neither." Her grip relaxed a little. "Is that what you'd like to do? Really?"

"Well." He leaned back against the hard wall beside the bunk. "I hadn't thought about it a lot," he mused, "but I've been alone for a long time. Really. Before this job. I need—" He shut his eyes. "Shit. What I mean to say is, I need to get out of this job for a while. I want a year or two off, to pull myself together and find out who I am again. A change and a rest. And if you're thinking about that, too, then—"

"You sound overworked." She shivered. "Someone just walked over my grave. You and me both, Martin, you and me both. Something about the New Republic uses you up, doesn't it? Listen, I've got about two years' accumulated leave waiting for me, after I get home. If you want to go somewhere together, to get away from all this—"

"Sounds good to me," he said quietly. "But right now . . ." He trailed off, with a glance at the cabin door.

There was a moment's frozen silence: "I won't let you down," she said softly. She hugged him briefly, then let go and stood up. "You're right. I really shouldn't be here, I've got a room to go to, and if they're still watching me—well."

She took her cap from the upper bunk, carefully placed it on her head, and opened the door. She looked back at him and, for a moment, he thought about asking her to stay, even thought about telling her everything; but then she was gone, out into the red-lit passages of the sleeping ship.

"Damn," he said softly, watching the door in mild disbelief. "Too late, too late. Damn . . ."

the shooting began with a telegram.

Locked in a loose formation with six other capital ships, the *Lord Vanek* hurtled toward the heliopause, where the solar wind met the hard vacuum of interstellar space. Wolf Depository lay five light-years ahead, and almost five years in the future—for the plan was that fleet would follow a partially closed timelike path, plunging deep into the future (staying within the scope of a light cone with its apex drawn on New Prague at the time of first warning of attack), then use the black boxes attached to their drive modules to loop back into the past. Without quite breaking the letter of the Eschaton's law—*Thou shalt not globally violate causality*—the fleet would arrive in orbit around Rochard's World just after the onslaught of the Festival, far faster than such a task force would normally cover the eight hops separating them from the colony world. In the process, it would loop around any forces sent by the enemy to intercept a straightforward counterstrike—and pick up a time capsule containing analyses of the battle written by future historians, the better to aid the Admiral's planning.

At least, that was what theory dictated. Get there implausibly fast, with more firepower than any attacker could possibly expect, and with advance warning of the attacker's order of battle and defensive intentions. What could go wrong?

The operations room was a hive of concentration as the gold team officers—the crew shift who would be on duty at the time of the forthcoming first jump, the one that would take the fleet into the future, as well as out into deep space—ran through their set-up checklists.

Captain Mirsky stood at the rear of the room, next to the heavy airtight door, watching his officers at their posts: a running display of telemetry from the ship's battle management systems ran up the main wall-screen. The atmosphere was tense enough to cut with a knife. It was the first time any warship of the New Republic had engaged a high-technology foe; and no one, to the best knowledge of Commodore Bauer's staff, had ever tried to pull off this tactical procedure before. Anything could be waiting for them. Five years into the future was as far as they dared probe in one jump; in theory, there should be a navigation beacon awaiting them, but if something went awry, the enemy might be there instead. Mirsky smiled thinly. *All the more reason to get it right,* he reasoned. *If we mess it up, there won't be a second time.*

The military *attaché* from Earth had invited herself in to rubberneck at the proceedings and presumably report back to her masters in due course. Not that it made any difference at this point, but it annoyed Mirsky's sense of order to have a tourist along, let alone one whose loyalty was questionable. He resolved to ignore her—or, if that became impossible, to eject her immediately.

"First breakpoint in five-zero seconds," called the flight engineer. "Slaved to preferential-frame compensation buffers. Range to jump initiation point, six-zero seconds." More jargon followed, in a clipped, tense voice; the routine stock-in-trade of a warship, every phrase was defined by some procedural manual.

Gunnery one: "Acknowledged. Standing by to power up laser grid." A mass of lasers—more than a million tiny cells scattered across the skin of the ship, able to operate as a single phased array—cycled through their power-up routines and reported their status. The ship was nearing the jump point; as it did so, it sucked energy out of the energized, unstable vacuum ahead of it and stored it by spinning up its drive kernel, the tiny, electrically charged black hole that nestled at the heart of the engine room containment sphere.

Engineering: "Main inertial propulsion holding at minus two seconds. Three-zero seconds to jump."

The ship drifted closer to the lightspeed transition point. The rippled space ahead of it began to flatten, bleeding energy into the underlying vacuum state. Six more huge warships followed behind at five-minute intervals; Squadron Two, the light screen of fast-movers who had set off behind the *Lord Vanek,* had overhauled them the day before and jumped through six hours ago.

Comms: "Telegram from the flag deck, sir."

"Read it," called Mirsky.

"Telegram from Admiral Kurtz, open, all ears. Begins: Assume enemy warships ahead, break. Initiate fire on contact with hostiles, break. For the glory of the empire. Ends. Sent via causal channel to all sister ships." The causal channels between the ships would die, their contents hopelessly scrambled, as soon as the ships made their first jump between equipotential points: quantum entanglement was a fragile phenomenon and couldn't survive faster-than-light transitions.

Mirsky nodded. "Acknowledge it. Exec, bring us battle stations." Alarms began to honk mournfully throughout the ship.

"Reference frame trap executed." Relativistics. "Jump field engaged. We have a white box in group B, repeat, white box in B." A captive reference frame meant the ship had mapped the precise space-time location of its origin perfectly. Using the newly installed drive controllers, the *Lord Vanek* could return to that point in time from some future location, flying a closed timelike loop.

Mirsky cleared his throat. "Jump at your convenience."

No lights dimmed, there was no sense of motion, and virtually nothing happened—except for a burst of exotic particles injected into the ergo-sphere of the quantum black hole in the ship's drive module. Nevertheless, without any fuss, the star patterns outside the ship's hull changed.

"Jump confirmed." Almost everybody breathed a slight sight of relief.

"Survey, let's see where we are." Mirsky showed no sign of stress, even though his ship had just jumped five years into its own future, as well as a parsec and a half out into the unknown.

"Yes, sir: laser grid coming up." About two gigawatts of power—enough to run a large city—surged into the laser cells in the ship's skin: if there was one thing a starship like the *Lord Vanek* had, it was electricity to burn. The ship lit up like a pulsar, pumping out a blast of coherent ultraviolet light powerful enough to fry anyone within a dozen kilometers. It stabilized, scanning rapidly in a tight beam, quartering the space ahead of the ship. After a minute it shut down again.

Radar: "No obstructions. We're well clear." Which was to be expected. Out here, fifteen to fifty astronomical units away from the primary, you could travel for 100 million kilometers in any direction without meeting anything much larger than a snowball.

The intense UV lidar pulse would propagate for minutes, then hours, before returning the faint trace of a skin signature.

"Very good. Conn, take us forward. One gee, total delta of one-zero k.p.s." Mirsky stood back and waited as the helm officer punched in the maneuver. Ten k.p.s. wasn't much speed, but it would take the *Lord Vanek* comfortably away from its point of emergence without emitting too much drive noise, leaving room for the rest of the flotilla behind them. A lidar pulse in the depths of the halo could only signify a warship on the prowl, and it would be extremely unhealthy to stay too close to its point of origin. In the Oort cloud of an industrialized system, even the snowballs could bite.

"Ping at nine-two-six-four!" crowed Radar Two. "Range four-point-nine M-klicks, bearing one by seven-five by three-three-two. Lots of hot one-point-four MeV gammas—they're cooking on antimatter!"

"Acceleration?" asked Mirsky.

"Tracking... one-point-three gees, confirmed. No change. Uh, wait—"

"Comms bulletin from the *Kamchatka,* sir."

"Comms, call it."

"Message reads, quote, under attack by enemy missile layers break. Situation serious break. Where are the BBs, break. All units please respond, ends."

Mirsky blinked. *Enemy warships? This soon?* Wolf Depository was right on the New Republic's doorstep, a mining system owned and exploited by the rich, heavily industrialized Septagon Central. What on earth were they doing allowing alien warships—

"Second burst at nine-two-six-four," called Radar One. "Same emission profile. Looks like we scared up a swarm!"

"Wait," grated Mirsky. He shook himself, visibly surprised by the news. "Wait, dammit! I want to see what else is out there. Comms, do not, under any circumstances, respond to signals from the *Kamchatka,* or anybody who came through ahead of us without clearing it with me first. If there are enemy ships out here, we've got no way of knowing whether our signals have been compromised."

"Aye aye, sir. Signal silence on all screening elements."

"Now." He bent his head, pondering the screen ahead. "If it *is* an ambush..."

The gamma-ray traces lit up on the main screen, labeled icons indicating their position and vector relative to the system ahead.

One-point-three gees wasn't particularly fast, but it was enough to send cold shudders up Mirsky's spine: it meant serious high-delta-vee propulsion systems, fusion or antimatter or quantum gravity induction, not the feeble ion drive of a robot tug. That could mean a number of things: sublight relativistic bombers, missile buses, intrasystem interceptors, whatever. The *Lord Vanek* would have to skim past them to get to the next jump zone. Which could give them a passing shot at over 1000 k.p.s.... a speed at which it took very little, maybe a sand grain, to total a ship. If it was an ambush, it had probably nailed the entire task force cold.

"Radar," he said, "give me a second lidar pulse, three-zero seconds. Then plot a vector intersect on those bogies, offset one-zero kiloklicks at closest pass, acceleration one-zero gees, salvo of two SEM-20s one-zero-zero kiloklicks out."

"Aye aye, skipper."

"Missiles armed, launch holding at minus one-zero seconds." Commander Helsingus, stationed at Gunnery One.

"I want them to get a good look at our attack profile," murmured the Captain. "Nice and close." Ilya Murametz glanced at him sidelong. "Keep the boys on their toes," Mirsky added, meeting his eye. Ilya nodded.

"Gamma burst!" called Radar Two. "Burst at one-four-seven-one. Range one-one point-two M-klicks, bearing one by seven-five by three-three-two. Looks like shooting, sir!"

"Understood." Mirsky clasped his hands together: Murametz winced as he cracked his knuckles. "Hurry up and wait. Helm: How's the attack course?"

"We're prepping it now, sir."

"Forward lidar. Looks like we are in a shooting war. And they know we're here by now. So let's get a good look at them."

Comms: "Sir, new message purportedly from the *Kamchatka*. Message from the *Aurora*, too."

"Read them."

Mirsky nodded at the comms station, where the petty officer responsible read from a punched paper tape unreeling from the brass mouth of a dog's head. "*Kamchatka* says, quote, engaged by enemy missile boats break we are shooting back break enemy warships astern painting us with target designation radar break situation desperate where are you. Ends. *Aurora* says, quote, no contact with enemies break *Kamchatka* off course stand by for orbital elements correction break what is all the shooting about. Ends."

"Oh bloody hell." Murametz turned red.

"Indeed," Mirsky said drily. "The question is, whose? TacOps: what's our status?"

"Target acquired, sir. Range down to four-point-eight M-klicks, speed passing one-zero-zero k.p.s. Engagement projected within two-point-four kiloseconds."

"We have a ... three-zero-zero-second margin," said Mirsky, checking the clock display. "That should be plenty. We can get a look at the closest one without getting so close their launch base can shoot at us if it's a missile bus. Everyone clear? Guns: I want real-time logging of those birds. Let's see how they perform. Radar: Can you lock a spectroscope on the target?"

"At three K-klicks per second, from one-zero K-klicks away? I think so, sir, but we'll need a big fat beacon to spot against."

"You'll have one." Murametz smiled widely. "Guns: dial those birds down to point-one of a kiloton before you fire them. Standard MP-3 warheads?"

"Yes, sir."

"Good. Keep 'em."

Standing at the back of the bridge, Rachel tried not to wince. Wearing her arms inspectorate hat, she was all too familiar with the effects of americium bombs: nuclear weapons made with an isotope denser and more fissile than plutonium, more stable than californium. Just good old-fashioned fission bombs, jacketed with a high-explosive shaped charge and a lens of pre-fragmented copper needles—shrapnel that, in a vacuum engagement, would come spalling off the nuclear fireball in a highly directional cone, traveling at a high fraction of lightspeed.

The next thirty minutes passed in tense silence, broken only by terse observations from Radar One and Two. No more targets burst from hiding; there might well be others in the Kuiper belt, but none were close enough to see or be seen by the intense lidar pulses of the warship. In that time, passive sensors logged two nuclear detonations within a range of half a light-hour; someone was definitely shooting. And behind them, the telltale disturbances of six big ships emerged from jump, then powered up their combat lidar and moved out.

"Launch point in six-zero seconds," called Helsingus. "Two hot SEM-20s on the rail."

"Fire on schedule," said Mirsky, straightening his back and looking directly ahead at the screen. The green arrow showing the *Lord Vanek*'s vector had grown until it was beginning to show the purple of relativistic distortion around its sensitive extrapolative tip: the ship was already nearing half a percent of lightspeed, a dangerous velocity. Too high a speed and it might not be able to track targets effectively: worse, it wouldn't be able to dodge or change its vector fast, or jump safely.

"Three-zero seconds. Arming birds. Birds show green, sir."

"I'm getting emissions from the target," called Radar Two. "Lots of—looks like jamming, sir!"

"Laser grid. Illuminate the target," said Mirsky. "Guns, set to passive."

"Aye aye, sir." Under passive homing mode, the missiles would lock onto the target, illuminated by the *Lord Vanek*'s laser battery, and home in on its reflection.

"Target still accelerating slowly," said Radar One. "Looks like a missile boat."

"One-zero seconds. Launch rails energized."

"You have permission to fire at will, Commander," said the Captain.

"Yes, sir. Eight seconds. Navigation updated. Inertial platforms locked. Birds charged, warheads...green. Five seconds. Launch commencing, bird one. Gone." The deck shuddered briefly: ten tons of missile hurtled the length of the ship in the grip of a coilgun, ejected ahead of the starship at better than a kilometer per second. "Lidar lock. Drive energized. Bird one main engine ignition confirmed. Bird two loaded and green...launch. Gone. Drive energized."

"Bingo," Ilya said quietly.

Red arrows indicating the progress of the missiles appeared on the forward screen. They weren't self-powered; nobody in his right mind would dare load a quantum black hole and its drive support mechanism into a robot suicide machine. Rather, the ship's phased-array lasers bathed them in a sea of energy, boiling and then superheating the reaction mass they carried until they surged forward far faster than the starship. Strictly a close-range low-delta-vee weapon, missiles were mostly obsolescent; their sole job was to get a nuclear device onto the right interception vector, like the "bus" on an ancient twentieth-century MIRV. They'd burn out after only thirty seconds, but by then the warheads would be closing the gap between the *Lord Vanek*'s projected course and the enemy ship itself. Shortly after the starship ran the gauntlet, its missiles would arrive—and deliver the killing blow.

"Radar One. Where are they?" Mirsky asked softly.

"Tracking as before," called the officer. "Still maintaining course and vector. And emitting loads of spam."

"Bird one MECO in one-zero seconds," said Helsingus. "They're trying to jam, sir. Nothing doing." He said it with heavy satisfaction, as if the knowledge that the anonymous victims of the attack were offering some token resistance reassured him that he was not, in fact, about to butcher them without justification. Even committed officers found the applied methods of three centuries of nuclear warfare hard to stomach at times.

Comms Two, voice ragged with tension: "Jamming stopped, sir! I'm receiving a distress beacon. Two—no, three! I say again, three distress beacons. It's like they're bailing out before we hit them."

"Too late," said Helsingus. "We'll have 'em in three-two seconds. They'll be inside the burst radius."

Rachel shuddered. Suddenly a horrible possibility began to rise to the surface of her mind.

Mirsky cracked his knuckles again, kneading his hands together. "Guns. I want a last-ditch evasion program loaded, activate at closest approach minus one-zero seconds if we're still here."

"Yes, sir," Helsingus said heavily. "Laser grid support?"

"Anything you like." Mirsky waved a hand magnanimously. "If we're still here to enjoy the light show."

Helsingus began flipping switches like a man possessed. On the screen, the outgoing birds passed their main engine cutout points and went ballistic; more enemy missiles began hatching like sinister blue fingers reaching out from the target point.

"Captain," Rachel said slowly.

"—One-zero seconds. They're jamming hard, sir, but the birds are still holding."

"What if *Kamchatka* is wrong? What if those are civilian mining ships?"

Captain Mirsky ignored her.

"Five seconds! Bird one ready to go—range down to one-zero K. Three. EMP lockdown is go. Sensor stepdown mag six is go. Optics shielded—bang. Sir, I confirm that bird one has detonated. Bang. Bird two is gone."

"Radar. What do you see?" asked Mirsky.

"Waiting on the fog to clear—ah, got sensors back sir. Incoming missiles still closing. Fireball remnants hashing up radar, lidar is better. Uh, the impact spectroscope has tripped, sir, we have a confirmed impact on the target alpha. Oxygen, nitrogen, carbonitrile emissions from the hull. I think we holed him, sir."

"We holed him—" Mirsky stopped. Turned to glance at Rachel. "What did you say?" he demanded.

"What if they're civilians? We have only *Kamchatka*'s word that they're under attack; no direct evidence other than bombs going off—which could be hers."

"Nonsense." Mirsky snorted. "None of our ships could make a mistake like that!"

"Nobody is actually shooting live missiles at us. The pre-jump briefing warned everyone to look out for enemy missile boats. How likely is it that the *Kamchatka* ran down a civilian mining ship by mistake and got a bit trigger-happy? And what you're seeing as an attack is actually just the cruiser screen shooting in the dark at anything that moves?"

Dead silence. Enlisted men and officers alike stared at Rachel disapprovingly: nobody spoke to the captain like that! Then from behind her: "Spallation debris on radar, sir. Target is breaking up. Uh, humbly reporting, Captain, we have distress beacons. Civilian ones..."

the *lord vanek* was going far too fast to slow down, and as flagship and lead element of the squadron, had a duty not to do so. Nevertheless, they signaled the squadron astern; and behind them, one of the elderly battleships peeled off to pick up any survivors from the disastrous attack.

The big picture, when it finally gelled some eight hours later, was very bad indeed. The "missile carriers" were actually refinery tugs, tending the migratory robot factories that slowly trawled the Kuiper-belt bodies, extracting helium 3 from the snowballs. Their sudden burst of speed had a simple explanation; seeing alien warships, they had panicked, dumping their cargo pods so that they could clear the area under maximum acceleration. One of the distant explosions had been the *Kamchatka,* landing a near miss on one of the "enemy battleships"—the cruiser *India.* (Minor hull damage and a couple of evacuated compartments had resulted; unfortunately, the cruiser's chaplain had been in one of the compartments at the time, and had gone to meet his maker.)

"Ser-erves 'em right for being in the way, dammit," quavered Admiral Kurtz when Commodore Bauer delivered the news in person. "Wha-what do they think this is?" He half rose to his feet, momentarily forgetting about his glass legs: "Simply appalling stupidity!"

"Ah, I believe we still have a problem, sir," Bauer pointed out as Robard tried to get his master settled down again. "This system is claimed by Septagon, and, ah, we have received signals as of half an hour ago indicating that they have a warship in the area, and it's engaging us on an intercept trajectory."

The Admiral snorted. "What can one warship d-do?"

Rachel, who had inveigled her way into the staff meeting on the grounds that, as a neutral observer, it was her duty to act as an intermediary in situations such as this one, watched Bauer spluttering with mordant interest. *Can he really be that stupid?* she wondered, glancing at the admiral, who hunched in his chair like a bald parrot, eyes gleaming with an expression of fixed mania.

"Sir, the warship that is signaling us is, ah, according to our most recent updates, one of their Apollo-class fleet attack carriers. Radar says they've got additional traces indicative of a full battle group. We outnumber them, but—"

Rachel cleared her throat. "They'll eat you for breakfast."

Bauer's head whipped around. "What did you say?"

She tapped her PA, where it lay on the table before her. "UN defense intelligence estimates suggest that Septagon's policy of building carriers, rather than the standard laser/missile platform that your navy has adopted, gives them a considerable advantage in the ability to cover an entire system. Simply put, while they lack short-range firepower, they're able to launch a swarm of interceptors that can pound on you from well outside your own engagement envelope. More to the point, they're frighteningly good, and unless I'm very much mistaken, that carrier, *on its own,* outmasses your entire fleet. I wouldn't want you to get the idea that I don't rate you against the Septagon Navy, but if you're planning on fighting them, do you think you could let me know in advance? I'd like a chance to grab a survival pod first."

"Well, we can't argue with the government of Earth's defense estimates, can we, Commander?" Bauer nodded pointedly at his executive officer.

"Ah, no, sir. The Colonel is quite correct." The young and somewhat flustered Lieutenant avoided looking at Rachel; it was a minor slight she was getting plenty of practice at ignoring.

"Damned newfangled inventions," mumbled Kurtz under his breath. "Blasted many-angled ones don't want us to succeed, anyway—per-per-perfidious technophiles!" Louder: "We must press on!"

"Absolutely." Commodore Bauer nodded sagely. "If we press on to Point Two on schedule, leaving the diplomatic niceties to the embassy—speaking of which—Lieutenant Kossov. What of the update? Where do we stand with respect to further information about this Festival, its order of battle and motives? What have we learned?"

"Ah." Lieutenant Kossov, removed and polished his pince-nez nervously. "Well, there's something of a problem. The deposition from the Admiralty doesn't seem to have arrived. We were supposed to be seeing an ordnance beacon, but although we quartered the designated orbital path, there's nothing there. Either they're late—or they never planted it."

"This orbital beacon." Rachel leaned forward. "A standard target buoy, right? With a diplomatic package containing anything the Republic's intelligence services have learned about the Festival in the five years since our jump?"

Kossov glanced warily at the Commodore, who nodded. "Yes, Colonel. What of it?"

"Well, if it isn't there, that can imply three things, can't it? Either it was there, but somebody else stole or disabled it. Or—"

"Perfidious Septagonians!" Robard hastily leaned over his charge, then looked up and shrugged, eloquently.

"Indeed, Admiral. Or, as I was saying, the second option is that it hasn't been put there yet—some miscalculation, or they couldn't determine any useful information about the enemy, or they forgot about us, or something."

The noise of Kurtz's snoring cut into her exposition. All eyes turned to the admiral; Robard straightened up. "I'm afraid the Admiral's legs have been paining him considerably of late, and the dosage of his medication is not conducive to lucidity. He may sleep for some hours."

"Well, then." Bauer looked around the conference table. "I believe if you would be so good as to return His Excellency to his cabin, I will continue as his proxy and prepare a minuted report of this meeting for him to review later, when he's feeling better. Unless anyone has any comments that specifically require the Admiral's ear?" Nobody demurred. "Very well then. Recess for five minutes."

Robard and an enlisted man gingerly rolled the Admiral's chair away from the table; then, using the lift just outside the room, disappeared with him in the direction of his quarters. Everybody stood, and saluted, while the snoring officer was wheeled out of the meeting. Rachel held her face expressionless, trying to conceal the disgust and pity the sight pulled from her. *He's young enough to be my grandson. How can they do this to themselves?*

Eventually, Bauer, assuming the admiral's position at the head of the table, rapped his hand on the brass bell. "Meeting will resume. The Terran attaché has the floor. You were saying?"

"The third possibility is that the New Republic no longer exists," Rachel said bluntly. She continued, ignoring the outraged gasps around the table. "You are facing an enemy about whose capabilities you are largely ignorant. I'm afraid to say, the UN knows little more about them than you do. As I noted, there are three reasons for the New Republic not to have contacted you, and their total defeat in the intervening time is only one of them, but not one it's safe to ignore. We're now in the outbound leg of a closed, timelike loop, which will eventually clip itself out of the world line of this universe if you succeed in looping back into our relative past—but the New Republic's absolute immediate future—and taking the intruders by surprise. This has some odd implications. History reaching us inside this loop may not bear any relationship to the eventual outcome we seek, for one thing. For another—" She shrugged. "If I'd been consulted prior to this expedition, I would have strongly counseled against it. While it is not technically a breach of the letter of Clause Nineteen, it is dangerously close to the sort of activity that has brought down intervention by the Eschaton in the past. The Eschaton really doesn't like time travel in the slightest, presumably because, if things go too far, someone might edit it out of existence. So there's the possibility that what you're up against isn't just the Festival, but a higher power."

"Thank you, Colonel." Bauer nodded politely, but his face was set in a mask of disapproval. "I believe that, for now, we shall disregard that possibility. If the Eschaton chooses to involve itself, there is nothing we can do in any case, so we must work on the assumption that it will not. And in that case, all we are up against is the Festival. Kossov. What did we know about it before we left?"

"Ah, um, well, that is to say—" Kossov looked around wildly, shuffled the papers on his blotter, and sighed. "Ah, good. Yes. The Festival—"

"I know what it's called, Lieutenant," the Commodore said reprovingly. "What is it and what does it want?"

"Nobody knows." Kossov looked at his supreme commander's deputy like a rabbit caught in the blinding headlights of an oncoming express train.

"So, Commissioner." Bauer cocked his head on one side and stared at Rachel, with the single-minded analytical purpose of a raptor. "And what can the esteemed government-coordinating body of Earth tell me about the Festival?" he asked, almost tauntingly.

"Uh." Rachel shook her head. Of course the poor kid had done his best—none of these people could know anything much about the Festival. Even *she* didn't. It was a big yawning blank.

"Well?" Bauer prodded.

Rachel sighed. "This is very provisional; nobody from Earth has had any direct contact with the agency known as Festival until now, and our information is, therefore, second-hand and unverifiable. And, frankly, unbelievable. The Festival does not appear to be a government or agency thereof, as we understand the term. In fact, it may not even be human. All we know is that something of that name turns up in distant settled systems—never closer than a thousand light-years, before now—and it, well, the term we keep hearing used to describe what happens next is 'Jubilee', if that makes any sense to you. Everything... stops. And the Festival takes over the day-to-day running of the system for the duration." She looked at Bauer. "Is that what you wanted to know?"

Bauer shook his head, looking displeased. "No it wasn't," he said. "I was after capabilities."

Rachel shrugged. "We don't know," she said bluntly. "As I said, we've never seen it from close-up."

Bauer frowned. "Then this will be a first for you, won't it? Which leads us to the next issue, updates to navigation plan Delta..."

a few hours later, Rachel lay facedown on her bunk and tried to shut the world out of her head. It wasn't easy; too much of the world had followed her home over the years, crying for attention.

She was still alive. She knew, somehow, that she should feel relieved about this, but what she'd seen in the briefing room screen had unnerved her more than she was willing to admit. The admiral was a senile vacuum at the heart of the enterprise. The intelligence staff were well-meaning, but profoundly ignorant: they were so inflexible that they were incapable of doing their job properly. She'd tried to explain how advanced civilizations worked until she could feel herself turning blue in the face, and they still didn't understand! They'd nodded politely, because she was a lady—even if a somewhat scandalous one, a lady *diplomat*—and immediately forgotten or ignored her advice.

You don't fight an infowar attack with missiles and lasers, any more than you attack a railway locomotive with spears and stone axes. You don't fight a replicator attack by throwing energy and matter at machines that will just use them for fuel. They'd nodded approvingly and gone on to discuss the virtues of active countermeasures versus low-observability systems. And they still didn't get it; it was as if the very idea of something like the Festival, or even the Septagon system, occupied a mental blind spot ubiquitous in their civilization. They could accept a woman in trousers, even in a colonel's uniform, far more easily than they could cope with the idea of a technological singularity.

Back on Earth, she had attended a seminar, years ago. It had been a weeklong gathering of experts; hermeneutic engineers driven mad by studying the arcane debris of the Singularity, demographers still trying to puzzle out the distribution of colony worlds, a couple of tight-lipped mercenary commanders and commercial intelligence consultants absorbed in long-range backstop insurance against a return of the Eschaton. They were all thrown together and mixed with a coterie of Defense SIG experts and UN diplomats. It was hosted by the UN, which, as the sole remaining island of concrete stability in a sea of pocket polities, was the only body able to host such a global event.

During the seminar, she had attended a cocktail party on a balcony of white concrete, jutting from a huge hotel built on the edge of the UN city, Geneva. She'd been in uniform at the time, working as an auditor for the denuclearization commission. Black suit, white gloves, mirrorshades pulsing news updates and radiation readings into her raw and tired eyes. Hyped up on a cocktail of alcohol antagonists, she sipped a bitter (and ineffective) gin with a polite Belgian cosmologist. Mutual incomprehension tinged with apprehension bound them in an uncomfortable Ping-Pong match of a conversation. "There is so much we do not understand about the Eschaton," the cosmologist had insisted, "especially concerning its interaction with the birth of the universe. The big bang." He raised his eyebrows suggestively.

"The big bang. Not, by any chance, an unscheduled fissile criticality excursion, was it?" She said it deadpan, trying to deflect him with humor.

"Hardly. There were no licensing bodies in those days—at the start of space-time, before the era of expansion and the first appearance of mass and energy, about a billionth of a billionth of a millionth of a second into the life of the universe."

"Surely the Eschaton can't have been responsible for that. It's a modern phenomenon, isn't it?"

"Maybe not responsible," he said, choosing his words carefully. "But maybe circumstances arising then formed a necessary precondition for the Eschaton's existence, or the existence of something related to but beyond the Eschaton. There's a whole school of cosmology predicated around the weak anthropic principle, that the universe is as it seems because, if it was any other way, we would not exist to observe it. There is a ... less popular field, based on the strong anthropic principle, that the universe exists to give rise to certain types of entity. I don't believe we'll ever understand the Eschaton until we understand why the universe exists."

She smiled at him toothily, and let a Prussian diplomat rescue her with the aid of a polite bow and an offer to explain the fall of Warsaw during the late unpleasantness in the Baltic. A year or so later, the polite cosmologist had been murdered by Algerian religious fundamentalists who thought his account of the universe a blasphemy against the words of the prophet Yusuf Smith as inscribed on his two tablets of gold. But that was typical of Europe, half-empty and prey to what the formerly Islamic world had become.

Somewhere along the line she, too, had changed. She'd spent decades—the best part of her second, early-twenty-second-century life—fighting the evils of nuclear proliferation. Starting out as a dreadlocked direct-action activist, chaining herself to fences, secure in the naive youthful belief that no harm could befall her. Later, she'd figured out that the way to do it was wearing a smart suit, with mercenary soldiers and the threat of canceled insurance policies backing up her quiet voice. Still prickly and direct, but less of a knee-jerk nonconformist, she'd learned to work the system for maximum effect. The hydra seemed halfway under control, bombings down to only one every couple of years, when Bertil had summoned her to Geneva and offered her a new job. Then she'd wished she'd paid more attention to the cosmologist—for the Algerian Latter-Day Saints had been very thorough in their suppression of the Tiplerite heresy—but it was too late, and in any event, the minutiae of the Standing Committee's investigations into chronological and probabilistic warfare beckoned.

Somewhere along the line, the idealist had butted heads with the pragmatist, and the pragmatist won. Maybe the seeds had been sown during her first marriage. Maybe it had come later; being shot in the back and spending six months recovering in hospital in Calcutta had changed her. She'd done her share of shooting, too, or at least directing the machinery of preemptive vengeance, wiping out more than one cell of atomic-empowered fanatics—whether central-Asian independence fighters, freelance mercs with a bomb too many in their basement, or on one notable occasion, radical pro-lifers willing to go to any lengths to protect the unborn child. Idealism couldn't coexist with so many other people's ideals, betrayed in their execution by the tools they'd chosen. She'd walked through Manchester three days after the Inter-City Firm's final kickoff, before the rain had swept the sad mounds of cinders and bone from the blasted streets. She'd become so cynical that only a complete change of agenda, a wide-angle view of the prospects for humanity, could help her retain her self-respect.

And so to the New Republic. A shithole of a backwater, in her frank opinion; in need of remodeling by any means necessary, lest it pollute its more enlightened neighboring principalities, like Malacia or Turku. But the natives were still people—and for all that they tampered with the machineries of mass destruction in apparent ignorance of their power, they deserved better than they'd receive from an awakened and angry Eschaton. They deserved better than to be left to butt heads with something they didn't understand, like the Festival, whatever it was: if they couldn't understand it, then maybe she'd have to think the unthinkable for them, help them to reach some kind of accommodation with it—if that was possible. The alarming aspect to the UN's knowledge of the Festival—the only thing she hadn't told Bauer about—was that antitech colonies contacted by it disappeared, leaving only wreckage behind when the Festival moved on. Just why this might be she didn't know, but it didn't bode well for the future.

nothing quite concentrates a man's mind like the knowledge that he is to be hanged in four weeks; unless it is possibly the knowledge that he has sabotaged the very ship he sails in, and he—along with everyone else in it—will be hanged in three months. For while the execution may be farther away, the chances of a reprieve are infinitely lower.

Martin Springfield sat in the almost-deserted wardroom, a glass of tea at his hand, staring absently at the ceiling beams. A nautical theme pervaded the room; old oak panels walled it in, and the wooden plank floor had been holystone-polished until it gleamed. A silver-chased samovar sat steaming gently atop an age-blackened chest beneath a huge gilt-framed oil painting of the ship's namesake that hung on one wall. *Lord Vanek* leading the cavalry charge at the suppression of the Robots' Rebellion 160 years ago—destroying the aspirations of those citizens who had dreamed of life without drudge-labor in the service of aristocrats. Martin shivered slightly, trying to grapple with his personal demons.

It's all my fault, he thought. *And there's nobody else to share it with.*

Comfortless fate. He sipped at his glass, felt the acrid sweet bite of the rum underlying the bitterness of the tea. His lips felt numb, now. *Stupid,* he thought. It was too late to undo things. Too late to confess, even to Rachel, to try to get her out of this trap. He should have told her right at the beginning, before she came on board. Kept her out of the way of the Eschaton's revenge. Now, even if he confessed everything, or had done so before they tripped the patch in the drive kernel controllers, it would only put him on a one-way trip to the death chair. And although the sabotage was essential, and even though it wouldn't kill anyone directly—

Martin shuddered, drained the glass, and put it down beside his chair. He hunched forward unconsciously, neck bowed beneath the weight of a guilty conscience. *At least I did the right thing,* he tried to tell himself. *None of us are going home, but at least the homes we had will still be there when we're gone.* Including Rachel's unlived-in apartment. He winced. It was next to impossible to feel guilt for a fleet, but just knowing about her presence aboard the ship had kept him awake all night.

The mournful pipes had summoned the ship to battle stations almost an hour ago. Something to do with an oncoming Septagonese carrier battle group, scrambled like a nest of angry hornets in response to the fiasco with the mining tugs. It didn't make any difference to Martin. Somewhere in the drive control network, an atomic clock was running slow, tweaked by a folded curl of space-time from the drive kernel. It was only a small error, of course, but CP violation would amplify it out of all proportion when the fleet began its backward path through space-time. He'd done it deliberately, to prevent a catastrophic and irrevocable disaster. The New Republican Navy might think a closed timelike loop to be only a petty tactical maneuver, but it was the thin end of a wedge; a wedge that Herman said had to be held at bay. He'd made his pact with a darker, more obscure agency than Rachel's. From his perspective, the UN DISA people merely aped his employer's actions on a smaller scale—in hope of pre-empting them.

Good-bye, Belinda, he thought, mentally consigning his sister to oblivion. *Good-bye, London.* Dust of ages ate the metropolis, crumbled its towers in dust. *Hello, Herman,* to the steady tick of the pendulum clock on the wall. As the flagship, *Lord Vanek* provided a time signal for the other vessels in the fleet. Not just that; it provided an inertial reference frame locked to the space-time coordinates of their first jump. By slightly slowing the clock, Martin had ensured that the backward time component of their maneuver would be botched very slightly.

The fleet would travel forward into the light cone, maybe as much as four thousand years; it would rewind, back almost the whole distance—but not quite as far as it had come. Their arrival at Rochard's World would be delayed almost two weeks, about as long as a rapid crossing without any of the closed timelike hanky-panky the Admiralty had planned. And then the Festival would—well, what the Festival would do to the fleet was the Festival's business. All he knew was that he, and everyone else, would pay the price.

Who did they think they were kidding, anyway? Claiming they planned to use the maneuver just to reduce transit time, indeed! Even a toddler could see through a subterfuge that transparent, all the way to the sealed orders waiting in the admiral's safe. *You can't fool the Eschaton by lying to yourself.* Maybe Herman, or rather the being that hid behind that code name, would be waiting. Maybe Martin would be able to get off the doomed ship, maybe Rachel would, or maybe through a twist of fate the New Republican Navy would defeat the Festival in a head-to-head fight. And maybe he'd teach the horse to sing . . .

He stood up, a trifle giddily, and carried his glass to the

samovar. He half filled it, then topped it up from the cut-glass decanter until the nostril-prickling smell began to waft over the steam. He sat down in his chair a bit too hard, numb fingertips and lips threatening to betray him. With nothing to do but avoid his guilt by drinking himself into a paralytic stupor, Martin was taking the easy way out.

Presently, he drifted back to more tolerable memories. Eighteen years earlier, when he was newly married and working as a journeyman field circus engineer, a gray cipher of a man had approached him in a bar somewhere in orbit over Wollstonecroft's World. "Can I buy you a drink?" asked the man, whose costume was somewhere between that of an accountant and a lawyer. Martin had nodded. "You're Martin Springfield," the man had said. "You work at present for Nakamichi Nuclear, where you are making relatively little money and running up a sizable overdraft. My sponsors have asked me to approach you with a job offer."

"Answer's no," Martin had said automatically. He had made up his mind some time before that the experience he was gaining at NN was more useful than an extra thousand euros a year; and besides, his employing combine was paranoid enough about some of its contracts to sound out its contractor's loyalties with fake approaches.

"There is no conflict of interest with your current employers, Mr. Springfield. The job is a nonexclusive commission, and in any event, it will not take effect until you go freelance or join another kombinat."

"What kind of job?" Martin raised an eyebrow.

"Have you ever wondered why you exist?"

"Don't be—" Martin had paused in midsentence. "Is this some religious pitch?" he asked.

"No." The gray man looked him straight in the eye. "It's exactly the opposite. No god exists yet, in this universe. My employer wishes to safeguard the necessary preconditions for God's emergence, however. And to do so, my employer needs human arms and legs. Not being equipped with them, so to speak."

The crash of his glass hitting the floor and shattering had brought Martin to his senses. "Your employer—"

"Believes that you may have a role to play in defending the security of the cosmos, Martin. Naming no names"—the gray man leaned closer—"it is a long story. Would you like to hear it?"

Martin had nodded, it seeming the only reasonable thing to do in a wholly unreasonable, indeed surreal, situation. And in doing so, he'd taken the first step along the path that had brought him here, eighteen years later: to a drinking binge alone in the wardroom of a doomed starship, only weeks left to play out the end of its role in the New Republican Navy. Minutes, in the worst possible case.

Eventually, he would be reported lost, along with the entire crew of the *Lord Vanek*. Relatives would be notified, tears would be shed against the greater backdrop of a tragic and unnecessary war. But that would be no concern of his. Because—just as soon as he finished this drink—he was going to stand up and weave his way to his cabin and lie down. Then await whatever would follow over the next three months, until the jaws of the trap sprang shut.

it was hot, and somewhat stuffy, in Rachel's room, despite the whirring white noise of the ventilation system and the occasional dripping of an overflow pipe behind the panel next to her head. Sleeping wasn't an option; neither was relaxation. She found herself wishing for someone to talk to, someone who would have an idea what was going on. She rolled over on her back. "PA," she called, finally indulging an urge she'd been fighting off for some time. "Where's Martin Springfield?"

"Location. Ship's wardroom, D deck."

"Anyone with him?"

"Negative."

She sat up. The crew were at their action stations: what on earth was Martin doing there on his own?

"I'm going there. Backdoor clause: as far as the ship is concerned, I am still in my cabin. Confirm capability."

"Affirmative. Backdoor tracking master override confirmed." They might have rebuilt the ship's fire control and propulsion systems, but they'd left the old tab/badge personnel tracking grid in place—unused, probably, because it reduced the need for tyrannical petty officers. Rachel pulled on her boots, then stood up and grabbed the jacket that lay on the upper bunk. She'd take a minute to look presentable, then go and find Martin. She was irresponsible to leave her airtight cabin while the ship was cleared for action—but so was he. What was he thinking of?

She headed for the wardroom briskly. The access spaces of the warship were eerily quiet, the crew all locked down in airtight compartments and damage control stations. Only the humming of the ventilation system broke the silence; that, and the ticking of the wardroom clock as she opened the door.

The only occupant of the room was Martin, and he looked somewhat the worse for wear, slumped in an overstuffed armchair like a rag doll that had lost its stuffing. A silver-chased tea glass sat on the table in front of him, half-full of a brown liquid which, if Rachel was any judge of character, was not tea. He opened his eyes to watch her as she entered, but didn't say anything.

"You should be in your cabin," Rachel observed. "The wardroom isn't vacuum-safe, you know."

"Who cares?" He made a rolling motion of one shoulder, as if a shrug was too much effort. "Really don't see the point."

"I do." She marched over and stood in front of him. "You can go to your cabin or come back to mine, but you *are* going to be in a cabin in five minutes!"

"Don't remember signing a contractual...of employment with you," he mumbled.

"No, you didn't," she said brightly. "So I'm not doing this in my capacity as your employer, I'm doing it as your government."

"Whoa—" Rachel heaved. "But I don't have a gummint." Martin stumbled out of the chair, a pained expression on his face.

"The New Republic seems to think you have, and I'm the best you'll find around here. Unless you'd prefer the other choice on offer?"

Martin grimaced. "Hardly." He staggered. "Got some 4-3-1 in left pocket. Think I need it." He staggered, fumbling for the small blister pack of alcohol antagonists. "No need to get nasty."

"I wasn't getting nasty; I was just providing you with an inertial reference frame for your own good. 'Sides, I thought we were going to look out for each other. And I wouldn't be doing my job if I didn't get you out of here and into a cabin before someone notices. Drunkenness is a flogging offense, did you know that?" Rachel took him by one elbow and began gently steering him toward the door. Martin was sufficiently wobbly on his legs to make this an interesting experience; she was tall, and had boosters embedded in her skeletal muscles for just such events, but he had the three advantages of mass, momentum, and a low center of gravity. Together, they described a brief drunkard's walk before Martin managed to fumble his drug patch onto the palm of one hand, and Rachel managed to steer the two of them into the corridor.

By the time they reached her cabin, he was breathing deeply and looking pale. "In," she ordered.

"I feel like shit," he murmured. "Got any drinking water?"

"Yup." She pulled the hatch shut behind them and spun the locking wheel. "Sink's over there; I'm sure you've seen one before."

"Thanks, I think." He ran the taps, splashed water on his face, then used the china cup to take mouthful after mouthful. "Damned alcohol dehydration." He straightened up. "You think I should have more sense than to do that?"

"The thought had crossed my mind," she said drily. She crossed her arms and watched him. He shook himself like a bedraggled water rat and sat down heavily on Rachel's neatly folded bunk.

"I needed to forget some things very badly," he said moodily. "Maybe too badly. Doesn't happen very often but, well, being locked up with nobody for company but my own head isn't good for me. All I get to see these days are cable runs and change schematics, plus a few naive young midshipmen at lunch. That spook from the Curator's Office is hanging around all the time, keeping an eye on me and listening to whatever I say. It's like being in a fucking prison."

Rachel pulled out the folding chair and sat on it. "You've never been in prison, then. Consider yourself lucky."

His lips quirked. "You have, I suppose? The public servant?"

"Yeah. Spent eight months inside, once, banged up for industrial espionage by an agricultural cartel. Amnesty Multinational made me a prisoner of commerce and started up a trade embargo: that got me sprung pretty quick." She winced at the memories, grey shadows of their original violent fury, washed out by time. It wasn't her longest stretch inside, but she had no intention of telling him that just yet.

He shook his head and smiled faintly. "The New Republic is like a prison for everyone, though. Isn't it?"

"Hmm." She stared through him at the wall behind. "Now you mention it, I think you could be stretching things a bit far."

"Well, you'll at least concede they're all prisoners of their ideology, aren't they? Two hundred years of violent suppression hasn't left them much freedom to distance themselves from their culture and look around. Hence the mess we're in now." He lay back, propping his head against the wall. "Excuse me; I'm tired. I spent a double shift on the drive calibration works, then four hours over on *Glorious,* troubleshooting its RCS oxidant switching logic."

"You're excused." Rachel unbuttoned her jacket, then bent down and slid off her boots. *"Ow."*

"Sore feet?"

"Damned Navy, always on their feet. Looks bad if I slouch, too."

He yawned. "Speaking of other things, what do you think the Septagon forces will do?"

She shrugged. "Probably track us the hell out of here at gunpoint, while pressing the New Republic for compensation. They're pragmatists, none of this babble about national honor and the virtues of courage and manly manhood and that sort of thing."

Martin sat up. "If you're going to take your boots off, if you don't mind—"

She waved a hand. "Be my guest."

"I thought I was supposed to be your loyal subject?"

She giggled. "Don't get ideas above your station! Really, these damned monarchists. I understand in the abstract, but how do they put up with it? I'd go crazy, I swear it. Within a decade."

"Hmm." He leaned forward, busy with his shoes. "Look at it another way. Most people back home sit around with their families and friends and lead a cozy life, doing three or four different things at the same time—gardening, designing commercial beetles, painting landscapes, and bringing up children, that sort of thing. Entomologists picking over the small things in life to see what's twitching its legs underneath. Why the hell aren't we doing that ourselves?"

"I used to." He glanced up at her curiously, but she was elsewhere, remembering. "Spent thirty years being a housewife, would you believe it? Being good God-fearing people, hubby was the breadwinner, two delightful children to dote over, and a suburban garden. Church every Sunday and nothing—nothing—allowed to break with the pretense of conformity."

"Ah. I thought you were older than you looked. Late-sixties backlash?"

"Which sixties?" She shook her head, then answered her own rhetorical question: "Twenty-sixties. I was born in forty-nine. Grew up in a Baptist family, Baptist town, quiet religion—it turned inward after the Eschaton. We were all so desperately afraid, I think. It was a long time ago: I find it hard to remember.

One day I was forty-eight and the kids were at college and I realized I didn't believe a word of it. They'd gotten the extension treatments nailed down by then, and the pastor had stopped denouncing it as satanic tampering with God's will—after his own grandfather beat him at squash—and I suddenly realized that I'd had an empty day, and I had maybe a million days just like it ahead of me, and there were so many things I hadn't done and couldn't do, if I stayed the same. And I didn't really *believe:* religion was my husband's thing, I just went along with it. So I moved out. Took the treatment, lost twenty years in six months. Went through the usual Sterling fugue, changed my name, changed my life, changed just about everything about me. Joined an anarchist commune, learned to juggle, got into radical antiviolence activism. Harry—no, Harold—couldn't cope with that."

"Second childhood. Sort of like a twentieth-century teenage period."

"Yes, exactly—" She stared at Martin. "How about you?"

He shrugged. "I'm younger than you. Older than most everyone else aboard this idiotic children's crusade. Except maybe the admiral." For an instant, and only an instant, he looked hagridden. "You shouldn't be here. *I* shouldn't be here."

She stared at him. "You've got it bad?"

"We're—" He checked himself, cast her a curious guarded look, then started again. "This trip is doomed. I suppose you know that."

"Yes." She looked at the floor. "I know that," she said calmly. "If I don't broker some sort of cease-fire or persuade them not to use their causality weapons, the Eschaton will step in. Probably throw a comet made of antimatter at them, or something." She looked at him. "What do you think?"

"I think—" He paused again and looked away, slightly evasively. "If the Eschaton intervenes, we're both in the wrong place."

"Huh. That's so much fun to know." She forced a grin. "So where do you come from? Go on, I told you—"

Martin stretched his arms and leaned back. "I grew up in a Yorkshire hill farming village, all goats and cloth caps and dark satanic mills full of God-knows-what. Oh yes, and compulsory ferret-legging down the pub on Tuesday evenings, for the tourist trade tha' knows."

"Ferret-legging?" Rachel looked at him incredulously.

"Yup. You tie your kilt up around your knees with duct tape—

as you probably know, no Yorkshireman would be seen dead wearing anything under his sporran—and take a ferret by the scruff of his neck. A ferret, that's like, uh, a bit like a mink. Only less friendly. It's a young man's initiation rite; you stick the ferret where the sun doesn't shine and dance the furry dance to the tune of a balalaika. Last man standing and all that, kind of like the ancient Boer aardvark-kissing competition." Martin shuddered dramatically. "I hate ferrets. The bloody things bite like a cask-strength single malt without the nice after-effects."

"That was what you did on Tuesdays," Rachel said, slowly beginning to smile. "Tell me more. What about Wednesdays?"

"Oh, on Wednesdays we stayed home and watched reruns of *Coronation Road*. They remixed the old video files to near-realistic resolution and subtitled them, of course, so we could understand what they were saying. Then we'd all hoist a pint of Tetley's tea and toast the downfall of the House of Lancaster. Very traditional, us Yorkshirefolk. I remember the thousandth-anniversary victory celebrations—but that's enough about me. What did *you* do on Wednesdays?"

Rachel blinked. "Nothing in particular. Defused terrorist A-bombs, got shot at by Algerian Mormon separatists. Uh, that was after I kicked over the traces the first time. Before then, I think I took the kids to soccer, although I'm not sure what day of the week that was." She turned aside for a moment and rummaged in the steamer trunk under her bunk. "Ah, here it is." She pulled out a narrow box and opened it. "You know what? Maybe you shouldn't have used that sober patch." The bottle gleamed golden beneath the antiseptic cabin lights.

"I'd be lousy company though. I was getting all drunk and depressed on my own, and you had to interrupt me and make me sober up."

"Well, maybe you should just have tried to find someone to get drunk with instead of doing it on your own." Two small glasses appeared. She leaned close. "Do you want it watered?"

Martin eyed the bottle critically. Replicated Speyside fifty-year malt, a cask-strength bottling template. If it wasn't a nanospun clone of the original, it would be worth its weight in platinum. Even so, it would be more than adequately drinkable. "I'll take it neat and report to sick bay for a new throat tomorrow." He whistled appreciatively as she poured a generous measure. "How did you know?"

"That you'd like it?" She shrugged. "I didn't. I just grew up on corn liquor. Didn't meet the real thing till a job in Syrtis—" Her face clouded over. "Long life and happiness."

"I'll drink to that," he agreed after a moment. They sat in silence for a minute, savoring the afterbloom of the whisky. "I'd be happier right now if I knew what was going on, though."

"I wouldn't be too worried: either nothing, or we'll be dead too fast to feel it. The carrier from Septagon will probably just make a fast pass to reassure itself that we're not planning on spreading any more mayhem, then escort us to the next jump zone while the diplomats argue over who pays. Right now, I've got the comms room taking my name in vain for all it's worth; hopefully, that'll convince them not to shoot at us without asking some more questions first."

"I'd be happier if I knew we had a way off this ship."

"Relax. Drink your whisky." She shook her head. "We don't. So stop worrying about it. Anyway, if they do shoot us, wouldn't you rather die happily sipping a good single malt or screaming in terror?"

"Has anyone ever told you you're cold-blooded? No, I take it back. Has anyone ever told you you've got a skin like a tank?"

"Frequently." She stared into her glass thoughtfully. "It's a learned thing. Pray you never have to learn it."

"You mean you had to?"

"Yes. No other way to do my job. My last job, that is."

"What did you do?" he asked softly.

"I wasn't joking about the terrorist A-bombs. Actually, the bombs were the easiest bit; it was finding the assholes who planted them that was the hard part. Find the asshole, find the gadget, fix the gadget, fix the dump they sprang the plute from. Usually in that order, unless we were unlucky enough to have to deal with an unscheduled criticality excursion in downtown wherever without someone mailing in a warning first. Then if we found the asshole, our hardest job would be keeping the lynch mob away from them until we could find out where they sourced the bang-juice."

"Did you ever lose any?" he asked, even more quietly.

"You mean, did I ever fuck up and kill several thousand people?" she asked. "Yes—"

"No, that's not what I meant." He reached for her free hand gently. "I know where you've been. Any job I do—if it doesn't work, somebody pays. Possibly hundreds or thousands of somebodies. That's the price of good engineering; nobody notices you did your job right."

"Nobody's actually trying to stop you doing your job," she challenged.

"Oh, you'd be surprised."

The tension in her shoulders ebbed. "I'm sure you've got a story about that, too. You know, for someone who's no good at dealing with people, you're not bad at being a shoulder to cry on."

He snorted. "And for someone who's a failure at her job you're doing surprisingly well so far." He let go of her hand and rubbed the back of her neck. "But I think you could do with a massage. You're really tense. Got a headache yet?"

"No," she said, slightly reluctantly. Then she took another sip of her whisky. The glass was nearly empty now. "But I'm open to persuasion."

"I know three ways to die happy. Unfortunately, I've never tried any of them. Care to join me?"

"Where did you hear about them?"

"At a séance. It was a good séance. Seriously, though. Dr. Springfield prescribes another dose of Speyside life-water, then a lie down and a neck massage. Then, even if the many-angled ones decide to come in shooting, at least fifty percent of us get to die happy. How's that sound?"

"Fine." She smiled tiredly and reached for the bottle, ready to top his glass up. "But you know something? You were right about the not knowing. You can get used to it, but it doesn't get any easier. I wish I knew what they were thinking..."

bronze bells rolled on the bridge of the Fleet attack carrier *Neon Lotus*. Incense smoldered in burners positioned above air inlet ducts; beyond the ornate gold-chased pillars marking the edges of the room, the brilliant jewels of tracking glyphs streamed past against a backdrop consisting of infinite darkness. Shipboard Facilities Coordinator Ariadne Eldrich leaned back in her chair and contemplated the blackness of space. She stared intently at the cluster of glyphs that intersected her vector close to the center of the wall. "Cultureless fools. Just what did they think they were doing?"

"Thinking probably had very little to do with it," Interdictor Director Marcus Bismarck noted drily. "Our Republican neighbors seem to think that too much mind-work rots the brain."

Eldrich snorted. "Too true." A smaller cloud of diadems traced a convergent path through the void behind the New Republican battle squadron; a wing of antimatter-powered interceptors, six hours out from the carrier and accelerating on a glare of hard gamma radiation at just under a thousand gees. Their crew—bodies vitrified, minds uploaded into their computational matrices— watched the intruders, coldly alert for any sign of active countermeasures, a prelude to attack. "But who did they think they were shooting at?"

A new voice spoke up. "Can't be sure, but they say they're at war." A soft soprano, Chu Melinda, shipboard liaison with the Public Intelligence Organization. "They say they mistook the mining tugs for enemy interceptors. Although what enemy they expected to meet on *our* turf—"

"I thought they weren't talking directly to us?" asked Bismarck.

"They aren't, but they've got a halfway-sensible diplomatic expert system along. Says it's a UN observer and authenticates as, uh, a UN observer. It vouches for their incompetence, so unless the Capitol wants to go accusing the UN of lying, we'd better take it at face value. Confidence factor is point-eight plus, anyway."

"Why'd they give it access to their shipboard comms net?"

"Who but the Eschaton knows? Only, I note with interest that all but one of those craft was built in a Solar shipyard."

"I can't say I'm best pleased." Eldrich stared at the screen moodily. The ship sensed some of her underlying mood: a target selection cursor ghosted briefly across the enemy glyphs, locking grasers onto the distant projected light cones of the enemy flotilla. "Still. As long as we can keep them from doing any more damage. Any change in their jump trajectory?"

"None yet," Chu commented. "Still heading for SPD-47. Why would anybody want to go there, anyway? It's not even on a track for any of their colonies."

"*Hmm.* And they came out of nowhere. That suggest anything to you?"

"Either they're crazy, or maybe the UN inspector is along for a purpose," mused Bismarck. "If they're trying to make a timelike runaround on some enemy who's—" His eyes widened.

"What is it?" demanded Ariadne.

"The Festival!" he exclaimed. His eyes danced. "Remember that? Five years ago? They're going to attack the Festival!"

"They're going to attack?" Ariadne Eldrich spluttered. "A *Festival?* Whatever for?"

A brief glazed look crossed Chu's face, upload communion

with a distributed meme repository far bigger and more powerful than every computer network of pre-Singularity Earth. "He's right," she said. "The rejectionists are going to attack the Festival as if it's a limbic-imperialist invader."

Ariadne Eldrich, Shipboard Facilities Coordinator and manager of more firepower than the New Republican Navy could even dream of, surrendered to the urge to cackle like a maniac. "They must be mad!"

telegram from the dead _____

before the singularity, human beings living on Earth had looked at the stars and consoled themselves in their isolation with the comforting belief that the universe didn't care.

Unfortunately, they were mistaken.

Out of the blue, one summer day in the middle of the twenty-first century, something unprecedented inserted itself into the swarming anthill of terrestrial civilization and stirred it with a stick. What it was—a manifestation of a strongly superhuman intelligence, as far beyond an augmented human's brain as a human mind is beyond that of a frog—wasn't in question. Where it was from, to say nothing of *when* it was from, was another matter.

Before the Singularity, developments in quantum logic had been touted as opening the door to esoteric breakthroughs in computational artificial intelligence. They'd also been working on funneling information back in time: perhaps as a route to the bulk movement of matter at faster-than-light speeds, although that was seen as less important than its application to computing. General relativity had made explicit, back in the twentieth century, the fact that both faster-than-light and time travel required a violation of causality—the law that every effect must have a prior cause. Various defense mechanisms and laws of cosmic censorship were proposed and discarded to explain why causality violation didn't lead to widespread instability in the universe—and all of them were proven wrong during the Singularity.

About nine billion human beings simply vanished in the blink of an eye, sucked right out of the observable universe with nothing to show where they had gone. Strange impenetrable objects—

tetrahedrons, mostly, but with some other platonic solids thrown in, silvery and massless—appeared dotted across the surface of the planets of the inner solar system. Networks crashed. One message crystallized out in the information-saturated pool of human discourse:

I am the Eschaton. I am not your god.
I am descended from you, and I exist in your future.
Thou shalt not violate causality within my historic light cone.
Or else.

It took the stunned survivors twenty years to claw back from the edge of disaster, with nine-tenths of the work force gone and intricate economic ecosystems collapsing like defoliated jungles. It took them another fifty years to reindustrialize the inner solar system. Ten more years and the first attempts were made to apply the now-old tunneling breakthrough to interstellar travel.

In the middle of the twenty-second century, an exploration ship reached Barnard's Star. Faint radio signals coming from the small second planet were decoded; the crew of the research mission learned what had happened to the people the Eschaton had removed. Scattered outside the terrestrial light cone, they'd been made involuntary colonists of thousands of worlds: exported through wormholes that led back in time as well as out in space, given a minimal support system of robot factories and an environment with breathable air. Some of the inhabited worlds, close to Earth, had short histories, but farther out, many centuries had passed.

The shock of this discovery would echo around the expanded horizons of human civilization for a thousand years, but all the inhabited worlds had one thing in common: somewhere there was a monument, bearing the injunction against causality violation. It seemed that forces beyond human comprehension took an interest in human affairs, and wanted everyone to know it. But when a course of action is explicitly forbidden, somebody will inevitably try it. And the Eschaton showed little sign of making allowances for the darker side of human nature...

the battlecruiser lay at rest, bathed in the purple glare of a stellar remnant. Every hour, on the hour, its laser grid lit up, sending a pulse of ultraviolet light into the void; a constellation of small interferometry platforms drifted nearby, connected by high-bandwidth laser links. Outside, space was hot: although no star gleamed in the center of the pupillary core, something in there was spitting out a rain of charged particles.

Elements of the battle fleet lay around the *Lord Vanek,* none of them close enough to see with the naked eye. They had waited here for three weeks as the stragglers popped out of jump transition and wearily cruised over to join the formation. Over the six weeks before that, the ship had made jump after jump—bouncing between the two components of an aged binary system that had long since ejected its planets into deep space and settled down to a lonely old age. Each jump reached farther into the future, until finally the ships were making millennial hops into the unknown.

The atmosphere in the wardroom was unusually tense. Aboard a warship under way, boredom is a constant presence: after nearly seven weeks, even the most imperturbable officers were growing irritable. Word that the last of the destroyers had arrived at the rendezvous had spread like wildfire through the ship a few hours earlier. A small cluster of officers huddled together in a corner, cradling a chilled bottle of schnapps and talking into the small hours of the shipboard night, trying desperately to relax, for tomorrow the fleet would begin the return journey, winding back around their own time line until they overhauled their own entry point into this system and became an intrusion into the loose-woven fabric of history itself.

"I only joined the Navy to see the fleshpots of Malacia," Grubor observed. "Spend too long nursing the ship's sewage-processing farm and before long the bridge crew starts treating you like a loose floater in free fall. They go off to receptions and suchlike whenever we enter port, but all I get is a chance to flush the silage tanks and study for the engineering board exams."

"Fleshpots!" Boursy snorted. "Pavel, you take your prospects too seriously. There're no fleshpots on Malacia that you or I would be allowed anywhere near. Most places I can't so much as breathe without Sauer taking notes on how well I've polished my tonsils; and then the place stinks, or it's full of evil bugs, or the natives are politically unsound. Or weird. Or deformed, and into hideous and unnatural sexual perversions. You name it."

"Still." Grubor studied his drink. "It would have been nice to get to see at least *one* hideous and unnatural sexual perversion."

Kravchuk twisted the lid off the bottle and pointed it in the direction of their glasses. Grubor shook his head; Boursy extended his for a top-up. "What I want to know is how we're going to get back," Kravchuk muttered. "I don't understand how we can do that. Time only goes one way, doesn't it? Stands to reason."

"Reason, schmeason." Grubor took a mouthful of spirit. "It doesn't have to work that way. Not just 'cause you want it to." He glanced around. "No ears, eh? Listen, I think we're in it up to our necks. There's this secret drive fix they bought from Lord God-knows-where, that lets us do weird things with the time axis in our jumps. We only headed out to this blasted hole in space to minimize the chances of anyone finding us—or of the jumps going wrong. They're looking for some kind of time capsule from home to tell us what to do next, what happened in the history books. Then we go back—farther than we came to get here, by a different route—and get where we're going before we set off. With me so far? But the real problem is God. They're planning on breaking the Third Commandment."

Boursy crossed himself and looked puzzled. "What, disrespecting the holy father and mother? My family—"

"No, the one that says thou shalt not fuck with history *or else,* signed Yours Truly, God. That Third Commandment, the one burned into Thanksgiving Rock in letters six feet deep and thirty feet high. Got it?"

Boursy looked dubious. "It could have been some joker in orbit with a primary-phase free-electron laser—"

"Weren't no such things in those days. I despair of you sometimes, I really do. Look, the fact is, we don't know what in hell's sixteen furnaces is waiting for us at Rochard's World. So we're sneaking up on it from behind, like the peasant in the story who goes hunting elephants with a mirror because he's never seen one and he's so afraid that—" Out of the corner of his eye, Grubor noted Sauer—unofficially the ship's political officer—walk in the door.

"Who are you calling a cowardly peasant?" rumbled Boursy, also glancing at the door. "I've known the Captain for eighty-seven years, and he's a good man! And the Admiral, are you calling the Admiral a fairy?"

"No, I'm just *trying* to point out that we're all afraid of one thing or another and—" Grubor gesticulated in the wrong direction.

"Are you calling me a poof?" Boursy roared.

"No, I'm not!" Grubor shouted back at him. Spontaneous applause broke out around the room, and one of the junior cadets struck up a stirring march on the pianola. Unfortunately his piano-playing was noteworthy more for his enthusiasm than his melodious harmony, and the wardroom rapidly degenerated into a heckling match between the cadet's supporters (who were few) and everyone else.

"Nothing can go wrong," Boursy said smugly. "We're going to sail into Rochard's system and show the flag and send those degenerate alien invaders packing. You'll see. Nothing will, er, did, go wrong."

"I dunno about that." Kravchuk, normally tight-lipped to the point of autism, allowed himself to relax slightly when drinking in private with his brother officers. "The foreign bint, the spy or diplomat or whatever. She's meant to be keeping an eye on us, right? Don't see why the Captain's going so easy on 'em, I'd march 'er out the dorsal loading hatch as soon as let 'er keep breathing our good air."

"She's in this too," said Boursy. "Bet you she wants us to win, too—look pretty damn stupid if we didn't, what? Anyway, the woman's got some kind of diplomatic status; she's allowed to poke her nose into things if she wants."

"Huh. Well, the bint had better keep her nose out of *my* missile loaders, less she wants to learn what the launch tubes look like from inside."

Grubor stretched his legs out. "Just like Helsingus's dog, huh."

"Helsingus has a pet dog?" Boursy was suddenly all ears.

"He *had* a dog. Past tense. A toy schnauzer this long." Grubor held his hands improbably close together. "Little rat-brained weasel of an animal. Bad-tempered as hell, yapped like a bosun with a hangover, and it took to dumping in the corridor to show it owned the place. And nobody said anything—nobody *could* say anything."

"What happened?" asked Boursy.

"Oh, one day it picked the wrong door to crap outside. The old man came out in a hurry and stepped in it before the rating I'd sent to follow the damn thing around got there to mop up. I heard about this, but I never saw the animal again; I think it got to walk home. And Helsingus sulked for weeks, I can tell you."

"Dog curry in the wardroom," said Kravchuk. "I had to pick hairs out of my teeth for days."

Boursy did a double take, then laughed hesitantly. Slugging back his schnapps to conceal his confusion, he asked: "Why did the Captain put up with it that long?"

"Who knows, indeed? For that matter, who the hell knows

why the Admiral puts up with the foreign spy?" Grubor stared into
his glass and sighed. "Maybe the Admiral actually *wants* her
along. And then again, maybe he's just forgotten about her..."

"beg to report, I've got something, sir," said the sensor op.
He pointed excitedly at his plot on the bridge of the light cruiser
Integrity.

Lieutenant Kokesova looked up, bleary-eyed. "What is it now,
Menger?" he demanded. Six hours on this interminable dog-
watch was getting to him. He rubbed his eyes, red-rimmed, and
tried to focus them on his subordinate.

"Plot trace, sir. Looks like...hmm, yes. It's a definite return,
from the first illumination run on our survey sector. Six-point-
two-three light-hours. Er, yes. Tiny little thing. Processing now...
looks like a metal object of some kind, sir. Orbiting about two-
point-seven billion kilometers out from the, uh, primary, pretty
much at opposition to us right now, hence the delay."

"Can you fix its size and orbital components?" asked the Lieutenant, leaning forward.

"Not yet, but soon, sir. We've been pinging on the hour; that
should give me enough to refine a full set of elements pretty
soon—say when the next response set comes in. But it's a long
way away, 'bout four-zero astronomical units. Um, preliminary
enhancement says it's about five-zero meters in diameter, plus or
minus an order of magnitude. Might be a lot smaller than that if
it's got reflectors."

"Hmm." Kokesova sat down. "Nav. You got anything else in
this system that fits the bill?"

"No, sir."

Kokesova glanced up at the forward screen; the huge red-
rimmed eye of the primary glared back at him, and he shuddered,
flicked a hand gesture to avert the evil eye. "Then I think we may
have our time capsule. Menger, do you have any halo objects?
Anything else at all?"

"No, sir." Menger shook his head. "Inner system's clean as a
slate. It's unnatural, you ask me. Nothing there except this object."

Kokesova stood again and walked over to the sensor post.
"One of these days you're going to have to learn how to complete
a sentence, Menger," he said tiredly.

"Yes, sir. Humbly apologize for bad grammar, sir."

All was silent in the ops room for ten minutes, save for the scribble of Menger's stylus on his input station, and the clack of dials turning beneath skillful fingertips. Then a low whistle.

"What is it?"

"Got confirmation, sir. Humbly report you might want to see this."

"Put it on the main screen, then."

"Aye aye." Menger pushed buttons, twisted knobs, scribbled some more. The forward screen, previously fixed on the hideous red eye, dissolved into a sea of pink mush. A single yellow dot swam in the middle of it; near one corner, a triangle marked the ship's position. "This is an unenhanced lidar map of what's in front of us. Sorry it's so vague, but the scale is huge—you could drop the whole of home system into one quadrant, and it's taken us a week to build this data set. Anyway, here's what happens when I run my orbital-period filter in the plane of the ecliptic."

He pushed a button. A green line rotated through the mush, like the hour hand of a clock, and vanished.

"I thought you said you'd found something." Kokesova sounded slightly peeved.

"Er, yes, sir. Just a moment. Nothing there, as you see. But then I reran the filter for inclined circular orbits." A green disc appeared near the edge of the haze, and tilted slowly. Something winked violet, close to the central point, then vanished again. "There it is. Really small, orbit inclined at almost nine-zero degrees to the plane of the ecliptic. Which is why it took us so long to spot it."

"Ah." Kokesova stared at the screen for a moment, a warm glow of satisfaction spreading through him. "Well, well, well." Kokesova stared at the violet dot for a long time before he picked up the intercom handset. "Comms: get me the Captain. Yes, I know he's aboard the Lord Vanek. I have something I think the brass will want to hear about . . ."

procurator vassily muller paused outside the cabin door and took a deep breath. He rapped on the door once, twice: when there was no response he tried to turn the handle. It refused to budge. He breathed out, then let a fine loop of stiff wire drop down his right sleeve and ran it into the badge slot. It was just like the training school: a momentary flash of light and the handle rotated freely. He tensed instinctively, fall-out from the same conditioning (which had focused on search and seizure ops, mist and night abductions in a damp stone city where the only constants were fear and dissent).

The cabin was tidy: not as tidy as a flyer's, policed by sharp-tongued officers, but tidy enough. The occupant, a creature of habit, was at lunch and would not be back for at least fifteen minutes. Vassily took it all in with wide eyes. There were no obvious signs of fine wires or hairs anchored to the doorframe: he stepped inside and pulled the door to.

Martin Springfield had few possessions on the *Lord Vanek*: symptomatic of his last-minute conscription. What he had was almost enough to make Vassily jealous: his own presence here was even less planned, and he'd a lot of time to bitterly regret having misunderstood the Citizen's Socratic warning ("What have you forgotten?" to a man searching a ship about to depart!); nevertheless, he had a job to do, and enough residual professionalism to do it properly. It didn't take Vassily long to exhaust the possibilities: the only thing to catch his attention was the battered grey case of the PA, sitting alone in the tiny desk drawer beneath the cabin's workstation.

He turned the device over carefully, looking for seams and openings. It resembled a hardback book: microcapsules embedded in each page changed color, depending what information was loaded into it at the time. But no book could answer to its master's voice, or rebalance a ship's drive kernel. The spine—he pushed, and after a moment of resistance it slid upward to reveal a compartment with some niches in it. One of them was occupied.

Nonstandard extension pack, he realized. Without thinking, he pushed on it; it clicked out and he pocketed it. There'd be time enough to put it back later if it was innocent. Springfield's presence on the ship was an aching rasp on his nerves: the man had to be up to something! The Navy had plenty of good engineers; why could they want a foreigner along? After the events of the past couple of weeks, Vassily could not accept that anything less than sabotage could be responsible. As every secret policeman knows, there is no such thing as a coincidence; the state has too many enemies.

He didn't linger in the engineer's cabin but paused to palm an inconspicuous little bead under the lower bunk bed. The bead would hatch in a day or so, spinning a spiderweb of receptors; a rare and expensive tool that Vassily was privileged to own.

The doorway clicked locked behind him; amnesiac, it would not report this visit to its owner.

Back in his cabin, Vassily locked his door and sat down on his own bunk. He loosened his collar, then reached into a breast pocket for the small device he had taken. He rolled it over in his fingers, pondering. It could be anything, anything at all. Taking a small but powerful device from his inventory of tools—one forbidden to any citizen of the Republic except those with an Imperial warrant to save the state from itself—he checked it for activity. There was nothing obvious: it wasn't emitting radiation, didn't smell of explosives or bioactive compounds, and had a standard interface.

"Riddle me this: an unknown expansion pod in an engineer's luggage. I wonder what it is?" he said aloud. Then he plugged the pod into his own interface and started the diagnostics running. A minute later, he began to swear quietly under his breath. The module was totally randomized. Evidence of misdoing, that was sure enough. But what *kind* of misdoing?

burµa rubenstein sat in the Ducal palace, now requisitioned as the headquarters of the Extropians and Cyborgs' Soviet, sipping tea and signing proclamations with a leaden heart.

Outside the thick oak door of his office, a squad of ward-geese waited patiently, their dark eyes and vicious gunbeaks alert for intruders. The half-melted phone that had started the revolution sat, unused, on the desk before him, while the pile of papers by his left elbow grew higher, and the unsigned pile to his right shrank. It wasn't a part of the job that he enjoyed—quite the opposite, in fact—but it seemed to be necessary. Here was a soldier convicted of raping and looting a farmstead who needed to be punished. There, a teacher who had denounced the historical processes of Democratic Transhumanism as misguided technophile pabulum, encouraging his juvenile charges to chant the Emperor's birthday hymn. Dross, all dross—and the revolution had no time to sift the dross for gold, rehabilitating and re-educating the fallen: it had been a month since the arrival of Festival, and soon the Emperor's great steel warships would loom overhead.

If Burya had anything to do with it, they wouldn't find anyone willing to cooperate in the subjugation of the civil populace, who were now fully caught up in the processes of a full-scale economic singularity. A singularity—a historical cusp at which the rate of change goes exponential, rapidly tending toward infinity—is a terrible thing to taste. The arrival of the Festival in orbit around the pre-industrial colony world had brought an economic singularity; physical wares became just so many atoms, replicated to order by machines that needed no human intervention or maintenance. A hard take-off singularity ripped up social systems and economies and ways of thought like an artillery barrage. Only the forearmed—the Extropian dissident underground, hard men like Burya Rubenstein—were prepared to press their own agenda upon the suddenly molten fabric of a society held too close to the blowtorch of progress.

But change and control brought a price that Rubenstein was finding increasingly unpalatable. Not that he could see any alternatives, but the people were accustomed to being shepherded by father church and the benign dictatorship of the little father, Duke Politovsky. The habits of a dozen lifetimes could not be broken overnight, and to make an omelet it was first necessary to crack some eggshells.

Burya had a fatal flaw; he was not a violent man. He resented and hated the circumstances that forced him to sign arrest warrants and compulsory upload orders; the revolution he had spent so long imagining was a glorious thing, unsullied by brute violence, and the real world—with its recalcitrant monarchist teachers and pigheaded priests—was a grave disappointment to him. The more he was forced to corrupt his ideals, the more he ached inside, and the more it grieved him, the more he hated the people who forced him to such hideous, bloody extremity of action— until they, in turn, became grist for the machinery of revolution, and subsequently bar stock for the scalpel blades that prodded his conscience and kept him awake long into the night, planning the next wave of purges and forcible uploads.

He was deep in his work, oblivious to the outside world, depressed and making himself more so by doing the job that he had always wanted to do but never realized would be this awful— when a voice spoke to him.

"Burya Rubenstein."

"What!" He looked up, almost guiltily, like a small boy discovered goofing off in class by a particularly stern teacher.

"Talk. We. Must." The thing sitting in the chair opposite him was so nightmarish that he blinked several times before he could make his eyes focus on it. It was hairless and pink and larger-than-human-sized, with stubby legs and paws and little pink eyes—and four huge, yellowing tusks, like the incisors of a rat the size of an elephant. The eyes stared at him with disquieting intelligence as it manipulated an odd pouch molded from the belt that was its only garment. "You talk. To me."

Burya adjusted his pince-nez and squinted at the thing. "Who are you and how did you get in here?" he asked. *I haven't been sleeping enough,* part of his mind gibbered quietly; *I knew the caffeine tablets would do this eventually...*

"I am. Sister of Stratagems. The Seventh. I am of the clade of Critics. Talk to me now."

A look of extreme puzzlement crossed Rubenstein's craggy face. "Didn't I have you executed last week?"

"I very much doubt. It." Hot breath that stank of cabbage, corruption and soil steamed in Burya's face.

"Oh, good." He leaned back, light-headed. "I'd *hate* to think I was going mad. How did you sneak past my guards?"

The thing in the chair stared at him. It was an unnerving sensation, like being sized up for a hangman's noose by a man-eating saber-toothed sausage. "You guards are. Nonsapient. No intentional stance. Early now, you learn lesson of not trusting unsapient guards to recognize threat. I made self nonthreat within their— you have no word for it."

"I see." Burya rubbed his forehead distractedly.

"You do *not.*" Sister Seventh grinned at Rubenstein, and he recoiled before the twenty-centimeter digging fangs, yellow-brown and hard enough to crack concrete. "Ask no questions, human. I ask, are you sapient? Evidence ambiguous. Only sapients create art, but your works not distinctive."

"I don't think—" He stopped. "Why do you want to know?"

"A question." The thing carried on grinning at him. "You asked. A question." It rocked from side to side, shivering slightly, and Rubenstein began feeling cautiously along the underside of his desk, for the panic button that would set alarm bells ringing in the guardroom. "Good question. I Critic am. Critics follow Festival for many lifetimes. We come to *Criticize.* First want I to know, am I Criticizing sapients? Or is just puppet show on cave wall of reality? Zombies or zimboes? Shadows of mind? Amusements for Eschaton?"

A shiver ran up and down Burya's spine. "I *think* I'm sapient," he said cautiously. "Of course, I'd say that even if I wasn't, wouldn't I? Your question is unanswerable. So why ask it?"

Sister Seventh leaned forward. "None of your people *ask* anything," she hissed. "Food, yes. Guns, yes. Wisdom? No. Am beginning think you not aware of selves, ask nothing."

"What's to ask for?" Burya shrugged. "We know who we are and what we're doing. What should we want—alien philosophies?"

"Aliens want *your* philosophy," Sister Seventh pointed out. "You give. You not take. This is insult to Festival. *Why?* Prime interrogative!"

"I'm not sure I understand. Are you complaining because we're not making demands?"

Sister Seventh chomped at the air, clattering her tusks together. "Ack! Quote, the viability of a postsingularity economy of scarcity is indicated by the transition from an indirection-layer-based economy using markers of exchange of goods and services to a tree-structured economy characterized by optimal allocation of productivity systems in accordance with iterated tit-for-tat prisoner's dilemma. Money is a symptom of poverty and inefficiency. Unquote, the Marxist-Gilderist manifesto. Chapter two. Why you not performing?"

"Because most of our people aren't ready for that," Burya said bluntly. A tension in his back began to relax; if this monstrous Critic wanted to debate revolutionary dialectic, well of course he could oblige! "When we achieve the post-technological utopia, it will be as you say. But for now, we need a vanguard party to lead the people to a full understanding of the principles of ideological correctness and posteconomic optimization."

"But Marxism-Gilderism and Democratic Extropianism is anarchist aesthetic. Why vanguard party? Why committee? Why revolution?"

"Because it's traditional, dammit!" Rubenstein exploded. "We've been waiting for this particular revolution for more than two hundred years. Before that, two hundred years back to the first revolution, this is how we've gone about it. And it works! So why shouldn't we do it this way?"

"Talk you of tradition in middle of singularity." Sister Seventh twisted her head around to look out the windows at the foggy evening drizzle beyond. "Perplexity maximizes. Not understand singularity is discontinuity with all tradition? Revolution is necessary; deconstruct the old, ring in the new. Before, I questioned your sapience. Now, your sanity questionable: sapience not. Only sapient organism could exhibit superlative irrationality!"

"That may be true." Rubenstein gently squeezed the buzzer under his desk edge for the third time. *Why isn't it working?* He wondered. "But what do you want here, with me?"

Sister Seventh bared her teeth in a grin. "I come to deliver Criticism." Ruby teardrop eyes focused on him as she surged to her feet, rippling slabs of muscle moving under her muddy brown skin. A fringe of reddish hair rippled erect on the Critic's head. "Your guards not answer. I Criticize. You come: now!"

the operations room on board the *Lord Vanek* was quiet, relaxed by comparison with the near panic at Wolf Depository; still, nobody could have mistaken it for a home cruise. Not with Ilya Murametz standing at the rear, watching everything intently. Not with the old man dropping by at least twice a day, just nodding from inside the doorway, but letting them know he was there. Not with the Admiral's occasional presence, glowering silently from his wheelchair like a reminder of the last war.

"Final maneuver option in one hour," announced the helm supervisor.

"Continue as ordered."

"Continue as ordered, aye. Recce? Your ball."

"Ready and waiting." Lieutenant Marek turned around in his chair and looked at Ilya inquiringly. "Do you want to inspect the drone, sir?"

"No. If it doesn't run, I'll know whom to blame." Ilya smiled, trying to pull some of the sting from his words; with his lips pulled back from his teeth, it merely made him look like a cornered wolf. "Launch profile?"

"Holding at minus ten minutes, sir."

"Right, then. Run the self-test sequence again. It can't hurt." Everyone was on edge from not knowing for sure whether the metallic reflector they'd picked up was the time capsule from home. Maybe the drone would tell them, and maybe not. But the longer they waited, the more edgy everyone got, and the edgier they were, the more likely they were to make mistakes.

"Looks pretty good to me. Engine idle at about one percent, fuel tanks loaded, ullage rail and umbilical disconnects latched and ready, instrument package singing loud on all channels. I'm ready to begin launch bay closeout whenever you say, sir."

"Well then." Ilya breathed deeply. "Get on the blower to whoever's keeping an eye on it. Get things moving."

Down near the back end of the ship, far below the drive compartment and stores, lay a series of airlocks. Some of them were small, designed for crew egress; others were larger, and held entire service vehicles like the station transfer shuttle. One bay, the largest of all, held a pair of reconnaissance drones: three-hundred-tonne robots capable of surveying a star system or mapping a gas giant's moons. The drones couldn't carry a gravity drive (nothing much smaller than a destroyer could manage that), but they could boost at a respectable twentieth of a gee on the back of their nuclear-electric ion rocket, and they could keep it up for a very long time indeed. For faster flybys, they could be equipped with salt-water-fueled fission rockets like those of the *Lord Vanek*'s long-range torpedoes—but those were dirty, relatively inefficient, and not at all suited to the stealthy mapping of a planetary system.

Each of the drones carried an instrument package studded with more sensors than every probe launched from Earth during the twentieth century. They were a throwback to the *Lord Vanek*'s nominal design mission, the semi-ironic goal inscribed on the end-user certificate: to boldly go where no man had gone before, to map new star systems on long-duration missions, and claim them in the name of the Emperor. Dropped off in an uninhabited system, a probe could map it in a couple of years and be ready to report in full when the battlecruiser returned from its own destination. They were a force multiplier for the colonial cartographers, enabling one survey ship to map three systems simultaneously.

Deep in the guts of the *Lord Vanek,* probe one was now waking up from its two-year sleep. A team of ratings hurried under the vigilant gaze of two chief petty officers, uncoupling the heavy fueling pipes and locking down inspection hatches. Sitting in a lead-lined coffin, probe one gurgled and pinged on a belly full of reaction mass and liquid water refrigerant. The compact fusion reactor buzzed gently, its beat-wave accelerators ramming a mixture of electrons and pions into a stream of lithium ions at just under the speed of light; neutrons spalled off, soaked into the jacket of water pipes, warming them and feeding pressure waves into the closed-circuit cooling system. The secondary solar generators, dismounted for this mission because of their irrelevance, lay in sheets at one end of the probe bay.

"Five minutes to go. Launch bay reports main reactor compartment closeout. Wet crew have cleared the fueling hoses, report tank pressure is stable. I'm still waiting on telemetry closeout."

"Carry on." Ilya watched patiently as Marek's team monitored progress on the launch. He looked around briefly as the ops room door slid open; but it wasn't the Captain or the Commodore, just the spy—no, the diplomatic agent from Earth. Whose presence was a waste of air and space, the Commander opined, although he could see reasons why the Admiral and his staff might not want to impede her nosy scrutiny.

"What are you launching?" she asked shortly.

"Survey drone."

"What are you surveying?"

He turned and stared at her. "I don't remember being told you had authority to oversee anything except our military activities," he commented.

The inspector shrugged, as if attempting to ignore the insult. "Perhaps if you told me what you were looking for, I could help you find it," she said.

"Unlikely." He turned away. "Status, lieutenant?"

"Two minutes to go. Telemetry bay closeout. Ah, we have confirmation of onboard control. It's alive in there. Waiting on ullage baffle check, launch rail windup, bay depressurization coming up in sixty seconds."

"There's the message capsule," the inspector said quietly. "Hoping for a letter from home, Commander?"

"You are annoying me," Ilya said, almost casually. "That's a bad idea. I say, over there! Yes, you! Status please!"

"Bay pressure cell dump in progress. External launch door opening... launch rail power on the bus, probe going to internal power, switch over now. She's on her own, sir. Launch in one minute. Final pre-flight self-test in progress."

"It's my job to ask uncomfortable questions, Commander. And the important question to ask *now* is—"

"Quiet, please!"

"—Was the artifact you're about to prod placed there by order of your Admiralty, or by the Festival?"

"Launch in three-zero seconds," Lieutenant Marek announced into the silence. He looked up. "Was it something I said?"

"What are you talking about?" asked Ilya.

Rachel shook her head. Arms crossed: "If you don't want to listen, be my guest."

"One-zero seconds to launch. Ullage pressure jets open. Reactor criticality coming up. Muon flux ramp nominal, accelerator gates clear. Um, reactor flux doubling has passed bootstrap level. Five seconds. Launch rail is go! Main heat pump is down to operating temperature!" The deck began to shudder, vibrating deep beneath the soles of their feet. "Two seconds. Reactor on temperature. Umbilical separation. Zero. We have full separation now. Probe one is clear of the launch bay. Doors closing. Gyrodyne turn in progress, ullage pressure maximal, three seconds to main engine ignition." The shudder died away. "Deflection angle clear. Main engine ignition." In the ops room, nothing stirred; but bare meters away from the ship, the probe's stingerlike tail spat a red-orange beam of heavy metal ions. It began to drop away from the battlecruiser: as it did so, two huge wings, the thermal radiators, began to extend from its sides.

Ilya came to a decision. "Lieutenant Marek, you have control," he said. "Colonel. Come with me."

He opened the door; she followed him into the passage outside. "Where are we going?" she asked.

"We're going to have a little talk," he said. Hurrying along toward the conference suite, he didn't wait for her to keep up. Up the elevator, along the next passage, and into a room with a table and chairs in it; thankfully unoccupied. He waited for her to enter, then shut the door. "Sit down," he said.

The inspector sat on the edge of a chair, leaning forward, looking up at him with an earnest expression.

"You think I'm going to tear a strip off you," he began. "And you're right, but for the wrong reason."

She raised a hand. "Let me guess. Raising policy issues in an executive context?" She looked at him, almost mockingly. "Listen, Commander. Until I came on the deck and saw what you were doing, I didn't know what was happening either, but now I do I think you *really* want to hear what I've got to tell you, then tell it to the Captain. Or the Commodore. Or both. Chains of command are all very well, but if you're going to retrieve that orbiting anomaly, then I think we may have less than six hours before all hell breaks loose, and I'd like to get the message across. So if we can postpone the theatrics until we've got time to spare, and just get on with things . . . ?"

"You're trying to be disruptive," Ilya accused.

"Yes." She nodded. "I make a career of it. I poke into corners and ask uncomfortable questions and stick my nose into other people's business and find answers that nobody realized were there. So far, I've saved eight cities and seventy million lives. Would you like me to be less annoying?"

"Tell me what you know. Then I'll decide." He said the words carefully, as if making a great concession to her undisciplined refusal to stick to her place.

Rachel leaned back. "It's a matter of deduction," she said. "It helps to have a bit of context. For starters, this ship—this fleet—didn't just accidentally embark on a spacelike trip four thousand years into the future. You are attempting a maneuver that nearly, but not quite, violates a number of treaties and a couple of laws of nature that are enforced by semidivine fiat. You're not going to go into your own past light cone, but you're going to come very close indeed—dive deep into the future to circumvent any watchers or eaters or mines the Festival might lay in your path, jump over to the target, then reel yourselves back into the past and accidentally come out not-quite-before the Festival arrives. You know what that suggests to me? It suggests extreme foolhardiness. Rule Three is there for a reason. You're banging on the Eschaton's door if you test it."

"I had that much already," Ilya acknowledged. "So?"

"Well, you should ask, what should we have expected to find here? We get here, and we're looking for a buoy. A time capsule with detailed tactical notes from our own past light cone—an oracle, in effect, telling us a lot about the enemy that we can't possibly know yet because our own time line hasn't intersected with them. Yet more cheating. But we're alive."

"I don't understand. Why wouldn't we be?"

"Because—" She stared at him for a moment. "Do you know what happens to people who use causality violation as a weapon?" she asked. "You're incredibly close to doing it, which is crazy enough. And you got away with it! Which simply isn't in the script, unless the rules have changed."

"Rules? What are you talking about?"

"Rules." She rolled her eyes. "The rules of physics are, in some cases, suspiciously anthropic. Starting with the Heisenberg Principle, that the presence of an observer influences the subject of observation at a quantum level, and working from there, we can see a lot of startling correlations in the universe. Consider the ratio of the strong nuclear force to the electromagnetic force, for example. Twiddle it one way a little, and neutrons and protons wouldn't react; fusion couldn't take place. Twiddle it in a different direction, and the stellar fusion cycle would stop at helium—no heavier nuclei could ever be formed. There are so many correlations like this that cosmologists theorize we live in a universe that exists specifically to give rise to our kind of life, or something descended from it. Like the Eschaton."

"So?"

"So you people are breaking some of the more arcane cosmological laws. The ones that state that any universe in which true
causality violation—time travel—occurs is *de facto* unstable. But
causality violation is only possible when there's a causal agent—
in this case an observer—and the descendants of that observer
will seriously object to causality violation. Put it another way: it's
accepted as a law of cosmology because the Eschaton won't put
up with idiots who violate it. That's why my organization tries to
educate people out of doing it. I don't know if anyone told your
Admiralty what happened out in the back of beyond, in what is
now the Crab Nebula: but there's a pulsar there that isn't natural,
let's put it that way, and an extinct species of would-be galactic
conquerors. Someone tried to bend the rules—and the Eschaton
nailed them."

Ilya forced himself to uncurl his fingers from the arms of his
chair. "You're saying that the capsule we're about to retrieve is a
bomb? Surely the Eschaton would have tried to kill us by now, or
at least capture us—"

She grinned, humorlessly. "If you don't believe me, that's
your problem. We've seen half a dozen incidents like this
before—the UN Defense Intelligence Causal Weapons Analysis
Committee, I mean—incidents where one or another secret
attempt to assemble a causality-violation device came to grief.
Not usually anything as crude as your closed timelike flight path
and oracle hack, by the way; these were real CVDs. History edi-
tors, minimax censors, grandfather bombs, and a really nasty toy
called a spacelike ablator. There's a whole ontology of causality-
violation weapons out there, just like nukes—atom bombs,
fission-boosted fusion bombs, electroweak imploders, and so on.

"Each and every one of the sites where we saw CVDs
deployed had been trashed, thoroughly and systematically, by
unidentified agencies—but agencies attributable to the Eschaton.
We've never actually *seen* one in the process of being destroyed,
because the big E tends toward overkill in such cases—the small-
est demolition tool tends to be something like a five-hundred-
kilometer asteroid dropped on the regional capital at two hundred
kilometers per second.

"So I guess the big surprise is that we're still alive." She
glanced around at the vacant chairs, the powered-down workstation on the table. "Oh, and one other thing. The Eschaton always
wipes out CVDs just before they go live. We figure it knows where
to find them because it runs its own CVD. Sort of like preserving

a regional nuclear hegemony by attacking anyone who builds a uranium enrichment plant or a nuclear reactor, yes? Anyway. You haven't quite begun to break the law *yet*. The fleet is assembling, you've located the time capsule, but you haven't actually closed the loop or made use of the oracle in a forbidden context. You might even get away with it *if* you hop backward but don't try to go any earlier than your own departure point. But I'd be careful about opening that time capsule. At least, do it a sensible distance away from any of your ships. You never know what it might contain."

Ilya nodded reluctantly. "I think the Captain should be aware of this."

"You could say that." She looked at the console. "There's another matter. I think you need all the advantages you can get your hands on right now, and one of them is spending most of his time sitting in his cabin twiddling his thumbs. You might want to have a word with Martin Springfield, the dockyard engineer. He's an odd man, and you'll need to make more allowances in his direction than you'd normally be inclined to, but I think he knows more than he's letting on—much more, when it comes to propulsion systems. MiG wasn't paying him two thousand crowns a week just because he has a pretty face. When MiG sold your Admiralty this bird, it was also betting on a fifty-year maintenance and upgrade contract—probably worth more revenue than the initial sale, in fact."

"What are you trying to say?" Ilya looked irritated. "Engineering issues aren't up to me, you should know that already. And I'll thank you for not telling me my—"

"*Shut up.*" She reached over and grabbed his arm—not hard, but firmly enough to shock him. "You really don't understand how an arms cartel works, do you? Look. MiG sold your government a ship to perform to certain specifications. Specifications that could fulfill the requirements your Admiralty dreamed up. The specs they *designed* it to are a different matter—but they certainly intended to charge for upgrades throughout its life. And they've probably got more experience of real-world interstellar combat requirements than your Admiralty, which—unless I'm very much mistaken—has never before fought a real interstellar war as opposed to sending a few gunboats to intimidate stone-age savages. Be nice to Springfield, and he may surprise you. After all, his life depends on this ship doing its job successfully." She let go.

Ilya stared at her, his expression unreadable. "I will tell the

Captain," he murmured. Then he stood. "In the meantime, I would appreciate it if you would stay out of the operations room while I am in charge—or hold your counsel in public. And not to lay hands on any officer. Is that understood?"

She met his gaze. If his expression was unreadable, hers was exactly the opposite. "I understand perfectly," she breathed. Then she stood and left the room without another word, closing the door softly as she left.

Ilya stared after her and shuddered. He shook himself angrily; then he picked up the telephone handset and spoke to the operator. "Get me the Captain," he said. "It's important."

it was a time capsule, pitted and tarnished from four thousand years in space. And it contained mail.

The survey drone nudged up to it delicately, probing it with radar and infrared sensors. Drifting cold and silent, the capsule showed no sign of life save for some residual radioactivity around its after end. A compact matter/antimatter rocket, it had crossed the eighteen light-years from the New Republic at a sublight crawl, then decelerated into a parking orbit and shut down. Its nose cone was scratched and scarred, ablated in patches from the rough passage through the interstellar medium. But behind it waited a silvery sphere a meter in diameter. The capsule was fabricated from sintered industrial diamond five centimeters thick, a safety-deposit box capable of surviving anything short of a nuclear weapon.

The mail was packed onto disks, diamond wafers sandwiching reflective gold sheets. It was an ancient technology, but incredibly durable. Using external waldoes, ratings controlling the survey drone unscrewed the plug sealing the time capsule and delicately removed the disk stacks. Then, having verified that they were not, in fact, explosives or antimatter, the survey drone turned and began to climb back out toward the *Lord Vanek* and the other ships of the first battleship squadron.

The discovery of mail—and surely there was too much of it to only be tactical data about the enemy—put the crew in a frenzy of anticipation. They'd been confined to the ship's quarters for two months now, and the possibility of messages from families and loved ones drove them into manic anticipation that alternated, individually, with deep depression at the merest thought that they might be forgotten.

Rachel, however, was less sanguine about the mail: the chances of the Admiralty having let her employers message her under diplomatic cypher were, in her estimation, less than zero. Martin didn't expect anything, either. His sister hadn't written to him back in New Prague; why should she write to him now? His ex-wife, he wouldn't want to hear from. In emotional terms, his closest current relationship—however unexpectedly it had dawned upon him—was with Rachel. So while the officers and crew of the *Lord Vanek* spent their off hours speculating about the letters from home, Rachel and Martin spent their time worrying about exposure. For, as she had pointed out delicately, he didn't have diplomatic papers: and even leaving matters of Republican public morality aside, it would be a bad idea if anyone were to decide that he was a lever to use against her.

"It's probably not a good idea for us to spend too much time together in private, love," she'd murmured at the back of his shoulder, as they lay together in his narrow bunk. "When everybody else is at action stations, they're not liable to notice us—but the rest of the time—" His shoulders went tense, telling her that he understood.

"We'll have to work something out," he said. "Can't we?"

"Yes." She'd paused to kiss his shoulder. "But not if it risks some blue-nosed bigot locking you up for conduct unbecoming, or convinces the admiral's staff that I'm a two-kopek whore they can grope or safely ignore, which isn't too far from what some of them think already."

"Who?" Martin rolled over to face her, his expression grim. "Tell me—"

"*Ssh.*" She'd touched a finger to his lips, and for a moment, he'd found her expression almost heartbreaking. "I don't need a protector. Have their ideas been rubbing off on you?"

"I hope not!"

"No, I don't think so." She chuckled quietly and rolled against him.

Martin was sitting alone in his cabin some days later, nursing wistful thoughts about Rachel and a rapidly cooling mug of coffee, when somebody banged on the hatch. "Who's there?" he called.

"Mail for the engineer! Get it in the purser's office!" Feet hurried away, then there was a cacophony from farther down the corridor.

"Hmm?" Martin sat up. *Mail?* On the face of it, it was improbable. Then again, everything about this voyage was improbable. Startled out of his reverie, he bent down and hunted for his shoes, then set out in search of the source of the interruption.

He didn't have any difficulty finding it. The office was a chaotic melee of enlisted men, all trying to grab their own mail and that of anyone they knew. The mail had been copyprinted onto paper, sealed in neat blue envelopes. Puzzled, Martin hunted around for anyone in charge.

"Yes?" The harassed petty officer in charge of the sorting desk looked up from the pile he was trying to bundle together for transfer to the His Majesty's courier ship *Godot*. "Oh, you. Over there, in the unsorted deck." He pointed at a smallish box containing a selection of envelopes; missives for the dead, the mad, and the non-naval.

Martin burrowed through the pile, curious, until he came to an envelope with his name on it. It was a rather fat envelope. *How odd,* he thought. Rather than open it on the spot, he carried it back to his cabin.

When he opened it, he nearly threw it away immediately: it began with the dreaded phrase, "My dear Marty." Only one woman called him that, and although she was the subject of some of his fondest memories, she was also capable of inspiring in him a kind of bitter, anguished rage that made him, afterward, ashamed of his own emotions. He and Morag had split eight years ago, and the recriminations and mutual blame had left a trench of silence between them.

But what could possibly have prompted her to write to him now? She'd always been a very verbal person, and her e-mails had tended to be terse, misspelled sentences rather than the emotional deluges she reserved for face-to-face communications.

Puzzled, Martin began to read.

> My Dear Marty,
>   It's been too long since I last wrote to you; I hope you'll forgive me. Life has been busy, as they say, and doubly so, for I have also had Sarah to look after. She's growing very tall these days, and looks just like her father. I hope you'll be around for her sixteenth birthday . . .

He stopped. This had to be an elaborate joke. His ex-wife seemed to be talking about a child—their child—who didn't exist.

And this was nothing like her style! It was almost as if someone else, writing from a dossier of his family history, was trying to—
He began to read again, this time acutely alert for hidden messages.

Sarah is studying theology at college these days. You know how studious she's always been? Her new teacher Herman seems to have brought her out of her shell. She's working on a dissertation about Eschatology; she insisted that I enclose a copy for you (attached below).

The rest of the letter was filled with idle chatter about fictional friends, reminiscences about trivial and entirely nonexistent shared memories and major (presumably well-documented) ones, and—as far as Martin could see—a content-free blind.

He turned to the "dissertation." It was quite long, and he pondered Herman's wisdom in sending it. Did New Republican schoolchildren write eight-page essays about God? And about God's motives, as far as they could be deduced from the value of the cosmological constant? It was written in a precious, somewhat dull style that set his teeth on edge, like an earnest student essay hunting for marks of approval rather than a straight discursive monograph asserting a viewpoint. Then his eyes caught the footnotes:

1. Consider the hypothetical case of a power that intends to create a localized causality violation that does not produce a light cone encompassing its origin point. (We are implicitly assuming a perfectly spherical zone of sinfulness expanding at velocity c with origin at time $T0$.) If the spherical volume of sinfulness does not intersect with the four-space trajectory of the power's initial location, we are not dealing with an original sin. Consequently we do not expect the Eschaton to condemn the entire sinful civilization to damnation, or a Type II supernova; redemption is possible. However, damnation of the sinful agency that causes the causality violation is required.

He skipped down the page and began underlining significant words and phrases.

2. Does the Eschaton always intervene destructively? The
    answer is probably "no". We see the consequences of
    intervention in issues of original sin, but for every such
    intervention there are probably thousands of invisible
    nudges delivered to our world line with subtlety and
    precision. The agency by which such nudges are deliv-
    ered must remain unknown for them to be effective.
    They probably flee the scene after intervention, hiding
    themselves in the teeming masses. The agency may
    even work in concert with our own efforts, as
    Eschaton-fearing human beings, to ensure no viola-
    tions exist. It is possible that some Eschatologically
    aware government agencies may assist the Eschaton's
    secret friends, if they are aware of their presence. Oth-
    ers, secret agents of sinful powers, may attempt to
    identify them by evidence and arrest them.

Well, that was all fairly instructive. Steganographic back
channels generally irritated Martin, with their potential for misunderstandings and garbled messages, but in this instance, Herman
was being quite clear. Distrust the New Republican secret police.
Possible help from other agencies—did that mean Rachel? No
retaliation against the New Republic itself: that was a big weight
off his conscience, for however much he might dislike or despise
their social affairs, they didn't deserve to die because of their
leader's inability to deal with an unprecedented problem. However, one last footnote remained impenetrable, however he tried to
understand it:

3. Of course, few people would contemplate breaking the
    law of causality without at least a very major apparent
    threat. One wonders what the invisible helpers of the
    Eschaton might do when confronted with the need to
    prevent a causality violation in the face of such a
    threat? At that point, they may find themselves with
    split loyalties: on the one hand, to defend the prime law
    of the anthropic cosmos, while at the same time, not
    wanting to surrender their misguided but nevertheless
    human peers into the claws of a great evil. Under these
    circumstances, I feel sure the Eschaton would tell its
    agents to look to their fellow humans' interests imme-
    diately after preventing the rupture of space-time itself.

The Eschaton may not be a compassionate God, but it is pragmatic and does not expect its tools to break in its service. However, the key issue is determining which side is least wrong. This leads us deep into the forest of ethics, wherein there is a festival of ambiguity. All we can do is hope the secret helpers make the right choices—otherwise, the consequences of criticism will be harsh.

Martin sat back and scratched his head. "Now what the hell does *that* mean?" he muttered to himself.

a semiotic war

the admiral was having a bad day.

"Damn your eyes, man, g-g-get your hands off me!" he croaked at his batman. Robard ignored him and carried on lifting; Kurtz's frail body wasn't capable of resisting as he sat the old man up and plumped up the pillows behind him. "I'll have you taken out and shot!"

"Certainly, sir. Would that be before or after breakfast?"

The Admiral growled, deep in the back of his throat, then subsided into a rasping pant. "'M'not well. Not like I used to be. Dammit, I hate this!"

"You're getting old, sir. Happens to us all."

"Not that blas-asted Terran attaché, dammit. He doesn't get old. I remember him back on Lamprey. Took lots of daguerreotypes of me standing by a hill of skulls we built in the public square of New Bokhara. Had to do something with the rebel prisoners, after all, no Jesus to make the quartermaster's loaves go further, ha-ha. Said he'd hang me, but never got around to it, the bastard. Wry cove, that wet fish. Could have sworn he was a female impersonator. What d'ye think, Kurt? Is he a shirt-lifter?"

Robard coughed and slid a bed table bearing cup of weak tea and a poached egg on toast in front of the Admiral. "The UN inspector is a lady, sir."

Kurtz blinked his watery eyes in astonishment. "Why, bless my soul—what a surprise!" He reached for the teacup, but his hand was shaking so much he could barely lift it without slopping the contents. "I thought I *knew* that," he accused.

"You probably did, sir. You'll feel better after you've taken your medicine."

"But if he's a girl, and he was at First Lamprey, that means—" Kurtz looked puzzled. "Do you believe in angels, Robard?" he asked faintly.

"No, sir."

"Well, that's alright then, she must be a devil. Can deal with those, y'know. Where's my briefing?"

"I'll fetch it right after your breakfast, sir. Commodore Bauer said to tell you he's looking after everything."

"Jolly good."

Kurtz concentrated on assaulting his egg. Presently, when he had accepted its surrender, Robard removed the table. "We'd better get you dressed and up, sir. Staff meeting in thirty minutes."

Thirty-five minutes later, the Admiral was ready to meet his staff in the huge conference room adjoining his suite. Donning a uniform and taking his medication seemed to have removed a decade from his shoulders; he shuffled into the room under his own power, leaning heavily on his canes, although Robard discreetly helped when the Admiral tried to return the assembled officers' salute (and nearly caught a walking stick in one eye).

"Good evening, gentlemen," began the Admiral. "I gather the rail packet has been me—I'm sorry. I gather the r-r—mail packet has been received. Lieutenant Kossov. What word of our dispatches?"

"Er—" Kossov looked green. "We have a problem, sir."

"What do you mean, a problem?" demanded the Admiral. "We're not supposed to have problems—that's the enemy's job!"

"There was a stack of twenty disks in the time capsule—"

"Don't give me disks, give me answers! What word of the enemy?"

Commodore Bauer leaned forward. "I think what the Lieutenant is trying to say," he interrupted, "is that the dispatches were damaged." Kossov eyed the Commodore with embarrassingly transparent gratitude.

"That's exactly right, sir. The private mail was intact, for the most part, but there was damage to the time capsule at one side— a micrometeoroid impact—and three of the disks were fragmented. We've retrieved a partial copy of a tenth of our orders from the remaining disks, but most of what came through consists of supply manifests for the quartermaster and a suggested menu for the Emperor's Birthday Commemoration Dinner. No details of the enemy, order of battle, force dispositions, diplomatic analysis, intelligence, or anything remotely useful. It's all shattered." "I see." The Admiral looked deceptively calm; Kossov quailed. "So our intelligence about the enemy disposition is absent. Ah, that-t makes life easier." He turned to Bauer. "Then we shall have to proceed in accordance with Plan B in order to accomplish a successful attack! Every man shall do his duty, for right is on our side. I ex-expect you have incontin-gency plans for dealing with in-insurgents on the ground? Good, very good. The Festival we shall meet in orbit and, having destroyed their ships, we shall work on the assumption that there is an aspiration to depose His Majesty among the rebels on the ground and their allies from the enemy camp! Commodore. You will supervise our approach to the target system. Colonel von Ungern—Sternberg? Plans for the disposition of your marines and the re-re-reimposition of order once we arrive, if you please. Captain Mirsky, you will coordinate the, ah, la-la—maneuvers of the flotilla. Report to Midshipman Bauer if you please."

The Admiral rose, shakily, and made no protest when Robard held him by one arm. "Diss-diss-missed!" he snapped and, turning, hobbled out of the room.

ProcuraTor MuLLer was bored. Bored and, furthermore, somewhat annoyed. Apart from the evidence of misconduct over a *weissbier* back in New Prague, there wasn't anything he could hang on the engineer. Just the fact that he was a foreigner who espoused radical opinions liable to encourage moral turpitude among the lumpenproletariat—which put him in the company of roughly ninety percent of the population of the known universe. Admittedly, there had been the nonstandard plug-in from the man's PA, but that wasn't conclusive. Was it?

He'd spent nearly two months of his life getting this much information. Much of the time, he was bored to tears; the crew and officers wouldn't speak to him—he was one of the Curator's men, charged with the preservation of society, and, like all police posts, this attracted some degree of suspicion—and hc had long since exhausted the small wardroom library. With no duties but covert surveillance of a suspect who knew he was under suspicion, there was little for him to occupy his time with except idle fantasies about his forthcoming meeting, when they arrived on Rochard's

World. But there were only a finite number of words he could think of to address his father with—and small consolation in imagining himself saying them.

However, one evening, it occurred to Vassily that there was another avenue he could follow in his exploration of the subject's movements. Wasn't Springfield spending an unhealthy amount of time in company with the foreign diplomat?

Now there was a shady case! Vassily's nostrils flared whenever he thought about her. If she hadn't had diplomatic papers, he'd have had her in an interrogation room in a trice. Springfield might be a radical, but Colonel Mansour wore *trousers*—enough to get her arrested for indecency on the streets of the capital, special credentials or no. The woman was a dangerous degenerate; obviously of depraved tastes, a male impersonator, probably an invert, and liable to corrupt anyone she came into contact with. Indeed, her very presence on this warship was a threat to the moral hygiene of the crew! That the engineer spent much of his time with her was obvious (Vassily had seen the surveillance recordings of him slipping in and out of her cabin), and the question of where the incriminating evidence was kept seemed fairly clear-cut. Springfield was a dangerous anarchist spy, and she must be his evil scheming control; a secretive mistress of the art of diplomatic seduction, mad, bad, and dangerous to know.

Which was why he was about to burgle her cabin and search her luggage.

It had taken Vassily nearly two weeks to reach this decision, from the moment he determined that Martin's nonstandard PA module was, not to put too fine a point on it, toast. It was a week and a half since the fleet had begun its momentous homeward voyage, first jumping across to the unpopulated binary system code-named Terminal Beta, then successively hopping from one star to the other, winding back more than a hundred years every day. Another four weeks and they would arrive at their destination; nevertheless, Vassily had taken his time. He'd have to be delicate, he realized. Without proof of treason he couldn't act against either of them, and the proof was obviously under diplomatic lock and key. Whatever he did would be ultimately deniable—get caught and, well, burgling a diplomat's luggage was about as infra dig as you could get. If anyone found him, he'd be thrown to the wolves—probably not literally, but he could look forward to a long career auditing penguins at the south polar station.

He picked an early evening for his raid. Martin was in the

wardroom, drinking schnapps and playing dominoes with Engineering Commander Krupkin. Sitting on in Lieutenant Sauer's security wardroom, Vassily waited until Colonel Mansour left her room for some purpose; his monitors tracked her down the corridor to the officer's facilities. Good, she'd be at least ten minutes in the shower, if she stuck to her usual timetable. Vassily tiptoed out of his cubbyhole and scampered toward the lift shaft, and thence, the passage into officer country.

Pulling her cabin door shut behind him, he looked around cautiously. In almost every respect, her room was just like that of any other officer. Built like a railway couchette, there were two bunks; the upper one configured for sleeping, and the lower currently rolled upside down on its mountings to serve as a desk. Two lockers, a tiny washstand sink, mirror, and telephone completed the fittings. One corner of a large trunk protruded from under the desk. The inspector didn't travel as light as a naval officer, that was for sure.

First, Vassily spent a minute inspecting the chest. There were no signs of fine hairs or wires glued across the lid, and nothing complicated in the way of locks. It was just a slightly battered leather-and-wood trunk. He tried to lever it out from under the bunk, but rapidly realized that whatever was in it was implausibly heavy. Instead, he unlatched the desk/bunk and folded it upward against the bulkhead. Exposed to the light, the chest seemed to smile at him, horrible and faceless.

Vassily sniffed and reached for his pick gun. Another highly illegal tool of the Curator's Office, the pick gun was an engineering miracle: packed with solenoid-controlled probes, electronic sensors, and transmitters, even a compact laser transponder, it could force just about any lock in a matter of seconds. Vassily bent over the chest. Presently he confirmed that UN diplomatic luggage was no more immune to a pick gun than any other eight-barrel mortise lock with a keyed-frequency resonance handshake and a misplaced faith in long prime numbers. The lid clicked and swung upward.

The lid held toiletries and a mirror; after a brief inspection, Vassily turned to the interior and found himself confronted with a layer of clothing. He swallowed. Unmentionables mocked him: folded underskirts, bloomers, a pair of opera gloves. He carefully moved them aside. Beneath them lay a yellow silk gown. Vassily flushed, deeply embarrassed. He picked up the gown, unfolding it in the process; confused, he stood up and shook it out. It was, he thought, wholly beautiful and feminine, not what he'd expected of the corrupt and decadent Terrestrial agent. This whole fishing expedition wasn't turning out they way he'd imagined. He shook his head and laid the gown on the upper bunk, then bent back to the chest.

There was a black jumpsuit beneath it, and an octagonal hatbox. He tried to pick up the hatbox, and found that it wouldn't move. It was solid, as heavy as lead! Encouraged, he picked up the suit and draped it over a chair. Beneath it he found a slick plastic surface with lights glowing within it. The chest was only six inches deep! The entire bottom half of it lay below the surface on which the false hatbox rested, and was doubtless full of contraband and spying apparatus.

Vassily poked at the plastic panel. It reminded him of a keyboard, but lacking ivory and ebony keys, and with nowhere to feed the paper tapes in. It was all disturbingly alien. He poked at the panel, hitting an obvious raised area: runes blinked. ACCESS FORBIDDEN: GENEPRINT UNRECOGNIZED.

Damn.

Sweat poured off his neck as he considered his options. Then his eyes turned to the contents of the trunk he'd heaped beside it. It wanted a familiar skin sample? Hmm. Gloves. He held them up. Long women's gloves. They smelt faintly of something—yes. Vassily rolled one inside-out over his right hand, up his arm. He touched the raised plinth: PROCESSING... AUTHORIZED. A human body sheds five million skin particles per hour; Rachel had worn these very gloves, therefore—

A menu appeared. Vassily prodded at it blindly. Option one said SEARS FOUNDATION DESIGN CATALOG, whatever that meant. Below it, FREE HARDWARE FOUNDATION GNU COUTURIER 15.6; then DIOR HISTORICAL CATALOG. He scratched his head. No secret code books, no hidden weapons, no spy cameras. Just incomprehensible analytical engine instructions! He thumped the plinth in frustration.

A deep humming filled the room. He jumped backward, knocking over the chair. A slot opened in the top of the hatbox. A demented clicking rattled from it and something spat out. Something red that landed on his head—a wisp of lace with two leg holes. *Scandalous!* With a grinding clank, the hatbox extruded in short order a shimmering tulle ball gown, a pair of spike-heeled ankle boots, and a pair of coarse-woven blue shorts. All the clothing was hot to the touch and smelled faintly of chemicals.

"Stop it," he hissed. "Stop it!" In reply, the trunk ejected a stream of stockings, a pair of trousers, and a corset that threatened any wearer with abdominal injury. He thumped at the control panel in frustration and, thankfully, the trunk stopped manufacturing clothing. He looked at it dizzily. *Why bring a trunk of clothing if you can bring a trunk that can manufacture any item of clothing you want to wear?* he realized. Then the trunk made an ominous graunching sound and he stared at it in ontological horror. *It's a cornucopia!* One of the forbidden, mythological chimeras of history, the machine that had brought degradation and unemployment and economic downsizing to his ancestors before they fled the singularity to settle and help create the New Republic.

The cornucopia grunted and hummed. Thoroughly spooked, Vassily looked to the door. If Rachel was on her way back—

The hatbox opened. Something black and shiny peeped forth. Antennae hummed and scanned the room; articulated claws latched onto the side of the box and levered.

Vassily took one look at the monster and cracked. He left the door swinging ajar behind him in his helpless flight down the corridor, disheveled and wild-eyed, wearing an inside-out opera glove on one hand.

Behind him, the freshly manufactured spybot finished surveying the insertion zone. Primitive programs meshed in its microprocessor brain: no operational overrides were present, so it established a default exploration strategy and prepared to reconnoiter. It grabbed the nearest non-fixed item of camouflage and, stretching it protectively over its crablike carapace, headed for the ventilation shaft. Even as it finished removing the grille, the hatbox clanked again: the second small robospy was born just in time to see the yellow gown disappearing into the air-conditioning duct. And then the luggage clanked again, preparing to hatch yet another...

By the time Rachel returned, her trunk was half-empty—and almost all her ready-made clothing had escaped.

"ᑌᴏᑌ ᑕOᗰᕮ ᗯITᕼ me," Sister Seventh told Burya. "See situation. Explain why is bad, and understand."

Wind whispered through the open window, carrying grey clouds across the city, as Novy Petrograd burned in an inferno of forbidden technology. Houses crumbled and grew anew, extrusions pushing up like mushrooms from the strange soil of men's dreams. Trees of silver rose from the goldsmith's district, their harsh, planar surfaces tracking the cumulus-shrouded sun. The hairless alien wobbled forward onto the balcony and pointed her tusks at the fairground on the other side of town: "This is not the Festival's doing!"

Helplessly, Burya followed her out onto the rooftop above the Duke's ballroom. A cloacal smell plugged his nostrils, the distant olfactory echo of the corpses swinging from the lampposts in the courtyard. Politovsky had disappeared, but his men had not gone quietly, and the mutinous troops, frenzied and outraged, had committed atrocities against the officers and their families. The ensuing reprisals had been harsh but necessary—

Javelins of light streaked across the cloudscape overhead. Seconds later, the rumble of their passage split the cold evening air. Thunder rattled and echoed from the remaining windows of the town.

"Festival does not understand humans," Sister Seventh commented calmly. "Motivation of fleshbody intelligences bereft of real-time awareness not simulatable. Festival therefore assumes altruist aesthetic. I ask: Is this a work of art?"

Burya Rubenstein stared at the city bleakly. "No." The admission came hard. "We hoped for better. But the people need leadership and a strong hand; without it they run riot—"

Sister Seventh made a strange snuffling noise. Presently he realized that she was laughing at him.

"Riot! Freedom! End of constraint! Silly humans. Silly notorganized humans, not smell own place among people, need to sniff piss in corner of burrow, kill instead. Make military music. Much marching and killing by numbers. Is comedy, no?"

"We will control it ourselves," Burya insisted trenchantly. "This chaos, this is not our destiny. We stand on the threshold of utopia! The people, once educated, will behave rationally. Ignorance, filth, and a dozen generations of repression are what you see here—this is the outcome of a failed experiment, not human destiny!"

"Then why you not a sculptor, cut new flesh from old?" Sister Seventh approached him. Her snuffling cabbage breath reminded him of a pet guinea pig his parents had bought him when he was six. (When he was seven there had been a famine, and into the cook pot she went.) "Why not you build new minds for your people?"

"We'll fix it," Burya emphasized. Three more emerald-colored diamonds shot overhead: they zipped in helices around one another, then turned and swerved out across the river like sentient shooting stars. *When in doubt, change the subject:* "How did your people get here?"

"We Critics. Festival has many mindspaces spare. Brought us along, like the Fringe and other lurkers in dark. Festival must travel and learn. *We* travel and change. Find what is broken and Criticize, help broken things fix selves. Achieve harmonious dark and warm-fed hiveness."

Something tall and shadowy slid across the courtyard behind Burya. He turned, hurriedly, to see two many-jointed legs, chicken-footed, capped by a thatch of wild darkness. The legs knelt, lowering the body until an opening hung opposite the balcony, as dark and uninviting as a skull's hollow nasal cavity.

"Come, ride with me." Sister of Stratagems the Seventh stood behind Burya, between him and his office. It was not an offer but an instruction. "Will learn you much!"

"I—I—" Burya stopped protesting. He raised a hand to his throat, found the leather thong he wore around it, and yanked on the end of it. "Guards!"

Sister Seventh rolled forward, as ponderous and irresistible as an earthquake; she swept him backward into the walking hut, making that odd snuffling noise again. A furious hissing and quacking broke out behind her, followed by erratic gunfire as the first of the guard geese shot their way through the study door. Rubenstein landed on the floor with two hundred kilos of mole rat on top of him, holding him down; the floor lurched then rose like an elevator, dropped, and accelerated in a passable imitation of the fairground ride at a winter festival. He choked, trying to breathe, but before he could suffocate Sister Seventh picked herself up and sat back on what appeared to be a nest of dried twigs. She grinned at him horribly, baring her tusks, then pulled out a large root vegetable and began to gnaw on it.

"Where are you taking me? I demand to be put down—"

"Plotsk," said the Critic. "To learn how to understand. Want a carrot?"

ᴛʜᴇʏ ᴄᴀᴍᴇ ꜰᴏʀ Martin as he lay sleeping. The door of his cabin burst open and two burly ratings entered; the light came on. "What's up?" Martin asked fuzzily.

"On your feet." A petty officer stood in the entrance.

"What—"

"On your feet." The quilt was pulled back briskly; Martin found himself dragged halfway out of bed before he had quite finished blinking at the brightness. "At the double!"

"What's going on?"

"Shut up," said one of the ratings, and backhanded him casually across the face. Martin fell back on the bed, and the other rating grabbed his left arm and slipped a manacle over his wrist. While he was trying to reach his mouth—sore and hot, painful but not badly damaged—they snagged his other wrist.

"To the brig. At the double!" They frog-marched Martin out the door, naked and in handcuffs, and hurried him down to the level below the engineering spaces and drive kernel. Everything passed in a painful blur of light; Martin spat and saw a streak of blood dribble across the floor.

A door opened. They pushed him through and he fell over, then the door clanged shut.

Shock finally cut in. He slumped, rolled to his side, and dry-heaved on the floor. From start to finish, the assault had taken less than two minutes.

He was still lying on the floor when the door opened again. A pair of boots entered his field of vision.

Muffled: "Get this mess cleared up." Louder: "You—on your feet."

Martin rolled over, to see Security Lieutenant Sauer staring down at him. The junior officer from the Curator's Office stood behind him, along with a couple of enlisted men. Martin began to sit up.

"*Out*," Sauer told the guards. They left. "On your feet," he repeated.

Martin sat up and pushed himself upright against one wall.

"You are in *big* trouble," said the Lieutenant. "No, don't say anything. You're in trouble. You can dig yourself in deeper or you can cooperate. I want you to think about it for a while." He held up a slim black wafer. "We know what this is. Now you can tell us all about it, who gave it to you, or you can let us draw our own conclusions. This isn't a civil court or an investigation by the audit bureau; this is, in case you hadn't worked it out, a military-intelligence matter. How you decide to deal with us affects how we will deal with you. Understood?"

Martin blinked. "I've never seen it before," he insisted, pulse racing.

Sauer looked disgusted. "Don't be obtuse. It was in your gadget. Naval regulations specify that it's an offense to bring unauthorized communications devices aboard a warship. So what was it doing there? You forgot to take it out? Whom does it belong to, anyway?"

Martin wavered. "The shipyard told me to carry it," he said. "When I came aboard I didn't realize I'd be on board for more than a shift at a time. Or that it was a problem."

"The shipyard told you to carry it." Sauer looked skeptical. "It's a dead causal channel, man! Have you any idea how much one of those things is worth?"

Martin nodded shakily. "Have you any idea how much this *ship* is worth?" he asked. "MiG put it together. MiG stands to make a lot of money selling copies: more if it earns a distinguished combat record. Has it occurred to you that my primary employers—the people you rented me from—have a legitimate interest in seeing how you've changed around the ship they delivered to you?"

Sauer tossed the cartridge on Martin's bunk. "Plausible. You're doing well, so far: don't let it go to your head." He turned and rapped on the door. "If that's your final story, I'll pass it on to the Captain. If you have anything else to tell me, let the supervisor know when he brings your lunch."

"Is that all?" Martin asked as the door opened.

"Is that all?" Sauer shook his head. "You confess to a capital offense, and ask if that's *all?*" He paused in the doorway and stared at Martin, expressionless. "Yes, that's all. Recording off."

Then he was gone.

υassilυ had gone to Lieutenant Sauer immediately after the abortive search through Rachel's luggage: badly frightened, needing advice. He'd poured everything out before Sauer, who had nodded reassuringly and calmed him down before explaining what they were going to do.

"They're in it together, son, that much is clear. But you should have talked to me first. Let's see this gadget you took from him, hmm?" Vassily had passed him the cartridge he'd stolen from Martin's PA. Sauer took one look at it and nodded to himself. "Never seen one of these before, have you? Well, don't worry; it's just the lever we need." He tapped the exhausted causal channel significantly. "Don't know why he had this on board, but it was bloody stupid of him, clear breach of His Majesty's regulations. You could have come to me with it immediately, no questions asked, instead of digging around the woman's luggage. Which, of course, you didn't do. Did you?"

"Uh—no, sir."

"Jolly good." Sauer nodded to himself again. "Because, if you had, I'd have to arrest you, of course. But I suppose, if she left her door unlocked and some enlisted man tried to help himself to her wardrobe, well, we can investigate it..." He trailed off thoughtfully.

"Why can't we arrest the woman, sir? For, um, possession of illicit machinery?"

"Because"—Sauer looked down his nose at Vassily—"she's got a diplomatic passport. She's *allowed* to have illegal machinery in her luggage. And, frankly, far as I can tell, she's got an excuse. Would you be complaining if she had a sewing machine? That's what she'll say it is; a garment fabricator."

"But I saw these *things* coming out of there, with too many legs! They were after me—"

"Nobody else has seen them," Sauer said in a soothing tone of voice. "I believe you; you probably *did* see something. Spy robots, perhaps. But good ones, good enough to hide—and without evidence—" He shrugged.

"What are you going to do, then, sir?"

Sauer glanced away. "I think we're going to pay Mr. Springfield a visit," he murmured. "We'll take him away. Stick him in the cells for a bit. And then"—he grinned, unpleasantly—"we'll see which way our diplomat jumps. Which should tell us what all this means, shouldn't it?"

Neither of them noticed the pair of polka-dotted knickers hiding behind the ventilation duct overhead, listening patiently and recording everything.

the *lord vanek* accelerated at an economical two gees, using its drive kernel to curve the space-time ahead of it into a valley into which it slid easily, without imposing punishing stress on crew or machinery. Ninety-two thousand tonnes of warship (with an eight-billion-tonne black hole at her core) took a lot of moving, but once set in motion, it could go places fast. It would take days to cross the vast gulf that separated *Lord Vanek*'s parking station from the first jump point on the return leg of its timelike path—but nothing like the years that humanity's earliest probes had taken to cover similar distances.

The ships of the fleet had traveled barely twenty light-years from the New Republic, but in the process, they had hopped forward in time by four thousand years, zigzagging between the two planetless components of the binary system in an attempt to outrun any long-term surveillance that the Festival might have placed on them. Soon the spacelike component of the voyage would commence, with a cruise to a similar system not far from Rochard's World; then the fleet would pursue a bizarre trajectory, looping back into the past of their own world line without actually intersecting that of their origin point.

Along the way, the fleet tenders would regularly top up the warships with consumable provisions, air and water and food; no less than eight merchant ships would be completely stripped and abandoned to fall forever between the stars, their crews doubled up aboard other vessels. The voyage would strain the Navy's logistic system beyond the point of failure: something had to give, and an entire year's shipbuilding budget would go into the supply side of this operation alone.

As they cruised between jumps, the warships exercised continually. Tentative lidar pulses strobed at the deep vacuum beyond the heliopause as officers sought firing solutions on the ships of the other squadrons; missile and torpedo trajectories were plotted, laser firing solutions entered into the tireless gear mills of the analytical engines. Tracking ships at long range was difficult, for they didn't emit much detectable radiation. Radar was hopeless: to pump out sufficient energy to get a return, the *Lord Vanek* would have produced enough waste heat to broil her crew alive. As it was, only her vast radiator panels, spread to the stars and now glowing a dull red, allowed them to run the lidar at high intensity for short periods of time. (Vacuum is a most effective insulator— and active sensors capable of reaching out across billions of kilometers run hot.)

Martin Springfield knew nothing of this. Lying in his cell he'd spent the past two days in despondent boredom, alternating between depression and guarded optimism by turns. *Still alive,* he thought. Then: *Not for long.* If only there was something he could do! But on board a starship, there was nowhere to run. He was enough of a realist to understand this: if they ran out of options here, he was dead. He'd simply have to hope that they hadn't worked out what he'd done, and would release him rather than antagonizing the shipyard.

He was sitting on the bunk one evening when the door opened. He looked up at once, expecting Sauer or the Curator's kid spook. His eyes widened. "What are you doing here?"

"Just visiting. Mind if I sit down?"

He nodded uneasily. Rachel sat on the edge of the bunk. She was wearing a plain black jumpsuit and had tied her hair back severely; her manner was different, almost relaxed. It wasn't a disguise, he realized; she wasn't acting the part of a woman of easy virtue or a diplomat posted to a banana republic, or anyone else, for that matter. She was being herself—a formidable figure. "I thought they'd have locked you up, too," he said.

"Yes, well..." She looked distracted. "One moment." She glanced at her pocket watch. "*Ah.*" She leaned over toward the head end of his bunk and placed something small and metallic on it.

"I already spiked the bugs," he said. "They won't hear much." She glared at him. "Thanks for nothing."

"What—"

"I want the truth," she said flatly. "You've been lying to me. I want to know why."

"Oh." He tried not to cringe. Her expression was unnaturally controlled, the calm before a storm.

"You've got only one chance to tell the truth," she said, pitching her voice in conversational tones that were belied by a brittle edge in it. "I don't think they know you're lying yet, but when we get back—well, they're not dummies and you're digging yourself in deeper. The Curator's Office will be watching. If you act guilty, the boy wonder will draw the only available conclusion."

He sighed. "And what if the conclusion is right? What if I *am* guilty?" he asked.

"I trusted you," she said flatly. "As yourself. *Not* as a player. I don't like being lied to, Martin. In business or my personal life, whichever."

"Well." He contemplated the shiny jammer she'd placed on his pillow. It was easier than facing her anger and hurt. "If I said they told me they were the shipyard, would that satisfy you?"

"No." She shook her head. "You're not dumb enough to fall for a cover story, anyway." She looked away. "I don't like being lied to," she said bitterly.

He looked at her. Rachel was an up-to-date professional, unlike the bumbling amateurs of the New Republic; she'd have speech analysis reflexes, lie detectors, any number of other gadgets trained on him, *if* this was business, and if she hadn't completely lost it. If she had—well, he could hardly blame her for being mad at him. In her place, he'd be angry, too. And hurt. "I don't like telling lies," he said, which was true enough. "Not without an overriding reason," he admitted.

She took a deep breath, visibly steeling herself. "I'm the nearest thing to a lawyer you're going to get here, Martin. I'm the nearest representative of your government—what they think is your government—within four thousand years and a two-hundred-light-year radius. They have a legalistic system of government, for all that they're medieval throwbacks, and they let me visit you as your advocate. I can plead your case if it comes up to a court-martial because you're a civilian, and I *might* be able to deflect things short of that. But only if you tell me everything, so I know what I'm defending."

"I can't talk about it," he said uncomfortably. He picked up his book, half trying to shelter his guilty conscience behind it. "I'm not allowed to. I thought you of all people would be able to understand that?"

"Listen." Rachel glared at him. "Remember what I told you about trust? I'm really disappointed. Because I *did* trust you, and it seems to me that you betrayed that trust. As it is, I'm going to have to do a lot of fast talking if I'm going to try to get your ass off the hook you're caught on, or at least get you out of here alive. And before I do that, I want to know what you've been lying to me *about*."

She stood up. "I'm a fool. And a damned fool for trusting you, and a worse fool for getting involved with you. Hell, I'm an unprofessional fool! But I'm going to ask you again, and you'd better answer truthfully. There are a lot of lives at stake this time, Martin, because this is not a game. Who the fuck are you working for?"

Martin paused a moment, dizzy with a sense of events moving out of control. *Can't tell her, can't not tell her*—he looked up, meeting her eyes for the first time. It was the hurt expression that made his mind up for him: no amount of rationalization would help him sleep that night if he left her feeling like this. Feeling betrayed by the only person she'd been able to trust within a radius of light-years. One moment of unprofessionalism deserved to be answered by another. His mouth felt dry and clumsy as he spoke: "I work for the Eschaton."

Rachel sat down heavily, her eyes wide with disbelief. "*What?*"

He shrugged. "You think the E's only way of dealing with problems is to drop a rock on them?" he asked.

"Are you kidding?"

"Nope." He could taste bile in the back of his throat. "And I believe in what I'm doing, else I wouldn't be here now, would I? Because truly, the alternative is to drop a planet-buster on the problem. The Eschaton finds that easier. And it makes the appropriate noises. It *scares* people. But really—most of the time, the E likes to solve problems more quietly through people like me."

"How long?"

"About twenty years." He shrugged again. "That's all there is to it."

"Why?" She buried her hands between her knees, holding them together tightly, looking at him with a miserably confused expression on her face.

"Because—" He tried to drag his scattered thoughts together.

"Believe me, the Eschaton prefers it when people like you do the job first. It saves a lot of pain all around. But once the fleet moved, and you lost the argument with them, there was no alternative. You didn't really think they'd set up the prerequisites for a closed timelike path and not follow it through to the logical end?" He took a deep breath. "That's the sort of job I do. I'm a plumber, for when the Eschaton wants to fix a leak quietly."

"You're an agent, you mean."

"Yes," he agreed. "Like you."

"Like me." She made a croaking noise that sounded as if it might have been intended as a laugh. "Shit, Martin, that is *not* what I was expecting to hear."

"I wish this hadn't happened. Especially with—well, us. In the middle."

"Me too, with brass knobs on," she said shakily. "Was that all there was?"

"*All* there was? That's all I was holding out on you, honest."

A long pause. "Alright. It was, uh, purely professional?"

He nodded. "Yes." He looked at her. "I don't like lying. And I haven't been lying, or withholding the truth, about anything else. I promise."

"Oh. Okay." She took a deep breath and grinned tiredly, simultaneously looking amused and relieved.

"It's really been eating you, hasn't it?" he asked.

"Oh, you could say that," she said, with heavy irony.

"Um." He held out a hand. "I'm sorry. Truly."

"Apology accepted—conditionally." She squeezed his hand, briefly, then let go. "Now, are you going to tell me what the Eschaton has in mind for us?"

Martin sighed. "Yes, inasmuch as I know. But I've got to warn you, it's not good. If we can't get off this ship before it arrives, we're probably going to die . . ."

time travel destabilizes history.

History is a child of contingency; so many events depend on critical misunderstandings or transient encounters that even the apocryphal butterfly's wing is apt to stir up a storm in short order. A single misunderstood telegram in June of 1917 permitted the Bolshevik revolution to become a possibility; a single spy in 1958 extended the Cold War by a decade. And without both such events, could a being like the Eschaton ever have come to exist?

Of course, in a universe which permits time travel, history itself becomes unstable—and the equilibrium can only be restored when the diabolical mechanism edits itself out of the picture. But that's scant comfort for the trillions of entities who silently cease to exist in the wake of a full-blown time storm.

It's hardly surprising that, whenever intelligent beings arise in such a universe, they will seek to use closed timelike curves to prevent their own extinction. Faster-than-light travel being possible, general relativity tells us that it is indistinguishable from time travel; and this similarity makes the technologies of total annihilation dreadfully accessible. In the small, stupid little organizations like the New Republic seek to gain advantage over their contemporaries and rivals. In the large, vast, cool intellects seek to stabilize their universe in the form most suitable to them. Their tampering may be as simple as preventing rivals from editing them out of the stable historical record—or it may be as sophisticated as meddling with the early epochs of the big bang, back before the Higgs field decayed into the separate fundamental forces that bind the universe together to ensure just the right ratio of physical constants to support life.

This is not the only universe; far from it. It isn't even the only universe in which life exists. Like living organisms, universes exist balanced on the edge of chaos, little bubbles of twisted ur-space that pinch off and bloat outward, expanding and cooling, presently giving birth to further bubbles of condensed space-time; a hyperdimensional crystal garden full of strange trees bearing stranger fruit.

But the other universes are not much use to us. There are too many variables in the mix. As the initial burst of energy that signals the birth of a universe cools, the surging force field that drives its initial expansion becomes tenuous, then breaks down into a complex mess of other forces. The constants that determine their relative strengths are set casually, randomly. There are universes with only two forces; others, with thousands. (Ours has five.) There are universes where the electron is massive: nuclear fusion is so easy there that the era of star formation ends less than a million of our years after the big bang. Chemistry is difficult there, and long before life can evolve, such universes contain nothing but cooling pulsars and black holes, the debris of creation brought to a premature end.

There are universes where photons have mass—others where there is too little mass in the universe for it to achieve closure and collapse in a big crunch at the end of time. There are, in fact, an infinity of universes out there, and they are all uninhabitable. There is a smaller infinitude of possibly habitable ones, and in some of them, intelligent life evolves; but more than that we may never know. Travel between universes is nearly impossible; materials that exist in one may be unstable in another. So, trapped in our little fishbowl of space we drift through the crystal garden of universes—and our own neighborly intelligences, beings like the Eschaton, do their best to prevent the less-clever inmates from smashing the glass from within.

The man in gray had explained all this to Martin at length, eighteen years ago. "The Eschaton has a strong interest in maintaining the integrity of the world line," he had said. "It's in your interest, too. Once people begin meddling with the more obscure causal paradoxes, all sorts of lethal side-effects can happen. The Eschaton is as vulnerable to this as any other being in the universe—it didn't create this place, you know, it just gets to live in it with the rest of us. It may be a massively superhuman intelligence or cluster of intelligences, it may have resources we can barely comprehend, but it could probably be snuffed out quite easily; just a few nuclear weapons in the right place before it bootstrapped into consciousness, out of the pre-Singularity networks of the twenty-first century. Without the Eschaton, the human species would probably be extinct by now."

"Epistemology pays no bills," Martin remarked drily. "If you're expecting me to do something risky..."

"We appreciate that." The gray man nodded. "We need errands run, and not all of them are entirely safe. Most of the time it will amount to little more than making note of certain things and telling us about them—but occasionally, if there is a serious threat, you may be asked to act. Usually in subtle, undetectable ways, but always at your peril. But there are compensations."

"Describe them." Martin put his unfinished drink down at that point.

"My sponsor is prepared to pay you very well indeed. And part of the pay—we can smooth the path if you apply for prolongation and continued residency." Life-extension technology, allowing effectively unlimited life expectancy beyond 160 years, was eminently practical, and available on most developed worlds. It was also as tightly controlled as any medical procedure could be. The controls and licensing were a relic of the Overshoot, the brief period in the twenty-first century when Earth's population blipped over the ten-billion mark (before the Singularity, when the Eschaton bootstrapped its way past merely human intelligence and promptly rewrote the rule book). The after-effects of overpopulation still scarred the planet, and the response was an ironclad rule—if you want to live beyond your natural span, you must either demonstrate some particular merit, some reason why you should be allowed to stay around, or you could take the treatment and emigrate. There were few rules that all of Earth's fractured tribes and cultures and companies obeyed, but out of common interest, this was one of them. To be offered exemption by the covert intervention of the Eschaton—

"How long do I have to think about it?" asked Martin.

"Until tomorrow." The gray man consulted his notepad. "Ten-thousand-a-year retainer. Ten thousand or more as a bonus if you are asked to do anything. And an essential status exemption from the population committee. On top of which, you will be helping to protect humanity as a whole from the actions of some of its more intemperate—not to say stupid—members. Would you care for another drink?"

"It's alright," said Martin. *They're willing to pay me? To do something I'd volunteer for?* He stood up. "I don't need another day to think about it. Count me in."

The gray man smiled humorlessly. "I was told you'd say that."

the gold team was on full alert. Not a head moved when the door opened, and Captain Mirsky walked in, followed by Commodore Bauer and his staff. "Commander Murametz, please report."

"Yes, sir. Time to jump transition, three-zero-zero seconds. Location plot confirmed, signals operational. All systems running at an acceptable level of readiness for engagement plan C. We're ready to go to battle stations whenever you say, sir."

Mirsky nodded. "Gentlemen, carry on as ordered." The Commodore nodded and quietly instructed his adjutant to take notes. Elsewhere on the ship, sirens blatted: the clatter of spacers running to their stations didn't penetrate the bulkheads, but the atmosphere nevertheless felt tense. Low-key conversations started at the various workstations around the room as officers talked over the tactical circuits.

"Ready for jump in two-zero-zero seconds," called Relativistics.

Rachel Mansour—wearing her disarmament inspector's uniform—sat uncomfortably close to one of the walls, studying a packed instrument console over the shoulder of a petty officer. Brass handles and baroque red LEDs glowed at her; a pewter dog's head barked silently from an isolation switch. Someone had spent half a lifetime polishing the engravings until they gleamed as softly as butter. It seemed a bitter irony, to observe such art in a place of war; the situation was, she thought, more than somewhat repulsive, and finding anything even remotely beautiful in it only made things worse.

The Festival: of all the stupid things the New Republic might attack, the Festival was about the worst. She'd spoken to Martin about it, piecing together his information with her own. Together they'd pieced together a terrifying hypothesis. "Herman was unusually vague about it," Martin admitted. "Normally he has a lot of background detail. Every word means something. But it's as if he doesn't want to say too much about the Festival. They're—he called them, uh, glider-gun factories. I don't know if you know about Life—"

"Cellular automata, the game?"

"That's the one. Glider guns are mobile cellular automata. There are some complex life structures that replicate themselves, or simpler cellular structures; a glider-gun factory is a weird one. It periodically packs itself into a very dense mobile system that migrates across the grid for a couple of hundred squares, then it unpacks itself into two copies that then pack down and fly off in opposite directions. Herman said that they're a real-space analogue: he called them a Boyce-Tipler robot. Self-replicating, slower-than-light interstellar probes that are sent out to gather information about the universe and feed it back to a center. Only the Festival isn't just a dumb robot fleet. It carries upload processors, thousands of uploaded minds running faster than real time when there are resources to support them, downloaded into long-term storage during the long trips."

Rachel had shuddered slightly at that, and he hugged her, misapprehending the cause of her distress. She let him, not wanting him to realize he had upset her. She'd dealt with uploads before. The first-generation ones, fresh from the meat puppet universe, weren't a problem: it was the kids that got her. Born—if you could call it that—in a virtual environment, they rapidly diverged from any norm of humanity that she could see. More seriously, their grasp of the real world was poor. Which was fine as long as they didn't have to deal with it, but when they did, they used advanced nanosystems for limbs and they sometimes accidentally *broke* things—planets, for instance.

It wasn't intentional malice; they'd simply matured in an environment where information didn't go away unless someone wanted it to, where death and destruction were reversible, where magic wands worked and hallucinations were dangerous. The real universe played by different rules, rules that their horrified ancestors had fled as soon as the process of migrating minds into distributed computing networks had been developed.

The Festival sounded like a real headache. On the one hand, an upload civilization, used to omnipotence within its own pocket universe, had decided for no obvious reason to go forth and play the galactic tourist. On the other hand, physical machinery of vast subtlety and power was bound to do their bidding at each port of call. Bush robots, for example: take a branching tree of fronds. Each bough split into two half-scale branches at either end, with flexible joints connecting them. Repeated down to the molecular level, each terminal branch was closed off with a nanomanipulator. The result was a silvery haze with a dumbbell-shaped core, glittering with coherent light, able to change shape, dismantle and reassemble physical objects at will—able to rebuild just about anything into any desired physical form, from the atomic scale up. Bush robots made the ultimate infantry; shoot at them, and they'd eat the bullets, splice them into more branches, and thank you for the gift of metals.

"I'm worried about what will happen when we arrive," Martin admitted. He'd wrung his hands while he spoke, unconsciously emphasizing his points. "I don't think the New Republicans can actually comprehend what's going on. They see an attack, and I can understand why—the Festival has destroyed the political and social economy on one of their colonies as thoroughly as if it had nuked the place from orbit—but what I can't see is any possible avenue to a settlement. There's not going to be any common ground there. What does the Festival want? What could make them go away and leave the Republic alone?"

"I thought you didn't like the New Republic," Rachel challenged.

He grimaced. "And I suppose you do? I don't like their system, and they know it. That's why I'm sitting in this cell instead of in my cabin, or on the engineering deck. But—" He shrugged. "Their social system is one thing, but people are people everywhere you go, just trying to get along in this crazy universe. I don't like them as individuals, but that's not the same as wanting them dead. They're not monsters, and they don't deserve what's coming to them, and life isn't fair, is it?"

"You did your bit to make it that way."

"Yes." He dropped his gaze to the floor, focusing intently on something invisible to her. "I wish there was an alternative. But Herman can't just let them get away with it. Either causality is a solid law, or—things break. Far better for their maneuver simply to fail, so the whole voyage looks like a cack-handed mess, than for it to succeed, and encourage future adventurers to try for a timelike approach on their enemies."

"And if you're lashed to the mast as the ship heads for the maelstrom?"

"I never said I was omniscient. Herman said he'd try to get me out of here if I succeeded; I wish I knew what he had in mind. What are *your* options like?"

Her lips quirked. "Maybe he nobbled my boss—he taught me never to travel at sea without a lifeboat."

Martin snorted, obviously misunderstanding: "Well, they say a captain always goes down with his ship—shame they never mention the black gang drowning in the engine room!"

An announcement from the helm brought Rachel back to the present: "Jump in one-zero-zero seconds."

"Status, please," said Commander Murametz. Each post called out in order; everything was running smoothly. "Time to transition?"

"Four-zero seconds. Kernel spin-down in progress; negative mass dump proceeding." Far beneath their feet, the massive singularity at the core of the drive system was spooling down, releasing angular momentum into the energetic vacuum underlying space-time. There was no vibration, no sense of motion: nor could there be. Spin, in the context of a space drive, was a property of warped patches of space, nothing to do with matter as most people understood it.

"Commander Murametz, proceed." The Captain stood back, hands clasped behind his back. "Commodore, by your leave?"

Bauer nodded. "Proceed on your initiative."

"Transition in progress...we're clear. Reference frame locked."

"No obstructions," called Radar One. "Um, looks like we're on the nail."

"One-zero gees, straight in on the primary," said Ilya. He looked almost bored; they'd rehearsed this a dozen times in the past three days alone. "Confirm positional fix, then give me a passive scan. Standard profile."

"Aye aye, sir. Nav confirmation; we have a star fix. Yes, we're a good bit closer to the bucket than last time. I see a waste heat dump from *Chancellor Romanoff;* they're through." That cheered them up; even at ten gees constant acceleration, a miss of a couple of astronomical units could take hours or days to make up. "Nothing else in view."

"Give me a lidar shout, then. Chirped, if you please, frontal nine-zero degrees."

"Emission starting—now. Profile steady." The main screen of the simulation showed megawatts of laser light pouring out into the depths of space, mostly hard ultraviolet tagged with the sawtooth timing pulses of the ship's clock. "Scan closure. Lidar shutdown."

Radar Two: "I've got backscatter! Range—Holy father! Sir, we're right on top of them! Range six-zero K-kilometers, looks like metal!"

Bauer smiled like a shark.

"Helm: take us to full military power in one-zero seconds. Course plus one-zero, minus four-zero."

"Aye aye, sir, bringing course to plus one-zero minus four-zero. Two-one one gees coming up in five...three...now." Like most regional powers, the New Republican Navy had adopted the Terran standard gee—ten meters per second squared. At full military power, *Lord Vanek* could go from a standing start to planetary escape velocity in less than sixty seconds; without a delicate balancing act, trading off the drive kernel's spin against the curvature of space around the ship, the crew would be squashed flat and broken on the floor. But carrying a drive kernel had its price—a non-FTL, fission-powered missile could, at short range, outrun or out-turn a warship hobbled by the mass of a mountain.

"Radar, get me some details on that bounce." Mirsky leaned forward.

"Aye aye, sir." A plot came up on the forward display. Rachel focused on the readouts, looking over the razor-scarred rolls at the base of Petty Officer Borisovitch's skull. "Confirming..."

Radar Two: "More contacts! Repeat, I have multiple contacts!"

"How far?" demanded the captain.

"They're—too close! Sir, they're very faint. Took a few seconds for the analysis grid to resolve them, in fact. They've got to be black body emitters with stealth characteristics. Range nine-zero K, one-point-three M, seven M, another at two-five-zero K... we're in the middle of it!"

Rachel closed her eyes. A chill ran up her spine as she thought about small robot factories, replicators, the swarm of self-replicating weapons breeding in low orbit around a distant gas giant moon. She breathed deeply and opened her eyes.

Radar Two interrupted her reverie: "Target! Range six-point-nine M-klicks, big emission profile. Course minus five-five, plus two-zero."

Mirsky turned to his executive officer: "Ilya, your call."

"Yes, sir. Designate the new contact as target alpha. Adopt convergent course for alpha, closest pass at three-zero K, full military power."

"Aye aye, targeting alpha."

"You expect something, sir," Ilya said quietly. Rachel tilted her head slightly, to let her boosted hearing focus on the two senior officers at the back of the room.

"Damn right I do. Something wiped out the system defense flotilla," Mirsky murmured. "Something that was sitting there, waiting for them. I don't expect anything except hostile contacts as soon as we come out of jump."

"I didn't expect them to be this close, though." Murametz looked troubled.

"I had to do some digging, but thanks to Inspector Mansour"—the Captain nodded in her direction—"we know a bit about their capabilities, which are somewhat alarming. It's not in the standard intelligence digest because the fools didn't think it worth mentioning. We're up against cornucopiae, you see, and nobody back at Naval Intel bothered asking what a robot factory can do tactically."

Commander Murametz shook his head. "I don't know. Sir? Does it have any military bearing?"

"Yes. You see, robots can *breed*. And spawn starwisps."

"Starwisps—" Enlightenment dawned. Ilya looked shocked. "How big would they be?" he asked the captain.

"About half a kilogram mass. You can cram a lot of guidance circuitry into a gram of diamond-substrate nanomachinery. The launchers that fire them probably mass a quarter of a tonne each—but a large chunk of that is stored antimatter to power the neutral particle beam generators. At a guess, there could be a couple of thousand out here; that's probably what those low aspect contacts are. If you trip-wire one of them, and it launches on you, expect the starwisp riding the beam to come out at upward of ten thousand gees. But of course, you probably won't even see it unless it gets lock-on and you get some side-scattered radiation from the beam. Basically, we're in the middle of a minefield, and the mines can shoot relativistic missiles at us."

"But—" Ilya looked horrified. "I thought this was a standard firing setup!"

"It is, Commander," Bauer said drily.

"Ah." Ilya looked slightly green at the edges.

"Backscatter!" It was Radar Three. "I have backscatter! Something is launching from target alpha, acceleration one-point-three—no, one-point-five gees. Cooking off gammas at one-point-four MeV."

"Log as candidate one," said Ilya. Urgently: "Sir, humbly request permission to resume immediate control?"

"Granted," snapped the Captain.

Rachel glanced around at the ops room stations. Officers hunched over their workstations, quietly talking into headset microphones and adjusting brass-handled dials and switches. Mirsky walked over to the command station and stood at Ilya's shoulder. "Get radar looking for energy spikes," he commented. "This is going to be difficult. If I'm right, we're in the middle of a minefield controlled by a central command platform; if we leak again, we're not getting out of here." Rachel leaned forward too, focusing on the main screen. It was, she thought, remarkable: if this was typical of their teamwork, then with a bit of luck they might even make it into low orbit around Rochard's World.

The tension rose over the next ten minutes, as the *Lord Vanek* accelerated toward the target. Its singularity drive was virtually undetectable, even at close range (spotting the mass of a mountain at a million kilometers defied even the most sensitive gravity-wave detectors), but all the enemy strongpoint had to do was switch on a pulse-doppler radar sweep and the battlecruiser would show up like a sore thumb. The first rule of space warfare—and the ancient submarine warfare that preceded it—was, "If they can see you, they can kill you."

On the other hand, the enemy base couldn't be sure exactly where the ship was right now; it had changed course immediately after shutting down its search lidar. Four more brief lidar pulses had swept across the ship's hull, as other members of the squadron dropped in and took their bearings: since then, nothing but silence.

"Second trace!" called Radar One. "Another live bird moving out. Range on this one is four-seven M-klicks, vector toward lidar source three, the *Suvaroff*."

"Confirm course and acceleration," ordered Ilya. "Log it as candidate two."

"Confirm three more," said Radar Two. "Another source, um, range nine-zero M-klicks. Designation beta. They're thick around here, aren't they?"

"Watch out for a—"

"Third echo from local target alpha," called Radar Two. "Scattering relative to candidates one and two. Looks like a third missile. This one's heading our way."

"Give me a time to contact," Mirsky said grimly. Rachel studied him: Mirsky was a wily old bird, but even though he'd figured out what was going on, she couldn't see how he planned to pull their chestnuts out of the fire. At any moment she expected to hear the shriek of alarms as one or another observer picked up the telltale roar of a relativistic particle stream, with a beam-riding starwisp hurtling toward them on top of it, armed with a cargo of antimatter.

Of course, it was too much to expect the New Republic's government to realize just how thoroughly they were outclassed; their cultural bias was such that they couldn't perceive the dangers of something like the Festival. Even their best naval tacticians, the ones who understood forbidden technologies like self-replicating robot factories and starwisps, didn't comprehend quite what the Festival might do with them.

The *Lord Vanek*'s chances of surviving this engagement were thin. In fact, the entire expedition was predicated on the assumption that what they were fighting was sufficiently human in outlook to understand the concept of warfare and to use the sort of weapons overeducated apes might throw at one another. Rachel had a hopeless, unpleasant gut feeling that acting without such preconceptions, the Festival would be far deadlier to the New Republican expeditionary force than they could imagine. Unfortunately, it appeared she was going to be around when they learned the hard way that interstellar wars of aggression were much easier to lose than to win.

"More backscatter. Target gamma! We have another target—range two-seven-zero M-klicks. Ah, another missile launching."

"That's—" Ilya paused. "One base per cubic AU? One M bases, if they're evenly distributed through the outer system." He looked stunned.

"You don't think you're fighting *people,* do you?" asked Mirsky. "This is a fully integrated robot defense network. And it's big. Mind-bogglingly big." He looked almost pleased with his own perspicacity. "The Admiralty didn't listen when I explained it to them the first time, you know," he added. "Eighteen years ago. One of the reasons I never made flag rank—"

"I listened," Bauer said quietly. "Proceed, Captain."

"Yes sir. Solution on target alpha?"

Fire control: "Time to range on target alpha, two-zero-zero seconds, sir."

"Hmm." Mirsky contemplated the display. "Commander. Your opinion."

Ilya swallowed. "I'd get in close and use the laser grid."

Mirsky shook his head, slightly. "You forget they may have X-ray lasers." Louder: "Relativity, I want you ready to give me a microjump. If I give the word, 1 want us out of here within five seconds. Destination can be anywhere within about one-zero AUs, I'm not fussy. Can you do that?"

"Aye aye, sir. Kernel is fully recharged; we can do that. Holding at T minus five seconds, now."

"Guns: I want six SEM-20s in the tube, armed and ready to launch in two minutes. Warheads dialed for directional spallation, two-zero degree spread. Three of them go to alpha target; hold the other three in reserve ready for launch on five seconds' notice. Next, load and arm two torpedoes. I want them hot and ready when I need them."

"Aye aye, sir. Three rounds for alpha, three in reserve, and two torpedoes. Sir, six birds on the rail awaiting your command. The hot crew is fueling the torpedoes now; they should be ready in about four minutes."

"That's nice to know," Mirsky said, a trifle too acid; the lieutenant at the gunnery console flinched visibly. "As you were," added the Captain.

"Proximity in one-two-zero seconds, sir. Optimum launch profile in eight-zero."

"Plot the positions of the nearest identified mines. Show vectors on command station alpha, assuming they fire projectiles holding a constant acceleration of ten kilo-gees. Can they nail us in just four-zero seconds?"

"Checking, sir." Navigation. "Sir, they can't nail us before we take out that command post, unless target alpha also has a speed demon or two up his sleeve. But they'll get us one-five seconds later."

Mirsky nodded. "Very good. Guns: we launch at four-zero seconds to target. Helm, relativity: at contact plus five seconds, that's five seconds *after* our fire on target, initiate that micro-jump."

"Launch T minus five-zero seconds, sir... mark."

Rachel watched the display, a fuzzball of red pinpricks and lengthening lines. Their own projected vector, in blue, stretched toward one of the red dots, then stopped abruptly. Any second now, she guessed, something nasty was bound to happen.

Guns: "T minus three-zero. Birds warm. Launch grid coming up to power now. T minus two-zero."

Radar One interrupted: "I'm picking up some fuzz from astern."

"One-zero seconds. Launch rails energized," added the gun-nery post.

"Fire on schedule," said the captain.

"Yes, sir. Navigation updated. Inertial platforms locked. Birds charged, warheads green."

"Light particles!" yelled Radar One. "Big explosion off six M-klicks, bearing six-two by five-nine! Looks like—damn, one of the cruisers bought it. I'm getting a particle stream from astern! Bearing one-seven-seven by five, sidescatter, no range yet—"

"Five seconds to launch. Launch commencing, bird one run-ning. Lidar lock. Drive energized. Bird one main engine ignition confirmed. Bird two loaded and green... running. Gone. Drive energized. Bird three running—"

"Radar One, I have a lidar lock! ECM engaged from directly astern! Someone's painting us. I have a range—five-two K—and—"

Mirsky stepped forward. "Guns. I want all three spare missiles ejected straight astern now. Passive seekers, we will illuminate the targets for them."

"Aye aye, sir. Bird four, coming up... green. Bird four run-ning. Five, green, running."

"Radar Two, we have a seeker on our tail. Range four-five K, closing at—Holy Mother of God, I don't believe it!"

"Bird six running astern. What do you want me to lock on?"

"Radar Two, feed your plot to gunnery for birds four through six to target. Guns, shoot as soon as you see a clear fix—buy us some time."

"Aye aye, sir." The Lieutenant, ashen-faced, hunched over his console and pushed buttons like a man possessed.

"Range to firing point on alpha?" asked Mirsky.

"Three-zero seconds, sir. You want to push the attack?" The nav officer looked apprehensive. Every watt of power they pumped at the attack salvo via the laser grid was one watt less to point at the incoming interceptor.

"Yes, Lieutenant. I'll trust you not to tell me my job." The nav officer flushed and turned back to his console. "Guns, what's our situation?"

"I've pumped the forward birds right up, sir, maximum acceleration the warheads will take. MECO is in one-five seconds. Soon as that happens I'll divert power to our trailers. Ah, bird one burnout in one-zero seconds."

Rachel nodded to herself. Remembering lectures on the basics of relativistic physics, strategy in the post-Einsteinian universe, and the implications of a light cone expanding across an evenly spaced grid of points. *Any moment now the fossil light from the next shell of interceptors should reach us...*

"Holy Father!" shouted Radar Three. "I have beam spillover on all sides! We're boxed!"

"Control yourself," snapped Mirsky. "How many sources?"

"They—they—" radar punched buttons. Red lines appeared on the forward screen. "One-six of 'em, coming in from all points!"

"I see." Mirsky stroked his moustache. "Helm, are you ready with that microjump?"

"Yes, sir."

"Good." Mirsky smiled, tight-lipped. "Guns, status."

"Bird one burnout. Boosting bird four. Bird two, bird three, burnout. I'm diverting all propulsion beam power to the second salvo. Salvo time to target, one-five seconds. Ah, we have one-seven inbound aggressors. Three outbound antimissiles."

"Hold further fire," ordered the Captain. "How long until the first hostile is in range?"

"Should happen at—oh. Two seconds postcontact, sir."

"Nav! Pull the jump forward five seconds. We'll not stay around to count coup."

"Aye aye."

Radar One: "More scattering! Sir, I have... no, they're not going to get us in time."

"How many, Lieutenant?"

"We're boxed. Incoming beamriders in all directions, at long range. I count—"

"Bird one detonating now! Bird two, detonating. Bird three gone. Sir, three detonations on target."

"Jump in five. Four—"

"One-eight-point-nine K—no, one-nine K beamriders incoming!"

"Incoming number one, range one-two K and closing—"

"Confirmed kill on target alpha, oxygen, nitrogen in emission spectra."

"Two."

"Nine K."

"Three-two K incoming hostiles! No, three-two and—"

"One. Jump commit."

The red emergency lights dimmed as the main overhead lights came up. There was silence on the bridge for a moment, then Commodore Bauer cleared his throat. "Congratulations, gentlemen," he announced to Mirsky and his stunned ops crew. "Of all the ships in the squadron who have run that tape so far, you are the only one to have escaped at all, much less to have taken any of the enemy down. There will be a meeting in my office at 1600 to discuss the assumptions underlying this exercise and explain our new tactical doctrine for dealing with situations like this—massively ramified robot defense networks with fire control mediated by causal channel. Then we'll run it again tomorrow and see how well you do with your eyes open..."

diplomatic behavior _____

Meanwhile, two thousand years away, a small boy lay curled in darkness, whimpering in the grip of a dream of empire.

Felix moaned and shivered and dragged the tattered blanket closer around his shoulders. The abandoned hayloft was unheated, and the gaps between the log walls admitted a furious draft, but at least it was a roof over his head. It was warmer than the stony ground. Wolves roamed the untamed wilderness, and for a lad to sleep beneath the stars at this time of year was hazardous even in normal times.

Raven roosted on the thick oak beam above Felix's head, his long black beak tucked under one wing. Occasionally, he would wake for a moment, shake his feathers out, shuffle from one foot to the other, and glance around. But as long as the door stayed barred, nothing could reach them that he couldn't deal with; and so he would rejoin his master in sleep.

Rain battered on the roof, occasionally leaking through the sods that covered the rough-cut timber, dripping to the floor in thin cold streams. The smell of half-decayed hay hung heavy in the air. Felix hadn't dared light a fire after Mr. Rabbit pointed out how dangerous that could be. There were things out there that could see heat, silent things without mouths. Things that liked to eat little boys' brains.

Felix dreamed of Imperial orders, men in shiny uniforms, and women in silky gowns; of starships and cavalry parades and ceremonies and rituals. But his dreams were invaded by a tired and pervasive cynicism. The nobles and officers were corrupt hangers-on, their women grasping harpies searching for security. The ceremonies and rituals were meaningless and empty, a charade concealing a ghastly system of institutional injustices orchestrated to support the excesses of the rulers. Dreaming of New Prague, he felt himself to be a duke or prince, mired in a dung heap, chained down by responsibility and bureaucracy, unable to move despite the juggernaut of decaying corruption bearing down on him.

When he twitched and cried out in his dream, Mr. Rabbit crawled closer and sprawled against him, damp fur rising and falling with his breath. Presently Felix eased deeper into sleep, and Mr. Rabbit rolled away, curling nose to tail to resume his nightly regurgitation and cud-chewing. If it was hard being a small boy in a time of rapid change, it was a doubly hard burden to be a meter-tall rabbit cursed with human sentience and cunicular instincts.

In the early-morning light, Felix yawned, rubbed his eyes, and stretched stiffly, shivering with cold. "Rabbit?"

"Caaaw!" Raven flapped down from overhead and hopped closer, head cocked to one side. "Rabbit gone to vill-lage."

Felix blinked, slowly. "I wish he'd waited." He shivered, feeling a sense of loneliness very alien to a nine-year-old. He stood up and began to pack his possessions into a battered-looking haversack; a blanket, a small tin can, a half-empty box of matches, and one of the curious metal phones by which the Festival communicated with people. He paused over the phone for a moment, but eventually his sense of urgency won, and he shoved it into the pack. "Let's play *hunt the wabbit*," he said, and opened the door.

It was a cold, bright morning, and the ground in the abandoned farmyard was ankle deep in squelching mud. The blackened ruin of the house squatted on the other side of the quagmire like the stump of a tree struck by lightning, the Holy Father's fire. Behind it, a patch of dusty gray mud showed the depletion layer where the Festival's nanosystems had sucked the soil dry of trace elements, building something huge; it was almost certainly connected with the disappearance of the farmer and his family.

The village lay about two kilometers downhill from the farmhouse, around a bend in the narrow dirt track, past a copse of tall pine trees. Felix shrugged on his backpack and, after a brief pause to piss against the fire-blackened wall of the house, slowly headed down the road. He felt like whistling or singing, but kept his voice to himself; there was no telling what lived in the woods hereabouts, and he wasn't inclined to ignore Mr. Rabbit's warnings. He was a very serious little boy, very grown-up.

Raven hopped after him, then flapped forward heavily and landed in the ditch some way down the path. His head ducked repeatedly. "Brrrreak-fast!" he cawed.

"Oh, good!" Felix hurried to catch up, but when he saw what Raven had found to eat he turned away abruptly and pinched the bridge of his nose until the tears came, trying not to gag. Tears came hard; a long time ago, a very long distance away, Nurse had told him, "Big boys don't cry." But he knew better now. He'd seen much bigger boys crying, men even, as they were stood up against the bullet-pocked wall. (Some of them didn't cry, some of them held themselves stiffly upright, but it made no difference in the end.) "Sometimes I hate you, Raven."

"Caaww?" Raven looked up at him. The thing in the ditch was still wearing a little girl's dress. "Hungrrry."

"You might be—but I we've got to find Pyotr. Before the Mimes catch us."

Felix looked over his shoulder nervously. They'd been running scared, one jump ahead of the Mimes, for the past three days. The Mimes moved slowly, frequently fighting an invisible wind or trying to feel their way around intangible buildings, but they were remorseless. Mimes never slept, or blinked, or stopped moving.

A hundred meters closer to the village, the phone woke up. It chirped like a curious kitten until Felix rummaged through his bag and pulled it out. "Leave me alone!" he exclaimed, exasperated.

"Felix? It's Mr. Rabbit."

"What?" He looked at the phone, startled. Chrome highlights glinted beneath grubby oil-slick fingerprints.

"It's me. Your flop-eared friend. I'm in the village. Listen, don't come any closer."

"Why not?" He frowned and carried on walking.

"They're here. My luck ran out; don't think I can get away. You—" The giant lagomorph's voice broke into something utterly inhuman for a moment, a rodent squeal of rage and fright. "—Behind you, too! Go cross-country. *Run, boy.*"

The phone buzzed, disconnected. Felix raised it angrily, meaning to dash it to the ground, then stopped. Ahead of him, Raven stared at him, beady-eyed and bloody-beaked. "Fly over the village," Felix ordered the bird. "Tell me what you see."

"Caaaw!" Raven took a running leap into the air, lumbering heavily over the grass, then climbing up over the treetops. Felix looked at the phone again, mingled rage and grief in his eyes. It wasn't fair. Nothing was fair! All he wanted was to be young and carefree, and to have fun. The companions came later; at first there had been Mrs. Hedgehog as well, but she'd been killed by a random Fringe performance, electrical discharges flashing to ground from an ionosphere raped by induced solar flares. The Fringe was like that; a mindless thing, infinitely dangerous and fickle, as trustworthy as a venomous snake but sometimes capable of producing works of great beauty. (The auroral displays had lasted for weeks.)

Felix looked around, nervously. Over the hedgerow, back down the road, something seemed to move. He held the phone to his cheek. "Somebody talk to me?"

"Will you entertain us?"

"I don't know how!" he burst out.

"Tell story. Provide entertaining formal proof of correctness. Sing, dance, clap your hands."

"What will you do for me in return?"

"What do you require?" The voice on the other end of the line sounded tinny, distant, compressed through the bandwidth ligature of a causal channel.

"Bad men are after me. They throw custard pies, turn me into one of them. Can you stop them? Protect me from the Mimes?"

"Tell story." It wasn't a statement or a question, it was an order.

Felix took a deep breath. He glanced up and saw Raven circling overhead. He jumped the ditch, then ducked under the first branches and began to weave his way into the woods. He talked as he walked. "In the beginning there was a duke who lived in a palace, on the banks of the river, overlooking the only city on the world. He wasn't a very wise duke, but he did what he thought was best for his people. Then one morning, it began to rain telephones, and the world changed. This is the duke's story."

It was a long and rambling story, and it went on for some time. How the duke's palace had been besieged by anarchist terrorists, who unleashed chaos and plastic cutlery on the town. All his soldiers deserted after looting the palace and the zoo; he escaped through a secret passage under the Curator's waiting rooms in the sub-sub-basement. The elderly duke had escaped with three trusty retainers. Grief-stricken, he had barely been able to understand what had happened to his world. Why had everything changed? A telephone chirped at him, like a curious kitten, from the rubbish in a back alley. He bent to pick it up and the motion saved his life for two renegade soldiers shot at him with their rifles. They killed Citizen Von Beck, but not before the Citizen marked them with his slow gun—for the Citizens of the Curator's Office were allowed to use forbidden weapons in the course of their duties. (Bullets from a slow gun flew on hummingbird wings, seeking their prey wherever they might flee. Bullets from a slow gun killed by stinging with their neurotoxin barbettes, like wasps with secret police insignia. They were a terror weapon, to demonstrate the horrors of unrestricted technology.)

Felix slipped down a root-woven embankment and crossed a clearing studded with green-sprouting stumps as he continued. The duke talked to the phone in his despair, and it offered him three wishes. He asked to be made young again, thinking it a bitter joke; to his surprise, his youth was magically restored. Next, he asked for companions; and he was given friends, wonderful friends, who would do anything for him and ask nothing in return. Even the third wish, the little-boy wish made in the first flush of restored youth, had been granted. None of which was exactly what he'd wanted, or would have asked for had he not been in a very disturbed state of mind at the time, but it was better than the wishes some people he'd met subsequently had made. (The kulak whose wish had been a goose that laid golden eggs, for example. It was a wonderful animal, until you held it close to a railway man's dosimeter and discovered the deluge of ionizing radiation spewing invisibly from the nuclear alchemist's stone in its gizzard. Which you only thought to do when the bloody stools became too much to bear, and your hair began to fall out in clumps.)

The duke-turned-child had walked across three hundred kilometers in the past month, living from hand to mouth. His friends had looked after him, though. Raven, who could see over and around things, told him of traps or ambushes or deadfalls before he walked into them. Mr. Rabbit hopped along at his side, and with his acute hearing, nose for trouble, and plain, old-fashioned common sense, kept him from starving or freezing to death. Mrs. Hedgehog had helped, too, bustling around, cooking and cleaning and keeping camp, occasionally fending off beggars and indigent trash with her bristles and sharp teeth. That was before the lightning storm took her.

But somewhere along the way, the little duke had begun to regain his sense of purpose—and with it, a great depth of despair. Everywhere he looked, crops rotted in the fields. Once-sober peasants upped stakes and took to the skies in mile-high puffball spheres of spun-sugar glass and diamond. Wisewomen aged backward and grew much wiser, unnaturally so—wise until their wisdom leaked out into the neighborhood, animating the objects around them with their force of will. Ultimately, the very wise lost their humanity altogether and fled their crumbling human husks, migrating into the upload afterlife of the Festival. Intelligence and infinite knowledge were not, it seemed, compatible with stable human existence.

The little duke had talked to some of the people, tried to get them to understand that this wasn't going to last forever; sooner or later, the Festival would be over, and there would be a dreadful price to pay. But they laughed at him, calling him names when they discovered who he had been in his previous existence. And then someone set the Mimes on him.

A crash of branches and a caw of alarm; Raven crunched down onto his shoulder, great claws gripping his arm hard enough to draw blood. "Mimes!" hissed the bird. "Nevermore!"

"Where?" Felix looked around, wide-eyed.

Something crackled in the underbrush behind him. Felix turned, dislodging Raven, who flapped heavily upward, cawing in alarm. A human shape lurched into view on the other side of the clearing. It was male, adult in size, powdery white in color from head to foot. It moved jerkily like damaged clockwork, and there was no mistaking the circular, yellowish object it held in its right hand.

"Pie-ie-ie!" croaked Raven. "Time to die!"

Felix turned away from the Mime and put his head down. He ran blindly, branches tearing at his head and shoulders, shrubbery and roots trying to trip him up. Distantly, he heard the screaming and cawing of Raven mobbing the Mime, flapping clear of the deadly flan and pecking for eyes, ears, fingers. Just one sticky strand of orange goo from the pie dish would eat clear through bone, its disassembly nanoware mapping and reintegrating neural paths along its deadly way, to convert what was left of the body into a proxy presence in realspace.

The Mimes were broken, a part of the Fringe that had swung too close to a solar flare and succumbed to bit rot several Festival visits ago. They'd lost their speech pathways, right down to the Nucleus of Chomsky, but somehow managed to piggyback a ride on the Festival starwisps. Maybe this forcible assimilation was their way of communicating, of sharing mindspace with other beings. If so, it was misguided at best, like a toddler's attempt to communicate with a dog by hitting it; but nothing seemed to deter them from trying.

A wordless scream from behind told him that Raven had certainly distracted that particular Mime. But Mimes traveled in packs. Where were the others? And where was Mr. Rabbit, with his trusty twelve-bore and belt of dried farmer's scalps?

Noise ahead. Felix staggered to a stop. He was still holding the phone. "Help," he gasped into it.

"Define help parameters."

A fuzzy white shape moved among the trees in front of him. It had once been a woman. Now it was powder white, except for blood-red lips and bobble nose: layers of white clothing shrouded its putrefying limbs, held together with a delicate lacework of silvery metallic vines that pulsed and contracted as it moved. It swayed from side to side as it approached, bending coquettishly at the hips, as if the base of its spine had been replaced by a universal joint. It clutched a large pie dish in both bony hands. Collapsed eye sockets lined with black photoreceptive film grinned at him as it bowed and extended the bowl, like a mother offering her spoiled son his favorite dessert.

Felix gagged. The smell was indescribable. "Kill it. Make it go away," he whimpered. He fell back against a tree. "Please!"

"Acknowledged." The Festival voice remained dusty and distant, but somehow its tone changed. *"Fringe security at your service. How may we be of assistance?"*

The Mimes were closing in. "Kill them!" Felix gasped. "Get me out of here!"

"Target acquisition in progress. X-ray laser battery coming on-line. Be advised current orbital inclination is not favorable for surgical excision. Cover your eyes."

He threw an arm across his face. Bones flashed in red silhouette, followed a split second later by a crash of thunder and a blast of heat, as if someone had opened the oven door of hell right in front of his face. His skin prickled as if Mrs. Hedgehog was embracing him, only all over. Trees falling in the forest, a flapping of panic-stricken wings. The flash and bang repeated itself a second later, this time behind him; then three or four more times, increasingly distant.

"Incident Control stand down. Threat terminated. Be advised you have received an ionizing radiation dose of approximately four Greys, and that this will be life-threatening without urgent remediation. A medical support package has been dispatched. Remain where you are, and it will arrive in twenty-two minutes. Thank you for your custom, and have a nice day."

Felix lay gasping at the base of his tree. He felt dizzy, a little sick: afterimages of his femur floated in ghostly purple splendor across his eyes. "I want Mr. Rabbit," he mumbled into the phone, but it didn't answer him. He cried, tears of frustration and loneliness. Presently, he closed his eyes and slept. He was still asleep when the spider slipped down from the stars and wove him into a cocoon of silvery not-silk to begin the task of dissolving and reforming his radiation-damaged body yet again. This was the third time so far; it was all his own fault for making that third wish. Youth, true friends... and what every little boy wished for in his heart, without quite grasping that an adventure-filled life isn't much fun when you're the person who has to live it.

Martin sat on the thin mattress in his cell, and tried to work out how many days he had left before they executed him.

The fleet was six days out from the final jump to Rochard's World. Before that, they'd probably transfer supplies from the remaining support freighters and put any supernumeraries—conscripts who'd gone mad, contracted crippling diseases, or otherwise become superfluous to requirements—on board. Maybe they'd move him over and send him back with the basket cases, back to the New Republic to face trial on the capital charge of spying in the dockyard. Somehow, he doubted that his defense (of shipyard necessity) would do him much good; that snot-nosed assistant from the Curator's Office had it in for him, quite obviously, and would stop at nothing to see him hang.

That was one option. Another was that he'd be kept in the brig aboard ship until it arrived. At which point they'd realize that the cumulative clock-delay he'd bodged into the *Lord Vanek*'s fourspace guidance system had screwed the pooch, completely buggering their plan to sneak up on the Festival via a spacelike trajectory. In which case, they'd logically assume sabotage, and they'd have the saboteur already in the cells, trussed like a turkey for Thanksgiving.

Somehow, the fact that he'd succeeded, that his mission was accomplished and the threat of a wider causality violation averted, did not fill Martin with happiness. There might, he supposed, be heroes who would go to the airlock with a spring in their step, but he wasn't one of them; he'd rather be opening Rachel's bedroom door than opening that other door, learning to breathe in her muff rather than learning to inhale vacuum. It was, he supposed dismally, typical of the pattern of his life to fall in love—the kind of annoying obsession that won't go away—just before stumbling irremediably into the shit. He'd been around enough to think he had few illusions left; Rachel had edges rough enough to use as a nail file, and in some ways, they had very little in common. But being banged up alone in a tiny cell was a frighteningly lonely experience, all the lonelier for knowing that his lover was almost certainly less than thirty meters away—and completely unable to help him. Probably under suspicion herself. And however much he needed her, he didn't, in all honesty, want her in here with him. He wanted to be with her on the outside—preferably somewhere many light-years from the New Republic, acquiring a long history of having absolutely nothing to do with it.

He lay back, rolled over on his stomach, and closed his eyes. Then the toilet began talking to him in a faint, buzzing voice.

"If you can hear me, tap one finger on the deck next to the base of the toilet, Martin. Just one."

I've lost it, he thought. *They won't bother executing me; they'll put me in one of their psychiatric zoos and let the children throw bananas.* But he reached out a hand and tapped at the base of the stainless-steel toilet that extruded from the wall of his cell.

"That's—" he sat up, and the voice went away abruptly.

Martin blinked and looked around. No voices. Nothing else had changed in the cell; it was still too hot, stuffy, with a constant background smell of bad drains and stale cabbage. (The cabbage was inexplicable; the menu had long since shifted to salt beef and ship's biscuit, a recipe perversely retained by the New Republic's Navy despite the ready availability of vacuum and extreme cold millimeters beyond the outer pressure hull of the ship). He lay down again.

"—just one. If you can—"

He closed his eyes and, as if at a séance, rapped once, hard, on the base of the toilet.

"Received. Now tap—" The voice paused. "Tap once for each day you've been in the tank."

Martin blinked, then rapped out an answer.

"Do you know Morse code?"

Martin racked his brains. It had been quite a long time— "yes," he tapped out. A mostly obsolete skill, that low-bandwidth serial code set, but one that he *did* know, for a simple reason: Herman had insisted he learn it. Morse was human-accessible, and a sniff for more sophisticated protocols might easily miss something as mundane as the finger-tapping back channel in a video call.

"If you lie with your head up against the side of the toilet bowl, you will hear me better."

He blinked. *Bone conduction?* No, something else. The induction wires around his auditory nerves—some high-frequency source must be shorting out against the metal of the toilet, using it as an antenna! Inefficient, but if it wouldn't carry far...

"Identify yourself," he signaled.

The reply came in Morse. "AKA Ludmilla. Who watched us over dinner?"

"The boy wonder," he tapped out. He slumped against the floor, shivering in relief. Only two people could reasonably be on the other side of the pipe, and the Curator's Office wasn't likely to authenticate his identity that way. "What's your relay?"

"Spy drone in sewage system jammed against effluent valve. One of batch accidentally released by idiot subcurator. Told them to find you. Fuel cells in drone very low, drained by conduction telephone. Prefer Morse. Martin, I am trying to get you out. No luck so far."

"How long till arrival?" he tapped urgently.

"Ten days to low-orbit arrival. If not released first, expect rescue day of arrival. Attempting to assert diplomatic cover for you."

Ten days. Rescue—if they didn't stick him on a freighter under armed guard and ship him back to execution dock, and if Rachel wasn't whistling in the face of a storm. "Query rescue."

"Diplomatic life belt big enough for two. Power level approaching shutdown: will try to send another relay later. Love you. Over."

"I love you, too," he tapped hopefully, but there was no reply.

a MЧГiad OҒ tiny gears whirred, clucked, and buzzed in a background hum of gray noise beneath a desktop. Optical transducers projected a magic-lantern dance of light on the wall opposite. The operator, gold-leafed collar unbuttoned, leaned back in his chair and dribbled smoke from his nostrils: a pipe dangled limply between his knuckles as he stared at the display.

There was a knock on the door.

"Come in," he called. The door opened. He blinked: came to his feet. "Ah, and what can I do for you, Procurator?"

"A m-moment of your time if I may, sir?"

"By all means. Always a pleasure to be of service to the Basilisk. Have a seat?"

Vassily settled down behind the desk, visibly uncomfortable. The shadow play of lights danced on the wall, thin blue smoke catching the red-and-yellow highlights and coiling lazily in midair. "Would this be the, ah, our state vector?"

For a moment Security Lieutenant Sauer considered hazing the lad; he reluctantly shelved the idea. "Yes. Not that there's much to be made of it, unless you're interested in the topology of five-dimensional manifolds. And it's only theoretical, until we arrive at the far end and relativistics come out with a pulsar map to confirm it. I'm trying to study it; promotion board ahead you know, once this affair is straightened out."

"Hmm." Vassily nodded. Sauer wasn't the only Navy officer expecting a promotion to come out of this campaign. "Well, I suppose you could look on the bright side; we're most of the way there now."

Sauer pursed his lips, raised his pipe, and sucked. "I would never say that. Not until we know the enemy's dead and buried at a crossroads with a mouthful of garlic."

"I suppose so. But your lads will take care of that, won't they? Meanwhile it's my people who have to come in afterward and do the tidying up, keep this sort of thing from happening again."

Sauer looked at the young policeman, maintaining a polite expression despite his mild irritation. "Is there something I can help with?"

"Er, yah, I think so." The visitor leaned back. He reached into his tunic pocket and withdrew a cigar case. "Mind if I smoke?"

Sauer shrugged. "You're my guest."

"Thank you!"

For a minute they were silent, lighters flaring briefly and blue-gray clouds trailing in the airflow to the ceiling vents. Vassily tried to suppress his coughing, still not quite accustomed to the adult habit. "It's about the engineer in the brig."

"Indeed."

"Good." *Puff.* "I was beginning to wonder what is going to happen to him. I, er, gather that the last supply ships will be dropping off their cargo and heading home in a couple of days, and I was wondering if . . . ?"

Sauer sat up. He put his pipe down; it had flamed out, and though the bowl was hot to the touch, it held nothing but white-stained black shreds. "You were wondering if I could sign him over to you and put you on the slow boat home with your man in tow."

Vassily half smiled, embarrassed. "Exactly right, I'm sure. The man's guilty as hell, anyone can see that; he needs to be sent home for a proper trial and execution—what do you say?"

Sauer leaned back in his chair and contemplated the analytical engine. "You have a point," he admitted. "But things aren't quite so clear-cut from where I'm sitting." He relit his pipe.

"Nice tobacco, sir," ventured Vassily. "Tastes a bit funny, though. Very relaxing."

"That'll be the opium," said Sauer. "Good stuff, long as you don't overdo it." He puffed contentedly for a minute. "Why do you think Springfield's in the brig in the first place?"

Vassily looked puzzled. "It's obvious, isn't it? He violated Imperial regulations. In fact, that's just what I'd been looking for."

"Executing him isn't going to make it easy for the Admiralty to convince foreign engineers to come work for us, though, is it?" Sauer sucked on his cigar. "If he was a spacer, lad, he'd have done the frog kick in the airlock already. I'll tell you what. If you insist on dragging him home on the basis of what you found on him, all that will happen is that the Admiralty will sit on it for a few months, hold an inquiry, conclude that no real harm was done, court-martial him for something minor, and sentence him to time served—on general principles, that is—and leave you looking like an idiot. You don't want to do that; trust me, putting a blot on your record card at this stage in the game is a bad move."

"Ah, so what do you suggest, sir?"

"Well." Sauer stubbed out his cigar and looked at it regretfully. "I think you're going to have to decide whether or not to have a little flutter on the horses."

"Horses, sir?"

"Gambling, Mr. Muller, gambling. Double or quits time. You *have* decided that this engineer is working for the skirt from Earth, no? It seems a justifiable suspicion to me, but there is a lack of firm evidence other than the disgraceful way she plays for him. Which, let us make no mistake, could equally well be innocent— disreputable but innocent of actual criminal intent against the Republic, I say. In any event, she has made no sign of wrongdoing, other than possessing proscribed instruments in her diplomatic bag and generally being detrimental to morale by virtue of her rather unvirtuous conduct. We have no grounds for censure, much less for declaring her *persona non grata*. And irritating though she may be, her presence on this mission was decreed by His Excellency the Archduke. So I think the time has come for you to either shit or get off the can. Either accept that Mr. Springfield is probably going to waltz free, or shoot for the bigger target and hope you find something big to pin on her so that we can overcome her immunity."

Vassily turned pale. Perhaps it hadn't really sunk in until now; he'd overstepped his authority already, rummaging in Rachel's cabin, and either he must find a justification, or his future was in jeopardy. "I'll gamble, sir. Do you have any recommendations, though? It seems like an awfully big step; I wouldn't want to make any mistakes."

Sauer grinned, not unpleasantly. "Don't worry, you won't. There're others who want her out of the way and are willing to stick their necks out a bit to help. Here's how we'll flush her cover..."

a ragged row of crucifixes capped the hill overlooking the road to Plotsk. They faced the narrow river that ran along the valley, overlooking Boris the Miller's waterwheel: their brown-robed human burdens stared sightlessly at the burned-out shell of the monastery on the other bank. The abbot of the Holy Spirit had gone before his monks, impaled like a bird on a spit.

"Kill them all, God will know his own," Sister Seventh commented mockingly as she turned the doorway to face the grisly row. "Not is what their nest father-mother's said in times gone before?"

Burya Rubenstein shivered with cold as the bird-legged hut strode along the road from Novy Petrograd. It was a chilly morning, and the fresh air was overlaid with a tantalizingly familiar odor, halfway between the brimstone crackle of gunpowder and something spicy-sweet. No smell of roast pork: they'd burned the monastery after killing the monks, not before. "Who did this?" he asked, sounding much calmer than he felt.

"You-know-who," said the Critic. "Linger not thisways: understand Fringe performers hereabout more so deranged than citywise. Mimes and firewalker bushbabies. *Very* dangerous."

"Did they—" Burya swallowed. He couldn't look away from the fringe on the hilltop. He was no friend of the clergy, but this festival of excess far outstripped anything he could have condoned. "Was it the Fringe?"

Sister Seventh cocked her head on one side and chomped her walrus tusks at the air. "Not," she declared. "This is human work.

But headlaunchers have herewise been seeding corpses with further life. Expect resurrection imminently, if not consensually."

"Headlaunchers?"

"Fringeoids with fireworks. Seed brainpan, cannibalize corpus, upload and launch map containing mindseeds to join Festival in orbit."

Burya peered at the row of crosses. One of them had no skull, and the top of the crucifix was charred. "'M going to be sick—"

He just made it to the edge of the hut in time. Sister Seventh made it kneel while he hung head down over the edge, retching and dry-heaving on the muddy verge below.

"Ready to continue? Food needed?"

"No. Something to drink. Something stiff." One corner of the hut was stocked with a pyramid of canned foodstuffs and bottles. Sister Seventh was only passingly familiar with human idiom; she picked up a large tin of pineapple chunks, casually bit a hole in it, and poured it into the empty can that Burya had been using as a cup for the past day. He took it silently, then topped it up with schnapps from his hip flask. The hut lurched slightly as it stood up. He leaned against the wall and threw back the drink in one swallow.

"Where are you taking me now?" he asked, pale and still shivering with something deeper than a mere chill.

"To Criticize the culprits. *This* is not art." Sister Seventh bared her fangs at the hillside in an angry gape. "No esthetics! Zip plausibility! Pas de preservatives!"

Rubenstein slid down the wall of the hut, collapsing in a heap against the pile of provisions. Utter despair filled him. When Sister Seventh began alliterating she could go on for hours without making any particular sense.

"Is it anyone in particular this time? Or are you just trying to bore me to death?"

The huge mole-rat whirled to face him, breath hissing between her teeth. For a moment he flinched, seeing grinning angry death in her eyes. Then the fire dimmed back to her usual glare of cynical amusement. "Critics know who did this thing," she rasped. "Come judge, come Criticize."

The walking hut marched on, carrying them away from the execution ground. Unseen from the vestibule, one of the crucified monk's habits began to smolder. His skull exploded with a gout of blue flame and a loud bang as something the size of a fist flew up from it, a glaring white shock contrail streaming behind. One more monk's mind—or what had been left of it after a day of crucifixion, by the time the headlaunch seed got to it—was on its way into orbit, to meet the Festival datavores.

The hut walked all day, passing miracles, wonders, and abominations on every side. Two thistledown geodesic spheres floated by overhead like glistening diadems a kilometer in diameter, lofted by the thermal expansion of their own trapped, sun-heated air. (Ascended peasants, their minds expanded with strange prostheses, looked down from their communal eyrie at the ground dwellers below. Some of their children were already growing feathers.) Around another hill, the hut marched across a spun-silver suspension bridge that crossed a gorge that had not been there a month before—a gorge deep enough that the air in its depths glowed with a ruddy heat, the floor obscured by a permanent Venusian fog. A rhythmic thudding of infernal machinery echoed up from the depths. Once, a swarm of dinner-plate-sized, solar-powered silicon butterflies blitzed past, zapping and sputtering and stealing any stray electrical cabling and discrete components in their path: a predatory Stuka the size of an eagle followed them, occasionally screaming down in a dive that ended with one of their number crumpled and shredded in the claws sprouting from its wheel fairings. "Deep singularity," Sister Seventh commented gnomically. "Machines live and breed. Cornucopia evolution."

"I don't understand. What caused this?"

"Emergent property of complex infocology. Life expands to fill environmental niches. Now, machines reproduce and spawn as Festival maximizes entropy, devolves into way station."

"Devolves into—" He stared at the Critic. "You mean this is only a *temporary* condition?"

Sister Seventh looked at him placidly. "What made you think otherwise?"

"But—" Burya looked around. Looked at the uncared-for fields, already tending toward the state of weed banks, at the burned-out villages and strange artifacts they were passing. "Nobody is prepared for that," he said weakly. "We thought it would last!"

"Some will prepare," said the Critic. "Cornucopiae breed. But Festival moves on, flower blossoming in light of star before next trip across cold, dark desert."

Very early the next day, they came within sight of Plotsk.

Before the Festival incursion, Plotsk had been a sleepy ginger-bread market town of some fifty thousand souls, home to a regional police fortress, a jail, two cathedrals, a museum, and a zeppelin port. It had also been the northernmost railhead on the planet, and a departure point for barges heading north to the farms that dotted the steppes halfway to the Boreal Ocean.

Plotsk was barely recognizable today. Whole districts were burned-out scars on the ground, while a clump of slim white tow-ers soared halfway to the stratosphere from the site of the former cathedral. Burya gaped as something emerald green spat from a window halfway up a tower, a glaring light that hurtled across the sky and passed overhead with a strange double boom. The smell, half gunpowder and half orchids, was back again. Sister Seventh sat up and inhaled deeply. "One loves the smell of wild assem-blers in the morning. Bushbot baby uploads and cyborg militia. Spires of bone and ivory. Craving for apocalypse."

"What are you talking about!" Burya sat on the edge of the pile of smelly blankets from which the Critic had fashioned her nest.

"Is gone nanostructure crazy," she said happily. "Civilization! Freedom, Justice, and the American Way!"

"What's a merkin way?" Burya asked, peeling open a fat garlic bratwurst and, with the aid of an encrusted penknife, chopping large chunks off it and stuffing them into his mouth. His beard itched ferociously, he hadn't bathed in days, and worst of all, he felt he was beginning to understand Sister Seventh. (Nobody should have to understand a Critic; it was cruel and unusual punishment.)

A bright green glare flashed on above them, shining starkly in through the doorway and lighting up the dingy corners of the hut. "*Attention! You have entered a quarantined area! Identify your-selves immediately!*" A deep bass humming shook Burya to his bones. He cringed and blinked, dropping his breakfast sausage.

"Why not you answer them?" Sister Seventh asked, unreason-ably calmly.

"Answer them?"

"*ATTENTION! Thirty seconds to comply!*"

The hut shook. Burya stumbled, treading on the wurst. Losing his temper, he lurched toward the doorway. "Stop that racket at once!" he yelled, waving a fist in the air. "Can't a man eat his breakfast in peace without you interfering, you odious rascals? Cultureless imbeciles, may the Duke's whore be taken short and piss in your drawers by mistake!"

The light cut out abruptly. "*Oops*, sorry," said the huge voice. Then in more moderate tones, "*Is that you, Comrade Ruben-stein?*"

Burya gaped up at the hovering emerald diamond. Then he looked down. Standing in the road before him was one of Timoshevski's guards—but not as Burya had known him back in Novy Petrograd.

rachel sat on her bunk, tense and nervous. Ignoring the banging and clattering and occasional disturbing bumps from the rear bulkhead, she tried desperately to clear her head. She had a number of hard decisions to make—and if she took the wrong one, Martin would die, for sure, and more than that, she might die with him. Or worse, she might be prematurely bugging out, throwing away any chance of fulfilling her real mission. Which made it all the harder for her to think straight, without worrying.

Thirty minutes ago an able flyer had rapped on her door. She'd hastily buttoned her tunic and opened it. "Lieutenant Sauer sends his compliments, ma'am, and says to remind you that the court-martial convenes this afternoon at 1400."

She'd blinked stupidly. "What court-martial?"

The flyer looked nonplussed. "I don't know, ma'am. He just told me to tell you—"

"That's quite alright. Go away."

He'd gone, and she'd hurriedly pulled her boots on, run a comb through her hair, and gone in search of someone who knew.

Commander Murametz was in the officers' wardroom, drinking a glass of tea. "What's all this about a court-martial?" she demanded.

He'd stared at her, poker-faced. "Oh, it's nothing," he said. "Just that engineer who's under arrest. Can't have him aboard when we go into battle, so the old man scheduled a hearing for this afternoon, get the business out of the way."

"What do you mean?" she asked icily.

"Can't go executing a man without a fair trial first," Ilya said, barely bothering to conceal his contempt. He rapped his glass down next to the samovar. "Trial's in this very room, this afternoon. Be seeing you."

The next thing she knew she was back in her cabin. She couldn't remember getting there; she felt cold and sick. *They want to kill Martin,* she realized. *Because they can't get at me any other way.* She cursed herself for a fool. Who was behind it, how many enemies had she racked up? Was it the Admiral? (Doubtful, he didn't need the formality of a trial if he wanted to have someone shot.) Or Ilya—yes, there was someone who'd taken against her. Or the kid spook, the wet-behind-the-ears secret policeman? Or maybe the Captain? She shook her head. Someone had decided to get her, and there were no secrets aboard the ship; however discreet she and Martin had thought they'd been, someone had noticed.

The cold emptiness in her stomach congealed into a knot of tension. This whole voyage was turning into a fiasco. With what she'd learned from Martin—including his mission—there was no way the Navy could make a success of it; in fact, they'd probably all be killed. Her own role as a negotiator was pointless. You negotiate with human beings, not with creatures who are to humans as humans are to dogs and cats. (Or machines, soft predictable machines that come apart easily when you try to examine them but won't fit back together again.) Staying on was useless, it wouldn't help her deliver the package for George Cho, and as for Martin—

Rachel realized she had no intention of leaving him behind. With the realization came a sense of relief, because it left her only one course of action. She leaned forward and spoke quietly. "Luggage: open sesame. Plan Titanic. You have three hours and ten minutes. Get started." Now all she had to do was work out how to get him from the kangaroo court in the wardroom to her cabin; a different, but not necessarily harder task than springing him from the brig.

The trunk silently rolled forward, out from under her bunk, and its lid hinged back. She tapped away at the controls for a minute. A panel opened, and she pulled out a reel of flexible hose. That went onto the cold-water tap on her tiny sink. A longer and fatter hose with a spherical blob on the end got fed down the toilet, a colonoscopy probing the bowels of the ship's waste plumbing circuit. The chest began to hum, expelling pulses of viscous white liquid into the toilet tube. Thin filaments of something like plastic began to creep back up the bowl of the toilet, forming a tight seal around the hose; a smell of burning leaked into the room, gunpowder and molasses and a whiff of shit. Rachel checked a status indicator on the trunk; satisfied, she picked up her gloves, cap, anything else she would need—then checked the indicator again, and hastily left the room.

The toilet rumbled faintly, and pinged with the sound of expanding metal pipework. The vent pipe grew hot; steam began to hiss from the effluent tube, and was silenced rapidly by a new growth of spiderweb stuff. An overhead ionization alarm tripped, but Rachel had unplugged it as soon as she arrived in her cabin. The radiation warning on the luggage blinked, unseen, in the increasingly hot room. The diplomatic lifeboat was beginning to inflate.

"don't worry, son. It'll work." Sauer slapped Procurator Muller on the back.

Vassily forced a wan smile. "I hope so, sir. I've never attended a court-martial before."

"Well." Sauer considered his words carefully. "Just think of this as an educational experience. And our best opportunity to nail the bitch legally..."

Truth be told, Sauer felt less confident than he was letting on. This whole exercise was more than slightly unauthorized; it exceeded his authority as ship's security officer, and without the active support of Commander Murametz, first officer, he wouldn't have dared proceed with it. He certainly didn't have the legal authority to convene a court-martial on his own initiative in the presence of superior officers, much less to try a civilian contractor on a capital charge. What he *did* have was a remit to root out subversion by any means necessary, including authorized deception, and a first officer willing to sign on the dotted line. Not to mention an institutional enthusiasm to show the Curator's agent up for the horse's ass that he was.

They were short of time. Since coming out of their jump on the edge of the inner system, the heavy squadron had been running under total radio silence at a constant ten gees, the heavy acceleration compensated for by the space-time-warping properties of their drive singularities. (Ten gees, without compensation, would be enough to make a prone man black out; bone-splintering, lung-crushing acceleration.) There had apparently been some sort of navigation error, a really bad one which had the admiral's staff storming about in a black fury for days, but it hadn't betrayed them to the enemy, which was the main thing.

Some days ago, the squadron had flipped end over end and

executed a deceleration sequence to slow them down to 100 k.p.s. relative to Rochard's World. In the early hours of this morning, they had reached engagement velocity; they would drift the last thirty light-seconds, resuming acceleration (and increasing their visibility) only within active radar range of the enemy. Right now, they were about two million kilometers out. Some time around midnight, shipboard time, they would begin their closest approach to the planet, go to full power, and engage the enemy ships—assuming they were willing to come out and fight. (If they didn't, then the cowards had conceded control of the low orbital zone to the New Republic, tantamount to abandoning their ground forces.) In any event, any action against the UN inspector had to be completed before evening, when the ship would lock down for battle stations—assuming they didn't run into anything before then.

In Sauer's view, it was a near miracle that Ilya had agreed to join in this deception. He could easily have scuppered it, or referred it to Captain Mirsky, which would have amounted to the same thing. This close to a major engagement, just detaching himself plus a couple of other officers who didn't have active duty stations to prepare was enough of a wonderment to startle him.

Sauer walked up to the table at the front of the room and sat down. It was actually the officer's dining table, decked out in a white tablecloth for the occasion, weighted down with leather-bound tomes that contained the complete letter of the Imperial Articles of War. Two other officers followed him; Dr. Hertz, the ship's surgeon, and Lieutenant Commander Vulpis, the relativist. They looked suitably serious. Sauer cleared his throat. "Court will come to order," he intoned. "Bring in the accused."

The other door opened. Two ratings marched in, escorting Martin Springfield who, being hobbled and handcuffed, moved rather slowly. Behind them, a door banged. "Ah, er, yes. Please state your name for the court."

Martin looked around. His expression was pale but collected. "What?" he said.

"Please state your name."

"Martin Springfield."

Lieutenant Sauer made a note on his blotter. Irritated, he realized that his pen held no ink; no matter. This wasn't an affair that called for written records. "You are a civilian, subject of the United Nations of Earth. Is that correct?"

A look of irritation crept over Martin's face. "No it bloody isn't!" he said. "I keep telling you people, the UN is not a government! I'm affiliated to Pinkertons for purposes of legislation and insurance; that means I obey their rules and they protect me against infringers. But I've got a backup strategic infringement policy from the New Model Air Force which, I believe, covers situations like this one. I've also got agreements with half a dozen other quasi-governmental organizations, but none of them is entitled to claim sovereignty over me—I'm not a slave!"

Dr. Hertz turned his head and looked pointedly at Sauer; his pince-nez glinted beneath the harsh glare of the tungsten lamps. Sauer snorted. "Let it be entered that the accused is a subject of the United Nations of Earth," he intoned.

"No he isn't." Heads turned. While Martin had been speaking, Rachel Mansour had slipped in through a side door. Her garb was even more scandalous than usual; a skintight white leotard worn beneath various items of padding and a bulky waistcoat resembling a flak jacket. *Almost like a space suit liner,* Sauer noted, puzzled. "The United Nations is not a—"

"Silence!" Sauer pointed at her. "This is a court of military justice, and I do not recognize your right to speak. Stay silent, or I'll have you thrown out."

"And create a diplomatic incident?" Rachel grinned unpleasantly. "Try it, and I'll make sure you regret it. In any event, I believe the accused is permitted to retain an advocate for the defense. Have you advised him of his rights?"

"Er—" Vulpis looked down.

"Irrelevant. The trial will continue—"

Martin cleared his throat. "I'd like to nominate Colonel Mansour as my advocate," he said.

It's working. Sauer made a pretense of scribbling on his blotter. At the back of the room, he could see Vassily's sharp intake of breath. The young whippersnapper was getting his hopes up already. "The court recognizes UN inspector Mansour as the defendant's counsel. I am obliged to warn you that this trial is being conducted under the Imperial Articles of War, Section Fourteen, Articles of Combat, in view of our proximity to the enemy. If you are ignorant of those rules and regulations, you may indicate so and withdraw from the trial now."

Rachel's smile broadened. "Defense moves for an adjournment in view of the forthcoming engagement. There will be plenty of time for this after the battle."

"Denied," Sauer snapped. "We need a fair trial on the record before we can execute the sentence." *That* made her smile slip. "Court will go into recess for five minutes to permit the defendant to brief his advocate, and not one minute longer." He rapped on the table with his fist, stood, and marched out of the room. The rest of the tribunal followed suit, trailed by a paltry handful of spectators, leaving Rachel, Martin, and four ratings standing guard on the doors.

"you know this is just a rubber stamp? They want to execute me," Martin said. His voice was husky, a trifle unsteady; he wrung his hands together, trying to stop them from shaking.

Rachel peered into his eyes. "Look at me, Martin," she said quietly. "Do you trust me?"

"I—yes." He glanced down.

She reached a hand out, across the table, put it across the back of his left wrist. "I've been reading up on their procedures. This is well out of order, and whatever happens I'm going to lodge an appeal with the Captain—who should be chairing this, not some jumped-up security officer who's also running the prosecution." She glanced away from him, looking for the air vents; simultaneously, she tapped the back of his hand rapidly. He tensed his wrist back in a well-understood pattern, message understood: *Next session. See me blink three times you start hyperventilating. When I blink twice hold breath.*

His eyes widened slightly. "There won't be time for them to do anything before perigeon, anyway," she continued verbally. "We're about two astronomical units out and closing fast; engagement should commence around midnight if there's to be a shooting war." *Got lifeboat,* she added via Morse code.

"That's—" he swallowed. *How escape?* he twitched. "I'm not confident they're going to observe all the niceties. This kangaroo court—" He shrugged.

"Leave it all to me," she said, squeezing his hand for emphasis. "I know what I'm doing." For the first time, there was hope in his expression. She broke contact and leaned back in her chair. "It's stuffy in here," she complained. "Where's the ventilation?"

Martin looked past her head. She followed his gaze: grilles in the ceiling. She closed her eyes and squeezed shut; green raster images like a nightmare vision of a jail cell pasted themselves across the insides of her eyelids. The spy drones, remnant of the flock Vassily had unleashed, waited patiently behind the vents. They'd followed her to this room, loaded up with a little something to add interest to the proceedings. *Serve the little voyeur right,* she thought bitterly about the spy. "I'll get you out of this," she told Martin, trying to reassure him.

"I understand." He nodded, a slight inclination of his head. "You know what I, uh, I'm not so good at people things—"

She shook her head. "They're doing this to get me to compromise myself. It's not about you. It's nothing personal. They just want me out of the way."

"Who?"

She shrugged. "The midranking officers. The ones who figure a short victorious war is a ticket up the promotion ladder. The ones who don't think I should be here in the first place, much less reporting back. Not after First Lamprey. I was Red Cross agent-in-place there, you know? Investigating the war crimes. Didn't leave anybody looking too good, and I think they know it. They don't want a negotiated settlement, they want guts and glory."

"If it's just you, why's the chinless wonder from the Curator's Office in here?" asked Martin.

She shrugged. "Two birds, one stone. Don't sweat it. If they screw this up, they can blame the Curator's cat's-paw, make the enemy within look bad. There's no love lost between Naval Intelligence and the civil secret police. If it works, they get us both out of the way. Reading the regs, they don't have authority to pull this stunt, Martin. It takes a master and commander to issue a capital sentence except in the face of the enemy, so if they do execute you, it's illegal enough to hang them all."

"That's a great reassurance." He forced a smile, but it came out looking decidedly frightened. "Just do your—hell. I trust you."

"That's good."

Then the doors opened.

"it's working," sauer commented. "She's come out to defend her minion. Now we need to maneuver her into outright defiance. Shouldn't be too hard; we have the bench."

"Defiance?" Vulpis raised an eyebrow. "You said this was a trial."

"A trial of wits, ours against hers. She's consented to defend him; that means she's acting as an officer of the court. Article

Forty-six states that an officer of the court is subject to the discipline of the Articles and may himself be arraigned for malfeasance or contempt of court. By agreeing to serve before our court, she's abandoning her claim of diplomatic immunity. It gets better. In about two hours, we go to stations. While we may be a charade right now, at that point *any* commissioned officer is empowered to pass a capital sentence—or even order a summary execution—because it's classified under Article Four, Obedience in the Face of the Enemy, Enforcement Thereof. Not that I'm *planning* on using it, but it does give us a certain degree of cover, no?"

Dr. Hertz removed his pince-nez and began to polish them. "I'm not sure I like it," he said fussily. "This smells altogether too much of the kind of trickery the Stasis like handing down. Aren't you concerned about playing for the Curator's brat?"

"Not really." Sauer finally grinned. "Y'see, what I really plan on doing is to get our new advocate so thoroughly wound up she's insubordinate or something—but for the defendant himself, I'm thinking of an absolute discharge or a not guilty verdict." He sniffed. "It's quite obvious he didn't know he was breaking any regulations. Plus, the device he had in his possession was inactive by the time it was discovered, so we can't actually prove it was in a state fit for use at any time when he was aboard the ship. And the Admiralty will be angry if we make it hard for them to hire civilian contractors in future. I'm hoping we can keep her rattled enough not to realize there's no case to answer until we've got her out of the way; then we discharge Springfield. Which will make our young Master Muller look like a complete and total idiot, not to mention possibly supplying me with cause to investigate *him* for suspicion of burglary, pilferage of personal effects, violation of a diplomat's sealed luggage, immoral conduct, and maybe even deserting his post." His grin became sharklike. "Need I continue?"

Vulpis whistled quietly in awe. "Remind me *never* to play poker with you," he commented.

Dr. Hertz reinstalled his spectacles. "Shall we resume the circus, gentlemen?"

"I think so." Sauer drained his glass of tea and stood up. "After you, my brother officers, then send in the clowns!"

the shipping trunk in Rachel's cabin had stopped steaming some time ago. It had shrunk, reabsorbing and extruding much of its contents. A viscous white foam had spread across the fittings of the cabin, eagerly digesting all available hydrocarbons and spinning out a diamond-phase substrate suitable for intensive nanomanufacturing activities. Solid slabs of transparent material were precipitating out of solution, forming a hollow sphere that almost filled the room. Below the deck, roots oozed down into the ship's recycling circuits, looting the cesspool that stored biological waste during the inbound leg of a journey. (By long-standing convention, ships that lacked recyclers only discharged waste when heading away from inhabited volumes of space; more than one unfortunate orbital worker had been gunned down by a flash-frozen turd carrying more kinetic energy than an armor-piercing artillery shell.)

The self-propelled trunk, which was frozen into the base of the glassy sphere, was now much lighter than it had been when Rachel boarded the ship. Back then, it had weighed the best part of a third of a tonne: Now it massed less than fifty kilos. The surplus mass had mostly been thick-walled capillary tubes of boron carbide, containers for thin crystals of ultrapure uranium-235 tetraiodide, and a large supply of cadmium; stuff that wasn't easy to come by in a hurry. The trunk was capable of manufacturing anything it needed given the constituent elements. Most of what it wanted was carbon, hydrogen, and oxygen, available in abundance in the ship's sewage-processing plant. But if a diplomat needed to get away in a real hurry and didn't have a potent energy source to hand ... well, fission, an old and unfashionable technology, was eminently storable, very lightweight, and didn't usually go bang without a good reason. All you needed was the right type of unobtanium to hand in order to make it work. Which was why Rachel had been towing around enough uranium to make two or three good-sized atom bombs, or the core of a nuclear saltwater rocket.

A nuclear saltwater rocket was just about the simplest interplanetary propulsion system that could fit in a steamer trunk. On the other side of the inner pressure hull from Rachel's cabin, the trunk had constructed a large tank threaded through with neutron-absorbing, boron-lined tubes: this was slowly filling with water containing a solution of near-critical uranium tetraiodide. Only a thin layer of carefully weakened hull plates and bypassed cable ducts held the glassy sphere and its twenty-tonne saltwater fuel tank on the other side of the bulkhead, inside the warship. The hybrid structure nestled under the skin of the ship like a maggot feeding on the flesh of its host, preparing to hatch.

Elsewhere in the ship, toilets were flushing sluggishly, the officer's shower cubicle pressure was scandalously low, and a couple of environment techs were scratching their heads over the unexpectedly low sludge level in the number four silage tank. One bright spark was already muttering about plumbing leaks. But with a full combat engagement only hours away, most attention was focused on the ship's weapons systems. Meanwhile, the luggage's fabricator diligently churned away, extruding polymers and component materials to splice into the lifeboat it was preparing for its mistress. With only a short time until the coming engagement, speed was essential.

"court will reconvene." Sauer rapped on the tabletop with an upturned glass. "Defendant Martin Springfield, the charges laid against you are that on the thirty-second day of the month of Harmony, Year 211 of the Republic, you did with premeditation carry aboard the warship *Lord Vanek* a communications device, to wit a causal channel, without permission from your superior officer or indeed any officer of that ship, contrary to Article Forty-six of the Articles of War; and that, furthermore, you did make use of the said device to communicate with foreign nationals, contrary to Article Twenty-two, and in so doing, you disclosed operational details of the running of the warship *Lord Vanek* contrary to Section Two of the Defense of the Realm Act of 127, and also contrary to Section Four of the Articles of War, Treachery in Time of War. The charges laid against you therefore constitute negligent breach of signals control regulations, trafficking with the enemy, and treason in time of war. How do you plead?"

Before he could open his mouth, Rachel spoke up. "He pleads not guilty to all charges. And I can prove it." There was a dangerous gleam in her eyes; she stood very straight, with her hands clasped behind her back.

"Does the accused accept that plea?" Vulpis intoned.

"The colonel speaks for me," said Martin.

"First, evidence supporting the charges. Item: on the thirty-second day of the month of Harmony, year 211 of the Republic, you did with premeditation carry aboard the warship *Lord Vanek* a communications device, to wit a causal channel, without permission from your superior officer or indeed any officer of that ship, contrary to Article Forty-six. Clerk, present the item."

A rating stepped forward, stony-faced, bearing a small paper bag. He shook the contents out over the tabletop; a small, black memory cartridge. "Item one: a type twelve causal channel, embedded within a standard model CX expansion cartridge as used by personal assist machines throughout the decadent Terran sphere. The item was removed from defendant's personal assist machine by Junior Procurator Vassily Muller, of the Curator's Office on assignment to monitor the conduct of the defendant, on the thirty-second day of Harmony as noted. A sworn deposition by the Procurator is on record. Does anyone contest the admissibility of this evidence? No? Good—"

"*I* do." Rachel pointed at the small black cartridge. "Firstly, I submit that the Junior Procurator's search of the defendant's personal property was illegal and any evidence gained from it is inadmissible, because the defendant is a civilian and not subject to the waiver of rights in the oath of allegiance sworn by a serving soldier—his civil rights, including the right to property, cannot be legally violated without a judicial warrant or an order from an official vested with summary powers subject to Article Twelve. Unless the Junior Procurator obtained such an order or warrant, his search was illegal and indeed may constitute burglary, and any information gathered in the process of an illegal search is not admissible in court. Secondly, if that thing is a causal channel, I'm a banana slug. That's a standard quantum dot storage card; if you get a competent electronic engineer in, they'll tell you the same. Thirdly, you don't have authority to hold this charade of a trial; I've been checking in the Articles, and they state quite clearly that courts-martial can only be convened by order of the senior officer present. Where's your written order from the Admiral?"

She crossed her arms and stared at the bench.

Sauer shook his head. "The Junior Procurator has standing orders to investigate Springfield; that makes anything he does legal in the eyes of the Curator's Office. And I must register my extreme displeasure at the defense's imputation that I do not have authority to convene this court. I *have* obtained such authority from my superior officer and will use it." Carefully, he avoided specifying precisely what kind of authority he had. "As for the item of evidence being misidentified, we have on record a statement by the defendant to the effect that it is a causal channel, which he was asked to carry aboard by foreign parties, to wit the dockyard. As the Articles concern themselves specifically with intent, it does not matter whether the item is in fact a banana slug: the defendant is still guilty of thinking he was carrying a communications device."

He paused for a moment. "Let it be entered that the item of evidence was admitted." He glared at Rachel: *Got you, you bitch. Now what are you going to do?*

Rachel glanced at Martin and blinked rapidly. Then she turned back to face the bench. "A point of law, sir. As it happens, thinking is not generally considered the same as doing. Indeed, in this nation, which refuses to even consider the use of thought-controlled machinery, the distinction is even sharper than in my own. You appear to be attempting to try the defendant for his opinions and beliefs rather than his actions. Do you have any evidence of his actually passing on information to a third party? If not, there is no case to answer."

"I have *exactly* that." Sauer grinned savagely. "You should know who he's been passing on information to." He pointed at her. "You are a known agent of a foreign power. Defendant has been communicating freely with you. Now, since you consented to defend him, you are acting as an officer of this court. I refer you to Article Forty-six: 'Any person deputized to act as an officer of the court is subject to the discipline of the Articles.' I conclude that you have courageously agreed to waive your diplomatic immunity in order to attempt to rescue your spy from the hangman's noose."

For a moment, Rachel looked confused; she looked at Martin again, blinking rapidly. Then she turned back to the bench. "So you rigged this whole kangaroo court as an attempt to work around my immunity? I'm impressed. I really didn't think you'd be quite this stupid—*Utah!*"

Everything happened very quickly. Rachel dropped to her knees behind her makeshift desk; Sauer made a motion toward the ratings at the back of the room, intending to have them arrest the woman. But before he could do more than open his mouth, four sharp bangs burst around the room. The overhead air-conditioning ducts split open; *things* dropped down, complex and many-armed things squirting pale blue foam under high pressure. The foam stuck to everything it touched, starting with the judge's bench and the guards at the back of the makeshift courtroom: it was lightweight but sticky, rapidly setting into a hard foam matrix.

"Get her!" Sauer shouted. He grabbed for his pistol, but somewhere along the way a huge gobbet of blue foam engulfed his arm and cemented it to his side. A strong chemical odor came from the foam, something familiar from childhood visits to the dentist. Sauer breathed deeply, struggling to dislodge the sticky mass, and the fruity, sickly stench cut into his lungs; then the world turned hazy.

rachel knew things were going to turn pear-shaped from the moment she walked into the room. She'd seen judges in hanging mode before, back on Earth, and on a dozen assignments since then. You could almost smell it, an acrid and unreasoning eagerness to order an execution, like the stench of death itself. This board had it—and something else. A sly reserve, a smug sense of anticipation; as if the whole thing was some kind of tremendous joke, with a punch line she could only guess at.

When the security lieutenant delivered it—a half-formed, inadequate punch line, in her opinion, obviously something he'd stitched up on an *ad hoc* basis to fit the occasion—she glanced around at Martin. *Please be ready.* She blinked three times and saw him stiffen, then nod; the prearranged signal. She turned back to the bench, blinking again: green lights rippled behind her eyelids. "State two," she subvocalized, the radio mike in her throat relaying the command to the drones waiting in the ventilation ducts. She turned back to the bench. The three officers sat there, glowering at her like thunderclouds on a horizon. *Buy time.*

"A point of law, sir. As it happens, thinking is not generally considered the same as doing.—" She carried on, wondering how they'd react to effectively being accused of rigging this charade; either they'd back down, or—

"I have exactly that." The political officer in the middle, the hatchet-faced one, grimaced horribly. "You should know who he's been passing on information to." He pointed straight at her. *Here it comes,* she thought. Subvocalizing again: "Luggage. Query readiness state."

"Lifeboat closed out for launch. Fuel storage subcritical and ready. Spare reaction mass loaded. Oxygen supply nominal. Warning, delta-vee to designated waypoint New Peterstown currently 86 k.p.s., decreasing. Total available maneuvering margin 90 k.p.s." That would do, she decided. The saltwater rocket was nearly as efficient as an old-fashioned fusion rocket; back home, it

would do for an Earth–Mars return trip, surface to surface. This was pushing it a bit—they wouldn't be able to ride it back up into orbit without refueling. But it would do, as long as—

"—I conclude that you have courageously agreed to waive your diplomatic immunity in order to attempt to rescue your spy from the hangman's noose."

She swallowed, glanced at Martin and blinked twice, the signal for "hold your breath." *"Luggage: prep for launch. Expect crew arrival from one hundred seconds. Launch hold at T minus twenty seconds from that time."* Once they burned that particular bridge and jumped overboard, all she could do was pray that the bridge crew wouldn't dare light off their radar—and risk warning the Festival—in order to find her and kill her. The lifeboat was a soap bubble compared to the capital ships of the New Republican naval force.

Rachel turned her attention back to the bench and took a deep breath, tensing. "So you rigged this whole kangaroo court as an attempt to work around my immunity? I'm impressed. I really didn't think you'd be quite this stupid—*Utah!*"

She ducked. The last word was a shout, broadcast to the drones through her throat mike. A simultaneous crackle told her the shaped-charge cutters had blown. She yanked the transparent breather hood over her face and choked it shut, then powered up her cellular IFF.

The drones swarmed in through holes in the ceiling. Spiders and crabs and scorpions, all made of carbon polymers—recycled sewage, actually—they sprayed sticky antipersonnel foam everywhere, releasing anesthetic trichloromethane vapor wherever anyone struggled. A rating made a move toward her, and her combat implants took over; he went down like a sack of potatoes before she consciously noted his existence, rabbit-punched alongside the head by an inhumanly fast fist. Everything narrowed into the gap between herself and Martin, standing wide-eyed behind a table, his arms half-raised toward her and a rating already beginning to steer him toward the door.

Rachel went to combat speed, cutting her merely human nervous system out of the control loop.

Time slowed and light dimmed; the chains of gravity weakened, but the air grew thick and viscous around her. Marionettes twirled in slow motion all around as she jumped over a table and ran at Martin. His guard began to turn toward her and throw up an arm. She grabbed it and twisted, feeling it pop out of its socket.

She threw a brisk left-handed punch at the other guard; ribs snapped like brittle cardboard, and a couple of the fine bones in the back of her hand fractured with the impact. It was hard to remember—hard to think—but her own body was her worst enemy, more fragile than her reflexes would admit.

She grabbed Martin with one arm, handling him delicately as bone china; the beginning of an *oof* of air from his lungs told her she'd winded him. The door wasn't locked, so she kicked it open and dragged Martin through before it had time to rebound closed. She dropped him and spun in place, slammed it shut, then grabbed in a vest pocket for a lump of something like putty. *"Omaha,"* she shouted into her throat mike. Strobing patterns of red-and-yellow light raced over the surface of the putty—visible in her mechanized vision—and she jammed it into the doorframe and spat on it. It turned blue and began to spread rapidly, a wave of sticky liquid rushing around the gap between door and wall, setting hard as diamond.

Between the glued door, the severed intercom cables, and the chloroform and antipersonnel foam, it might be a minute or two before anyone in the room managed to raise the alarm.

Martin was trying to double over and gasp. She picked him up and ran down the corridor. It was like wading through water; she rapidly discovered it was easier to kick off with one foot, then the other, like low-gee locomotion.

A red haze at the edge of her vision told her she was close to burnout. Her peripheral nervous system might have been boosted, but for this sort of speed, it relied on anaerobic respiration, and she was exhausting her reserves frighteningly fast. At the next intersection, a lift car stood open: she lurched into it, dragging Martin behind, and tapped the button for the accommodation level in officer country. Then she dropped back to normal speed.

The doors slid shut as the lift began to rise, and Martin began to gasp. Rachel slumped against the far wall, black spots hazing her vision as she tried to draw air into straining lungs. Martin was first to speak. "Where—did you learn—"

She blinked. A clock spiraled in the left upper quadrant of her vision. Eight seconds since she'd yelled Utah—eight seconds? Minutes, maybe. She drew a deep breath that turned into a yawn, flushing the carbon dioxide from her lungs. All her muscles ached, burning as if there were hot wires running down her bones. She felt sick, and her left hand was beginning to throb violently. "Special. Implants."

"Think you nearly broke a—rib, back there. Where are we going?"

"Life. Boat." *Gasp.* "Like I said."

A light blinked above them. They'd crawled up one floor. One more to go.

The door opened on the right level. Rachel staggered upright. Nobody there, which was a blessing; in her present state, she didn't know if she could put a hamster in its place, much less a soldier. She stepped out of the lift, Martin following. "My room," she said quietly. "Try to look at ease."

He raised his wrists. "Wearing these?"

Shit. Should have ripped them apart before running out of boost. She shook her head and hunted in her hip pocket, pulled out a compact gray tube. "Stun gun."

They ran out of luck halfway down the last corridor. A door opened and a petty officer stepped out; he moved to give them room to pass, then his jaw dropped as he realized what he was see-ing. "Hey!"

Rachel shot him. "Hurry," she hissed over her shoulder, and stumbled ahead. Martin followed her. Her door was ahead, just around a curve in the corridor. "*Gold,*" she called to the waiting lifeboat.

Red lights flashed overhead: the PA system piped up, a war-bling alert noise. "Security Alert! Green deck accommodation sector B, two armed insurgents on the loose. Armed and danger-ous. Security to Green deck accommodation B. Alert!"

"Shit," Martin mumbled. A pressure door began to rumble shut ten meters ahead of them.

Rachel went to combat speed again, her vision greying almost immediately. She threw herself forward: stood directly beneath the door and thrust straight up at the descending pressure barrier. Martin moved forward with glacial slowness as she felt the motors bear down on her, trying to crush her in half. He ducked and swam under the barrier. She followed him, letting go, and stayed fast, even though her hands and feet were becoming numb and a deadly warning pincushion sensation pricked at her face. The door to her cabin was two meters away. "*Juno!*" she yelled at it through her throat mike, the word coming out in a high-pitched gabble that sounded like the croaking of an aged dinosaur to her ears.

The door swung open. Martin ran through inside, but it was too late for Rachel: she couldn't see, and her knees were begin-

ning to give way. The combat acceleration stopped, and she felt
herself floating, a bruised impact along one side.

Someone was dragging her over gravel and it hurt like hell.

Her heart sounded as if it was about to explode. She couldn't
get enough air.

Sound of a door slamming.

Darkness.

the committee for the Revolution had taken over the onion-domed orthodox cathedral in Plotsk, making it the headquarters of the Commissariat for Extropian Ideology. All those who rejected the doctrine of revolutionary optimization and refused to flee the town were dragged before the tribunal and instructed boringly and at length about the nature of their misdemeanor; then they were shot, minds mapped and uploaded into the Festival, and sentenced to corrective labor—usually all at once. There weren't many of them; for the most part, the population had fled into the wilderness, transcended, or happily adopted the revolutionary cause.

Sister Seventh's hut, spun from local memories of myth and legend uploaded into the noosphere of the Festival, squatted in the courtyard outside the Revolutionary Commissariat and defecated massively. Presently, the house stood and ambled in the direction of the cherry trees that fringed the square: it was hungry, and the Bishop's liking for cherry blossom wouldn't stop it eating.

Sister Seventh wrinkled her snout with displeasure and ambled indoors. The floor of the church was full of plaintiffs, queuing to demand this or appeal that. They stood before a kitchen table parked in the middle of the nave, behind which sat half a dozen bored-looking revolutionary functionaries. The small, frenetic human called Rubenstein waved his arms and exhorted their chairman, who was so heavily augmented with mechanical add-ons that he clanked when he walked. The subject of the exhortation seemed to be something to do with the need to reverse the previous policy of destroying the artistically illiterate.

True, that priority rated low in the estimates of the Critics—after all, you can't win an argument over esthetics with a corpse—but Rubenstein's willingness to change his mind after only a day or two in her company didn't commend his artistic integrity to her. These curious, lumpen humans were so impossibly gnomic in their utterances, so lacking in consistency, that sometimes she despaired of understanding their underlying esthetic.

Sister Seventh lost herself for a while in the flux of knowledge from the Festival. It let a filtered feed of its awareness escape, titillating the Critic colony in orbit, who relayed choice tidbits her way. The Festival propagated by starwisp, that much was true. It also relied on causal channels to relay its discoveries home. Now, great Higgs boson factories were taking shape in the rings of machinery orbiting Sputnik, icy gas and dust congealing into beat-wave particle accelerators on the edge of planetary space. Thousands of huge fusion reactors were coming on-stream, each pumping out enough energy to run a continental civilization. The first batch of new starwisps was nearing readiness, and they had a voracious appetite, a tonne of stabilized antimatter each; then there were the causal channels, petabytes and exabytes of entangled particles to manufacture and laboriously, non-observationally, separate into matching batches. The first starwisps would soon take on their payloads, point their stubby noses at the void, and accelerate at nearly half a million gees, sitting atop the neutral particle beams emitted by vast launch engines in high orbit above Rochard's World. Their primary destinations were the last two stops on the Festival's route, to deliver fresh channels and a detailed report on the current visit; their other destinations—well, the Festival had been encamped for three months. Soon the traders would arrive.

Traders followed the Festival everywhere. A self-replicating, natural source of causal channels, the Festival laid down avenues of communication, opening up new civilizations to trade—civilizations which, in the wake of a visitation, were usually too culture-shocked to object to the Traders' abstraction of the huge structures the Festival had constructed and abandoned for its own purposes. More than a thousand megafortunes had been made by natives of dirt-based trader civilizations with FTL ships and just enough nous to follow the trail of the Festival; like birds in the wake of a plow turning over rich farm soil, they waited to pounce on juicy nuggets of intellectual property turned up by the passing farmer.

Now something new tickled Sister Seventh's hindbrain. She stopped beside a font and stooped to drink. A message from She Who Observes the First. *Ships coming. Festival notices. Many ships coming in silence.* Now *that* was interesting; normally, the traders would appear like a three-ring circus, flashing lights and loud music playing on all available wavelengths, trying to attract attention. Stealth meant trouble. *Forty-two vessels itemized. All with drive kernels, all with low emissions: query thermal dump to stern, reduce visibility from frontal aspect. Range seven light-seconds.*

How peculiar. Sister Seventh straightened up. Someone—no, some construct of the Festival, human-child-high, but with long, floppy ears and a glossy fur coat, eyes mounted on the sides of its rodent face—was coming in through the side door. *Sister mine. What reflex of Festival?* she asked silently. Hardwired extensions patched her through the Festival's telephonic nervous system, building a bridge to her sibling.

Festival has noticed. Current activities not over; will not tolerate interference. Three Bouncers have been dispatched.

Sister of Stratagems the Seventh shivered and bared her teeth. There were few things about the Festival that scared her, but Bouncers were second on the list, right behind the Fringe. The Fringe might kill you out of random pique. The Bouncers were rather less random...

The leporine apparition in the aisle bounced toward her, a panicky expression on its face. Burya stopped lecturing Timoshevski and looked around. "What is it?" he demanded.

Timoshevski rumbled forward. "Am thinking is rabbit stew for dinner."

"No! Please, sirs! Help!" The rabbit stopped short of them, pushing two aggrieved babushkas aside, and held out its front limbs—arms, Sister Seventh noticed, with disturbingly human hands at their extremities. It was wearing a waistcoat that appeared to consist entirely of pockets held together by zip fasteners. "Master in trouble!"

"Are no masters here, comrade," said Timoshevski, apparently categorizing the supplicant as inedible. "True revolutionary doctrine teaches that the only law is rationalism and dynamic optimism. Where are you from, and where is your internal passport?"

Rabbits have little control over their facial muscles; nevertheless, this one made a passable show of being nonplussed. "Need *help*," it bleated, then paused, visibly gathering self-control. "My master is in trouble. Mime hunt! They got between us, a village ago; I escaped, but I fear they're coming this way."

"Mimes?" Timoshevski looked puzzled. "Not clowns?" A metallic tentacle tipped in gun-muzzle flanges uncurled from his back, poked questing into the air. "Circus?"

"Circus of death," said Sister Seventh. "Fringe performance, *very* poor. If coming this way, will interfere with popular acclaim of your revolution."

"Oh, how so?" Timoshevski focused on Sister Seventh suspiciously.

"*Listen* to her, Oleg," growled Burya. "She came with the Festival. Knows what's going on." He rubbed his forehead, as if the effort of making that much of a concession to her superior knowledge was painful.

"Oh?" Wheels turned slowly behind Timoshevski's skull; evidently his plethora of augmentations took a goodly amount of his attention to run.

Sister Seventh stamped, shaking the floor. "Mimes are boring. Say help rabbit. Learn something new, maybe stage rescue drama?"

"If you say so." Burya turned to Oleg. "Listen, you're doing a reasonable job holding things down. I'd like to take six of your finest—who do I talk to?—and go sort these Mimes out. We really don't need them messing things up; I've seen what they do, and I don't like it."

A sallow-faced commissar behind Oleg shouldered his way forward. "I don't see why we should listen to you, you pork-fed cosmopolitan," he snarled in a thick accent. "This isn't your revolution; this is the independent Plotsk soviet soyuz community, and we don't take any centralist reactionary shit!"

"Quiet, Babar," said Oleg. The tentacle sticking out of his back rotated to face the easterner: a dim red light glowed from its tip. "Burya is good comrade. If wanted force centralism on us, am thinking he would have come with force, no?"

"He did," said Sister Seventh, but the revolutionaries ignored her.

"He go with detachment of guards. End to argument," Oleg continued. "A fine revolutionary; trust him do right by this—rabbit."

"You better be right, Timoshevski," grunted Babar. "Not fools, us. Am not tolerating failure."

sauer was out of the wardroom and into the security watch office less than a minute after regaining consciousness, cursing horribly, blinking back a painful chloroform headache, and tugging creases from his rumpled and spattered tunic. The petty officer on duty sprang to his feet hastily, saluting; Sauer cut him off. "General security alert. I want a full search for the UN spy and the shipyard engineer immediately, all points. Pull all the surveillance records for the UN spy in the past hour on my workstation, soon as you've got the search started. I want a complete inventory on all off-duty personnel as soon as you've done that." He flung himself down behind his desk angrily. He ran fingers through his razor-cut hair and glared at the screen set into his desktop, then hit the switchboard button. "Get me the duty officer in ops," he grunted. Turning around, "Chief, what I said—I need it now. Grab anyone you need."

"Yes, sir. Excuse me, sir, beg permission to ask—what are we expecting?"

"The Terran diplomat is a saboteur. We flushed her, but she ran, taking the engineer with her. Which might have done us all a favor, except, firstly, they're still loose, and, secondly, they're armed and aboard this ship right now. So you're to look for crazed foreign terrorists with illegal off-world technology lurking in the corridors. Is that clear?"

"Yes, sir." The flyer looked bemused. "Very clear, sir."

The workstation bonged. Sauer turned to face it. Captain Mirsky stared at him inquiringly; "I thought you were busy keeping an eye on that damned chinless wonder from the Curator's Office," he commented.

"Sir!" Sauer sat bolt upright. "Permission to report a problem, sir!"

"Go ahead."

"Security violation." Sweat stood out on Sauer's forehead. "Suspecting a covert agenda on the part of the Terran diplomat, I arranged a disinformation operation to convince her we had her number. Unfortunately, we convinced her too well; she escaped from custody with the shipyard engineer and is loose on the ship right now. I've started a search and sweep, but in view of the fact that we appear to have armed hostiles aboard, I'm recommending a full lockdown and security alert."

The Captain didn't even blink. "*Do it.*" He turned around, out of camera view for a few seconds. "The operations room is now sealed." Beyond the sound-insulating door of the security office, a siren began to wail. "Report your status."

Sauer looked around; the rating standing by the door nodded at him. "Beg to report, sir, security office is sealed."

"We're locked down in here, sir," said Sauer. "The incident only began about three minutes ago." He leaned sideways. "Found the records yet, Chief?"

"Backtracking now, sir," said the Chief Petty Officer. "Ah, found external—*damn.* Begging your pardon, sir, but twelve minutes ago the surveillance cameras in Green deck, accommodation block—that's where her quarters are—were disabled. An internal shutdown signal via the maintenance track, authorized by—ah. Um. The shutdown signal was authorized under your ID, sir."

"Oh." Sauer grunted. "Have you traced off-duty crew dispositions?"

"Yes, sir. Nobody was obviously out of bounds during the past hour. 'Course that doesn't mean anything—worst thing a sneak would normally get for being caught without a tracking badge would be a day or two in the brig."

"You don't say. Get a team down there now, I want that corridor covered!"

Sauer didn't remember the open phone channel until the Captain cleared his throat. "I take it you're secure for the time being," he said.

"Yes, sir." The Lieutenant's ears began to turn red. "Someone disabled the sensors outside the inspector's cabin, using my security authentication. Sir, she's really put one over on us."

"So what are you going to do about it?" Mirsky raised an eyebrow. "Come on. I want a solution."

"Well—" Sauer stopped. "Sir, I believe I've located the saboteurs. Permission to go get them?"

Mirsky grinned humorlessly. "Do it. Take them alive. I want to ask them some questions." It was the first time Sauer had seen his captain look angry, and it made his blood run cold. "Yes, make sure they're alive. I don't want any accidents. Oh, and Sauer, another thing."

"Sir?"

"When this is over I want a full, written report explaining how and why this whole incident happened. By yesterday morning."

"*Yes, sir.*" The Captain cut the connection abruptly; Sauer stood up. "You heard the man," he said. "Chief, I'm taking a pager. And arms." He walked over to the sealed locker and rammed his thumb against it; it clicked open, and he began pulling equipment out. "You're staying here. Listen on channel nineteen. I'm going to be heading for the cabin. Keep an eye on my ID. If you see it going somewhere I'm not, I want you to tell me about it." He pulled on a lightweight headset, then picked up a taser, held it beside his temple while the two computers shook hands, then rolled his eyes to test the target tracking. "Is that clear?"

"Yes, sir. Should I notify the red tabs on green deck?"

"Of course." Sauer brought the gun to bear on the door. "Open the hatch."

"Aye aye, sir." There was a click as latches retracted; the rating outside nearly dropped his coffee tray when he saw the Lieutenant.

"You! Maxim! Dump that tray and take this!" Sauer held out another firearm, and the surprised flyer fumbled it into place. "Stick to channel nineteen. Don't speak unless you're spoken to. Now follow me." Then he was off down the corridor, airtight doors scissoring open in front and slamming closed behind him, turning the night into a jerky red-lit succession of tunnels.

the first thing she realized was her head hurt. The second . . .

She was lying in an acceleration couch. Her feet and hands were cold. "Rachel!"

She tried to say "I'm awake," but wasn't sure anything came out. Opening her eyes took a tremendous effort of will. "Time. Wassat? How long—?"

"A minute ago," said Martin. "What's happened in here?" He was in the couch next to her. The capsule was claustrophobically tiny, like something out of the dawn of the space age. The hatch above them was open, though, and she could just see the inner door of her cabin past it. "*Hatch, close.* I said I had a lifeboat, didn't I?"

"Yeah, and I thought you were just trying to keep my spirits up." Martin's pupils were huge in the dim light. Above him, the roof of the capsule began to knit itself together. "What's going on?"

"We're sitting on top of—" She paused to pant for breath. "Ah. *Shit.* On top of—a saltwater rocket. Fission. Luggage full of—of uranium. And boron. Sort of unobtanium you need in 'mergency, stuff you can't find easily. My little insurance policy."

"You can't just punch your way out of an occupied space-ship!" Martin protested.

"Watch me." She grimaced, lips pulling back from her teeth. "Sealed—bulkheads. Airtight cocoon 'round us. Only question is—"

"*Autopilot ready,*" announced the lifeboat. An array of emergency navigation displays lit up on the console in front of them.

"Whether they shoot at us when we launch."

"Wait. Let me get this straight. We're less than a day out from Rochard's World, right? This—thing—has enough legs to get us there? So you're going to punch a neat hole in the wall and eject us, and they're just going to let us go?"

"'S about the size of it," she said. Closing her eyes to watch the pretty blue displays projected on her retinas: "About ten thousand gee-seconds to touchdown. We're about forty thousand seconds from perigee right now. So we're going to drift like a turd, right? Pretend to be a flushed silage tank. If they light out their radar, they give themselves away; if they shoot, they're visible. So they'll let us go, figure to pick us up later 's long as we get there after they do. If we try to get there first, they'll shoot..."

"You're betting the Festival will finish them off."

"Yup," she agreed.

"*Ready to arm initiator pump,*" said the autopilot. It sounded like a fussy old man.

"M' first husband," she said. "He always nagged."

"And here was me thinking it was your favorite pet ferret." Martin busied himself hunting for crash webbing. "No gravity on this crate?"

"'S not a luxury yacht."

Something bumped and clanked outside the door. "Oh shit."

"We launch in—forty-two seconds," said Rachel.

"Hope they give us that long." Martin leaned over and began strapping her into the couch. "How many gees does this thing pull?"

She laughed: it ended in a cough. "Many as we can take. Fission rocket."

"Fission?" He looked at her aghast. "But we'll be a sitting duck! If they—"

"Shut up and let me work." She closed her eyes again, busy with the final preparations.

Sneak was, of course, of the essence. A fission rocket was a sitting duck to a battlecruiser like the *Lord Vanek;* it had about four hours' thrust, during which time it might stay ahead—if the uncompensated acceleration didn't kill its passengers, and if the ship didn't simply go to full military power and race past it—but then it was out of fuel, a ballistic casualty. To make matters worse, until she managed to get more than about ten thousand kilometers away from the *Lord Vanek,* she'd be within tertiary laser defense range—close enough that the warship could simply point its lidar grid at the lifeboat and curdle them like an egg in a microwave oven.

But there was a difference between *could* and *would* which, Rachel hoped, was big enough to fly a spaceship through. Activating the big warship's drive would create a beacon that any defenders within half a light-minute or so might see. And torching off the big laser sensor/killer array would be like lighting up a neon sign saying INVADING WARSHIP—COME AND GET ME. Unless Captain Mirsky was willing to risk his Admiral's wrath by making a spectacle of himself in front of the Festival, he wouldn't dare try to nail Rachel so blatantly. Only if she lit off her own drive, or a distress beacon, would he feel free to shoot her down—because she would already have given his position away.

However, first she had to get off the ship. Undoubtedly, they'd be outside her cabin door within minutes, guns and cutters in their hands. The weakened bulkheads between the larval lifeboat and the outer pressure hull were all very well, but how to achieve a clean separation without warning them?

"Mech one. Broadcast primary destruct sequence."

"Confirm. Primary destruct sequence for mech one."

"*Sword.* Confirm?"

"Confirmed."

The transponder in her luggage was broadcasting a siren song of destruction, on wavelengths only her spy mechs—those that were left—would be listening to. Mech one, wedged in a toilet's waste valve in the brig, would hear. Using what was left of its feeble power pack, it would detonate its small destruct charge. Smaller than a hand grenade—but powerful enough to rupture the toilet's waste pipe.

WARSHIPS CAN'T USE gravity-fed plumbing; the *Lord Vanek*'s sewage-handling system was under pressure, an intricate network of pipes connected by valves to prevent backflow. The *Lord Vanek* didn't recycle its waste, but stored it, lest discharges freeze to shrapnel, ripping through spacecraft and satellites like a shotgun loaded with ice. But there are exceptions to every rule; holding waste in tanks to reduce the risk of ballistic debris creation was all very well, but not at the risk of shipboard disaster, electrical short circuit, or life-support contamination.

When Rachel's makeshift bomb exploded, it ruptured a down pipe carrying waste from an entire deck to the main storage tanks. Worse, it took out a backflow valve. Waste water backed up from the tank and sprayed everywhere, hundreds of liters per second drenching the surrounding structural spaces and conduits. Damage control alarms warbled in the maintenance stations, and the rating on duty hastily opened the main dump valves, purging the waste circuit into space. The *Lord Vanek* had a crew of nearly twelve hundred, and had been in flight for weeks; a fire spray of sewage exploded from the scuppers, nearly two hundred tonnes of waste water purging into space just as Rachel's lifeboat counted down to zero.

In the process of assembling her lifeboat, the robot factory in Rachel's luggage had made extensive—not to say destructive—changes to the spaces around her cabin. Supposedly solid bulkheads fractured like glass; on the outer hull of the ship, a foam of spun diamond half a meter thick disintegrated into a talc-like powder across a circle three meters in diameter. The bottom dropped out of Rachel's stomach as the hammock she lay in lurched sideways, then the improvised cold-gas thrusters above her head kicked in, shoving the damply newborn lifeboat clear of its ruptured womb. Weird, painful tidal stresses ripped at her; Martin grunted as if he'd been punched in the gut. The lifeboat was entering the ship's curved-space field, a one-gee gradient dropping off across perhaps a hundred meters of space beyond the hull; the boat creaked and sloshed ominously, then began to tumble, falling end over end toward the rear of the warship.

On board the *Lord Vanek,* free-fall alarms were sounding. Cursing bridge officers yanked at their seat restraints, and throughout the ship, petty officers yelled at their flyers, calling them to crash stations. Down in the drive maintenance room, Commander Krupkin was cursing up a blue streak as he hit the scram switch, then grabbed his desk with one hand and the speaking tube to the bridge with the other to demand an explanation.

Without any fuss, the warship's drive singularity entered shutdown. The curved-space field that provided both a semblance of gravity and shielding against acceleration collapsed into a much weaker spherical field centered on the point mass in the engine room—just in time to prevent two hundred tons of bilgewater, and a twenty-tonne improvised lifeboat, from hammering into the rear of the *Lord Vanek*'s hull and ripping the heat exchangers to shreds.

In the Green deck accommodation block corridor, a nightmare cacophony of alarms was shrilling for attention. Lights strobed overhead, blue, red, green; blow-out alarm, gravity failure alarm, everything. Lieutenant Sauer cursed under his breath and grappled with an emergency locker door; "Help me, you idiot!" he shouted at Able Flyer Maxim Kravchuk who, whey-faced with fear, was frozen in the middle of the corridor. "Grab this handle and pull for your life!"

Farther up the corridor, damage control doors were sliding shut; as they closed, struts extended from their inner surfaces and extended bright orange crash nets. Maxim grabbed the handle Sauer pointed him at and yanked. Together they managed to unseal the stiff locker door. "Get *inside,* idiot," Sauer grunted. The blow-out alarm, terror of all cosmonauts, stopped strobing, but now he could feel the keening of the gravity failure siren deep in his bones—and the floor was beginning to tilt. Kravchuk tumbled inside the locker and began to belt himself to the wall, hands working on instinct alone. Sauer could see the whites of the man's terrified eyes. He paused in the entrance, glancing up the corridor. The UN bitch's cabin was in the next segment—he'd have to secure this one and get breathing apparatus before he could go and find out what she'd done to his ship. *It's not just the skipper who'll be asking questions,* he thought bitterly.

Sauer clambered into the locker even as the floor began to tilt sideways; but the tilt stabilized at a relatively tolerable thirty degrees. He began to feel light on his feet. *Drive must be going into shutdown,* he realized. Leaving the door open—it would close automatically if there was a pressure drop—he began systematically to pull on an emergency suit. The emergency suit was basically a set of interconnected transparent bags, with enough air to last six hours in a backpack, no good for EVA but a lifesaver inside a breached hull. "You get dressed," he told the frightened rating. "We're going to find out what caused this."

Four minutes later, Chief Molotov and four armed red-tab police arrived, laboriously cycling through the sealed-off corridor segments; the young Procurator tagged along behind them, face flushed, evidently struggling with the unfamiliar survival suit. Sauer ignored him. "Chief, I have reason to believe there are armed saboteurs inside the next corridor segment, or the third compartment in it. When I give the signal, I want this door open and the corridor behind it cleared. I don't know what the occupants have by way of defenses, but they're definitely armed, so I suggest you just saturate with taser fire. Once we've done that, if it's empty, we move on the compartment. Got that?"

"Aye," said Molotov. "Any idea who's inside?"

Sauer shrugged. "My best bet is the engineer, Springfield, and the woman from Earth. But I could be wrong. How you handle it is your call."

"I see." Molotov turned. "You and you; either side of the door. When it opens, shoot anything that moves." He paused. "Remote override on the cabin door?"

"It's locked. Manual hinges only, too."

"Right you are." Molotov unslung a knapsack, began unrolling a fat cable. "You'll want to stand back, then." He grabbed the emergency door override handle. "On my mark! Mark!"

The emergency door hummed up into the ceiling, and the ratings tensed, but the corridor was empty. "Right. The cabin, lads."

He approached the cabin door carefully. "Says it's open to vacuum, sir," he said, pointing to the warning lights on the door frame.

"Bet you it's a pinhole leak she's rigged to keep us out. Just get everyone into suits before we blow it." Sauer approached and watched as Molotov attached the cable of rubbery cord to the door frame, running it alongside the hinges and then around the door handle and lock, holding it in place with tape. "I'm going to use cutting cord. Better tell Environment to seal this corridor for a pressure drop-off until we repressurize this compartment."

"Sir—" It was Muller, the cause of this whole mess.

"What is it?" Sauer snapped, not bothering to conceal his anger.

"I, uh—" Vassily recoiled. "Please be careful, sir. She—the inspector—isn't a fool. This makes me nervous—"

"Keep pestering me, and I'll make you nervous. Chief, if this man makes a nuisance of himself, feel free to arrest him. He caused this whole fiasco."

"He did, did he?" Chief Molotov glared at the Subcurator, who wilted and retreated down the passage.

"I'll get Environment to seal us off." Sauer was on the command channel again, as Molotov retrieved some wires and a detonator, and began cabling up the explosives. Finally, he retreated a few paces down the corridor and waited. "All clear," said Sauer. "Okay. Is everybody ready?" He backed up until he stood beside Molotov. "Are you ready?" The chief nodded. "Then *go.*"

There was a loud whip crack, and smoke jetted from the sides of the door. Then there was an unbelievably loud bang, and Sauer's ears popped. The doorway was gone. Behind it, a rolling darkness dragged at him with icy claws, howling and sucking the others out into the void. *Not a pinhole?* He tried to grab at the nearest emergency locker door, but it was already slamming shut, and he was dragged down the corridor. Something thumped him hard between the shoulders, so hard that he couldn't breathe. Everything was dark, and the pain was unbelievable. A dark cylinder spun before his eyes, and there was a ringing whistling in his ears. Plastic flapped against his face. *Must have ripped my suit,* he thought vaguely. *I wonder what happened to...* Thinking was hard work; he gave up and fell into a doze, which spiraled rapidly down into dreamless silence.

Vassily Muller, however, was luckier.

the admiral sat at his desk and squinted.

Commodore Bauer cleared his throat. "If I may have your attention, sir."

"Huh? Speak up-up, young man!"

"We enter terminal engagement range with the enemy tonight," Bauer said patiently. "We have to hold the final pre-approach session, sir, to articulate our immediate tactical situation. I need you to sign off on my orders if we are to conduct the battle."

"Very well." Admiral Kurtz tried to sit up in his chair; Robard's helping hands behind his frail shoulders steadied him. "You have them?"

"Sir." Bauer slid a slim folder across the polished oak. "If you would care to see—"

"No, no." The Admiral waved a frail hand. "You're a sound man. You give-ive those natives jolly what for, won't you?"

Bauer stared at his commander in mixed desperation and relief. "Yes, sir, I will," he promised. "We will be in lidar range of the planetary surface in another hour, then we should be able to establish their order of battle fairly accurately. Task Group Four will illuminate and take the first blood, while the heavies stay under emission control and punch out anything we can identify after we get within close broadside range. I have the destroyer squadrons ready to go after any fixed emplacements we find in GEO, and the torpedo boats are tasked with high-delta-vee intercepts on anything fleeing—"

"Give the natives what-ho," Kurtz said dreamily. "Make a hill of skulls in the town square. Volley fire by platoons. Bomb the bastards!"

"Yes, sir. If you'd be so good as to sign here—"

Robard put the pen between the Admiral's fingers, but they shook so much that his crimson signature on the orders was almost completely obscured by a huge blot, like fresh blood.

Bauer saluted. "Sir! With your permission I will implement these orders forthwith."

Kurtz looked up at the Commodore, his sunken eyes glowing for a split second with an echo of his former will. "Make it so! Victory is on-on our side, for our Lord will not permit his followers to come to—" A look of vast puzzlement crossed his wrinkled face, and he slumped forward.

"Sir! Are you—" The Commodore leaned forward, but Robard had already pulled the Admiral's chair back from the table.

"He's been overwrought for days," Robard commented, reclining his charge's chair. "I shall take him back to his bedchamber. As we approach the enemy—" He tensed. "Would sir please accept my apologies and call the ship's surgeon?"

Half an hour later, ten minutes late for his own staff meeting, Commodore Bauer surged into the staff conference room. "Gentlemen. Please be seated."

Two rows sat before him, before the podium from which the Admiral commanding could address his staff and line officers. "I have a very grave announcement to make," he began. The folio under his right arm bent under the tension with which he gripped it. "The Admiral—" A sea of faces upturned before him, trusting, waiting. "The Admiral is indisposed," he said. Indisposed indeed, if you could call it that, with the ship's surgeon in attendance and giving him a ten percent chance of recovery from the cerebral hemorrhage that had struck him down as he signed the final order. "Ahem. He has instructed me to proceed with our prearranged deployment, acting as his proxy while he retains overall control of the situation. I should like to add that he asked me to say, he knows every man will do his duty, and our cause will triumph because God is on our side."

Bauer shuffled his papers, trying to dismiss his parting image of the Admiral from his awareness; lying prone and shriveled on his bed, the surgeon and a loblolly boy conferring over him in low voices as they awaited the arrival of the ship's chaplain. "First, to review the situation. Commander Kurrel. What word on navigation?"

Commander Kurrel stood. A small, fussy man who watched the world with sharp-eyed intelligence from behind horn-rimmed glasses, he was the staff navigation specialist. "The discrepancy is serious, but not fatal," he said, shuffling the papers in front of him. "Evidently Their Lordships' projected closed timelike path was more difficult to navigate than we anticipated. Despite improvements to the drive timebase monitors, a discrepancy of no less than sixteen million seconds crept in during our traversal—which, I might add, is not entirely inexplicable, considering that we have made a grand total of sixty-eight jumps spaced over some 139 days, covering a distance of just over 8053 light-years; a new and significant record in the history of the Navy."

He paused to adjust his spectacles. "Unfortunately, those sixteen mega-seconds lay in precisely the worst possible direction—timewise, into the domain within which the enemy occupied our territory. Indeed, we would have done little worse had we simply made the normal five-jump crossing, a distance of some forty-four light-years. A full pulsar map correlated for spin-down indicates that our temporal displacement is some three million seconds into the future of our origin point, when it is extrapolated to the destination's world line. This is confirmed by classical planetary ephemeris measurements; according to local history, the enemy—the Festival—has been entrenched for thirty days."

A single intake of breath rattled around the table, disbelief and muted anger mingling. Commodore Bauer watched it sharply. "*Gentlemen.*" Silence resumed. "We may have lost the anticipated tactical benefits of this hitherto untried maneuver, but we have not entirely failed; we are still only ten days in the future of our own departure light cone, and using a conventional path we wouldn't be arriving for another ten days or so. As we have not heard anything from signals intelligence, we may assume that the enemy, although entrenched, are not expecting us." He smiled tightly. "An inquiry into the navigation error will be held after the victory celebrations." That statement brought a brief round of "ayes" from the assembly. "Lieutenant Kossov. General status report, if you please."

"Ah, yes, sir." Kossov stood. "All ships report ready for battle. The main issues are engineering failures with the *Kamchatka*—they report that pressure has been restored to nearly all decks, now—and the explosion in the waste-disposal circuits of this ship. I understand that, with the exception of some cabins on Green deck, and localized water damage near the brig, we are back to normal; however, several persons are missing, including Security Lieutenant Sauer, who was investigating some sort of incident at the time of the explosion."

"Indeed." Bauer nodded at Captain Mirsky. "Captain. Anything to report?"

"Not at this time, sir. Rescue parties are currently busy trying to recover those who were expelled from the ship during the decompression incident. I don't believe this will affect our ability to fight. However, I will have a full and detailed report for you at your earliest convenience." Mirsky looked grim; and well he might, for the Flag Captain's ship was not expected to disgrace the fleet, much less to lose officers and crew to some sort of plumbing accident—if indeed it was an accident. "I must report, sir, that the Terran diplomat is among those listed as missing following this incident. Normally, I would conduct a search for survivors, but in the current situation—" His shrug was eloquent.

"Let me extend my sympathies, Captain; Lieutenant Sauer was a fine officer. Now, as to our forthcoming engagement, I have decided that we will deploy in accordance with attack plan F. You've gamed it twice in exercises; now you get a chance to play it for real, this time against a live but indeterminate foe—"

a bUMpIng on the hull brought Martin to his senses.

He blinked, hair floating in front of his eyes, and stared at the wall in front of him. It had slid past his eyes as the cold-gas thrusters tried to yank him into the ceiling, turning from solid gray into a sheet of blackness stippled with the glaring diamond dust of stars. The tides of the *Lord Vanek* had tried to yank his arms and legs off; he ached with a memory of gravity. Rachel lay next to him, her lips twitching as she communed with the lifeboat's primitive brainstem. Huge gray clouds blocked the view directly overhead, waste water from the scuppers. As he looked, yellow beacons flashed in it, rescue workers searching for something.

"You alright?" he croaked.

"Just a minute." Rachel closed her eyes again and let her arms float upward until they almost touched the glassy overhead screen—which was much, much closer than Martin had originally thought. The capsule was a truncated cylinder, perhaps four meters in diameter at the base and three at the top, but it was less than two meters high; about the same volume as the passenger compartment of a hackney carriage. (The fuel tanks and motor beneath it were significantly larger.) It hummed and gurgled quietly with the rhythm of the life-support pipework, spinning very slowly around its long axis. "We're making twelve meters per second. That's good. Puts us a kilometer or so from the ship . . . damn, what's going on back there?"

"Somebody on EVA? Looking for us."

"Seems like more than one of 'em. Almost like a debris cloud." Her eyes widened in horror as Martin watched her.

"Whatever happened, it happened after we left. If you'd triggered a blowout, we'd be surrounded by debris, wouldn't we?"

She shook her head. "We should go back and help. We've got a—"

"*Bullshit.* They've got EVA teams suited up all the time they're at battle stations, you know that as well as I do. It's not your problem. Let me guess. Someone tried to get into your cabin after we left. Tried a bit too hard, by the look of it."

She stared at the distant specks floating around the rear of the warship, a stubby cylinder in the middle distance. "But if I hadn't—"

"I'd be on my way to the airlock with my hands taped behind my back, and you'd be under arrest," he pointed out. Tired, cold, rational. His head ached; this capsule must be at a lower pressure than the ship. His hands were shaking and cold in reaction to the events of the past five minutes. Ten minutes. However long it had been. "You saved my life, Rachel. If you'd stop kicking yourself over it for a minute, I'd like to thank you."

"If there's anyone out there and we leave them—"

"The EVA crew will get them. Trust me on this, I figure they tried to blow their way into your cabin. Didn't check that it wasn't open to space first, and got blown a bit farther than they expected. That's what warships have away teams and jolly boats for. What we should be worrying about now is hoping nobody notices us before the final event."

"Um." Rachel shook her head: her expression relaxed slightly, tension draining. A certain darkness seemed to lift. "We're still going to be entirely too close for my liking. We've got another cold-gas tank, that'll give us an extra ten meters per second; if I use it now that means we'll have drifted about 250 kilometers from the ship before perigee, but before then, they should begin maneuvering and widen the gap considerably. We've got enough water and air for a week. I was figuring on a couple of full-on burns to take us downside while they're busy paying attention to the enemy defenses, whatever they turn out to be. If there are any."

"I'm betting on eaters, shapers." Martin nodded briefly, then held his head still as the world seemed to spin around him. Not spacesickness, surely? The thought of being cooped up in this cubbyhole for a week with a bad case of the squirts was too revolting to contemplate. "Maybe antibodies. Nothing the New Republic understands, anyway. Probably easy enough for us to avoid, but if you go in shooting—"

"Yeah." Rachel yawned.

"You look exhausted." Concern filled him. "How the hell did you do that? I mean, back on the ship? It must take it out on you later—"

"It does." She bent forward and fumbled with a blue fishnet, down around what would have been the floor of the cabin. Surprisingly homely containers of juice floated out, tumbling in free fall. She grabbed one and began to suck on the nozzle greedily. "Help yourself."

"Not that I'm ungrateful or anything," Martin added, batting a wandering mango and durian fruit cordial out of his face, "but—why?" She stared at him for a long moment. "Oh," he said.

She let the empty carton float free and turned to face him. "I'd prefer to give you some kind of bullshit about trust and duty and so on. But." She shrugged uncomfortably in her seat harness. "Doesn't matter." She held out a hand. Martin took it and squeezed, wordlessly.

"You didn't blow your mission," he pointed out. "You never had a mission out here. Not realistically, anyway, not what your boss, what was his name?"

"George. George Cho."

"—George thought. Insufficient data, right? What would he have done if he'd known about the Festival?"

"Possibly nothing different." She smiled bleakly at the empty juice carton, then plucked another from the air. "You're dead wrong; I still have a job to do, if and when we arrive. The chances of which have just gone down by, oh, about fifty percent because of this escapade."

"Huh. Let me know if there's anything I can do to help, alright?" Martin stretched, then flinched with a remembered pain. "You wouldn't have seen my PA would you? After—"

"It's bagged under your chair, along with a toothbrush and a change of underwear. I hit your cabin after they pulled you in."

"You're a star," he exclaimed happily. He bent double and began fishing around in the cramped space under the control console. "Oh my—" Straightening up, he opened the battered gray book. Words and pictures swam across the pages in front of him. He tapped an imaginary keyboard; new images gelled. "You need any help running this boat?"

"If you want." She drained the second container, thrust both the empties into the bag. "Yes, if you want. You've flown before?"

"Spent twelve years at L5. Basic navigation, no problem. If it's got a standard life-support module, I can program the galley, too. Traditional Yorkshire habit, that, learning how to cook black pudding in free fall. The trick is to spin the ship around the galley, so that the sausage stays still while the grill rotates—"

She chuckled; a carton of cranberry juice bounced off his head. "Enough already!"

"Alright." He leaned back, the PA floating before him. Its open pages showed a real-time instrument feed from the lifeboat's brain. (A clock in one corner spiraled down the seconds to Rachel's first programmed deceleration burn, two thousand seconds before perigee.) Frowning, he scribbled glyphs with a stylus. "We should make it. Assuming they don't shoot at us."

"We've got a Red Cross transponder. They'd have to manually override their IFF."

"Which they won't do unless they're *really* pissed off. Good." Martin tapped a final period on the page. "I'd be happier if I knew what we were flying into, though. I mean, if the Festival hasn't left anything in orbit—" They both froze.

Something scraped across the top of the escape capsule, producing a sound like hollow metal bones rattling against a cage.

the rabbit snarled and hefted his submachine gun angrily. Ears back and teeth visible, he hissed at the cyborg.

Sister Seventh sat up and stared at the confrontation. Everyone else except Burya Rubenstein ducked; Burya stepped forward into the middle of the clearing. "Stop this! At once!"

For a long moment the rabbit stood, frozen. Then he relaxed his stiff-backed pose and lowered his gun muzzle. "He started it."

"I don't care what he started: we have a job to do, and it does not require shooting each other." He turned to the cyborg whom the rabbit had confronted. "What did you say?"

The revolutionary looked bashful; her fully extended claws retracted slowly. "Is not good extropian. This *creature*—" her gesture at the rabbit brought another show of teeth—"believe cult of personality! Is counterrevolutionary dissident. Headlaunch now! Headlaunch now!"

Burya squinted. Many of the former revolutionaries had gone overboard on the personal augmentations offered by the Festival, without realizing that it was necessary to modify their central nervous systems in order to run them. This led to a certain degree of confusion. "But, comrade, you have a personality, too. A sense of identity is a necessary precondition to consciousness, and that, as the great leaders and teachers point out, is the keystone upon which the potential for transcendence is built."

The cyborg looked puzzled. Mirror-finished nictitating membranes flashed across her eyeballs, reflecting inner thoughts. "But within society of mind there is no personality. Personality arises from society; therefore, individual can have no—"

"I think you misunderstand the great philosophers," Rubenstein said slowly. "This is not a criticism, comrade, for the philosophers are, of their essence, very brilliant and hard to follow; but by 'society of mind', they were referring to the arrival of consciousness within the individual, arising from lesser pre-conscious agents, not to society outside the person. Thus, it follows that being attached to one's own consciousness is not to follow a cult of personality. Now, following another's—" He broke off and looked sharply at the rabbit. "I don't think we will pursue this question any further," he said primly. "Time to move on."

The cyborg nodded jerkily. Her fellows stood (or in one case, uncoiled) and shouldered their packs; Burya walked over to Sister Seventh's hut and climbed inside. Presently the party moved off.

"Not understand revolutionary sense," commented the Critic, munching on a sweet potato as the hut bounced along the dirt track behind the detachment from the Plotsk soviet. "Sense of identity deprecated? Lagomorph Criticized for affinity to self? Nonsense! How appreciate art without sense of self?"

Burya shrugged. "They're too literal-minded," he said quietly. "All doing, no innovative thinking. They don't understand metaphors well; half of them think you're Baba Yaga returned, you know? We've been a, ah, stable culture too long. Patterns of belief, attitudes, get ingrained. When change comes, they are incapable of responding. Try to fit everything into their preconceived dogmas." He leaned against the swaying wall of the hut. "I got so tired of trying to wake them up..."

Sister Seventh snorted. "What you call *that?*" she asked, pointing through the door of the hut. Ahead of them marched a column of wildly varied cyborgs, partially augmented revolutionaries frozen halfway beyond the limitations of their former lives. At its head marched the rabbit, leading them into the forest of the partially transcended wilderness.

Burya peered at the rabbit. "I'd call it anything it wants. It's got a gun, hasn't it?"

By noon, the forest had changed beyond recognition. Some strange biological experiment had warped the vegetation. Trees and grass had exchanged leaves, so that now they walked on a field of spiny pine needles, while flat blades waved overhead; the leaves were piebald, black and green, with the glossy black spreading. Most disturbingly of all, the shrubbery seemed to be blurring at the edges, species exchanging phenotypic traits with unnatural promiscuous abandon. "What's responsible for this?" Burya asked Sister Seventh, during one of their hourly pauses.

The Critic shrugged. "Is nothing. Lysenkoist forestry fringe, recombinant artwork. Beware the Jabberwocky, my son. Are there only Earth native derivations in this biome?"

"You asking me?" Rubenstein snorted. "I'm no gardener."

"Guesstimation implausible," Sister Seventh replied archly. "In any event, some fringeworks are recombinant. Non humancentric manipulations of genome. Elegant structures, modified for non-purpose. This forest is Lamarckian. Nodes exchange phenotype-determinant traits, acquire useful ones."

"Who determines their usefulness?"

"The Flower Show. Part of the Fringe."

"What a surprise," Burya muttered.

At the next stop, he approached the rabbit. "How far?" he demanded.

The lagomorph sniffed at the breeze. "Fifty kilometers? Maybe more?" It looked faintly puzzled, as if the concept of distance was a difficult abstraction.

"You said sixty kilometers this morning," Burya pointed out, "We've come twenty. Are you sure? The militia doesn't trust you, and if you keep changing your mind, I may not be able to stop them doing something stupid."

"I'm just a rabbit." Ears twitched backward, swiveling to either side to listen for threats. "Know where master is, *was*, attacked by Mimes. Haven't heard much from him since, you bet. Always know where he is, don't know how—but can't tell you how far. Like fucking compass in my head, mate, you understand?"

"How long have you been a rabbit?" asked Rubenstein, an awful suspicion coming to mind.

The rabbit looked puzzled. "I don't rightly know. I think I once—" He stopped talking. Iron shutters came down, blocking the light behind his eyes. "No more words. Find master. Rescue!"

"Who is your master?" Burya demanded.

"Felix," said the rabbit.

"Felix . . . Politovsky?"

"Don't know. *Maybe.*" Rabbit twitched his ears right back and bared his teeth. "Don't want to talk! We there tomorrow. Rescue master. Kill the Mimes."

vassily looked down at the stars wheeling beneath his feet. *I'm going to die,* he thought, swallowing acrid bile.

When he closed his eyes, the nausea went away a little. His head still hurt where he'd thumped it against the wall of the cabin on his way through; everything had blurred for a while, and he'd caught himself floating away on a cloud of pain. Now he had time to reflect, the pain seemed like an ironic joke; corpses didn't hurt, did they? It told him he was still alive. When it stopped hurting—

He relived the disaster again and again. Sauer checking everybody was suited up. "It's just a pinhole," someone said, and it had seemed so plausible—the woman had let some air out of her cabin to trip the decompression interlocks—and then the bright flash of the cutting cord proved him wrong. The howling maelstrom had reached out and yanked the lieutenant and the CPO right out of the ship, into a dark tunnel full of stars. Vassily had tried to catch a door handle, but the clumsy mitten hands of his emergency suit wouldn't grip. They'd left him tumbling over and over like a spider caught in the whirlpool when a bath plug is pulled.

Stars whirled, cold lights like daggers in the night outside his eyelids. *This is it. I'm really going to die. Not going home again. Not going to arrest the spy. Not going to meet my father and tell him what I really think of him. What will the Citizen think of me?*

Vassily opened his eyes. The whirling continued; he must be spinning five or six times a minute. The emergency suit had no thrusters, and its radio had a pathetic range, just a few hundred meters—more than enough for shipboard use, perhaps enough to make a beacon if anyone came looking for him. But nobody had. He was precessing like a gyroscope; every couple of minutes, the ship swam briefly into view, a dark splinter outlined against the diamond dust of the heavens. There'd been no sign of a search party heading his way; just that golden fog of waste water spreading out around the ship, which had been over a kilometer away before he first saw it.

It looked like a toy; an infinitely desirable toy, one he could pin all his hopes of life and love and comradeship and warmth and happiness on—one that hung forever out of reach, dangling in a cold wasteland he couldn't cross.

He glanced at the crude display mounted on his left wrist, watching the air dial tick down the hours left in his oxygen bottle. There was a dosimeter there, too, and this wasteland was hot, charged particles streaming through it at a rate that might suffice to prevent his mummified corpse decaying.

Vassily shuddered. Bitter frustration seized him: *Why couldn't I do something right?* he wondered. He'd thought he was doing the right thing, enlisting in the Curator's Office, but when he'd pridefully shown his mother the commission, her face had closed like a shop front, and she'd looked away from him in that odd manner she used when he'd done something wrong but she didn't want to chastise him for it. He'd thought he was doing the right thing, searching the engineer's luggage, then the diplomat's—but look where it had taken him. The ship beneath his shoes was a splinter against the dark, several kilometers away and getting farther out of reach all the time. Even his presence aboard the ship—if he was honest, he'd have done better to stay at home, wait for the ship (and the engineer) to return to New Prague, there to resume his pursuit. Only the news from Rochard's World, the place of exile, had filled him with a curious excitement. And if he hadn't wanted to go along, he wouldn't be here now, spinning in a condemned man's cell of memories.

He tried to think of happier times, but it was difficult. School? He'd been bullied mercilessly, mocked because of who and what his father was—and was not. Any boy who bore his mother's name was an object of mockery, but to have a criminal for a father as well, a notorious criminal, made him too easy a target. Eventually he'd pounded one bully's face into pulp, and been caned for it, and they'd learned to avoid him, but it hadn't stopped the whispering and sniggering in quiet corners. He'd learned to listen for that, to lie in wait after classes and beat the grins off their faces, but it hadn't gained him friends.

Basic training? That was a joke. A continuation of school, only with sterner taskmasters. Then police training, and the cadet's college. Apprenticeship to the Citizen, whom he strived to impress because he admired the stern inspector vastly; a man of blood and iron, unquestionably loyal to the Republic and everything it stood for, a spiritual father whom he'd now managed to disappoint twice.

Vassily yawned. His bladder ached, but he didn't dare piss—not in this suit of interconnected bubbles. The thought of drowning was somehow more terrifying than the idea of running out of air. Besides, when the air went—wasn't this how they executed mutinous spacers, instead of hanging?

A curious horror overtook him, then. His skin crawled; the back of his neck turned damp and cold. *I can't go yet,* he thought. *It's not fair!* He shuddered. The void seemed to speak to him. *Fairness has nothing to do with it. This will happen, and your wishes are meaningless.* His eyes stung; he squeezed them tightly shut against the whirling daggers of night and tried to regain control of his breathing.

And when he opened them again, as if in answer to his prayers, he saw that he was not alone in the deep.

high in orbit above Rochard's World, the Bouncers were stirring.

Two kilometers long, sleek and gray, each of them dwarfed the incoming naval task force. They'd been among the first artifacts the newly arrived Festival manufactured. Most of the Bouncers drifted in parking orbits deep in the Oort cloud, awaiting enemies closing along timelike attack paths deep in the future of the Festival's world line; but a small detachment had accompanied the Festival itself, as it plunged deep into the inner system and arrived above the destination world.

Bouncers didn't dream. Bouncers were barely sentient special units, tasked with the defense of the Festival against certain crude physical threats. For denial of service, decoherence attacks, and general spoofing, the more sophisticated antibodies could be relied on; for true causality-violation attacks, the Festival's reality-maintenance crew would be awakened. But sometimes, the best defense is a big stick and a nasty smile—and that was what the Bouncers were for.

The arrival of the New Republic task force had been noted four days earlier. The steady acceleration profiles of the incoming warships stuck out like a sore thumb; while His Majesty's Navy thought in terms of lidar and radar and active sensors, the Festival used more subtle instruments. Localized minima in the outer system's entropy had been noted, spoor of naked singularities, echoes of the tunneling effect that let the conventional starships jump from system to system. The failure of the incoming fleet to signal told its own story; bouncers knew what to do without being told.

The orbiting Bouncer division began to accelerate. There were no fragile life-forms aboard these craft—just solid slabs of impure diamond and ceramic superconductors, tanks of metallic hydrogen held under pressures that would make the core of a gas giant planet seem like vacuum, and high-energy muon generators to catalyze the exotic fusion reactions that drove the ships. Also, of course, the fractal bushes that were the Bouncers' cargo: millions of them clinging like strange vines to the long spines of the ships.

Fusion torches providing thrust in accordance with Newtonian laws might seem quaint to the New Republic Admiralty, who had insisted on nothing but the most modern drive singularities and curved-space engines for their fleet; but unlike the Admiralty, the Festival's Bouncers had some actual combat experience. Reaction motors had important advantages for space-to-space combat, advantages that gave an unfair edge to a canny defender; a sensible thrust-to-mass ratio for one thing, and a low degree of observability for another. Ten-billion-tonne virtual masses made singularity-drive ships incredibly ponderous: although able to accelerate at a respectable clip, they couldn't change direction rapidly, and to the Festival, they were detectable almost out to interstellar ranges. In contrast, a gimbaled reaction motor could change thrust vector fast enough to invite structural breakup if the ship wasn't built to withstand the stresses. And while a fusion torch seen from astern was enough to burn out sensors at a million kilometers, the exhaust stream was very directional, with little more than a vague hot spot visible from in front of a ship.

With the much larger infrared emitter of the planet behind them, the Bouncers accelerated toward the New Republic first squadron at a bone-crushing hundred gees. Able to triangulate on the enemy by monitoring their drive emissions, the Bouncers peaked at 800 k.p.s., then shut down their torches and drifted silently, waiting for the moment of closest approach.

the operations room of the *Lord Vanek* was tense and quiet.

"Gunnery Two, ready a batch of six SEM-20s. Dial them all to one-zero-zero kilotonnes, tune the first two for maximum EMP, next three for spallation debris along main axis. Gunnery One, I want two D-4 torpedoes armed for passive launch with a one-minute motor-on delay inlined into them."

Captain Mirsky sat back in his chair. "Prediction?" he muttered in the direction of Commander Vulpis.

"Holding ready, sir. A bit disturbing that we haven't seen anything yet, but I can give you full maneuvering power within forty seconds of getting a drive signal."

"Good. Radar. Anything new?"

"Humbly report nothing's new on passive, sir."

"Deep joy." They were two hours out from perigee. Mirsky had to fight to control his impatience. Tapping his fingers on the arm of his chair, he sat and waited for a sign, anything to indicate that there was life elsewhere in this empty cosmos. The fatal ping of a lidar illuminator glancing off the *Lord Vanek*'s stealthed hull, or the ripple of gravitomagnetic waves; anything to show that the enemy was out there, somewhere between the battle ship squadron and its destination.

"Any thoughts, Commander Vulpis?"

Vulpis's eyes flickered around the fully manned stations in front of him. "I'd be a lot happier if they were making the effort to paint us. Either we've taken 'em completely by surprise, or ...."

"Thank you for that thought," Mirsky commented under his breath. "Marek!"

"Sir!"

"You've got a rifle. It's loaded. Don't shoot till you see the whites of their eyes."

"Sir?" Vulpis stared at his Captain.

"I will be in my cabin if anything happens," Mirsky said lightly. "You have the helm, pending Commander Murametz's or my own return. Call me at once if there's any news."

Down in his stateroom, directly under the ops room, Mirsky collapsed into his chair. He sighed deeply, then poked at the dial of his phone. "Switchboard. My compliments to the Commodore and if he has a spare moment? Jolly good." A minute later, the phonescreen dinged. "Sir!"

"Captain." Commodore Bauer wore the expression of a very busy, very tired manager.

"I have a report for you on the, ah, annoyance. If you have time for it now."

Bauer made a steeple of his fingers. "If you can keep it short," he said gloomily.

"Not difficult." Mirsky's eyes glittered in the gaslight. "It was all the fault of my idiot of an intelligence officer. If he hadn't managed to kill himself, I'd have him in irons." He took a deep breath. "But he didn't act alone. As it is, sir, in confidence, I would recommend a reprimand for my FO, Fleet Commander Murametz, if not formal proceedings—except that we are so close to the enemy that—"

"Details, Captain. What did he do?"

"Lieutenant Sauer exceeded his authority by attempting to draw out the Terran spy—the woman, I mean—by means of a faked trial. He somehow convinced Commander Murametz to cover him, damned error of judgment if you ask me: he had no job making a mess in diplomat territory. Anyway, he pushed too hard, and the woman panicked. Ordinarily this would be no problem, but she somehow—" He coughed into his fist.

Bauer nodded. "I think I can guess the rest. Where is she now?"

Mirsky shrugged. "Outside the ship, with the dockyard contractor. Missing, probably suited up, don't know where they are, don't know what in *hell* they thought they were doing—the Procurator's missing too, sir, and there's an embarrassing hole in our side where there used to be a cabin."

Slowly, the Commodore began to smile. "I don't think you need waste any time searching for them, Captain. If we found them, we'd only have to throw them overboard again, what? I suppose the Procurator had a hand in this kangaroo court, didn't he?"

"Ah, I suppose so, sir."

"Well, this way we don't have to worry about the civilians. And if they get a little sunburned during the engagement, no matter. I'm sure you'll take care of everything that needs doing."

"Yes, sir!" Mirsky nodded.

"So," Bauer said crisply, "that's tied down. Now, in your analysis, we should be entering the enemy's proximity defense sphere when?"

Mirsky paused for thought. "About two hours, sir. That's assuming that our emcon was sufficient and the lack of active probes is a genuine indication that they don't know we're out here."

"I'm glad you added that qualifier. What's your schedule for working up to stations?"

"We're ready right now, sir. That is, there are some inessential posts that won't lock down for another hour or so, but the ops crew and black gang are already on combat watch, and gunnery is standing by the weapons. The mess is due to send around some hot food, but in principle, we're ready for action at a moment's notice."

"Very good." Bauer paused and glanced down at his desk. Rubbed the side of his nose with one long, bony finger. Then he glanced up. "I don't like this silence, Captain. It stinks of a trap."

Martin and rachel glanced up in reflexive terror, seeking the source of the noise.

Aboard a spacecraft, any noise from outside spells trouble— big trouble. Their lifeboat was drifting toward Rochard's World at well over solar escape velocity; a BB pellet stationary in their path would rip through them with the force of an antishipping missile. And while warships like the *Lord Vanek* could carry centimeters of foamed diamond armor and shock bumpers to absorb spallation fragments, the lifeboat's skin was thin enough to puncture with a penknife.

"Masks," snapped Rachel. A mess of interconnected transparent bags with complex seals and some sort of gas tank inside coiled from the console opposite Martin and bounced into his lap; for her part, she reached behind her seat and pulled out a helmet. Yanking it on over her head, she let its rim melt into her leotard, dripping sealant down her neck. Crude icons blinked inside the visor. She breathed out, relieved, hearing the fan whine behind her right ear. Beside her, Martin was still stuffing himself into the transparent cocoon. She looked up. "Pilot. Topside sensor view, optical, center screen."

"Oh shit," Martin said indistinctly.

The screen showed an indistinct blur that moved against a backdrop of pinprick stars. As they watched, the blur receded, dizzyingly fast, and sharpened into a recognizable shape. Moving.

She turned and stared at Martin. "Whoever he is, we can't leave him out there," he said.

"Not with a rescue beacon," she agreed grimly. "Pilot. Oxygen supply. Recalculate on basis of fifty percent increase in consumption. How does it affect our existing survival margin?"

An amber GANT chart flickered across the screen. "Bags of room," Martin commented. "What about landfall? Hmm." He prodded at his PA. "I think we can make it," he added. "Mass ratio isn't so much worse."

"Think or know?" she replied pointedly. "If we get halfway

down and run out of go-juice, it could put a real damper on this day-trip."

"I'm aware of that. Let me see . . . yeah. We'll be okay, Rachel. Whoever designed this boat must have thought you'd be carrying one hell of a diplomatic bag with you. More like a wardrobe."

"Don't *say* that." She licked her lips. "Question two. We take him on board. How are we going to stop him if he decides to get in the way?"

"I think you get to use your feminine wiles on him," Martin deadpanned.

"I should have known you'd come up with something like that." Wearily, she groped for the stun gun. "This won't work in vacuum, you know? And it's not a good idea to use the sucker in a confined space either."

"Talking of confined spaces." Martin pointed to the rather basic mass detector display. "Twelve kilometers and drifting. We don't want to be this close when they spin up for combat."

"No, we don't," Rachel agreed. "Okay. I'm as ready as I'll ever be. You got confirmation on suit integrity? Once we vent, you won't be able to move much." Martin nodded, held up a balloon-bloated glove. Rachel cranked open her oxygen regulator and yawned, deliberately, hunting the roof of the cabin for an attachment point for her survival tether. "Okay. Pilot, EVA cycle. Prepare to depressurize cabin."

an alarm pinged in the operations room.

"Contact." Lieutenant Kokesova leaned over his subordinate's shoulder and stared at the gauges on his console. Lights blinked violet and green. "I say again, contact."

"Accepted." Lieutenant Marek swallowed. "Comms, please signal captain to the ops room and condition red."

"Aye aye, sir." A red light began to strobe by the doorway. "Any specifics?" asked Marek.

"Tracking. I have a definite fusion source, came up about two-zero seconds ago. I thought at first it was a sensor malfunction but it's showing blue-shifted Balmer lines, and it's bright as hell— black body temperature would be in the five-zero-zero M-degree range. Traveling at well above local stellar escape velocity."

"Very good." Marek tried to lean back in the command chair but failed, unable to force himself to relax that much. "Time to get a solution on it?"

"Any minute." Lieutenant Kokesova, tech specialist, demonstrating his proficiency once again. "I'll see if I can pickle some neutrinos for you."

The door opened, and the guard beside it came to attention. Lieutenant Marek spun around and saluted stiffly. "Sir!"

"What's the situation?"

"Humbly report we have a provisional fix on one incoming, sir," said Marek. "We're still waiting for a solution, but we have a blue-shifted fusion torch. Looks like we're looking straight up their endplate mirror."

Mirsky nodded. "Very good, Lieutenant. Is there anything else?"

"Anything else?" Marek was flustered. "Not unless something's come up—"

"Contact!" It was the same sensor op. He looked up apologetically. "Begging your pardon, sir."

"Describe." It was the Captain's turn.

"Second fusion source, about two M-kilometers above and south of the first. It's tracking on a parallel course. I have a preliminary solution, looks like they're vectoring to pass us at about one-zero-zero K-klicks, decelerating from eight-zero-zero k.p.s. Time to intercept, two K-seconds."

"Any other activity?" asked Mirsky.

"Activity, sir?"

"You know. Anomalous lateral acceleration. Jamming, comms traffic, luminous pink tentacles, whatever. Anything else?"

"No, sir."

"Well, then." Mirsky stroked his beard thoughtfully. "Something doesn't add up."

The door to the bridge opened again; Lieutenant Helsingus came in. "Permission to take fire control, sir?"

"Do it." Mirsky waved his hand. "But first, riddle me this: Why by the Emperor's beard can we see two drive torches, but nothing else?"

"Ah—" Marek shut up.

"Because," Commander Vulpis said over Mirsky's shoulder, "it's an entrapment, Captain."

"I don't know how you could possibly imagine such a thing; they're obviously inviting us to a dinner dance." Mirsky grinned nastily. "Hmm. You think they ditched a bunch of mines before they fired up the torches?"

"Quite possibly." Vulpis nodded. "In which case, we're going to get hit in about"— he punched at his board—"two-five-zero seconds, sir. We won't be in range of anything you can cram on a mine for very long, but at this speed, even a cloud of sand would make a mess of us."

Mirsky leaned forward. "*Guns.* Point defense to automatic! Comms, please request an ack from the commodore's staff, and from *Kamchatka* and *Regina.* Make sure they're watching for mines." He smiled grimly. "Time to see what they're made of, I think. Comms, my compliments to the Commodore, and please say that I am requesting permission to terminate emission control for defensive reasons."

"Aye aye, sir."

Emission controls were desperately important to a warship. Active sensors like radar and lidar required an echo from a foreign body to confirm its presence; but a sufficiently distant (or stealthed) body wouldn't return an echo loud enough to pick up. Sending out the initial pulse gave away a ship's position with great accuracy to any enemy who happened to be stooging around outside the return range but within passive detection range. By approaching Rochard's World under emission control, the battle squadron had attempted to conceal themselves. The first ship to start actively radiating would make its presence glaringly obvious—painting a target on itself in the process of lighting up the enemy.

"Sir?"

"Yes, Lieutenant Marek?"

"What if there are more than two ships out there? I mean, we carry probes and a shuttle. What if we're up against some kind of larger force, and the two we can see are just a decoy?"

Captain Mirsky grinned humorlessly. "That's not a possibility, Lieutenant, it's a near certainty."

"Mine intercept waypoint one, four minutes." Vulpis read off timings from the glowing nixie tubes before him. He glanced up at the command chair; Captain Mirsky, seated there, nodded.

"Weapons, arm torpedoes, stand by on missiles. Remotes, status on red, blue, orange." Mirsky was calm and collected, and his presence was a settling influence on the otherwise tense ops room crew.

The red telephone rang, jangling. Mirsky listened, briefly, then replaced the handset. "Radar. You have permission to radiate."

Radar One: "Going active now, sir. One-zero-second pulse-doppler train, four octave agile spread, go to jamming sequence alpha afterward. Decoys, sir?"

"You may launch decoys." Mirsky folded his hands in his lap and gazed straight ahead at the main screen. Beneath the calm exterior, he was seriously worried; he was gambling his life and his ship—and all those aboard her—on a hypothesis about the nature of their pursuers. He wasn't confident, but he was sufficiently well informed to make an educated guess about what was after them. *Maybe the UN woman had the right idea,* he thought gloomily. He glanced around the ops room. "Commander Helsingus. Status, please?"

The bearded gunnery officer nodded. "First four rounds loaded as per order, sir. Two self-propelled torpedoes with remote ignition patches on my board, followed by six passive-powered missiles rigged for EMP in a one-zero-degree spread. Laser grid programmed for tight point-defense. Ballistic point-defense programs loaded and locked."

"Good. Helm?"

"Holding steady on designated fleet approach pattern, sir. No evasion authorized by staff."

"Radar?"

Lieutenant Marek stood up. He looked tense and drawn, new lines forming around his eyes. "Humbly report, sir, active is on cold clamp. Passive shows nothing yet, except on infrared trace, but that should give us a fix in"—he glanced down—"about three minutes and counting. Decoy is overboard, running out to radiation rangepoint one." The decoy—a small unpowered drone trailing behind the warship on a ten-kilometer-long tether—was preparing to radiate an EM signature identical to that of the ship: synchronized by interferometer with the active sensors aboard the *Lord Vanek,* it would help confuse any enemy sensors as to the exact position of the battlecruiser.

"Good." Mirsky looked at the clock beside the main forward display, then glanced down at the workstation before him. Time for the checklist. "At waypoint one, be prepared to commence burn schedule one on my word. That's four-zero gees continuous until we build up to six-zero k.p.s. then shut down, full damping, course three-six-zero by zero by zero on current navigation lock. Comms, notify all elements of squadron one. Guns, at time zero plus five seconds, be prepared to drop torps one and two, on my word. Comms, signal torpedo passive drop to Squadron One. Please confirm."

"Aye aye, sir. One and Two"—Helsingus snapped a brass switch over—"are armed for passive drop at time plus five."

"Good."

"Time to possible mine intercept, two minutes, sir."

"Thank you Nav Two, I can see the clock from here." Mirsky gritted his teeth. "Helm, status."

"Program locked. Main engine is available for burn in five-zero seconds, sir."

"Radar, update."

"We should pick 'em up in about two minutes, sir. No emissions—" Lieutenant Marek stopped. "What's that?"

Radar Two: "Contact, sir! Lidar registers ping one. Waiting for—"

An alarm shrilled. "Something just pinged us, sir," said Marek.

Everybody except the radar techs were staring at Mirsky. He caught Helsingus's eye and nodded. "Track beta."

"Aye aye, sir. Guns Two, track beta." An almost imperceptible thump shuddered through the structure of the battlecruiser as the main axial launch coil spat twenty tonnes of intricately machined heavy metal and fuel out through the nose of the ship. A second bump signaled the release of the second torpedo. Drifting unpowered, cold but for their avionics packages, they would wait behind when the *Lord Vanek* began to accelerate.

"Minus three-zero seconds," called Nav Two.

"Beg to report on the contact, sir," said Marek.

"Speak, Nav."

"We managed to get a look at the pulse train on the contact, and it looks, um, strange. Noisy, if you follow my meaning; they've done a good job of concealing their recognition signature."

"One-zero seconds."

"All posts switch to plan two," said Captain Mirsky. "Nav, pass that contact info on to *Kamchatka* and *Ekaterina*. Get anything you can off them." He picked up the phone to notify his squadron captains of the impending change of plan.

"Aye aye, sir. Plan two burn commencing in five . . . two, one, now." There was no change evident in the ops room, no shaking or shuddering or sudden leaden-limbed feeling of acceleration, but inside the guts of the starship, the extremal black hole twisted in sudden torment; the *Lord Vanek* fell forward at full military acceleration, four hundred meters per second squared, more than forty gees.

Another alarm trilled. Nav: "Full scan running." Twenty giga-watts of laser light beamed out in all directions, a merciless glare bright enough to melt steel at a range of kilometers. Down in the bowels of the ship, heat exchanges glowed red-hot, flashing water into saturated high-pressure steam and venting it astern; this close to combat, running out the huge, vulnerable heat exchangers would be suicidal.

Guns: "Track beta launch commencing." This time a real bump-and-grind made the ship shudder; the two missiles Helsin-gus had preloaded back when they'd been on the track alpha head-ing. As they hurtled ahead of the ship, a tenth of its total laser output focused up their tails, energizing their reaction mass.

This was the time of maximum danger, and Mirsky did his best to maintain a confident demeanor for the benefit of his crew. As the Commodore had put it in the privacy of his staff briefing room: "If they're smart, they'll send out just enough assets to make us reveal ourselves, then use whatever they've got in orbit to dump a snowstorm of mines in our path. They know where we're going; that's half the problem of pinpointing us. When we start radiating they'll get their solution—and it'll be a question of how much pounding they can hand out, and how much we can take."

Attacking a fixed point—in this case, the low-orbit installa-tions around a planet—was traditionally reputed to be the hardest task in deep-space warfare. The defenders could concentrate forces around it and rapidly bring defensive missile and laser screens to bear on anyone approaching; and if the attackers wanted to know just what they were attacking, they'd have to hang out high-energy signposts for the defenders to take aim on.

Seconds later, Mirsky breathed a quiet sigh of relief. "Point defense reports all quiet, sir. We're inside their envelope, but they don't seem to have dropped a minefield." Drifting mines wouldn't follow the deceleration curve of the enemy ships; they'd come slamming in way ahead of the warships that had dropped them overboard at peak velocity.

"That's good," Mirsky murmured. His eyes focused on the two red points on the main plotting screen. They were still decelerat-ing, painfully fast; almost as if they were aiming for a zero-relative-velocity slugging match. The *Lord Vanek*'s two missiles crawled toward them—in reality, boosting at a savage thousand gees, already over 1000 k.p.s. Presently, they shut down and coasted, retaining only enough reaction mass for terminal maneuvering when they got within ten seconds of the enemy. Ahead of the *Lord Vanek,* the glinting purple crosses of the unpowered torpedoes fell forward toward the enemy.

A minute later, Gunnery Two spoke up. "I've lost missile one, sir. I can ping it, but it doesn't respond."

"Odd—" Mirsky's brow furrowed; he glanced at the doomsday clock. The battlecruiser was closing on the destination at a crawl, just 40 k.p.s. The enemy was heading toward them at better than 200 k.p.s., decelerating, but their thrust was dropping off—if this continued, closing unpowered at 250 k.p.s., their paths would intersect in about 500 seconds, and they'd be within missile-powered flight range 200 seconds before that. These long, ballistic shots weren't expected to cause real damage, but if they came close, they would force the enemy to respond. But missile one had been more than 50,000 kilometers from the target—

"Humbly reporting, I've lost missile two as well, sir."

"That doesn't make sense," muttered Helsingus. He glanced at the plot: a flurry of six more missiles, all fired from the *Kamchatka,* was closing in on their target: ranging shots all, with little chance of doing any damage, but—

Point Defense: "Sir, problem on deck one. Looks like—humbly report a debris impact, sir, lost a scattering of eyeballs on the lidar grid but nothing broke the inner pressure hull."

"Looks like they've got bad dandruff," Mirsky commented. "But their point defense is working. Torpedoes?"

"Not yet, sir," said Helsingus. "They've only got about five-zero-zero k.p.s. of delta-vee. Won't be in position to light off for, ah, eight-zero more seconds." Drifting toward the enemy almost 100 k.p.s. faster than the warship that had launched them, the torpedoes nevertheless had relatively short legs. Unlike the missiles, they had their own power plant, radar, and battle control computers, which made them valuable assets in event of an engagement—but they accelerated more slowly and had a lower total acceleration budget.

Radar Two: "Humbly report I think I spotted something, sir. About one-zero-zero milliseconds after missile two dropped off, detector three trapped a neutrino pulse; impossible to say for sure whether it came from the target or the missile, but it looked fairly energetic. Ah, no sign of any other radiation."

"Most peculiar," Mirsky murmured under his breath: an extreme understatement. "What's our range profile?"

"Torpedo range in six-zero seconds. Active gunnery range in one-five-zero seconds; contact range in four-zero-zero seconds. Closest pass two-zero K-kilometers, speed on the order of two-six-zero k.p.s. assuming no maneuvering. Range to target is one-zero-five K-kilometers on my mark, now."

"Hah." Mirsky nodded. "Gentlemen, this may look preposterous, but I have a problem with the way things are going. Helsingus, your two torpedoes—torch 'em off straight at bogey one."

"But they'll go ballistic short of—"

Mirsky raised a warning hand. "Just do it. Helm, option three-two. Signal all ships." Once again, he picked up the phone to the Commodore's battle room to confer with his flag officer.

"Aye aye, sir." The display centered on Rochard's World shifted, rolling; the orange line representing *Lord Vanek*'s course, hitherto straight in toward the planet, began to bend, curving away from the planet. The red lines showing the course of the two incoming enemy ships were also bending, moving to intercept the *Lord Vanek* and her five sister ships; meanwhile the twelve dots of blue, representing the torpedoes the squadron had dropped overboard almost two minutes earlier, began to grow outward.

Live torpedoes were not something any starship captain wanted to get too close to. Unlike a missile—essentially a tube full of reaction mass with a laser mirror in its tail and a warhead at the other end—a torpedo was a spacecraft with its own power plant, an incredibly dirty fission rocket, little more than a slow-burning atom bomb, barely under control as it spewed a horribly radioactive exhaust stream behind it. It was also the most efficient storable-fuel rocket motor available, without the complexity of fusion reactors or curved-space generators. Before the newer technologies came along, early-twenty-first-century pioneers had used it for the first crewed interplanetary missions.

"Fish are both running, sir. Ours are making nine-six and one-one-two gees respectively; general squadron broadside averages ninety-eight. They should burn out and switch to sustainer in one-zero-zero seconds and intersect bogeys one and two if they stay on current course in about one-five-zero seconds. Guidance pack degradation should still be under control by then, we should be able to do terminal targeting control."

"Good," Mirsky said shortly. Heading in on the *Lord Vanek* on a reciprocal course, the enemy ships might well be able to start shooting soon: but the torpedoes would get in the way nicely, messing up the clear line of sight on the *Lord Vanek* while threatening them. Which was exactly what Mirsky was hoping for.

There was something extremely odd about the two ships, he noted. They weren't following any kind of obvious tactical doctrine, just accelerating in a straight line, pulsing with lidar as they came—homing in blindly. There was no sign of sneaky moves. They'd lurched out and begun pinging away like drunken fools playing a barroom computer game, throwing away the advantage of concealment that they'd held. *Whoever was driving those birds is either a fool or—*

"Radar," he said softly. "Saturation cover forward and down. Anything there?"

"I'll look." Marek gulped, getting the Captain's drift immediately. If these two were hounds, flushing their game out of hiding, something would be drifting in quietly from ahead. Not mines dropped at peak velocity, but something else. Maybe something worse, like a brace of powered torpedoes. "Um, humbly suggest optical scan as well, sir?"

"It can't fix us for them any better," Mirsky grunted. "They know where we are."

Radar Two: "Sir, nothing on mass. Nothing within two light-seconds ahead or down. Small amount of organic debris—we passed through a thin cloud of it back at waypoint one, picked up a couple of scratches on the nose—but no sign of escorts or weapons."

"Sir, we are all clear ahead," said Lieutenant Marek.

"Well, keep looking then." Mirsky looked down at his hands. They were tightly entwined in his lap, veins standing out on their backs, old hands, the fine hair at his wrists turning gray. "How did I get this far?" he asked himself quietly.

His workstation pinged. "Incoming call for you, sir," it said.

"Damn." He punched up the image. It was Commodore Bauer.

"I'm busy," he said tersely. "Torpedo run. Can it wait?"

"I don't think so. There is something very flaky going on. Why do you think they aren't shooting?"

"Because they've already shot at us, but the bullets haven't arrived yet," Mirsky said through gritted teeth.

Bauer stared at his Flag Captain for a moment, wordless agreement written on his face. Then he nodded. "Get us the hell out of here, Captain. I'll tell the rest of the squadron to follow your lead. Just give me as much delta-vee as you can between us and those—whatever."

Radar Two: "Time to torpedo closest approach, eight-zero seconds. Sir, there are no signs that wolf one or two has seen the fish. But they're well within sensor range if they're using something equivalent to our G-90s."

"Understood." Mirsky paused. Something was nagging at the back of his mind; a nasty sense of having forgotten something. That neutrino pulse, that was it. Neutrinos meant strong nuclear force. So why no flash? "Guns, load up twelve SEM-20s for tail drop at shortest intercept course. Assuming they come in from behind." He glanced back at his screen, but the commodore had hung up on him without waiting.

"Aye aye. Birds loaded." Helsingus seemed almost happy, twitching levers and adjusting dials. It was the nearest thing to pleasure Mirsky remembered the dour gunnery officer showing since his dog had disappeared. "Ready at minus one-zero seconds."

"Helm." Mirsky paused. "Prepare to execute plan bugout on my command."

An alarm warbled at the radar desk. "Beg to report sir," began the petty officer on duty, face whey-pale: "I've lost *Prince Vaclav.*"

Faces looked up in shock all around the room. "What do you mean, lost it?" snapped Vulpis, bypassing the operational pecking order. "You didn't just lose a battlecruiser—"

"Sir, she's stopped responding. Stopped accelerating, too. I can see her on plot, but there's something wrong with her—" The radar operator paused. "Sir, I can't get an IFF heartbeat out of her. And she's reflecting way too much energy—something must have ripped the front off her emission control coating."

"Helm. Execute plan bugout," Mirsky snapped in the sudden silence that followed the report.

"Aye aye, sir, bugout it is." Lieutenant Vulpis began flipping switches in a frenzy.

A fundamental problem with combat in space was that if things began to go wrong, they could do so with dizzying speed—and to make matters worse, catastrophe would only become visible to a ship that was so deep into the enemy's powered-missile envelope that escape was nearly impossible. Mirsky had gamed this situation repeatedly with Bauer and the other fleet captains; plan bugout was the result. It was a lousy plan, the only thing to commend it being the fact that all the alternatives were worse. Something had just reached out across ninety thousand kilometers and bushwhacked a battlecruiser. This wasn't entirely unexpected; they were here to fight, after all. But they hadn't seen any missiles, only their own birds and the debris from the blow-out drifting in ahead of them, and the fine drizzle of organic "dandruff" from the enemy ships—and in active mode, the *Lord Vanek*'s lidar could pin down a missile at almost a light-second, three hundred thousand kilometers. If the enemy had a beam weapon of some kind that was capable of trashing a capital ship at that range, nearly two orders of magnitude greater than their own point-defense energy weapons, they were already too damned close. All they could do was turn side-on and go to emergency thrust, generating a vector away from the enemy before they could respond.

Radar Two: "Torpedo intersect in four-zero seconds. Wolves one and two still tracking on course, acceleration down to one gee."

"Well, that's nice to know. Mr. Helsingus, I would appreciate it if you'd be so good as to prepare a warm welcome for anything our friends try to send after us. I don't know just what they threw at *Prince Vaclav*, but I don't propose to give them time to show us. And if you gentlemen will excuse me for a minute, I have a private call to make." Mirsky pulled on his headset and pushed down on the antisound lever. "Comms, get me the Commodore." His earpieces clicked. "Sir?"

"Have you started bugout?"

"Yes, sir. The *Prince Vaclav*—"

The screech of the decompression alarm cut through his ears like a knife. "By the numbers, damn you!" yelled Mirsky. "Suit up!" He yanked off his headset. Officers and men dashed to the emergency locker at the rear of the compartment and pulled their gear on, stumbled back to man posts while their backups followed suit. The ops room had already cycled onto its emergency supply, along with all the main nerve centers of the ship, but Mirsky wasn't one to take chances. Not that being suited up would count for much protection in ship-to-ship combat, but decompression was another threat entirely, one dreaded aboard any starship almost as much as fire or Hawking radiation. "Damage control, talk to me," he grunted. A passing CPO held out a suit for him; he stood up and pulled it on slowly, making sure to double-check its status display.

"Humbly report a big pressure drop on A deck, sir. Critical

decompression, we're still venting air. Ah, humbly report there appears to be some damage to lidar emitter quadrant three."

"You make sure everybody's buttoned down. Guns, Radar, where do we stand?"

Radar One: "Torpedo intercept in one-five seconds. Bogey holding course, due to pass inside our terminal engagement envelope for two-zero seconds in one-two-zero then drop behind."

Helsingus nodded. "All tubes loaded," he reported.

"Damage Control: Patch into life support and find out what the hell is loose."

"Got it already, sir. I've got some kind of contamination, source inside life support one: weird organic molecules, low concentration. Also, er, localized outbreaks of fire. It's mostly around A deck. The lidar grid damage is localized, around where the debris strike happened. Ah, I have one-six crew marked down on the status board. A deck segment two is open to space, and they were all inside at the time."

Gunnery: "Five seconds to torpedo terminal boost phase."

"Let's dazzle 'em now," said Helsingus. "Grid to full power."

"Aye aye, sir, full multispectral shriek in progress."

Helsingus leaned sideways and muttered into his headset; Radar One muttered back. There was some mutual adjustment of switches as radar relinquished priority control on the huge phased-array laser grid that coated the warship, then Helsingus and his two assistants began entering instructions.

The *Lord Vanek* boosted at right angles to the two enemy craft, accelerating away from the two silent pursuers on a ripple of warped space-time. The two saltwater-fission torpedoes, bright sparks behind, accelerated toward the enemy warships like a pair of nuclear fireworks. Now the tight-packed mosaic of panels that covered much of the *Lord Vanek*'s cylindrical bulk began to glow with the intense speckled purity of laser light. A thousand different colors appeared, blending and clashing and forming a single brilliant diadem of light; megawatts, then gigawatts of power surged out, the skin of the ship burning like a directional magnesium flare. The glow built up, and most of it flowed out in two tightly controlled beams, intense enough to cut through steel plate like a blowtorch at a range of a thousand kilometers.

Simultaneously, the flight of torpedoes throttled up to maximum thrust, weaving erratically as they closed the final three thousand kilometers to the onrushing enemy ships. Hurtling in ten times faster than an ICBM of the pre–space age, the rockets jinked and wove to avoid the anticipated point-lasers, relying on passive sensors and sophisticated antispoofing algorithms to cut through the expected jamming and countermeasures of the enemy ships. They took barely thirty seconds to close the distance, and found the enemy point defense to be almost nonexistent.

From the ops room of the *Lord Vanek,* the engagement was undramatic. One of the pursuer points simply disappeared, replaced by an expanding shell of spallation debris and hot gases energized by an incandescent point far brighter than any conventional fission explosion; with the ship's hull blown wide and drive mountings shattered, the antimatter bottle spilled its contents into a soup of metallic hydrogen, triggering a mess of exotic subnuclear reactions. But only one of the torpedoes struck home; the other eleven winked out.

"Humbly report got more neutrino pulses, sir," called the radar op. "Not from the one we nailed—"

Mirsky stared at the main screen. "Damage control. What about A deck?" he demanded. "Helm. Everyone else running on bugout?"

"A deck is still empty to space, sir. I sent a control team, but they aren't reporting back. Pressure's dropping in the number four recycler run, no sign of external venting. Um, I'm showing a major power drain on the grid, sir, we're losing megawatts somewhere."

"Bugout message was sent a minute ago, sir. So far they're all—" Vulpis cursed. "Sir! *Kamchatka*'s gone!"

"Where, dammit?" Mirsky leaned forward.

"Another IFF drop-off," called radar. "From—" The man paused, eyes widening with shock. "*Kamchatka,*" he concluded. On the main plot at the front of the bridge, the Imperial ships' vectors were lengthening, up to 300 k.p.s. now and creeping up steadily. The target planet hung central, infinitely far out of reach.

Mirsky glanced at his first officer. Ilya stared back apprehensively.

"With respect, sir, they're not fighting any way we know—"

Red lights. Honking sirens. Damage Control shouting orders into his speaking horn. "Status!" roared Mirsky. "What's going on, dammit?"

"Losing pressure on B deck segment one, sir! No readings anywhere on segment three from A down to D deck. Big power fluctuations, distribution board fourteen compartment D-nine-five is on fire. Ah, I have a compartment open to space and another compartment on fire in B-four-five. I can't get through to damage control on B deck at all and all hell has broken loose on C deck—"

"Seal off everything above F," ordered Mirsky, his face white. "Do it *now!* Guns, prep decoys two and three for launch—"

But he was already too late to save his ship; because the swarm of bacteria-sized replicators that had slammed into A deck at 600 k.p.s.—cushioned in a husk of reinforced diamond—and eaten their way down through five decks into the ship, were finally arriving in the engineering spaces. And eating, and breeding...

vassily's voice quavered with a nervous, frightened edge that would have been funny under other circumstances. "I am arresting you for sabotage, treason, unlicensed use of proscribed technologies, and giving aid and comfort to the enemies of the New Republic! Surrender now, or it will be the worse for you!"

"Shut up and grab the back of that couch unless you want to walk home. Martin, if you wouldn't mind giving him a leg down—that's right. I need to get this hatch shut—"

Rachel glanced around disgustedly. There was a beautiful view; stars everywhere, a terrestrial planet hanging huge and gibbous ahead, like a marbled blue-and-white hallucination—and this idiot child squawking in her ear. Meanwhile, she was clinging with both hands to the underside of the capsule lid, and with both feet to the pilot's chair, trying to hold everything together. When she'd poked her head up through the hatch and seen who was clinging to the low-gain antenna, she'd had half a mind to duck back inside again and fire up the thrusters to jolt him loose; a stab of blind rage made her grind her teeth together so loudly a panicky Martin had demanded to know if her suit had sprung a leak. But the red haze of anger faded quickly, and she'd reached out and grabbed Vassily's arm, and somehow shoved his inflated emergency suit in through the hatch.

"I'm coming down," she said. Clenching her thighs around the back of the chair, she clicked the release catch on the hatch and pulled it down as far as she could, then locked it in position. The cabin below her was overfull: Vassily obviously didn't have a clue about keeping himself out of the way, and Martin was busy trying to squirm into the leg well of his seat to make room. She yanked on her lifeline, dropped down until she was standing on the seat of her chair, then grabbed the hatch and pulled it the rest of the way shut. She felt the solid ripple-click of a dozen small catches locking home on all four sides. "Okay. Autopilot, seal hatch, then repressurize cabin. Martin, not over there—that's the toilet, you really don't want to open that—yes, that's the locker you want." Air began hissing into the cabin from vents around the ceiling; white mist formed whirlpool fog banks that drifted across the main window. "That's great. You, listen up: you aren't aboard a Navy ship here. Shut up, and we'll give you a lift downside; keep telling me I'm under arrest, and I might get pissed off enough to push you overboard."

"Urp."

The Junior Procurator's eyes went wide as his suit began to deflate around him. Behind the seats, Martin grunted as he rifled through the contents of one of the storage lockers. "This what you want?" He punted a rolled-up hammock at Rachel. She rolled around in her seat and stuck one end of it to the wall behind her, then let it unroll back toward Martin. He drifted out of the niche, narrowly avoided kicking their castaway in the head, and managed to get the other end fastened. "You. Out of that suit, into this hammock. As you may have noticed, we don't have a lot of room." She pressed the release stud, and her helmet let go of her suit and drifted free; catching it, she shoved it down behind her seat, under the hammock. "You can unsuit now."

Martin peeled halfway out of his own suit, keeping his legs and lower body in the collapsed plastic bag. Vassily floated out of his niche, struggling with the flaccid bladder of his helmet: Martin steered him into the hammock and managed to get his head out of the bag before he managed to inhale it. "You're—" Vassily stopped. "Er, thank you."

"Don't even *think* about hijacking us," Rachel warned darkly. "The autopilot's slaved to my voice, and neither of us particularly wants to take our chances with your friends."

"Er." Vassily breathed deeply. "Um. That is to say—" He looked around wildly. "Are we going to die?"

"Not if I have anything to do with it," Rachel said firmly.

"But the enemy ships! They must be—"

"It's the Festival. Have you got any idea what they are?" asked Martin.

"If you know anything about it, you should have told the Admiral's staff. Why didn't you tell them? Why—"

"We *did* tell them. They didn't listen," Rachel observed.

Vassily visibly struggled to understand. Ultimately, it was easier to change the subject than think the unthinkable. "What are you going to do now?"

"Well." Rachel whistled tunelessly through her front teeth. "Personally, I'd like to land this lifeboat somewhere near, say, Novy Petrograd, book the honeymoon suite in the Crown Hotel, fill the bathtub with champagne, and lie in it while Martin feeds me caviar on black bread. However, what we actually do next really depends on the Festival, hmm? If Martin is right about it—"

"Believe it," Martin emphasized.

"—the Navy force is going to quietly disappear, never to be seen again. That's what comes of assuming that everyone plays by the same set of rules. We're just going to drift on through, then fire up our motor for a direct landing, meanwhile squawking that we're neutral at the top of our voices. The Festival isn't what your leaders think it is, kid. It's a threat to the New Republic—they got that much right—but they don't understand what *kind* of threat it is, or how to deal with it. Going in shooting will only make it respond in kind, and it's better at it than your boys."

"But our Navy is good!" Vassily insisted. "They're the best navy within twenty light-years! What would you anarchists do? You don't even have a strong government, much less a fleet!"

Rachel chuckled. After a moment, Martin joined in. Gradually their laughter mounted, deafening in the confined space.

"Why are you laughing at me?" Vassily demanded indignantly.

"Look." Martin hunched around in his chair until he could lock eyes with the Procurator. "You've grown up with this theory of strong government, the divine right of the ruling class, the thwack of the riding crop of firm administration on the bare buttocks of the urban proletariat and all that. But has it occurred to you that the UN system also works, and has maybe been around for twice as long as the New Republic? There's more than one way to run a circus, as I think the Festival demonstrates, and rigid hierarchies like the one you grew up in are lousy at dealing with change. The UN system, at least after the Singularity and the adoption of the planetary unconstitution—" He snorted.

"Once, the fringe anarchists used to think the UN was some kind of quasi-fascist world government. Back in the twentieth and twenty-first centuries, when strong government was in fashion because the whole planetary civilization was suffering from future shock, because it was approaching a Singularity. After that passed, though—well, there weren't a lot of viable authoritarian governments left, and the more rigid they were, the less well they could deal with the aftereffects of losing nine-tenths of their populations overnight. Oh, and the cornucopiae: it can't be pleasant to run a central bank and wake up one morning to discover ninety percent of your taxpayers are gone and the rest think money is obsolete."

"But the UN is a government—"

"No it isn't," Martin insisted. "It's a talking shop. Started out as a treaty organization, turned into a bureaucracy, then an escrow agent for various transnational trade and standards agreements. After the Singularity, it was taken over by the Internet engineering task force. It's not the government of Earth; it's just the only remaining relic of Earth's governments that your people can recognize. The bit that does the common-good jobs that everyone needs to subscribe to. World-wide vaccination programs, trade agreements with extrasolar governments, insurer of last resort for major disasters, that sort of thing. The point is, for the most part, the UN doesn't actually *do* anything; it doesn't have a foreign policy, it's just a head on a stick for your politicians to rant about. Sometimes somebody or another uses the UN as a front when they need to do something credible-looking, but trying to get a consensus vote out of the Security Council is like herding cats."

"But you're—" Vassily paused. He looked at Rachel.

"I *told* your Admiral that the Festival wasn't human," she said tiredly. "He thanked me and carried right on planning an attack. That's why they're all going to die soon. Not enough flexibility, your people. Even trying to run a minor—and horrendously illegal—causality-violation attack wasn't that original a response." She sniffed. "Thought they'd turn up a week before the Festival, by way of that half-assed closed timelike path 'to avoid mines and sleepers.' As if the Eschaton wouldn't notice, and as if the Festival was just another bunch of primitives with atom bombs."

A red light winked on the console in front of her. "Oh, look," said Martin.

"It's beginning. Better strap yourself in—we're way too close for comfort."

"I don't understand. What's going on?" asked Vassily.

Martin reached up to adjust a small lens set in the roof of the cabin, then glanced over his shoulder. "Can you juggle, kid?"

"No. Why?"

Martin pointed at the screen. "Spine ships. Or antibodies. Subsentient remotes armed with, um, you don't want to know.

Eaters and shapers and *things*. Nasty hungry little nanomachines. Gray goo, in other words."

"Oh." Vassily looked ill. "You mean, they're going to—"

"Come out to meet the fleet and take a sniff, by the look of it. Unfortunately, I don't think Commodore Bauer realizes that if he doesn't make friendly noises, they're all going to die; he still thinks it's a *battle,* the kind you fight with missiles and guns. If they *do* decide to talk—well, the Festival is an infovore. We're perfectly safe as long as we can keep it entertained and don't shoot at it. Luckily, it doesn't understand humor; finds it fascinating, but doesn't quite get it. As long as we keep it entertained it won't eat us; we may even be able to escalate matters to a controlling intelligence that can let us off the Bouncers' hook and let us land safely." He reached into the bag of equipment he'd dredged out of the locker behind the seats. "Ready to start broadcasting, Rachel? Here, kid, put this on. It's showtime."

The red nose floating in the air in front of Vassily's face seemed to be mocking him.

the telephone repairman

sitting in a highly eccentric polar orbit that drifted almost sixty thousand kilometers above the provincial township of Plotsk, the Festival's prime node basked fat and happy at the heart of an informational deluge. The pickings in this system were sparse compared to some of the previous ports of call on its itinerary, but Rochard's World was still unusual and interesting. The Festival had chanced upon few primitive worlds in its travel, and the contrast with its memories of them was great.

Now, as the first starwisps departed—aimed forward at new, unvisited worlds, and back along its track to the hot-cores of civilization where it had stopped before—the Festival took stock. Events on the ground had not gone entirely satisfactorily; while it had accrued a good body of folklore, and not a little insight into the social mores of a rigidly static society, the information channels on offer were ridiculously sparse, and the lack of demand for its wares dismaying. Indeed, its main source of data had been the unfortunate minds forcibly uploaded by some of the more dissolute, not to say amoral, fringe elements. The Critics, with their perennial instinct to explain and dissect, were moaning continuously—something about the colony succumbing to a disastrous economic singularity—but that sort of thing wasn't the Festival's problem. It would soon be time to move on; the first tentative transmissions from Trader clades had been detected, burbling and chirping in the Oort cloud, and the job of opening up communications with this civilization was nearly done.

Each of the hundreds of starwisps the high-orbit launchers were dispatching carried one end of a causal channel: a black box containing a collection of particles in a quantum-entangled state with antiparticles held by the Festival. (By teleporting the known quantum state of a third particle into one of the entangled particles, data could be transmitted between terminals infinitely fast, using up one entangled quantum dot for each bit.) Once the starwisps arrived at their destinations, the channels would be hooked into the communications grid the Festival's creators had set out to construct. No longer limited by the choke point of the Festival's back channel to its last destination, the population of Rochard's World would be exposed to the full information flow of the polity it belonged to.

Out toward Sputnik, the Festival took note of some activity by Bouncers. They seemed to be clearing up a small mess: a handful of slow, inefficient ships that had approached without warning and opened fire on the Bouncers with primitive energy weapons. The Bouncers responded with patient lethality; anything that menaced them died. Some small craft slipped by, evidently not involved in the assault; a number of the second wave broke and ran, and they, too, were spared. But for the most part, the Festival ignored them. Anyone so single-mindedly hostile as to attack the Festival was hardly likely to be a good source of information: as for the others, it would have a chance to talk to them when they arrived.

Lhe air in the lifeboat was foul with a stench of sweat and stale farts. Rachel sat hunched over her backup console, staring unblinkingly at the criticality monitors while the rocket howled and rumbled beneath them: while a single output jitter might kill them before she could even blink, it made her feel better to go through the motions. Besides, she was totally exhausted: as soon as they touched down she had every intention of sleeping for three days. It had been fourteen hours since they escaped from the *Lord Vanek;* fourteen hours on top of a day and a sleepless night before. If she stopped making the effort to stay awake—

"Riddle this interrogative." The creature on the screen snapped its tusks, red light gleaming off fangs like blood. "Why not you Bouncers accept?"

"I couldn't possibly place myself further in their debt," she said as smoothly as she could manage. *Neutron flux stable at ten kilobecquerels per minute,* warned her implants. A hundred chest X rays, in other words, sustained for four hours during the deceleration cycle. The lifeboat's motor shuddered beneath her like something alive. Vassily's hammock swung behind her. He'd fallen asleep surprisingly fast once she convinced him they weren't going to throw him overboard, exhausted by the terror of four hours adrift spent waiting to die. Martin snored softly in the dim red light of the comms terminal, similarly tired. *Nothing like learning you aren't about to die to make you relax,* she thought. Which was why she couldn't sleep yet—

"No debt for payment in kind," said the strange creature. "You bear much reduction of entropy."

"Your translation program is buggy," she muttered.

"Is so interrogative? Suppose, we. Reiterate and paraphrase: question why you do not attack Bouncers like other ships?"

Rachel tensed. "Because we are not part of their expedition," she said slowly. "We have different intentions. We come in peace. Exchange information. We will entertain you. Is that understood?"

"Ahum. *Skreee*—" the thing in the screen turned its head right around to look over its shoulder. "We you understand. Will Bouncers of notify peaceful intent. You part are not of not-old administrative institution territoriality of planet?"

"No, we're from Earth." Martin stopped snoring: she glanced sideways. One eye was open, watching her tiredly. "Original world of humans," she clarified.

"Know about Dirt. Know about you-mans, too. Information valuable, tell all!"

"In due course," Rachel hedged, acutely aware of the thickening air in the capsule. "Are we safe from the Bouncers?"

"Am not understanding," the thing said blandly. "We are will notify Bouncers of your intent. Is that not safety?"

"Not exactly." Rachel glanced at Martin, who frowned at her and shook his head slightly. "If you notify the Bouncers that we are not attacking them, will that stop them from eating us?"

"Ahum!" The creature blinked at her. "Maybe not."

"Well, then. What *will* stop the Bouncers from attacking us?"

"*Skree*—why worry? Just talk."

"I'm not worrying. It's just that I am not going to tell you everything you want to know about me until I am no longer at risk from the Bouncers. Do you understand that?"

"Ha-*frumph*! Not entertaining us. Humph. A-okay, Bouncers will *not* eat you. We have dietary veto over theys. Now tell all?"

"Sure. But first—" She glanced at the autopilot monitor. "We're running low on breathable air. Need to land this ship. Is that possible? Can you tell me about conditions on the ground?"

"Sure." The creature bounced its head up-down in a jerky parody of a nod. "You not problem, land. May find things changed. Best dock here first. We Critics."

"I'm looking for a man," Rachel added, deciding to push her luck. "Have you installed a communications net? Can you locate him for us?"

"May exist. Name?"

"Rubenstein. Burya Rubenstein." A noise behind her; Vassily rolling over, his hammock swinging in the shifting inertial reference frame of the lifeboat.

"Excuse." The creature leaned forward. "Name Rubenstein? Revolutionary?"

"Yes." Martin frowned at her inquiringly: Rachel glanced sideways. *I'll explain later,* she thought at him.

"Knows Sister Burya. Sister Seventh of Stratagems. You business with have the Extropian Underground?"

"That's right." Rachel nodded. "Can you tell me where he is?"

"Do better." The thing in the screen grinned. "You accept orbital elements for rendezvous now. We take you there."

Behind her, Vassily was sitting up, his eyes wide.

ᴛʜᴇ ᴀᴅᴍɪʀᴀʟ ᴅɪᴅɴ'ᴛ want to board the lifeboat.

"D-d-d-d-" he drooled, left eye glaring, right eye slack and lifeless.

"Sir, please don't make a fuss. We need to go aboard now." Robard looked over his shoulder anxiously, as if half-expecting red-clawed disaster to come stooping and drooling through the airlock behind him.

"N-ever surrr—" Kurtz found the effort too much; his head flopped forward onto his chest.

Robard hefted his chair, and pushed forward, into the cramped confines of the boat. "Is he going to be alright?" Lieutenant Kossov asked fussily.

"Who knows? Just show me somewhere to lash his chair and we'll be off. More chance of getting help for him down—"

Sirens honked mournfully in the passage outside, and Robard winced as his ears popped. Kossov reached past another officer wearing the braid of a lieutenant commander and yanked the emergency override handle: the outer door of the lifeboat hissed shut. "What's going on?" someone called from up by the cockpit.

"Pressure breach in this section! Doors tight!"

"Aye, doors tight. Is the Admiral aboard?"

"Yes to that. You going?"

In answer, the deck heaved. Robard grabbed a stanchion and held on one-handed, bracing the Admiral's wheelchair with another hand as the lifeboat lurched. A rippling bang of explosive bolts severed its umbilical connection to the stricken warship, then it was falling—falling through a deliberately opened gap in the ship's curved-space field, which was otherwise strong enough to rip the small craft apart. Officers and a handful of selected enlisted men struggled to seize anchor points as whoever was in the hot seat played a fugue on the attitude thrusters, rolling the lifeboat out from behind the warship. Then the drive cut in with a gentle buzzing hiss from underfoot, and a modicum of weight returned them to the correct plane.

Robard bent to work on the wheelchair with a length of cable. "Someone help me with the Admiral," he asked.

"What do you need?" Lieutenant Kossov peered at him, owlish behind his pince-nez.

"Need to tie this chair down. Then—where are we landing? Is there a doctor aboard this boat? My master really needs to be taken to a hospital, as soon as possible. He's very ill."

"Indeed." The Lieutenant glanced at him sympathetically, then his gaze wandered to the somnolent Admiral. "Give me that."

Robard passed him the other end of the cable, and together they secured the wheelchair to four of the eye bolts that dotted the floor. Around them, the other surviving officers were taking stock of the situation, neatly unfolding emergency deceleration hammocks from overhead lockers and chatting quietly. The atmosphere aboard the lifeboat was subdued, chastened; they were lucky to be alive, ashamed not to be aboard the stricken battlecruiser. The fact that most of the survivors were officers from the admiral's staff didn't go amiss; the real warriors remained at their posts, trying valiantly to halt the plague that was eating the ship around them. In one corner, a junior lieutenant was sobbing inconsolably at the center of an embarrassed circle of silence.

The Admiral, oblivious to everything around him, mumbled and coughed querulously. Kossov leaned forward attentively. "Is there anything I can do for you, my Admiral?" he asked.

"I fear he's beyond our help," Robard said sadly. He rested a gentle hand on Kurtz's shoulder, steadying the Admiral in his chair. "Unless the surgeons can do something—"

"He's trying to talk," Kossov snapped. "Let me listen." He leaned close to the old warrior's face. "Can you hear me, sir?"

"A-a—" The Admiral gargled in the back of his throat.

"Don't excite him, I implore you! He needs rest!"

Kossov fixed the servant with a baleful eye. "Be silent for a minute."

"—Aah, arr—we—'oing?"

Robard started. "Humbly report we are on our way down to the planetary surface, sir," said the Lieutenant. "We should be arriving in the capital shortly." Nothing about the rest of the fleet, the disposition of which was anything but likely to arrive in the colonial capital.

"'Ood." The Admiral's face relaxed, eyelids drooping. "'Amprey. 'Ive'm wha' for." He subsided, evidently exhausted by the effort of speaking.

Robard straightened up: his eyes met those of the Lieutenant. "He never gives up," he said calmly. "Even when he ought to. It'll be the death of him one of these days . . ."

riding a chicken-legged hut through a wasteland that had recently gone from bucolic feudalism to transcendent posthumanism without an intervening stage, Burya Rubenstein drifted through a dream of crumbling empires.

The revolutionaries were ideologically committed to a transcendence that they hadn't fully understood—until it arrived whole and pure and incomprehensible, like an iceberg of strange information breaking the surface of a frozen sea of entropy. They hadn't been ready for it; nobody had warned them. They had hazy folk memories of Internets and cornucopiae to guide them, cargo-cult assertions of the value of technology—but they hadn't felt the elephant, had no sense of the shape the new phenomena took, and their desires caused new mutant strains to congeal out of the phase space of the Festival machinery.

Imagine not growing up with telephones—or faxes, video conferencing, on-line translation, gesture recognition, light switches. Tradition said that you could send messages around the world in an eyeblink, and the means to do so was called e-mail. Tradition didn't say that e-mail was a mouth morphing out of the nearest object and speaking with a friend's lips, but that was a more natural interpretation than strange textual commands and a network of post-office routers. The Festival, not being experienced in dealing with Earth-proximate human cultures, had to guess at the nature of the miracles being requested. Often, it got them wrong.

Burya knew all about communications; his grandfather had dandled him on his knee and passed on legends his own grandfather had told him, legends about management information systems that could tell the management everything they could possibly know about the world and more, legends about the strange genii of human resources that could bring forth any necessary ability at will. Some of the more wired dissidents of Novy Petrograd had cobbled together something which they, in turn, called a management information system: cameras squatted with hooded cyclopean eyes atop the garrets and rooflines of the city, feeding images into the digital nervous system of the revolution.

Before he'd left Plotsk, Burya had spent some time with Timoshevski. Oleg had applied the leeches to Burya's engorged sense of importance, reminding him that he was only a high official within the Novy Petrograd soviet, that the soviet, in turn, was only a benign parasite upon the free market, a load-balancing algorithm that would be abandoned when the true beauty of the level playing field could be established. Oleg had also applied the worms, which itched furiously (and occasionally burned) as they established contact with Burya's nervous system. He'd had to inquire pointedly as to the origins of Burya's strange sense of bourgeois incrementalism in order to goad his erstwhile colleague into accepting the upgrade, but in the end, Rubenstein had seen no alternative. Given his currently peripatetic occupation, he'd be sidelined by the Central Committee if he stayed out of touch much longer. And so it was that his head itched abominably, and he was plagued by strange visions as the worms of the Committee for State Communications forged a working relationship with his brain.

When Burya slept, he dreamed in rasterized false-color images, scanned from the rooftops of the capital. The revolution, eternally vigilant, multitasked on his lateral geniculate body, rousting slumbering synapses to recognize suspicious patterns of behavior. Burya found it both disturbing and oddly reassuring to see that the city, for all the changes wrought by the revolution, continued. Here a youth darted from shadow to shadow, evidently on a midnight assignation with his sweetheart; there a grimmer kind of conspiracy fomented, dogs fighting over the bones of temporal responsibility as a block warden stalked a resented house-owner with murder in his eye. Houses grew and fissioned in slow motion, great sessile beasts prodded hither and yon by their internal symbionts. It was all unspeakably alien to him: an eerie half-life crawling over the once-familiar city, echoes of the way he'd lived for years, lying like a corpse in an open casket. Even the searing light of a nighttime shuttle landing at the field outside the city couldn't bring it back to a semblance of the life he'd known.

Burya dreamed, too, of his own family; a wife he hadn't seen in fourteen years, a five-year-old son whose chubby face blurred with distance. (Internal exile was not a sentence of exclusion from family, but she came from solid middle-class stock, had disowned him upon hearing of his sentence and been granted a legal separation.) A helpless, weak loneliness—which he cursed whenever he noticed it in waking life—dogged his heels. The revolutionary junta had barely affected the course of events; it provided a nucleus for the wilder elements to coagulate around, a lens to focus the burning rays of resentment on the remains of the ancien régime, but in and of itself, it had achieved little. People suddenly gifted with infinite wealth and knowledge rapidly learned that they didn't need a government—and this was true as much for members of the underground as for the workers and peasants they strove to mobilize. Perhaps this was the message that the Critic had been trying to drum into him ever since his abduction from the offices of the revolutionary soviet—the revolution he had been striving for didn't need him.

On the second morning of the search for Felix, Burya awakened exhausted, limbs aching and sore, feet half frozen, in one corner of the walking hut. Sister Seventh was elsewhere, snuffling and crashing in the undergrowth beside the path. Bright polymer-walled yurts clung to the fringes of the clearing they'd camped in. A growth of trees around them struggled defiantly beneath huge shelf fungi that threatened to turn them into many-colored outcroppings. All around them grew gigantic ferns and purple-veined cycads, interstellar colonists planted by the unseen gardeners of the Festival fleet. Small mouselike creatures tended the ferns, bringing them scraps of decaying matter and attaching them to the sundewlike feeding palps that sprouted from their stems.

According to the presingularity maps, they should have passed a village two kilometers ago, but they'd seen no sign of it. Instead, they'd passed beneath a huge drifting geodesic sphere that had turned the sunset to flame overhead, making one of the cyborg militia shout and fire wildly into the air until Sergeant

Lukcas yelled at him and took his gun away. "It's a farm, pighead," he'd explained with heavy-handed irony, "like what you grew up on, only rolled into a ball and flying around the sky. And if you don't stop shooting at it, we'll use your head the same way." Some of the guards had muttered and made signs to avert the evil eye—in one case using a newly functional set of mandibles—and the rabbit walked with his ears laid flat along his head for half a kilometer before they made camp, but there were no further untoward incidents before the end of the road. But now the road had definitely come to an end.

The posse had made good progress along the Emperor's metaled highways to reach this point; but ahead of them, the Lysenkoist forest was attempting to assimilate the road. Small, eyeless rodents with fine pelts gnawed mindlessly at the asphalt surface, extruding black pellets that were swarmed over by notants the size of grasshoppers. Tall clay structures not unlike termite mounds dotted the open spaces between the ferns: they hummed quietly with a noise like a million microscopic gas turbines.

The campfire crackled ominously and belched steam as Mr. Rabbit threw scraps of dead, fungus-riddled wood on it. Burya yawned and stretched in the cold air, then stumbled off to find a tree to piss behind. Bedrolls stirred on the ground, militiamen grumbling and demanding coffee, food, and sexual favors from a nonexistent cook. There was a gout of flame and the rabbit jumped backward, narrowly missing a soldier who howled curses; the road castings were highly inflammable.

After pissing, Burya squatted. It was in this undignified position that Sister Seventh, in an unusually avuncular mood, found him.

"Greetings of morning and good micturations to you! News of outstandingness and grace bring I."

"Harrumph." Burya glared at the giant rodent, his ears meanwhile flushing red with the effort of evacuation. "Has anybody told you it isn't polite to stare?"

"At what?" Sister Seventh looked puzzled.

"Nothing," he muttered. "What's this news?"

"Why, of importance nothing." The Critic turned away innocently. "Of pleasing symmetry—"

Burya gritted his teeth, then began fumbling about for leaves. (This was something that had never been mentioned in the biographies of the famous revolutionaries, he noted vaguely; being attacked by bears and pursued by bandits or Royal mounted police was all very exciting and noteworthy, but the books never said anything about the shortage of toilet paper in the outback, or the way there were never any soft leaves around when you needed them.) "Just the facts."

"Visitors! My sibling's nest overflows with a bounty of information."

"Visitors? But—" Burya stopped. "Your siblings. In *orbit?*"

"Yes!" Sister Seventh rolled forward and over, waving her stubby legs in the air briefly before tumbling over with a loud thud. "Visitors from space!"

"Where from?" Burya leaned forward eagerly.

"The New Republic." Sister Seventh grinned amusedly, baring huge, yellowed tusks. "Sent fleet. Met Bouncers. There were survivors."

"Who, dammit!" He gritted his teeth angrily as he yanked his trousers up.

"Ambassador from Earth-prime. One other-else-who component-wise is part of her hive. And ambiguosity. They inquire for you, yourself. Want to meet?"

Burya gaped. "They're coming *here?*"

"They land at our destination. Soon."

the lifeboat was dark, hot, and stank of methane; the waste gas scrubber had developed an asthmatic wheeze. By any estimate, the life-support loop was only good for another day or so of breathable air before they had to retreat into their suits—but long before then, the passengers would have to face the perils of reentry.

"Are you sure this is safe?" asked Vassily.

Rachel rolled her eyes. "Safe, he asks," muttered Martin. "Kid, if you wanted safe, you should have stayed home when the fleet left port."

"But I don't understand—you've been talking to those aliens. They're the enemy! They just killed half our fleet! But you're taking orbital elements and course correction advisories from them. Why are you so trusting? How do you know they won't kill us, too?"

"They're not the enemy," Rachel said, patiently prodding away at the autopilot console. "They never were the enemy—at least, not the kind of enemy the Admiral and his merry band expected."

"But if they're not your enemy, you must be on their side!" Vassily glanced from one of them to the other, thoroughly spooked now.

"Nope." Rachel carried on prodding at the autopilot. "I wasn't sure before, but I am, now: the Festival isn't anything like you think it is. You guys came out here expecting an attack by a foreign government, with ships and soldiers, didn't you? But there are more things out in this universe than humans and their nations and multinational organizations. You've been fighting a shadow."

"But it destroyed all those ships! It's hostile! It—"

"Calm down." Martin watched him cautiously. *Ungrateful little shit: or is he just terminally confused?* Rachel's easy conversation with the Critics had unsettled Martin more than he liked to admit, almost as much as her unexpectedly successful rescue attempt. There were wheels within wheels here, more than he'd expected. "There are no sides. The Critics aren't enemies; they aren't even part of the Festival. We tried to tell your people to expect something totally alien, but they wouldn't listen."

"What do you mean?"

"The Festival isn't human, it isn't *remotely* human. You people are thinking in terms of people with people-type motivations; that's wrong, and it's been clear that it's wrong from the start. You can no more declare war on the Festival than you can declare a war against sleep. It's a self-replicating information network. Probe enters a system: probe builds a self-extending communications network and yanks the inhabited worlds of that system into it. Drains all the information it can get out of the target civilization, then spawns more probes. The probes carry some parasites, uploaded life-forms that build bodies and download into them whenever they reach a destination—but that's not what it exists for."

Vassily gaped. "But it attacked us!"

"No it didn't," Martin replied patiently. "It isn't intelligent; analyzing its behavior by adopting an intentional stance is a mistake. All it did was detect an inhabited planet with no telephone service at a range of some light-years and obey its instructions."

"But the instructions—it's war!"

"No, it's a bug fix. It turns out that the Festival is just a—a telephone repairman. Like a robot repairman. Only it doesn't repair mere telephones—it repairs holes in the galactic information flow." Martin glanced sideways at Rachel. She was wrestling with the autopilot, getting the landing burn sequence keyed in. It was a bad idea to distract her at a time like this; better keep the young nuisance occupied.

"Civilizations rise and fall from time to time; the Festival is probably a mechanism set in place a few millennia ago to keep them in touch, built by an interstellar culture back in the mists of time. When it detected a hole in the net it maintains, it decided to fix it, which is why it set up to do business in orbit around Rochard's World, which is about as isolated and cut off as it's possible to be."

"But we didn't ask for it," Vassily said uncertainly.

"Well, of course not. Actually, I think it's strayed outside its original maintenance zone, so every system it discovers in this sector warrants a repair job: but that's not necessarily all there is to it. Part of the repair process is a rapid exchange of information with the rest of the network it connects to, a flow that runs in two directions. Over time, the Festival has become more than a mere repair service; it's become a civilization in its own right, one that blooms like a desert flower—briefly flourishing in the right environment, then curling up into a seed and sleeping as it migrates across the deserted gulf light-years between oases. Telephone switches and routers are some of the most complicated information-processing systems ever invented—where do you think the Eschaton originally came from?

"When the Festival arrived at Rochard's World, it had a 250-year communications deficit to make good. That repair—the end of isolation, arrival of goods and ideas restricted by the New Republic—caused a limited local singularity, what in our business we call a consensus reality excursion; people went a little crazy, that's all. A sudden overdose of change; immortality, bioengineering, weakly superhuman AI arbeiters, nanotechnology, that sort of thing. It isn't an attack."

"But then—you're telling me they brought unrestricted communications with them?" he asked.

"Yup." Rachel looked up from her console. "We've been trying for years to tell your leaders, in the nicest possible way: information wants to be free. But they wouldn't listen. For forty years we tried. Then along comes the Festival, which treats censorship as a malfunction and routes communications around it. The Festival won't take no for an answer because it doesn't have an opinion on anything; it just *is*."

"But information isn't free. It can't be. I mean, some things— if anyone could read anything they wanted, they might read things that would tend to deprave and corrupt them, wouldn't they? People might give exactly the same consideration to blasphemous pornography that they pay to the Bible! They could plot against the state, or each other, without the police being able to listen in and stop them!"

Martin sighed. "You're still hooked on the state thing, aren't you?" he said. "Can you take it from me, there are other ways of organizing your civilization?"

"Well—" Vassily blinked at him in mild confusion. "Are you telling me you let information circulate freely where you come from?"

"It's not a matter of permitting it," Rachel pointed out. "We had to admit that we couldn't prevent it. *Trying* to prevent it was worse than the disease itself."

"But, but lunatics could brew up biological weapons in their kitchens, destroy cities! Anarchists would acquire the power to overthrow the state, and nobody would be able to tell who they were or where they belonged anymore. The most foul nonsense would be spread, and nobody could stop it—" Vassily paused. "You don't believe me," he said plaintively.

"Oh, we believe you alright," Martin said grimly. "It's just— look, change isn't always bad. Sometimes freedom of speech provides a release valve for social tensions that would lead to revolution. And at other times, well—what you're protesting about boils down to a dislike for anything that disturbs the *status quo*. You see your government as a security blanket, a warm fluffy cover that'll protect everybody from anything bad all the time. There's a lot of that kind of thinking in the New Republic; the idea that people who aren't kept firmly in their place will automatically behave badly. But where I come from, most people have enough common sense to *avoid* things that'd harm them; and those that don't, need to be taught. Censorship just drives problems underground."

"But, terrorists!"

"Yes," Rachel interrupted, "terrorists. There are always people who think they're doing the right thing by inflicting misery on their enemies, kid. And you're perfectly right about brewing up biological weapons and spreading rumors. But—" She shrugged. "We can live with a low background rate of that sort of thing more easily than we can live with total surveillance and total censorship of everyone, all the time." She looked grim. "If you think a lunatic planting a nuclear weapon in a city is bad, you've never seen what happens when a planet pushes the idea of ubiquitous surveillance and censorship to the limit. There are places where—" She shuddered.

Martin glanced at her. "You've got somewhere specific in mind to—"

"I don't want to talk about it," she said tersely. "And you should be ashamed of yourself, winding the boy up like that. Either of you two noticed the air stinks?"

"Yeah." Martin yawned widely. "Are we about—"

"—I am not a—" A thundering chorus of popping noises sounded outside the cabin. "—boy!" Vassily finished with a squeak.

"Belt up, kid. Main engine coming on in five seconds."

Martin tensed, unconsciously tightening his belt. "What's our descent curve?"

"Waypoint one coming up: ten-second course adjustment, one-point-two gees. We sit tight for four minutes or so, then we hit waypoint two, and burn for two hours at two and a quarter gees— this ends 'bout four thousand klicks elevation relative to planetary surface, and we'll hit atmosphere sixteen minutes later at about four k.p.s. We'll have some reaction mass left, but I really don't want to power up the main engine once we're in air we'll have to breathe afterward; so we're going to drop the propulsion module once we're suborbital and it'll kick itself back into a graveyard orbit with the last of its fuel."

"Er." Vassily looked puzzled. "Four k.p.s. Isn't that a bit fast?"

"No it's—" A high-pitched roar cut into Rachel's explanation, jolting everything in the capsule back toward the rear bulkhead. Ten seconds passed. "It's only about Mach 12, straight down. And we'll have dropped the engines overboard, first. But don't worry, we'll slow up pretty fast when we hit the atmosphere. They used to do this sort of thing all the time during the Apollo program."

"The Apollo program? Wasn't that back in the days when space travel was *experimental?*" Martin noticed that where Vassily was gripping the back of his chair, the lad's knuckles had turned white. *How interesting.*

"Yeah, that was it," Rachel said casually. "'Course, they didn't have nuclear power back then—was it before or after the Cold War?"

"Before, I think. The Cold War was all about who could build the biggest refrigerator, wasn't it?"

"Cold War?" piped Vassily.

"Back on Earth, about four, five hundred years ago," Rachel explained.

"But they were doing this, and they couldn't even build a steam engine?"

"Oh, they could build steam engines," Martin said airily. "But they powered them by burning rock oil under the boilers. Fission reactors were expensive and rare."

"That doesn't sound very safe," Vassily said dubiously. "Wouldn't all that oil explode?"

"Yes, but Earth is an early population three planet, and quite old; the isotope balance is lousy, not enough uranium-235."

"Too damn much if you ask me," Rachel muttered darkly.

"I think you're trying to confuse me, and I really don't like that. You think you're so sophisticated, you Terrans, but you don't know everything! You still can't keep terrorists from blowing up your cities, and for all your so-called sophistication you can't control your own filthy impulses—meddling fools by politics, meddling fools by nature!"

Another burp from an attitude control thruster. Rachel reached over and grabbed Martin's shoulder. "He's got us nailed."

"Aye up, 'e's got us bang to rights. It's a fair cop, guv."

Vassily glanced from one of them to the other in bewilderment; his ears began to glow bright red. Rachel laughed. "If that's meant to be a Yorkshire accent, I'm a Welsh ferret, Martin!"

"Well, I'd be pleased to stuff you down my trousers any day of the week, my dear." The engineer shook his head. Out of the corner of his eye, he noted Vassily's glow spreading from ears to neck. "You've got a lot to learn about the real world, kid. I'm surprised your boss let you out on your own without a minder."

"Will you stop calling me a child!"

Rachel hunched around in her chair and stared at him. "But you are, you know. Even if you were sixty years old, you'd still be a child to me. As long as you expect someone or something else to take responsibility for you, you're a child. You could fuck your way through every brothel in New Prague, and you'd *still* be an overgrown schoolboy." She looked at him sadly. "What would you call a parent who never let their children grow up? That's what we think of your government."

"But that's not why I'm here! I'm here to protect the Republic! I'm here because—"

The main motor went critical and spooled up to full power with a deep bass roar, rattling the capsule like a tin can in a hurricane. Vassily was shoved back into his hammock, gasping for breath; Rachel and Martin subsided into their seats, slugged by a solid twenty meters per second of acceleration—not the five-hundred-kilo chest-squishing gorilla of re-entry, but enough force to make them lie back and concentrate on breathing.

The engine burned for a long time, carrying them away from the drifting wreckage of battle, toward an uncertain rendezvous.

the husks of two spent Bouncer ships drifted toward the edge of the system, tumbling end over end at well over stellar escape velocity. They didn't matter anymore; they'd done their job.

Behind them, the wreckage of the New Republican home fleet scattered like ashes on a searing hot wind. Two-thirds of the ships bubbled and foamed, engineering segments glowing red-hot as the disassembler goop stripped them down; bizarre metallic fuzz sprawled across their hulls, like fungal hyphae drilling through the heart of dead and rotting trees. Almost all of the other warships were boosting at full power, pursuing escape trajectories that would take them back into deep space. The space around Rochard's World was full of screaming countermeasure signals, jammers and feedback howlers and interferometry decoys and penaids that—unknown to their owners—were proving as effective as shields slung over the backs of tribesmen fleeing in the face of machine-gun fire. A scattering of much smaller, slower ships continued to decelerate toward the planet ahead, or coasted slowly in. For the most part the remaining Bouncers ignored these: lifeboats weren't generally troublemakers. Finally, coasting in from a range of astronomical units, came the first trade ships of the merchant fleet that followed the Festival around. Their signals were gaily entertaining, flashy and friendly: unlike the New Republic, these were not ignorant of the Festival, its uses and hazards.

But the Festival barely noticed the approaching trade fleet. Its attention was directed elsewhere: soon it would give birth to its next generation, wither, and die.

Antimatter factories the size of continents drilled holes in the fiery solar corona, deep in the curved-space zone just outside the photosphere of Rochard's star. Huge accelerator rings floated behind their wake shields, insulated by kilometers of vacuum; solar collectors blacker than night soaked up solar energy, megawatts per square meter, while masers dumped waste heat into the interstellar night overhead. Every second, milligram quantities of antimatter accumulated in the magnetic traps at the core of the accelerators. Every ten thousand seconds or so, another hazardous multigram payload shipped out on a beam-riding cargo pod to the starwisp assembly zone around Sputnik. There were a hundred factories in all; the Festival had dismantled a large Kuiper body to make them and placed the complex barely a million kilometers above the stellar surface. Now the investment was paying off in raw energy, a million times more than the planetary civilization had been able to muster.

The starwisps weren't the Festival's only cargo, nor were the Fringe and the Critics the only passengers to visit the planetary surface. Deep in the planetary biosphere, vectors armed with reverse transcriptase and strange artificial chromosomes were at work. They'd re-entered over the temperate belt of the northern continent, spreading and assimilating the contents of the endogenous ecology. Complex digestive organs, aided by the tools of DNA splicing and some fiendishly complicated expression control operons, assimilated and dissected chromosomes from everything the package's children swallowed. A feedback system—less than conscious but more than vegetable—spliced together a workable local expression of a design crafted thousands of years ago; one that could subsist on locally available building blocks, a custom saprophyte optimized for the ecology of Rochard's World.

Huge Lamarckian syncitia spread their roots across the pine forest, strangling the trees and replacing them with plants shaped like pallid pines. They were fruiting bodies, mushrooms sprouting atop the digested remains of an entire ecosystem. They grew rapidly; special cells deep in their cores secreted catalytic enzymes, nitrating the long polysaccharide molecules, while in the outer bark long, electrically conductive vessels took shape like vegetable neurons.

The forest parasite grew at a ferocious rate, fruiting bodies sprouting a meter a day. It was a much longer-term project than the rewiring of the incommunicado civilization that the Festival had stumbled across; and one more grand than any of the sentient passengers could have imagined. All they were aware of was the spread of intrusive vegetation, an annoying and sometimes dangerous plague that followed the Festival as closely as did the Mimes and other beings of the Fringe. Come the dry season, and the Festival forest would become a monstrous fire hazard; but for now, it was just a sideshow, still sprouting slowly toward its destiny, which it would reach around the time the Festival began to die.

Fifty kilometers above the ocean, still traveling at twelve times the speed of sound, the naval lifeboat spread its thistledown rotors behind the shock front of re-entry and prepared to autorotate.

"Makes you wish the Admiralty'd paid for the deluxe model," Lieutenant Kossov muttered between gritted teeth as the capsule juddered and shook, skipping across the ionosphere like a burning sodium pellet on a basin of water. Commander Leonov glared at him: he grunted as if he'd been punched, and shut up.

Thirty kilometers lower and fifteen hundred kilometers closer to the coast of the northern continent, the plasma shock began to dissipate. The rotors, glowing white at their tips, freewheeled in the high stratosphere, spinning in a bright blurring disk. Lying in an acceleration couch in the cockpit, the flight crew grappled with the problem of landing a hypersonic autogyro on an airfield with no ground control and no instrument guidance, an airfield that was quite possibly under siege by hostiles. Robard's blood ran cold as he thought about it. Reflexively, he glanced sideways at his master: a life dedicated to looking after the Admiral had brought him to this fix, but still he looked to him for his lead, even though the old warhorse was barely conscious.

"How does he look?" Robard asked.

Dr. Hertz glanced up briefly. "As well as can be expected," he said shortly. "Did you bring his medications with you?"

Robard winced. "Only his next doses. There are too many pill bottles—"

"Well then." Hertz fumbled with his leather bag, withdrew a pre-loaded syringe. "Was he taking laudanum? I recall no such prescription, but . . ."

"Not to my knowledge." Robard swallowed. "Diabetes, a

dyskinesia, and his um, memory condition. Plus his legs, of course. But he was not in *pain*."

"Well, then, let's see if we can wake him up." Hertz held up the syringe and removed the protective cap. "I would not normally so brutalize an old man before landing, especially one who has suffered a stroke, but under the circumstances—"

Twelve kilometers up, the autogyro dropped below Mach 2. Rotors shedding a disk of thunderous lightning, its ground track angled across the coast; where it passed, animals fled in panic. The lifeboat continued to lose altitude while Hertz administered his wake-up injection. Less than a minute later, the craft dropped to subsonic speed, and a new keening note entered the cabin. Robard glanced up instinctively.

"Just restarting the aerospikes," Kossov mumbled. "That way we can make a powered touchdown."

The Admiral groaned something inarticulate, and Robard leaned forward. "Sir. Can you hear me?"

The lifeboat flew sideways at just under half the speed of sound, a bright cylinder of fire spurting from the tips of the rotor disk that blurred around its waist. The copilot repeatedly tried to raise Imperial Traffic Control, to no avail; he exchanged worried glances with his commander. Trying to land under the missile batteries of the Skull Hill garrison, with no word on who was holding the city below, would be nerve-racking enough. To do so in a lifeboat short on fuel, with a desperately sick admiral aboard—

But there was no breath of search radar bouncing off the lifeboat's hull. Even as it rose over the castle's horizon, drifting in at a sedate four hundred kilometers per hour, there was no flicker of attention from the ground defense batteries. The pilot keyed his intercom switch. "The field's still there even though nobody's talking to us. Visual approach, stand by for a bumpy ride."

The Admiral muttered something incoherent and opened his eyes. Robard leaned back in his seat as the rotor tip aerospikes quietened their screeching roar, and the pilot fed the remaining power into the collective pitch, trading airspeed against altitude. "Urk." Lieutenant Kossov looked green.

"*Hate* 'copters," mumbled the Admiral.

The motors shut down, and the lifeboat dropped, autorotating like a fifty-ton sycamore seed. There was a brief surge of upward acceleration as the pilot flared out before touchdown, then a bone-jarring crunch from beneath the passenger compartment. A screech of torn metal told its own story; the lifeboat tilted alarmingly, then settled back drunkenly, coming to rest with the deck tilted fifteen degrees.

"Does that mean what I think it means?" asked Robard.

"Shut up and mind your business," grated Commander Leonov. He hauled himself out of his couch and cast about. "You! Look sharp, man the airlock! You and you, break open the small-arms locker and stand by to clear the way." He began to clamber down the short ladder to the flight deck, hanging on tight despite the fifteen-degree overhang, still barking out orders. "You, Robot or whatever your name is, get your man ready to move, don't know how long we've got. Ah, Pilot-captain Wolff. I take it we're on the field. Did you see any sign of a welcoming committee?"

The pilot waited while Leonov backed down the ladder, then followed him down to the deck. "Sir, humbly report we have arrived at Novy Petrograd emergency field, pad two. I was unable to contact traffic control or port air defense control before landing, but nobody shot at us. I didn't see anyone standing around down there, but there are big changes to the city—it's not like the briefing cinematograph. Regret to report that on final approach we ran a little short of fuel, hence the bad landing."

"Acceptable under the circumstances." Leonov turned to the airlock. "You there! Open the hatch, double quick, ground party will secure the perimeter immediately!"

The Admiral seemed to be trying to sit up. Robard cranked up the back of his wheelchair, then leaned down to release the cables securing it in place. As he did so, the Admiral made a curious chuckling noise.

"What is it, sir?"

"Heh—'omit commit. Heh!"

"Absolutely, sir." Robard straightened up. Fresh air gusted into the confines of the lifeboat; someone had tripped the override on the airlock, opening both hatches simultaneously. He could smell rain and cherry blossoms, grass and mud.

Lieutenant Kossov followed the ground party through the airlock, then ducked back inside. "Sir. Humbly report, ground party has secured the site. No sign of any locals."

"Hah, good. Lieutenant, you and Robot can get the old man down. Follow me!" Leonov followed the last of the officers—the flight crew and a couple of lieutenant commanders Robard didn't recognize, members of the Admiral's staff or the bridge crew—into the airlock.

Together, Robard and Lieutenant Kossov grunted and sweated

the Admiral's wheelchair down a flimsy aluminum stepladder to the ground. Once his feet touched concrete, Robard breathed in deeply and looked around. One of the lifeboat's three landing legs looked wrong, a shock absorber not fully extended. It gave the craft an oddly lopsided appearance, and he knew at once that it would take more than a tankful of fuel to get it airborne again, much less into orbit. Then his eyes took in what had happened beyond the rust-streaked concrete landing pad, and he gasped.

The landing field was less than two kilometers from the brooding walls of the garrison, on the outskirts of the scantily settled north bank of the river. South of the river, there should have been a close-packed warren of steep-roofed houses, church spires visible in the distance before a knot of municipal buildings. But now the houses were mostly gone. A cluster of eldritch silvery ferns coiled skyward from the former location of the town hall, firefly glimmerings flickering between their fractally coiled leaves. The Ducal palace showed signs of being the worse for wear; one wall looked as if it had been smashed by a giant fist, the arrogant bombast of heavy artillery.

The Admiral slapped feebly at the arm of his chair. "'Ot right!"

"Absolutely, my lord." Robard looked around again, this time hunting the advance landing party. They were halfway to the control tower when something that glowed painfully green slashed overhead, making the ground shake with the roar of its passage.

"Enemy planes!" shouted Kossov. "See, they've followed us here! We must get the Admiral to cover, fast!" He pushed Robard aside and grabbed the handles of the wheelchair, nearly tipping it over in his haste.

"I say!" Robard snapped, angry and disturbed at his position being usurped. He cast a worried glance at the sky and decided not to confuse the issue further; the Lieutenant's behavior was unseemly, but the need to get the admiral to safety was pressing. "I say, there's a path there. I'll lead. If we can reach the tower—"

"You! Follow us!" Kossov called to the perimeter guards, confused and worried ratings who, thankful at being given some direction, shouldered their carbines and tagged along. It was a warm morning, and the Lieutenant wheezed as he pushed the wheelchair along the cracked asphalt path. Robard paced along beside him, a tall, sepulchrally black figure, hatchet-faced with worry. Weeds grew waist high to either side of the path, and other signs of neglect were omnipresent; the field looked as if it had been abandoned for years, not just the month since the invasion. Bees and other insects buzzed and hummed around, while birds squawked and trilled in the distance, shamefully exposing the locals' neglect of their DDT spraying program.

A distant rumble prompted Robard to glance over his shoulder. Birds leapt into the sky as a distant green brightness twisted and seemed to freeze, hovering beneath the blind turquoise dome of the sky. "Run!" He dashed forward and threw himself into the shade of a stand of young trees.

"What?" Kossov stopped and stared, jaw comically dropping. The green glare grew with frightening, soundless rapidity, then burst overhead in an emerald explosion. A noise like a giant door slamming shut pushed Robard into the grass: then the aircraft thundered past, dragging a freight train roar behind it as it made a low pass over the parked lifeboat and disappeared toward the far side of the city. Bees buzzed angrily in his ears as he picked himself up and looked wildly around for the Admiral.

The Lieutenant had been knocked off his feet by the shock wave; now he was sitting up, cradling his head gingerly. The wheelchair had remained upright, and a loud but slurred stream of invective was flowing from it. "'Orson swiving 'role'erian cocksu'ing *ba-a-stards!*" Kurtz raised his good arm and shook a palsied fist at the sky. "You 'evolushunary shit'll get yours! Ouch!" The arm flopped.

"Are you alright sir?" Robard gasped nervously.

"'Astard *stung* me," Kurtz complained, drooling on the back of his wrist. "Damn bees." An angry buzzing veered haywire around Robard, and he whacked at it with his dirt-stained gloves.

"I'm sure you'll be alright, sir, once we get you to the control tower and then the castle." He inspected the mashed insect briefly, and froze. Red, impact-distorted letters ridged its abdomen with unnatural clarity. He shuddered and smeared the back of his glove on the ground. "We'd better move fast, before that plane decides we're the enemy."

"You take over," said Kossov, clutching a reddened handkerchief to his forehead. "Let's go." Together they turned and pushed on toward the control tower, and beyond it the uncertainties of the Ducal palace and whatever had become of the capital city under the new order.

eighty kilometers away, another lifeboat was landing. Rachel shook herself groggily and opened her eyes. It took her a moment to realize where she was. Re-entry had been alarmingly bumpy; the capsule was swinging back and forth with a regular motion that would have made her nauseous if her vestibular dampers hadn't kicked in. There was a moan from behind her seat and she glanced sideways. Martin was waking up visibly, shaking his head, his face going through a horrible series of contortions and twitches. Behind her, Vassily moaned again. "Oh, that was terrible."

"Still alive, huh?" She blinked at the viewscreen. Black smears obscured much of it, remnants of the ablative heat shield that had melted and streaked across the cameras on the outside of the hull. The horizon was a flat blue line, the ground half-hidden beneath a veil of clouds as they descended beneath the main parasail. An altimeter ticked down the last two thousand meters. "Say yes if you can wriggle your toes."

"Yes," said Martin. Vassily just moaned. Rachel didn't bother to inquire further after their health; she had too many things to do before they landed. It could all get very messy very fast, now they didn't have an engine.

Pilot: Plot range and heading to rendezvous waypoint omega. A map overlay blinked on the viewscreen. They were coming down surprisingly close, only a few kilometers out from the target. *Pilot: Hard surface retromotor status, please.* More displays; diagnostics and self-test maps of the landing motor, a small package hanging in the rigging halfway between the rectangular parachute and the capsule roof. Triggered by radar, the landing turbine would fire a minute before touchdown, decelerating the capsule from a bone-crushing fifty-kilometer-per-hour fall and steering them to a soft touchdown.

"I could do with a drink," said Martin.

"You'll have to wait a minute or two." Rachel watched the screen intently. One thousand meters.

"I can't feel my toes," Vassily complained.

Oh shit. "Can you wriggle them?" asked Rachel, heart suddenly in her mouth. She'd never expected a third passenger, and if the hammock had landed him with a spinal injury—

"Yes."

"Then why the fuck did you say you couldn't feel them?"

"They're cold!"

Rachel yawned; her ears popped. "I think we just depressurized. You must have your toes on top of the vent or something."

The outside grew hazy, whited out. Ten more seconds, and the wispy cloud thinned, peeling back to reveal trees and rivers below. A dizzying view, the ground growing closer. She gritted her teeth. Next to her, Martin shuffled for a better view.

"*Attention. Landing raft inflation.*" A yellow python wrapped itself around the bottom of the capsule and bloated outward, cutting off her view of the ground directly below. Rachel cursed silently, looked for a clearing in the trees. The forest cover was unusually dense, and she tensed.

"Over there." Martin pointed.

"Thanks." Using the side stick, she pointed out the opening to the autopilot. *Pilot: make for designated landing ground. Engage autoland on arrival.*

"*Attention. Stand by for retromotor ignition in five seconds. Touchdown imminent. Three seconds. Main canopy separation.*" The capsule dropped sickeningly. "*Motor ignition.*" A loud rumbling from above, and the fall stopped. The clearing below lurched closer, and the rumbling grew to a shuddering roar. "*Attention. Touchdown in ten seconds. Brace for landing.*"

Trees slid past the screen, implacable green stems exfoliating purple-veined leaves the size of books. Martin gasped. They dropped steadily, like a glass-walled elevator on the side of an invisible skyscraper. Finally, with a tooth-rattling bump, the capsule came to rest.

Silence.

"Hey, guys." Rachel shakily pushed the release buckle on her seat belt. "Thank you for flying Air UN, and may I take this opportunity to invite you to fly with us again?"

Martin grunted and stretched his arms up. "Nope, can't reach it from here. Got to unbelt first." He let his arms flop down again. "Feel like lead. Funny."

"All it takes is eight hours in zero gee." Rachel rummaged in the storage bins next to her leg well.

"I think I understand you Terrans now," Vassily began, then paused to let the tremor out of his voice before continuing. "You're all mad!"

Martin looked sidelong at Rachel. "He's only just noticed."

She sat up, clutching a compact backpack. "Took him long enough."

"Well. What do we do now? Make with the big tin opener, or wait for someone to pass by and yank the ring pull?"

"First"—Rachel tapped icons busily on the pilot's console—

"we tell the Critics that we're down safely. She said she'd try to help us link up. Second, I do *this.*" She reached up and grabbed the top edge of the display screen. It crumpled like thin plastic, revealing the inner wall of the capsule. A large steamer trunk was half-embedded in the bulkhead, incongruous pipes and cables snaking out of its half-open lid.

"I knew it!" Vassily exclaimed. "You've got an illegal—"

"Shut up." Rachel leaned forward and adjusted something just inside the lid. "Right, now we leave. Quickly." Standing up, she unlocked the overhead hatch and let it slide down into the capsule, taking the place of the screen. "Give me a leg up, Martin."

"Okay." A minute later, all three of them were sitting on top of the lander. The truncated cone sat in a puddle of yellow inflatable skirts, in the middle of a grassy meadow. To their left, a stream burbled lazily through a thick clump of reeds; to their right, a row of odd, dark conifers formed a wall against the light. The air was cold and fresh and smelled unbearably clean. "What now?" asked Martin.

"I advise you to surrender to the authorities." Vassily loomed over him. "It will go badly with you if you don't cooperate, but if you surrender to me I'll, I'll—" He looked around wildly.

Rachel snorted. "What authorities?"

"The capital—"

Rachel finally blew her top. "Listen, kid, we're stuck in the back of beyond with a dead lifeboat and not a lot of supplies, on a planet that's just been hit by a type three singularity, and I have just spent the past thirty-six hours slaving my guts out to save our necks—all of them, yours included—and I would appreciate it if you would just *shut up* for a while! Our first priority is survival; my second priority is linking up with the people I've come here to visit, and getting back to civilization comes third on the list. With me so far? Because there are *no* civil authorities right now, not the kind you expect. They've just been dumped on by about a thousand years of progress in less than a month, and if your local curator's still sitting at his desk, he's probably catatonic from future shock. This planetary civilization has *transcended.* It is an ex-colony; it has ceased to be. About the only people who can cope with this level of change are your dissidents, and I'm not that optimistic about them, either. Right now, *we* are your best hope of survival, and you'd better not forget it." She glared at Vassily, and he glared right back at her, obviously angry but unable to articulate his feelings.

Behind her, Martin had clambered down to the meadow. Something caught his attention, and he bent down. "Hey!"

"What is it?" Rachel called. The spell was broken: Vassily subsided with a grumble and began hunting for a way down off the capsule. Martin said something indistinct. "What?" she called.

"There's something wrong with this grass!"

"Oh shit." Rachel followed Vassily down the side of the pod— two and a half meters of gently sloping ceramic, then a soft landing on a woven spider-silk floatation bed. "What do you mean?"

Martin straightened up and wordlessly offered her a blade of grass.

"It's—" She stopped.

"Rochard's World is supposed to have an Earth-normal biosphere, isn't it?" Martin watched her curiously. "That's what it said in my gazetteer."

"What *is* that?" asked Vassily.

"Grass, or what passes for it." Martin shrugged uncomfortably. "Doesn't look very Earth-normal to me. It's the right color and right overall shape, but—"

"Ouch. Cut myself on the damned thing." Rachel dropped it. The leaf blade fluttered down, unnoticed: when it hit the ground it began to disintegrate with eerie speed, falling apart along radial seams. "What about the trees?"

"There's something odd about them, too." A crackling noise from behind made Martin jump. "What's that?"

"Don't worry. I figured we'd need some ground transport, so I told it to make some. It's reabsorbing the capsule—"

"Neat luggage," Martin said admiringly. The lifeboat began to crumple inward, giving off a hot, organic smell like baking bread.

"Yeah, well." Rachel looked worried. "My contact's supposed to know we're here. I wonder how long . . ." She trailed off. Vassily was busily tramping toward the far side of the clearing, whistling some sort of martial-sounding tune.

"Just who is this contact?" Martin asked quietly.

"Guy called Rubenstein. One of the more sensible resistance cadres, which is why he's in internal exile here—the less sensible ones end up dead."

"And what do you want with him?"

"I'm to give him a package. Not that he needs it anymore, if what's happened here is anything to go by."

"A package? What kind of package?"

She turned and pointed at the steamer trunk, which now rested on the grass in the middle of a collapsing heap of structural trusses, belching steam quietly. *"That* kind of package."

"That kind of—" His eyes gave him away. Rachel reached out and took his elbow.

"Come on, Martin. Let's check out the tree line."

"But—" He glanced over his shoulder. "Okay."

"It's like this," Rachel began, as they walked. "Remember what I said about helping the people of the New Republic? A while ago—some years, actually—some people in a department you don't really need to know much about decided that they were ripe for a revolution. Normally we don't get involved in that kind of thing; toppling regimes is bad ju-ju even if you disapprove of them or do it for all the right moral reasons. But some of our analysts figured there was a chance, say twenty percent, that the New Republic might metastasize and turn imperial. So we've been gearing up to ship power tools to their own home-grown libertarian underground for a decade now.

"The Festival . . . when it arrived, we didn't know what it was. If I'd known what you told me once we were under way, back at Klamovka, I wouldn't be here now. Neither would the luggage. Which is the whole point of the exercise, actually. When the aristocracy put down the last workers' and technologists' soviet about 240 years ago, they destroyed the last of the cornucopiae the New Republic was given at its foundation by the Eschaton. Thereafter, they could control the arbeiter classes by restricting access to education and tools and putting tight bottlenecks on information technology. This luggage, Martin, it's a full-scale cornucopia machine. Design schemata for just about anything a mid-twenty-first-century postindustrial civilization could conceive of, freeze-dried copies of the Library of Congress, all sorts of things. Able to replicate itself, too." The tree line was a few meters ahead. Rachel stopped and took a deep breath. "I was sent here to turn it over to the underground, Martin. I was sent here to give them the tools to start a revolution."

"To start a—" Martin stared at her. "But you're too late."

"Exactly." She gave him a moment for it to sink in. "I can still complete my mission, just in case, but I don't really think . . ."

He shook his head. "How are we going to get out of this mess?"

"Um. Good question." She turned and faced the melting re-entry capsule, then reached into a pocket and began bringing out some spare optical spybots. Vassily was aimlessly circling the perimeter of the clearing. "Normally, I'd go to ground in the old town and wait. In six months, there'll be a merchant ship along. But with the Festival—"

"There'll be ships," Martin said with complete assurance. "And you've got a cornucopia, you've got a whole portable military-industrial complex. If it can make us a lifeboat, I'm sure I can program it to manufacture anything we need to survive until we've got a chance to get off this godforsaken hole. Right?"

"Probably." She shrugged. "But first I really ought to make contact, if only to verify that there's no point in handing the luggage over." She began to walk back toward the lander. "This Rubenstein is supposed to be fairly levelheaded for a revolutionary. He'll probably know what—" There was a distant cracking sound, like sticks breaking. At the other side of the clearing, Vassily was running back toward the luggage. "Shit!" Rachel dragged Martin to the ground, fumbled for the stunner in her pocket.

"What is it?" he whispered.

"I don't know."

"Damn. Well, looks like they've found us, whoever they are. Nice knowing you." A large, hunched thing, hugely, monstrously bipedal, lurched into the clearing: a vast mouth like a doorway gaped at them.

"Wait." Rachel held him down with one hand. "*Don't* move. That thing's wired like a fucking tank, sensors everywhere."

The thing swung toward the lander, then abruptly squatted on its haunches. A long, flat tongue lolled groundward; something big appeared at the top of it and stepped down to the meadow. It swept its head from side to side, taking in the decrepitating lifeboat, Vassily hiding behind it, the rest of the clearing. Then it called out, in a surprisingly deep voice. "Hello? We arrive not-warfully. Is there a Rachel Mansour here?"

Well, here goes. She stood up and cleared her throat. "Who wants to know?"

The Critic grinned at her, baring frighteningly long tusks: "I am Sister Seventh. You come in time! We a crisis have!"

people began gathering outside the Ducal palace around evening. They came in ones and twos, clumped shell-shocked beneath the soot-smeared outer walls. They looked much like any other citizens of the New Republic; perhaps a bit poorer, a bit duller than most.

Robard stood in the courtyard and watched them through the gates. Two of the surviving ratings stood there, guns ready, a relic of temporal authority. Someone had found a flag, charred along one edge but otherwise usable. The crowd had begun to form about an hour after they raised it to fly proudly in the light breeze. The windows might be broken and the furniture smashed, but they were still soldiers of His Imperial Majesty, and by God and Emperor there were standards, and they would be observed—so the Admiral had indicated, and so they were behaving.

Robard breathed in deeply. Insect bite? A most suspicious insect, indeed. But since it had stung the Admiral, his condition had improved remarkably. His left cheek remained slack, and his fingers remained numb, but his arm—

Robard and Lieutenant Kossov had borne their ancient charge to the control tower, cursing and sweating in the noonday heat. As they arrived, Kurtz had thrown a fit; choking, gasping, choleric, thrashing in his wheelchair. Robard had feared for the worst, but then Dr. Hertz had come and administered a horse syringe full of adrenaline. The Admiral subsided, panting like a dog: and his left eye had opened and rolled sideways, to fix Robard with a skewed stare. "What is it, sir? Is there anything I can get you?"

"Wait." The Admiral hissed. He tensed, visibly. "'M all hot. But it's so clear." Both hands moved, gripping the sides of his wheelchair, and to Robard's shock the old man rose to his feet. "My Emperor! I can walk!"

Robard's feelings as he caught his employer were impossible to pin down. Disbelief, mostly, and pride. The old man shouldn't be able to do that; in the aftermath of his stroke, he'd been paralyzed on one side. Such lesions didn't heal, the doctor had said. But Kurtz had risen from his chair and taken a wobbly step forward—

From the control tower to the castle, events had moved in a dusty blur. Requisitioned transport, a bouncing ride through a half-deserted town, half the houses in it burned to the ground and the other half sprouting weird excrescences. The castle, deserted. Get the Admiral into the Duke's bedroom. Find the kitchen, see if there's anything edible in the huge underground larders. Someone hoisted a flag. Guards on the gate. Two timid serving women like little mice, scurrying from hiding and curtsying to the service they'd long since been broken to. A cleaning detail, broken furniture ruthlessly consigned to the firewood heap that would warm the grand ballroom. Emergency curtains—steel-mesh and spidersilk—furled behind the tall and shattered windows. Guards on the gate, with guns. Check the water pipes. More uniforms moving in the dusty afternoon heat. Busy, so busy.

He'd stolen a minute to break into Citizen Von Beck's office. None of the revolutionary cadres had got that far into the castle, or survived the active countermeasures. All the Curator's tools lay handy; Robard had paused to check the emergency causal channel, but its entropy had been thoroughly maximized even though the bandwidth monitor showed more than fifty percent remaining. His worst suspicions confirmed, he made liberal use of the exotic insecticides Von Beck had stocked, spraying his person until the air was blue and chokingly unbreathable. Then he pocketed a small artifact—one that it was illegal on pain of death for anyone not of the Curator's Office to be in possession of—left the room, locked it behind him, and returned to the duties of the Admiral's manservant.

The aimless cluster outside the Ducal palace had somehow metamorphosed into a crowd while he'd been busy. Anxious, pinched faces stared at him: the faces of people uncertain who they were, bereft of their place in the scheme of things. Lost people, desperately seeking reassurance. Doubtless many would have joined the dissident underground; many more would have made full use of the singular conditions brought about by the arrival of the Festival to maximize their personal abilities. For years to come, even if the Festival vanished tomorrow, the outback would be peopled by ghouls and wizards, talking animals and sagacious witches. Some people didn't want to transcend their humanity; a life of routine reassurance was all they craved, and the Festival had deprived them of it. Was that an army greatcoat lurking at the back of the square? A sallow-faced man, half-starved, who in other circumstances Robard would have pegged for a highwayman; here he was just as likely to be the last loyal dregs of a regiment that had deserted *en masse*. Snap judgments could be treacherous.

He looked farther. Dust, rising in the distance, perhaps half a mile away. *Hmm.*

The grand hallway opened from the front doors and led to the main staircase, the ballroom, and numerous smaller, more discreet destinations. Normally, a manservant would have used a small side entrance. Today, Robard strode in through the huge doors that normally would have welcomed ambassadors and knights of the realm. Nobody watched his dusty progress across the floor, treading dirt into shattered tiles and bypassing the shattered chandelier. He didn't stop until he reached the entrance to the Star Chamber.

"—other leg of lamb. Damn your eyes, can't you knock, man?"

Robard paused in the doorway. The Admiral was sitting at the Governor's desk, eating a platter of cold cuts—very cold, preserved meats and pickles from the cellar—with Commander Leonov and two of the other surviving staff officers standing attentively by. "Sir. The revolutionary guards are approaching. We have about five minutes to decide whether to fight or talk. Can I suggest you leave the rest of your meal until after we have dealt with them?"

Leonov rounded on him. "You bounder, how dare you disturb the Admiral! Get out!"

Robard raised his left hand and turned it over, revealing the card he held. "Have you ever seen one of these before?"

Leonov turned white. "I—I—"

"I don't have time for this," Robard said brusquely. To the Admiral; "My lord?"

Kurtz stared at him with narrowed eyes. "How long?"

Robard shrugged. "All the time I've been with you, my lord. For your own protection. As I was saying, a crowd is moving in our direction from the south bank, over the old bridge. We have about five minutes to decide what to do, but I doubt we will make any friends by shooting at them."

Kurtz nodded. "I will go and talk to them, then."

Now it was Robard's turn to stare. "Sir, I believe you should be in a wheelchair, not arguing with revolutionaries. Are you quite sure—"

"Haven't felt this good in, oh, about eight years, young feller. The bees around here pack a damned odd sting."

"Yes, you could say that. Sir, I believe you may have been compromised. The Festival apparently has access to a wide range of molecular technologies, beyond the one that's done such a sterling job on your cerebrovascular system. If they wanted—"

Kurtz raised a hand. "I know. But we're at their mercy in any event. I will go down to the people and talk. Were any of the crowd old?"

"No." Robard puzzled for a moment. "None that I saw. Do you suppose—"

"A cure for old age is a very common wish," Kurtz observed. "Dashed slug-a-beds want to be shot by a jealous husband, not a nurse bored with emptying the bedpan. If this Festival has been granting wishes, as our intelligence put it . . ." He stood up. "Get me my dress uniform, Rob—oh. You, yes you, Kossov. You're my batman now Robard here outranks you all. And my medals!"

Leonov, white as a sheet, still hadn't stopped shaking. "It's alright," Robard said sepulchrally. "I don't usually have people executed for being rude to me."

"Sir! Ah—yes, sir! Um, if I may ask—"

"Ask away."

"Since when is an Invigilator of the Curator's Office required to disguise himself as a manservant?"

"Since"—Robard pulled out his pocket watch and glanced at it—"about seven years and six months ago, at the request of the Archduke. Really. Nobody *notices* a servant, you know. And His Excellency—" Kossov returned bearing the trappings of high office. Leonov ushered Robard out onto the landing while the Admiral dressed. "His Excellency is not in *direct* line to the throne. If you take my meaning." Leonov did, and his sharp intake of breath—combined with the stress analyzers wired into his auditory nerves—told Robard everything he needed to know. "No, His Majesty had no expectation of a coup; the Admiral is unquestionably loyal. But his personal charisma, fame as a hero of the Republic, and wide popularity, made his personal safety a matter of some importance. We can use him here."

"Oh." Leonov thought for a while. "The revolutionaries?"

"If he pushes them, they'll crumble," Robard said decisively. "All their strongest supporters have long since fled; that's the nature of a singularity. If they don't"—he tapped his pocket—"I am licensed to take extraordinary measures in the defense of the Republic, including the use of proscribed technologies."

Leonov dabbed at his forehead with a handkerchief. "Then it's all over. You'll break the revolutionaries by force or by politics, install His Excellency as governor pro tem, and in six months time it will all be over, bar the shouting."

"I wouldn't say that. Even if the woman from Earth was right—and I am inclined to think she was telling the truth about the Festival not being interested in planetary conquest as we understand it, in which case this whole expedition has been a monstrously expensive mistake—we've lost two-thirds of the population. We can never get rid of the pernicious virus of band-width that they've infected this planet with; we may have to abandon the colony, or at the very least institute quarantine procedures. The bloody revolutionaries have *won,* here, the djinn is well and truly out of the bottle. Everything our ancestors fought for, torn up and scattered to the winds! A virus of eternal youth is loose in the bees, and the streets are paved with infinite riches. It devalues everything!" He stopped and took a deep breath, disturbed by the degree of his own agitation. "Of course, if we can suppress the revolutionary cadres here in New Petrograd, we can mop up the countryside at our leisure . . ."

The door to the Star Chamber opened to reveal Admiral Kurtz standing there, resplendent in the gold braid, crimson sash, and chestful of medals that his rank dictated. He looked a decade younger than his age, not two decades older: patrician, white-haired, the very image of a gentleman dictator, reassuringly authoritarian. "Well, gentlemen! Shall we review the crowds?" He did not stride—wasted leg muscles saw to that—but he walked without a hand at either elbow.

"I think that would be a very good idea, sir," said Robard.

"Indeed." Leonov and the senior Curator fell into step behind the admiral as he walked toward the staircase. "The sun is setting on anarchy and disarray, gentlemen. Only let my tongue be silver and tomorrow will once again be ours."

Together, they stepped into the courtyard to address the sheep who, did they but know it, had already returned to the fold.

an amber teardrop the size of a charabanc perched on the edge of a hillside covered in the mummified bones of trees. Ashy telegraph poles coated in a fine layer of soot pointed at the sky; tiny skeletons crunched under Burya Rubenstein's boots as he walked among them, following a man-sized rabbit.

"Master in *here,*" said Mr. Rabbit, pointing at the weirdly curved lump.

Rubenstein approached it cautiously, hands clasped behind his back. Yes, it was definitely amber—or something closely resembling it. Flies and bubbles were scattered throughout its higher layers; darkness shrouded its heart. "It's a lump of fossilized vegetable sap. Your master's dead, rabbit. Why did you bring me here?"

The rabbit was upset. His long ears tilted backward, flat along the top of his skull. "Master *in* here!" He shifted from one foot to the other. "When Mimes attack, master call for help."

Burya decided to humor the creature. "I see—" He stopped.

There *was* something inside the boulder, something darkly indistinct. And come to think of it, all the trees hereabouts were corpses, fried from the inside out by some terrible energy. The revolutionary guards, already spooked by the Lysenkoist forest, had refused to enter the dead zone. They milled about downslope, debating the ideological necessity of uplifting non-human species to sapience—one of them had taken heated exception to a proposal to giving opposable thumbs and the power of speech to cats—and comparing their increasingly baroque implants. Burya stared closer, feeling himself slip into a blurred double vision as the committee for state communications' worms fed their own perspective to him. There was something inside the boulder, and it was thinking, artlessly unformed thoughts that tugged at the Festival's cellular communications network like a toddler at its mother's skirt.

Taking a deep breath, he leaned against the lump of notamber. "Who are you?" he demanded noiselessly, feeling the smooth warm surface under his hands. Antennae beneath his skin radiated information into the packetized soup that flooded in cold waves through the forest, awaited a reply.

"Me-Identity: Felix. You-Identity: ???"

"Come out of there with your hands above your head and prepare to submit your fate to the vanguard of revolutionary justice!" Burya gulped. He'd meant to send something along the lines of "Can you come out of there so we can talk?", but his revolutionary implants evidently included a semiotic de-referencing stage that translated anything he said—through this new cyberspatial medium—into Central Committee sound bites. Angry at the internal censorship, he resolved to override it next time.

"Badly hurt. No connection previous incarnation. Want/need help metamorphosis."

Burya turned and leaned his back against the boulder. "You. Rabbit. Can you hear any of this?"

The rabbit sat up and swallowed a mouthful of grass. "Any of what?"

"I've been talking to, ah, your master. Can you hear us?"

One ear flicked. "No."

"Good." Burya closed his eyes, settled back into double vision, and attempted to communicate. But his implant was still acting up. *"How did you get here? What are you trying to achieve? I thought you were in trouble"* came out as "Confess your counterrevolutionary crimes before the tribunal! What task are you striving to accomplish in the unceasing struggle against reactionary mediocrity and bourgeois incrementalism? I thought you were guilty of malicious hooliganism!"

"Fuck," he muttered aloud. "There's got to be a bypass filter—" Ah. *"Sorry about that, my interface is ideologically biased. How did you get here? What are you trying to achieve? I thought you were in trouble."*

An answer slowly burbled up and out of the stone; visual perceptions cut in, and for a few minutes Burya shook in the grip of a young lad's terrified flight from the Fringe.

"Ah. So. The Festival mummified you pending repairs. And now you're ready to go somewhere else—where? What's that?"

Another picture. Stars, endless distance, tiny dense and very *hot* bodies sleeping the dreamless light-years away. Bursting in a desert storm of foliage on a new world, flowering and dying and sleeping again until next time.

"Let me get this straight. You used to be the governor. Then you were an eight-year-old boy with some friendly talking animals under some kind of geas to 'lead an interesting life' and have lots of adventures. Now you want to be a starship? And you want me, as the nearest delegate of the Central Committee for the revolution, to help you?"

Not exactly. Another vision, this time long and complex, burdened by any number of political proposals that his implant irritatingly attempted to convert into plant-yield diagrams indicating the progress toward fruition of an agricultural five-year plan. "You want me to do *that?*" Burya winced. "What do you think I am, a free agent? Firstly, the Curator's Office would shoot me as soon as look at me, much less listen to what they'd view as treason. Secondly, you're not the governor anymore, and even if you were and proposed something like this, they'd sack you faster than you can snap your fingers. In case you didn't notice those fireworks yesterday, that was the Imperial fleet—what's left of it—shooting it out with the Festival. Thirdly, the revolutionary committee would be queuing up to shoot me, too, if I proposed something like this. Never underestimate the intrinsic, as opposed to ideological, conservatism of an idea like revolution once it's got some momentum behind it. No, it's not practical. I really don't see why you wasted my time with such a stupid proposal. Not at—"

He stopped. Something downslope was making a lot of noise, thrashing through the kill zone left by the X-ray laser battery.

"Who's there?" he asked, but Mr. Rabbit had vanished in a tuft of panicky white tail fur.

A telephone-pole tree toppled slowly over before the thrashing, and a strange, chicken-legged mound lurched into view. Sister Seventh sat in the hut's doorway, glaring intently at him. "Burya Rubenstein!" she yelled. "Come here! Resolution achieved! Cargo retrieved! You have visitors!"

ехресting а момеntоus meeting, Rachel cast her eyes around the hillside: they took to the air and flew on insectile wings, quartering the area for threats.

The trees hereabouts were dead, charred by some terrible force. Martin watched anxiously as she rummaged in the corpulent steamer trunk. "What's that?" he asked.

"Cornucopia seed," she said, tossing the fist-sized object at him. He caught it and inspected it curiously.

"All engineering is here," he marveled. "In miniature." Several million billion molecular assemblers, a kilowatt of thin-film solar cells to power them, thermodynamic filtration membranes to extract raw feedstocks from the environment, rather more computing power than the whole of the pre-Singularity planetary Internet. He pocketed the seed, then looked at her. "You had a reason...?"

"Yup. We're not going to have the original for much longer. Don't let the kid see it, he might guess what it is and flip his lid." She continued forward. There was some kind of boulder near the crest of the hill, and a man was leaning against it. The Critic's house lurched forward, crashing and banging toward it. "If that's who I hope it is—"

They started up the rise. The trees hereabouts were all dead. Martin stumbled over a rounded stone and kicked at it, cursing: he stopped when it revealed itself to be a human skull, encrusted with metallic fibrils. "Something bad happened here."

"Big surprise. Help me steer this thing." The steamer trunk, now running on fuel cells, was proving balky and hard to control on the grassy slope: half the time they had to drag it over obstacles. "You got any holdouts?"

Martin shrugged. "Do I look like a soldier?"

She squinted at him for a moment. "You've got enough hidden depths, dearie. Okay, if it turns nasty, I'll handle things."

"Who's this guy you're supposed to be seeing, anyway?"

"Burya Rubenstein. Radical underground journalist, big mover and shaker in the underground. Ran a soviet during a major worker's strike some years ago; got himself exiled for his pains, lucky they didn't shoot him."

"And you're planning to hand—" Martin stopped. "Ah, so that's what you were planning. That's how you were going to start a revolution here, before the Festival made it all last year's news." He glanced over his shoulder, but Vassily was nowhere to be seen.

"Not exactly. I was just going to give them the tools to do so if they wanted to." She wiped her forehead on the back of a hand. "Actually, it's been a contingency plan for years, only we never quite had a good enough reason to do it—initiation of force, that kind of thing. Now, well, the whole game's changed. Far as I can tell, Rubenstein's lot survived the transition to a postscarcity economy; they may be the nearest thing to civil authorities on this two-bit backwater colony right now. When the Festival gets bored and moves on, they may not be able to survive without a cornucopia. Assuming, of course, that they didn't ask the Festival for one straight off." The luggage surged forward, getting a grip on the ground, and she stopped talking for a while to concentrate on steering it up the hill.

"So what was your exit strategy?" Martin asked, walking along behind her.

"Exit strategy? We don't need no stinking exit strategy! Just— deliver this. Then melt into the chaos. Find somewhere to live. Settle down till trade resumes. Ship out. You?"

"About the same. Herman has a way of catching up after a while. Uh, did you have anywhere in mind to—"

"Small town called Plotsk." She jerked her head sharply. "First things first. I need to deliver the package. Then we need to ditch laughing boy somewhere safe where he can't follow us, hmm? Aside from that, I was wondering if—well. About us."

Martin reached out and took her free hand. "Wondering if you were going to get rid of me?"

She stared at him. "Mm. Why—am I going to have to?"

Martin took a deep breath. "Do you *want* to get rid of me?"

She shook her head.

Martin gently pulled her toward him, until she leaned against him. "Me neither," he murmured in her ear.

"Two of us stand a better chance than one, anyway," she rationalized. "We can watch each other's backs, it's going to be hairy for a while. Plus, we may be stuck here for some time. Years, even."

"Rachel. Stop making excuses."

She sighed. "Am I that transparent?"

"You've got a worse sense of duty than—" She pulled back a little, and he stopped, seeing the warning glint in her eyes. Then she began to laugh quietly, and after a moment he joined her.

"I can think of much worse people to be stranded with in the middle of a backwater recovering from a revolution, Martin, believe me—"

"Okay, I believe you, I believe you!" She leaned forward and kissed him, hard, then let go with a smile.

The luggage was rolling smoothly now, and the slope of the ground was flattening out. The boulder above them glowed yellow in the afternoon light; and the man who'd been leaning against it was deep in animated arm-waving conversation with the huge Critic. As they approached, he turned to face them: a wiry, short man with bushy hair, a goatee, and the antique affectation of pince-nez. Judging by the state of his clothing he'd been on the road for some time. "Who are you?" he demanded aggressively.

"Burya Rubenstein?" Rachel asked tiredly.

"Yes?" He glared at her suspiciously. "You have countermeasures!"

"Parcel for Burya Rubenstein, care of the Democratic Revolutionary Party, Rochard's World. You wouldn't believe how far it's come or how many hoops I've had to jump through to get it to you."

"Ah—" He stared at the trunk, then back at Rachel. "Who did you say you were?"

"Friends from Old Earth," Martin grunted. "Also hungry, dirty, shipwrecked survivors."

"Well, you won't find any decent hospitality here." Rubenstein swept a hand around the clearing. "Old Earth, did you say? Now that *is* a long way to come with a parcel! Just what exactly is it?"

"It's a cornucopia machine. Self-replicating factory, fully programmable, and it's yours. A gift from Earth. The means of production in one handy self-propelled package. We hoped you might feel like starting an industrial revolution. At least we did before we found out about the Festival." Rachel blinked as Rubenstein threw back his head and laughed wildly.

"Just what exactly is that meant to mean?" she demanded irritably. "I've come forty light-years, at not inconsiderable risk, to deliver a message you'd have murdered for six months ago. Don't you think you could explain yourself?"

"Oh, madam, please accept my apologies. I do you a disservice. If you'd delivered this even four weeks ago, you'd have changed the course of history—of that I have no doubt! But you see"—he straightened up and his expression grew sober—"we have had such devices since the first day of the Festival. And for all the good they've done us, I'd just as soon never have set eyes on one."

She looked back at Rubenstein. "Well, that confirms it. I suppose you've got time to fill me in on what's been going on here while I've been engaged in this fool's errand?" she demanded.

"We held the revolution about, ah, three weeks ago." Burya circled the steamer trunk, inspecting it. "Things did not go according to plan, as I'm sure our friend the Critic here will explain." He sat down on the chest. "Eschaton only knows what the Critics are doing here in the first place, or indeed the Festival. We—nobody—was ready for what happened. My dreams are co-opted by committee meetings, did you know that? The revolution ran its course in two weeks: that's how long it took for us to realize nobody *needed* us. Emergent criticality. The Sister here has been showing me the consequences—bad consequences." He hung his head. "Survivors of the fleet have landed at the capital, they tell me. People are flocking to them. They want security, and who can blame them?"

"So let me get this straight." Rachel leaned against the huge amber boulder. "You changed your mind about wanting to change the system?"

"Oh no!" Burya stood up agitatedly. "But the system no longer exists. It wasn't destroyed by committees or soviets or worker's cadres; it was destroyed by people's wishes coming true. But come, now. You look as if you've been through a battle! There are refugees everywhere, you know. Once I sort out my business here, I will return to Plotsk and see what I can do to ensure stability. Perhaps you'd like to come along?"

"Stability," Martin echoed. "Um, what business? I mean, why are you here? We seem to be quite a way from civilization." That was a huge understatement, as far as Rachel could see. She leaned back and looked down at the forest dispiritedly. To come all this distance, only to find that she was three weeks too late to change history for the better: that the Festival had dropped an entire planetary society, such as it was, into an informational blender and dialed the blades to FAST; it was all a bit too much to appreciate. That, and she was *tired,* mortally tired. She'd done her best, like Martin. Three weeks. *If Martin had failed...*

"There's someone inside that boulder," said Rubenstein.

"What?" A complex three-dimensional model of the hillside spread out before Rachel's distributed spy-eyes. There was Vassily, working his way up the far side of the slope. Here was Martin. And the boulder—

"The occupant." Burya nodded. "He's still alive. Actually, he wants to join the Festival as a passenger. I can see why; from his point of view, it makes sense. But I think the emergency committee might disagree—they'd rather see him dead. The reactionary forces in the capital would disagree for other reasons: they'd want him back. He used to be the planetary governor, you see, until too many of his private, personal wishes came true. Dereliction of duty." Rubenstein blinked. "I wouldn't have believed it, but."

"Ah. So what's the real problem with him joining the Festival?"

"Getting their attention. The Festival trades information for services. He's told it everything he knows. So have I. What are we to do?"

"That's preposterous," said Martin. "You mean, the Festival will only accept fare-paying passengers?"

"Strange as this may seem, it's how the Fringe and the Critics first came aboard. The Critics still pay their way by providing higher-level commentary on whatever they find." Burya sat down again.

Martin yelled. "Hey! Critic!"

On the lower slopes of the hill, Sister Seventh sat up. "Question?" she boomed.

"How are you going home?" Martin shouted at her.

"Finish Critique! Exchange liftwise."

"Can you take a passenger?"

"Ho!" Sister Seventh ambled up the slope of the hill. "Identity interrogative?"

"Whoever's in this vitrification cell. Used to be the planetary governor, I'm told."

The Critic shambled closer. Rachel tried not to recoil from her clammy vegetable-breathy presence. "Can take cargo," Sister Seventh rumbled. "Give reason."

"Um." Martin glanced at Rachel. "The Festival assimilates

information, no? We came from the fleet. I have an interesting story to tell."

Sister Seventh nodded. "Information. Useful, yes, low entropy. Is passenger—"

"Vitrified," Burya interrupted. "By the Festival, apparently. Please be discreet. Some of my colleagues would disapprove, and as for the reactionaries—"

Some sixth sense made Rachel turn around. It was Vassily: he'd circled around the far side of the hill for some reason, and now she saw that he was clutching a seemingly bladeless handle. His expression was wild. "Burya Rubenstein?" he gasped.

"That's me. Who are you?" Rubenstein turned to face the new arrival.

Vassily took two steps forward, half-staggering, like a marionette manipulated by a drunk. "I'm your son, you bastard! Remember my mother yet?" He raised his power knife.

"Oh *shit.*" Rachel suddenly noticed the fuzz of static that was even now plucking at her implants, trying to tell them this wasn't happening, that there was nobody there. Things became clearer, much clearer. She wasn't the only person with high-level implants hereabouts.

"My son?" Rubenstein looked puzzled for a moment, then his expression cleared. "'Milla was allowed to keep you after I was exiled?" He stood up. "My son—"

Vassily swung at Rubenstein, artlessly but with all the force he could muster. But Burya wasn't there when the knife came down; Martin had tackled him from behind, ramming him headfirst into the ground.

With a shrill screech, the power knife cut into the lid of the cornucopia, slicing through millions of delicate circuits. A numinous flickering light and a smell of fresh yeast rose up as Vassily struggled to pull the blade out. A superconducting monofilament, held rigid by a viciously powerful magnetic field, the knife could cut through just about anything. Martin rolled over on his back and looked up just as Vassily, his face a slack mask, stepped toward him and raised the knife. There was a brief buzzing sound, and his eyes rolled up: then Vassily collapsed across the chest.

Arms and chest burning, Rachel lowered the stun gun and dropped back into real-world speed. Panting, heart racing. *Do this too often and die.* "Bloody hell, wasn't there *anybody* aboard the fleet without a covert agenda?" she complained.

"Doesn't look like it." Martin struggled to sit up.

"What happened?" Burya looked around, dazed.

"I think—" Rachel looked at the trunk. It was outgassing ominously: the power knife had cut through a lot of synthesis cells, and evidently some of the fuel tanks were leaking faster than the repair programs could fix them. "It could be a bad idea to stay here. Talk about it on the road to Plotsk?"

"Yes." Burya rolled Vassily off the trunk and dragged him a few paces. "Is he really my son?"

"Probably." Rachel paused to yawn for air. "I wondered a bit. Why he was along. Couldn't have been a mistake. And then, the way he went for you—programmed, I think. Curator's Office must have figured, if revolution, you'd be central. Bastard child, disgraced mother, easily recruited. Credible?"

Sister Seventh had ambled up and was sniffing at the vitrification cell occupied by the nearly late Duke Felix Politovsky. "I told Festival passenger upload now-soon," she rumbled. "You tell story? Honor credit?"

"Later," said Martin.

"Okay." Sister Seventh gnashed at the air. "You got overdraft at the mythology bank. I fix. Go Plotsk, now-soonish?"

"Before the luggage goes bang," Martin agreed. He stood up a trifle drunkenly, winced as he transferred his weight onto one knee. "Rachel?"

"Coming." The dark spots had almost vacated her visual field. "Okay. Um, if we can tie him up and put him in that walking hut of yours, we can work on his brainwashing later. See if there's anything more to him than a programmed assassin."

"I agree." Burya paused. "I didn't expect this."

"Neither did we," she said shortly. "Come on. Let's get away before this thing blows."

Together they stumbled away from the fizzing revolutionary bomb and the last unchanging relic of the ancien régime, back down the hillside that led toward the road to Plotsk.

ONCE NEWS OF Admiral Kurtz's miraculous appearance in the Ducal palace spread into the city, a tenuous curtain of normality began to assert itself. The revolutionary committees centered on the Corn Exchange watched the situation with alarm, but the common people were less unenthusiastic. Most of them were bewildered, disoriented, and deeply upset by the strangeness of the times. Those who weren't had for the most part already left the city; the survivors huddled together for comfort amidst the ruins of their certainties, eating manna from the Festival's machines and praying.

Kurtz's mysterious burst of good health continued; as Robard had noticed earlier, diseases of senescence were extremely rare among the survivors of the Festival, and for good reason. Acting on the Curator's advice, the Admiral magnanimously announced an amnesty for all progressive elements and a period of reconstruction and collective introspection. Many of the remaining revolutionaries took the opportunity to melt into the crowded camps or leave the city, in some cases taking cornucopia seeds with them. Rochard's World was thinly colonized, an almost unknown wilderness starting just three hundred kilometers beyond the city. Those who could not stand to watch a return to the old *status quo* took to the roads.

Also at the behest of the Curator's Office, the Admiral made no attempt to send militia forces after them. There would be time for dealing with miscreants later, Robard pointed out. Time enough after they'd starved through the coming winter.

A few more lifeboats made it down intact, cluttering the landing field behind the palace. Regular light shows lit up the sky with blue streaks of light; departing spawn of the Festival. Babushkas in the street looked up, made the sign of the evil eye, and spat in the gutter as the evil time passed. Some of the passing wisps bore the encoded essence of the old Duke; but few people knew and fewer cared. Gradually, the Festival's orbiting factories reached the end of their design life and shut down: slowly, the telephones stopped ringing. Now, people used them to call each other up. It was good to talk, and scattered families and friends rediscovered one another through the directionless medium of the phone network. The Curator fretted, and finally concluded that there was nothing to be done about it. Not until contact with the father planet resumed, in any event.

things happened differently in Plotsk. The outlying township lay cut off from the capital by landslides and bizarre, dangerous structures that had rendered the roads impassable. Here, the revolutionary committee wound down until it was now a local provisional council, now a town governance. Peasants began to squat in the many abandoned farms around the town, second and third sons gifted by a sudden superfluity of soil. Strangers drifted in, fleeing chaos in smaller settlements, and there was space for everybody. Comrade Rubenstein of the Central Committee announced his intention to settle; after a heated row with the governance, he agreed to stick to publishing a newsletter and leave matters of ideology to less mercurial souls. He moved into Havlicek the Pawnbroker's apartment above the gutted shop on Main Street, along with a young man who said little and was not seen in public for the first week, providing much fertile material for wagging tongues. Strange structures burbled and steamed in the small courtyard behind the shop, and rumor had it that Rubenstein dabbled in the strange arts of technological miracle-working that had so upset the state sometime ago—but nobody disturbed him, for the local constabulary were in the pay of the governance, who had more sense than to mess with a dangerous wizard and revolutionary ideologue.

Another strange couple took over a tenement above Markus Wolff's old hardware store. They didn't talk much, but the bearded man demonstrated a remarkable aptitude with tools. Together they rebuilt the store, then opened for business. They kept a small stock of locks and clocks and rebuilt telephones and more exotic gadgets, racked in the age-blackened oak cabinets within the shop. These they traded for food and clothing and coal, and tongues wagged about the source of the miraculous toys that they sold so cheap—items that would have cost a fortune in the capital of the father world, never mind a backwoods colonial town. The supply seemed never-ending, and the sign they hung from the shop front was daringly close to subversive: access to tools and ideas. But this didn't provoke as much comment as the conduct of his partner; a tall, thin woman with dark hair cut short, who sometimes went about bareheaded and unaccompanied, and frequently ran the shop when her husband was absent, even serving strangers on her own.

Back before the Festival, their conduct would have been sure to arouse comment, perhaps even a visit by the police and a summons to the Curator's Office. But in these strange times, nobody seemed to care: and the radical Rubenstein was a not-infrequent visitor to their shop, procuring interesting components for his printing mechanism. They evidently had dangerous friends, and this was enough to deter the neighbors from snooping too much—except for the widow Lorenz, who seemed to feel it was her duty to pick a quarrel with the woman (who she suspected of being a Jewess, or unwed, or something equally sinister).

Over the nine months following the Festival, summer slid into the cold, rainy depths of autumn: the sun hid its face, and winter settled its icy grip into the ground. Martin spent many evenings rooting through the supply of metal bar stock he'd collected during the summer, feeding pieces to the small fabricator in the cellar, trying his hand at toolmaking with the primitive mechanical equipment to hand. Diamond molds, electric arc furnace, numerically controlled milling machine—these, his tools, he spun from the fabricator, using them in turn to make artifacts that the farmers and shopkeepers around him could understand.

While Martin worked at these tasks, Rachel kept house and shop together, rooted out clothing and food, bought advertising space in Rubenstein's broadsheet, and kept her ears to the ground for signs of trouble. They lived together as man and wife, meeting nosy neighborly inquiries with a blank stare and a shrug meaning *mind your own business*. Life was primitive, their resources and comfort limited both by what was available and by the exigencies of leading an inconspicuous existence; although after winter began to bite, Martin's installation of insulating foam and heat pumps kept them so warm that one or two of the more daring neighbors developed an unwelcome tendency to hang around the shop.

One chilly morning, Martin awoke with a headache and a dry mouth. For a moment he couldn't recall where he was: he opened his eyes and looked up at a dingy white curtain. Someone murmured sleepily and rolled against him. *How did I get here? This isn't my shop. This isn't my life*—the sense of alienation was profound. Then memory came sluicing back like a flash flood, damping down the dusty plains. He rolled over and reached out an arm, hugged her sleeping shoulders against his chest. Distant emitters twittered to the back of his head: all the wards were in place. Rachel muttered and twitched, yawning. "Awake?" he asked softly.

"Yeah. Ah. What time is it?" She blinked against the morning light, hair tousled and eyes puffy with sleep, and a stab of affection thrilled through him.

"After dawn. Bloody cold out here. 'Scuse me." He hugged her once, then slid feet first through the bed-curtains, out into the frigid bedroom. The frost had scrawled its runes inside the windowpanes. Trying to keep his feet off the wooden floor, he twitched on his felt slippers then pulled out the chamber pot and squatted. He pulled on chilly outerwear from the clothesline inside the canopy bed, then went down into the cellar to inspect the charcoal burner that still glowed, peltier cells generating power for the small manufacturing plant's overnight milling run. Draw water, boil it, and soon they'd have coffee—a miraculous luxury, notwithstanding that it was ersatz, produce of a cornucopia machine. Maybe in a week or two the geothermal tap would be providing a bit more heat; for now, any temperature above freezing was a win in the face of the fierce steppe winter.

Rachel was up, floor creaking underfoot, yawning as she pulled on her chemise and underskirts. He stomped downstairs to rake out the oven and light a new fire; his hands were too cold, and he rubbed them hard to get the circulation going. *Morning market, isn't it?* He thought. *Lots of farmers. Maybe make some sales.* Then he almost pinched himself. *What am I turning into?* Cold ashes tumbling into a tin bucket as he scraped behind the fire grate. Something rustled behind him. He glanced around. Rachel was clad for outdoors: her voluminous brown dress covered her to the soles of her boots, and she'd tied her hair up in a head scarf, knotted tightly under her chin after the local fashion. Only her face was exposed. "You going out?" he asked.

"Market this morning. I want to buy some bread, maybe a chicken or two. They're not going to be so easy to come by if we leave it any longer." She glanced away. "Brr. Cold today, isn't it?"

"We should be warming up in here by the time you get back." He finished laying coals in the grate and used a small, familiar piece of magic: light blossomed fast, spread hungrily across the anthracite surfaces. He turned his back to the oven. "Should be a lot of sales today. Money—"

"I'll draw some from the till." She leaned close, and he wrapped his arms around her. Reassuring and solid, embedded within the guise of a local artisan's wife. She leaned her chin on his shoulder with long familiarity.

"You're looking good this morning. Wonderful."

She smiled a little, and shivered. "Flatterer. I wonder how much longer we're going to be able to stay here?"

"Be able to? Or have to?"

"Um." She considered for a moment. "Is it getting to you?"

"Yes. A bit." He chuckled quietly. "I caught myself thinking like a shopkeeper this morning, while I was cleaning out the grate. It'd be so easy to slip into a routine. It's what, eight months now? Living the quiet life. I could almost see us settling down here, raising a family, sinking into obscurity."

"It wouldn't work." She tensed under his hands, and he rubbed at her shoulders. "We wouldn't age right. They'll open up travel again in the new year, and then, well. I've done child rearing, too. It wouldn't work, trust me. Be glad of that reversible vasectomy. Or had you thought what it'd be like to be on the run with a baby in tow?"

"Oh, I know about that." He carried on moving his hands in small circles until she relaxed slightly. Thick fabric moved under his fingertips, many layers of it against the cold. "I know. We need to move on, sooner rather than later. It's just so...quiet. Peaceful."

"Graveyards are quiet, too." She pulled back to arm's length and stared at him, and once again he held his breath: because when she did this, he found her unbearably beautiful. "That's what the New Republic is all about, isn't it? This isn't a good place to live, Martin. It isn't safe. The town's in shock; collectively they're all in a fit of denial. All their wishes granted, for three months, and it wasn't enough! When they wake up, they'll reach for the security blanket. The place will be crawling with Curator's Office informers, and this time you don't have an Admiralty contract and I don't have a diplomatic passport. We'll have to move on."

"And your employers—" He couldn't continue.

"Easy come, easy go." She shrugged. "I've taken leave of absence before. This isn't leave; it's lying low, waiting to exit a hot zone. But if we could only make it back to Earth, there are lots of things I'd like to do with you. Together. There'll be room to make plans, then. Here, if we stay, someone else will plan everything for us. Along with everybody else."

"Alright." He turned back to the cooker: a healthy red glow rippled beneath the coals that the adiabatic heater had goosed into combustion. "Today, the market. Maybe this evening we can think about when to—"

There was a pounding at the front door.

"What is it?" Martin shouted. Leaving the stove, he shambled through into the cold, dark shop: paused at the door. Opened the letterbox. "Who's there?"

"Telegram!" piped a breathless voice. "Telegram for Master Springburg!"

With a rattle of bolts, Martin slid the door ajar. Blinding white snow, and a red-uniformed post office runner boy who stood staring up at him. "Telegram? For the toolsmith?"

"That'd be me," he said. The boy waited: Martin fumbled for a tip, a few kopecks, then closed the door and leaned against it, heart pounding. *A telegram!*

"Open it!" Rachel loomed over him, eyes anxious with hope and surprise. "Who is it from?"

"It's from Herman—" he opened the envelope and, mouth dry, began to read aloud:

TO: MARTIN SPRINGFIELD AND RACHEL MANSOUR,
   CONGRATULATIONS ON YOUR BABY.

   I UNDERSTAND THE CHILD WAS BORN IN ORBIT AROUND ROCHARD'S WORLD, AND SHORTLY DEPARTED IN VARIOUS DIRECTIONS. WHILE I APPRECIATE THAT YOU ARE BOTH TIRED, YOU MIGHT BE INTERESTED TO KNOW THAT I HAVE AN IMPORTANT BUSINESS VENTURE OPENING BACK HOME. IF YOU'D LIKE TO BE INVOLVED, TWO TICKETS ARE WAITING FOR YOU AT THE CENTRAL POST OFFICE IN NOVY PETROGRAD.

   PS: I GATHER SPRING IS AN UNHEALTHY SEASON IN PLOTSK. PLEASE DON'T TARRY.

Later that day, the old Wolff hardware store caught fire and burned down to the ground—the victim, local rumor had it, of neglect by its feckless owner. He had last been seen leaving town in a hired sleigh, accompanied by his fancy woman and a small carpetbag. They were never seen again in Plotsk, but vanished into the capital city like a drop of ink in the blue ocean: lost in the turbulence and excitement surrounding the arrival of the first civilian starship since the Festival departed, a tramp freighter from Old Calais.

They weren't really lost: but that, as they say, is another story. And before I recount it, I have some wishes I would like you to grant me . . .

iron sunrise

contents

For Olivia and Howard

ACKNOWLEDGMENTS

Thanks due to: Emmett O'Brien, Caitlin Blasdell, Andrew Wilson, Simon Bisson, Cory Doctorow, Ken McLeod, and James Nicoll. In particular I'd like to single out Emmett, for going far beyond where any reader might be expected to; Caitlin, my agent, for asking the questions that needed asking; and Geoff Miller, for an inspiring quote.

prologue: wednesday child _____

wednesday ran through the darkened corridors of the station, her heart pounding. Behind her, unseen yet sensed as a constant menacing presence, ran her relentless pursuer—a dog. The killhound wasn't supposed to be here: neither was she. Old Newfoundland Four was in the process of final evacuation, the last ship supposed to have undocked from bay green fourteen minutes ago—an icon tattooed on the inside of her left eye showed her this, time counting negative heading out for the nearest flat space-time for the jump to safety. The launch schedule took no notice of tearaway teens, crazed Dresdener captains with secret orders, and gestapo dogs with murder burning in their gunsight eyes. She panted desperately, nerves straining on the edge of panic, lungs burning in the thin, still air. Sixteen years old and counting, and if she didn't find a way to elude the dog and climb back to the docking hub soon—

She didn't want to be there when the wavefront arrived.

Three-point-six light years away, and almost three-point-six years ago, all two hundred million inhabitants of a nondescript McWorld called Moscow had died. Moscow, an introverted if not entirely rural polity, had been in the midst of political upheavals and a nasty trade dispute with New Dresden, something boring to do with biodiversity and free trade, engineering agribusiness and exchange rate controls. Old Newfoundland Four, Portal Station Eleven, was the last remaining sovereign territory of the Federal Republic of Moscow. They'd hauled down the flag in the hub concourse four hours ago, sounded the last retreat with a final blare of brass trumpetry, and marched slowly to the docking hub. Game over, nation dissolved. There'd been a misunderstanding, and Dresdener warships had impounded a freighter from Moscow. Pistol shots fired across a crowded docking hub. Then someone— to this day, the successor Dresdener government hotly denied responsibility, even though they'd executed their predecessors just to be sure—had hit Moscow Prime with a proscribed device.

Wednesday didn't remember Moscow very clearly. Her father was a nitrogen cycle engineer, her mother a protozoan ecology specialist: they'd lived on the station since she was four, part of the team charged with keeping the life-support heart of the huge orbital complex pumping away. But now the heart was still. There was no point in pretending anymore. In less than a day the shock front of Moscow Prime's funeral pyre would slam past, wreaking havoc with any habitat not shielded by a good thirty meters of metal and rock. Old Newfie, drifting in stately orbit around a planetless brown dwarf, was simply too big and too flimsy to weather a supernova storm at a range of just over a parsec.

Wednesday came to a crossroads. She stopped, panting, and tried to orient herself, biting back a wail of despair. Left, right, up, or down? Sliding down to the habitat levels of the big wheel had been a mistake. There were elevators and emergency tunnels all the way up to the hub, and all the way down to the heavy zone. The central post office, traffic control, customs, and bioisolation were all located near the maintenance core at the hub. But the top of the pressurized wheel rim was sixty meters above her, then there was another hundred meters of spoke to climb before she could get to the hub, and the dog would sense her if she used the lifts. There was too much centrifugal force down here, dragging at her like real gravity; she could turn her head sharply without feeling dizzy, and her feet felt like lead. Climbing would be painfully slow at first, the Coriolis force a constant tug trying to pull her sideways off the ladder to safety.

Dim lighting panels glowed along the ceiling, turned down to Moonlight Seven. The vines in the small hubgarden at the center of the crossroads drooped, suffering already from eighteen hours of darkness. Everything down here was dead or dying, like the body she'd found in the public toilet two decks up and three segments over. When she realized the dog was still on her tail she'd headed back home to the apartment she'd shared with her parents and younger brother, hoping the scent would confuse the hound while she sneaked away onto one of the other evacuation ships. But now she was trapped down here with it, and what she should

really have done was head for the traffic control offices and barri-
cade the doors—

Her training nudged her forward. This sector was given over
to administration offices, station police, customs and trade monitors, and the small clump of services that fed them during their
work shifts. Darkened office doorways hung open, unattended,
dust already gathering on chairs and desks. Very deliberately, she
stepped into the police station. Behind the counter a public notice
poster scrolled endlessly, STATION CLOSED. Grunting with effort, she
clambered over the chest-high barrier, then rolled down behind it.

The antique leather satchel Herman had told her to take
banged against her hip; she cursed it and what it had brought her
to. It was half-full of paper: rich, slightly creamy fabric-weave
paper, written on with real ink that didn't swim and mutate into
different fonts when you stroked the margin. Dumb matter, the
sort of medium you used when you really, *really* didn't want some
tame infowar worm to unpick your traffic. Nestled at the bottom
of the bag was a locked cassette full of molecular storage—
records from the station customs post. Records that somebody
thought were important enough to kill for.

She twitched a ring, dialing the lights up to Twilight Three, and
looked around the cop shop. She'd been there once before, when
Constable Barca had given her year a tour of the premises. That had
been a pointed adult hint about how to stay out of trouble. Things
were different now, the offices and detention areas and waiting
rooms all gaping like empty sockets in a skull. The administration
thought they knew all about teenagers, but they were wrong. She'd
seen the locked cupboard in the ready room and got Pete to front a
question about it: sticky foam and pepper gas, breathing masks and
handcuffs in case of civil disorder. *In case of riot, break glass.* Old
Newfie was mostly peaceful; there'd been just one murder and only
a handful of fights in the past thirty years. Admin thought a SWAT
team was what you sent to deal with a wasp's nest in a ventilation
duct. She paused at the locked cabinet, dumped the satchel, and
grabbed something that looked more useful.

Claws rattled on the floor outside the office, and paused.

IMPACT: T plus 1392 days, 17 hours, 30 minutes

"What do you mean, she's missing?" Constable Ito said irritably.
"Can't you keep your children under—"

The tall, stooped man ran his fingers through his thinning hair. "If you had kids—no, I'm sorry! Look, she's not here. I know she has a shipboard badge because I pinned it on her jacket myself, all right? She's not here, and I'm afraid she might have gone back home or something."

"Home?" Ito pushed his visor up and stared at the worried father. "She couldn't be that stupid. Could she?"

"Kids!" It came out like a curse, though it wasn't intended as one. "No, I don't think she's that stupid. But she's not on the ship, either, or at least she's turned off her implants—Constable Klein sent out a broadcast ping for her an hour ago. And she seemed upset about something this morning."

"Shit. Implants, huh? I'll put out a notice, all right? Things are insane around here right now. Have you any idea what it's like trying to rehouse fifteen thousand people? She'll probably turn up somewhere she isn't meant to be, crew service areas or something. Or decided to hitch a lift on *Sikorsky's Dream* for the hell of it, before she undocked. She'll turn up, that I promise you. Full ID, please?"

"Victoria Strowger. Age sixteen. ID 3 of that name."

"Ah, okay." Ito made an odd series of gestures with the rings on his right hand, tracing runes in copspace. "Okay, if she's somewhere aboard this pile of junk, that should find her. If not, it'll escalate to a general search in about ten minutes. Now if you'll excuse me until then—"

"Certainly." Morris Strowger sidled away from the Constable's desk. "She's probably just dropped her badge down the toilet," he muttered to himself. Behind him the next in the queue, an elderly woman, was haranguing the Constable about the size of her accommodation module: she refused to believe that her apartment—one human-sized cell in a five-thousand-person honeycomb of refugee pods slung in the cargo bay of the New Dresden freighter *Long March*—was all any of them would get until arrival in the nearest Septagon system. The relocation was paid for, gratis, courtesy of the (new) New Dresden government, and the residual assets of the Republic of Moscow's balance of trade surplus, but the pods weren't exactly the presidential suite of a luxury liner. *I hope Vicki gets tired of hiding soon. Maybe it'll do her some good if the Constabulary find her first and run her in. Teach her not to go looking for trouble in the middle of an emergency...*

Take a girl like *that*. Pallid complexion, cropped mop of black hair, pale blue eyes: waif or demon? She was a bit of a loner. Preternaturally smart for her age: her parents planned her, used a sensible modicum of predictive genomics to avoid the more serious pitfalls. Paid for the most expensive interface implants they could buy, imported from Septagon: they wanted only the best for her. She was seventeen and sullen, going through one of those phases. Refusing to wear anything but black, spending her free time poking around in strange service ducts, training an eighteen-million-synapse nerve garden in her bedroom (parents didn't even want to think about what she might be training it to dream of). She grew plants: deadly nightshade, valerian, aconite, hemlock—and what were they going to do with the latter when it reached full height? (Nobody knew. Nobody knows.) She liked listening to depressing music in her room with the door shut. Her anxious parents shoehorned her into the usual healthy outdoor pursuits—climbing lessons, solar sailing, karate—but none of them took a grip on her imagination. Her legal forename was Victoria, but the other teens all called her Wednesday; she hated it, but not as much as she hated her given name.

Wednesday was a misfit. Like misfits from time immemorial, she'd had an invisible friend since she was young: they played together, exploring the espionage envelope. Elevator surfing. Duct diving—with an oxy mask; you could never tell what might be on the other side of a sealed bulkhead. But most kids didn't have invisible friends who talked back via the expensive net implants their parents had shelled out for, much less taught them skills like steganography, traffic analysis, tail spotting, and Dumpster diving. And most kids grew out of having invisible friends, whereas Wednesday didn't. That was because most misfit kids' invisible friends were imaginary. Wednesday's wasn't.

When she was younger she'd told her brother Jeremy about her friend, who was called Herman: but Jerm had blabbed to Mum, and the result was a tense inquisition and trips to the network engineers, then the counselor's office. When she realized what was expected of her she denied everything, of course, but not abruptly; Herman told her how to do it so as to allay their suspicions. *You're never alone with schizophrenia,* he'd joked mordantly, annoying her because she knew that schizophrenia was nothing to do with having multiple personalities, and everything to do with hearing voices in her head. When she'd first learned about it she'd dialed chlorpromazine and flupenthixol up from the kitchen pharm, and staggered around in a haze for days while Herman witheringly explained how she might have poisoned herself: Parkinson's was a not-unknown side effect of primitive neuroleptics. It wasn't a word she'd known before he used it.

Everyone had known evacuation day was coming for months. They'd known about it to the day, to the hour in fact, since a couple of weeks after the Incident. The ships began to arrive a week ahead of zero hour. Normally Old Newfie only received one liner a month, clearing via customs to transfer passengers and cargo to the short-haul local freighters that bounced back and forth across the last parsec. But right now all the docking bays on the hub were extended, piers pressurized like great gray hagfish sucking the guts out of the station.

The surviving in-system freighters had come home for the final time two weeks earlier, rerigged with ferry tanks for the final flight. Everyone huddled together on the one station, thirty thousand souls drifting above the ecliptic of a gloomy red gas giant eight times the mass of Jupiter. They had fuel—that was what Old Newfoundland Four was in the business of selling—six hundred megatons of refined methane ice bunkered in a tank farm streaming kilometers behind the axle of the big wheel. And they were close enough to one of the regular trade routes between Septagon system and the core worlds to pick up passing trade, close enough to act as an interchange for local traffic bound for Moscow. They were still profitable and self-sufficient, had been even since before the disaster. But they couldn't stay there—not with the iron sunrise coming.

The liner *Sikorsky's Dream* nuzzled up to the hub, taking VIPs and the governor and his staff. Behind it hung two freighters from New Dresden, sent in yet another symbolic gesture of reconciliation. They looked like pregnant midwife toads, blistered with bulky refugee pods hanging from their cargo spines, steerage for tens of thousands of passengers on the three-week, forty-light year journey to Septagon for resettlement.

Even Septagon would be uncomfortably close to the shock front, but it was the best relocation center on offer. There was money enough to house and reskill everyone, and a governing polity that actively courted immigration. It would be a chance to draw a line under the incident, to look to the future, and to turn away from the dull despair and the cloud of mourning that had hovered over the station since news of the Zero Incident arrived three and a half years ago. There had been suicides then, and more than one near riot; the station was haunted by a thousand ghosts for every one alive. It was no fit place to raise a child.

Dad and Mum and Jeremy had moved aboard the *Long March* two days ago, dragging Wednesday along in their glassy-eyed optimistic undertow. There were holes in the facade, empty figures in the family photograph. Cousin Jane, Uncle Mark, Grandpa and Grandma weren't coming. At least, not in the living flesh; they were dust now, burned by the godwind that would blow past the station in four days' time.

Harried wardens had shown Wednesday and her family to their deck, corridor, segment, and cell. They had a family space: four sleeping pods and a two-by-three living room with inflatable furniture. It would be home for the voyage. They were to eat in the canteen on Rose Deck, bathe in the communal hygiene unit on Tulip, and count themselves lucky for being alive at all—unlike Mica and her husband, friends and neighbors who'd been home on a month's leave for the first time in five years when the Incident took place.

Within hours, Wednesday had been bored silly. Her plants were dead, her nerve garden shut down for cold storage, and they had been ordered to remain in steerage until after departure, with nothing but the inane prattle of the entertainment net and the ship's lobotomized media repository for company. Some budding genius from New Dresden— a more regimented society than Moscow's—had decided that horror interactives and books were unfit for minors, and slapped a parental control on that section of the database. Her friends—those she counted as friends—were mostly on the other ships. Even Herman had told her he'd be unable to talk after the ship's first jump. It would have been more fun if they'd had cold sleep tankage, but there was no way that the station's facilities could process more than a couple of hundred at a time: so Wednesday was to be a martyr to boredom for the next week.

The only consolation was that she had a whole new world to explore—a starship. She hadn't been on a ship since she was eight, and the itch to put learning into practice was irresistible. Besides, Herman said he knew and could show her the layout of this particular vessel. It was a late-model Backhoe series heavy lifter fabricated in the yards over Burgundy, with life-support superstructure by Thurn und Taxis Pty of New Dresden. It was just a trash hauler—fusion rockets, contrarotating spin wheels— nothing as sophisticated as a momentum transfer unit or grav generators. Its jump module was a sealed unit purchased from some-place where they knew how to make such things; neither Dresden nor Moscow had the level of tech infrastructure necessary to throw naked singularities around. But Herman knew his way around the ship, and Wednesday was bored. So obviously it was time to go exploring; and when she told him, he had some inter-esting suggestions for where to go.

Wednesday was lousy at staying out of locked rooms. Her second-year tutor had summed it up: "She's like a cat—takes a shut door as a personal insult." She took her pick gun and tablet with her as a matter of course, not out of malice or a desire to bur-gle, but simply because she couldn't abide not knowing what lay on the far side of a door. (The ship had a double-walled hull, and the only doors that breached into vacuum were airlocks. Unless she was stupid enough to pick a door with flashing pressure warn-ing lights, heavy gaskets, and mechanical interlocks, she wasn't running any risks. Or so she thought...)

The ship wasn't exactly off-limits to passengers, but she had a feeling her presence would be discouraged if anyone noticed her. So she sneaked up into the central service axis and back down into the crew ring the smart way: sitting on the roof of a powered ele-vator car, her stiction pads locked to the metal as it swam up the tunnel, decelerating and shedding angular momentum. She rode it up and down twice, searching for ventilation ducts with the aid of a torch, before she made her move. She swam through darkened service shafts, down another tube, hitched a lift on the roof of a passenger car, and surfed all the way into one of the main ventila-tion bronchi. The maintenance moles in the airflow system left her alone, because she was alive and moving, which was just as well, really. After an hour of hobbiting around in the ducts she was tired and a bit disoriented—and it was then that she came across the fil-tration hood that Herman had told her to expect.

It sat in the floor of a cramped duct, humming softly to itself, laminar pumps blurring quietly in the twilight. A faint blue glow of ultraviolet lamps shone from the edges. Fascinated, she bent close to inspect it. *Sterilizers aboard a starship?* Only in the life-support system, as a rule. But this was the accommodation deck, so what was it doing here? A quick once-over of the mounting bolts revealed another anomaly—a fine wire leading down through a hole in the floor of the duct. It was obviously an alarm cable. Not the sort of unreliable IR sensor that might be set off by a passing maintenance pig, nor a nerve garden eyeball sensor to be bamboozled by shadows, but an honest old-fashioned burglar alarm! She attacked it with her multitool and the compact maintenance kit she'd acquired a few months ago. Wires were easy—

A minute later she had the filtration hood unbolted and angled up at one side. Dropping an eyeball through was the work of seconds. Her camera-on-a-thread—disguised as a toy spider—swam in dizzy circles, revealing a cramped room, locked inner door, shelves with boxes secured to four of the walls. Purser's office or captain's locker? Wednesday couldn't tell, but it was obviously where they kept the high-value cargo, anything compact that had to be shipped in a safe under lock and key, accessible for inspection during the voyage. Deeds. Share certificates. Papers, orders, DNA samples, cypher keys, the odd rare piece of proprietary software. *"Why don't you go look?"* a familiar voice prodded her. Herman blinked a schematic behind her eyes. *"Observe: according to this original blueprint this room should be part of the Captain's quarters."*

"Think I'll find any treasure inside?" asked Wednesday, already looking for an attachment point for her rope. The lure of forbidden fruit was more than she'd ever been able to resist.

Locked doors. A teenage girl going through one of those phases. Modifications to a standard lifesystem. Stop all the clocks: a star has died. Blue plastic toy spiders. Confidential orders handwritten on dumb paper. Invisible playmates. Badge dropped down lift shaft. Respiration stops: the universe holds its breath. And . . .

IMPACT: T zero

just outside the expanding light cone of the present a star died, iron-bombed. *Something*—some exotic force of unnatural origin—twisted a knot in space, enclosing the heart of a stellar furnace. A huge loop of superstrings twisted askew, expanding and contracting until the core of the star floated adrift in a pocket universe where the time-like dimension was rolled shut on the scale of the Planck length, and another dimension—one of the closed ones, folded shut on themselves, implied by the standard model of physics—replaced it. An enormous span of time reeled past within the pocket universe, while outside a handful of seconds ticked by.

From the perspective of the drifting core, the rest of the universe appeared to recede to infinity, vanishing past an event horizon beyond which it was destined to stay until the zone of expansion collapsed. The blazing ball of gas lit up its own private cosmos, then slowly faded. Time passed, uncountable amounts of time wrapped up in an eyeblink from the perspective of the external universe. The stellar core cooled and contracted, dimming. Eventually a black dwarf hung alone, cooling toward absolute zero. Fusion didn't stop but ran incredibly slowly, mediated by quantum tunneling under conditions of extreme cold. Over a span billions of times greater than that which had elapsed since the big bang in the universe outside, light nuclei merged, tunneling across the high quantum wall of their electron orbitals. Heavier elements disintegrated slowly, fissioning and then decaying down to iron. Mass migrated until, by the end of the process, a billion trillion years down the line, the star was a single crystal of iron crushed down into a sphere a few thousand kilometers in diameter, spinning slowly in a cold vacuum only trillionths of a degree above absolute zero.

Then the external force that had created the pocket universe went into reverse, snapping shut the pocket and dropping the dense spherical crystal into the hole at the core of the star, less than thirty seconds after the bomb had gone off. And the gates of hell opened.

Iron doesn't fuse easily: the process is endothermic, absorbing energy. When the guts were scooped out of the star and replaced with a tiny cannonball of cold degenerate matter, the outer layers of the star, held away from the core by radiation pressure, began to collapse inward across a gap of roughly a quarter million kilometers of cold vacuum. The outer shell rushed in fast, accelerating in the grip of a stellar gravity well. Minutes passed, and from the outside the photosphere of the star appeared to contract slightly as huge vortices of hot turbulent gas swirled and fulminated across it. Then the hammerblow of the implosion front reached the core...

There was scant warning for the inhabitants of the planet that had been targeted for murder. For a few minutes, star-watching satellites reported an imminent solar flare, irregularities leading to atmospheric effects, aurorae, and storm warnings for orbital workers and miners in the asteroid belt. Maybe one or two of the satellites had causal channels, limited bandwidth instantaneous communicators, unjammable but expensive and touchy. But there wasn't enough warning to help anyone escape: the satellites simply went off-line one by one as a wave of failure crept outward from the star at the speed of light. In one research institute a meteorologist frowned at her workstation in bemusement, and tried to drill down a diagnostic—she was the only person on the planet who had time to realize something strange was happening. But the satellites she was tracking orbited only three light minutes closer to the star than the planet she lived on, and already she had lost two minutes chatting to a colleague about to go on her lunch break about the price of a house she would never buy now, out on the shore of a bay of lost dreams.

The hammerfall was a spherical shock wave of hydrogen plasma, blazing at a temperature of millions of degrees and compressed until it had many of the properties of metal. A hundred times as massive as the largest gas giant in the star system, by the time it slammed into the crystal of iron at the heart of the murdered star it was traveling at almost 2 percent of lightspeed. When it struck, a tenth of the gravitational potential energy of the star was converted into radiation in a matter of seconds. Fusion restarted, exotic reactions taking place as even the iron core began to soak up nuclei, building heavier and hotter and less stable intermediaries. In less than ten seconds, the star burned through a visible percentage of its fuel, enough to keep the fires banked for a billion years. There wasn't enough mass in the G-type dwarf to exceed the electron degeneracy pressure in its core, collapsing it into a neutron star, but nevertheless a respectable shock front, almost a hundredth as potent as a supernova, rebounded from the core.

A huge pulse of neutrinos erupted outward, carrying away much of the energy from the prompt fusion burn. The neutral particles didn't usually react with matter; the average neutrino could zip through a light year of lead without noticing. But there were so many of them that, as they sluiced through the outer layers of the star, they deposited a good chunk of their energy in the roiling bubble of foggy plasma that had replaced the photosphere. Not far behind them, a tidal wave of hard gamma radiation and neutrons a billion times brighter than the star ripped through the lower layers, blasting them apart. The dying star flashed a brilliant X-ray pulse like a trillion hydrogen bombs detonating in concert: and the neutrino pulse rolled out at the speed of light.

Eight minutes later—about a minute after she noticed the problem with the flare monitors—the meteorologist frowned. A hot, prickling flush seemed to crawl across her skin, itching: her vision was inexplicably streaked by crawling purple meteors. The desk in front of her flickered and died. She inhaled, smelling the sharp stink of ozone, looked round shaking her head to clear the sudden fog, and saw her colleague staring at her and blinking. "Hey, I feel like somebody just walked on my grave—" The lights flickered and died, but she had no trouble seeing because the air was alive with an eerie glow, and the small skylight window cast razor-sharp shadows on the floor. Then the patch of floor directly illuminated by the window began to smoke, and the meteorologist realized, fuzzily, that she wasn't going to buy that house after all, wasn't going to tell her partner about it, wasn't ever going to see him again, or her parents, or her sister, or anything but that smoking square of brilliance that was slowly growing as the window frame burned away.

She received a small mercy: mere seconds later the upper atmosphere—turned into an anvil of plasma by the passing radiation pulse—reached the tropopause. Half a minute later the first shock wave leveled her building. She didn't die alone; despite the lethal dose they all received from the neutrino pulse, nobody on the planet lived past the iron sunrise for long enough to feel the pangs of radiation sickness.

IMPACT: T plus 1392 days, 12 hours, 16 minutes

Wednesday hid under the desk, heart pounding with terror, clutching a stubby cylinder. She'd seen the body of the customs officer stuffed inside the darkened kitchen; realized he was dead, like the handwritten instructions in the diplomatic pouch said. Now the thing that did it was coming for her, and she wished—
     There was a scratching click of claws on polycellulose flooring. *I don't want to be here,* she prayed, fingers slipping around the sweat-lubed cylinder. *This isn't happening to me!* She could see the hellhound outside, imagining it in her mind's eye: jaws like diamond saw blades, wide-set eyes glowing with the overspill from its phased-array lidar. She could see the small, vicious gun implanted in its hollow skull, its brains governed by a set of embedded computers to override its Doberman instincts. Fist-sized overlapping bald patches, psoriatic skin thickening over diamond mesh armor. It could smell her fear. She'd read the papers in the strong room, realized how important they must be, and pushed the door ajar, thinking to leave—yanked it shut barely ahead of the snarl and the leap. Acrid smoke had curled up from the hinges as she scrambled into the ductwork, fled like a black-clad spider into the service axis and through the pressurized cargo tunnel and the shadows of the almost-empty dock, panting and crying as she went. Always hearing a scrabble of diamond-tipped claws on the floor behind her. *I don't exist. You can't smell me!*
     Herman—as usual, when she needed him most—wasn't talking.
     The dog could smell her—or smell someone. She'd tabbed into a public term and watched the dog, or one of its cousins, stalk across the loading bay like the spectral, elongated shadow of a wolf—something born in frozen forests beneath a midnight sun, evolved to lope across the cyborg-infested tundra of an alien world. It had glanced at the hidden camera with glowing eyes, a glow that spun into static as it locked on and fired. It could sneeze

nerve gas and shit land mines, if you believed her kid brother Jerm's cheap third-person scripted arcventures; a product of a more sophisticated technosphere than Moscow's, its muscles didn't run on anything as primitive as actin/myosin contraction, and its bones were built for leverage—a hellhound running at full power hissed like a primitive locomotive, dissipating waste heat as steam hot enough to scald anyone who got too close.

She raised the riot cartridge, fingers tightening on the trigger switch, and pointed it at the doorway. Dim shadow of legs, *too many legs*. They paused, and the shadow swung across the wall, homing in. She squished down on the trigger and the canister kicked back at her hands as a terrible clatter rushed towards her and the air in front turned black. *No, blue: like the dead man's tongue, lying there.* The paper said all but one copy of the data cartridge containing the customs transfer log were to be destroyed, and anyone who knew was to die. A tenuous aerogel foam bubbled and farted, rushing out into a ballooning mass as the dog lunged forward, teeth snapping, making a soft growling sound deep in its throat. It thumped against her feet in a soap-bubble cocoon, the growl turning into a deafening moaning howl of frustration.

Shuddering, Wednesday shuffled backward, pushing the heavy desk over as she stood up. She looked around wildly. The dog's hind legs scrabbled at the floor, driving it after her. She could see a glow of rage in its eyes as it struggled with the sticky antipersonnel foam. "Good doggie," she said vacuously, backing away, wondering inanely if she should hit it. But no, if a hellhound thought you had won, it would blow itself up, wouldn't it? They always did that in the arcventures—

Something cold and wet stubbed itself against the back of her neck, and snuffled damply. She sagged, her knees and stomach turning to sacks of ice water; paw-fingers like bone clamped tight on her shoulders, holding her upright. Her eyelid monitor flickered, then died as the lights came up. The hound on the floor seemed to grin up at her—no, *past* her. When he spoke, his voice was surprisingly human, a deep gravelly growl converging from three directions. "Victoria Strowger, this is emergency police pack four-alpha. By order of Captain Mannheim, superintending evacuation process for Old Newfoundland, we are placing you under arrest. You will return with us to the main hub traffic bay to await uplift. I must caution you that any resistance you offer may be dealt with using weapons of nonlethal intent. Running back aboard this habitat was a senseless waste of police time." Two of the voices fell silent, but a third continued: "And while we're about it, why *were* you running away?"

Twenty-two minutes past departure time and the dogs had rounded up the last stray lamb, herding her into the service lock. Captain Mannheim had other things to worry about this instant, like topping off the number four tank and making sure Misha vented the surplus ullage pressure and kept the flow temperature within good limits. Then he was going to run the launch plan and get the hell out of this ghost system before the storm front blew in, and once clear he'd have it out with the guard dogs. (And why had they let some interfering punk kid sneak around the service core in the first place?) And then...

Twenty-two minutes! More than a thousand seconds overdue! There was room for slippage on the critical path—nobody would be insane enough not to make some allowances—but with five thousand passengers, twenty-two minutes meant all of five person-years of consumables gone just like that, virtually in an eyeblink. The refugee pods had an open-loop life-support system, there being no room for recycling tankage on this relief flight, so the whole exercise was running into millions, tens of millions. Some dumb kid had just cost the burghers of New Dresden about, oh, two thousand marks, and Captain Mannheim about two thousand extra gray hairs.

"What's our criticality profile looking like?" he demanded, leaning over to glare at Gertrude's station.

"Ah, all nominal, sir." Gertrude stared fixedly ahead, refusing to meet his eye.

"Then keep it that way," he snapped. "Misha! That tank of yours!"

"Vented and closed out within tolerances." Misha grinned breezily from across the bridge. "The load-out is looking sweet. Oh, and for once the toilet plumbing on number two isn't rattling."

"Good." Mannheim sniffed. The number two reaction motor's mass-flow plumbing suffered from occasional turbulence, especially when the hydrogen slurry feeding it went over sixteen degrees absolute. The turbulence wasn't particularly serious unless it turned to outright cavitation, with big bubbles of supercooled gases fizzing inside the pipes that fed reaction mass to the fusion rockets. But *that* was potentially catastrophic, and they didn't have any margin for repairs. Not for the first time, Mannheim's thoughts turned enviously to the beautiful, high-tech liner from Novya Romanov that had pulled out six hours ago on an invisible wave of curved space-time, surfing in the grip of an extremal singularity. No messing with balky, mass-guzzling antiquated fusion rockets for *Sikorsky's Dream!* But the *Long March* was as sophisticated a ship as anything the Dresdener merchant syndicate could afford, and he'd do as well with it as was humanly possible. "Ship! What's our sequence entry status?"

The robotically smooth voice of the autopilot rolled across the bridge. "Kerberos unit and final passenger boarding notified two minutes ago and counting. Critical path elements in place. Entry status green, no exceptions raised—"

"Then commence launch cycle immediately."

"Aye. Launch cycle commencing. Station power and utility disconnect proceeding. Station mass transfer disconnect proceeding. Boarding pier disconnect proceeding. Main engine spin-up engaged, station one. Live cargo systems spin-down engaged, station two."

"I hate live cargo," Gertrude muttered. "Live cargo spin-down notification going out." Fingers tapped invisible cells in the air in front of her face. "Hub lift interlocks to safe—"

Mannheim stared at the complex web of dependencies that hovered over the blank wall of the bridge, a meter in front of his nose. Slowly, red nodes blinked to green as the huge starship prepared to cast free of the station. It was supposed to be the last ship ever to sail from this port. From time to time, he prodded a station glyph and spoke quietly to whoever's voice answered from the thin air: loadmasters and supercargo and immigration control officers and civil polizei, Jack in the drive damage control center and Rudi in the crow's nest. Once he even talked to Traffic Control. The station's robot minders plodded on imperturbably, unaware that the end of their labor was in sight, coursing toward them on an expanding shock front of radiation-driven plasma. An hour went by. Someone invisible placed a mug of coffee at his right hand, and he drank, carried on talking and watching and occasionally cursing in a quiet voice, and drank again and it was cold.

Finally, the ship was ready to depart.

Moscow system died at the speed of light, death rippling outward on a tsunami of radiation.

First to die were the weather satellites, close in on the star, watching for solar flares and prominences. Buoys built to track breezes were ripped adrift by the tornado blast of the artificially induced nova, not so much disabled as evaporated, adding their stripped nuclei to the boiling fury of the iron sunrise.

Seconds later the radiation pulse melted the huge, flimsy solar collectors that glided in stately orbit half an astronomical unit out, feeding power to antimatter generators a hundred kilometers in diameter. Robot factories unattended by humans passed unmourned and unnoticed. The gamma pulse shed by their tons of stored anti-hydrogen added a candle glow to the hurricane.

Eight minutes after detonation, the radiation front reached the innermost human habitat in the system: the world called Moscow. The neutrino flux was high enough to deliver a rapidly lethal radiation dose even after traveling right through the planet. The night-side fluoresced, atmosphere glowing dimly against the unbearably bright background. The gamma pulse, close behind it, flashed the dayside atmosphere to plasma and slammed it into the already melting rock. Supersonic tornadoes rippled around the daylight terminator, scouring the surface down to bedrock.

Half an hour into the nova, the process of planetary disintegration was well under way. On the dayside, Moscow's atmospheric pressure dropped drastically, and the primary gaseous constituents were hydrogen and oxygen radicals stripped from the boiling fog that had been the boreal ocean. Cloud top temperatures were already in the thousands of degrees, while Mach waves rippled through the turgid troposphere on the nightside, crushing houses like matchwood kindling to become pyres for the dying bodies of their occupants. The night receded before a ghastly daylight, the sullen glare of an exploding star reflected off the planet's own comet trail of air. To an observer at ground level Moscow Prime would have covered half the sky, a magnesium flare of radiant energy that would still be bright enough to burn out eyeballs tens of trillions of kilometers away. The main shock wave of the explosion was approaching by then, a wave of plasma flash-heated to hundreds of millions of degrees, barely less dense than the dissipated atmosphere and traveling outward at 20 percent of light-speed. When it arrived, Moscow vanished—swallowed like a watermelon at ground zero in the expanding fireball of an atomic explosion.

Sixty minutes: the radiation pulse ghosted through the rings of Siberia, a huge green ice giant with attendant moons strung around it like lucent pearls. They flashed briefly and sprouted streamers of glowing gas as the rings flared violet, forming a huge glowing disk of light that jetted outward from the star, consuming the mass of a small moon in seconds. Siberia absorbed a huge pulse of energy, sufficient to melt the tundra at its core and spawn gigantic storms. Hurricanes the size of Moscow raced toward the nightside of the giant planet as it, too, sprouted a glowing cometary tail. Unlike the inner bodies, Siberia was too huge to evaporate entirely. Though it glowed white-hot and molten, and its orbital track was distorted by the tremendous shock wave of the stellar explosion, the innermost core of nickel-iron remained—a gravestone marker that would take millions of years to cool in the twilight emptiness of Moscow system.

The first survivor weathered the blast at a range of ninety-eight light minutes.

Sleeping in deep orbit around the outer gas giant Zemlya, a robot beacon blinked awake at the first harsh glare of energy. The beacon carried huge reserves of coolant within its faceted black-armored carapace. Designed to withstand direct hits from a battle-ship's laser grid, it weathered the storm—although it was sent tumbling, blasted right out of its seventy-year orbit by the surge of heavy charged particles. The beacon was 118 years old, one of 750 in its series. Code-named TALIGENT SPARROW, it was part of the early warning system of the Strategic Retaliation Command of the recently vaporized Moscow Foreign Office.

TALIGENT SPARROW blinked and took stock. The stars were occluded by glowing gas and debris, some of them its own ablated skin. No matter: it had a task. Deep memory remembered the pattern of the seasons and turned sensors in search of Moscow. It tried vainly to swivel a high-gain antenna that had been reduced to a crumpled mass of molten tissue. Other sensors tried to distinguish the gamma flux of inbound relativistic missiles and failed, over-loaded. A primitive expert system plumbed the depths of its decision tree and determined that something unknown had attacked it. Qubits trickled into entropy as taligent sparrow powered up its causal channel and shrieked murder at the uncaring stars.

Somebody heard.

The police drone was robotically curt. "We've found your daughter. Please come to deck G-red, zone two meeting point, and collect her."

Morris Strowger stood up and glanced at his wife. He smiled. "I told you they'd find her." The smile slowly faded.

His wife didn't look up. With her bony fingers thrust together between her knees and her bowed head, Indica Strowger's shoulders shook as if she'd grabbed hold of a live power supply. "Go away," she said very quietly, her voice hard and controlled. "I'll be all right."

"If you're sure—" Already the police drone was moving off. He glanced back uncertainly at her hunched form, then followed the insect away through crowded, human-smelling partition-runs, runs that were already deteriorating into a high-tech slum patrolled by bees with stun guns. Something about their departure, perhaps the final grim reality of dispossession, had snapped a band of tension that had held everyone together through the dark years just ended, and the solid ground of depression was giving way to a treacherous slurry of despair, hysteria, and uncertainty about the future. Dangerous times.

Wednesday was waiting at the meeting point just as the bee had said. She looked alone and afraid, and Morris, who had been thinking of harsh words, suddenly found himself unable to speak. "Vicki—"

"Dad!" She buried her chin in his shoulder, sharp-jawed like some young feral predator. She was shaking.

"Where've you been? Your mother's been going crazy!" That wasn't the half of it. He hugged her, firmly, feeling a terrible sense of hollow unease ebb away. His daughter was back, and he was angry as hell at her—and unspeakably relieved.

"I wanted to be alone," she said very quietly, voice muffled. He tried to step back, but she refused to let go. A pang: she did that when she didn't want to tell him something. She was no good at dissembling, but her sense of privacy was acute. An old woman behind him was raising a fuss at the harassed constable, something about a missing boy—no, her pet dog. Her son, her Sonny. Wednesday looked up at him. "I needed time to think." The lie solidified in a crystal moment, and he didn't have the heart to call her on it. There'd be time for that, and to tell her about the official reprimand later: trespassing off-limits on board a ship wasn't the same as exploring the empty quadrants of a station. She didn't know how lucky she was that the Captain was understanding—and that unusual allowances were being made for stressed-out adults, never mind kids leaving home for the first time they could remember.

"Come on." He turned her away from the desk, rubbed her shoulder. "Come on. Back to our, uh, cabin. Ship's undocking soon. They'll be widecasting from the bridge. You don't want to miss that?"

She looked up at him, an unreadable, serious expression on her face. "Oh, no."

IMPACT: T plus 4 hours, 6 minutes

Two hundred and forty-six minutes after the Zero Incident, the freighter *Taxis Pride* congealed out of empty space, forty-six degrees out of the plane of the ecliptic, six light hours away from its final destination. Brad Mornington, skipper, was on the flight deck, nattering with Mary Haight, the relativistics op. *Taxis Pride* was a three-point shuttle, connecting Moscow to Iceland Seven station, thence to the Septagonese trans-shipment outpost at Blaylock B. Brad had made this zone transfer eighteen times in the past seven years, and it was as routine as the mug of strong, heavily sugared coffee that Alex placed by his elbow before the jump countdown commenced, which was just then cooling down enough to drink.

Brad put out the standard navigation squawk and waited for a detailed flight path. In the meantime he pondered the food situation: the kitchen was getting somewhat monotonous, and the downside ferry would give him a chance to stretch his legs and reacquaint himself with clouds and sky again. *Taxis Pride* was a fast freighter, built to carry time-critical physical mail and perishables. The extremal singularity in her drive core let her accelerate in real space as rapidly as some warships: six light hours was a one-week cruise for her, not the painful odyssey an old hydrogen burner would have to endure. Mary concentrated on a backup star fix—routine, in case the traffic controllers were on strike again, just to keep her professional certification up to date. In her spare moments she was wondering if there'd be time to drop in on an old friend while they were docked for their cargo load cycle.

Then the bridge screamer went off.

"What the—get that!" Brad's coffee went flying as he scrambled for the comm terminal. Mary jolted upright, whey-faced.

"Got it. That's not traffic—"

"Hello, this is flight Echo Gold Nine Zero responding to broadcast squawk from, ah, Delta X-ray Zeus Seven, we have handshake. What's the—"

"Something flaky here, boss—"

Red flashing lights blinked on the conference circuit. There was a thirty-second delay while they waited tensely for a reply.

"Echo Gold Nine Zero this is Delta X-ray Zeus Seven, emergency relay service. Admiralty signal blue four, authentication follows message. This is a systemwide military emergency. Moscow is under quarantine—the whole system is under lockdown, no exceptions. Evacuate immediately. I emphasize, get your kernel spun up and get out of here immediately! Please acknowledge."

Brad flushed, furious. "This is some sort of fucking joke!" He waved off the authentication code and punched in the waypoint series for Moscow. "When I find the asshole—"

"Brad. Come here." He looked round sharply. Mary was leaning over the repeater from Wang's crow's nest downstairs. She looked sick.

"What is it?"

"Here." She pointed to a plot that had just shown up. *Taxis Pride* was a fleet auxiliary, liable for mobilization in event of war: it carried near-military-grade passive sensors. "Gamma plot, classic proton-antiproton curve, about two AUs out. It's redshifting on us. I got a fix on that relay service buoy, Brad: it's at the origin point for that . . . burn."

"Shit!" The screen swam in front of Brad's eyes. All of a sudden he remembered what it was like when he was nine, when his father told him his dog had died. "*Shit!*" Positronium was an unstable intermediate created during some matter-antimatter reactions. Redshifted, it was moving away from the reference frame of the observer at some fraction of the speed of light. Out from the star, it could mean only one thing—slower-than-light antimatter rockets, relativistic retaliation bombers cranking up for a kamikaze run on someone's home world. "They've *launched.* They've fucking launched the deterrent fleet!"

They were a long-practiced team: he didn't have to tell Mary what to do. She was already bringing back up the gravitational potential maps he'd need for the jump. Brad canceled his half-planned course and fed in the return journey jump coordinates. "Hello Delta X-ray Zeus Seven, this is flight Echo Gold Nine Zero acknowledging. We are preparing to return to Iceland Seven soonest. Can you clarify the situation for us. Other shipping may be in the queue and need warning off. Do you need assistance? Over." Then he got on the blower to Liz, down in kernel monitoring, explaining to her that, no, this wasn't a joke, and yes, he was going to overrun the drive maintenance cycle, and yes, it was going to put the *Pride* in the dock for a month and there was a good reason for it all—

"Echo Gold Nine Zero, departure cleared. This is Delta X-ray Zeus Seven, relaying through NavServ buoy six-nine-three via causal channel. Situation as follows: inner system exterminated by surprise attack using weapons of mass destruction approximately two-seven-zero minutes ago absolute time. Your range three-six-zero light minutes considered marginal for survival: the star's gone. We're assuming one hundred percent fatalities on Moscow, repeat, *one hundred percent*. V-force has launched, but we've got no idea who did it. As of two hours ago, Moscow system is under complete interdict. Wait—" for a moment the steady voice wavered. "Oh. Oh my! That felt weird." A pause. "Echo Gold Nine Zero, we've just taken a core radiation pulse. Funny, two kilometers of rock shielding outside us. Ah, shit. Off the scale. Neutrinos, has to be. Echo Gold Nine Zero, this is Delta X-ray Zeus Seven, there's—I don't think there's anything you can do for us. Get the hell out while you still can—warn everybody off. Signing off now."

Brad stared at the comm status display without seeing it. Then he mashed his palm down on the general channel glyph. "Crew, captain speaking." He glanced at Mary and saw her staring back at him. Waiting. "We have a situation. Change of plan." Glancing down at his panel he blinked and dragged the urgent course correction into the flight sequence. "We're not going home. *Ever.* "

Taxis Pride was the first ship to leave Moscow system after the explosion. Another two ships made it out, one of them badly damaged by jumping into the tail of the shock wave. Word of the explosion filtered out: several freighters were saved from jumping into a fiery grave by dint of a massive and well-coordinated emergency alert. Over the next few weeks, the inhabitants of the Iceland Seven refinery station—a mere eight light months from Moscow—were evacuated to Shenjen Principality, and as the shock wave rolled outward, more vulnerable habitats were evacuated in turn. The nearest populated planetary system, Septagon Central, was far enough away to be saved by the heavy radiation shielding on its orbital republics. Meanwhile, years would pass before another starship visited the radiation-scarred corpse of Moscow system.

"What's your finding?" demanded the Captain.

The three dogs grinned at him from their positions around his cramped day cabin. One of them bent to lick at a patch of blue foam sticking to its left hind leg. The foam hissed and smoked where saliva ran. "There is nothing to report on the first incident, the customs officer. We regret to inform you that he must be classed as missing, presumed dead, unless we subsequently learn that he boarded one of the other ships. The second incident was a juvenile delinquent escapade committed by an asocial teenager. No trusted subsystems appear to have been compromised. I have no direct access to the cargo carried in the security zone, but you have assured me yourself that none of the black manifest packages are missing. The recorded history of the delinquent is consistent with this event, as is her subsequent behavior, and a search of the documentation corpus pertaining to socialization of juvenile adults in prewar New Moscow society indicates that territorial escapades of this kind are a not-infrequent response to environmental stress."

"Why did she get in there in the first place?" Mannheim leaned forward, glaring at the lead hellhound with a mixture of anxiety and distrust. "I thought you were supposed to be guarding—"

"In my judgment her actions are compatible with typical human adolescent dysfunctional behavior. This search-and-rescue security unit is not authorized to use lethal force to protect bonded cargo, Captain. A secondary consideration was that her absence had been noticed by familial parties and formally reported after she was officially transferred aboard the evacuation ferry. Remanding the delinquent into the care of her parents, with subsequent monitoring and supervision for the duration of the voyage, will prevent repetition and will not invite further attention."

The dog that had been talking jerked its head pompously. One of its fellows padded over and sniffed at its left ear. Mannheim watched them nervously. Police dogs, incredibly expensive units bought from some out-system high-tech polity, programmed for loyalty to the regime: he'd never even seen any before this voyage, was startled to learn the government owned any, much less that they'd see fit to deploy them on something as mundane as an evacuation run. And then, one of them claimed to be a Foreign Office dog, loaded onto his ship along with orders—sealed orders handwritten on paper for his eyes only—to be turned loose on the ship. Uplifted dogs designed for security and search-and-rescue, a pack hiding one member capable of killing. Exotic sapient weapons.

"Did you carry out your mission?"

Number one dog looked at him. "What are you talking about?"

"Eh?" Mannheim straightened up. "Now look here," he began angrily, "this is my ship! I'm responsible for everyone and everything on it, and if I need to know something I—"

The dogs stood up simultaneously, and he realized they had him surrounded. Gun-muzzle faces pointed at him, a thousand-yard stare repeated three times over. The FO dog spoke up: the others seemed to be under its control in some way. "We could tell you, Captain, but then we would have to silence you. Speculation on this matter by parties not authorized by the Ministry of War is deemed to be a hostile act, within the meaning of section two, paragraph four-three-one of the Defense of the Realm Act. Please confirm your understanding of this declaration."

"I—" Mannheim gulped. "I understand. No more questions."

"Good." The number two dog sat down again, and unconcernedly set about licking the inside of its right hind leg. "The other units of this pack are not cognizant of these affairs. They're just simple secret police dogs. You are not to trouble them with unpleasant questions. This debriefing is at an end. I believe you have a ship to run?"

IMPACT: T plus 1393 days, 02 hours, 01 minutes

Wednesday watched the end of the world with her parents and half the occupants of the Rose Deck canteen. The tables and benches had been deflated and pushed back against one wall while the ship was under boost. Now a large screen had been drawn across the opposite wall and configured with a view piped down from the hub sensor array. She had wanted to watch on her own personal slate, but her parents had dragged her along to the canteen: it seemed like most people didn't want to be alone for the jump. Not that anybody would know it had happened—contrary to dramatic license, there was absolutely no sensation when a starship tunneled between two equipotent locations across the light years—but there was something symbolic about this one. A milestone they'd never see again.

"Herman?" she subvocalized.

"I'm here. Not for much longer. You'll be alone after the jump."

"I don't understand. Why?" Jeremy was staring at her so she grimaced horribly at him. He jumped back, right into the wall, and his mother glared at him.

"Causal channels don't work after a jump outside their original light cone: they're instantaneous communicators, but they don't violate causality. Move the entangled quantum dots apart via FTL and you break the quantum entanglement they rely on. As I speak to you through one that is wired into your access implant, and that is how you speak to me, I will be out of contact for some time after you arrive. However you are in no danger as long as you remain in the evacuation area and do nothing to attract attention."

She rolled her eyes. As invisible friends went, Herman could do an unpleasantly good imitation of a pompous youth leader. Dark emptiness sprinkled with the jewel points of stars covered the far wall, a quiet surf of conversation rippling across the beach of heads in front of her. A familiar chill washed through her: too many questions, too little time to ask them. "Why did they let me go?"

"You were not recognized as a threat. If you were, I would not have asked you to go. Forgive me. There is little time remaining. What you achieved was more important than I can tell you, and I am grateful for it."

"So what did I accomplish? Was it really worth it for those papers?"

"I cannot tell you yet. The first jump is due in less than two minutes. At that point we lose contact. You will be busy after that: Septagon is not like Old Newfoundland. Take care: I will be in touch when the time is right."

"Is something wrong, Vicki?" With a start she realized her father was watching her.

"Nothing, Dad." Instinctive dismissal: *Where did he learn to be so patronizing?* "What's going to happen?"

Morris Strowger shrugged. "We, uh, have to make five jumps before we arrive where we're going. The first—" He swallowed.

"Home, uh, the explosion, is off to one side. You know what a conic section is?"

"Don't talk down to me." She nearly bit her tongue when she saw his expression. "Yes, Dad. I've done analytic geometry."

"Okay. The explosion is expanding in a sphere centered on, on, uh, home. We're following a straight line—actually, a zigzag around a straight line between equipotent points in space-time—from the station, which is outside the sphere, to Septagon, which is outside the sphere of the explosion but on the other side. Our first jump takes us within the sphere of the explosion, about three light months inside it. The next jump takes us back out the other side."

"We're going into the explosion?"

Morris reached out and took her hand. "Yes, dear. It's—" He looked at the screen again, ducking to see past one of the heads blocking the way. Mum, Indica, was holding Jeremy, facing the screen: she had her hands on his shoulders. "It's not dangerous," he added. "The really bad stuff is all concentrated in the shock front, which is only a couple of light days thick. Our shielding can cope with anything else; otherwise, Captain Mannheim would be taking us around the explosion. But that would take much longer, so—" He fell silent. A heavily accented voice echoed from the screen.

"Attention. This is your captain speaking. In about one minute we will commence jump transit for Septagon Central. We have a series of five jumps at seventy-hour intervals except for the fourth, which will be delayed eighteen hours. Our first jump takes us inside the shock front of the supernova: religionists may wish to attend the multifaith service of remembrance on G deck in three hours' time. Thank you."

The voice stopped abruptly, as if cut off. A stopwatch appeared in one corner of the wall, counting down the seconds. "What will we do now?" Wednesday asked quietly.

Her father looked uncomfortable. "Find somewhere to live. They said they'd help us. Your mother and I will look for work, I suppose. Try to fit in—"

The black-jeweled sky shimmered, rainbow lights casting many-colored shadows across the watchers. A collective sigh went up: the wall-screen view of space was gone, replaced by the most insanely beautiful thing she had ever seen. Great shimmering curtains of green and red and purple light blocked out the stars, gauzy shrouds of fluorescent silk streaming in a wild breeze. At their heart, a brilliant diamond shone in the cosmos, a bloodred dumb-bell of light growing from its poles. "Herman?" she whispered to herself. "Do you see that?" But there was no reply: and suddenly she felt empty, as hollow as the interior of the baby nebula the ship now floated in. "All gone," she said aloud, and suddenly there were tears in her eyes: she made no protest when her father gathered her in his arms. He was crying, too, great racking sobs making his shoulders shake: she wondered what he could be missing for a moment, then caught its palest shadow and shuddered.

"May i ask what I'm accused of?" Rachel asked for the third time. *Don't let them get to you,* she told herself, forcing her face into a bland smile: *One slip and they'll hang you out to dry.*

The daylight filtering through the window-wall was tinted pale blue by the slab of dumb aerogel, the sky above the distant mountains dimmed to a remote purple. Behind the heads of her inquisitors she focused on the contrail of a commuter plane scratching its way across the glass-smooth stratosphere.

"There are no *charges,*" the leader of the kangaroo court said, smiling right back at her. "You haven't broken any regulations, have you?" The man next to her cleared his throat. "Well, none of *ours,*" she added, her exaggeratedly dyed lips curling minutely in distaste. Rachel focused on her hairline. Madam Chairman was dressed in an exaggeratedly femme historical style—perhaps to add a touch of velvet and lace to her S&M management style—but a ringlet of hair had broken free of whatever chemical cosh she used to discipline it, and threatened to flop over one razor-finished eyebrow in a quizzical curl.

"The excursion to Rochard's World was not my initiative, as I pointed out in my report," Rachel calmly repeated, despite the urge to reach across the table and tweak Madam Chairman's hairdo. *Damn, I'd like to see* you *manage a field operation gone bad,* she thought. "George Cho got the run-around from the New Republican government, the idiots had *already* decided to violate the Third Commandment before I arrived on the scene, and if I hadn't been in position, there wouldn't have been *anybody* on the ground when the shit hit the fan. So George sent me. As I think

I've already stated, you're not cleared to read the full report. But that's not what this is about, is it?"

She leaned back and took a sip from her water glass, staring at the chief mugger through half-closed eyes. Madam Chairman the honorable Seat Warmer, who evidently rejoiced under the name of Gilda something-or-other, took advantage of the pause to lean sideways and whisper something in Minion Number One's ear. Rachel put her glass down and smiled tightly at Madam Chairman. She had the soul of an auditor and a coterie of gray yespeople; she'd come for Rachel out of nowhere the day before, armed with a remit to audit her and a list of questions as long as her arm, mostly centering on Rachel's last posting outside the terrestrial light cone. It had been clear from the start that she didn't know what the hell Rachel did for the diplomatic service, and didn't care. What she was pissed off about was the fact that Rachel was listed on the budget as an entertainments officer or cultural attaché—a glorified bribe factor for the department of trade—and that this was *her* turf. The fact that Rachel's listing was actually a cover for a very different job clearly didn't mean anything to her.

Rachel fixed Madam Chairman with her best poker face. "What you're digging for is who it was that authorized George to send me to Rochard's World, and who ordered the budget spend. The long and the short of that is, it's outside your remit. If you think you've got need to know, take it up with Security."

She smiled thinly. She'd been assigned to Cho's legation to the New Republic on the Ents payroll, but was really there for a black-bag job; she answered to the Black Chamber, and Madam Chairman would run into a brick wall as soon as she tried to pursue the matter there. But the Black Chamber had to maintain Rachel's official cover—the UN had an open hearings policy on audits to reassure its shareholders that their subscriptions were being spent equitably—and she was consequently stuck with going through the motions. Up to and including being fired for misappropriation of funds if some bureaucratic greasy-pole climber decided she was a good back to stab on the way up. It was just one of the risks that went with the job of being a covert arms control inspector.

Gilda's own smile slid imperceptibly into a frown. Her politician-model cosmetic implant didn't know how to interpret such an unprogrammed mood: for a moment, bluish scales hazed into view on her cheeks, and her pupils formed vertical slits. Then the lizard look faded. "I disagree," she said airily, waving away the objection. "It was your job, as officer on-site, to account for expenditure on line items. The UN is *not* made of money, we all have a fiduciary duty to our shareholders to ensure that peace-keeping operations run at a profit, and there is a *small* matter of eighty kilograms of highly enriched—weapons grade—uranium that remains unaccounted for. Uranium, my dear, does not grow on trees. Next, there's your unauthorized assignment of a diplomatic emergency bag, class one, registered to this harebrained scheme of Ambassador Cho's, to support your junket aboard the target's warship. The bag was subsequently expended in making an escape when everything went wrong—as you predicted at the start of the affair, so you should have known better than to go along in the first place. And then there's the matter of you taking aboard *hitchhikers*—"

"Under the terms of the common law of space, I had an *obligation* to rescue any stranded persons I could take on board." Rachel glared at Minion Number One, who glared right back, then hastily looked away. *Damn, that was a mistake,* she realized. *A palpable hit.* "I'll also remind you that I have a right under section two of the operational guidelines for field officers to make use of official facilities for rescuing dependents in time of conflict."

"You weren't married to him at the time," Madam Chairman cut in icily.

"Are you sure it wasn't a marriage of convenience?" Minion Number Two chirped out, hunting for an opportunistic shot.

"I would say the facts *do* tend to support that assumption," Minion Number One agreed.

"The facts of the matter are that you appear to have spent *a great deal* of UN *money* without achieving *anything* of any significance," Madam Chairman trilled in a singsong. She was on a roll: she leaned forward, bosom heaving with emotion and cheeks flushed with triumph as she prepared for the kill. "We hold you to account for this operation, Junior Attaché Mansour. Not to put too fine a point on it, you wasted more than two million ecus of official funds on a wildcat mission that didn't deliver any measurable benefits you can point to. You're on the personnel roster under *my* oversight, and your screwup makes Entertainments and Culture look bad. Or hadn't you realized the adverse impact your spy fantasies might have on the serious job of marketing our constituent's products abroad? I can find *some* minor contributions to the bottom line on your part in the distant past, but you're very short on mitigating factors; for that reason, we're going to give you twenty-seven—"

"Twenty-six!" interrupted Minion Number Two.

"—Twenty-six days to submit to a full extradepartmental audit with a remit to prepare a report on the disposition of funds during operation Mike November Charlie Four Seven-slash-Delta, and to evaluate the best practices compliance of your quality outcome assurance in the context of preventing that brushfire conflict from turning into a full-scale interstellar war." Madam Chairman simpered at her own brilliance, fanning herself with a hard copy of Rachel's public-consumption report.

"A full-scale audit?" Rachel burst out: "You stupid, *stupid,* desk pilot!" She glanced round, fingering the control rings for her personal assist twitchily. A security guard would have gone for the floor at that point, but Rachel managed to restrain herself even though the adrenaline was flowing, and the upgrades installed in her parasympathetic peripheral nervous system were boosting her toward combat readiness. "Try to audit me. Just try it!" She crossed her arms tensely. "You'll hit a brick wall. Who's in your management matrix grid? Do you think we can't reach all of them? Do you really want to annoy the Black Chamber?"

Madam Chairman rose and faced Rachel stiffly, like a cobra ready to spit. "You, you slimy little minx, you *cowboy*—" she hissed, waving a finger under Rachel's nose—"I'll see you on the street before you're ever listed under Entertainments and Culture again! I know your game, you scheming little pole-climber, and I'll—"

Rachel was about to reply when her left earlobe buzzed. "Excuse me a moment," she said, raising a hand, "incoming." She cupped a hand to her ear. "Yeah, who is this?"

"Stop that at once! This is *my* audit committee, not a talking shop—"

"*Polis dispatch. Are you Rachel Mansour? SXB active three-zero-two? Can you confirm your identity?*"

Rachel stood up, her pulse pounding, feeling weak with shock. "Yes, that's me," she said distantly. "Here's my fingerprint." She touched a finger to her forehead, coupling a transdermal ID implant to the phone so that it could vouch for her.

"Someone stop her! Philippe, can't you jam her? This is a disgrace!"

"*Voiceprint confirmed. I have you authenticated. This is the* Fourth Republican Police Corporation, dispatch control for

Geneva. You're in the Place du Molard, aren't you? We have an urgent SXB report that's just across the way from you. We've called in the regional squad, but it's our bad luck that something big's going down just outside Brasilia, and the whole team is out there providing backup. They can't get back in less than two hours, and the headcase is threatening us with an excursion in only fifty-four minutes."

"Oh. Oh, hell!" Situations like this tended to dredge up reflexive blasphemies left over from her upbringing. Rachel turned toward the door, blanking on her surroundings. Sometimes she had nightmares about this sort of thing, nightmares that dragged her awake screaming in the middle of the night, worrying Martin badly. "Can you have someone pick me up in the concourse? Brief me on the way in. You know I haven't handled one of these in years? I'm on the reserve list."

"Stop that now!" Madam Chairman was in the way, standing between Rachel and the doorway. She pouted like a fighting fish faced with a mirror, bloodred lips tight with anger and fists balled. "You can't just walk out of here!"

"What are you going to do, slap me?" Rachel asked, sounding amused.

"I'll bring charges! You arranged this distraction—"

Rachel reached out, picked Madam Chairman up by her elbows, and deposited her on the conference table in a howl of outrage and a flurry of silk skirts. "Stick to minding your desk," Rachel said coldly, unable to resist the urge to rub it in. "The adults have got important work to be getting on with."

Rachel just about had the shakes under control by the time she reached the main exit. *Stupid, stupid!* she chided herself. Blowing up at Madam Chairman could only make things worse, and with the job ahead she needed desperately to cultivate a calm head. A police transporter was waiting for her in the landscaped courtyard outside the UN office dome, squatting in the shadow of a giant statue of Otto von Bismarck. "Suspect an unemployed artist and recluse believed to be named Idi Amin Dadaist," the police dispatcher told her via her bonephone, simultaneously throwing a bunch of images at the inside of her left eyelid. "No previous record other than minor torts for public arts happenings with no purchase of public disturbance and meme pollution rights, and an outstanding lawsuit from the People's Republic of Midlothian over his claim to the title of Last King of Scotland. He's—"

The next words were drowned out by the warble of alarm

sirens. Someone in the headquarters bubble had been told what was going down a few blocks away. "I haven't even done a training update for one of these in three years!" Rachel shouted into the palm of her hand as she jogged toward the transporter. She climbed in, and it surged away, meters ahead of the human tide streaming out of the building toward the nearest bomb shelters. "Don't you have anyone who's current?"

"You used to be full-time with SXB, that's why we've still got you flagged as a standby," said the dispatcher. A worried-looking cop glanced round from the pilot's seat, leaving the driving to the autopilot. "The regulars, like I said, they're *all* en route from Brasilia by suborbital. We're a peaceful city. This is the first bomb scare we've had in nearly twenty years. You're the only specialist—active or reserve—in town today."

"Jesus! So it *had* to happen when everyone was away. What can you tell me about the scene?"

"The perp's holed up in a refugee stack in Saint-Leger. Says he's got an improv gadget, and he's going to detonate it in an hour minus eight minutes unless we accede to his demands. We're not sure what kind it is, or what his demands are, but it doesn't really matter—even a pipe bomb loaded with cobalt sixty would make a huge mess of the neighborhood."

"Right." Rachel shook her head. "'Scuse me, I've just come from a meeting with a bunch of time-wasters, and I'm trying to get my head together. You're saying it's going to be a hands-on job?"

"He's holed up in a cheap apartment tree. He's indoors, well away from windows, vents, doors. Our floor penetrator says he's in the entertainment room with something dense enough to be a gadget. The stack is dusted, but we're having fun replaying the ubiquitous surveillance takes for the past month—seems he started jamming before anything else, and his RFID tag trace is much too clean. Someone has to go inside and talk him down or take him out, and you've got more experience of this than any of us. It says here you've done more than twenty of these jobs; that makes you our nearest expert."

"Hell and deviltry. Who's the underwriter for this block?"

"It's all outsourced by the city government—I think Lloyds has something to do with it. Whatever, *you* bill *us* for any expenses, and we'll sort them out. Anything you need for the job is yours, period."

"Okay." She sighed, half-appalled at how easy it was to slip back into old ways of thinking and feeling. Last time, she'd sworn it would be her last job. Last time she'd actually tried to slit her wrists afterward, before she saw sense and realized that there were easier ways out of the profession. Like switching to something even more dangerous, as it turned out. "One condition: my husband. Get someone to call him, right now. If he's in town tell him to get under cover. And get as many people as possible into bunkers. The older apartments are riddled with the things, aren't they? There is no guarantee that I'm going to be able to pull this off on my own without a support and planning backstop team, and I don't want you to count on miracles. Have you got a disaster kit standing by?"

"We're already evacuating, and there'll be a disaster kit waiting on-site when you arrive," said the dispatcher. "Our normal SXB team are on the way home, but they won't be able to take over for an hour and a half, and they'll be into re-entry blackout in about ten minutes—I think that means they won't be much help to you."

"Right." Rachel nodded, redundantly. She'd dressed for the office, but unlike Madam Chairman, she didn't go in for retrofemme frills and frou-frou: she'd had enough of that in the year she'd spent in the New Republic. *What does the bitch have against me, anyway?* she asked herself, making a mental note to do some data mining later. She dialed her jacket and leggings to sky blue—calming colors—and settled back in the seat, breathing deeply and steadily. "No point asking for armor, I guess. Do you have any snipers on hand?"

"Three teams are on their way. They'll be set up with crossfire and hard-surface-penetrating sights in about twenty minutes. Inspector MacDougal is supervising."

"Has he evacuated the apartments yet?"

"It's in progress. She's moving in noisemakers as her people pull the civilians. Orders are to avoid anything that might tip him off that we've got an operation in train."

"Good. Hmm. You said the perp's an artist." Rachel paused. "Does anyone know what *kind* of artist?"

The transporter leaned into the corner with the Boulevard Jacques, then surged down the monorail track. Other pods, their guidance systems overridden, slewed out of its way: two police trucks, bouncing on their pneumatic tires, were coming up fast behind. The buildings thereabouts were old, stone and brick and wood that had gone up back before the Diaspora and gone out of fashion sometime since, lending the old quarter something of the air of a twenty-first-century theme park far gone in ungenteel decay. "He's an historical reenactor," said the dispatcher. "There's something here about colonies. Colonialism. Apparently it's all to do with reenacting the historic process of black liberation before the holocaust."

"Which holocaust?"

"The African one. Says here he impersonates a pre-holocaust emperor called Idi Amin, uh, Idi Amin Dada. There's a release about reinterpreting the absurdist elements of the Ugandan proletarian reformation dialectic through the refracting lens of neo-Dadaist ideological situationism."

"Whatever that means. Okay. Next question, where was this guy born? Where did he come from? What does he *do*?"

"He was born somewhere in Paraguay. He's had extensive phenotype surgery to make himself resemble his role model, the Last King of Scotland or President of Uganda or whoever he was. Got a brochure from one of his performances here—says he tries to act as an emulation platform for the original Idi Amin's soul."

"And now he's gone crazy, right? Can you dig anything up about the history of the original Mister Amin? Sounds Islamicist to me. Was he an Arab or something?"

The transporter braked, swerved wildly, then hopped off the monorail and nosed in between a whole mass of cops milling around in front of a large, decrepit-looking spiral of modular refugee condominiums hanging off an extruded titanium tree. A steady stream of people flowed out of the block, escorted by rentacops in the direction of the Place de Philosophes. Rachel could already see a queue of lifters coming in, trying to evacuate as many people as possible from the blocks around ground zero. It didn't matter whether or not this particular fuckwit was competent enough to build a working nuke: if the Plutonium Fairy had been generous, he could make his gadget fizzle and contaminate several blocks. Even a lump of plastique coated with stolen high-level waste could be messy. Actinide metal chelation and gene repair therapy for several thousand people was one hell of an expensive way to pay for an artistic tantrum, and if he *did* manage to achieve prompt criticality . . .

The officer in charge—a tall blond woman with a trail of cops surrounding her—was coming over. "You! Are you the specialist dispatch has been praying for?" she demanded.

"Yeah, that's me." Rachel shrugged uncomfortably. "Bad

news is, I've had no time to prep for this job, and I haven't done one in three or four years. What have you got for me?"

"A real bampot, it would seem. I'm Inspector Rosa MacDougal, Laughing Joker Enforcement Associates. Please follow me."

The rentacop site office was the center of a hive of activity, expanding to cover half the grassed-over car park in front of the apartment block. The office itself was painted vomit-green and showed little sign of regular maintenance, or even cleaning. "I haven't worked with Laughing Joker before," Rachel admitted.

"First, let me tell you that as with all SXB ops, this is pro bono, but we expect unrestricted donations of equipment and support during the event, and death benefits for next of kin if things go pear-shaped. We do *not* accept liability for failure, on account of the SXB point team usually being too dead to argue the point. We just do our best. Is that clear with you?"

"Crystal." MacDougal pointed at a chair. "Sit yourself down. We've got half an hour before it goes critical."

"Right." Rachel sat. She made a steeple of her fingers, then sighed. "How sure are you that this is genuine?"

"The first thing anyone knew about it was when the building's passive neutron sniffer jumped off the wall. At first the block manager thought it was malfing, but it turns out yon Idiot was tickling the dragon's tail. He'd got a cheap-ass assembler blueprint from some anarchist phile vault, and he's been buying beryllium feedstock for his kitchen assembler over the past six months."

"Shit. Beryllium. And nobody noticed?"

"Hey." MacDougal spread her hands. "Nobody *here* is paying us for sparrowfart coverage. Private enterprise doesn't stretch to ubiquitous hand-holding. We go poking our noses in uninvited, we get sued till we bleed. It's a free market, isn't it?"

"Huh." Rachel nodded. It was an old, familiar picture. With nine hundred permanent seats on the UN Security SIG, the only miracle was that anything ever got done at all. Still, if anything could stimulate cooperation, it was the lethal combination of household nanofactories and cheap black-market weapons-grade fissiles. The right to self-defense did not, it was generally held, extend as far as mutually assured destruction—at least, not in built-up areas. Hence the SXB volunteers, and her recurring nightmares and subsequent move to the diplomatic corps' covert arms control team. Which was basically the same job on an interstellar scale, with the benefit that governments usually tended to be more rational about the disposition of their strategic interstellar deterrents than bampot street performers with a grudge against society and a home brew nuke.

"Okay. So our target somehow scored twelve kilos of weapons-grade heavy metal *and* tested a subcritical assembly before anybody noticed. What then?"

"The block management 'bot issued an automatic fourteen-day eviction notice for violation of the tenancy agreement. There's a strict zero-tolerance policy for weapons of mass destruction in this town."

"Oh, sweet Jesus." Rachel rubbed her forehead.

"It gets better," Inspector MacDougal added with morbid enthusiasm. "Our bampot messaged the management 'bot right back, demanding that they recognize him as President of Uganda, King of Scotland, Supreme Planetary Dictator, and Left Hand of the Eschaton. The 'bot told him to fuck right off, which probably wasnae good idea: that's when he threatened to nuke 'em."

"So, basically it's your routine tenant/landlord fracas, with added fallout plume."

"That's about the size of it."

"Shit. So what happened next?"

"Well, the management 'bot flagged the threat as being (a) a threat to damage the residential property, and (b) subtype, bomb hoax. So it called up its insurance link, and *our* 'bot sent Officer Schwartz round to have a polite word. And that's when it turned intae the full-dress faeco-ventilatory intersection scene."

"Is Officer Schwartz available?" asked Rachel.

"Right here," grunted what Rachel had mistaken for a spare suit of full military plate. It wasn't: it was SWAT-team armor, and it was also occupied. Schwartz turned ponderously toward her. "I was just up-suiting for to go in."

"Oh." Rachel blinked. "Just what's the situation up there, then?"

"A very large man, he is," said Schwartz. "High-melatonin tweak. Also, high-androgenic steroid tweak. Built like the west end of an eastbound panzer. Lives like a pig! Ach." He grunted. "He is an *artiste*. This does not, I say, entitle one to live like ani-mal."

"Tell her what happened," MacDougal said tiredly, breaking off from fielding a call on her wristplant.

"Oh. This artist demands to be crowned King of Africa or some such. I tell him politely no, he may however he crowned king of the stretch of gutter between numbers 19 and 21 on the

Rue Tabazan if he wishes to not leave quietly. I was not armored up at that time, so when *monsieur l'artiste* points a gun at me, I leave quietly instead and thank my fate for I am allowed to do so."

"What kind of gun?"

"Database says it is a historical replica Kalashnikov mechanism."

"Did you see any sign of his bomb?" asked Rachel, with a sinking sensation.

"Only the dead man's trigger strapped to his left wrist," said Officer Schwartz, a glint in his eyes just visible through the thick visor of his helmet. "But my helmet detected slow neutron flux. He says it is a uranium-gun design, by your leave."

"Oh *shit!*" Rachel leaned forward, thinking furiously: *Nuclear blackmail. Fail-hard switch. Simple but deadly uranium-gun design. Loon lies bleeding, in the distance the double flash of the X-ray pulse burning the opaque air, plasma shutter flickering to release the heat pulse. Idi Amin Dadaist impersonating a dead dictator to perfection. Fifty-one minutes to detonation, if he has the guts to follow through. The performance artist scorned. What would an artist do?*

"Give him half a chance and an audience, he'll push the button," she said faintly.

"I'm sorry?"

She looked out of the window at the steady stream of poor evacuees being shepherded away from the site. They were clearly poor; most of them had lopsided or misshapen or otherwise ugly, natural faces—one or two actually looked *aged.* "He's an artist," she said calmly. "I've dealt with the type before, and recently. Like the bad guy said, never give an artist a Browning; they're some of the most dangerous folks you can meet. The Festival fringe—shit! Artists almost always want an audience, the spectacle of destruction. That name—Dadaist. It's a dead giveaway. Expect a senseless act of mass violence, the theater of cruelty. About all I can do is try and keep him talking while you get in position to kill him. And don't give him anything he might mistake for an audience. What kind of profile match do you have?"

"He's a good old-fashioned radge. That is to say, a dangerous fuckwit," said MacDougal, frowning. She blinked for a moment as if she had something in her eye, then flicked another glyph at Rachel. "Here. Read it fast, then start talking. I don't think we've got much time for sitting around."

"Okay." Rachel's nostrils flared, taking in a malodorous mixture of stale coffee, nervous sweat, the odor of a police mobile incident room sitting on the edge of ground zero. She focused on the notes—not that there was much to read, beyond the usual tired litany of red-lined credit ratings, public trust derivatives, broken promises, exhibitions of petrified fecostalagmites, and an advanced career as an art-school dropout. Idi had tried to get into the army, any army—but not even a second-rate private mercenary garrison force from Wichita would take him. *Nutty as a squirrel cage,* said a telling wikinote from the recruiting sergeant's personal assist. MacDougal's diagnosis was already looking worryingly plausible when Rachel stumbled into the docs covering his lifelong obsession and saw the ancient photographs, and the bills from the cheapjack body shop Idi—his real name of record, now he'd put his dismal family history behind him—spent all his meager insurance handouts on. "*Treponema pallidum* injections—holy shit, he paid to be infected with syphilis?"

"Yeah, and not just any kind—he wanted the fun tertiary version where your bones begin to melt, your face falls off, and you suffer from dementia and wild rages. None of the intervening decades of oozing pus from the genitals for our man Idi."

"He's mad." Rachel shook her head.

"I've been telling you that, yes. What I want to know is, can you take him?"

"Hmm." She took stock. "He's big. Is he as hard as he looks?"

"No." This from Schwartz. "I could myself have easily taken him, without armor. Only he had a gun. He is ill, an autosickie."

"Well then." Rachel reached a decision. "We've got, what? Forty-four minutes? When you've got everybody out, I think I'm going to have to go in and talk to him face-to-face. Keep the guns out of sight but if you can get a shot straight down through the ceiling that—"

"No bullets," said MacDougal. "We don't know how he's wired the dead man's handle, and we can't afford to take chances. We've got these, though." She held up a small case: "Robowasps loaded with sleepy-juice, remotely guided. One sting, and he'll be turned off in ten seconds. The hairy time is between him realizing he's going down and the lights going out. Someone's got to stop him yelling a detonation command, tripping the dead man's handle, or otherwise making the weasel go pop."

"Okay." Rachel nodded thoughtfully, trying to ignore the churning in her gut and the instinctive urge to jump up and run—anywhere, as long as it was away from the diseased loony with the

Osama complex and the atom bomb upstairs. "So you hook into me for a full sensory feed, I go in, I talk, I play it by ear. We'll need two code words. 'I'm going to sneeze' means I'm going to try to punch him out myself. And, uh, 'That's a funny smell' means I want you to come in with everything you've got. If you can plant a lobotomy shot on him, do it, even if you have to shoot through him. Just try to miss my brain stem if it comes down to it. That's how we play this game. Wasps would be better, though. I'll try not to call you unless I'm sure I can immobilize him, or I'm sure he's about to push the button." She shivered, feeling a familiar rush of nervous energy.

"Are you about that certain?" Schwartz asked, sounding dubious.

Rachel stared at him. "This fuckwit is going to maybe kill dozens, maybe hundreds of people if we don't nail him *right now*," she said. "What do you think?"

Schwartz swallowed. MacDougal shook her head. "What is it you do for a living, again?" she asked.

"I reach the parts ordinary disarmament inspectors don't touch." Rachel grinned, baring her teeth at her own fear. She stood up. "Let's go sort him out."

earth, seen from orbit in the twenty-fourth century, was a planet harrowed by technological civilization, bearing the scars left by a hatchling transcendence. Nearly 10 percent of its surface had been concreted over at one time or another. Whole swaths of it bore the suture marks of incomplete reterraforming operations. From the jungles of the Sahara to the fragile grassland of the Amazon basin it was hard to find any part of the planetary surface that hadn't been touched by the hand of technology.

Earth's human civilization, originally restricted to a single planet, had spread throughout the solar system. Gas giants in the outer reaches grew strange new industrial rings, while the heights of Kilimanjaro and central Panama sweated threads of diamond wire into geosynchronous orbit. Earth, they had called it once; now it was Old Earth, birth-world of humanity and cradle of civilization. But there was a curious dynamic to this old home world, an uncharacteristically youthful outlook. Old Earth in the twenty-fourth century wasn't home to the oldest human civilizations. Not even close.

For this paradoxical fact, most people blamed the Eschaton. The Eschaton—the strongly superhuman AI product of a technological singularity that rippled through the quantum computing networks of the late twenty-first century—didn't like sharing a planet with ten billion future-shocked primates. When it bootstrapped itself to weakly godlike intelligence it deported most of them to other planets, through wormholes generated by means human scientists still could not fathom even centuries later. Not that they'd had much time to analyze its methods in the immediate aftermath—most people had been too busy trying to survive the rigors of the depopulation-induced economic crash. It wasn't until well over a hundred years later, when the first FTL starships from Earth reached the nearer stars, that they discovered the weirdest aspect of the process. The holes the Eschaton had opened up in space led back in time as well, leading a year into the past for every light year out. And some of the wormhole tunnels went a very great distance indeed. From the moment of the singularity onward, SETI receivers began picking up strong signals; hitherto silent reaches of space echoed with the chatter and hum of human voices.

By the third century after the immense event, the polities of Earth had largely recovered. The fragmented coalitions and defensive microeconomies left behind by the collapsing wake of the twenty-first century's global free-trade empire re-formed as a decentralized network able to support an advanced economy. They even managed to sustain the massive burden of the reter-raforming projects. Some industries were booming; Earth was rapidly gaining a reputation as *the* biggest, most open trading hub within a hundred light years. The UN—even more of a deafening echo chamber talking shop than the first organization to bear that name—also included nontribal entities. Restructured to run on profit-making lines, it was amassing a formidable reputation for mercantile diplomacy. Even the most pressing problem of the twenty-second century, the population crash that followed in the wake of the singularity, had been largely averted. Cheap anti-aging hacks and an enlightened emigration policy had stabilized the population at mid-twentieth-century levels, well within the carrying capacity of the planet and in the numbers required to support advanced scientific research again. It was, in short, a time of optimism and expansion: a young, energetic, pluralistic plane-tary patchwork civilization exploding out into the stellar neigh-borhood and rediscovering its long-lost children.

None of which made for a bed of roses, as Rachel Mansour—who had been born on this same planet more than a hundred years previously—probably appreciated more than most.

i'M readu to go in," she said quietly, leaning against the wall next to the cheap gray aerogel doorslab. She glanced up and down the empty corridor. It smelled damp. The thin carpet was grimy, burdened by more dirt than its self-cleaning system could cope with, and many of the lighting panels were cracked. "Is everyone in position?"

"We've got some heavy items still assembling. Try not to call a strike for at least the first ten seconds. After that, we'll be ready when you need us."

"Okay. Here goes." For some reason she found herself wishing she'd brought Madam Chairman along to see the sort of jobs her diplomatic entertainment account got spent on. Rachel shook herself, took a deep breath, and knocked on the door. Madam Chairman could read all about it in the comfort of her committee room when the freelance media caught on. At the moment, it was Rachel's job, and she needed to keep her attention 101 percent locked on to it.

"Who is that?" boomed a voice from the other side of the partition.

"Police negotiator. You wanted to talk to someone?"

"Why are you waiting then? You better not be armed! Come in and listen to me. Did you bring cameras?"

Uh-oh. "Schwartz is right," Rachel muttered to her audio monitor. "You going to take off now?"

"Yes. We're with you." MacDougal's voice was tinny and hoarse with tension in her left ear.

Rachel took hold of the doorknob and pushed, slowly. The rentacops had applied for the emergency override, and the management had switched off all the locks. The door opened easily. Rachel stood in the doorway in full view of the living room.

"Can I come in?" she asked, betraying no sign of having noticed the whine of insect wings departing her shoulders as the door swung wide.

The apartment was a one-room dwelling: bed, shower tray, and kitchen fab were built to fold down out of opposite walls of the entertainment room. A picture window facing the front door showed a perpetual view of Jupiter as seen from the crust of smoking, yellow Io. It had once been a cheap refugee housing module (single, adult, for the use of), but subsequent occupants had *nested* in it, allowing the basic utility structures to wear out and trashing the furnishings. The folding furniture was over-extended, support struts bent and dysfunctional. The wreckage of a hundred ready-meals spilled across the worn-out carpet. The sickly sweet smell of decaying food was almost masked by the stench of cheap tobacco. The room reeked of cigarette smoke—a foul, contaminated blend, if Rachel was any judge, although she'd given up the habit along with her third pair of lungs, many years ago.

The man sprawled in the recliner in the middle of the room made even the mess around him look like an example of good repair. He was nearly two meters tall and built like a tank, but he was also clearly ill. His hair was streaked with white, his naked belly bulged over the stained waistband of his sweats, and his face was lined. He swiveled his chair toward her and beamed widely. "Enter my royal palace!" he declared, gesturing with both hands. Rachel saw the dirty bandage wrapped around his left wrist, trailing a shielded cable in the direction of a large crate behind the chair.

"Okay, I'm coming in," she said as calmly as she could, and stepped inside the room.

A hoarse robot voice burbled from the crate: "T minus thirty-five minutes and counting. Warning: proximity alert. Unidentified human at three meters. Request permission to accelerate detonation sequence?"

Rachel swallowed. The man in the chair didn't seem to notice. "Welcome to the presidential palace of the Once and Future Kingdom of Uganda! What's your name, sweetie? Are you a famous journalist? Did you come here to interview me?"

"Um, yes." Rachel stopped just inside the doorway, two meters away from the sick man and his pet talking nuke. "I'm Rachel. That's a very nice bomb you've got," she said carefully.

"Warning: proximity alert. Unidentified human at—"

"Shut the fuck up," the man said casually, and the bomb stopped in midsentence. "It *is* a lovely bomb, isn't it?"

"Yes. Did you make it yourself?" Rachel's pulse raced. She blipped her endocrine overrides, forcing the sweat ducts on the palms of her hands to stop pumping and her stomach to cease trying to flip out through the nearest window.

"*Moi?* Do I resemble a weapons scientist? I bought it off the shelf." He smiled, revealing the glint of a gold tooth—Rachel managed to keep a straight face, but her nostrils flared at the unmistakable odor of dental decay. "Is it not great?" He held up his wrist. "If I die, *poof!* All funeral expenses included!"

"How big is it?" she ventured.

"Oh, it's *very* big!" He grinned wider and spread his legs suggestively, rubbing his crotch with one hand. "The third stage dials all the way to three hundred kilotons."

Rachel's stomach turned to ice. *This isn't your run-of-the-mill black-market bomb,* she subvocalized, hoping MacDougal would be listening carefully. "That must have cost you a lot of money," she said slowly.

"Oh yes." The grin faded. "I had to sell everything. I even gave up the treatments."

"Which treatments?"

Suddenly he was on his feet and ranting. "The ones that make me Idi Amin! King of Scotland, Victoria Cross, KBE, MBE, Governor of Kiboga and Mayor of Bukake! I am the President! Respect me and fear me! You chickenshit white Europeans have oppressed the people of Africa long enough—it's time for a new world of freedom! I stand for Islamic values, African triumph, and freedom from the oppressors. But you don't give me no respect! Nobody listens when I tell them what to do. It's time for punishment!" Spittle filled the air in front of her. Rachel tried to take a step forward without attracting his attention, but the bomb noticed.

"Alert: close proximity alert! Unidentified human, believed hostile, at—"

"Don't move," MacDougal whispered tinnily in her ear. *"The fucking thing just armed itself. If you get any closer without him telling it you're friendly, it could blow."*

A bead of sweat trickled down the side of Rachel's face. She forced herself to smile. "That's really impressive," she said slowly. Insects whined softly overhead, police wasps circling his head, waiting for an opportunity to strike safely. A thought dug its unwelcome claws into her mind: *Got to get closer! But how?* "I *like* impressive men," she cooed. "And you're really impressive, Mister President."

I'm going to try to get close enough to immobilize him, she subvocalized. *Tell me exactly what your bugs are loaded with again.*

"Glad you think so, little lady," said the Last King of Scotland, rubbing his crotch. *Isn't priapism a late-stage symptom?* she subvocalized, staring at his dirty sweats and forcing herself to lick her suddenly dry lips.

"They're loaded with a really strong serotonin antagonist targeted on his reticular activating system. Ten seconds and he'll be in a coma. We just need to stop him telling the bomb to go bang after it goes in and before he nods off. And, uh, yes, it is a symptom."

"Your little king looks like he wants to hold court." Rachel smiled invitingly, dry-swallowing and steeling herself for the next step. *First get his confidence, then abuse it...* "What's the protocol for approaching a President, Mister President?"

"You do it naked. Naked folks are my *friends.* Naked people don't have no guns. You hear that, bomb? Naked women are my *friends.* Naked bitches. My special friends." He seemed to have calmed down a bit, but the set of his jaw was still tense, and he squinted angrily, as if he had a bad sinus headache. "You going to get *naked,* bitch?"

"If you say so, Mister President." Rachel locked her jaw muscles in a painful rictus that imitated a smile as she unsealed her jacket and slowly shrugged her way out of it. *Did you hear that?* she subvocalized as she rolled her leggings down around her ankles and stepped out of them. She stood in front of him and held the forced grin, trying to look inviting, willing her endocrine override to give her a flush of subcutaneous blood vessels and a crinkling of nipples. Trying to fake arousal, to do anything to keep the sad bastard distracted from the prospect of wanking his way into nuclear oblivion, taking half a city with him. *Anything* to let her get closer to the trigger—

"You may approach the throne," declared Field Marshal Professor President Doctor Idi Amin Dadaist, spreading his legs. With a moue of vague disgust he yanked his pants open. His penis was indeed large and stiff: it also bore several weeping sores, like a blighted aubergine. "Kneel to kiss your emperor!"

Rachel saw his hands raised above his head. His right fingertips brushed against the dead man's wristband as he smiled lazily. She knelt before him, tensing. "I can do good things with my hands," she offered as she reached toward his crotch, her skin crawling.

"Then do so," he said magisterially. "Remember, as your President I hold the power of life and death over you."

Rachel nodded and gently stroked his glans. She could see a vein pulsing in it. She leaned closer, trying to judge the distance, swallowing bile. "May I kiss you, Mister President? You're a very powerful man. Would you like that? I'm your loyal subject. Will you let me kiss you on the mouth?"

The Field Marshal and Professor sat up slightly. "Certainly," he said, mustering up a slightly pathetic gravitas: his breath caught as she stroked him.

"Hey, that's a funny smell," Rachel said quickly. Then she leaned forward and clamped her mouth down onto his lips, tongue questing, fingers busy with his shaft. He tensed slightly, back arching, and she reached up to grab his right arm by the wrist. Something insectoidal flickered past her eyes in a blur of wings as he spasmed and pumped a ropy stream of hot imperial semen across her thigh. His jaws flexed: she stuck her tongue into his mouth as far as she could, squeezing her eyes shut, holding her breath, and prayed that he wouldn't have a seizure as he bucked and jerked against her. The President for Life twitched a couple of times: then his eyes rolled up and he slumped backward in the recliner. His right arm fell sideways as she let go of it. She straightened up, gasping, and managed to turn aside. She spat, trying to get the taste of decaying teeth out of her mouth, then doubled over and vomited noisily across the would-be dictator's feet.

After a few seconds, she felt strong arms around her shoulder. "Come on," said MacDougal. "Let's get you out an' away. It's all under control."

"Under—" Rachel moved to wipe the tears from her eyes, then realized her hand was sticky. "Ugh. It's over?"

The room was filling up with naked policewomen toting toolboxes and talking into throat mikes. "Ordinary bomb team's already here to take over—half of it, anyways. You can come away now." Without her uniform and body armor, Inspector MacDougal had the most remarkable tattoos Rachel had seen in a long time: angel wings on her shoulder blades, a snake around her narrow waist. She pointed at the four nude women who were leaning over the bomb with instruments and neutron counters. "That was inspirational, Colonel! 'Naked women are my friends.'"

Rachel shook her head. An insect buzzed overhead. Not police issue, it was probably the first harbinger of a swarm of journalists. "I'm not really a colonel, I just play one in the banana republics." She shuddered. "I needed to get close enough to gag him and hold his arm out of the way. Whatever it took."

"Well, if it was up to me, you'd get a medal." MacDougal looked hard at the recliner and shook her head. "Took guts. Some assholes will do *anything* for a handjob."

"Need water," Rachel gasped, feeling another wave of nausea coming on.

Someone passed her a bottle. She rinsed and spat, rhythmically, until the bottle was empty, trying to remind herself how much worse it could have been. She could have had her tongue bitten off if he'd into a seizure. Or he might have wanted something worse. Another bottle appeared, and she poured half of it over her left hand and thigh. "I need a shower. Antibiotics. *Lots* of antibiotics. How long does that shot put him out for?"

"How long?" MacDougal sounded puzzled, then spotted the insects: she straightened up, tried to look severe, and went into press-management mode. "Laughing Joker Security takes WMD incursions extremely seriously. In accordance with our zero tolerance of nuclear sidearms policy, we deployed a destroyer payload targeted on the offender's reticular activating system. He hasn't got one anymore—he'll stay asleep until the rest of his cerebellum fails." Which, judging from the way she glanced at the erratically snoring figure, would be sooner rather than later. Impromptu art happenings involving nuclear weapons tended to get a bad press even in the laid-back Republique et Canton Geneve.

There was a shrill beeping from the pile of discarded clothes near the doorway. Rachel was leaning over it and fumbling for her interface rings before she realized she'd moved. "Yes?" she said hoarsely.

"You haven't heard the last of this!" Judging from her hectoring tone, Madam Chairman had been following events on multicast, and she was royally pissed off at something—probably the fact that Rachel was still alive. "I know about you and your cronies in the enforcement branch! Don't think you can get out of the audit hearing the same way!"

"Oh, fuck off!" said Rachel, killing the call. *I'll get you later,* she thought dizzily, leaning against the doorframe. *Find out what your game is and beat you* ... She tried to get a grip, paranoia running out of control. "Inspector, can you see I get home? I think I'm about to collapse." She slid down the wall, laughing and crying at the same time. On the other side of the room a naked lady held up something like a fat shotgun cartridge in both hands, triumphantly. Everyone else seemed to be cheering, but for the life of her Rachel couldn't see why.

More than a year earlier, in the middle of a field mission that was rapidly falling apart in all directions simultaneously, Rachel had struck a bargain with the devil. She'd made a deal with something that was indeed perfectly capable of destroying worlds: and much to her disquiet, she discovered afterward that she did not regret it.

In the wake of the singularity, the Eschaton had apparently vanished from the Earth, leaving behind a crippled network, depopulated cities, the general aftermath of planet-shaking disaster—and three commandments engraved on a cube of solid diamond ten meters on a side:

1. I am the Eschaton. I am not your god.

2. I am descended from you and I exist in your future.

3. Thou shalt not violate causality within my historic light cone. Or else.

Some people claimed to understand what this meant, while others said they were imbeciles or charlatans. The First Reformed Church of Tipler, Astrophysicist, battled it out in the streets with the Reformed Latter-Day Saints. Islam mutated out of recognition, other religions curled up and died. Computer scientists—the few who were left; for some reason the Eschaton seemed to select them preferentially—came out with crazy hypotheses. The Eschaton was a chunk of software that had, by way of who-knew-what algorithm, achieved computational sentience. It had rapidly boot-strapped itself across the Internet, achieving in minutes or hours as much thinking time as a human might attain in a million years. Then it had transcended, achieving a level of intelligence that simply could not be speculated on, an intellect that compared to human thought as a human might compare to a frog. What it did then, it did for motives that no human being was likely to guess, or understand. How it opened macroscopic wormholes in space-time—something human scientists had no clue how to do—remained a mystery.

Bizarre references to the light cone made no sense at all for more than a hundred years, until the first successful construction of a faster-than-light spacecraft. Then it began to fit into a big picture. The universe was seething with human-populated worlds, the dumping grounds where the Eschaton had deposited the nine billion or so people it had abducted in the course of a single frantic day. The wormholes covered immense distances in time as well as space, opening a year back in time for every light year out in distance. Astrophysicists speculated blatantly about the computational implications of causality violation, until silenced in a bizarre jihad by a post-Christian sect from North Africa.

The human consequences of the singularity reverberated endlessly, too. The exiles hadn't simply been dumped on any available world; in almost all cases, they'd been planted in terrain that was not too hostile, showing crude signs of recent terraforming. And the Eschaton had given them gifts: cornucopias, robot factories able to produce any designated goods to order, given enough time, energy, and raw materials. Stocked with a library of standard designs, a cornucopia was a general-purpose tool for planetary colonization. Used wisely, they enabled many of the scattered worlds to achieve a highly automated postindustrial economy within years. Used unwisely, they enabled others to destroy themselves. A civilization that used its cornucopia to produce nuclear missiles instead of nuclear reactors—and more cornucopias—wasn't likely to outlast the first famine, let alone the collapse of civilization that was bound to follow when one faction or another saw the cornucopia as a source of military power and targeted it. But the end result was that, a couple of hundred years after the event, most worlds that had not retreated to barbarism had achieved their own spacegoing capabilities.

Military strategists puzzled endlessly over the consequences of being able to attack an enemy with total surprise, until reminded of the third commandment. One or two of them, it transpired, had tried just that; the typical consequence was that a bizarre accident would befall whoever planned such an attack. Interestingly, even the most secretively prepared attempts to use time travel as a military tactic seemed to be crushed, just before they could actually take place.

Rachel had discovered the hard way just why this was the case. The Eschaton was still a factor in human affairs; reclusive and withdrawn it might be, but it still kept a watchful eye open for trouble. It intervened, too, for its own reasons. Causality violation—time travel—if allowed to flourish without check, offered an immediate threat to its existence; sooner or later somebody would try to grandfather it out of history. Various other technological possibilities also threatened it. AI research might generate a competitor for informational resources; nanotechnology developments might achieve the same results through alternative pathways. Hence the third commandment—and the existence of an army of covert enforcers, saboteurs, and agents of influence working on its behalf.

Two years before, Rachel had met one of those agents. She'd been politically compromised, a witness to his activities: a fifteen-microsecond-induced error in a clock which sealed the fate of a fleet and the interstellar empire that had dispatched it to recapture a planet that hadn't been lost in the first place. She'd stayed quiet about it, tacitly accepting the abhuman intervention in diplomatic affairs. The Eschaton hadn't destroyed a civilization this time; it had simply caused an invasion fleet to arrive at its destination too late to alter history, and in so doing had triggered the collapse of an aggressive militaristic regime. It was the job she'd been sent to do herself, by her controllers in the Black Chamber.

In fact, it had been a very happy coincidence from her point of view, because not only had she met an agent of the Eschaton: she'd married him. And sometimes, on good days, on days when she wasn't being hauled over the coals by bureaucratic harridans or called in to deal with hideous emergencies, she thought that the only thing she was really afraid of was losing him again.

On good days . . .

rachel had been lying in bed for an hour, showered and bathed to squeaky cleanliness and dosed up with a wide-spectrum phagebot and a very strong sedative, when Martin came home.

"Rachel?" she heard him call, through a blanket of thick, warm, lovely lassitude. She smiled to herself. He was home. *I can come down now,* she thought, *if I want.* The thought didn't seem to mean anything.

"Rachel?" The bedroom door slid open. "Hey." She rolled her eyes to watch him, feeling a wave of semisynthetic love.

"Hi," she mumbled.

"What's—" His gaze settled on the bedside stand. "Oh." He dropped his bag. "I see, you've been hitting the hard stuff." The next moment, he was sitting beside her, a hand on her forehead. "The polis called," he said, face clouded with worry. "What happened?"

Time to come down, she realized reluctantly. Somehow she dredged up the energy to point at the A/D patch sitting by the discarded wrapper. It was the hardest thing she'd ever done, harder than wrapping her fingers around—

"Oh. Yeah." Nimble digits, far nimbler than hers, unpeeled the backing and smoothed the patch onto the side of her neck. "Shit, that's strong stuff you're on. Was it really that bad?"

Speech was getting easier. "You have no idea," she mumbled. At the edge of her world a tidal wave of despair was gathering, ready to crash down on her as the synthetic endorphin high receded before the antidote patch. Dosing herself up had seemed like a good idea while she was alone and his flight was in plasma blackout on the way down, but now she was coming out from it she wondered how she could have done something so stupid. She reached out and grabbed his wrist. "Go. Fetch a couple of bottles of wine from the kitchen. Then I'll tell you."

He was gone a long time—possibly minutes, although it felt like hours—and when he came back he'd shed most of his outerwear, acquired a bottle and two glasses, and his face was pale and drawn. "Shiva's balls, Rachel, how the fuck did you let yourself get roped into something like that?" Clearly the media had caught up with him in the kitchen. He put the glasses down, sat beside her, and helped her sit up. "It's all over the multis. That fucking *animal*—"

His arm was round her shoulders. She leaned against him. "Lunatic squad," she said hoarsely. "Once in, never out. I'm a negotiator, remember? There was nobody else here who could do it, so—" She shrugged.

"But they shouldn't have called you—" His arm tensed.

"You. Listen." She swallowed. "Open the bottle."

"Okay." Martin, wisely sensing that this wasn't a good place to take the conversation, shut up and poured her a glass of wine. It was a cheap red Merlot, and it hadn't had time to breathe, but she didn't want it for the flavor. "Was it true you were the only one they could call? I mean—"

"Yes." She drained the glass, then held it out for more. He poured himself one, then refilled hers. "And no, I don't think there was anyone else who could do the job. Or any other way. Not with the resources to hand. This is a peaceful 'burg. No WMD team on twenty-four-by-seven standby, just a couple of volunteers. Who were on a training course in Brasilia when the shit hit the fan."

"It was—" He swallowed. "There were camera flies all over the place. I saw the feed downstairs."

"How was Luna?" she asked, changing the subject pointedly.

"Gray and drab, just like always." He took a sip, but didn't meet her eyes. "I've... Rachel, please don't change the subject."

"No?" She stared at him until he looked away.

"At least try to give me some warning next time."

"I tried to get a message to you," she replied irritably. "You were in re-entry blackout. It all blew up really fast." She pulled a face, then sniffed again. "Jesus, I'm crying," she said, half-disgusted. "This isn't like me."

"Everyone does that sooner or later," he said. She put the glass down, and Martin stroked the side of her arm, trying to soothe her.

"Asshole thought he could use me as a public convenience," she said quietly. "Someone holds a gun to your head and tells you to fuck, most legal codes call that rape, don't they? Even if the gun is actually a bomb, and you get to use your hands instead of your mouth or cunt." She took a deep breath. "But I'm not a victim." She held out her glass. "Give me a refill. The fucker's sleeping with the donor organs tonight, while *I* shall be getting drunk. All right?" She took another deep breath. Everything was getting easier, now Martin was here, and the alcohol was taking effect. "Because when I walked through that door I had a good idea what could happen, and I also knew what was at stake, and I did it of my own free will." Stray drops of wine fell on the comforter, spreading out in a wide stain. "I've been in worse situations. And in the morning I will be sober, and he'll still be fucking ugly. And dead." She giggled. "But y'know what I want right now?"

"Tell me?" he asked, uncertainly.

She sat up, throwing the comforter on the floor. "I want another bath," she announced. "With my favorite bath toy: you.

Lots of oil, foam, and stuff. Some good wine this time, not this crap. And I want one of your back rubs. I want to feel your hands all over me. And once I'm relaxed I want to hit up a couple of lines of something to turn me on, and then I want to fuck you until we're both exhausted. And raw." She sat up, unsteadily, and leaned on Martin as she tried to get out of bed. "Then tomorrow, or sometime whenever, I'm going to go and piss on the fuckwit's grave. You coming with me?"

Martin nodded, uncertain. "Promise me you'll try to get your name off the register?" he asked.

"I'll try," she said, abruptly sober. She shuddered. "Whether I'll succeed is another matter, though. It's a dirty job, but *some-one*'s got to do it. And most people are too smart to volunteer in the first place."

she returned to consciousness slowly, half-aware of a pounding headache and a nauseated stomach, in conjunction with sore leg muscles and crumpled bedding. A feeling that she was far too dirty to have just had two baths preoccupied her for a moment until another thought intruded—where was Martin?

"Ow," she moaned, opening her eyes. Martin was sitting up on the other side of the bed, watching her with a quizzical expression. He seemed to be listening to something.

"It's George Cho," he said, sounding puzzled. "I thought you had your phone blocked?"

"George?" She struggled to sit up. "What time is it?" An icon blinked into view, hovering in front of the wardrobe. "Oh shit." *Three in the morning. What does George want with me at three o'clock?* she wondered. "Nothing good ... pass the call?"

"Rachel? No video?"

"We're in *bed,* George," she said indistinctly. "It's the middle of the night. What the hell did you think?"

"Oh, I'm sorry." A picture blinked into view on the flat surface of the wardrobe. George was one of the few mainstream career diplomats senior enough to know what her real job description was. Normally dapper, and cultivating a bizarre facsimile of old age that some of the more primitive polities seemed to mistake for *distinguished,* George currently looked worried and unkempt. "It's a code red," he said apologetically.

Rachel sat up as fast as she could. "Hold on a minute," she said. "Where'd you put the hangover juice, Martin?"

"Bathroom, left cupboard, top shelf," he said.

"Give me a minute," she told George. "Okay?"

"Er, yes indeed." He nodded, looking worriedly at the pickup.

It took her one minute precisely to grab a bathrobe, a glass of water, and the bottle of wakeup juice. "This had better be good," she warned George. "What's the hurry?"

"Can you be ready to move in half an hour?" asked Cho, looking nervous. "It's a full dress team op. I've been trying to get through to you for hours. You weren't at the office this afternoon—what happened?"

Rachel glared at the camera: "You were too busy to notice some asshole trying to blow up the whole of Geneva?"

"You were involved in that?" George looked astonished. "I assure you, I didn't know—but this is far more important."

"Don't." She yawned. "Just spill it."

"I'll be giving everybody the full briefing en route—"

"*Everybody?* How many people are you bringing in? What do you mean by en route—and how long is this going to take?"

George shrugged uncomfortably. "I can't tell you that. Just plan for at least a month."

"A month. Shit." Rachel frowned at Martin's expression of dismay. "This would be out-of-system, then?"

"Er, I can't confirm or deny, but that's a good guess."

"Open-ended."

"Yes."

"Diplomatic. Black-bag. Or you wouldn't want me along."

"I-can-neither-confirm-nor-deny-that. At this time. Obviously."

"You *bastard!*" she breathed. "No, not you, George." She shook her head. "You realize I'm due about six years' sabbatical, coming up in three months? Do you *also* realize I got married a couple of months ago and we're planning on starting a family? What about my partner?"

George took a deep breath. He looked unhappy. "What do you want?"

"I want a—"

Rachel stopped dead for a moment. *Code red,* she thought, an icy sense of dread insinuating itself into her tired head. *That's really serious, isn't it?* Code red was reserved for war alerts—not necessarily ones that would bring the Security Council into play, but the code didn't get used if shots weren't about to be fired. Which meant...

"—I want a double berth," she snapped. "I come back from a year-long clusterfuck in the New Republic, get hauled over the coals by some harpy from head office because of the *hospitality* budget, have to deal with the mess when some lunatic is visited by the Plutonium Fairy and tries to landscape downtown Geneva by way of an art happening because he can't get a handjob, and now you want to drag me away from home and hearth on a wild goose chase into the back of nowhere: I figure a double berth is the least you can do for me."

"Oh." George held up his right hand. "Excuse me, just a moment." His eyes flickered with laser speckle as some urgent news beamed straight onto his retinas. "You haven't registered a change of status. I didn't realize—"

"Damn right you didn't realize. No long solo postings anymore, George, not for the foreseeable and not without planning."

"Well." He looked thoughtful. "We need you right now. But..." He rubbed his chin. "Look, I'll try to get your husband or wife a diplomatic passport and a ticket out to, er, the embassy destination on the next available transport. But we need *you, now,* no messing."

Rachel shook her head. "Not good enough. Martin comes along, or I don't go."

Across the bedroom, Martin crossed his arms, shrugged, miming incomprehension. Rachel pretended not to see.

"If that's your final word," George said slowly. He thought for a minute. "I think I can manage that, but only if your husband consents to sign on as a staff intern. There's a fast courier ship waiting in orbit; this isn't a joyride. Are you willing to do that?"

Rachel glanced sidelong at Martin. "Are you?"

He raised an eyebrow, then after a moment he nodded. "It'll do. I've got nothing coming up in the next month, anyway. If you think...?"

"I do." She forced herself to smile at him, then glanced back in-field at George. "He'll take it."

"Good," George said briskly. "If you can be ready to travel in an hour, that would be good. No need to bring clothing or supplies—there's a budget for that en route. Just bring yourselves. Um, this child—it hasn't been fertilized yet? Neither you nor your husband is pregnant, I hope?"

"No." Rachel shook her head. "You want us in one hour? You can't even hint what this is about?"

For a moment Cho looked haggard. "Not until we're under

way," he said quietly. "It's a maximum-security issue. But... about today. How many lives did you save?"

"Um. Three hundred kilotons would be... all of Geneva, if you want to look at it like that. About half a million people. Call it half of them dead, the other half homeless, if our little friend had got his shit together. Why?"

"Because about a thousand times that many people will die if we don't pull this one off," George said with quiet vehemence. "And that's just for starters..."

another day, another editorial _____

The Times of London—*thundering the news since 1785! Now brought to you by Frank the Nose, sponsored by Consolidated Vultee Interstellar, Mariposa Interstructures, Bank Muamalat al-Failaka, CyberMouse™, and The First Universal Church of Kermit.*

LEADER
I want to talk to you about the disaster in New Moscow. Even if you phrase it in the morally bankrupt language of so-called objective journalism, this is a truly sickening mess, the kind of colossal eight-way clusterfuck that exists to keep angels, warbloggers, and every other species of disaster whore as happy as a wino in a whisky barrel. Like most people downline in this venerable organ's light cone, you probably think New Moscow is someone else's headache—a two-cow backwater McWorld populated by sinister sheep-swivers who tried messing around with godbreaker tech and got whacked, hard, by the Eschaton. A bit of hard gamma, a pretty new nebula, and it'll all blow over in a couple more years. A recent flash survey commissioned by this blog found that 69 percent of earthworms had never heard of New Moscow; of those who had, 87 percent were sure that it has nothing to do with Terrestrial politics, and by the way, blow jobs aren't really sexual intercourse, that old pervert Santa Claus comes down your chimney every December 25, and the Earth is flat.

Well, now is the time to peel back the foreskin of misconception and apply the wire brush of enlightenment to this mass of sticky half-truths and lies. The truth hurts, but not as much as the consequences of willful ignorance.

I was on New Moscow nine years ago, doing the usual peripatetic long-haul circuit climb out through the fleshpots of Septagon, the rural sprawl of Two Rivers, and whatever wild overgeneralizations you prefer to pin on places like Al-Assad, Brunei, and Beethoven. New Moscow was—I tell you three times—*not* a bucolic rural backwater. It's kind of hard to be a bucolic rural backwater planet when you've got six continental-scale state governments participating in a planetary federation, cities the size of Memphis, Ajuba, and Tokyo, and an orbital infrastructure capable of building fusion-powered interplanetary freighters.

Insular is a word you might want to try pinning on New Moscow—how cosmopolitan can you be, with only two hundred million citizens and no shipyards capable of manufacturing FTL drive kernels?—but they maintained their core industrial competences better than many postintervention colonies, and they lived pretty well. Just because your ancestors came from Iowa and Kansas and you talk like you're yawning the whole time, it does not follow that you are stupid, primitive, inbred, or a mad imperialist set on galactic conquest. I found the people of New Moscow to be generally as tolerant, friendly, open-minded, outward-looking, energetic, funny and humane as any other people I've known. If you were looking for the stereotypical McWorld, Moscow would be it: settled by unwilling refugees from the twenty-first-century Euro-American mainstream culture, people who took enlightenment values, representative democracy, mutual tolerance, and religious freedom as axioms, and built a civilization on that basis. A McWorld, we call them—bland, comfortable, tolerant, heirs to the Western historical tradition. Another description that fits would be: boring.

Except, someone fucking murdered them.

"Edbot: tweak my scat-profile down to point seven. I think I'm laying it on a bit heavily here."

Shocked at the bad language? Good: I wanted to get your attention. What happened on New Moscow is shocking because it could have happened anywhere. It could have happened right here, on Earth—where you probably are right now, seeing how 70 percent of you readers are left-behinds—or on Marid's world. It could even have happened to the obnoxious imperialist fuckwits from Orion's Law or the quiet enlightened muslim technocrats of Bohraj. We are *all* vulnerable, because whoever vaped New Moscow has gotten clean away with a monstrous crime, and as long as there's no formal investigation, they're going to think maybe they can do it again. And I'm telling you now, whoever they are they are not a Muscovite.

The *Times* has managed to secure exclusive access to the Sixfold State Commission's last available internal government budget, passed just under two years before the Zero Incident. (The most recent budget was not publicly released prior to the disaster.) We believe these data to be accurate, and I can assure you that military spending which might have provoked an Eschatological incursion was not even on the radar. A detailed audit *[Edbot: add hyperlinks for supplementary material]* shows that the official military spend was 270 million a year on maintaining the STL deterrent fleet, and another 600 mil on civil defense: mostly against natural disasters. There was not enough slack in the budget to buy more than another 100 mil in black project spend, and New Moscow's shipyards—crucially—lacked the expertise and tooling to build or repair FTL fabrications. No causality-violation warfare here, folks, there's nothing to see, nothing that might have caught the attention of the big E, no infrastructure for developing forbidden weapons or violating Rule Three. Accusing these guys of secretly building a causality-violation weapon just doesn't hold water. On the other hand, they *had* just signed a cooperation and collaboration treaty with their nasty neighbors in Newpeace, which suggests several unpleasant possibilities, but nothing firm enough to print in a newsblog. At least, not yet.

Bottom line, someone did it *to* them. Probably some nasty sneaky human faction with weapons of mass destruction and an axe to grind against Moscow's government, a perceived grudge that drove them to massacre millions of innocents purely to avenge some slight inflicted, no doubt, in complete ignorance of the fact that it *was* a slight. In other words, an act of genocide.

Finally: to the gradgrind scum in the feedback forum who says that the destruction of New Moscow by Act of Weakly Godlike Being means we should withhold funds from the aid and hardship budget to help resettle the refugees, all I can say is fuck off and die. You fill me with contempt. I am so angry that I shouldn't really be writing this; I'm surprised the keyboard isn't melting under my fingertips. I'm appalled that the question ever arose in the first place. You aren't fit to be allowed to read the *Times,* and I'm canceling your subscription forthwith. You are a disgrace to the human species—kindly become extinct.

Ends (*Times* Leader)

Frank stubbed out his cigar angrily, grinding what was left of it into the ashtray with his thumb. "Fuck 'em," he grumbled to himself. "Fuck 'em." He took a deep breath, sucking in the blue soup that passed for air in his cramped stateroom. Sooner or later he'd have to turn the ventilation back on and pull down the plastic film he'd spread all over the smoke detector—otherwise, the life-support stewards would come round and give him their usual patronizing-but-polite lecture on shipboard life-support systems—but for now he took an obscure comfort in his ability to inhale the smog of his choice. Everything else about this ship was out of his grasp, locked down like a mobile theme park, and as a compulsive control-twiddler, Frank was pathologically uncomfortable with any environment he couldn't mess up to his heart's content.

Frank was pissed. He was so angry he had to get up and walk, before he gave in to the temptation to start banging his head on the bulkhead. It was one of his biggest problems, he admitted: he had an appalling capacity to feel other people's pain. If he'd been able to have it surgically removed, he'd have done so—maybe he'd then have been able to make a career for himself in politics. But as it was, given his vocation, it just gave him violent conscience-aches. Especially when, as on this cruise, he was going to have to exorcise some of his own ghosts. So he blinked away the work-flow and copy windows, folded up his keyboard and dropped it in a pocket, stood up, took a final deep breath of the blue toxic waste cloud—then opened the door for the first time in nearly twenty-four hours.

Somewhere in the crew quarters of the *Romanov* an alarm siren was probably whooping: "Danger! The troll in suite B312 has emerged! Send deodorant spray and prepare to decontaminate corridor B3! Danger! Danger! Chemical warfare alert!" He sniffed the unnaturally pure air, nostrils flaring. A big man, with a beetling brow and an expressive nose, one of his ex-lovers had described him as resembling a male silverback gorilla, a resemblance that his silver-and-black close-cropped hair only emphasized. Right then his skin glowed with youthful vigor, and he was almost vibrating with energy: he'd had his first telomere reset and aging fix only six months before, and was filled with a restless teenage exuberance that he'd almost forgotten existed. It was overflowing into his work by way of pugnacious editorials and take-no-prisoners prose, and after a few hours of writing it nearly had him bouncing off the ceiling.

The corridor was lined with doorways and walled with plush beige carpet, recessed handholds, and safety nets ready to turn it into a series of safety cubes in event of off-axis acceleration. Here and there, recessed false windows looked out onto scenes of bucolic harmony, desert sunsets and sandy beaches, vying with lush tropical rain forests and breathtaking starscapes. Indirect lighting turned it into a shadowless tube, bland as a business hotel and twice as boring. And it smelled of synthetic pine.

Frank snorted as he ambled along the corridor. He detested and despised this aspect of interstellar travel. What was the point of embarking on a perilous journey to far-off worlds if the experience was much like checking into one of those expensively manicured racks of self-contained service apartments designed to appeal to the lowest-common-denominator shit-for-brains salesdrone? Hotels with carefully bland hand-painted artwork on the walls, a cupboard where the ready-meal of your choice would appear in a prepack ready to eat, and the ceiling above the emperor-sized bed was ready to screen a hundred thousand crap movies or play a million shit immersives.

Well, fuck 'em! Fuck the complacent assholes, and their trade-mission-to-the-stars quick buck mentality. Inward-looking, pampered, greedy, and unwilling to look at anything beyond the end of their noses that doesn't come with a reassuringly expensive price tag attached. Fuck 'em and their consumer demand for bland, boring flying hotels with supercilious or patronizing hired help, and absolutely nothing that might give them any sign they weren't in Kansas anymore, Toto, that they might actually be aboard a million tons of smart matter wrapped around a quantum black hole slipping across the event horizon of the observable universe on a wave of curved space-time. Gosh, if they realized what was happening, they might be *disturbed, frightened,* even! And that might make them less inclined to buy a ticket with WhiteStar in future, thus impacting the corporate bottom line, so...

Frank had traveled by oxcart. He'd traveled on antiquated tramp freighters that had to spin their crew quarters like a wheel to provide a semblance of gravity. He'd spent one memorable night huddling with other survivors on the back of an armored personnel carrier thundering across desert sands, neck itching in the edgily imagined sights of the victor's gunships, and he'd spent a whole week huddled in the bottom of a motorized vaporetto in a swampy river delta near the town of Memphis, on Octavio. Compared to any of those experiences this was the lap of luxury. It was also puerile, bland, and—worst of all—characterless.

At the end of the gently curving corridor Frank pushed through a loose curtain that secured access onto a landing that curved around the diamond-walled helix of a grand staircase, spacecraft-style. The staircase itself was organic, grown painstakingly from a single modified mahogany tree that had been coaxed into a spiral inside its protective tube, warped into a half-moon cross-section, then brutally slain and partially dissected by a team of expert carpenters. It led up through the eleven passenger decks of the ship, all the way to the stellarium with its diamond-phase optically clean dome—covered, now, because the aberration of starlight from the ship's pilot wave had dimmed everything except gamma-ray bursters to invisibility. He glanced around, puzzled by the lack of passengers or white-suited human stewards, then did a double take as he checked his watch. "Four in the morning?" he grunted at nobody in particular. "Huh." Not that the hour meant much to him, but most people lived by the ship's clocks, trying to keep a grip on the empire time standard that bound the interstellar trading circuits together, which meant they'd be asleep, and most of the public areas would be shut for maintenance.

The night bar on F deck was still open, and Frank was only slightly breathless from hauling himself round fifteen hundred degrees of corkscrewing staircase when he arrived, pushed through the gilt-and-crystal doors, and looked around.

A handful of night owls hung out in the bar even at this late hour: one or two lone drinkers grimly tucked away the hard stuff, and a circle of half a dozen chattering friends clustered around a table in the corner. It was often hard to judge people's age, but there was something that looked young about their social interaction. Maybe they were students on the Grand Tour, or a troupe of workers caught up in one of those unusual vortices of labor market liquidity that made it cheaper to take the workers where the work was rather than vice versa. Frank had seen *that* before—he'd been on the receiving end himself once, back when he was young and clueless. He snorted to himself and slouched onto one of the barstools. "I'll have a Wray and Nephew on ice, no mixer," he grunted at the bartender, who nodded silently, realized that Frank didn't want a whole lot of chatter with his drink, and turned away to serve it up.

"Good voyage so far, eh, what-what?" chirped a voice from somewhere by his left shoulder.

Frank glanced round. "Good for some," he said, biting back his first impulsive comment. You never could tell who you'd run across in a bar at four in the morning, as at least one senior government bureaucrat had discovered after being mugged by the *Times* and left for dead in the Appointments pages. Frank had no intention of giving anything away, even to an obvious weirdo. Which this guerrilla conversationalist clearly was, from the tips of his ankle boots—one of which was red, and the other green—to the top of his pointy plush skull cap (which was electric blue with a dusting of holographic stars). Soulfully deep brown eyes and crimson moustache notwithstanding, he looked like an escapee from a reeducation camp for fashion criminals. "You'll pardon me for saying this, but I didn't come down here for a co-therapy session," Frank rumbled. The bartender punctuated his observation with a clink of crystal on teak; Frank picked up his shot glass and sniffed the colorless liquid.

"That's all right, I didn't come here for a good laugh, either." The colorful squirt nodded in exaggerated approval then snapped his fingers at the bartender. "I'll have one of whatever he's having," he piped.

Frank stifled a sigh and glanced at the gaggle of youths. They had a depressingly clean-cut, short-haired, brutally scrubbed look: there was not a single piercing, chromatophore, braid, or brand among the whole lot. It reminded him of something disturbing he'd seen somewhere, but in thirty-odd years of traveling around the settled worlds he'd seen enough that the specifics were vague. They seemed suspiciously healthy in a red-cheeked outdoors kind of way. Probably Dresdener students, children of the hereditary managementariat, off on their state-funded *wanderjahr* between high gymnasium studies and entry into the government bureaucracy. They all wore baggy brown trousers and gray sweaters, as identically cut as a uniform, or maybe they just came from a world where fashion victims were run out of town on a rail. There was just enough variation to suggest that they'd actually chosen to dress for conformity rather than having it thrust upon them. He glanced back at the technicolor squirt. "It's cask-strength," he warned, unsure why he was giving even that much away.

"That's okay." The squirt took a brief sniff, then threw back half the glass. "Whee! Hey, I'll have another of these. What did you say it was called?"

"Wray and Nephew," Frank said wearily. "It's an old and horribly expensive rum imported direct from Old Earth, and you are going to regret it tomorrow morning. Um, evening. Or whenever you get the bill."

"So?" The paint factory explosion picked up his glass, twirled it around, and threw the contents at the back of his throat. "Wow. I needed that. *Thank you* for the introduction. I can tell we're going to have a long and fruitful relationship. Me and the bottle, I mean."

"Well, so long as you don't blame me for the hangover..." Frank took a sip and glanced around the bar, but with the exception of the Germanic diaspora clones there didn't seem to be any prospect of rescue.

"So where are you going, what-what?" asked the squirt, as the bartender planted a second glass in front of him.

"Septagon, next." Frank surrendered to the inevitable. "Then probably on to New Dresden, then over to Vienna—I hear they've taken in some refugees from Moscow. Would you know anything about that? I'm skipping Newpeace." He shuddered briefly. "Then when the ship closes the loop back to New Dresden, I'm coming aboard again for the run back to Septagon and Earth, or wherever else work takes me."

"Ah! Hmm." A thoughtful look creased the short guy's face. "You a journalist, then?"

"No, I'm a warblogger," Frank admitted, unsure whether to be irritated or flattered. "What are you here for?"

"I'm a clown, and my stage name's Svengali. Only I'm off duty right now, and if you ask me to crack a joke, I'll have to make inquiries as to whether your home culture permits dueling."

"Erm." Frank focused on the short man properly, and somewhere in his mind a metaphorical gear train revolved and locked into place with a *clunk*. He took a big sip of rum, rolled it around his mouth, and swallowed. "So. Who are you *really?* Uh, I'm not recording this—I'm off duty too."

"A man after my own heart." Svengali grinned humorlessly. "There's nothing funny about being a clown, at least not after the first six thousand repetitions. I can't even remember my own name. I'm working my way around the fucking galaxy entertaining morons who live in shitholes and stashing away all the *blat* I can manage. People who don't live in shitholes I don't perform for because I might want to retire to a non-shithole one of these days."

"Oh. So you're working for WhiteStar?"

"Yes, but strictly contract. I don't hold with industrial serfdom."

"Oh. So is there much call for clowns on a liner?"

Svengali took another sip of rum before replying in a bored monotone: "The WhiteStar liner *Romanov* carries 2,318 passengers, 642 cabin crew, and 76 engineering and flight crew. By our next port of call, in eleven days' time, that number will have increased by one—two births and, according to the actuaries, there's a 70 percent probability of at least one death on this voyage, although there hasn't been one yet. There are thirty-one assorted relatives and hangers-on of crew members aboard, too. Now, most of this mob are well into their extended adulthood, but of the total, 118 are prepubertal horrors suffering from too much adult attention—they're mostly single children, or have siblings more than twenty years older than them, which makes for much the same species of spoiled brat. Someone has to keep the yard apes entertained, and they're far more demanding than adults: cheap passives and interactives only go so far. In fact"—Svengali raised his glass and tipped the bartender a wink—"they're exhausting. And that's before you get me started on the so-called adults."

Frank put his glass down. "The revue," he said. "That damn cabaret act that keeps spamming me with invitations. Is that anything to do with you?"

Svengali looked disturbed. "Don't blame me," he said. "It's

official company Ents policy to rape the nostalgia market for all it's worth. Consider yourself, a business traveler who can use his time productively on the journey: you're an exception to the general rule, which is that most travelers are bored silly and can't do anything about it. People travel to arrive at a destination. So, why would they want to stay awake through weeks of boredom, eating their heads off in an expensive stateroom when they could be tucked up in a vitrification pod in the cargo bay? Deadheads in steerage consume no oxygen, don't get bored, and buy no expensive meals or entertainments en route. So the company has to lay on *diversions* and *novelties* if they are to extract the maximum revenue from their passengers. Do you realize that the Ents manager on this ship outranks the chief engineer? Or that there's an unofficial revenue enhancement target of 50 percent over the bare room and board tariff per waking passenger?" He nodded slyly at Frank's refilled glass of rum. "For all you know, I could be a revenue protection officer and this glass of mine is drinking water. I'm here to keep you drinking in this bar until you collapse under the table, to the greater glory of WhiteStar's bottom line."

"You wouldn't do that," Frank said with a degree of magisterial assurance that came from three shots of cask-strength rum and a finely tuned bullshit detector. "You're a fucking anarchist, and your next drink's on me, right?"

"Um." Svengali sighed. "You're making presumptions on my honesty, and I've only known you for five minutes, but I thank you from the bottom of my bitter and twisted little ventricles. What kind of blogger *are* you, to be giving precious alcohol away?"

"One who wants to get drunk as a skunk, in company. Hard fucking editorial, the copy fought back, and there are no politicians to go beat up on until we get wherever it is that we're going. My momma always told me that drinking on your own was bad, so I'm doing my best to live up to her advice. Really, you won't like me anymore when you get to know me; I'm heartless when I'm sober."

"Hmm, I may be able to help you. I've got the heart of an eight-year-old boy; I keep it in a jar of formaldehyde in my luggage. Er, please excuse me—if that's funny I'm supposed to bill you."

"Don't worry, it was dead on arrival."

"That's all right then."

"Make mine a Tallisker," said Frank, turning to the bartender. "What cigars have you got?"

"Cigars, you say?" asked Svengali: "I'm fresh out of bangers."

"Yeah, cigars." In the far corner the clean-living crew began singing something outdoors-ish and rhythmic in what sounded to Frank's ear to be a dialect descended from German. Much thumping of beer glasses ensued. Svengali winced and took two fat Havanas from the offered humidor, then passed one to Frank. "Hey, you got a light?" Svengali shrugged and snapped his fingers. Flame blossomed.

"Thanks." Frank took an experimental puff, winced slightly, and took another. "That's better. Whisky and cigars, what else is there to life?"

"Good sex, money, and the death of enemies," said Svengali. "Not right now, I hasten to add: experience and honesty compels me to admit that mixing shipboard life with sex, money, and murder is generally a bad idea. But once I get off at New Dresden— end of this circuit, for now, for me—I confess I might just indulge in one or the other preoccupation."

"Not murder, I hope."

Svengali grinned humorlessly. "And what would a simple clown have to do with that? The only things I murder are straight lines."

"I'm glad to hear it." Frank took another puff from his cigar and let the smoke trickle out in a thick blue stream. He pretended not to notice the bartender surreptitiously inserting a pair of nose plugs. "Did you ever run into any refugees from Moscow?"

"Hmm, that would be about, what, four years ago indeed?"

"About that," Frank agreed. "The event itself happened"—he paused to check his watch—"about four years and nine months ago, normalized empire time."

"Hmm." Svengali nodded. "Yes, there were outlying stations weren't there? I remember that." He put his cigar down for a moment. "It really bit the flight schedules hereabouts. Every ship had to stand to arms for rescue missions! Indeed it did. However, I was working for a most malignant circus impresario at the time, groundside on Morgaine—a woman by the name of Eleanor Ringling. She had this strange idea that clowning was in the nature of unskilled labor, and used us harder than the animals. In the end I actually had to *escape* from that one, false papers and cash down for a freezer ticket off planet because she was trying to tie me up in court over an alleged bond of indenture she'd faked my spittle on." He snorted. "Think I'll stay on the rum, what?"

"Be my guest." Frank puffed on his cigar, which, while not on a par with his private supply, was well within the remit of various arms control committees and definitely suitable for a public drinking establishment. "Hmm. Ringling. Name rings a bell, I think. Didn't she turn up dead under peculiar circumstances a couple of years ago? Caused a scandal or something."

"I couldn't possibly comment. But it wouldn't surprise me if an elephant sat on her—the woman had a way of making enemies. If I'm ever on the same continent, I think I'll make a point of visiting her grave. Just to make sure she's dead, you understand."

"You must have got on like a house on fire."

"Oh we did, we did," Svengali said fervently. "She was the arsonist and I was the accelerant: her predilection for being tied up and sat on a butt plug while being beaten with sausages by a man wearing a rubber nose was the ignition source. We—" He stopped, looking at something behind Frank.

"What is"—Frank turned round—"it?" he finished, looking up, and up again, at the silent and disapproving face of one of the youths from the other table. He was blond, lantern-jawed, and built like a nuclear missile bunker. He was so tall that he even succeeded in looking over Frank.

"You are poisoning the air," he said, icily polite. "Please cease and desist at once."

"Really?" Frank switched on his shit-eating grin: *There's going to be trouble.* "How strange, I hadn't noticed. This is a public bar, isn't it?"

"Yes. The matter stands. I do not intend to inhale your vile stench any further." The kid's nostrils flared.

Frank took a full mouthful of smoke and allowed it to dribble out of his nostrils. "Hey, bartender. Would you care to fill laughing boy here in on shipboard fire safety?"

"Certainly." It was the first thing he'd heard the bartender say since he arrived. She looked like the strong, silent type, another young woman working her way around the worlds to broaden her horizons on a budget. One side of her head was shaven to reveal an inset intaglio of golden wires; her shoulder muscles bulged slightly under her historically inauthentic tank top and bow tie. "Sir, this is a general intoxicants bar. For passengers who wish to smoke, drink, and inject. It's the only part of this ship they're allowed to do that in, on this deck."

"So." Frank glared at the fellow. "What part of that don't you understand? This is the smoking bar, and if you'd like to avoid the smell, I suggest you find a *non*smoking bar—or take it up with the Captain."

"I don't think so." For a moment square-jaw looked mildly annoyed, as if a mosquito was buzzing around his ears, then an instant later Frank felt a hand like an industrial robot's grab him by the throat.

"Hans! No!" It was one of the women from the table, rising to her feet. "I forbid it!" Her voice rang with the unmistakable sound of self-assured authority.

Hans let go instantly and took a step back from Frank, who coughed and glared at him, too startled to even raise a fist. "Hey, asshole! You looking for a—"

A hand landed on his shoulder from behind. "Don't," whispered Svengali. "Just *don't.*"

"Hans. Apologize to the man," said the blonde. "*At once.*"

Hans froze, his face like stone. "I am sorry," he said tonelessly. "I did not intend to lay hands on you. I must atone now. Mathilde?"

"Go—I think you should go to your room," said the woman, moderating her tone. Hans turned on his heel and marched toward the door. Frank stared at his back in gathering fury, but by the time he glanced back at the table the strength-through-joy types were all studiously avoiding looking in his direction.

"What the fuck was that about?" he demanded.

"I can call the purser's office if you'd like an escort back to your room," the bartender suggested. She finally brought both hands out from below the bar. "That guy was *fast.*"

"Fast?" Frank blinked. "Yeah, I'd say. He was like some kind of martial arts—" He stopped, rubbed his throat, glanced down at the ashtray. His cigar lay, half-burned, mashed flat as a pancake. "Oh fuck. *That* kind of fast. Did you see that?" he asked, beginning to tremble.

"Yeah," Svengali said quietly. "Military-grade implants. I think my friend here could do with that escort," he told the bartender. "Don't turn your back on that guy if you see him again," he added in a low conversational tone, pitched to avoid the other side of the room.

"I don't understand—"

"This drink's on me. One for you, too," Svengali told the bartender.

"Thanks." She poured them both a shot of rum, then pulled out a bottle of some kind of smart drink. "Sven, did my eyes fool me, or did you have some sort of gadget in your hand?"

"I couldn't possibly comment, Eloise." The clown shrugged, then knocked back half the glass in one go. "Hmm. That must be my fifth shot this evening. Better crank up my liver."

"What *was* that about—"

"We get all types through here," said Eloise the bartender. She leaned forward on the bar. "Don't mess with these folks," she whispered.

"Anything special?" asked Svengali.

"Just a feeling." She put the bottle down. "They're flakes."

"Flakes? I've done flakes." Svengali shrugged. "We've got fucking Peter Pans and Lolitas on the manifest. Flakes don't go crazy over a little cigar smoke in a red-eye bar."

"They're not *normal* flakes," she insisted.

"I think he'd have killed me if she hadn't stopped him," Frank managed to say. His hand holding the glass was shaking, rattling quietly on the bar top.

"Probably not." Svengali finished his shot glass. "Just rendered you unconscious until the cleanup team got here." He raised an eyebrow at Eloise. "Is there a panic button under the bar, or were you just masturbating furiously?"

"Panic button, putz." She paused. "Say, nobody told me about any ersatz juvies. How do I tell if they come in my bar?"

"Go by the room tag manifest for their ages. Don't assume kids are as young as they look. Or old folks, for that matter. You come from somewhere that restricts life extension rights, don't you?" Svengali shrugged. "At least most of the Lolitas have a handle on how to behave in public, unlike dumb-as-a-plank there. Damn good thing, that, it can be really embarrassing when the eight-year-old you're trying to distract with a string of brightly dyed handkerchiefs turns out to have designed the weaving machine that made them. Anyway, who *are* those people?"

"One minute." Eloise turned away and did something with the bar slate. "That's funny," she said. "They're all from someplace called Tonto. En route to Newpeace. Either of you ever heard of it?"

There was a dull *clank* as Frank dropped his glass on the floor.

"Oh shit," he said.

Svengali stared at him. "You dropped your drink. Funny, I had you pegged for a man with bottle. You going to tell me what's bugging you, big boy?"

"I've met people from there before." He glanced at the mirror behind the bar, taking in the table, the five clean-cut types playing cards and studiously ignoring him, their quasi-uniform appearance and robust backwoods build. "Them. Here. Oh *shit.* I thought the *Romanov* was only making a refueling stop, but it must be a real port of call."

An elbow prodded him in the ribs; he found Svengali staring up at him, speculation writ large on the off-duty clown's face. "Come on, back to my room. I've got a bottle stashed in my trunk; you can tell me all about it. Eloise, room party after your shift?"

"I'm off in ten minutes, or whenever Lucid relieves me," she said. Glancing at him, interestedly: "Is it a good story?"

"A story?" Frank echoed. "You could say." He glanced at the table. A flashback to icy terror prickled across his skin, turned his guts to water. "We'd better leave quietly." The woman, Mathilde, the one in charge, was watching him in one of the gilt-framed mirrors. Her expression wasn't so much unfriendly as disinterested, like a woman trying to make up her mind whether or not to swat a buzzing insect. "Before they really notice us."

"Now?" Svengali hopped down off his stool and got an arm under Frank's shoulder. He'd had rather a lot to drink, but for some reason Svengali seemed almost sober. Frank, for his part, wasn't sober so much as so frightened that it felt like it. He let Svengali lead him through the door, toward a lift cube, then from it down a narrow uncarpeted corridor to a small, cramped crew stateroom. "Come on. Not much farther," said Svengali. "You want that drink?"

"I want—" Frank shivered. "Yeah," he said. "Preferably somewhere where they don't know it's my room."

"Somewhere." Svengali keyed the door open, waved Frank down at one end of the narrow bunk, and shut the door. He rummaged in one of the overhead lockers and pulled out a metal flask and a pair of collapsible shot glasses. "So how come you know those guys?"

"I'm not sure." Frank grimaced. "But they're from Tonto, and going to Newpeace. I had a really bad time on Newpeace once..."

Frank and alice watched the beginnings of the demonstration from the top of the Demosthenes Hotel in downtown Samara. The top of the hotel was a flat synrock expanse carpeted in well-manicured grass, now browning at the edges. The swimming pool and bar in the center of the lawn was drained, water long since diverted for emergency irrigation. In fact, most of the hotel staff had gone—conscripted into the Peace Enforcement Organization, fled to the hills, joined the rebels, who knew what.

It wasn't quite Frank's first field job, but it was close enough that Alice, a tanned, blond, hard-as-nails veteran of many botched campaigns, had taken him under her wing and given him a clear-cut—some would say micromanaged—set of instructions for how to run the shop in her absence. Then she'd taken off into the heart of darkness in search of the real story, leaving Frank to cool his heels on the roof of the hotel. She'd returned from her latest expedition three days earlier, riding the back of a requisitioned militia truck with a crateful of camera drones and a magic box that took in water at one end and emitted something not entirely unlike cheap beer at the other—as long as the concentrate cans held out. Frank welcomed her back with mixed emotions. On the one hand, her tendency to use him as a gofer rankled slightly; on the other, he was slowly going out of his skull with a mixture of boredom and paranoia, minding the shop on his own and hoping like hell that nothing happened while the boss was away.

To get the hotel roof (right on the edge of City Square, empty and untended in the absence of foreign business travelers and visiting out-of-town politicos) they'd had to pay off the owner, a twitchy-eyelidded off-world entrepreneur called Vadim Trofenko, with untraceable slugs of buttery, high-purity gold. Nothing else would do in these troubled times, it seemed. Getting hold of the stuff had been a royal pain in the ass, and had entailed Alice going on a weeklong trip up to orbit, leaving Frank to mind the bureau all on his lonesome. But at least the agency's money was buying them the penthouse suite, however neglected it was. Most of the other hacks who'd descended like flies on the injured flank of the city of Samara to watch the much-ballyhooed descent into civil war at firsthand had discovered that they could find accommodation for neither love nor money.

Frank had hung in while his boss was away, hammering out hangovers and human-angle commentaries by day, and descending like some kind of pain-feeding vampire from his rooftop every night to walk the streets and talk to people in the cafes and bars and on boulevard corners, soaking up the local color and nodding earnestly at their grievances. Lately he'd taken to hanging out in the square with a recorder, where the students and unemployed gathered to chant their slogans at the uncaring ranks of police and the blank facade of the provincial assembly buildings. He did this long into the night, before staggering back to the big empty hotel bed to crash out. But not this morning.

"I've got a bad feeling, kid," Alice had told him. She stared pensively out at the square. "A *really* bad feeling. Look to the back door; you wouldn't want to catch your ass in it when they slam it shut. Somebody's going to blink, and when the shit hits the fan..." She gestured at the window, out at the huge poster that covered most of the opposite wall of the square. "It's the tension, mostly. It seems to be slackening. And that's always a bad sign."

Big Bill's avuncular face beamed down, jovial and friendly as anyone's favorite uncle, guarded from the protesters by a squad of riot police, day and night. Despite the sentries, someone had managed to fly a handheld drone into the dead politician's right eye, splashing a red paint spot across his iris in a grisly reminder of what had happened to the last elected President.

"I didn't exactly think things were getting better," Frank equivocated. "But isn't it just political chicken? Same old same old—they'll devalue the dollaro and get a public works program going, someone will go out into the outback and haggle with Commandante Alpha, and things'll begin working again. Won't they?"

Alice snorted. "You wish. It only seems to be lightening up because the jokers are getting ready to pull something serious."

Up top wasn't much different. "It's gonna burn," said Thelma, a short, deeply tanned woman who was related to one of the public bizintel agencies out around Turku in some obscurely mercenary way, and who'd weaseled her way into Alice's confidence by sharing her stash of fuel cells with her. She was working over one of Alice's tripod-mounted bug launchers when Frank came up onto the roof. The air still held the last of night's chill, but the vast glazed dome of the sky promised another skull baker of a day. "Did you hear about the mess down Cardinal's Way yesterday?"

"Nope. What happened?" Frank held a chipped coffee mug bearing the hotel's crest under the nozzle of Alice's fizzbeer contraption and pushed the button. It gurgled creakily and dribbled a stream of piss-colored fluid, propelled by whatever was left of the hotel's water tankage. The Peace Enforcement had turned off the water supply to the hotels in the business district two days before, officially in case they fell into the hands of subversive elements. In practice, it was a not-so-subtle "Fuck off, we've got business in hand" signal to the warblogger corps.

"Over by the homeless aid center on West Circular Four. Another car bomb. Anyway, the polis cordoned off the area afterward and arrested *everyone*. Thing is, the car that went bang was an unmarked polis car: one they used for disappearances until a resistance camera tagged it a week ago. The only people who got hurt were doalies queuing for their maintenance. I was on my way there to meet Ish—a source—and word is that before it went up, a couple of cops parked it, then walked away."

"Uh-huh." Frank passed her the mug of lukewarm fizzbeer. "Have you had any luck messaging off planet today?"

"Funny you should ask that." It was Alice, arriving on deck without warning. "Someone's been running all the outgoing imagery I sent via the post office through a steg-scrubber, fuzzing the voxels." She cast Frank a sharp look. "What makes you ask?"

"Well, I haven't had as much mail as usual..." he trailed off. "How do you know it's being tampered with?" he asked, curiosity winning out.

"How the fuck do you think Eric gets his request messages to me without the Peace Enforcement bugging the call? It's our little back channel." (Eric was their desk editor back home.)

"That makes sense." Frank was silent for a moment. "What's he saying?"

"Time to check our return tickets." Alice gave a tight little smile.

"Will you guys stop talking in code and tell me what you think's going on?" demanded Thelma.

"The cops are getting ready to break skulls, wholesale," said Alice, pointing at the far side of the square. "They've been piling on the pressure for weeks. Now they're lifting off, to let the protesters think they've got a bit of slack. They'll come out to complain, and the cops get to round them all up. If that's the right way to describe what's coming."

The situation on Newpeace—or, more accurately, in the provincial capitals of Redstone and Samara and Old Venice Beach—had been deteriorating for about three years, ever since the last elections. Newpeace had been settled by (or, it was more accurate to say, the Eschaton had dumped on the planet) four different groups in dispersed areas—confused Brazilian urbanites from Rio; ferocious, insular, and ill-educated hill villagers from Borneo; yet more confused middle-class urban stay-at-homes from Hamburg, Germany; and the contents of a sleepy little seaside town in California. Each colony had been plonked down in a different corner of the planet's one major continent—a long, narrow, skinny thing the shape of Cuba but nearly six thousand kilometers long—along with a bunch of self-replicating robot colony factories, manuals and design libraries sufficient to build and maintain a roughly late-twentieth-century tech level McCivilization, and a ten-meter-tall diamond slab with the Three Commandments of the Eschaton engraved on it in ruby letters that caught the light of the rising sun.

Leave a planet like that to mature and ferment for three centuries: the result was a vaguely federal system with six major provinces, three languages, a sizable Catholic community, and an equally sizable bunch of Eschaton-worshiping nutbars from the highlands who spent their surplus income building ten-meter-tall cargo cult diamond monoliths. It hadn't been entirely tranquil, but they hadn't fought a major war for nearly two hundred years—until now.

"But isn't most of the resistance out in the hills?" asked Frank. "I mean, they're not going to come down hard in the towns, are they?"

"They've got to do it, and do it soon," Alice said irritably.

"Running around the hills is hard work; at least in the city the pro-testers are easy to find. That's why I say they're going to do it here, and do it soon. You seen the latest on the general strike?"

"Is it going ahead?" Frank raised an eyebrow.

Thelma spat. "Not if the Peace Enforcement Organization scum get their way."

"Wrong." Alice looked grimly satisfied. "The latest I've got from the Transport Workers' collective, last time I spoke to them—Emilio was clear on it being a negotiating gambit. They don't expect actually to have to play that card: it would hurt them far more than it would hurt the federales. But the feds can act as if it's a genuine threat. The collective are playing into their hands. Watch my lips: there's going to be a crackdown. Ever since Friedrich Gotha bought the election after Wilhelm he's been creaming himself looking for an excuse to fuck the rebels hard. Did you hear about Commandante Alpha being in the area? That'd be a bad sign, you ask me. I've been trying to arrange an interview but—"

"Commandante Alpha does not exist," a woman's voice called from the staircase. Frank turned and squinted against the rising sun. Whoever she was, she'd come up the service stairs: despite the sun in his eyes he had a vague impression of a slightly plump ice blonde, dressed for knocking around the outback like all the other journalists and war whores thronging the city and waiting for the storm to break. Something about her nagged at him for a moment before he realized what it was; her bush jacket and trousers looked as if they'd been laundered less than five minutes earlier. They were crisp, video anchor crisp, militarily precise. *Whoever's paying for the live video bandwidth better have deep pockets,* he thought vaguely as she continued. "He's a psywar fab-rication. Doesn't exist, you see. He's just a totem designed to inspire support and loyalty to the resistance movement among confused villagers."

"Does it make any difference?" asked Alice. She was busy unpacking another drone as she talked. "I mean, the thing about a mass movement is, once it gets going it's hard to stop it. Even if you take down a charismatic leader, as long as the roots of the grievance remain, another fucking stupid hero will come along and pick up the flag. Leaders generate themselves. Once you get a cycle of revenge and retribution going..."

"Exactly." The new arrival nodded approvingly. "That's what's so interesting about it. Commandante Alpha is an idea. To dispose of him the PEO will have to do more than simply point out that he does not exist."

"Huh?" Frank heard a distant noise like the tide coming in; an impossibility, for they were more than three hundred kilometers from the sea, and besides, Newpeace had no moons large enough to raise tides. He pulled out his keyboard and tapped out a quick note to himself. "Who did you say you were?"

"I didn't." The woman stared at him. It was not a friendly expression. "You are Frank the Nose Johnson, correct?"

Something about her manner made him tense. "Who's asking?"

She ignored the question. "And *you* are Alice Spencer, so *you* must be Thelma Couper. Three little piggies, warbloggers united. It's your good luck that you're all very lazy little piggies, up here on the roof this historic morning rather than down on the streets with the unsuspecting mob. If you're *smart* little piggies, you'll stay here and not try to leave the building. Relax, watch the fireworks, drink your beer, and don't bother trying to get an outside line. I'll come for you later."

Alice grabbed hold of Frank's arm, painfully hard. He hadn't even noticed that he'd begun to move toward the stranger. "Who the fuck are you?" he demanded.

The woman ignored him, instead turning back to the staircase. "See you around," she called over her shoulder, a mocking smile on her face. Alice loosened her grip on Frank's elbow. She took two steps toward the stairwell, then froze. She slowly spread her arms and stepped backwards, away from the steps.

"What—"

"Don't," Alice said tightly. "Just don't. I think we're under house arrest."

Frank looked round the open doorway leading down to the penthouse.

"Hey, freak! Get back! Didn't you hear the boss-woman?"

Frank got. "Shit!"

"My thoughts exactly." Alice nodded. "Y'know what? I think they *want* witnesses. Just far away enough not to smell the tear gas."

Frank found that his hands were shaking. "That cop—"

"Smart guy." It was Thelma; she sounded mocking, but maybe it was simply nerves—his or hers, didn't matter. "How's he armed?"

Alice seemed mostly unaffected. "He's got body armor. Some

kind of riot gun." She paused. "Shit! He's in blue. Did you see that, Frank?"

Frank nodded. "So?"

"So, cops hereabouts wear black. Blue means army."

"Oh. *Oh!*"

The noise outside was getting louder.

"Does that sound like a demonstration to you?" asked Thelma.

"Could be the big one, for the land protesters they locked up last week." Alice started dictating names to her chunky plastic disposaphone—she'd had it for only three weeks, since she arrived on Newpeace, but the digits were already peeling off the buttons on its fascia—then frowned. "It keeps saying 'network congested.' Fuck it. You guys? Can you get through to anyone?"

"I can't be arsed trying," Thelma said disgustedly. "It's a setup. Leastways we're supposed to survive this one long enough to file our reports and get out. I think."

Frank looked at his own phone: it blinked its display at him in electronic perplexity, locked out of the network. He shook his head, unsure what to believe. Then there was a thud from behind him. He turned and saw that someone had come out of the stairwell and fallen over, right at the top. There was blood, bright on the concrete. It was Phibul, the small guy from Siam who was booked in one floor down. Frank knelt beside him. Phibul was breathing fast, bleeding messily from his head. "You!" Frank looked up and found himself staring up the barrel of a gun. He froze. "Get this sack of shit outa my face. You show your head, you bettah pray I don' think you doalie."

Frank licked his lips; they felt like parchment. "Okay," he said, very quietly. Phibul groaned. The guard took a step back, servos whining at knee and ankle. The gun barrel was flecked with red.

"Nothing happen' here," said the guard. "You unnerstand?"

"I—I understand." Frank blinked, humiliated and angry, but mostly just frightened. The guard took another step back, down the stairs, then another. Frank didn't move until he was out of sight at the bottom. Phibul groaned again and he looked down, then began fumbling in his pockets for his first-aid kit.

The surf-on-a-beach noise was joined by a distant hammering drone: the sound of drums and pipe, marching with the people.

"Let me help, dammit!" Frank looked up as Thelma knelt beside him. "Shit." She gently peeled back one of Phibul's eyelids, then the other. "Pupillary reflex is there, but he's gonna have some concussion."

"Fucker whacked him over the head with his gun barrel."

"Could be worse," she said tersely. "C'mon. Let's get him over to the sun lounger."

A couple of pops and whines came from the edge of the roof— Alice was sending bird-sized drones spinning through the air to orbit overhead, circling for perspective shots taking in the entire square. Frank took a deep breath, smelling hot blood, Thelma's sweat—surprisingly rank—and the stink of his own fear. A hot tangy undernote of dust rose from the soon-to-be-baking surface of the plaza. "I've got an open channel," Alice called over her shoulder. "One of the local streams is relaying some kind of federal announcement. Do me a favor, Frank, get it out of my face. Transcribe and summarize."

"Okay." Frank accepted the virtual pipe, let it stream through the corner of his left eye as he watched Thelma efficiently cut up a wound dressing and gum it down on the mess of blood and thin hair atop Phibul's head. Despite the fear he was glad they were facing this together—not alone and frightened, locked in their rooms or in a police cell. The distant surf had become an approaching roar of voices. Alice threw some output at him from two of her birds, and he shuffled them round until he could see the back of his own head, kneeling alongside the drained swimming pool next to an injured reporter and a busy woman. "This is—hey, everybody!"

He tweaked the stream over onto one of Alice's repeater screens. There was a background of martial music (which here-abouts sounded like classical heavy metal) and a pompous guy in midnight blue, lots of technicolor salad on his chest, sitting uneasily behind a desk. "In view of the state of emergency, the Peace Commission has instructed all loyal citizens to stay indoors wherever possible. In the affected cities of Samara and Redstone, a curfew came into effect as of 2600 hours yesterday. Anyone out-doors in the region of Greater Samara and Metropolitan Redstone must seek shelter immediately. Assembly in groups of more than four individuals is forbidden and, in accordance with the Suppres-sion of Terrorism Regulations, Peace Enforcement units will use lethal force if they consider themselves to be under threat—"

Thelma stood up. "I've got to get a channel off-world," she said tensely. "You guys up to helping me?"

"How do you propose to do that?" Alice asked mildly, turning round. She was wearing repeater glasses rather than using optic implants—a stupid retro affectation, in Frank's view—and they cast a crazy quilt of colored light across her eyes. "Didn't you hear? We're being routed around. If you try to crack their security, they'll probably point some of their infowar assets your way—"

"I've got a causal channel in my luggage," Thelma confessed, looking scared but determined. "It's on the second floor. If we could get past laughing boy downstairs—"

"You've got your own causal channel?" Frank asked, hope vying with disbelief.

"Yeah, one that goes straight home to Turku via a one-hop relay in Septagon. No worries." She turned her hands palms up. "Ask me no questions, I'll tell you no lies. But if I can't get a secure handshake with it, it's not a lot of use, is it?"

"What do you need?" Alice asked, suddenly intent. Frank focused on her expression in a sudden moment of scrutiny: eyes widening, cheekbones sharp under dark skin, breath speeding—

"I need the thing physically up here, so I can handshake with it. I didn't know we were going to be bottled up here when—" She shook her head in the direction of the stairwell.

"How big is it?" Alice demanded.

"Tiny—it's the second memory card in my camera." She held her thumb and forefinger apart. "Looks just like a normal solid-state plug. Blue packaging."

"Your camera doesn't do real time?" Frank asked.

"I've seen it and it does; it's got local memory backup against network outages," Alice said tersely. "Let me guess. You've got the channel in your camera so you can bypass local censorship, shoot in real time, and have the outtake saved straight to your editor's desk? That's got to be costing someone an arm and a leg. All right, this camera is where, exactly?"

"Room hundred and seventeen, floor two. Corner window with a balcony."

"Hmm. Did you leave the balcony door open?"

"I think so—why?"

Alice looked over the waist-high safety wall, then backed away from the edge. "I'm not climbing down there. But a bird—hmm. Think I've got a sampler head left. If it can eject the card... you want me to have a go? Willing to stake half your bandwidth to me if I can liberate it?"

"Guess so. It's got about six terabits left. Fifty-fifty split." Thelma nodded. "How about it?"

"Six terabits—" Frank shook his head in surprise. He hated to think how much it must have cost to haul those milligrams of entangled quantum dots across the endless light years between here and Turku by slower-than-light starwisp. Once used they were gone for good, coherence destroyed by the process that allowed them to teleport the state of a single bit between points in causally connected space-time. STL shipping prices started at a million dollaros per kilogram-parsec; it was many orders of magnitude more expensive than FTL, and literally took decades or centuries of advance planning to set up. But if it could get them a secure, instantaneous link out onto the interstellar backbone nets...

"Yeah, let's try it," said Alice. The noise from beyond the balcony was getting louder.

Frank saw that Alice was already rooting through her bag of tricks. She surfaced with a translucent disc the size of her hand, trailing short tentacles that disquietingly resembled those of a box jellyfish. "I think this should do the trick."

"Is it strong enough?" Thelma asked edgily. "If that thing drops it, we'll never—"

"It'll do," Alice called. She flipped it upside down and coupled it to its small propane tank. "With you in a minute, just as soon as I've gassed it up."

"Okay." Phibul groaned again, then groaned louder; Frank turned and knelt by him. "Easy, man. Easy. You're going to be all right. Phibul?"

"My—" Phibul tried to raise one hand. Frank caught it, torn between sympathy and a strong urge to go and take a look over the parapet at the plaza. The crowd noise was enormous. Alice had stopped tracking her airborne birds, and they'd wandered off-station; Frank had a dizzying, unstable view down side streets, watching a sea of heads flowing down the Unity Boulevard, then across the roofline of a bank to another road, where boxy gray vehicles were moving purposefully—

"Alice!" he shouted, sitting up: "Don't launch it!"

Alice looked at him abstractedly as she flipped the trigger on her tripod and sent the discus spinning into the air above the rooftop. "What did you say?" she called, and for a desperate moment Frank thought it meant that everything would be all right, that the gray-painted vehicles and the brightly spinning disc and the sunburst flashes in the corner of his eye didn't mean anything. But the window in his left eye disappeared, all the same. The laser beam skybounced from the antimissile battery to the fighting mirror above the bank building was invisible to the naked eye, and the fighting mirror sure didn't care about journalistic credentials or, indeed, who owned the recce drones floating high above the city. All it knew about was friend, enemy, and counterbattery fire. "Take cover!" Frank yelled, just as the top of Alice's head vanished in a spray of red mist with a horrible popping sound, like an egg exploding in a microwave oven.

For a minute or so Frank blanked. There was a horrible noise, a screeching roar in his ears—blood on his hands, blood on his knees, blood everywhere, an ocean to Phibul's dried-up creek. He was dizzy and cold and the hand holding his didn't seem to help. It seemed to want to let go. Alice in the bar downstairs. Alice explaining the facts of life to him after bribing a government official, joking about the honeymoon suite when they moved in. Alice flying drones over the cityscape far below, spotting traffic, spotting likely hot spots with a look on her face like—

There was shouting beyond the balcony. Shouting, and a grinding metallic squeal he'd heard before, down below. Alice was dead and he was stranded with a dried-up swimming pool, a stranger from Turku, and no way to make the fuckers pay. No real-time link.

"You can't do anything for her." There was a hand on his shoulder, small and hard—he shook it loose, then pushed himself to his knees dizzily.

"I know," he heard someone else say. "I wish—" His voice cracked. He didn't really know what that person wished anymore: it wasn't really relevant, was it? He hadn't been in love with Alice, but he'd *trusted* her; she was the brains of the operation, the wise older head who knew what the hell to do. This wasn't supposed to happen. The head of mission wasn't supposed to die in the field, brains splattered all over the roof by—

"Keep *down*," Thelma whispered. "I think they're going to start now."

"Start?" he asked, shivering.

A hush fell across the square, then the noise of the crowd redoubled. And there was another sound; a pattering, like rain falling onto concrete from a clear blue sky, accompanied by a crackling roar. Then the screams. "Alice was right," said Thelma, shuddering and crouching down below the parapet. Sweating and whey-faced, she looked the way Frank felt. "It's the season for bullets."

Below them, in the packed dusty square before the government buildings, the storm drains began to fill with blood.

svengali had drunk half a bottle of single malt by the time Frank reached the massacre. His throat was hoarse, but he hadn't stopped for long enough to ask for a refill. It hurt too much to pause. Now he held his glass out. "I don't know how your liver copes with that."

"He's got the guts of a rat," slurred Eloise: "hepatic alcohol dehydrogenase pathway and all." She stood up, wobbling slightly. "'Scuse me, guys, but this isn't my night for partying after all. Nice of you to invite me and maybe some other time and all, but I think I'm going to be having nightmares tonight." She hit the release button on the doorframe and was gone into the twilight of the ship's crew accommodation deck.

Svengali shook his head as he pulled the door shut. "And here I was, hoping for a threesome," he said. He tipped a generous measure into Frank's glass, then put the rapidly emptying bottle down. "So, the troops massacred the demonstrators. What has this got to do with those guys, whoever they are?"

"The—" Frank swallowed bile. "Remember the spook woman? She came back, after the massacre, with soldiers. And Thelma's camera. She let Thelma scan the courtyard, then the guards sat her down with a gun at her head and the spook dictated my copy to me. Which I signed and submitted under my own name."

"You—" Svengali's eyes narrowed. "Isn't that unethical?"

"So is threatening to execute hostages. What would you do in my shoes?"

"Hmm." The clown topped off his own glass and took a full mouthful. "So you sent it, in order to . . ."

"Yeah. But it didn't work." He fell silent. Nothing was going to make him go into the next bit, the way they'd cuffed him, stuck needles full of interface busters in his arm to kill off his implants, and flipped him on his stomach to convulse, unable to look away or even close his eyes while they gut-shot Phibul and left him to bleed out, while two of the soldiers raped Thelma, then cut off her screams and then her breasts with their bayonets. Of the three of them, only Frank's agency had bought him a full war correspondent's insurance policy.

It had been the beginning of a living nightmare for Frank, a voyage through the sewers of the New Settlement's concentration camps that only ended nine months later, when the bastards concluded that ensuring his silence was unnecessary and the ransom from his insurers was a bigger asset than his death through destructive labor. "I think they thought I was sleeping with her," he said fuzzily.

"So you got away? They released you?"

"No: I ended up in the camps. They didn't realize at first, the Newpeace folk who supported the Peace Enforcement, that those camps were meant for everyone, not just the fractious unemployed and the right-to-land agitators. But sooner or later everyone ended up there—everyone except the security apparat and the off-planet mercenaries the provisional government hired to run the machine. Who were all smartly turned-out, humorless, efficient, fast—like those kids in the bar. *Just* like them. And then there were the necklaces."

"Necklaces?" Svengali squinted. "Are you shitting me?"

"No." Frank shuddered and took a mouthful of whisky. "Try to pull it off, try to go somewhere you're not supposed to, or just look at a guard wrong, and it'll take your head off." He rubbed the base of his throat, unconsciously. *And then there was Processing Site Administrator Voss, but let's not go there.* "They killed three thousand people in the square, you know that? But they killed another two million in those camps over the next three years. And the fuckers *got away with it.* Because anyone who knows about them is too shit-scared to do anything. And it all happened a long time ago and a long way away. The first thing they did was pin down all the causal channels, take control of any incoming STL freighters, and subject all real-time communications in and out of the system to censorship. You can emigrate—they don't mind that—but only via slower-than-light. Emigrants talk, but most people don't pay attention to decades-old news. It's just not *current* anymore," he added bitterly. "When they decided to cash in my insurance policy they deported me via slower-than-light freighter. I spent twenty years in cold sleep: by the time I arrived nobody wanted to know what I'd been through."

And it had been a long time before he'd been ready to seek the media out for himself: he'd spent six months in a hospital relearning that if a door was open, it meant he could go through it if he wanted, instead of waiting for a guard to lock it again. Six months of pain, learning again how to make decisions for himself. Six months of remembering what it was to be an autonomous human being and not a robot made out of meat, trapped in the obedient machinery of his own body.

"Okay. So they...what? Go around conquering worlds? That sounds insane. Pardon me for casting aspersions on your good self's character, but it is absolutely ridiculous to believe anyone could do such a thing. Destroy a world, yes, easily—but conquer one?"

"They don't." Frank leaned back against the partition. "I'm not sure *what* they do. Rumor in the camps was, they call themselves the ReMastered. But just what that means...Hell, there are rumors about everything from brainwashing to a genetically engineered master race. But the first rule of journalism is you can't trust unsubstantiated rumors. All I know is, this ship is going to Newpeace, which they turned into a hellhole. And those guys are from somewhere called Tonto. What the fuck is going on?"

"You're the blogger." Svengali put the bottle down, a trifle unsteadily. He frowned. "Are you going to try to find out? I'm sure there's a story in it..."

in a stately home by the banks of a dried-up river on a world with two small moons, a woman with sea-green eyes and crew-cut black hair sat behind a desk, reading reports. The house was enormous and ancient, walls of stone supported by ancient oak timber beams, and the French windows were thrown wide open to admit a breeze from the terrace before the house. The woman, engrossed in her reading, didn't notice the breeze or even the smell of rose blossom wafting in on it. She was too busy paging through memoranda on her tablet, signing warrants, changing lives.

The door made a throat-clearing sound. "Ma'am, you have a visitor."

"Who is it, Frank?" She glanced at the brass terminal plaque that had been hacked into the woodwork by an overenthusiastic former resident.

"S. Frazier Bayreuth. He says he has some sort of personal report for you."

"Personal," she muttered. "All right. Show him in." She pushed her chair back, brushing imaginary lint from the shoulder of her tunic, and thumbed her tablet to a security-conscious screen saver.

The door clicked, and she rose as it opened. Holding out a hand: "Frazier."

"Ma'am." There was no click of heels—he wore no boots—but he bowed stiffly, from the neck.

"Sit down, sit down. You've been spending too much time in the New Republic."

S. Frazier Bayreuth sank into the indicated chair, opposite her desk, and nodded wearily. "They rub off on you."

"Hah." It came out as a grim cough. "How are the compatibility metrics looking?"

"Better than they were a year ago, better than anybody dared hope, but they won't be mature enough for integration for a long time yet. Reactionary buffoons, if you ask me. But that's not why I'm here. Um. May I ask how busy you are?"

The woman behind the desk stared at him, head slightly askew. "I can give you half an hour right now," she said slowly. "If this is urgent."

Bayreuth's cheek twitched. A wiry, brown-haired man who looked as if he was made of dried leather, he wore blue-gray seamless fatigues; battle dress in neutral, chromatophores and impact diffusers switched off, as if he'd come straight from a police action, only pausing to remove his armor and equipment webbing. "It's urgent all right." He glanced at the open window. "Are we clear?"

She nodded. "Nobody who overhears us will understand anything," she said, unsmiling, and he shivered slightly. In a ubiquitous surveillance society, any such bare-faced assertion of privacy clearly carried certain implications.

"All right, then. It's about the Environmental Service cleanup report on Moscow."

"The cleanup." She gritted her teeth. "What is it this time?"

"Arbeiter Neurath begs to report that he has identified auditable anomalies in the immigration trace left by the scram team as they cleaned up and departed. On at least three occasions over the three years leading up to the Zero Incident and the five years since then, personnel working in the Environmental Operations Team under U. Vannevar Scott failed to behave consistently in accordance with best practice guidelines for exfiltrating feral territory. *That,* in itself, I would not need to bring to your attention, my lady. The guilty parties have been reprocessed and their errors added to the documentation corpus *pour encourager les autres.* He cleared his throat. "But . . ."

The woman stared at him, her expression relaxed: Bayreuth tensed. When U. Portia Hoechst looked most relaxed she was at her most dangerous—if not to him, then to someone else, some designated enemy of the mission, roadkill on the highway to destiny. She might be thirty, or ninety—it was hard to tell with ReMastered, before the sudden unraveling of the genome that brought their long lives to an abrupt but peaceful close—but if asked to gamble Bayreuth would have placed his money at the higher end of the scale. Peaceful eyes, relaxed eyes, eyes that had seen too many horrors to tense and flicker at a death warrant.

"Continue," she said in a neutral tone of voice.

"Neurath took it upon herself to examine the detailed findings of U. Scott's team. She discovered further anomalies and brought them to my attention. I confirmed her observations and realized the issue must be escalated. In addition to the breakdown of operational discipline in the Moscow away team, there is some evidence that Scott has been, ah, relocating skeletons from the family closet into the oubliette, if you follow me."

"You have evidence."

"Indeed." Bayreuth suppressed an urge to shuffle. Hoechst made him nervous; she was far from the worst mistress he'd served—quite the contrary—but he'd never yet seen her *smile*. He had a horrible feeling that he was about to, and the consequences made him increasingly uneasy. Her dislike of U. Vannevar Scott needed no explanation—they were of different clades, and in no way compatible other than their service to the ultimate—but it was to be devoutly hoped that none of it rubbed off on him. The wars of the bosses at overstaffsupervisor level and above were best avoided if you wanted to keep your head, much less aspire to those heights yourself one day.

"Disclose it."

Bayreuth took a deep breath. *You can't back out now.* "A major weak link has come to light. It turns out that Scott's team established an MO by which all traffic to and from Moscow went through a single choke point. The theory was that in event of a leak, only the one location would require sanitizing. Leaving aside the question of backup routing and fail-over capacity, this means that the immigration desk at this one location held a complete audit trail of all our agents' movements in and out of the system."

U. Portia Hoechst frowned very slightly. "I do not follow your argument. Surely this would have been destroyed by the Zero Incident...?"

Bayreuth shook his head slowly and watched her eyes widen. "The bottleneck they picked was an isolated fuel dump and immigration post about a parsec from Moscow. It was evacuated some time ago, before the shock wave hit. U. Scott sent a proxy squad to tidy up any loose ends on the station, trash the immigration records, liquidate any witnesses, that sort of thing. Doubtless if it had worked properly it would have been an elegant and sufficient solution to the problem, but it would appear that a number of unexplained incidents occurred during the evacuation. Such as his *written instructions* to the agent on-site *going missing,* such as the failure to return all copies of the backup dumps from the sealed immigration desk, and possibly more. There is some question over a classified log of the experimental protocols that were then in progress, which appears to have been misplaced during the evacuation. The agent sent *dogs,* boss. State security dogs borrowed from the Dresdener Foreign Office. He seemed to think that sending a proper sterilization team to do the job by the book was unnecessary. All swept under the rug, of course, the evidence securely encrypted—that's why it's taken so long to come to light."

"Oh dear." Hoechst grinned at him. "Is that *all?*" she asked warmly, and Bayreuth shivered. From being cold as ice, suddenly Hoechst had warmed to him. "And he failed to report this?"

Bayreuth nodded. He didn't trust himself to speak right then.

"And your channel into Scott's department . . ." She raised an eyebrow.

"The channel is a *very personal* friend of Otto Neurath," he emphasized. "However you decide to act on this information, I would ask you to behave leniently in her case. I believe Otto shows a lot of potential for intelligent action in support of his superior's goals, and an indelicate response to his special friend might, ah, compromise his future utility. Parenthetically speaking."

"Oh, Georg. What kind of monster do you take me for?" The terrible smile disappeared. "I'm not stupid, you know. Or bloodthirsty. At least, not needlessly." She snorted. "Otto can keep his toy, once her loyalties have been retargeted on our team. I won't break her for him." Bayreuth nodded, relieved. Her restraint, for which he could claim responsibility, would only serve to bind Otto tighter to his rising faction. "As for you—" the terrifying grin was back—"how would you like to open discussions with Scott's department, about our forthcoming merger?"

"Me?" He blinked, shocked.

"Yes, you." She nodded. "I've been thinking you deserved the added opportunities that come with an elevated degree of responsibility for some time now, Georg. What was that phrase? A lot of potential for intelligent action in support of his superior's goals, I think you said."

"Why, I'm deeply grateful, but—"

"Don't be. Not yet." She gestured out through the window, at the terrace of rosebushes and the garden beyond the ha-ha, the walls and trees and the avenue leading uphill to the stately home. "If what you're telling me is correct, we have a serious leak to fix. And I think I may need to fix it on-site. I've been weaving destinies from behind a desk for too long, Georg. Scott's mistake is typical of what happens when you stay out of the field and lose touch with reality."

"Are you going to travel in person, then? What about your estates and committees—"

"They'll look after themselves. They'd better—they'll know I'll be back." Another smile, this time almost coy; if he hadn't known better, he'd have sworn she was *flirting* with him. "But seriously. I can combine the trip with a tour of the new candidates, consolidate my control over Scott's puppets in the field, and get back in touch with what it's really about. The great program, Georg. Fancy that!" She tapped her tablet. "Get me a full briefing. Then I'll arrange a session with Overdepartmentsecretary Blumlein, and obtain permission before issuing the formal denunciation by way of the Committee of Inquiry. After which we'll discuss how you're going to mind the shop for me while I'm gone."

He caught her eye. "Me? The whole thing?"

She didn't blink. "Did you have any other plans for tonight? No? Good, then I assume I can safely invite you to dine with me. We have a lot of things to discuss, Georg. Including how to ensure that you don't disappoint me the way U. Scott has ..."

the action went down hard and fast, once Hoechst had drawn certain facts to the elevated attention of Overdepartmentsecretary Blumlein. Blumlein had stared at her with those icy blue eyes, set just too close together: "Do it," he'd said, and that was all. Leaving her enough rope to hang herself with if it turned out she was wrong and U. Vannevar Scott's Subdepartment of External Environmental Control was, in fact, clean.

Walking in through the smashed glass doors of the office building in Samara, Hoechst nodded and smiled at the troops holding the front desk. *Show the flag,* as her creche-leader Fergus had exhorted her. One or two walking wounded waited stoically for the medevac truck to show up. A pile of pithed and drained bodies lay stacked like cordwood on the polished granite tiles at one side of the foyer, leaking blood from their ears and eyes, their minds already taken by the Propagators. Hoechst ignored them, concentrated on shaking hands and exchanging congratulations with her staff. *First things first.* Blood on the soles of her boots. She'd get to Scott in due course: *Damn him for forcing me to this!*

Of course, Scott's headquarters wasn't the only target of the action. Nodes had gone down all over the planetary net, branch offices off-lined and isolated during the mop-up. Out in the country, Peace Enforcement troops had punched in the doors of his harem, taken the puppets by the brain stem and turned them in for processing—those that weren't put down immediately as a poor cost/benefit risk for reclamation. It was all part and parcel of the messy business of taking down a ranking ubermensch who had been accused of malfeasance, and Hoechst hated him for it, hated him for forcing her to publicly expose a ReMastered who was less than adequate at his assigned role. But she had no real alternative. A failure to act right then might only encourage him, or worse, expose her own people to accusations of inadequacy; and in the long run it risked undermining the destiny of the people.

Troops in cream-and-beige office camouflage wedged fire and blast doors open for her as she walked through the administrative castle toward the executive service core. Her bodyguards kept pace with her, anonymous behind their masks. Staff officers followed in their wake, apprehensive and eager to serve her. There were few signs of damage, and little violence, for U. Scott's castle had been taken by stealth in the first instance. A scheduled movement of internal security troops had been replaced by Hoechst's own storm groups, welcomed with open arms by slack defenders who never suspected that their death warrant had been ordered by the planetary overdepartmentsecretary with a curt two-word phrase.

At the core of the building stood a secure zone, doors locked open by a treacherous override. Hoechst climbed the staircase, her mood bleak. At the top, a mezzanine floor looked out across Scott's control hub. He was one of those who seemed to thrive on oversight, she noted, as if he couldn't trust anything that happened outside the reach of his own senses. The doorway onto the mezzanine was splattered with drying clots of blood, brown and sharp-smelling beneath the emergency lights. Her guards waited at either corner. In the middle of the floor a curious triumvirate waited for her. In the big chair, U. Vannevar Scott himself, pithed and locked down, his limbs limp and his face an accusatory mask. Behind it, to either side, stood S. Frazier Bayreuth and another person, a woman in the robe and veil of the Propagators' Order.

"Vannevar, my dear. A shame we had to run into each other again under such distressing circumstances." Hoechst smiled at the man in the chair. His eyes tracked her slowly, barely able to move. "And yourself, Bayreuth. And to whom else do I have the pleasure?"

The strange woman inclined her head: "U. Doranna Mengele, your excellency. Here by order of the overdepartmentsecretary to pay witness to the proceedings and ensure that all is conducted in accordance with the best practices and customs of the enlightenment."

The body in the chair seemed to be agitated. Hoechst leaned close: "You should relax, Van. Struggling won't help. Those nerves won't grow back, you know." It was necessary for her image; inside, something was screaming, *You stupid unplanned bastard! What in the dead god's name did you think you were doing?* "We were given a warrant and we have executed it."

She glanced at Bayreuth. "Do you have an activation key?"

He turned and beckoned a guard over. "Switch this one back on for the supervisor," he said tersely. The Propagator cocked her head to one side and watched, silently. Hoechst tried not to pay any attention to her. There was no avoiding it. With a Propagator to witness everything, spooling the uploaded sensory take straight into the distributed network of her order, any attempt at dissembling—or mercy—would be exposed instantly.

The guard touched his wand to the back of U. Scott's neck, and some expression returned to the man's face. A finger twitched. He slurred something, fighting for control: "Portia. How could you?"

"Certain facts were drawn to my attention," she said drily, half-noticing the way Bayreuth had turned pale behind the chair. *Facts I could not ignore once they were on the record,* she added to herself, expanding the eulogy. "Sloppy procedures. Failure to abide by best practice and custom. Potential treason."

He closed his eyes. "I would never commit treason."

"Not through commission," she said, then damned herself for her weakness in conceding even that much in front of the Propagator's eyecams. "Nevertheless. A risk of exposure was noted—

and more importantly, swept under the rug." She leaned over him, rested a fine-boned hand on one immobile shoulder. "We couldn't ignore that," she said quietly.

"I was in the process of cleaning up." He sounded infinitely tired already; the upload bush would have digested his cerebellum, already be eating away at his thalamus, preserving him for posterity and the glory of the unborn god. Without the activator he'd soon be dead, not simply immobilized. Although he'd die soon enough, when the Propagator took his mind. "Didn't you know, Portia? I thought, you ... you ..."

"Booster." She snapped her fingers, fuming angrily. *Don't ghost out on me now!* His shoulder felt like a joint of uncooked meat, solid and immobile. There was a nasty stench in the air—if he'd lost bowel control already, that meant he was farther along than she'd wanted. "Witness for the Propagation, I request access to this one's lineage. While the instance vector has proven unreliable, I believe with suitable guidance the phenotype may prove stable and effective."

Bayreuth was blinking at her in surprise. The Propagator nodded. "Your request has been received," she said distantly. "A reproductive license is under consideration. Or were you thinking of a clone?"

"No, recombination only." Hoechst leaned closer, staring into U. Vannevar Scott's eyes, remembering earlier days, more innocent, both of them interns on the staff of an ubermensch—stolen nights, sleepless days, the guilt-free pleasure before responsibility became a curse. Politics. *What, thirty years? Thirty-seven years?* She could barely remember his body; some lovers were like that. Well, others you remembered for life. Scott ... Scott was history, in more than one way. "It will be something to recall him by."

"Your request will be considered by the Race Genome Improvement Committee," said the Propagator, placidly straightening her wimple. "Is there anything else?"

"Termination witness." She kept her hand on his shoulder while the guard administered the coup, switching the tree into uncontrolled dendritic mapping. His sightless eyes closed; presently a pale fluid began to leak from the back of his skull. The touch of dead meat; once she'd hated that ... now it just left her feeling glad it wasn't her turn. She smoothed his hair down, straightened up, and caught Georg Bayreuth's eye. "Have this taken away for recycling." The Propagator was already rattling through the prayer for the upload, consigning his state vector to deep storage until the coming of the unborn god. "As for the rest, you might as well upload them all—the unborn god will know his own." She sighed. "Now. Have we found where he kept his master list of puppets?"

well, portia. That brings me to the next question. How *is* your pet project going?"

Hoechst leaned back in the overstuffed velvet-lined recliner, and stared at the gold leaf intaglio on the ceiling. She took her time answering: it was all a little overpowering. Truth be told, she was unused to having the confidence of the Overdepartmentsecretariat, and U. Blumlein's avuncular tone put her on a defensive edge. It reminded her of one of her teachers, from the hazy years back in the creche, a fellow whose temperament alternated between confiding warmth and screaming tantrums—contrived, she later discovered while reading the creche's policy mandate, to teach the youngsters the benefits of close-lipped circumspection. She'd been a good pupil, perhaps too good, and it was unnerving to find that the kindly professor's object lesson in pain had such direct applicability to the upper reaches of the clade. It just went to show that *that which does not kill us makes us stronger* was more than just an empty platitude.

"I asked a question," her superior reminded her.

"I believe I have the basic issues under control," she said confidently, raising her glass and taking a cautious sip of almond liqueur to cover her moment of hesitation.

"The basic issues," Blumlein echoed, and smiled. He held out his glass and a moppet hastened to refill it. Hoechst shuffled slightly in her chair and ran a finger under the shoulder of her gown. She smiled back at him, although she was anything but relaxed.

An invitation into her superior's parlor for an evening's entertainment was normally public recognition, a sign of favored status within the clade. But a *private* invitation, to dinner for two, was something else again. The only people who'd see her were their bodyguards, private secretaries, and the service moppets, all of whom—apart from the secretaries—were disposables who counted as nothing in the sparse social networks of the ReMastered. What could he have in mind? Special orders? It certainly wasn't a seduction attempt—his tastes lay notoriously in other directions—and she couldn't see herself being important enough to cultivate for other reasons. One thing every ReMastered acquired early was a sensitive nose for relative status, and this discreet assignation simply didn't make sense from any angle she could think of. Unless he had, for some inexplicable reason, decided to assess her for the role of his public partner, a remarkable if knife-edged honor.

"I'd like you to recap the basic issues, Portia. In your own words and in your own time, if you please."

"Oh. Well." Portia shook herself. *Idiot!* She cursed. *What else could it be about?* "Scott failed miserably on Moscow. Or rather, he succeeded inappropriately. The result was, well, not what we anticipated. Sixteen ubermenschen dead, not to mention the loss of an entire client world that was less than eighteen months from open phase-two restabilization—that was a major setback in its own right. Worse, the weapons tests—the causality-violation devices his puppets were testing—have probably attracted the attention of the Enemy. Bluntly, he failed on *two* levels; his treason against his own kind failed, and worse, the weapons tests also failed catastrophically, leading to the loss of the system. It was, all told, a disaster, and Scott knew he would attract unwelcome attention if he could not provide a compensatory positive outcome."

"Hmmph." Blumlein grunted, something approximating a twinkle of amusement in his eyes. On the stage behind her, three or four moppets were performing some sort of erotic dance: Portia angled her chair so that she could watch sidelong, while keeping her attention on the planetary overdepartmentsecretary. "Juggling on the tightrope over the abyss is a long and honorable tradition, I suppose." He smiled, not unkindly. "What long-term plans did U. Scott intend to pursue?"

"I think he was going to take over New Dresden, but he didn't leave any written records." Portia sniffed. "Not surprising." His attitude encouraged her to return the smile as a peer—a gamble, but one that might bring serious advancement if it paid off.

"Absolutely." Blumlein's expression turned chilly. "How could he possibly have been so stupid?"

She shrugged, dismissively. "Scott has—well—never lacked for self-confident ambition." *You can say that again.* A brief flashback: lying in bed listening to him rant, plans to create his own clade, bring about the unborn god, steal whole worlds from the flock. "I worked closely with him for several years, when we were younger. It's probably a good thing time ran out on him; he wasn't keeping his eye on the fine detail, and if he'd gotten his plan past the second stage, the consequences could have been even worse than the slow-motion disaster he's left us with."

Blumlein put his glass down, leaned closer, his pupils dilating slightly. Portia mirrored his gestures, becoming the confidante. "Tell me what Scott was working on in that sector," he said quietly. "And what you think you might have done with it in his stead."

"The—" Her eyes swiveled sideways.

The overdepartmentsecretary caught her glance and nodded. "They won't remember any of this tomorrow," he said.

"Good. I'd hate to be responsible for spoiling such well-trained dancers."

"I thank you for your attentiveness to my estate, but would you mind returning to the matter in hand? We don't have all evening." There was an edge to his voice that hadn't been there a moment before, and Portia cursed silently, nodding.

"Very well. Scott's official task was to take over Moscow and divert it to serve the purposes of the Defense Directorate by developing munitions types forbidden to us by the Enemy. Then he was to prepare Moscow for assimilation. His agents infiltrated the government of Moscow quite effectively using only routine puppetry and a modicum of bribes. But in addition to the official project plan he paid special attention to their Defense Ministry. This paid off with the entire attack plan for the system's deterrent force, at which point Scott started getting ambitious. He got the lot—go codes, stop codes, waypoints, and insertion vectors for every possible target—and when the Zero Incident occurred that data was safely filed away in his office."

"Ah." Blumlein nodded and smiled, his expression thawing. "And now."

"Well." She considered her next words with care. "I trust the copies of the go codes and stop codes arrived at your office satisfactorily. And Moscow itself is a nonissue, thanks to the failure of certain technological initiatives. But there's still the issue of how to clean up after Scott's little adventure. Not to mention the issue of how you want to deal with the leverage this situation places in your hands with respect to the neighbors."

Blumlein nodded carefully. "In your assessment, how good was Scott's final plan?"

"The general theory is audacious—nobody has ever done anything quite like it before—but the substance I wouldn't touch with a pointy stick." The words came out automatically. "He got sloppy with Moscow, sloppy enough that he left loose ends dangling. Exfiltration witnesses, basically, but it could all unravel from there if somebody with enough time and resources got their hands on the details and backtracked to find out where the bodies were coming from, or going to."

She took a breath. "And while the basic scheme was interesting, his second-stage scheme relied too much on synchronicity— and took enormous risks. What makes it worse for us is that he'd actually begun to implement it. The moves against the Muscovite diplomatic team, for example—they're already in progress, if not completed. We can't tell until the telegrams come in, but my guess is that they'll succeed, and they'll make every chancellery within a hundred light years shit themselves. Not to mention what will happen when the High Directorate finds out. To take a whole planet for himself, then use its weapons of mass destruction to set himself up as an interplanetary emperor—it's insanely audacious, I'll grant you that. But his plan relied on the bystanders believing that a bunch of *democrats* would willingly do what he wanted. And I think it was only wishful thinking that made him contemplate such a dependency."

"Then that brings me to my next question." Blumlein paused for a moment, looking thoughtful, then snapped his fingers; a moppet minced forward, knelt to present a small silver box atop a velvet cushion. He took the box, flipped the lid open, and removed the inhaler within: "Dose?"

"Thank you kindly, no."

He nodded, then bent over it for a few seconds. "Ah, that's better." Cold blue eyes, pinprick pupils. "The core of the matter. In the hypothetical case that I was to charge you with implementing U. Scott's plan and carrying it to completion, for the greater good of the clade—" he sent a flickering glance in the direction of the stage, and at that moment Hoechst realized that despite every protestation of privacy, he believed the Propagators or the Arm might be watching, might have corrupted his own puppet master—"how would you go about it?"

Oh. Oh. Portia shivered, appalled by the vista of opportunities before her. This could mean her elevation to parity with Blumlein, to board level for an entire planet if she played her hand successfully. An almost sexual thrill: *Then nobody could touch me!* To be in control of the mechanics—she clamped down on the thought immediately, before it could form. *First things first.* The cost would be high, the temptation to Blumlein to have her executed before she could become a threat would be enormous...

Composing herself, she nodded slightly and picked up her glass. "I would first have to assure myself that I had the approval of the Directorate," she began, not glancing at the stage. "Then, once I had that, I'd pursue U. Scott's general plan, but directing events on-site in person rather than entrusting control to an extra layer of subordination. I don't believe you can have a sufficiently tight grasp on an action if you try to exercise remote control; every level of authority you delegate adds delay and an additional risk of failure, and the plan has too many contingencies to entrust command to a junior puppeteer who lacks the big picture. And I'd divert the target of his enterprise to a, ah, more acceptable one..."

CENTRIS MAGNA WAS a boringly average asteroid colony, built to a classic design that didn't rely on gravity generators: a diamond tube fifty kilometers along the main axis and eight kilometers in diameter, spinning within the hollowed-out husk of a carbonaceous chondrite somewhere in Septagon Four's inner debris belt. The inner core consisted of service facilities while the outer, high-gee levels were mostly zoned as parklands or recreational zones: the occupants lived in multilevel tenements in the mid-gee cylinders. It was a pattern repeated endlessly throughout the Septagon systems, among the hundreds of worldlets that made up the polity that had taken in most of the refugees from Moscow. And three years after her arrival, Wednesday had learned to hate it, and the grinding poverty it rubbed her nose in every minute of every day.

"Wednesday?" Her father's voice was attenuated by her barely open bedroom door: if she pulled it shut, she could block him out completely. But if she pulled it shut—

"Wednesday. Where are you?"

Biting her tongue in concentration she finished tying her bootlaces, getting them perfect. *There.* She stood up. Boots, new boots, nearly knee high, gleaming like black mirrors over her skintight cloned pantherskin leggings. "Here, Dad." Let him find her. A last look in the window, set to mirror-mode, confirmed that her chromatophores were toned in: blood-red lips, dead white skin, straight black hair. She picked up her jacket and stroked it awake, then held out her arms and waited for it to crawl into place and grip her tightly at elbows and shoulders. *Nearly ready—*

"Wednesday! Come here."

She sighed. "Coming," she called. Quietly, to herself: "Bye, room."

"Goodbye," said her bedroom, dimming the lights as she opened the door, feeling tall and slightly unbalanced in her new boots and headed through to the living room, where Dad would probably be waiting.

Morris was, as she'd expected, in the main room of the apartment. It was a big open space, a mezzanine floor upstairs on top of the dining room providing him with an office from which he could look down on the disordered chairs and multiforms of the communal area. Jeremy had been trying to undo amah's housekeeping again, building an intricate dust trap of brightly colored phototropic snowflakes in the middle of the antique dining table that Dad periodically insisted they sit around for formal meals. The dust trap writhed toward her when she opened the door. Her father had been watching a passive on the wall; it froze as he looked round at her, ancient avatars looking impossibly smooth and shiny in the perspective-bending depths. "What's *that* you're wearing?" he asked wearily.

"Sammy's throwing a party tonight," she said, annoyed. (She almost added, *How come* you *never go out?*—but thought better of it at the last minute.) "I'm going with Alys and Mira." Which was a white lie—she wasn't talking to Mira, and Alys wasn't talking to her—but they'd both be there, and anyway did it really matter who she went with when it would only take ten minutes and she'd be out all night? "First time out for my new boots!"

Dad sighed. He looked unwell, his skin pasty and bags under his eyes. Too much studying. Study, study, *study*—it was all he ever seemed to do, roosting up on top of the kitchen roof like a demented owl-bird. Smart drugs didn't seem to help; he was having real difficulties assimilating it all. "I was hoping to have some time to talk with you," he said tiredly. "Are you going to be out late?"

"All night," she said. A frisson of anticipation made her tap her toes, scuff the floor: they were remarkably fine boots, shiny, black, high-heeled and high-laced, with silver trim. She'd found the design in a historical costuming archive she'd Dumpstered, and spent most of a day turning them into a program for the kitchen fab. She wasn't going to tell him what the material had cost, real vat-grown leather like off a dead cow's skin made some people go "ick" when you told them what you were wearing. "I like dancing," she said, which was another little white lie, but Dad still seemed to harbor delusions of control, and she didn't want him to get any ideas about grounding her, so making innocent noises was a good idea.

"Um." Morris glanced away, worried, then stood up. "Can't wait," he mumbled. "Your mother and I are going to be away all day tomorrow. Sit down?"

"All right." Wednesday pulled out one of the dining table chairs and dropped onto it back to front, arms crossed across the back. "What is it?"

"We're—your mother and I, that is, uh—" Flustered, he ground to a halt. "Um. We worry about you."

"Oh, is that so?" Wednesday pulled a face at him. "I can look after myself."

"But can you—" He caught himself, visibly struggling to keep something in. "Your school report," he finally said.

"Yeah?" Her face froze in anticipation.

"You're not getting on well with the other children, according to Master Talleyrand. He, they, uh, the school social board, are worried about your, um, they call it 'acculturation'."

"Oh, great!" she snapped. "I've—" She stopped. "I'm going out," she said rapidly, her voice wobbling, and stood up before he could say anything.

"We'll have to talk about this sometime," he called after her, making no move to follow. "You can't run away from it forever!"

Yes I can: watch me. Three steps took her past the kitchen door, another hop and a skip—risking a twisted ankle in the new boots—took her to the pressure portal. Pulse hammering, she thumped the release plate and swung it open manually, then dived through into the public right-of-way with its faded green carpet and turquoise walls. It was dim in the hallway, the main lights dialed down to signify twilight, and apart from a couple of small maintenance 'bots she had the passage to herself. She began to walk, a black haze of frustration and anger wrapped tightly around her like a cloak. Most of the front doors to either side were sealed, opening onto empty—sometimes depressurized—apartments; this sub-level was cheap to live in, but only poor refugees would want to do so. A dead end, like her prospects. *Prospects—* what prospects? From being comfortably middle-class her family had sunk to the status of dirt-poor immigrants, lacking opportunities, looked down on for everything from their rural background to things like Wednesday's and Jerm's implants—which had cost

Morris and Indica half a year's income back on Old Newfie, only to be exposed as obsolete junk when they arrived here. "Fucking social board," she muttered to herself. "Fucking thought police."

Centris Magna had been good in some ways: they had a much bigger apartment than back home, and there was lots of stuff happening. Lots of people her age, too. But there were bad things, too, and if anyone had asked Wednesday, she'd have told them that they outweighed the good by an order of magnitude. Not that anyone *had* actually asked her if she wanted to be subjected to the bizarre cultural ritual known as "schooling," locked up for half her waking hours in an institution populated by imbeciles, sadistic sociopaths, bullies, and howling maniacs, with another three years to go before the Authorities would let her out. Especially because at fifteen in Moscow system she'd been within two years of adulthood—but in Septagon, you didn't even get out of high school until you were twenty-two.

Centris Magna was part of the Septagon system, a loosely coupled cluster of brown dwarf stars with no habitable planets, settled centuries ago. It was probably the Eschaton's heavy-handed idea of a joke: a group called the space settlers' society had found themselves the sole proprietors of a frigid, barely terraformed asteroid, with a year's supply of oxygen and some heavy engineering equipment for company. After about a century of bloodshed and the eventual suppression of the last libertarian fanatics, the Septagon orbitals had gravitated toward the free-est form of civilization that was possible in such a hostile environment: which meant intensive schooling, conscript service in the environmental maintenance crews, and zero tolerance for anyone who thought that hanging separately was better than hanging together. Wednesday, who had been one of the very few children growing up on a peripheral station supported by a planet with a stable biosphere, was not used to school, or defending the atmospheric commons, or to being expected to fit in. Especially because the education authorities had taken one look at her, pigeonholed her as a refugee from a foreign and presumably backward polity, and plugged her straight into a remedial school.

Nobody had inquired in her first year as to whether she was *happy*. Happy, with most of the people she knew light minutes away, scattered across an entire solar system? Happy, with the Bone Sisters ready to take any opportunity to commit surreptitious acts of physical violence against her? Happy when the first person she'd confided in had spread her private life around the commons like a ripped laundry bag? Happy fitting in like a cross-threaded screw, her dialect an object of mockery and her lost home a subject of dead yokel jokes? Happy to sit through endless boring lectures on subjects she'd taken a look at and given up on years ago, and through more boring lectures on subjects she was good at by teachers who didn't have a clue and frequently got things wrong? *Happy?*

Happy was discovering that the school surveillance net had been brainwashed to ignore people wearing a specific shade of chromakey green, and to track people wearing black. Happy was discovering that Ellis could be counted on to have a stash of bootleg happy pills and would trade them for help with the biochemistry courseware, which at age nineteen was still about three years behind where she'd got to on her own at age fifteen. Happy was finding a couple of fellow misfits who didn't have bad breath and boast about getting their ashes hauled the morning after. Happy was learning how not to get beaten up in camera blind spots by invisible assailants, and accused of confabulation and self-mutilation when she cried for help.

She didn't dare think about the kind of happy that might come from Mom or Dad finally reskilling to the point where they could land themselves some paid work, or being able to move out of this shithole of a slum tenement, or even able to emigrate to a richer, bigger hab. About not having to look forward to the prospect of being treated like a baby for more than two-thirds of her current life span, until she hit thirty—the age of majority in Septagon. Or about—

Oops, she thought, glancing around. *That wasn't very smart, was it?*

Introspection had distracted Wednesday as she left home. Which wasn't particularly bad, normally: even the sparsely inhabited subsidized apartment corridors had surveillance coverage and environmental support. But she'd turned two corners, taken a shortcut through a disused corporate warren with override-forced doors, and been heading farther toward the distal pole where the party supposedly was. Sammy and her gang (who were not the school bullies, but the arbiters of fashion and cool, and never let Wednesday forget how lucky she was to be invited) had done this before, taken over an abandoned apartment or office zone, or even a manufacturing cube, gutted it, brought in temporary infrastructure and bootleg liquor, and cranked up the music. Moving out into the distal zone was daring: the sub-basement there was some of the oldest housing in the colony, long abandoned and scheduled for restructuring and development some time in the next ten years or so.

Wednesday had been blindly running the inertial route map Johnny deWitt had nervously beamed her the day before, saved to her cache: a flashing ring on her index finger pointed the path out to her. In her self-absorbed haze she hadn't noticed how very deep the shadows were getting, nor how sparse the pedestrian traffic was, nor how many of the corridor lighting strips were smashed. Now she was alone, with nobody else in sight. There was detritus under foot, broken roofing panels, a stack of dusty utility hoses, missing doors gaping like rotten teeth in the walls—this whole sector looked unsafe, *leaky.* And now it occurred to her to start thinking. "Why Johnny?" she asked quietly. "Johnny?" Short, spotty, and ungifted with any sense of fashion, he'd have been the class nerd if he'd been smarter: as it was, he was simply a victim. And he hadn't beamed her the ticket with any obvious ulterior motive, no stammering invitation to hole up in a soft space for an hour—just plain nervous, staring over his shoulder all the time. *I could phone him and ask, but then I'd look like a fool.* Weak. But... *if I don't phone him, I'll* be *a fool.*

"Dial Johnny the Sweat," she subvocalized. *Connecting... no signal.* She blinked in disbelief. Surely there should be bandwidth down here? It was even more fundamental than oxygen. With bandwidth you could get rescue services or air, or find your way out of trouble. Without it, *anything* could happen.

There were rumors about these abandoned hab sectors. Dismembered bodies buried in the cable ducts, surveillance cams that would *look away* if you knew the secret gesture to bypass their programming, invitingly abandoned houses where one of the rooms was just a doorknob away from hard vacuum. But she'd never heard rumors of entire segments that were blacked out, where you couldn't call someone or talk to your agents or notepad, where maintenance 'bots feared to crawl. That was beyond neglect; it was actively dangerous.

She walked through a wide, low-ceilinged hall. From the rails along one side and the lack of decoration it looked to have been some kind of utility tunnel, back when people lived and worked there. Empty doorways gaped to either side, some of them fronted with rubble—crushed dumb aerogel and regolith bricks, twisted frameworks. Most of the lights were dead, except for a strip along the middle of the ceiling that flickered intermittently. The air was stale and smelled musty, as if nothing much stirred it. For the first time Wednesday was glad of her survival sensor, which would scream if she was in danger of wandering into an anoxic gas trap.

"This can't be right," she muttered to herself. With a twitch of her rings she brought up a full route map, zoomed to scale so that this corner of the colony's public spaces was on the display. (The rings were another thing that rubbed it in; back in Moscow's system they'd have been a bulky, boxy personal digital assistant, not a set of hand jewels connected to her nervous system by subtle implants.) The whole segment was grayed out, condemned, off-limits. Somewhere on the way she'd gone blundering through a doorway that was down on the map as a blank wall. "Bother." The party—she dumped her follow-me tag into the map—lay roughly a hundred meters outside the shield wall of the pressure cylinder. "Shit," she added, this time with feeling. Someone had put Johnny up to it, spiking her with a falsie—or, more subtly, run a middleman spoof on his hacked ring. She could see it in her mind's eye: a bunch of mocking in-things joking about how they'd send the little foreign bitch on a climb down into the dirty underbelly of the world. Something rattled in the rubbish at one side of the hall, rats or—

She glanced round, hastily. There didn't seem to be any cams down there, just hollow eye sockets gaping in the ceiling. Ahead, a dead zone sucked up the light: a big hall, ceiling so high it was out of sight, opened like a cavern off the end of the service tunnel. And she heard the noise again. The unmistakable sound of boots scuffing against concrete.

What do I—Old reflexes died hard: it took Wednesday a split second to realize that it was no good asking Herman for advice. She glanced around for somewhere to hide. If someone was stalking her, some crazy—more likely, a couple of Bone Sisters who'd lured her down there to whack her bad for wearing team invisicolors and carrying a cutter on their loop—she wanted to be way out of sight before they eyeballed her. The big cavern ahead looked like a good bet, but it was dark, too dark to see into, and if it was a dead end, she'd be bottled in. But the doorways off to the left looked promising; lots of housing modules, jerked airlocks gaping like eye sockets.

Wednesday darted sideways, trying to muffle her bootheels. The nearest door gaped wide, floor underlayers ruptured like decompressed intestines, revealing a maze of ducts and cables. She stepped over them delicately, stopped, leaned against the wall and forced herself to close her eyes for ten seconds. The wall was freezing cold, and the house smelled musty, as if something had rotted in there long ago. When she uncovered her eyes again, she could see some way into the gloom. The floor paneling resumed a meter inside the threshold, and a corridor split in two directions. She took the left fork hesitantly, tiptoeing quietly and breathing lightly, listening for the sound of pursuit. When it got too dark to see she fumbled her tracker ring round, and whispered, "I need a torch." The thin blue diode glow wasn't much, but it was enough to outline the room ahead of her—a big open space like her family's own living room, gutted and abandoned.

She looked around the room. A broken fab bulked in one corner next to an exposed access crawlway. A sofa, seat rotted through with age and damp, occupied the opposite wall. Holding her breath, she forced herself not to sneeze. Words came to her, unbidden, on the breeze: "—fuck da bitch go?"

"One o' these. Youse take starboard, I taken the port."

Male voices, with a really *strange* accent, harsh-sounding and determined. Wednesday shuddered convulsively. *Not the Sisters!* Bone Sisters were bad—you crossed them, they crossed you and you needed surgery—but the white sorority didn't hang out with—

Crunch. Cursing. Someone had stuck a foot in the open cable channel. Teetering on the edge of blind panic, Wednesday scurried toward the half-meter-high crawlway and scrambled along it on hands and knees, headfirst into a tube of twilight that stretched barely farther than arm's length. The tube kinked sharply upward, pipes bundled together against a carrier surface. She paused, forced herself to relax, and rolled over onto her back so that she could see round the bend. *Can I...?* Push from the knees, begin to sit up, stick boot toes into gaps in the carrier trunking, *push...*

Panting with effort, she levered herself up and out of view of the room. *Please don't have infrared trackers or dogs.* The thought of the dogs still woke her up in a cold, shivering sweat, some nights. *Please just be muggers.* Knowing her luck, she'd crossed paths with a couple of serial fuckmonsters, transgressive nonconsensuals looking for a meat puppet. And she didn't have a backup: that cost real money, the kind that Mom and Dad didn't have. She shuddered, forcing back panic, braced her elbows against the walls of the duct, and flicked her rings to shutdown. She switched off her implants—backup brain, retinal projectors, the lot. Completely *off.* She could die there and nobody would find the body until they tore down the walls. There could be a gas trap, and she'd never know. But then again, the hunters might be following her by tracking her emissions.

"She come 'ere? I not am 'inking 'dis." Scuffling and voices and, frighteningly, a faint overspill of light from a hand torch. A second voice, swearing. "Search'e floor! Have youse taken beneath dat?"

"I have. Tracer an' be saying she—shitting vanish. Tracer be losing she. Signal strong al'way from she's home. Prey be wise to sigint 'striction."

Not some girl gang shit: they were stalking her, had followed her all the way from home. Forget muggers, forget ordinary sickheads. Wednesday stifled a squeak of pure cold terror.

"I an' be checking over the way. You be clearing dis side an' if-neg we-all be waiting mid-way. If she be hiding, she-an be come out."

"An' we be dumping nitro down here? Bath she in unbreathable?"

The second one replied, contemptuous: "You-an' be finding rotten meat after, you be dumping 'de breathing mix. Contractees, t'ey wanting authentication." Footsteps clattered over the grating, stopped.

They're going to wait me out in the corridor? At least they weren't going to flood the entire sector with nitrogen, but even hearing them talking about it was frightening her. *Rotten meat. They want to* know *I'm dead,* she realized, and the dizzying sense of loss made her stomach heave. *How do I get out of this?*

Just asking the question helped; from somewhere she dredged up a memory of her invisible friend lecturing her, an elevator-surfing run during happier days back home. *The first step in evading a pursuit is to identify and locate the pursuers. Then work out what sort of map they're using and try to locate their blind spots.* Not to take the stairs or the elevator, but to go through a service hatch, carefully step onto the roof of a car, and ride it to safety—or as a training game, all the way to Docking Control and back down again without showing up anywhere on Old Newfie's security map. She'd learned to ghost through walls, disappear from tracking nets, dissolve in a crowd. Ruefully, Wednesday recalled Herman's first lesson: *When threatened, do not let yourself panic. Panic is the most likely thing to kill you.* At the time, it had been fun.

It still is *a game,* she realized suddenly. *A game for* them. *Whoever they are. But I don't have to play by their rules.* With that realization, she managed to recapture a tenuous sense of self-confidence. *Now where?*

The duct was pitch-black, but she vaguely recalled it leading upward before she'd switched her gear off. It looked like it had been a house once, a slum tenement for cheap labor—so cheap it didn't even have en suite bathrooms and automated amahs to do the cleaning. Apartments there were prefab assemblies: a bunch of sealed, airtight modules connected by pressure-tight doors, bolted together in a big empty space and linked to the pressurized support mains by service tunnels like this one. This duct had to run somewhere pressurized. The only question was whether there was room for her to follow it all the way.

Wednesday braced herself against the back of the tube and began to lever herself up. The pipes and cables with their regular ties and their support grid were nearly as good as a ladder, and their insulation was soft and friable with age, forming spongy hand-holds for her questing fingers. She paused every half meter to feel above her with one hand and tried not to think about her clothing: the boots were a miserable pain for climbing in, but she couldn't take them off, and as for what the duct was doing to her jacket...

Her questing hand found empty space. Gasping quietly she reached up, then felt the cables bend over in a curve onto what had to be the top of the rooms' outer gas containment membrane. A final convulsive heave brought her up and over, and left her dou-bled over across the cable support, panting for breath, her legs still dangling over three meters of air space. Now she risked turning on her locater ring for a moment, still dialed to provide a light glow. Glancing around, she felt an edgy bite of claustrophobia. The crawl space widened to almost a meter, but was still only half a meter high. Ahead, there was a darkness that might be a branch off to one side, in the direction of the front door *if* she hadn't lost her bearings. Wednesday pulled her legs up and crawled toward it.

She came to a branch point, an intersection with a duct that had been built with humans in mind. The ceiling rose to a meter, and another quick flash of the ring revealed lighting panels (dead and dusty) and a flat, clear crawlway. She worked her way round into it, and shuffled along on hands and knees as fast as she could go. After about six meters she came to a large inspection hatch and paused. *I'm over the road, aren't I?* She put her ear to the hatch and listened, trying to ignore the thudding of her pulse.

"—be not seeing any'ting." The voice was faint and tinny, but distinct.

"But she not being 'ere!" Protest, muted by metal. "'An being gone. Considered an' we tracer 'coy with 'an wall ghost? Be telling you not she'an 'ere."

"Tell you th'man she not being not here? I an' you wait."

Wednesday crept forward, taking shallow breaths and forcing herself not to move too fast. On the other side of the road there'd be another apartment module, and maybe a utility hub or a tunnel up to the next level, where she could get away from these freaks, whoever they were, with their weird dialect and frightening intent. She was still sick with fear, but now there was a hot ember of anger to go with it. *Who do they think they are?* Hunting her like dogs through the abandoned underbelly of the cylindrical city—the years fell away, bringing back the same stomach-churning fear and resentment.

Another node, another risky flash of light revealing another tunnel. This time she took the branch that headed toward the big empty cavern at the end of the passage. It ran straight for ten meters, then she flashed her ring again and saw a jagged edge ahead, dust and debris on the floor, what looked like the mummified turds of some tunnel-running animal and a pile of blown-out wall insulation. Beyond the ledge her light was swallowed by darkness and a distant dripping noise.

Shit. She knelt on the cold metal floor and glanced back. Below and behind her, two strange men were stalking her network shadow. Here in meatspace, though, she was blocked. Wasn't she? She crawled forward slowly and looked out into the cavern. There could be anything here: a gas trap full of carbon dioxide, or a cryogenic leak, insulation ripped and walls so cold you'd freeze to them on contact. She sniffed the air, edging close to panic again. *Herman would know* . . . But Herman wasn't there. Herman hadn't followed her from Old Newfie. He'd told her at the time: causal channels broke when you tried to move an end point faster than light, and the one his agent had planted on her—a pediatrician who'd spent an internship on the hab when she was twelve—was now corrupt. She'd have to figure it out for herself if she wanted to get to Sammy's party. Or anywhere. Home, even.

"An' chasing ghost." The voice was muffled, distant, echoing up the corridor below her. "If she here, how an' finding she? Dustrial yard my son, dustrial. An' ghost I telling." A light flickered across shadows in the gloom on the floor of the cavern and Wednesday held her breath.

"Terascan—"

"—Show none. See, titan alloy walls, you be seeing? She ghost decoy, an' I telling you."

"Yurg, he an' being not happy."

Titanium walls? She looked down. Metal ductwork. If they had a teraherz scanner, they'd find her in a flash—except these old dumb metal ducts, fabbed from junk metal ore left over from the quarrying of the asteroid, made an excellent Faraday cage. *No signal.* Her shoulders shook as she heard bootheels below her, stomp and turn.

"Me an' you, we be going back uplight her patch. Wait there an' she."

Stomp. Stomp. Angry footsteps, moving away down the corridor. Wednesday took a deep breath. *Can't hurt?* She twitched her rings back on for ten seconds and waited, then off again. The footsteps didn't return, nor the angry searching voices, but it was several minutes before she trusted herself to turn them back on again, and this time leave them glowing at her knuckles.

"Fuckmonsters," she mumbled. Not that Centris Magna was exactly overflowing with sex criminals, but it was easier to believe than—

Her phone squeaked for attention.

"Yes?" she demanded.

"Wednesday. This is Herman. Do you understand?"

"What—" Her head was reeling with coincidence. "It's been a long time!"

"Yes. Please pay attention. Your life is in danger. I am transferring funds to your purse for later retrieval. Keep your implants turned off: if you do that, I will be able to make it difficult for your pursuers to locate you. There is a ladder to one side of your current location; climb one floor, take the second exit on the left, first right, and keep going until you enter a densely populated area. Mingle with a crowd if you can find one. Do *not* go home, or you will endanger your family. I will contact you again shortly and provide directions. Do you understand?"

"Yes, but—" She was talking to herself.

"Fuckmonster," she snapped, trying to sound as if she meant it. *Herman?* After three years of silence she felt weak at the knees. *Did I imagine it?* She turned up the light on her finger, saw the piles of debris and the scuff marks on her oh-so-labor-intensive boots. "No." Saw the ladder running down to floor level and up to the next corridor up beside the platform. "Yes!"

for this party Sam had repoed a dead light industrial unit on the edge of the reclaim zone. Wednesday didn't go there immediately; she headed uplight a couple of levels to a boringly bourgeois housing arc, found a public fresher, and used the facilities. Besides getting the muck off her boots and leggings and telling her jacket to clean itself over the toilet, her hair was a mess and her temper was vile. *How dare those scumbags follow me?* She dialed her lips to blue and the skin around her eyes to angry black, got her hair back into a semblance of order, then paused. "Angry. *Angry!*"

She shook her head; the face in the mirror shook right back, then winked at her. "Can I recommend something, dear?" asked the mirror.

In the end she let it talk her into ordering up a wispy, colorful sarong, a transparent flash of silky rainbows to wrap around her waist. It didn't fit with her mood, but she had to admit it was a good idea—her jacket, picking up on her temper, had spiked up across her shoulders until she resembled an angry hedgehog, and without the softening touch she'd have people avoiding her all evening. *Then* she used the mirror to call Sam's receptionist and, swallowing her pride, asked for directions. The party was impromptu and semirandom; as good a place to hide out as anywhere, just as long as nobody tailed her there. And she had no intention of letting herself be tagged and followed twice in one night shift.

Sam had taken over an empty industrial module a couple of levels below the basement slums, spray-bombed it black, and moved in a bunch of rogue domestic appliances. Light pipes nail-gunned to rubbery green foam flared erratically at each corner of the room. The seating was dead, exotic knotworks of malformed calcium teratomas harvested from a biocoral tank, all ribs and jawbones. Loud waltz music shotgunned into screeching feedback by a buggy DJ-AI attacked her eardrums. There was a bar full of dumb and dumber, the robot waiter vomiting alcoholic drinks, and passing out joints and pink noise generators. Sameena knew how to run a party, Wednesday grudgingly acknowledged. Decriminalization lite, prosperity-bound urban youth experimenting with the modicum of risk that their subtly regimented society allowed them. A cat lay on top of a dead solvent tank, one foreleg hanging down, staring at everyone who entered. She grinned up at it. It lashed its tail angrily and looked away.

"Wednesday!" A plump boy, mirrored contact lenses, sweat gleaming red in the pit lights: Pig. He clutched a half-empty glass of something that might be beer.

"Pig." She looked around. Pig was wired. Pig was always wired, boringly religious about his heterocyclic chemistry: a bioresearch geek. Ten kilos of brown adipose cells full of the weirdest organic chemistry you could imagine boiled away beneath his skin. He kept trying to breed a better liposome for his gunge-phase experiments. Said it kept him warm: one of these days someone was going to light his joint, and he'd go off like one of those old-time suicide bombers. "Have you seen Fi?"

"Fi? Don't want hang round Fiona! She boring."

Wednesday focused on Pig for the first time. His pupils were pinpricks, and he was breathing hard. "What are you on?"

"Dumbers. Ran up a nice little hydroxylated triterpenoid to crank down the old ethanol dehydrogenase. Teaching m'self about beer 'n' hangovers. What did you bring?" He made as if to paw at her sleeve. She ducked round him gracefully.

"Myself," she said, evaluating and assessing. Pig, sober, would just about fill her needs. Pig, drunk, wasn't even on the cards. "Just my wonderful self, fat boy. Where's Fi?"

Pig grunted and took a big swig from his glass. Swaying, he spilled some of it down his chin. "Next cell over." Grunt. "Had bad day thinking too hard thismorn. 'M'I dumb yet?"

She stared at him. "What's the cube root of 2,362?"

"Mmm ... six-point-nine ... point-nine-seven ... point-nine-seven-one ..."

She left Pig slowly factoring his way out of her trap in a haze of Newtonian approximation and drifted on into the night, a pale-skinned ghost dressed in artful black tatters. Fancy dress, forgotten youthful death cults. She allowed herself to feel a bit more mellow toward Pig, even condescending to think fondly of him. Pig's wallowing self-abasement made her own withdrawn lack of socialization feel a bit less retarded. The world was full of nerds and exiles. The hothouse of forced brilliance the Septagon system produced also generated a lot of smart misfits, and even if none of them fit in individually, together they made an interesting mosaic.

There were people dancing in the next manufactory cell, accelerated bagpipes, feedback howls, a zek who'd hacked himself into a drum-machine trance whacking on a sensor grid to provide a hammering beat. It was an older crowd, late teens/early twenties, the tail end of high school. There were fewer fashion victims than you'd see at a normal high school hop, but wilder extremes; most people dressed—or didn't—as if they picked up whatever was nearest to their bed that morning, plus one or two exaggeratedly bizarre ego statements. A naked, hairless boy with a clanking crotch full of chromed chain links, dancing cheek to cheek with another boy, long-haired, wearing a swirling red gown that left his pierced and swollen nipples visible. A teenage girl in extreme fetish gear hobbled past; her wasp-waist corsetry, leather ball gag, wrist and ankle chains were all visible beneath a transparent, floor-sweeping dress. Wednesday ignored the exhibitionist extremals: they were fundamentally boring, attention-craving types who needed to be needed and were far too demanding to make good fuckfriends.

She headed for the back of the unit, hunting real company. Fiona was sitting on top of a dead cornucopia box, wearing black leggings and a T-shirt locked to the output from an entropy pool. She was chatting to a boy wearing a pressure suit liner with artfully slashed knees. The spod clutched a nebulizer, and was gesticulating dreamily. Fi looked up and called, "Wednesday!"

"Fi!" Wednesday leaned forward and hugged her. Fiona's breath was smoky. "What is this, downer city?"

Fi shrugged. "Sammy said make it dumb, but not everyone got it." (On the dance floor Miss Ball Gag was having difficulty communicating with some boy in a black rubber body-stocking who wanted to dance: their sign language protocols were incompatible.) Fi smiled. "Vinnie, meet Wednesday. You want a drink, Wednesday?"

"Yeah, whatever."

Fi snapped her fingers and Vinnie blinked slowly, then shambled off in the direction of the bar. "Nice guy, I think, under the dumb layer. I dunno. I didn't want to get wasted before everybody else, know what I mean?"

Wednesday hitched up her sarong and jumped up on the box beside Fi. "Ack. No uppers? No inverse-agonists?"

Fiona shook her head. "House rules. You want to come in, you check your IQ at the door. Hear the jammers?"

"No." When she said it, Wednesday suddenly realized that she could: the pink noise field was like tinnitus, scratching away at the edges of her implant perceptions. *Does Herman talk to Sam?* she wondered. "So that's what's got to Pig."

"Yeah. He's cute when he's thick, isn't he?" Fi giggled a bit and Wednesday smiled—sepulchrally, she hoped, because she didn't really know how Fi expected her to respond. "'Sa good excuse. Get dumb, get dumber, stop thinking, relax."

"You been at it already?" Wednesday kept her voice down.

"Yeah. Just a bit."

"Too bad. Was hoping to talk about—"

"Shh." Fi leaned against her. "I am going to get in Vinnie's pants tonight, see if I don't!" She pointed at the spod who was swaying back and forth, and working his way toward them. "Ass so tight you could drop him and he'd bounce."

The music was doing things to him and to Fi that sent a stab of jealousy all the way from Wednesday's amygdala to her crotch. She smoothed her skirt down. "What do you expect to find in his pants? A catfish?"

Fi giggled again. "Listen, just this once! Relax. Let go, ducky. Stop thinking, fuck like a bunny, learn the joy of grunt. Can't you switch off?"

Wednesday sighed. "I'll try." Vinnie was back. Wordlessly he held out a can of grinning neural death. She took it, hoisted a toast to higher cerebral shutdown, tried to chug it—ended up coughing. The night was young, the air full of augmentation jammers and neuroleptics and alcohol, and the party was just beginning to mix down to the right level of trancelike zombie heaven that high-pressure synthetic geniuses needed to switch off and groove.

A long way down to the unthinking depths. She briefly wondered if she'd meet Pig down there and find him attractive.

———

in the end it wasn't Pig; it was a boy called Blow, green skin and webbing between his fingers and toes—but not his cock and balls—and she ended up on his arm giggling at a string of inane puns. He'd slipped a hand into the slit in her skirt but politely gone no farther and left it to her to pop the question, which she did for reasons that escaped her in the morning except that he'd been clean and well-mannered, and none of her usual fuckfriends were around and free, and she felt so *tense*...

...and the poor lad had ended up staying with her half the night just to give her a back rub, after she'd finished screaming and clawing his buttocks in one of the antisound-curtained alcoves at the sides of the dance floor.

"You're *really* tight," he said in amazement, kneading away at one shoulder.

"Oh, you bet." Her jacket had crawled into one corner and curled protectively around the rest of her gear. She lay facedown on the pad, damp and sweaty and postorgasmic and a bit stoned, trying to let go and relax, as he worked on her upper back. "Aaah."

He paused. "Want to talk about it?" he asked.

"Not really," she mumbled.

After a moment he went back to prodding at the sore patch on her left shoulder blade. "You should relax." *Rub.* "It's a party. Was it someone here? Or someone else?"

"I said I don't want to talk about it," she said, and he broke off from trying to get her back to relax.

"If you don't want to talk about it, what do you want?" he asked, beginning to sound annoyed. "I could be out there." He didn't sound as if he believed it.

"Then go." She reached backward and grabbed his thigh blindly, contradicting herself. "Stay. I'm not sure." She was always bad at handling this, the difficult morning-after socializing that went with a one-off fuck with someone who she didn't know. "Why do you have to talk?"

"Because you're interesting." He sounded serious, which was a bad sign. "I haven't met you before. And I think I like you."

"Oh." She glanced over at the dance floor, legs moving in irregular strobing flashes of light only a meter or two from their sweaty nest. He smelled of some kind of musk, and the faint tang of semen. She rolled over on her back, fetching up against the padded back of the recess, and looked at him. "You got something else in mind?"

He stared at her sleepily. "If you want to swap links, maybe we could meet up some other time?"

I'm being propositioned! she realized, startled. Not just sex. "Maybe later." She looked him up and down, mentally dressing him, wondering what it would be like. *A boyfriend?* Tension clawed at her, an unscratchable itch. She glanced at her hand. "My phone's turned off, and I can't switch it back on."

"If that's—"

"No!" She grabbed his hand: "I'm really, not, uh, being—" She pulled him towards her. "Oh." *That wasn't the right answer, was it?* she thought, as the slide of hot skin against her—and the interesting drugs they'd been taking—made the breath catch in her throat and brought a twitch of life to his groin. She reached out and caught him in her hands. "No swapping links. Just tonight. Make it like it's your last, best time." Cunning fingers found a nipple. "Oh, that's too easy." And it was back into the unthinking depths, with a frogman called Blow to be her skin pilot and a nagging tension at the back of her skull, banished for the moment by an exchange of lust.

ᴡednesday came awake suddenly, naked and sticky and alone on the foam pad. It still smelled of Blow. The dance floor action was going, but more slowly, the music ratcheting toward a false dawn shutdown. She felt alone for a moment, then cold. *Damn,* she thought hazily. *He was good. Should have swapped—*

There was a set of rings on the pad next to her. And a self-heating coffee can set solicitously close to them.

"What the fuck?" She shook her head, taking stock. *What a guy.* She felt a momentary stab of loss: someone who'd take time out from a party to give her a back rub *after* making skinny, even if she hadn't wanted to talk...that was worth knowing. But he'd left a set of rings. She picked them up, puzzling. They looked to be about the right size. Still puzzled, she flipped the heater tab on the coffee and slid her own rings off, pulled the new set on, and twitched them alive. Instead of the half-expected authentication error, there was a tuneful chord and a smell of rose blossom as they glommed on to her implants and registered her as their rightful owner. Fully authenticated, with access to a whole bunch of stuff that was now instantiating itself in her implants from off a public server somewhere: "Wow! Hey, voice mail. Any word from Herman?" she asked.

"Retrieving. You have a noninteractive message. Hello,

Wednesday. This is Herman. Your instructions are as follows. Do not go home. Go to Transit Terminal B. There is a ticket waiting for you there, booked under the authority of professor-gymnast David Larsen, for your participation in a student work placement project. Collect the ticket and leave this hab immediately. Retain these rings, they're keyed to a new identity and set up to route packets to you via a deep market anonymizer. You cannot be traced through them. I will contact you in due course. Let me emphasize that you should not, under any circumstances, go home." *Click.*

She stared at her rings in astonishment. "Herman?" she asked, biting her lower lip. "Herman?" *Don't go home.* A cold chill brought up the gooseflesh on her back. *Oh shit.* She began fumbling with her pile of clothes. "*Herman...*"

Her invisible agents, the software ghosts behind the control rings and her implants and the whole complex of mechanized identity that was Wednesday's persona within the Septagon network, didn't reply. She dragged her leggings and boots on, shrugged into the spidersilk camisole, and held out her arms for the jacket; the sarong she stuffed in a temporary pocket. Jittery and nervous with worry, mouth ashy with the taste of overstewed Blue Mountain, she lurched out of the privacy niche and around the edge of the dance floor. Miss Ball Gag was gagged no longer, straddling the lap of Mister Latex, taking it hard and fast and letting the audience know about it with both lungs. *Exhibitionists.* Wednesday spared her a second's snort as she slid past the bar and round the corner and out along a corridor—then up the first elevator she came to. She had a bad feeling, and the sense of unease grew worse the farther she went. She felt dirty and tired and she ached, and a gnawing edge of guilt bit into her. Shouldn't she have called home, warned someone? Who? Mom or Dad? Wouldn't they think she—

"Holy shit."

She stopped dead and abruptly turned away from the through-route, heart hammering and palms sticky.

The corridor that led to her home run was blocked dead, the eery blue ghost glow of polis membrane slashed across it like a scar. Cops in full vacuum gear stood beside a low-loader with green-and-orange flashing spurs, pushing a mobile airlock toward the pressure barrier.

"Oh shit oh shit oh shit..." The seconds spurted through her fingers like grease. She ducked around another corner, opened her eyes, and began looking for a dead zone. *Fucking Bone Sisters…* well no, this wasn't their doing, was it? Dom games require a sub witness, a survivor. This was *Yurg, he an being not happy* and strangers' boot steps clicking in the cold, wet darkness behind her. And Herman on the phone for the first time in years. She found a corner, stopped, and massaged the pressure points in her jacket, the ones she'd spent so much time building into it. It clamped together around her ribs like a corset, then she reached over and pulled the hood over her head. The leggings were part of the same outfit; she rucked them up, then stretched the almost-liquid hem right over the outside of her boots, her beautiful dumb-matter platform-heeled lace-up air-leaking boots. "Pressurize," she said, then a moment later: "Fade." The jacket rubbed between her shoulder blades, letting her know it was active, and the opaque hood over her face flickered into transparency. Only the hissing of her breath reminded her that from then on in she was impregnable, hermetically sealed, and invisible so long as she danced through the Bone Sisters' blind spots.

There was a service passage one level up and two over, and she ghosted past the slave trolleys, trying to make no noise on the hard metal floor as she counted her way toward the door leading to—

"Shit and corruption." The door handle was sealed with the imperious flashing blue of a police warning. Below the handle, the indicator light glowed steady red, a gas trap alert. Panicky claustrophobia seized her. "Where the fuck is my family?" She brought up her rings and called up the home network. "Dad? Mom? Are you there?"

A stranger's voice answered her: "Who is this?"

She cut the link instantly and leaned against the wall. "Damn. *Damn!*" She wanted to cry. *Where are you?* She was afraid she knew. "Headlines, rings." *Anoxic sink hits residential street in sector green, level 1.24, six dead, eight injured.* "No!" The walls in front of her blurred; she sniffed, then rubbed her eyes through the smart fabric of her hood.

The door was sealed, but the bottom panel bulged about ten centimeters out of it—an emergency lock. She knelt and yanked the red handle, stood back as it inflated and unfolded from the door and bulged out, until it occupied half the corridor. Fumbling at the half-familiar lock tags with her gloves, she unzipped it halfway and scrambled in. She was beyond panic, by then, just a high voice at the back of her head crying *NoNoNoNoNo* continuously, weeping for her while she got on with the job. Rolling on her back and zipping the entrance panel shut, she kicked her way forward into the lock segment on the other side of the door and poked at the display on the other tag. "This can't be happening," someone said. The pressure outside was reading fifty millibars— not vacuum, but as close as made no difference. Even pure oxy wouldn't keep you alive at that. "If they're in there and running on house gas, they'll be safe until the cops reach them," the voice calmly told her, "but if the bad guys hacked the house gas reserve, then dumped pressure overnight, they're dead. Either way, you can't help them. And the bad guys were going to wait there for you." *ButButBut.*

Her fingers were buzzing, her rings calling. She held them to the side of her head. "I told you not to go home." It was Herman. "The police have noticed an airlock trip. You have three minutes at most to clear the area. They'll think you did it." *Silence.*

Wednesday could hear her heartbeat, the swish of blood in her ears. An impossible sense of loss filled her, like a river bursting its banks to sweep her away. "But Dad—"

The next thing she knew she was standing in the corridor beside a slowly deflating emergency airlock, walking round a bend back toward human territory, away from the blue-lit recesses of the service tunnel. "Jacket, back to normal." The hood dropped loose and she pushed it back, forming a snood; the leggings could wait. She walked away jerkily, tugging her gloves off and shoving them into a pocket, half-blind, almost walking into a support pillar. *Oh shit oh shit oh shit.* She slid back into the aimless stroll of a teen out for a walk, slowly reached up with a shaking hand to unfasten her jacket. It relaxed quickly, blousing out loosely around her. *Oh shit.*

Posessed by a ghastly sense of loss, Wednesday headed toward Transit Terminal B.

ᴄᴇɴᴛʀɪꜱ ᴍᴀɢɴᴀ ᴡᴀꜱ a small hab; its shuttle port wasn't designed to handle long-haul craft, or indeed anything except small passenger shuttles. Bulk freight traveled by way of a flinger able to impart up to ten klicks of delta-vee to payloads of a thousand tons or so—but it would be a very slow drift to the nearest ports of call. Only people traveled by fast mover. Consequently, the terminal was no bigger than the hub of Old Newfie, its decor dingy and heavily influenced by the rustic fad of a decade or so earlier. Wednesday felt a flicker of homesickness as she walked into the departure lounge, almost a relief after the sick dread and guilt that had dogged her way there.

She zeroed in on the first available ticket console. "Travel ticketing, please."

The console blinked sleepy semihuman eyes at her: "Please state your destination and your full name?"

"Vicky Strowger. Um, I have a travel itinerary on file with you for educational purposes? Reference, uh, David Larsen's public schedule."

"Is that Vocational Educator Larsen, or the David Larsen who paints handmade inorganic toys and designs gastrointestinal recycling worms for export to Manichean survivalists?"

"The former." Wednesday glanced around nervously, half-expecting blank-faced fuckmonsters with knives and manglers to lurch out at her from behind the soft furnishings. The wide hall was almost empty; grass, service trees, gently curling floor (it was so close to the axial end cap that the curvature was noticeable and the gravity barely a quarter of normal)—it was too big, positively threatening to someone who'd spent her youth on a cramped station.

"Paging. Yes, you have a travel itinerary. Payment is debited to the Outbound Project on—"

It's now or never. "I'd like to upgrade, please."

"Query?"

"Sybarite class, please, or the nearest thing to it you can find for me." She'd checked her credit balance and she was damned if she was going to hunch restlessly in a cattle class seat for the duration of the transfer flight.

The terminal mumbled to itself for a while. "Acknowledged. Annealing to determine how we can accommodate your wishes—confirmed. Departure from bay sixteen in two hours and four minutes, local shuttle to Centris Noctis orbital for transfer to luxury liner WSL *Romanov* for cycle to Minima Four. Your connection will be in twenty-eight hours. Which option would you like and how would you like to pay?"

"Whichever."

The terminal cleared its throat: "I'm sorry, I was unable to understand that. What economic system would you like to pay in? We accept money, approved modal barter, agalmic kudos metrics, temporal futures, and—"

"Check my purse, dammit!"

The terminal abruptly closed its eyes and opened its mouth. A small blue six-legged mouse poked its head out. "Hello!" it piped. "I am your travel voucher! Please allow me to welcome you to TransVirtual TravelWays on behalf of all our entities and symbionts! We hope your journey with us will be enjoyable and your business will be fruitful! Please keep your travel voucher in your possession at all times, and—*squeep*—"

Wednesday caught it.

"Shut the fuck up," she snarled. "I am not in the fucking *mood*. Just show me to my cabin and fuck off."

"—Please note that there is a security deposit for damage to TransVirtual TravelWays property, including fittings, fixtures, and emotivationally enhanced passenger liaison systems! We hope you have a pleasant voyage and a succulent profession! Please ensure your luggage remains under your control at all times, and proceed now to the green walkway under the cherry tree for transit to departure bay sixteen, where the VIP suite is awaiting your excellency's attention."

The mouse-ticket shut up once Wednesday transferred it to a pocket that didn't contain any power tools or high-density energy storage devices. The path winked green in front of her feet, red behind her, as it guided her round a couple of strategically placed cherry trees and into a blessedly spartan metal-walled walkway that curved up and over the departure hall like a socialist-realist rendering of a yellow brick road.

Three hours to go. What am I going to do? Wednesday wondered nervously. *Wait for Herman to phone?* If he could be bothered talking to her—for some reason he didn't seem to want to stay close. A twinge of loneliness made her clench her jaw. *What am I letting myself in for?* And then a stab of guilt so sharp she nearly doubled over fighting back the urge to vomit. *Mom! Dad!*

The VIP lounge was privacy-spoofed, a huge acreage of black synthskin and gleaming ivory patrolled by silent gray partition walls that flickered from place to place while her back was turned, ensuring that she could wander freely without seeing—or being seen by—the other transit passengers. A dumb waiter followed her around, all bright gleaming brass and scrollwork, eager to fulfill her every desire. "When do we board?" she asked.

"Ahem. If madam would follow me, her personal transshipment capsule is being readied now. If there are any special dietary or social or religious requirements—"

"Everything is just fine," Wednesday said automatically, her voice flat. "Just find me a sofa or something to sit on. Uh, maximum privacy."

"Madam will find one just behind her." Wednesday sat. The walls moved around her. A few meters away the floor was moving, too. It all happened too smoothly to notice by accident. Something in one of her pockets twitched, then began to recite brightly: "We provide a wide range of business services, including metamagical consultancy, stock trading and derivatives analysis systems, and a full range of communications and disinformation tools for the discerning corporate space warrior. If you would like to take advantage of our horizontally scalable—"

Wednesday reached into her pocket and picked up her travel voucher by the loose skin at the scruff of its neck. "Just shut up." It fell silent and drew its tail up, clutching it with all six paws. "I want a half hour call before boarding. Between now and then, I want total privacy—so private I could die and you wouldn't notice. No ears, no eyes, no breathing gas mixture analysis, nobody disturbs me. Got it?"

The voucher blinked its wide, dark, excessively cute eyes at her. "Good." She dropped it back in her pocket and stretched out on the huge expanse of padded cushions behind her. For a moment she wondered if she should have asked the voucher to leave her a bottle of something drinkable, then dismissed the thought. Privacy was more important just then, and besides, if there was something to drink, the way her luck was running right now she'd probably drink herself into a sodden stupor and choke on her own vomit. She held her hand to her face. "Get me Herman."

"I'm here." The voice was anonymous, bland.

"You corpsefucker," she hissed.

"I can tell you what is happening," said Herman.

After a moment, she made a noise.

"On Old Newfoundland, before the evacuation. I made a mistake, Wednesday."

"No shit."

"Like the mistake you made in attempting to return home. There were skin particles on the outside of your jacket, Wednesday. Both you and your friend. It will take at least four hours for the police forensics to identify your genome, but then you may be suspected of vandalism at best, conspiracy to commit murder at worst. Your friend will be eliminated from the investigation rapidly, but you may be unable to return home until the situation is resolved. Did you want that to happen to you?"

She couldn't see anything. Her rings, biting into the palm of her hand, were her only contact with reality.

"What did you say?"

"I said." She took a deep breath and tried to remember. "Meant to say. What makes you think this is home?"

"You live here."

"That's not good enough." She fell silent. Herman, too, fell silent for a few seconds. "I would have protected your family if I could."

"What do you mean, *if?*"

"I thought there were only two or three hunters. I was wrong. Earlier, I thought events were of no significance that were highly significant. I should not have left you alone here. I should not have let your family stay here, so close to the resettlement hub. I should not have let you settle in Septagon at all."

"What do you *want?*" Her voice rose to a squeak that she hated.

"I want you to be my helper again." Pause. "I want you to go on a voyage for me. You will be provided with money. There will be an errand. Then you can let go. It will take less than two hundred days, no longer."

"I want my family back. I want..." She couldn't go on.

"I cannot give you your parents." Herman sounded infinitely remote, flat, abhuman. "But if you work for me, the hunters who took them will suffer a setback. And they will never trouble you again."

Murder by Numbers

Forty light years from Earth, the yacht *Gloriana* congealed out of the cold emptiness between stars, emitting an electric blue flare of Cerenkov radiation. If it drifted at the residual velocity carried over from its last reference frame shift, it would take nearly two hundred years to cover the distance separating it from the star system it was heading for, but drifting wasn't the name of the game. After only a few minutes the ship's inertial transfer unit came online. Lidar probed the space ahead for obstacles as the yacht came under acceleration.

The *Gloriana* had started life as a billionaire's toy, but these days almost half the passenger volume was filled by the extensive diplomatic function spaces of a mobile embassy. The ship—and its three sisters—existed because it was cheaper for the UN to swallow the extra costs of running a starship than maintaining consulates on the couple of hundred planets that received visitors from Earth more than once in a decade but less than a thousand times a year. Now running between jump zones at full acceleration, *Gloriana* had been under way for a week; over the course of which time Rachel Mansour had become increasingly annoyed and worried by George Cho's refusal to disclose the purpose or destination of the mission.

Finally, however, it looked as if she was about to get some answers.

The conference room was walled in a false woodgrain veneer that hardly sufficed to cover the smart skin guts of the ship. Tricked out in natural surfaces, the whole thing was as artificial as a cyborg smile. Maybe the big boardroom table (carved in the ornate intricacies of the neo-retrogothic fad of a century earlier) was made of wood, but Rachel wasn't betting on it. She glanced round the occupied chairs as she sat down, recognizing Pritkin, Jane Hill, Chi Tranh, and Gail Jordan. *George's little munchkins are out in force,* she noted ironically. She'd worked with most of them in the past; the lack of new faces told its own story.

"I take it nothing's running to schedule, is it?"

"The best-laid plans of mice and men," Cho commented apologetically. "You can lock the door now," he told Pritkin. "I've got some papers for you, dumb hard copy only, and they do *not* leave this room." He reached under the desk and retrieved six fat files, their covers banded with red and yellow stripes, then tapped a virtual button on his pad. There was a faint hissing sound from the air conditioning. "We're now firewalled from the rest of the ship. No bandwidth, bottled air, and the ship itself isn't within hailing distance of anything else . . . you can't be too careful with this stuff."

Rachel's skin crawled. Last time she'd seen George put on the full-dress, loose-lips-sink-ships song and dance it had been the run in to the mess on Rochard's World. Which had involved dirty-tricks black ops that could have backfired to the extent of starting an interstellar war. "How does this rate with the last, uh, mission?" she asked.

"Messier. All turn to page 114." There was a rustle of dumb paper as everybody opened their files simultaneously. Someone whistled tunelessly, and Rachel glanced up in time to see Gail looking startled as she studied the page. Rachel began to read just in time for George to derail her concentration by talking. "Moscow. Named after the imperial capital of Idaho rather than the place in Europe, except Idaho didn't have an empire back when the Eschaton grabbed a million confused Midwesterners from the first republic and stuffed them through a wormhole leading to the planetary surface."

The words on the page swam before Rachel's eyes: *Bill of indictment in re: signatories of the Geneva Conventions on Causality Violation versus Persons Unknown responsible for the murder of—*

"Moscow was, bluntly, another boring McWorld. And a bit backward, even by those standards. But it had a single—and fairly enlightened—federal government, a single language, and no history of genocide, nuclear war, cannibalism, slavery, or anything else very unpleasant to explain it. It wasn't utopia, but neither was it hell. In fact, I'd have said the Muscovites were rather *nice*. Easygoing, friendly, laid-back, a little sleepy. Unlike whoever murdered them."

Rachel leaned back in her chair and watched George. Cho was a diplomat, and a polished and experienced gambler who liked nothing better than a game of three-stud poker—so the experience of seeing him actually looking angry and upset about something was a novelty in its own right. The wall behind him showed supporting evidence. Rippling fields of grain as far as the eyes could see, a city rising—if that was the word for an urban sprawl where only city hall was more than three stories high—from the feet of blue-tinted mountains, white-painted houses, huge automated factory complexes, wide empty roads stretching forever under a sky the color of bluebells.

"Not everyone on Moscow was totally laid-back," George continued, after taking a sip from his water glass. "They had a small military, mostly equipped for disaster relief work—and a deterrent. Antimatter-fueled, ramscoop-assisted bombers, hanging out in the Oort cloud, about twelve light hours out."

The wall dissolved into icy interstellar darkness and a close-up of a starship—not an elegant FTL yacht like this one, with the spherical bump of its drive kernel squatting beneath a tower of accommodation and cargo decks, but the evil angular lines of a planet-buster. Most of the slower-than-light bomber consisted of fuel containment vessels, and the huge inverted funnel of the ram field generator. Scooping up interstellar hydrogen for reaction mass, using antimatter to energize it, the warship could boost itself to more than 80 percent of lightspeed in a matter of weeks. Steering toward a target, it would then drift until it was time for terminal approach. Then, instead of decelerating, the crew and the ramscoop would separate and make their own way—leaving the remains of the ship to slam into the target planet.

"This is a reconstruction of a Muscovite Vindicator-class second-strike STL bomber. Our best intelligence gives it a maximum tau factor of point two and a dry rest mass of three kilotons—extremely high for the product of a relatively backward world—with an aggregate kinetic yield of 120 million megatons. It's probably designed to prefragment prior to impact, and coming in at 80 percent of lightspeed with several hundred penetration aids and a wake shield against ablator clouds, it would be able to saturate any reasonable planetary ballistic defense system. It would deliver about 20 percent more energy than the Chicxulub impactor that hit Earth 65 million years ago, enough to devastate a continent and trigger a dinosaur winter. In other words, it's a pretty typical second-strike slower-than-light deterrent for a planet that didn't have any enemies or major foreign policy engagements; an insurance policy against invaders.

"Moscow had four of these monsters, and we know for sure that the early warning system alerted them before the stellar shock front reached their firebases; we know at least three of them came under acceleration. What happened to the fourth ship is unclear at this time. They probably took some serious damage from the nova, but we have to assume that those four ships are engaged on a strike mission."

George sat down again and refilled his water glass. Rachel shivered slightly. *They launched? But where to?* The idea was disquieting, even revolting: "Has anyone ever actually launched an STL deterrent before, that you know of? I don't think I've ever heard of one being used..."

"May I?" It was Chi Tranh, lean-featured and quiet, the expert on weapons of mass destruction and, sometimes, her back-office researcher. Not a field agent, but George had evidently included him in the operation from the start, judging by the way he nodded along. "The answer is no," said Tranh. "We have *never* seen one of these weapons systems used in anger. Nobody can start a war using STL ships—it would give years for a pre-emptive retaliatory strike. The idea is simply to have a deterrent—a club up your sleeve that makes the cost of invading and occupying your world too expensive for an aggressor to bear. This is a first, at least within our light cone." He sat back and nodded at George.

"Who were they directed at?" Gail asked tentatively. "I mean, who would do such a thing? How are they controlled? Have they—" She looked bewildered, which gave Rachel little satisfaction: the easily flustered protocol officer wasn't her first choice of someone to bring into the inner circle. *What was George thinking?* she wondered.

"Peace." George made soothing gestures with his left hand. "We, um...at the time of the event, Moscow was engaged in heated and unpleasant trade discussions with New Dresden. That's in your briefing documents, too, by the way. A previous trade deal cemented between a Muscovite delegation and the central committee of the Balearic Federation collapsed when the, um,

Balearics were finally forced to sue for peace with the provisional government of Novy Srebrenicza. Prior to the peace of '62, the Balearics controlled the planet's sole surviving skyhook, which gave them a chokehold on the surface-to-orbit bulk freight trade. But after '62, the Patriotic Homeland Front was running the show. They decided to renegotiate several of their local bilateral trade arrangements—in their favor, of course—to help with the reconstruction. Things got extremely heated when they impounded a Muscovite starship and confiscated its cargo: differential levels of engineering support orbit-side in both systems meant that, although New Dresden had more turmoil and a war to recover from, heavy shipping was a proportionately much more expensive item on Moscow, which didn't have the tech base to fabricate drive kernels. The Muscovites' consulate was downsized to a negotiating core, and a large chunk of the Dresdener embassy was expelled a couple of weeks before the, ah, event."

"So the bombers launched, on New Dresden," Rachel concluded with a sinking feeling.

"We, um, think so," said George. "We're not sure. Tranh?"

"We can't track RAIR bombers once they go ballistic," said Tranh. "It's standard procedure to launch in a random direction at high delta-vee, crank up to about point one light, then shut down and drift for a bit before lining up on the real target and boosting steadily to cruise speed. The drive torch is highly directional, and if nobody is in line behind it to see the gamma signature, it's easy to miss. Especially as the bombers launch from out in the Oort cloud and aim their exhausts to miss the inner system completely during the initial boost phase. Once they're under way the crew, usually four or six of them, enter suspended animation for a month or more, then the Captain wakes up and uses the bomber's causal channel to establish contact with one of the remaining consulates or embassies. He or she also opens any sealed orders. In this case, we've been informed—through confidential channels, initially by the Muscovite embassy on Earth—that a week before Moscow was hit, the Governor-General's office updated the default fire plan for the V-force to target New Dresden. We don't know *why* she did that, but the trade dispute . . ." Tranh trailed off.

"That's the situation." George shook his head. "Doubtless the Muscovite government didn't expect to be attacked by New Dresden—but as a precaution they selected New Dresden as a default target, leaving the fallout for the diplomatic corps to deal with. New Dresden is thirty-six light years from Moscow, so at full bore the bombers can be there in forty years. Thirty-five now, and counting. New Dresden has a population of over eight hundred million. There is no way, even if we install extra skyhooks and obtain maximum cooperation from the neighbors, that we can evacuate nearly a billion people—the required cubage, over thirty million seats a year, exceeds the entire terrestrial registered merchant fleet's capacity. Never mind the refugee problem—who'd take them in?"

"I don't believe they could be so stupid!" Gail said vehemently. Rachel watched her cautiously. Gail might be good at organizing the diplomatic niceties, but in some respects she was very naive. "How could they? Is there a recall signal?"

"Yes, there's a recall code," George admitted. "The problem is getting the surviving members of the Muscovite diplomatic corps to send it."

Rachel flipped through the pages of her briefing document rapidly. *Ah, yes, I was* afraid *it would be something like this.* Background: the bombers communicated with the remaining embassies via causal channel. In the absence of a recall code, the bombers would proceed on a strike mission to the designated target, their crews in cold sleep for most of the voyage. After conducting the attack, the crew—with their ramscoops and life-support modules—could decelerate or cruise on to another system at near lightspeed. If a recall code was received first, standard procedure was for the crew to burn their remaining fuel, braking to a halt in deep space, and for the embassy to lay on a rescue ship to remove the crew, laying scuttling charges to decommission the bombers *in situ.*

"How is a recall code sent?" Rachel inquired.

"Via causal channel from one of the embassies," said Tranh. "Because the bombers are strictly STL, they maintain contact with the government-in-exile. The ambassadors possess authentication tokens that the bomber crews can use to confirm their identity. Having authenticated themselves, they have a vote code system—if two or more of them send a recall code, the bomber crews are required to stand down and disclose their position and vector for a decommissioning flight. But—and this is a *big* but— there's also a coercion code. It is known only to the ambassadors, like the recall code, and if three or more ambassadors send the coercion code, the bomber crews are required to destroy their causal channel and proceed to the target. The coercion code overrides the recall code; the theory is that it will only be used if an aggressor has somehow managed to lay his or her hands on an ambassador and is holding a gun to their head. The ambassadors can tell the black hats the wrong code and, if three or more of them are under duress, ensure that the strike mission goes forward."

"Oh. Oh." Gail shook her head. "Those poor people! How many ambassadors do we have to work on? With?"

George tapped the tabletop. "It's in your dossier. There were twelve full-dress embassies from Moscow in residence at the time of the disaster. Unfortunately, two of the ambassadors had been recalled for consultation immediately before the incident, and they are presumed dead. Of the remaining ten, one committed suicide immediately, one died in a vehicular accident six months later—it was ruled an accident; he seems to have fallen in front of a train—and, well, this is where it gets *interesting*. I hope you all have strong stomachs ..."

afƭer ƭhe meeƭing she caught up with Martin. He was idling on the promenade deck, playing with the image enhancement widgets on the main viewing window.

"How did it go?" he asked, glancing up at her from the chaise longue. He seemed to be treating the journey as an enforced vacation, she noticed; dressing casually, lounging around, catching up on his reading and viewing, spending his surplus energy in the gym. But he looked worried now, as if she'd brought a storm cloud of depression in with her.

"It's a lot to swallow. Budge over." He made some space for her to sit down. "I want a drink."

"I'll get you one. What do you—"

"No, don't. I said I *wanted* a drink, not that I'm going to have one."

She stared gloomily at the wall-sized expanse of darkness on the other side of the almost empty room. Something circular and penumbral, darker than the interstellar night, cut an arc out of the dusting of unwinking stars. "What's that?"

"Brown dwarf. Uncataloged, it's about half a light year away. I've got the window accumulating a decent visible light image of it right now."

"Oh, okay." Rachel leaned back against the wall. The designers had tricked out the promenade deck in a self-conscious parody of the age of steam. From the holystoned oak planking of the floor to the retro-Victoriana of the furniture, it could have been a slice out of some nuclear-powered liner from the distant planet-bound past, a snapshot of the *Titanic* perhaps, a time populated by women in bonnets and ballooning skirts, men in backward baseball caps and plus-fours, zeppelins and jumbos circling overhead. But it wasn't big enough to be convincing, and instead of a view across the sea, there was just a screen the size of a wall and her husband wearing a utility kilt with pockets stuffed with gadgets he never went anywhere without.

"How bad was it?" he asked quietly.

"Bad?" She shrugged. "On a scale of one to ten, with the New Republic an eight or nine, this is about an eleven. A chunk of it is die-before-disclosing stuff, but I guess there's no harm in letting you in on the public side. Which is bad enough." She shook her head. "What time is it?"

"Mm, about 1500, shipboard. There was some announcement about setting the clocks forward tonight, as well."

"Okay." She tapped her fingertips idly on the lacquered side table. "I think I *will* take you up on that drink, as long as there's some sober-up available just in case."

"Umph." Martin twisted one of his rings. "Pitcher of iced margaritas on the promenade deck, please." He watched her closely. "Is my ex-employer involved?"

"Hmm. I don't think so." Rachel touched his shoulder. "You haven't heard anything, have you?"

"I'm on the beach, I think." His cheek twitched. "And between contracts, so there's no conflict of interests."

"Good," she said, taking his free hand, *"good."*

"You don't sound happy."

"That's because—" She shook her head. "Why the *hell* are people so stupid?"

"Stupid? What do you mean?" He lifted her hand slightly, inspecting the back of her wrist intently.

"People." It came out as a curse. "Like that asshole in Geneva. Turns out there was a, a—" She swallowed, and before she could continue the dumb waiter beside the table dinged for attention. "And that bitch in Ents. I set a search going, by the way. Pulled some strings. I should have all the dirt on her when we get home." She turned to open the dumb waiter and found there was a tray inside. "That was fast." She removed two glasses, passing one to Martin.

"Where was I? Yes, stupid, wanton, destructive assholes.

About five years ago, that supernova out near the Septagon stars, a system called Moscow. Turns out it wasn't a natural event at all. Someone iron-bombed the star. That's a causality-violation device, and about as illegal as they come—also apparently unstable to build and hazardous as hell. I'd like to know why it didn't attract a certain local deity's attention. Anyway, the Moscow republic had a modest deterrent fleet in their Oort cloud, far enough out to just about survive the blast, and they were in the middle of a trade dispute. So they launched, and now we're trying to talk their diplomatic staff into calling off a strike on a planet with nearly a billion inhabitants who we are pretty damn sure had nothing to do with the war crime."

"Sounds bad." She watched him raise his glass, a guarded expression on his face.

"The headache is, the place they launched on—New Dresden—isn't squeaky clean. They had a series of really bloody civil wars over the past century or so, and what they're left with may be stable but isn't necessarily happy. Meanwhile, Moscow—damn!" She put the glass down. "Worlds with a single planetary government aren't *meant* to be peaceful and open and into civil rights! When I see a planet with just one government, I look for the mass graves. It's some kind of natural law or something—world governments grow out of the barrel of a gun."

"Um. You mean, the good guys are getting ready to commit genocide? And the bad guys are asking you in to talk them out of it? Is that the picture?"

"No." She took a quick pull of her ice-cold margarita. "If that was all it was, I think I could cope with it. Just another talk-down, after all. No, there's something much worse going on in here. A real stinking shitty mess. But George wants to keep a lid on it for the time being, so I can't dump it on your shoulder."

"So." One of the most soothing things about Martin was that he could tell when not to push her. This was one of those times: instead of shoving, he stretched his arm along the back of the sofa, offering her a shoulder. After a moment, she leaned against him. "Thanks."

"It's all right." He waited while she shifted to a more comfortable position. "What are we going to do, then? When we arrive? Dresden, did you say?"

"Well." She considered her words carefully. "I'm on the Ents budget listed as a cultural attaché. So I'm going to do some cultural attaché things. There's a memorial ceremony to attend, meetings, probably the usual bunch of diplomatic parties to organize. Luckily Dresden's relatively developed, socially and industrially, not like New Prague." She pulled a face. "You're probably going to have the wonderful, unmissable, once-in-a-lifetime chance to be my diplomatic wife for a few weeks. Once-in-a-lifetime's all you'll take before you flee screaming back to a shipyard, I promise you."

"Ten ecus says you're wrong." He hugged her.

"And fifty says you won't make it. Sucker." She kissed him, then pulled back to arm's length, smiling. Then her smile slipped. "I've got some other stuff to do," she said quietly, "and maybe a side trip. But I can't talk about it."

"Can't, or don't want to?"

"Can't." She emptied her glass and put it down. "It's the other I told you about. Sorry."

"I'm not pushing," he said slyly. "I just want to know every-thing you get up to when I'm not around!" He continued in a more serious tone of voice: "Promise me if it's anything like, uh, last week, you'll try to let me know in advance?"

"I—" She nodded. "I'll try," she said softly. "If it's remotely possible." Which was entirely true, and she hated herself for it—he meant well, and the idea that he might think she was lying to him stung her—but there were things she wasn't at liberty to talk about, just as there were topics Martin wouldn't raise within earshot of her coworkers. Serious, frightening, things. And if she didn't cooperate with Cho's covert agenda, she'd be gambling with other people's lives. Because, when she thought about it, she couldn't see any sane alternative to what George was proposing to do.

Flashback, one hour earlier

"Here's the Honorable Maurice Pendelton, ambassador of the Republic of Moscow to the court of Ayse Bayar, Empress of al-Turku."

George Cho stood up and fiddled with a control ring. The wall behind him flickered to a view of an office—ornately pan-eled in wood, gas-lit and velvet-draped, richly carpeted and dom-inated by a ponderous desk bearing an antique workstation. There was something else on the desk; for a moment Rachel couldn't quite work out what she was looking at, then she realized that it was a man, slumped across the green leather blotter. A timer counted down seconds in the top left corner of the display. In his back—

"Murder?" asked Jane, tight-lipped. Rachel hadn't seen much of her since the events back on New Prague, when Jane had uncomplainingly shouldered the burden of Rachel's research work inside the diplomatic compound. She wondered idly how Jane would cope with a field assignment if she couldn't even figure out a scene like this for herself.

"The inquisitor's report was very clear about the fact that his arms weren't long enough for him to stab himself in the back—at least, not with a sword," Tranh said drily. "Especially not with enough force to nail the torso to the tabletop. Proximate cause of death was a severed dorsal aorta and damage to the pericardium—he bled out and died within seconds, but most of the mess is behind the desk."

George fidgeted with his rings and the camera viewpoint slewed dizzyingly around the room. The scene behind the ambassador's desk was a mess. Blood had gouted from the wound in his back and splattered across his chair, pooling in viscid puddles beneath his desk. Footprints congealed in the rich carpet, an obscene trail leading toward the door.

"I take it this is important to our mission," said Rachel. "Do we have a full crime scene report? Was the killer apprehended?"

"No and no," Cho said with gloomy satisfaction. "The Office of the Vizier of Morning took control of the investigation outside the embassy, and while the Turku authorities have been polite and helpful to us, they have declined to give us full details of the killing, other than this diorama shot. Note, if you will, the theatrical red nose and bushy moustache a party or parties unknown applied to the Ambassador's face—after he was dead, according to the Vizier's Office. Oh, in case you were wondering, the killer wasn't apprehended. For the sake of face the Vizier's Office rounded up a couple of petty thieves, forced them to confess, then beheaded them in front of the public newsfeeds, but our confidential sources assure us that the real investigation is still continuing. Which brings me to incident number two."

Another wall-sized photograph of chaos. This time it was a roadside disaster—the wreckage of a large vehicle, obviously some sort of luxury people mover, lay scattered across a road, uniformed emergency crews and rescue vehicles all around it. Blue sheets covered misshapen mounds to either side. Much of the debris was scorched; some of it was still smoking.

"This was an embassy limousine, taking her excellency Simonette Black to a conference on resettlement policy for refugee populations in Bonn, the capital of the Frisian Foundation, a confederation of independent states on Eiger's World. Which, unlike al-Turku, is a Deutsch McWorld with no real history of political violence other than a couple of wars fought over oil fields and states' rights a century or two ago."

George pointed at some bushes to one side of the road, and the screen obligingly zoomed. Something gleamed: "*That* is a reflector post for an infrared beam. If we look at the source"—the viewpoint flipped dizzyingly into the sky then back down, 180 degrees away from the post—"we find *this*." A green box, with a round hole in its front, above a complex optical sight and some kind of rubber mat. The box, too, looked scorched. "I'm told that's a disposable antiarmor missile launcher, hypervelocity, with a two-stage penetrator jet designed to punch through ceramic armor or high-Tesla fields. The poor people in the limousine— Black, her wife, their driver, the chargé d'immigration, and two bodyguards—didn't stand a chance. It was stolen from an army depot one week before the incident. It was armed by remote control and rigged to fire when the beam was interrupted. I'm told that the plastic object underneath the missile launcher is an, ah, whoopee cushion. A rubber bladder that emits a flatulent sound when sat upon."

Rachel looked down at her pad. To her surprise, she realized she'd begun to doodle on it with her stylus in ink transfer mode. Pictures of mushroom clouds and Mach waves knocking over groundscrapers and arcologies. She glanced up. "Once is happenstance, twice is coincidence," she said. "Any more?"

George's shoulders fell. He looked very old for a moment, even though Rachel knew he was seven years her junior. "Yes," he said. Another diorama filled the wall. "I've been saving this until last. This is the Honorable Maureen Davis, ambassador to the United Nations of Earth in Geneva." Gail looked away, visibly upset, and Rachel wondered distantly if she was going to cry. Violent death didn't just strip the victims of their dignity, it insulted the survivors. And it was a personal insult to Rachel. *We were supposed to protect her!* An attack on a visiting diplomat reflected on the honor of the nation or coalition that played host to them. And this—

"Did we let this happen on our watch?" she demanded angrily. "*After* knowing that two other ambassadors had died in questionable circumstances?" She closed the dossier in front of her and flattened it against the table, pressing until her knuckles turned white.

"No." George took a deep breath. "She was the first to die— just the last for us to be aware of. At first we penciled it in as a simple murder—horrible, but not special. Unlike the other two incidents we have a complete crime scene breakdown and we're pursuing the murderer with every resource at our disposal. We are"—he took another breath—"appalled and outraged that this has happened. But more than that, we're very much afraid that it's going to happen again. Tranh, could you explain?"

Tranh stood up again and began to recite in a flat monotone that suggested that he, too, was trying to hold down the lid on his outrage. "Ambassador Davis was discovered in the state you see by a housekeeper maintenance contractor who called to deal with a fault alert by the house cleaning 'bot. The amah was confused by, well, a conflict between its recognizer for human beings and its garbage collection monitor. That doesn't happen very often these days, but Ambassador Davis had an antique that still had a heuristic support contract in force. Embassy security admitted the maintenance contractor and immediately discovered the ambassador in this state. They immediately requested our assistance— unlike their counterparts on Turku." His voice quivered with outrage as he added, "The killer used a bungee cord for a ligature."

Foul play? That's one way of putting it, Rachel observed. Ambassadors did not, as a rule, hang themselves in the stairwell of their own residences using rubberized ropes. Nor did they do so after pinioning their hands behind them, not to mention fracturing the backs of their skulls on mysteriously missing blunt objects.

"Ah yes, she shot herself three times in the back of the head and jumped out of the sixth floor window *just* to make us look bad," she muttered, drawing a wide-eyed look of confusion from Gail. "When did this happen relative to the others? In the empire time defined by the Moscow embassy causal channels, if you've got the figures. That might tell us something."

"The order was"—George flipped pages in a separate file— "Ambassador Davis at datum zero, followed by Simonette Black at T plus fourteen days, six hours, three minutes. Then Ambassador Pendelton thirty-four days, nineteen hours and fifty-two minutes later." He gazed at Rachel tiredly. "Any other questions?"

"Yes." She leaned back in her chair, tapping her stylus on the cover of her briefing file. "Are Turku and the, uh, Frisian Foundation coordinating their investigations? Are they even *aware* of the other assassinations?"

"No and no." George inclined his head slightly. "You have more questions. Let's hear them, and your reasoning."

"All right." Rachel sat up straight and looked at Gail. "You might not want to hear this."

"I can take it." She looked back, angry and bewildered. "I don't have to like it."

"Okay." Rachel tapped the file in front of her. "As the man said, once is happenstance, twice might be coincidence, but three times is enemy action. We have a very nasty situation evolving, in which there exists a dwindling pool of assets—ambassadors— such that if the total drops below three, 800 million people will die. From an initial nine survivors, three have been murdered in the past three months. I assume the rest are under heavy guard—"

"Wherever possible," George murmured.

"—But we basically have a crisis on our hands. Someone has figured out how to kill 800 million birds with just six stones. Leaving aside the killer's evident penchant for cruel practical jokes, we know absolutely nothing about who they are and what motivates them. In fact, what we appear to know may actually be deliberate deception. And we're the only people who are treating these assassinations as part of a big picture, rather than isolated killings."

"That's essentially correct," said Tranh. "There are other investigative measures we are taking, but"—he shrugged, looking unhappy—"it takes time."

"Well then." Rachel licked her lips, which had become unpleasantly dry. "As I see it, our ideal outcome is to convince them to issue the abort code to the bombers immediately, before any more of them die. But right now they'll probably view any such request with extreme suspicion—the murders could be seen as a conspiracy to force them to issue the code. Or we could prove to them that the New Dresdeners didn't do the dirty deed and show them who did—if we have any idea."

She nodded when Cho shook his head. "I was afraid of that. The other option is to stake out a goat, wait for the assassins to show up, and try to trace them back to their masters. But we have a mess of motives at work here. Someone seems to want to ensure that the Muscovite weapons destroy New Dresden, and I've got to ask, why? Who could possibly benefit from wiping out one—or maybe even two—planets?" She glanced around the table.

"That's essentially where we've got to," George said heavily, "except for the final part."

"Explain." She leaned forward attentively.

"We don't have time to stake them all out. Given the current attrition rate, we've got to face the risk of losing four more ambassadors in the next month. We haven't caught a single assassin, so we don't know who's doing it. So tell me what you deduce from that fact."

"That we're in the shit," Rachel said in a low monotone. She leaned forward tensely. "Let's look at this as a crime in progress. If we shelve the means and opportunity questions, who's got a motive? Who could possibly gain by arranging for Moscow to bomb the crap out of Dresden in thirty-five years' time?"

She held up a hand and began counting off fingers. "One: a third party who hates Dresden. I think we can take that as a non sequitur; nobody is ever crazy enough to want to exterminate an entire planet. At least, nobody who's that crazy ever gets their hands on the means to do it." *Well, virtually nobody,* she reminded herself, flashing back a week. *Idi would have done it—if he'd had an R-bomb. But he didn't. So...* "Two: a faction among the Muscovite exiles who really, really hates Dresden—enough to commit murder, murder of their own people, just to make sure. Three: someone who wants to strike a negotiating position of some kind. It could be blackmail, for example, and the ransom note hasn't arrived yet. Four: it's a continent smasher. Could be a *really* nasty bunch of folks have decided to make sure it goes home, as a prelude to a, uh, rescue and reconstruction mission of a rather permanent nature."

"You're saying it could be some other government that wants to take advantage of the situation?" Gail looked aghast.

"That's realpolitik for you." Rachel shrugged. "I'm not saying it is, but...do we have any candidates?" She raised an eyebrow at Tranh.

"Possibly." He frowned. "Among the neighbors...I can't see the New Republic doing that, can you?"

Rachel shook her head. "They're out for the count."

"Then, hmm. Forget Turku, forget Malacia, forget Septagon. None of them have an expansionist government except Septagon, and they're not interested in anything with a primary that masses more than point zero five of Sol or comes with inhabitable planets. There's Newpeace, but they're still in a mess from the civil war. And Eiger isn't likely. Tonto, that's another of those weird semiclosed dictatorships. They might have an angle on it. But it's not anything obvious, is it?"

Rachel frowned. "There seem to be a couple of dictatorships in this sector, aren't there? Funny: they aren't normally stable enough to last..."

"There's some kind of weird political ideology, calling themselves the ReMastered. Tonto went ReMastered forty or fifty years ago," offered Jane. "Don't know much about them: they're not nice people." She shivered. "Why do you ask?"

Rachel's frown deepened. "If you can dig anything up I'd appreciate hearing it. George, you're holding something back, aren't you?"

The ambassador sat up slightly, then nodded. "Yes, I am." He glanced round the table.

"You probably figured out why I wanted you; it's because none of you had any conceivable link either to Moscow or New Dresden. Which, incidentally, is where we're en route. It so happens that Ambassador Elspeth Morrow is in residence in Sarajevo, and Harrison Baxter, former trade minister of the Muscovite government—and the highest surviving government officer, he's also on the code schedule—is there, too. He was sent just before the incident, to attempt to resolve the trade dispute. I strongly suspect that they're the next logical target, being a two-for-one hit. Our cover story—for everyone outside this room—is that we're here to discuss the R-bomb situation with Morrow and Baxter.

"The real task in hand is somewhat different. It's to keep them alive and if possible capture one of the killers and backtrack to their masters. Which is where you come in, Rachel. Tranh, your job is to brief the embassy guard and the Dresdener Interior Ministry special security police and act as external security liaison. Gail, you and I are going to talk directly to the Minister and the Ambassador and impress the urgency of the situation upon them. You handle protocol, I'll handle diplomacy. Pritkin, you're our switchboard and front office. Jane, I need you on back office, coordinating any intel we get from home about the circumstances of the murders. Rachel, you've got a nasty, suspicious mind. I want you to try and set up a trap for the killers—assuming they surface. And I've, well, got a little surprise."

"Surprise," she mimicked. "Uh-huh. One of *those* surprises?"

"Those?" echoed Jane.

"Those." Rachel grimaced. "Spill it, George."

Cho took a deep breath. "For you, I've got a covert job in mind. You're about the same size and build as Ambassador Morrow. You fill in the dotted line."

"Oh. Oh no." Rachel shook her head. "You can't do this to me!"

"Oh yes?" Tranh's smile wasn't entirely friendly. "What was that you were saying earlier about wanting to nail the culprits?"

"Um." She nodded like a puppet with a blown feedback circuit. "*If* you're right about there being a hit planned."

"I think we're right." George nodded. "Because there's another datum I haven't given you."

"Oh yeah?"

"In addition to a time series on the murders, we ran a spatial map and a full shipping traffic analysis. It turns out that there are about three starships that called at each location a day or so before the hit, then moved on afterward. They're busy places, mostly. Anyway, one of those ships is a freighter, and none of the crew went down from orbit at any port on its cycle. Another is—well, if you want to accuse the Malacian Navy of trying to start a war with three of their neighbors by whacking diplomats, *you* draw their attention to the suspicious maneuvers of one of their cruisers. Whose flight plan for the current goodwill tour was finalized nearly a year before Ambassador Black arrived on Eiger's World. Which leaves just one suspect."

"Stop winding me up, George. Just tell it straight."

George looked at her, his expression one of wounded dignity. "My, my! Very well, then. It's the WhiteStar liner *Romanov,* outbound from Earth on a yearlong tour circuit. It was in orbit around Eiger's World when Ambassador Black was murdered. It was in orbit around Turku when Pendelton was murdered. And while it wasn't parked over Kilimanjaro when Ambassador Davis was murdered, the smoking gun is that it arrived a day later, then departed. That was the zero incident. The arrival times line up. It is in principle possible that an assassin joined the *Romanov* after killing Ambassador Davis, then traveled to Turku and Eiger's World to repeat the task."

Rachel knotted her fingers together. "Tell me it isn't calling at New Dresden next?"

"It's not. It's en route to Septagon Four—but first port of call after that is New Dresden, sure enough. We should get there a couple of weeks ahead of it. And that's basically why I wanted you on board. We'll show up as a special diplomatic team tasked with demonstrating that the Dresdener governments' hands are clean. You will be attached to our team—that's your cover story—but your real job will be to set up a trap in which you body double for Ambassador Morrow, a week before our killer turns up. And when they try to take you out, we'll have them. And then"—his expression was fierce—"let's hope we can get to the bottom of this before the assassins murder 800 million people."

wednesday was so busy working on a better way of expressing her rage that she didn't notice when the walls around her recliner softened and flowed, containerizing her in a lozenge of dark foam and dropping her through the floor of the terminal into the cargo mesh of an intrasystem freighter bound for Centris Noctis. "*Stupid* brainless unplanned intelligence, no, stupid brainless unplanned stupid—*what?*"

Her itinerary cleared its throat again: "Please hold on tight! Departure in three hundred seconds! Departure in—"

"I heard you the first time, fuckmonster." Anger was better than the gaping hole in her life, the absolute bitter despair she was trying so hard to ignore. The walls, flowing past and re-forming into the shape of a compact hexagonal cabin, did nothing to soothe her. "How long am I in transit?"

"Eep! Don't hurt me! TransVirtual TravelWays welcomes all passengers to the transit shuttle *Hieronymus B.,* departing Centris Magna hab four port authority bay sixteen for Centris Noctis hab eleven port authority bay sixty-two in four minutes and thirty seconds. Please familiarize yourself with our flight profile and safety briefing. After a few seconds of free fall, we will be under continuous acceleration at one-tenth of gee standard for eight hours, dropping to—"

Wednesday shut it out, nodding along vaguely and watching the blurred images in the wall through a thin haze of angry tears with her arms wrapped around her legs. *Fuckmonsters,* she thought vacantly. *Following me, vaccing out the apartment, Mom, Dad, Jerm*—The concrete horrors of the vision rubbed it all in, forcing it home. People chasing her, Herman admitting a mistake, unimaginable. Her credit balance when she'd checked it, *This has got to be a mistake*: there was enough money to buy a house, a good-sized cubic in an upmarket swing zone, never mind a ticket out of town on the next shuttle. "Give you a job." *Yeah, but how much use is it?* She'd give it all back in an instant to have the past day to run again with a different outcome. Just to be able to have that chat with Dad.

"How long?" she asked through her misery.

"Total transit time to Centris Noctis, currently six point one million kilometers distant, is sixteen hours and forty-one minutes. We hope you enjoy your flight and choose TransVirtual Travel-Ways again!"

The itinerary froze, motionless. Wednesday sighed. "Sixteen *hours?*" *I should have caught the high-delta service,* she realized. Not that she was used to flying anywhere at all, but this would take almost a day. "What shipboard facilities are available? Am I stuck in here for the whole trip?"

"Passengers are invited to remain in their seats for the duration of path injection maneuvering. Your seat is equipped to protect you from the consequences of local vertical variances. Eep! Please do not damage company assets willfully as these items are chargeable to your account. When the 'thrust' light is extinguished you may release your safety belt and walk around the ship. You are on A deck. B deck, C deck, and D deck are the other passenger decks on this flight. F deck provides a choice of entertainment arcades and the food court—"

"Enough." Wednesday's stomach lurched; she looked up in time to see the stylized thrust light in the ceiling flash urgently. Loops of safety webbing crawled out from the sides of her chair, wrapping around her securely as the gravity failed. "Oh, shit. Uh, how many other people are on this flight?"

"The manifest for this flight shows a total of forty-six passengers! You are one of five lucky Sybarite-class travelers! Below you in space, comfort, privacy, and our estimate are six Comfort class business passengers! The remainder are making use of our Basic-class package in common—"

"Shut up." Wednesday squeezed her eyes shut tiredly. "I'm trying to think. I *should* be thinking." Memories of lessons, way back in her early teens when Herman had first tempted her with strange adventure games. *Playing at spy versus spy?* She wouldn't put anything beyond him: clearly Herman wasn't simply a pet invisible friend, and equally clearly he had fingers in a lot of pies. All that stuff about evasion and tailing, how to locate surveillance nets and make use of blind spots, how to break relational integrity by finding camera overlaps and spoofing just one of them so the system interpolated an error... *Wear the black hat. I'm chasing me, Wednesday. Just killed*—her train of thought faltered for a moment, teetering on the edge—*and now I'm after her. Who, how, where, what?* "Can you stop listening until I call your name, ticket?"

"Madam is now in full privacy! All speech commands will be ignored until you unlock your suite. Call for 'Wendigo' when you want to discontinue privacy."

"Uh-huh." She glanced at the itinerary; it curled up, gripping the end of her recliner, and mimed mammalian sleep. "Hmm. At least two bad guys. If I'm lucky they think I was in the apartment when they, when they—" *Don't think about that.* "If not, what will they do? Worst case: they're covering the transit ferries so there's one aboard right now. Or they've got friends waiting for me at the other end. I can't evade that. But if they're limited to following me, then, then..."

She sighed. *Shit.* The prospect of spending nearly seventeen hours trapped in the recliner was already beginning to seem like hell. There was a quiet chime, and the thrust light went out. "Oh." It seemed to be taunting her. "Maybe they didn't cover the port. Maybe." She stared at it for another minute, then reached for the quick release on her safety belts and picked up her itinerary, stuffing it into a jacket pocket. "Wendigo. Open the door. There's a manual outside? Okay, close the door and go back to full privacy mode as soon as I've gone."

Outside the door of her room she found herself in a narrow circular corridor, with cabin doors spaced around the circumference and a twisting circular staircase leading down to the other decks. The ship hummed quietly beneath her as she took the steps six at a time, floating effortlessly down. The two lower passenger decks looked like open-plan seating, rows of recliners bolted side by side. As she passed she saw that most of them were empty. *Business must be down,* she decided.

The food court turned out to be a cramped circle of tables in the middle of a ring of food fabs programmed for different cuisines, a belt of arms waiting overhead to take orders. Wednesday found a small table at the edge and tapped it for the menu. She was just beginning to figure out her way around it when somebody sat down opposite her.

"Hi." She looked up, startled. He smiled shyly at her. *Wow!* Two meters tall, he had blue eyes, blond hair that looked so real it had to be a family heirloom—tied back in a ponytail—diamond earrings, not too much muscle or makeup, skin like—"I couldn't help noticing you. Are you traveling alone?"

"Maybe not." She found herself smiling right back. "I'm Wednesday."

"Leo. May I...?"

"Sure." She watched him sit down, graceful in the low-gee environment. "I was about to do lunch. Are you hungry?"

"I could be." *Beat.* He grinned. "Food, too."

Oh. Wednesday watched him, beginning to have second thoughts about the idea of a full stomach. He was gorgeous, and he was focused right at her. *Where were* you *at Sammy's party?* "Where are you traveling?" she asked aloud.

"Oh, I'm on vacation. Going to stay with my uncle." He shrugged. "Can I interest you in a drink?"

"What, you want to get me drunk and drag me off to my cabin?" She tapped on the tabletop for a bowl of miso soup and a hand roll. "Hmm. What kind of drink did you have in mind?"

"Something exquisite and bubbly, I guess. To fit in with the company." He leaned forward, close enough for her to inhale the faint scent of his skin: "If you're interested?"

"I think so." She waited a second, then leaned back, watching him with narrowed eyes. "Are you going to order anything?"

"Mm-hmm." She watched him as he scrolled the tabletop, jabbing at the wine submenu and ordering a plate of spiced noodles—*coordinated* and *confident,* she thought—and a bottle of something that was not only exquisite and bubbly, but also expensive. "Do you often go to stay with your uncle?" she asked, feeling idiotic, a conversational casualty in progress. "I don't mean to pry or anything—"

"Not really." The waitron was back, bearing a bottle with an intricate pressure-relief cork and a pair of fluted glasses. He took them and raised an eyebrow at her. "It's not like there are more than two flights a day between Magna and Noctis, is it?" He poured carefully, and handed her a nearly full glass. "To your very good...taste?"

Wednesday took a gulp of sparkling wine to hide her turmoil.

Everything about Leo was right, and he was an eminently eligible
choice for a friendly fuck to while away the journey—except that
he was *too* right. Too polished, too witty, too includable. He was
the sort of fashion accessory the "in" crowd always had on display. Why pick on her for an evening's dalliance? She glanced
around. There was a double handful of other passengers in the
food hall, mostly in groups, but there were one or two singles of
indeterminate age: well, maybe he was telling the truth. "To my
very good luck—in meeting you," she said, and knocked back the
rest of her glass. "I was really afraid today was going to be a dead
loss."

The food arrived, and Wednesday managed to drink her soup
without taking her eyes off him. Lust confused her. *What is it
about him?* she wondered. "Are you traveling in Comfort or Syb?"
she asked.

"Cattle class." He frowned momentarily. "All I get is a seat, a
curtain, and a boring neck massage. Why?"

"Oh, nothing," she said innocently. *My place or yours?* was a
no-brainer. In fact—

Her earlobe began to vibrate.

"'Scuse me a moment." She tapped the table for privacy, then
yet more privacy: everything around her went distant and fuzzy,
like being inside a velvet-lined black hole. "Yeah?" she demanded.

"Wednesday?" He sounded hesitant.

"Who—wait a minute. My phone was switched off!"

"You said if I was serious I should find your links myself?"

Well not exactly, but— She crossed her legs, uneasy. "Yeah,
you did, didn't you? Look, I'm going to be away for a while. You
were lucky to get me without a twenty-second lag. I won't be back
for months. Is there anything we need to say?"

"Uh, yes." Blow sounded hesitant at the end of the bitstream.
"I, uh, I wanted to apologize for being too talky last night. Uh, I
guess if you don't want to see me—"

"No, it's not that." Wednesday frowned minutely. Outside her
cone of silence she could see Leo watching her intently; she
moved instinctively to cover her mouth with the palm of her hand
as she spoke. "I really am going on a voyage right now. I know I
didn't want to get downheavy last night, but that was just the way
it was then. If you want to look me up when I get back, that would
be great. But I'm off-station already, so there's no chance to meet
up first."

"Are you in some kind of trouble?" he asked.

"No, I—yes. Shit! Yes, I'm in trouble." She caught Leo's gaze, rolled her eyes at him, lying with her face. He winked at her, and she forced a grin. The warmth in her belly turned to ice. *My rings. These are Herman's rings. The untraceable ones.* "Who told you?"

"This, uh, guy I sometimes work for, he called me up just now and told me you were in bad trouble and needed a friend. Is there anything I can do to help?"

Leo was pulling a face at her: Wednesday pulled a face right back. "I think you just did, just by calling. Listen, are *you* in trouble? Has anyone been round to talk to you? Cops?"

"Yes." His voice tended to break out into a croak when he was worried. "Said they just wanted to clear something up. Asked if I'd seen you. I said 'no'."

She relaxed slightly. "Your invisible friend, is he called Herman?"

A second's silence. "You know Herman?"

"Listen to him," she hissed, rolling her eyes some more and shrugging through the sound screen at Leo. "There's something bad going on. I'm being followed. Just stay out of this, all right?"

"Okay." He paused. "I want to ask you lots of questions sometime. Are you coming back?"

"I hope so." Leo was looking bored. "Listen, I've got to go. Problem to deal with. Thanks for talking—I've got your callback. Bye."

"I—uh. Bye."

"Privacy off." She grinned at Leo.

"Who was that?" he asked, curiously.

"Old friend," she said carelessly. "Didn't know I was leaving."

"Well, isn't that a shame?" He pointed at her place setting. "Your soup's cold."

"Oh well." She shrugged, then stood up, her heart beating fast. It wasn't arousal anymore, though. At least, it wasn't sexual arousal. Her palms were cold and her stomach threatening to twist itself into knots. "Where are you staying on Noctis?" she asked. "I was thinking, maybe I could come visit you?"

"Uh, I don't know. My uncle, he's got some pretty weird ideas," he said edgily. "How about we try your cabin? I've always wanted to see how the other half live."

Shit. He knew which class she was in. *Careless of him*—or he was overconfident. "Okay," she said lightly, smiling as he took her wrist and pulled her toward him. Another sniff of that enticing man-scent, something about his skin that made her want to slip her arm under his shirt and inhale. *That's something specific for your vomeronasal organ, something to go straight to your hypothalamus and get you wet, isn't it?* Her senses seemed to sharpen as she leaned against him. "Come on," she breathed in his ear, wondering how on earth she was going to get out of this mess. Her heart was pounding, and it *felt* like lust, or terror, or both. She was actually leaning against him, knees weak with something. *A neurotoxin?* she wondered, but no—that would be much too public if he was what she thought he might be. Probably just pheromone receptor blockers. "Come on."

On the staircase he paused for a moment and pulled her close. "Let me carry you?" he whispered in her ear. She nodded, dizzy with tension, and he picked her up, her head resting close to his ear as he climbed the stairs two steps at a time. A deck, the ring of Syb-class capsules. "Where's your—"

"Hold on, put me down, I'll find it." She smiled at him and leaned close. The corridor lights were dim, most of the other passengers snoozing their way through the flight. He smelled of fresh sweat and something musky, treacherously intoxicating. Herman had taught her a term for this: *Venus trap.* She grabbed him and pressed her lips against his in a kiss that he returned enthusiastically. Hips bumped. "Shit, not here." She tugged him along the corridor, nerves on fire. "Here." She tapped the door panel. "I need the rest room. You go on inside and make yourself at home. I won't be long."

"Really?" he asked, stepping inside her room.

"Yeah." She leaned close, nibbled him delicately on the neck. "I won't be a minute." Heart pounding, she stepped back and hit the door close button. Then she tapped the panel next to it, the privacy lock. Her heart was trying to climb out through her rib cage: "Did I *really* just do that?" she asked herself. "Wendigo. Suite, can you hear me?"

"Greetings, passenger Strowger! I can hear you." Its voice was tinny, coming to her through the external control plate.

"Please lock my suite door. Do not unlock the door until one hour after arrival. I want to sleep in. Divert all incoming calls, cancel outgoing routing. Maximum sound damping. Return to full privacy mode and add voiceprint authentication to keyword."

The simpleminded suite agent swallowed it. "Warning! Privacy may be overridden by authorized crew members in event of accident or medical emergency—"

"How many crew does this flight carry?" Her stomach lurched, icy cold soup sloshing.

"This is an unattended flight."

"Keep it that way. Now shut up and don't talk to anyone." There was a tentative knocking from inside the cabin, almost inaudible through the smart foam. Then a faint bump as if something massive had bounced off the inside of the door. Wednesday pouted at it, then headed for the staircase, a wistful urge to run back and apologize still fighting it out with her common sense. Sex on legs, packaged just for her? *Where were you during Sammy's party?* "Vacc'ing out Mom'n'Dad," she muttered to herself, half-blind with anger and loss as she hunted round C deck for an empty row to colonize. "Unless he's the best friendly fuck I've ever dropped by mistake..." She carried on arguing with herself for a long time before she dozed off, and by the time she was awake again the ferry had passed turnover and was nearly ready to dock.

oĸɑ띠 I'ᴍ ɦєᴦє. What do I do now?"

Noctis concourse wasn't built with fail-safe operation in mind. It was a product of the ebullient Septagonese economic miracle, so optimistic that nothing could possibly go wrong. Gravity thereabouts was a variable, vectored in whichever direction the architects had willed it. There were jungles on the walls, sand dunes on the ceiling, moebius walkways snaking through them for maximum visual impact.

Wednesday hurried along a strip locked to a steady half gee, trailing behind a flickering lightbug. She passed occasional clumps of other long-distance travelers—a mix of emigrants, merchants taking the long caravanserai, *wanderjahr* youth on the Grand Tour—and a variety of variously enticing and annoying shops disguised as environmental features. Butterflies the size of dinner plates flapped slowly past overhead, their wings flickering with historical docudramas. A small toroidal rain cloud spun slowly over a bright crimson nest of muddy-rooted mangroves, small lightning discharges clicking across its inner hole. Wednesday glanced past it, through a chink in the artistic foliage that led into a sudden perspective shift; stars glinted through diamond windows over a kilometer away. It was very Septagon, life defying vacuum, and for a moment she was dizzy with homesickness and the infinitely deep pool of depression that waited just beneath the thin ice of her self-control. *If we hadn't come here, Mom and Dad would still be alive. If. If.*

"Follow the lightbug to your connection with the liner *Romanov*. Once you reach the *Romanov*'s dock you should go aboard and remain in your stateroom until departure. Which is due in under six hours. I can cover for you for some time, but if you venture around the terminal, it is possible that a police agent will spot you and place you under volitional arrest. I believe there is a high probability that no charges will be brought, but you would miss the departure, and there is a high risk that the individuals pursuing you would locate you and make another attempt on your life. At the very least, they would be able to regain their lock on you. Good work with the suite, by the way."

"But what do I *do?*" she demanded nervously, stepping around a gaggle of flightless birds that had decided to roost in the middle of the footpath.

"Once you are on the liner and it is under way, they cannot reinforce their surveillance. I believe they are stretched thin, covering the orbitals around Centris Delta. There may be one or more aboard the ship, but you should be able to avoid them. Use the funds in your account to buy essentials aboard the ship; keep yourself alert. The next port of call is New Dresden, and I expect by that time to have fully identified your pursuers."

"Wait—you mean you *don't know* who they are? What *is* this?" Her voice rose.

"I believe them to be a faction of a group calling themselves the ReMastered. Whether they are an official faction, or a rogue splinter group, is unknown at this time. They may even be using the ReMastered as a cover: they've concealed their trail very effectively. If you go along with my suggestions, you will force them to expose themselves. Do you understand? I will have help waiting for you at New Dresden."

"You mean this ship is going to New Dresden? I—" She found herself talking into silence. "Shit. ReMastered." Whoever they were, at least she had a name, now. A name for something to hate.

The loop path branched, and her lightbug darted off to one side. Wednesday followed it tiredly. It was past midnight by her local time, and she badly needed something to keep her going. Here, the concourse took a turn for the more conventional. The vegetation thinned out, replaced by tiled blood diamond panes the size of her feet. Large structures bumped up from the floor and walls, freight lifts and baggage handlers and stairwells leading down into the docking tunnels that led out to the berthed starships. Some ships maintained their own gravity, didn't they? Wednesday wasn't sure what to expect of this one—wasn't it from Old Earth? She vaguely remembered lectures about the place, docutours and ecodramas. It had all sounded confusingly complicated and backward, and she'd been trying to keep Priz the Axe from cracking her tablet instead of listening to the professora. Was Earth a high-level kind of place, or backward like home had been?

The lightbug paused in front of her, then went dark. "Welcome to embarkation point four," piped her itinerary, somewhat muffled from inside a jacket pocket. "Please have your itinerary, identification documents, and skinprint ready for inspection!" The bug lit up again, darting back and forth between Wednesday and a powered walkway leading to the level below the concourse.

"Okay." Wednesday unsealed her pocket. "Uh, identification. Hmm." She fumbled with her rings for a moment. "Herman," she hissed, "do these rings authenticate me?"

Click. "Default identity, Victoria Strowger. Message from owner: Have fun with these, and remember to check the files I've stored in them under your alias." *Clunk.*

She blinked, bemused. "O-kay . . ."

Down below the wild efflorescences of the port concourse she found herself in a cool, well-lit departure hall fronting a boarding tunnel. A redheaded woman in some kind of ornate blue-and-gold uniform—*How quaint!* she thought—stood by the entrance. "Your papers, please?"

"Uh, Vicky Strowger." She held up her itinerary. "Have I come to the right place?"

The woman glanced aside at some kind of internal list. "Yes, we've been expecting you." She smiled with professional ease. "I see you've got a companiotronic guide. Would you like me to update it for shipboard use?"

"Sure." Wednesday handed the furry blue nuisance over to the woman. "If you don't mind me asking, who are you and what happens next?"

"Good questions," the woman said distractedly, stroking the back of the guide's skull while it spasmed in a fit of downloading. "I'm Elena, from the purser's office. If you have any questions later, feel free to ask room service to put you through to me. We're not scheduled to depart for another five and a half hours, but most passengers are already aboard, which is why— Ah, hello! Mr. Hobson? You're earlier than usual, sir. If you'd care to wait one second— Here you are, Victoria. If you'd like to go through into the elevator it will take you straight to the accommodation level you're on. Do you have any luggage?" She raised an eyebrow at Wednesday's small shake of the head. "All right. You're in Sybarite-class row four, Corridor C. There's a fab you can use for the basics in your room, and a range of boutiques two levels down and one corridor across from you if you want to shop for extras later. Anything else you need to know, feel free to ask for me. Bye!" She was already turning to deal with the unusually early Mr. Hobson as Wednesday slid the talking travel guide back into its pocket. She shook her head: *Too much, too fast.* So Earth had fabs? Then it wasn't a backwater like New Dresden—or home— and she wasn't going to have to camp out in a refugee cell for a week. Maybe the journey would turn out all right, especially if Herman had given her his usual thorough map of the service facilities...

the darkened tool storage pod hanging from the aircon stack at the top of ring J normally smelled of packing foam and damp. Now it stank of silicone lube grease and fear.

A quiet voice recited a list of sins. "Let me recap. You hired ordinary goons who tracked the kid as far as a dead zone, but they lost her inside a derelict housing module. She was on her way to a fucking party, but nobody thought to trace her friends, find out where it was, and go there. Meanwhile, your other proxies liquidated her family, thus losing all possible links to the primary target and simultaneously warning her that her life was in danger. So tell me, Franz, *how* does a nineteen-year-old refugee manage to outsmart a pair of even remotely professional gangsters? And why did her skin traces show up all over the *inside* of the emergency lock leading into the depressurized cell?"

Pause. "Uh, would you believe, shit happens?" A longer pause. "The goons were tracking her via her interface rings. It's my fault for not anticipating that she had evasion training; I expected it to be a straightforward track and tag. When she took off—"

U. Portia Hoechst sighed. "Give me some light in here, Jamil."

The interior of the service pod lit up.

"Are you going to kill me now?" asked Franz. He looked mildly apprehensive, as if steeling himself for an unpleasant dental procedure. He didn't have much of an alternative. Portia's bodyguard Marx had done a thorough job of trussing him to a couple of anchor beams.

"That depends." Portia tapped the end of her stylus against her front teeth thoughtfully as she stared at him. She narrowed her eyes. "There has been a culture of unacceptable slackness in this organization."

Franz opened his mouth as if about to say something, then shut it again, slowly. A bead of sweat jiggled on his forehead, just below the hairline. It was growing visibly bigger, as she watched, held in place by surface tension, unable to run away in the milligee environment.

"What did you do next?" she asked, almost kindly.

"Well, I concluded she'd run. Either to the authorities for protection or somewhere outside the hab. So I sent Burr, Samow, and Kerguelen off to grab seats on the next departing ferry shuttles to other habs, with orders to do a full cap routine on her if she showed up, and I took myself and Erica down to the local cop shop to puppetize our way into their holding tank in case she turned out to have stayed home. As we only had the one puppetry kit in the entire system..." His voice trailed off.

"What other resources did you have? You only covered three shuttle flights with one finger on each. Isn't that a bit thin?" Her voice was almost gentle.

"I was fully committed." Franz sounded tense. "I only have six residents here, including me! That isn't even enough to maintain a twenty-four-by-seven tail on a single individual, much less conduct a full penetration or cleanup. Why do you think I had to use paid muscle instead of properly programmed puppets? I've been requesting additional backup for months, but all that came down the line were orders to make better use of my resources and a 10 percent budget cut. Then your group..." He trailed off.

"Your requests. Were they at least acknowledged?"

"Yes." He watched her warily, unsure where this chain of inquiry was leading. She watched him watching her, speculating. Franz was the resident in Centris, a station chief left over from U. Vannevar Scott's operation, and therefore, automatically suspect. But he was also the only station chief in this entire system, the complex of orbital habs circling in the accretion belt around the brown dwarf at the heart of Septagon B. It was sheer luck that he'd even been able to move his team onto the right hab in the first place. If he was telling the truth, hung out to dry with six staff to pin down three hundred million people scattered through nearly five hundred orbital habitats and countless smaller stations and ships, he'd clearly been starved of support. While U. Scott had been pouring funds into his central security groups, snooping on his rivals within the Directorate.

Portia stared at him. "I will investigate this, you know."

Franz watched her unflinchingly, not even sparing a glance for Marx. Marx was the one who'd pith him if it came to it, or even kill him, simply wasting his memories, leaving everything that he was to drain into nothingness.

"Has your crew reported back about the loose end?"

Now his expression broke: irritation, even a spark of outright rebellion. "I'd be able to tell you if you'd unwrap me and give me a chance to find out," he said waspishly. "Or ask Erica. Assuming you haven't already decided she's a broken tool and discarded her."

Portia reached a decision. The practicalities of it were risky, but then so was life. "Release him," she told Jamil.

"Is this wise?" Marx grunted, keeping his eyes focused dead center on Franz's forehead. "We could repurpose him—"

"I prefer my subordinates to have free will." Her smile vanished abruptly. "Do you have a problem with that?"

"Just looking out for your safety, boss."

"I'm quite sure that U. Franz Bergman will remember whose purpose he serves now that External Environmental Control Four has been, ah, absorbed by Group Six."

Jamil produced a knife from somewhere and began slicing away at the tape fastening Franz's arms to the support bars.

Franz's eyes widened. "Did you say *absorbed?* What happened to Control Four?"

"U. Vannevar Scott has been an extremely naughty boy," Portia trilled. "So naughty that Overdepartmentsecretary Blumlein saw fit to take all his toys away." Slight emphasis on the *all,* a raised eyebrow, a pouting lip. "You're on the gray list." Gray, as opposed to black, whose status was *pith and reclaim with extreme prejudice.* "It's not very big, but you're on it. Who knows? If you work hard, you may even stay there."

Franz slumped slightly, floating free of the anchor beams, nervously apprehensive. "What do you want me to do?" he asked. "Nobody told us anything about—" He swallowed.

"Indeed." Portia nodded at Jamil, big and solidly muscled. "You and Jamil are going to go and do the rounds. You're going to give me a sitrep, and Jamil is going to sit on your shoulder and see how you go about it. Think of it as an entrance exam." She recognized his unspoken question. "You and your people, both."

"I'm, uh, very grateful—"

"Don't be." The brilliant smile was back. "I want to know what's going on out there in the wild. You've got two kiloseconds to find out. And believe me, until I decide to pass you, dying will seem like the easy option."

bᴜ the time he got back to the pod, Franz was truly frightened. As if the mess he'd been holding together for the past nine months wasn't bad enough, having the DepSec from hell descend on him with bodyguards and a full-dress away team was worse. Luckily Erica was with him, a calming influence. But the news—

He glanced over his shoulder at her. She stared back at him, trying to look unaffected. A competent deputy station chief, following her boss's lead. Jamil followed them both, imperturbable, threatening. "I'll handle this," he reassured her.

"I understand." He wanted to reach out and grab her hand, but he didn't dare. Not in front of Jamil. She looked rattled enough as it was. Maybe it was because she'd figured out where they stood for herself, but he couldn't be sure.

The DepSec was waiting for him like a spider at the center of her web, black and shiny and carnivorous when she smiled, disturbingly red lips parting to reveal perfect teeth. Sea-green eyes as cold as death watched him. Behind her, the bodyguard waited. "You made it with fifty seconds to spare!" She glanced at Erica. "So, you're U. Erica Blofeld?"

Franz noticed Erica nodding out of the corner of his eye. He could *smell* the DepSec, the warm mind-fuzzing sense of family coming off her in waves. He could feel Erica's nervousness. "Ye-es. Boss."

"Let her speak for herself," Hoechst said gently. "You can speak, can't you?" she added.

"Yes." Erica cleared her throat. "Yes, uh. Boss? Nobody told us anything."

"Jamil. Did U. Franz Bergman tell U. Erica Blofeld anything substantive about the change of management structure?"

"No, boss."

"Good." Hoechst focused on the woman. "What's the situation, Erica? Tell me."

"I—" She shrugged uncomfortably. "Burr and Samow drew a blank. Kerguelen messaged to say he'd found the target, in transit to Noctis hab in a first-class berth. Last he sent, he was closing on her to lay a honeypot and do a field-expedient pickup. Since then I've heard nothing. He last called in about eleven hours ago, and they should be arriving at Noctis real soon, but he's missed three checkpoints, and while I can think of several reasons for doing so, none of them are good." She watched Hoechst closely, eyes flickering back and forth between her face and her hands.

"Well, that is convenient." Hoechst's expression was bland. "Did it occur to any of you that the target of this action might be trained in evasion and self-defense?"

Franz tried to answer. "We didn't—"

"Shut up! That was a rhetorical question." Hoechst looked past him at the doorway. "You've told me what I needed to know, and I thank you," she said graciously, nodding to Erica. "Jamil, give U. Erica Blofeld coffee *now*."

Franz kicked off the floor, hit the ceiling and rolled, intending to bounce off it and take Jamil in the gut. Desperation triggered his boost reflexes, narrowing focus until the world was a graywalled tunnel. But Jamil had already brought up something like a silvery hand-sized Christmas tree, and he stabbed it toward the back of Erica's head. Erica's eyes bulged. She spasmed, beginning to turn as blood gouted—

Something hit Franz hard, in the small of his back.

can you hear me?"

"I think he's playing moppet, boss."

Not exactly. There was a searing pain in his back, and his head felt as if he had the worst hangover in human space. In fact, he felt sick. But that wasn't the worst part of it. The worst part of it was that he was conscious again, which meant that he was still alive, which meant...

"Listen to me, Franz. Your station deputy was on the black list. She reported to U. Scott's Countersubversion Department. I will ensure that her reclaimed state vector is dispatched to the Propagators with all due decency, and leave judgment of her soul up to the unborn god. But you *will* open your eyes within thirty seconds, or you'll join her. Do you understand?"

He opened his eyes. The twilight was painfully bright. A quivering black sphere of uncoagulated blood floated past, wobbling slowly in the direction of one of the extractor vents. Despair hit him like a velvet club.

"We were—" He paused, carefully, searched for an acceptable

word, unsure why it was so important to do so now that his real life was over before it had even begun. His throat was dry. "Close." *Close*, that was the word. It brought it all home, while revealing nothing.

"If you value your intimacy so highly, you're welcome to join her," hell's handmaiden told him half-seriously. She moved across the room in front of him, a blur before his eyes. He had to struggle to focus. "The ReMastered race doesn't need moral weaklings. Or were you naive enough to think you were *in love?*"

"I'm—" *angry*, he realized. "I feel ill. Dysfunctional." He was angrier than he'd ever been before—angry in his helplessness. He hadn't been angry when her bodyguard had stunned him and he'd awakened strapped to a set of beams; just frightened and apprehensive beyond all reason. But now, with the thought that he might survive, there was room for anger. *Erica's dead.* It shouldn't have meant that much to him, but they'd been living outside the Directorate for too long. They'd been a little reckless, adopting feral ways, naive native sentimentality. And now, naive native pain and loss.

"You're angry," Hoechst said soothingly. "It's a perfectly understandable human reaction. Something you thought was yours has just been taken away from you. I don't blame you for it, and if you want to yell at me later, you're welcome to. But right now Blumlein himself has given us a very important task, and if you get in my way, I'll have to crush you. Nothing personal. And just in case it hasn't sunk in, your friend was a *countersub* agent. Reporting directly to U. Scott's Office of Internal Inquiries. Programmed to execute you at the first sign of disloyalty to Scott." Franz found himself nodding, unconsciously agreeing; but all the time he was full of the scent of her skin, the memory of her laughter, their secret shared sin of commission, out here beyond the Directorate, where love wasn't a state of war and hate wasn't politics.

She wouldn't have given me away, he thought. *Not ever.* Because she'd told him all about her second job within a day of their first frantic assignation, holed up in a hotel, hungry to the point of starvation for intimacy. It had been their dirty little secret, a shared furtive fantasy about eloping, defecting, lighting out for the event horizon. Either Hoechst—in her capacity as death's angel—knew far less than she thought she did about the cell she was taking over, or the Directorate was rotten to the core anyway, and the unborn god a sick fantasy.

But you couldn't ever let yourself dream such thoughts when you were around other ReMastered, not if you wanted to live. So Franz bundled up his scream of loss and pain, and shoved it down a long way, deep down where he could curl up around it later and lick the suppurating wound—and forced himself to nod vigorously.

"I'll be all right soon," he said meekly: "It was just a shock." If he let them realize how deeply he and Erica had been involved...

"That's good," Hoechst said reassuringly. His nostrils flared, but he gave nothing away. Marx floated behind her like a lethal shadow, holding a spinal leech casually in one hand.

"What do you want me to do now?" he asked hoarsely.

"I want you to rest up and recover. We're going on a journey, soon as we gather up the rest of your cell."

"A journey—"

"New Dresden, via yacht." She pulled a face. "Some yacht— it's an old Heidegger-class frigate with its weapons systems ripped out and replaced with stores compartments and bunks. We've got about eight days to get there ahead of your runaway, who is traveling master class on a liner. When we get there, we're going to rescue the situation, nail down all the loose ends, and stop the avalanche U. Vannevar Scott set in motion. Got that?"

"I—" He flexed his left hand; a stabbing pain in his wrist made him gasp. "I think I damaged something."

"That's all right." She grinned at him with easy camaraderie: "You're going to damage lots more things before this is over..."

it took an entire week for Portia to get round to raping him. For Franz, most of the time passed in a blur as he worked like an automaton; he was too busy rounding up his remaining agents to notice the cool, speculative looks she was sending his way.

It happened after Hoechst dealt with Kerguelen. Missing his target might have been excusable if he hadn't already been on the gray list, and debatable even in spite of it, but he'd compounded the error by alerting the girl. She'd locked him in her own Syb-class cabin, turning the tables. Hoechst was incandescent with fury when she found out, and even Franz had felt an answering twinge of indignation through his haze of loss.

Portia collected Kerguelen from Noctis herself, ordering a diversion that cost the *DD-517* almost a day's headway while it stooged around pretending to be a luxury yacht. She wore a

watered silk gown of blue and violet to the police station where
the unfortunate Kerguelen was being held, along with a blond wig
and a king's ransom in precious stones; she had the mannerisms
and giggle down to perfection for her role as the second wife of a
rich ship-owning magnate from al-Turku. Franz and Marx and
Samow marched behind her stiffly, wearing the archaic uniforms
and pained air of superiority of her household retainers. The show
ended about five milliseconds after they got the anxiously grateful
Ker across the boarding tube threshold and behind a 'lock door.
Then she was at his throat.

"*Bastard!*" she hissed, wrist muscles standing out like steel
bands as she choked him. It was a deadly insult among the
ReMastered, but nobody was interested in Ker's reply. Marx and
Samow held his arms as he bucked and kicked against the bulkhead while she crushed his larynx. When he stopped moving,
Hoechst looked round their small circle, sparing Franz such a
malice-filled glare that he shuddered, sensing how close his own
neck was to those strong hands, but then she relaxed slightly and
nodded at him. "He showed me up," she said coolly. "Worse, he
made the Directorate look foolish. You also."

"I understand," he said woodenly, and that seemed to satisfy her.

"Samow, see that his neural map is reclaimed, then ditch the
remains. Marx, give my compliments to the pilot and tell her it's
time to execute Plan Coyote. U. Bergman, come with me." She
turned and stalked toward the lift up to the crew decks. Franz followed her, his mind blank. Kerguelen had worked for him for
three years, a happy-go-lucky youngster on his first out-of-system
assignment. He was prone to living it up, but not self-consciously
sloppy, and there seemed to be a serious ideological commitment
underlying his actions. His self-evident belief in the cause, in the
unborn god and the destiny of the ReMastered, had sometimes left
Franz feeling like a hollow fraud.

Kerguelen had lived life as large as he was allowed to, as if he
were working in the early days of a better universe. To see him
broken and discarded rubbed home Franz's own inadequacy. So
he didn't protest, but followed Hoechst, wafting in her trail of
rustling silks and expensive floral triterpenoids and volatile oils.
The faint smell of old-fashioned powder cosmetics stung his nose.

The DepSec's suite was larger than the cubbyhole Franz was
bunking in. It held a pair of chairs, a rolltop desk, and a separate
folding bed. Perhaps it had once been the friggatenführer's quarters, back when the yacht had been a warship. Hoechst shut the

door and waved him to a seat, but remained standing and busied herself with something at her table. He couldn't take his eyes off her. She was beautiful, in a feral, ex-Directorate sort of way, but also frightening. Intimidating. A predator, beautiful but deadly and incapable of behaving any other way. She eased her wig off and placed it on the desk, then ran her fingertips through her close-cropped pale hair. "You look as if you need a drink."

She was offering him a glass, he realized through a cloud of befuddlement. He accepted it instantly, his instinct for self-preservation kicking in. "Thank you." She poured herself another from a cut-crystal decanter, some kind of amber fluid that stank of alcohol and ashes. "Is this an imported whisky?"

She curled her lower lip thoughtfully, then replaced the decanter stopper and sat down on the chair opposite him. "Yes." She smoothed her gown over her knees and looked momentarily abashed, as if she couldn't remember how she came to be there, a fairy-tale princess aboard a warship of the ReMastered race. "You should try it."

He raised his glass, then paused, trying to remember the formula: "To your very good health." He silently appended a less flattering toast.

She raised her glass back to him. "And yours." Her cheek twitched. "If that's your idea of a toast to my health, I can't imagine what my painful death would warrant."

Her words struck home. "Boss, I—"

"Silence." She watched him over the rim of her glass, green eyes narrowed. Sweat-spiked black hair, high cheekbones, full red lips, narrow waist: a warrior's body held in a sheath of silk that had taken master couturiers a month to stitch. She had the inhumanly symmetrical features that only a first-line clade could afford to buy for the alpha instances of their phenotype. "I brought you here because I think we may have gotten off on the wrong foot when we were first introduced."

Franz sat frozen in his chair, the glass of scotch—worth a small fortune, for it had been imported across more than two hundred light years—clutched in his right hand. "I'm not sure I understand you."

"I think you do." Hoechst watched him, unblinking except for the occasional flicker of her nictitating membranes. "I've been following your profile. You would be surprised how much information on their subjects even the privacy fetishists of Septagon manage to collect. Our target refugee, for instance. I think I've got a handle on her—she made the mistake of talking to some friends after her unfortunate run-in with that waste of air, and I think I know where she's bound for. But she's not the only one."

Now it comes, he realized, the muscles in his neck tensing involuntarily. *She's going to—what?* If she wanted him dead, she could have executed him along with Ker.

She kept her eyes on him, avaricious for information: "You were 'in love' with U. Erica Blofeld, weren't you?"

A stab of unreasoning anger provoked him to speak frankly: "I'd rather not talk about it. You've got what you want, haven't you? My undivided attention and the liquidation of an elite countersub agent from Scott's personal cadre. Isn't that enough?"

"Perhaps not." Her cheek muscles tensed, pulling the sides of her mouth up into something that resembled a smile but didn't touch her eyes. "You've been in Septagon space for too long, Franz. In a way it's not your fault. It could happen to anyone, spending too long on their own without backup and indoctrination, forming their own little schismatic reality, wondering if perhaps the Directorate was really the only way of doing things, wondering if you could possibly ignore it and pretend it would go away. Isn't that it? You don't need to admit anything, by the way, this isn't an inquisition. I'm not going to feed you to the Propagators. But you can express yourself freely here. I don't mind. You have my permission to shout at me. Remember what I said earlier?"

"You..." His fingers tightened on the glass. For a despairing moment he thought about smashing it and going for her throat, before the reality of his situation struck home. "So what? Nothing I can say matters. You wouldn't believe my denials."

"Well then!" She smiled, and it filled him with anger, because her expression was so genuine—she looked joyously happy, and grief and envy said that *nobody* should be allowed to look that way, ever again—when Erica was dead. And even though he knew it was just his glands speaking, that this, too, would pass, it goaded him. "I have a problem," she said, continuing as if nothing was wrong. She rubbed her right knee through the sheer fabric of her gown. "We're about to go and close down some loose ends. If we succeed, the sky is the limit. Not only will everybody in this unit be rehabilitated, but I will be—well, promotion is not the most of it." She leaned toward him, confidingly. "At the higher levels, Franz, things are a little different. Unforgivable disciplinary errors become understandable personality flaws. The Propagators become tools with which the garden is teased into a pleasing shape: servants, not masters. Quite possibly, expedient termination orders become reversible."

He licked his lips. "Reversible?"

"I haven't sent U. Blofeld's state vector to the Propagators yet," she said softly, as if the very thought was new to her. "We don't have a Propagator with us, so I bear responsibility for life records and a memory diamond that is to be turned over to them only at the end of our mission. And I retained tissue samples."

Thoughtfully: "The sole complete upload image of her brain currently exists right here aboard this ship. And they need not end up with the Propagators, if a suitable alternative presents itself. What I do with them is still open. I'm short on personnel here— you were right about your mission being grossly underresourced. U. Scott was systematically overreporting his manifest, filtering people off your team for missions elsewhere, and maintaining two sets of books. I didn't bring enough support staff along, and I'm even shorter on people who understand the feral humans out here. I need someone who can act as my right hand while Bayreuth is holding things down back home."

She leaned toward him confidingly and took his left hand in hers: "If we succeed, I can give her back to you, Franz. There's a medical replicator in the medical suite aboard the *CG-52*. My support ship. It's expensive and against normal operational procedure, but they can clone her a new body and download her into it. You can have her back again if that's what you want. As long as you're willing to do some things for me."

"Things?" Franz felt himself leaning toward her, drawn by the terrible force of her will and by the abominable hope she dangled in front of him. *Bring Erica back? In return for... what?* His stomach churned with hope and dread.

"They're not the sort of jobs I can give an ordinary subordinate. They're jobs that only someone who's lived among feral humans for several years can do."

"What jobs?"

She pulled his hand close, placing it palm down on her thigh. "You fell in love, didn't you? That's still supposed to be possible for us, but I've never heard of two ReMastered who did it to each other at the same time. So you'll have a better grasp of how to use the phenomenon to manipulate ferals than anyone else here." She smelled of floral extracts, and something else: the musk of power, sebaceous glands expressing pheromones that were only switched on in alpha ReMastered.

It was exciting and frightening and made him angry. He dropped his glass and pulled back, away from her. "I don't want—"

She was on her feet, then leaning over him. "I don't care what you want," she said coolly. "Unless it's U. Erica. In which case you'll do as I say with a shit-eating grin for the next three months, won't you?"

He stared at her breasts. Under the thin layers of silk he could see her nipples, aureoles flushed and crinkled with dominance. The dizzying smell was getting to him. His own traitorous hope prevented him from resisting. "Love is a grossly underrated tool within the Directorate, Franz. You're going to teach me how to use it."

"How—"

"Hush." She pulled up the skirts of her gown, bunched them around her waist, and sat down on his lap. He couldn't get away, much less force himself not to respond to her dominance pheromones. He grew stiff and felt his face flush as she unbuttoned his comic-opera jacket and rubbed her breasts against him. "I want you to teach me about love. It's going to take a few sessions, but that's all right—we've got time for a first lesson right now. How did you do it with her? Did she start it, or did you, or was it something else?" She began to work at the buttons of his trousers. "If you want to see her again, you'll show me what you did for her . . ."

The Times of London—thundering the news since 1785! Now brought to you by Frank the Nose, sponsored by Thurn und Taxis Arbeitsgemeinschaft, Melting Clock Interstellar Scheduling Specialists PLC, Bank Muamalat al-Failaka, Capek Robotica Universuum, and The First Universal Church of Kermit.

LEADER

Let's talk some more about the Moscow disaster and its inevitable fallout—this time from the point of view of the people at ground zero, staring down the flight path of the oncoming bullets. These people are edgy and unhappy, and you should be, too—because what's sauce for the goose is sauce for the gander, and if we allow this slow-motion atrocity to set a precedent, we might be the next bird on the block.

New Dresden is not a McWorld: it's a shitty little flea hole populated by pathologically suspicious Serbs, bumptiously snobbish Saxons, three different flavors of Balkan refugee, and an entire bestiary of psychopathic nationalist loons. The planetary national sport is the grudge match, at which they are undisputed past masters. I say "past masters" for a reason—they're not as bad as they used to be. The planet has been unified for the past ninety years, since the survivors finished merrily slaughtering everyone else, formed a federation, had a nifty little planetary-scale nuclear war, formed another federation, and buried the hatchet (in one another's backs).

For most of the past forty years, New Dresden has been ruled by a sinister lunatic, Colonel-General Palacky, chairman of PORC, the Planetary Organization of Revolutionary Councils. Most of Palacky's policies were dictated by his astrologers, including his now-notorious abolition of the currency and its replacement with bills divisible by 9, his lucky number. Palacky was a raving egomaniac; he renamed the month of January after himself and fixed the rest of the calendar, too, except for November and December (his mother-in-law got August, for some reason). However, toward the end, he became a recluse, seldom venturing beyond the high iron gates of the presidential palace. There he presided over an endless party, providing fire-eaters, wrestlers, tribal dancers, drag queens, and prostitutes for his guests, while dwarfs balancing silver platters loaded with cocaine on their heads patrolled the corridors to ensure all his protégés had a good time. Needless to say, the palace gates were topped with the decaying skulls of those army officers and PORC delegates who disagreed with the Colonel-General over such fundamental policy issues as the need to feed the people.

The inevitable revolution—which finally came four years ago, in the wake of the Moscow scandal—saw Palacky thrown from his own executive ornithopter and installed a more pragmatic junta of bickering, but not entirely insane, PORC apparatchiks. Thus proving some point about it being bad form for any one PORCer to hog the entire trough.

Anyway, that's the dark picture. On the bright side, they're not as remorselessly reactionary as Gouranga, as totalitarian and oppressive as Newpeace, as boringly bucolic as Moscow used to be, as intolerantly Islamic as Al-Wahab, or... you get the picture. A planet is a big place, and even the excesses of the PORC junta can't really damage the economy too badly. Given a couple of decades of civilization and a few war crimes tribunals, New Dresden will be well on the way to being the sort of place that rational tourists don't automatically cross off their itineraries with a shudder.

In fact, as long as you don't question the political wisdom of a system with sixteen secret police forces, thirty-seven ministries with their own militias, four representative assemblies (three of which are run on single-party-state lines by *different* single parties and all of which have veto power over one another), and above all, as long as you *don't mention the civil war,* New Dresden can be a welcoming place for visitors. Just as long as your purpose in visiting is to buy the pretty rustic souvenirs and quaint quantum nanocomputers, ooh and aah at the wonderful reconstructed ethnic villages in Chtoborrh Province, and drink the fine laagered ales in the alpine coaching houses, you can't go wrong.

Life isn't that bad for the ordinary people, as near as I can tell. I couldn't get close enough to be sure, because to do that I'd have to spend twenty years as a deep-cover mole. I wasn't exaggerating the national suspicion toward strangers. It's a survival trait on New Dresden; they've been breeding for paranoia for centuries. But from outside, the standard of living is clearly rising and looks pretty damned good compared to a clusterfuck like the New Republic.

These people have got automobiles—real fuel-cell-powered people movers, no messing around with boilers or exploding piston motors—and they've got music-swapping networks and cosmetic surgery and package holidays on the moons and seven different styles of imported extraplanetary fusion cuisine. Wealthy people have less time and energy for shooting each other to bits, so mostly the grudges fester on in the form of elaborate social snubs rather than breaking out in revolutions. And there are only 800 million people, so they've got a lot of potential if they can break the violent cycle of the past two and a half centuries.

And there *are* signs of peace breaking out. These days the secret police spend most of their energy spying on each other. They leave the civilians alone and drink in the same bars at the weekend. There are actually homegrown independent journalists there these days. Who knows? Any day now the place might be civilized...

...Except that three faceless bureaucrats are about to murder everyone.

I'm talking, of course, about whichever of the surviving Muscovite diplomats put their fingers to the trigger and push simultaneously. As opposed to the two of them who *could,* if they had the bravery to concede that the game is not worth the candle, issue a reprieve to this promising planet of nearly a billion people who are, when you get right down to it, not that much different from the former citizenry of Moscow.

Intestinal fortitude, and the lack thereof. If you're going to appoint yourself supreme judge in a death penalty case, you should damn well make sure that you're prepared to pass judgment and live with the consequences. And I don't believe these cunts have got what it takes.

Which is why I'm on my way to New Dresden. I'm going to corner Ambassador Elspeth Morrow and Trade Minister Harrison Baxter and put the question to them—exactly why are they willing to execute 800 million people, in the absence of any evidence that they're responsible for the crime of which they are accused?

Watch this space.

Ends (*Times* Leader)

ϝrank stretched his arms toward the ceiling of the breakfast room and yawned tremendously. He had slept in, and had a mild hangover. Still, it was better than being hagridden by memories of the incident in the bar the night before. For which he was grateful.

The breakfast lounge was like the other dining rooms—only slightly smaller, with a permanent heated buffet and no bar or cabaret stage against the opposite wall. That late in the morning it was almost empty. Frank helped himself to a plate, loaded it down with hash browns and paprika-poached eggs, added a side order of hot blueberry bagels fresh from the fabricator, and hunted around for a free table. The sole steward on duty wasted no time in offering him a coffeepot, and as he dug into his food Frank tried to kick his tired brain cells into confronting the new day's agenda. *Item: Transfer point with Septagon Centris Noctis. Passengers departing and boarding. Hmm. Worth staking out the bulletin boards in case? Next item: See to transmitting latest updates. Spool incoming news, read and inwardly digest. Then . . . fuck it, eat first.* He poured a measured dose of cream into his breakfast coffee and stirred it. *Wonder if anything's happened since the last jump?*

It was the perpetual dilemma of the interstellar special correspondent—if you stayed in one place, you never got to see anything happen up close and personal, but you could stay plugged into the network of causal channels that spread news in empire time. If you traveled around, you were incommunicado from the instant the ship made its first jump until the moment it entered the light cone of the destination. But what the channels paid Frank for was his insights into strange cultures and foreign politics. You couldn't get those by staying at home; so every new port of call triggered a mad scramble for information, to be digested into editorials and opinion pieces and essays during the subsequent flight, and spat out at the net next time the ship arrived in a system with bandwidth to the outside universe.

Frank yawned and poured himself another cup of coffee. He'd had too little sleep, too much rum and whisky, and faced a day's work to catch up on preparation for the liner's arrival at New Dresden. Septagon was so connected and so well covered that there was no real point going ashore there: it was a major data exporter. But New Dresden was off the beaten track, and directly in jeopardy as a result of the slow-motion disaster unfolding from Moscow system. When he got there he faced four days of complete insanity, starting with a descent on the first available priority pod and ending with a last-minute dash back to the docking tunnel, during which he had to file copy written en route, gather material for two weeks' worth of features, and do anything else that needed attending to. He'd checked the timetables: he figured he could make the trip with two and a quarter hours to spare. Okay, make that three and a half days of buzzing around like a demented journalistic bluebottle, released on a ticket of leave in the middle of a promising field of diplomatic bullshit—it was a good thing that New Dresden wasn't uptight about pharmaceuticals, because by the time Frank was back in his stateroom he'd be ready for the biggest methamphetamine crash in journalistic history. Which was precisely what you deserved if you tried to cover four continents, eight cities, three diplomatic receptions, and six interviews in three days, but *c'est la vie.*

Stomach filled and coffee flask emptied, Frank pushed back from the table and stood up. "When do we push back?" he asked the air casually.

"Departure is scheduled in just under two thousand seconds," the ship replied softly, beaming its words directly into his ears. "Transition to onboard curved-space generator will be synchronized with the station, and there will be no free-fall lockdown. Acceleration to jump point will take a further 192,000 seconds approximately, and bandwidth access to Septagon switching will be maintained until that time. Do you have further requests?"

"No thank you," Frank replied, slightly spooked by the way the ship's expertise had anticipated his line of questioning. *Damn thing must be plugged in to the Eschaton,* he thought nervously. There were limits to what anyone sane would contemplate doing by way of artificial intelligence experiments—the slight ethical issue that a functioning AI would have a strong legal claim to personhood tended to put a brake on the more reckless researchers, even if the Eschaton's existence didn't hold a gun to their heads— but sometimes Frank wondered about the emergent smarts exhibited by big rule-driven systems like the ship's passenger assistance liaison. Somehow it didn't seem quite right for a machine he'd never met to be anticipating his state of mind.

He strolled distractedly around the promenade deck on C level, barely conscious of his surroundings. C deck by day shift was a different place to the darkened night-time corridors. Elegant plate-diamond windows to either side displayed boutiques, shops, beauty salons, and body sculptors. Whole trees, cunningly constrained in recessed tubs, grew at intervals in the corridor, their branches meshing overhead. Below them, tiny maintenance 'bots harvested browning leaves before they could fall and disturb the plush carpet.

The corridor wasn't empty, but passengers were thin on the ground—mostly they were still coming through the docking tube from Noctis orbital, the WhiteStar open port in Septagon system. Here went a young couple, perhaps rich honeymooners from Eiger's World strolling arm in arm with the total inattention of the truly in love. There went a stooped old man with lank hair, a facial tic that kept one cheek jumping, and the remains of breakfast matted in his beard, heading toward a discreet opium den with a dull look of anticipation in his eyes. A gamine figure in black stopped dead and gaped into the window of a very expensive jewelery studio as Frank stepped around her—him, it—and slid to one side to avoid a purposefully striding steward. The ship was a shopping mall, designed to milk idle rich travelers of their surplus money. Frank, being neither idle nor rich, focused on threading a path around the occasional window-shoppers.

The promenade deck stretched in a two-hundred-meter loop around the central atrium of the ship's passenger decks, an indoor waterfall and the huge sculptured staircases rising through it like glass-dressed fantasies. Halfway around it, Frank came to a gap in the shop fronts and a radial passage that led to a circular lounge, carpeted in red and paneled in improbably large sheets of ivory scrimshaw, with a stepped pit in the middle. It was almost empty, just a few morning folk sipping cups of coffee and staring into the inner space of their head-ups. Frank headed for a decadent-looking sofa, a concoction of goose-down cushions in cloned human leather covers, soft enough to swallow him and luxurious as a lover's touch. He sprawled across it and unpocketed his keyboard, expanded it to full size, and donned his shades. "Right. Priorities," he muttered to himself, trying to dismiss yet more intrusive memories from the night before at the caress of the leather. *Whom do I mail first, the embassy or the UN consulate? Hmm...*

He was half an hour into his morning correspondence when someone touched his left shoulder.

"Hey!" He tried to sit up, failed, flailed his arms for a moment, and managed to get a grip on the leading edge of the sofa.

"Are you Frank the Nose?" asked a female voice.

Frank pulled his shades right off, rather than dialing them back to transparency. "What the f— eh, what are you talking about?" he spluttered, reaching for his left shoulder with his left hand. It was the young woman he'd seen in the corridor. He couldn't help noticing the pallor of her skin and the fact that every item of her costume was black. She was cute, in a tubercular kind of way. *Elfin, that's the word,* he noted.

"I'm sorry to disturb you, it's, like, I was told you were a warblogger?"

Frank spent a moment massaging his forehead as, briefly, a number of responses flitted through his head.

"Who wants to know?" he finally asked, surprising himself with his mildness. *Click.* Physically young—either genuinely young, or just rejuved. Pale, dark hair currently a mess, high cheekbones on clear-skinned face, female. *Click.* Alone. *Click.* Asking for Frank the Nose by name. *Click.* Is there a story here? *Click.* Get the story ...

"A friend said I should get in touch with you," said the kid. "You're the journalist who's looking into the—the end of Moscow?"

"What if I am?" Frank asked. She looked tense, worried about something. But what?

"I was born there," she mumbled. "I grew up on Old Newfie, uh, portal station eleven. We were evacuated after—in time—"

"Have a seat." Frank gestured at the other side of the sofa, trying to keep his face still. She flopped down in a heap of knees and elbows and impossibly long limbs. *So what's she doing* here? "You said something about a friend?" he asked. "What's your name?"

"You can call me Wednesday," she said nervously. "Uh, there are people"— she glanced over her shoulder as if she expected assassins to come swarming out of the walls—"No, uh, no! That's not where to begin. Why can't I get this right?" She ended on a note of plaintive despair, as if she was about to start tugging her hair.

Frank leaned back, watching her but trying to give her some space to decompress in. She was tired and edgy. There was something indefinable about her, the insecurity of the exile. He'd seen it before. *She's from Moscow!* This could be good. If true, she'd make excellent local color for his dispatches—the personal angle, the woman in exile, a viewpoint to segue into for a situation report and editorial frame. Then he felt a stab of concern. *What's she doing here, looking for me? Is she in trouble?* "Why did you want to talk to me?" he asked gently. "And what are you doing here?"

She looked around again. "I—shit!" Her face fell. "I, uh, I have to give a message to you."

"A message." Frank had an itchy feeling in the palms of his hands. The lead item walking in off the street to spill his or her guts into the car of a waiting reporter, the exclusive waiting to happen, was a legend in the trade. It so rarely happened, vastly outnumbered by hoaxers and time-wasters, but when it did—*Let's not get ahead of the game,* he told himself sternly. He watched her eyes and she stared right back. "Begin with the beginning," he suggested. "Who's your message from? And who's it for?"

She huddled in the corner of the sofa as if it was the only stable place in her universe. "It's, um, going to sound crazy. But I shouldn't be here. On this ship, I mean. I mean, I've *got* to be here, because if I stayed behind I wouldn't be safe. But I'm not *supposed* to be here, if you see what I mean."

"Not supposed—do you have a ticket?" he asked. His brow wrinkled.

"Yes." She managed a faint flicker of what might have been an impish grin if she hadn't been so close to exhaustion. "Thanks to Herman."

"Uh-huh." *Is she a crazy?* Frank wondered. *This could be trouble*... He pushed the thought aside.

"The—information—I've got for you is that if you visit Old New—sorry, portal station eleven, and go down to cylinder four, kilo deck, segment green, and look in the public facility there you'll find a corpse with his head down the toilet. And, uh, behind the counter of the police station in cylinder six, segment orange, there's a leather attaché case with handwritten orders in, like, real ink on paper, saying that whoever the orders are for is to wipe all the customs records, trash the immigration tracking and control system—but bring a single copy home—and if necessary, kill anyone who looks like they're going to notice what's going on. Fat chance, as the customs and immigration cops were pulled out six months earlier, but the man in the toilet was in uniform—" She swallowed.

Frank realized that his fingers were digging into the arm of the sofa so tightly that the soft leather was threatening to rip. "Customs records?" he said mildly. "Who told you to tell me this?" he asked. "Your friend?"

"Herman," she said, deadpan. "My fairy godfather. Okay, my rich uncle then."

"Hmm." He gave her a long, cool stare. Is *she a crazy*? "This message—"

"Ah, shit." She waved a hand in front of her face. "I'm no good at lying," she said guiltily. "Listen, I need your help. Herman said you'd know what to do. They're, uh, he said the same people, the ones who killed the cop—he's down as missing in the evacuation, nobody wanted to go back for him—are looking for anyone who might be a witness. They tried—" she took a deep breath. "No, *someone* tried to mug me a few days ago. Or worse. I got away. They're looking for me because the shipboard security came back onto the station and found me and I'm one of the only loose ends, and now they're not panicking over the evacuation they're trying to tie everything up..." She subsided in confusion.

"Oh." *Oh very good, Frank,* he told himself sarcastically. *How very articulate of you!* He shook his head. "Let me get this straight. You're not alone. You ran across something on your station before the evacuation, right before it. Something you think is important. Now someone's trying to kill you, you think, so you hopped aboard this ship. Is that substantially correct?"

She nodded violently. "Yeah."

Okay. Heads she's a kook, tails she's tripped over something very smelly indeed. What should I do? Put that way, it was fairly obvious: run some background checks, try to prove she was a kook before accepting anything at face value. But she didn't *look* crazy. What she looked like was a tired, shaky young woman who'd been booted out of her life by forces beyond her control. Frank shuffled against the cushions, struggling to sit up. "Do you have any idea who the, uh, killers might be?"

"Well." She looked uncertain. "The ship that took us off was from Dresden. And the case with the orders was in the Captain's luggage store."

"It was—" Frank stared at her. "How did you get to see it then?"

"I guess you could say I broke in." She screwed her face into something that might have been meant to look like an embarrassed smile.

"You—" Frank stared some more. "I think you'd better tell me all about it," he said quietly. "By the way, the public spaces here are all monitored, all the time. But the staterooms are private. If you're going to say anything that might incriminate you, we ought to go somewhere that isn't being recorded. Do you have a room?"

"Uh, I guess so." She looked at him uncertainly. "My ticket says I do, but I didn't choose it. And I've only just come aboard." She glanced at the doorway self-consciously. "I haven't even bought any stuff yet. I was in a real hurry."

"Okay, we'll go wherever your ticket says. If you don't mind, I'd like to record an interview and check some facts out. Then—" A thought struck him. "Do you have any money?" he asked.

"I don't know." She looked even more uncertain. "My friend wired me some, I think."

"You think?"

"There are too many zeroes." Her eyes were wide.

"Hmm. Well, if that's a problem, I'll see what I can sort out for you. WhiteStar likes to soak you for extras, but at least on board this ship you won't want for complimentary scented Egyptian cotton towels and luxury pedicure kits. And if we're—" He paused. "Where did you friend buy you a ticket to?" he asked.

"Some place called, uh, Newpeace?"

Shit! An icy calm descended on Frank. "Well, I think we might just have to see about extending it a bit farther. All the way to Earth itself, and maybe back home afterward."

"Why?"

"Newpeace isn't somewhere I'd want to send my worst enemy. It's run by scum who call themselves the ReMastered."

"Oh no!"

Suddenly she was on her feet, looking alarmed. Frank blinked in surprise. "What have you heard about them?" he demanded.

"Herman said it was probably the ReMastered who killed my—" She choked up, her shoulders shaking.

"Let's go to my room," Frank said quietly, his pulse roaring in his ears. "We can talk about it there."

she'd gone to ground in the morning lounge on A deck, finding a niche between a potted coconut palm and a baby grand piano the color of stressed titanium. Eyes swiveling, refugee instincts humming. This wasn't anything like the trash hauler she'd been on, years ago. Everything around her screamed *luxury!* at high volume. *What am I meant to do here? If anyone finds me—* She had a ticket. Nobody was going to haul her off to the nearest airlock and make her walk home. Still, just being there felt profoundly wrong, and then there was whatever had happened to her family. Just trying not to think about it was a draining experience.

"Okay, Herman, what have you got me into?" she muttered angrily. A twist of her storage ring got her into the files he'd left her. They were copious, but at least he'd left an introduction.

"As soon as you're on board, search for Frank the Nose and tell him about the items you left aboard Old Newfie. Do so before the ship departs. That will give him time to file a news report, after which your pursuers will be unable to achieve their goal of concealing the existence of the items by killing you. Let me emphasize this: Until you publicize the existence of the sealed orders and the body, your life is in danger. Once you have done so, they can gain nothing by killing you and may only lend credence to your story. And here's a second point. Don't assume that all ReMastered are automatically members of the group hunting you. They're riddled with factions, and whoever is after you may even be using them as a cover. Don't assume *anything*.

"Once you have broken the story, remain aboard the liner. Enjoy the facilities. You are traveling in Sybarite class with a personal allowance suitable to an heiress of independent means. Consider this to be part payment for your earlier work on my behalf. If you become bored by the formal passenger facilities—the shops, the bars and dining rooms, the dances and other social events—feel free to use the attached technical schemata to discreetly explore the service and maintenance spaces of the liner. If anyone asks you, your cover story is that you are a rich, idle, bored heiress. The Moscow trust has paid up a dividend big enough that your parents have agreed to you undertaking a grand tour as a prelude to your coming out. Here's a hint: I don't mind if you're no good at spending money like water, but please find time to become bored. There will be an exam later.

"The next stop on your itinerary is New Dresden, for a four-and-a-half-day layover. The previous New Dresdener government is believed by many people to be responsible for the destruction of your home world. As you probably realize by now, that is untrue. Your layover coincides with the annual remembrance ceremony at the Muscovite embassy in the capital, Sarajevo. I would appreciate it if you would attend the ceremony. You might want to buy something more formal to wear before doing so.

"I will provide further instructions for you on arrival in New Dresden orbit. To recap: Find Frank the Nose and tell him about your adventure on Old Newfie. Doing so will ensure that you have an uneventful voyage. Feel free to explore the ship. On arrival, attend the remembrance ceremony at the embassy. *Bon voyage!*"

She shook her head in bafflement, but still began to do as he suggested. The ship hadn't even departed yet, and residual nerves kept Wednesday looking over her shoulder as the big guy took her straight to an elevator, tastefully hidden behind a trompe l'oeil painting on one wall. *What if Leo or whatever he's called followed me aboard?* But something about the hulking journalist made her feel safe: he looked like he could walk through walls, but he was mild enough toward her, clearly aware that his appearance tended to intimidate and trying not to look threatening.

The elevator car was narrow and sparse, polished metal with a button-laden control panel. "It's a crew car," he explained, finger-pecking at the panel. "Sven showed me how to use them. They don't just go up and down, they go—aha!" The car lurched sideways, began to ascend, then twirled back on its route for a while before coming to a halt. The doors opened on a dimly lit corridor that reminded Wednesday of a hotel her parents had once taken her and Jerm to, a couple of years ago. "Here we are."

Frank's stateroom reinforced the sense of being in a hotel suite—a rumpled, used one pervaded by a horrible, indefinable stink, as if something had died there. She wrinkled her nose as he closed the door and ambled over to the writing desk, feeling a momentary unease. It passed as he bent down and pulled out a compact multimedia recording deck and positioned it on the table. "Sit down," he invited. "Make yourself at home." He smiled alarmingly. "This is a recording cut. We'll do this once, then I'll mail it right back to Joe—she's my researcher and desk ed, back home—immediately. Joe can edit it into shape for a release. The sooner it hits the blog, the better. Comfortable? Okay. Let's start. Would you tell me your name? It'll go better if you look straight at the pickup..."

Almost an hour later, Wednesday was growing hoarse. On top of that, she was bone-tired and bored with repeating herself, not to say upset. While Frank was surprisingly gentle and understanding, having to relive the horror of those minutes in the corridor outside her home was disturbing, dredging up tears she'd thought she had under control. She'd managed to snatch a couple of hours of uneasy sleep in her stolen cattle-class seats aboard the ferry, but then she'd had the stress of finding her way to the ship and tracking down Frank. "I need something to drink," she said. "And—"

"I said I'd buy you breakfast, didn't I? I'm sorry, I got carried away." Frank sounded apologetic—and something else. He hauled out a pad and pointed it at her. "Pick anything on the menu—anything you like. Listen, that was a great interview." He frowned at the door. "Scum, like I said." Judging from his thunderous expression there ought to be a huge blackened hole in the wall. "Now, I'm going to put a cover on that interview and push it out right away as unsubstantiated rumor. I mean, you really don't want to leave this sitting around, do you? The sooner we get some physical corroboration, the better, though that might take a while. But the sooner this is out, the sooner the scum who killed your family are going to learn that trying to shut you up was a mistake." He was positively glowering.

"You said you knew something about the—the ReMastered?" she asked diffidently.

"I, I—" He closed his mouth and shook his head angrily, like a bear pestered by hornets. Then he sighed. "Yes, I know something about the ReMastered," he admitted. "Much more than I want to. I'm just surprised they're snooping around Septagon." He looked thoughtful. "Checking out your story about the station is going to cost real money. Need to charter a ship if I have to go poking around a hot station behind a supernova shock front. But the rest's easy enough. You want to order up some food and make yourself at home in here?"

"Mmph." Wednesday finger-shopped listlessly for agedashi tofu and tuna-skin hand rolls and sing chow noodles and a luminous green smart drink that promised to banish fatigue. "Food. I remember that."

"Chill out." Frank unpacked a battered-looking pocket keyboard of antique design and began typing like a machine gun. "When you're ready, give it to me and I'll put the order on my tab."

"Do you think I'm in danger?" she asked, her voice catching.

He looked her in the eye, and for the first time she realized that he looked worried. Fear didn't belong on that face, atop a gorilla of a man. It was just plain wrong. "Listen, the sooner this is on the net, the better for both of us," he said. "So if you don't mind—" He went back to hammering the keyboard.

"Sure." Wednesday sighed. She finished her menu selections and shoved the pad back at his side of the desk. "Journalists. Feh!" She spread her fingers out, admiring the rings on her left hand. Smart rings, untraceable fake rings, rings that claimed she was a rich bitch and came with sealed orders. *What's it really like to be rich?* she wondered.

The Times of London—*thundering the news since 1785! Now brought to you by Frank the Nose, sponsored by Thurn und Taxis Arbeitsgemeinschaft, DisneyMob Amusements, NPO Mikoyan-Gurevitch Spaceyards, Motorola Banking al-Failaka, Glossolalia Translatronics, and The First Universal Church of Kermit.*

EXCLUSIVE: Skullduggery in Septagon, Murderers in Moscow

The *Times* has obtained an exclusive interview with a young survivor of the destroyed Moscow system that suggests agents of an external power have something to hide—*after* the holocaust.

Wednesday Shadowmist (not her real name), 19, is a citizen of the former planetary republic of Moscow. She and her family survived the induced nova that destroyed their home world because they lived on Portal Station

Eleven, Old Newfie, a refueling and transfer station nearly a light year from the star. They were evacuated aboard a starship belonging to a Dresdener merchant agency and resettled in one of the Septagonese orbitals. For their safety, the *Times* is not disclosing which one.

Immediately prior to the evacuation, Wednesday returned to the portal station for her own reasons. While there, she discovered a body, believed to be that of Customs Officer Gareth Smaile, who was listed as "missing" after the evacuation. Officer Smaile is confirmed as having been one of the individuals responsible for maintaining immigration records for persons entering and leaving Moscow system via the portal station, before the holocaust. When Wednesday found him he appeared to have been murdered—a unique event on a small colony that averaged one violent crime every five years.

Abandoned by the body were written instructions to parties unknown requesting that all customs records relating to immigration be wiped prior to evacuation, save for a single copy that was to be returned to the author of the letter.

Taking this report at face value, someone wants to cover up the fact that they quietly entered or departed Moscow system through Portal Station Eleven shortly before the catastrophe. Whoever they were, they had an agent or agents aboard the Dresdener starship *Long March* when it called at Old Newfie to evacuate the survivors—an agent who was willing to commit murder.

If this is a hoax, it's a violent one. [Newshound: Trace police blotter report CM-6/9/312-04-23-19-24A, double murder.] Two hit men were sent after our informant; she evaded them, unlike the rest of her family, who woke up dead two days ago. Someone maliciously bypassed the gas-conditioning inlet to their home and disabled the alarms. Police crime investigation officer Robin Gough characterized the murder as an "extremely professional" hit, and says she's looking for two men [Newshound: Trace police arrest warrant W/CM-6/9/312-B4] wanted for murder. Here's a hint: Septagon police are efficient enough that if they haven't been found within half an hour, they're not going to be found at all because they're not on the station anymore.

The *Times* is not yet certain about what's going on, but

it appears to be a particularly nasty game of spy-versus-spy. The implication—that there is an attempt in progress to cover up the true story of the destruction of Moscow—appears compelling, and we will continue to investigate it. In the meantime, we are releasing this raw and uncooked interview in order to render pointless further attempts to maintain the cover by murdering the surviving witnesses.

The *Times* has this message for the culprits, whoever they are: The truth will out!

Ends (*Times* Editorial)

cymbals chimed: the floor gave a faint lurch, almost imperceptible, barely sufficient to rattle the china in the dining lounges as the huge liner cut over to onboard gravity. Junior Flight Lieutenant Steffi Grace shook her head. "That's not very good."

"It's within tolerances, but only just," agreed her boss, Flying Officer Max Fromm. He pointed at the big status board in front of her. "Want to tell me why?"

"Hmm. Kernel balance looks good. We've stabilized nicely, and the mass distribution is spot on—no problems there. Um. I don't see anything on board. But the station..." She paused, then brought up a map of the ambient gravity polarization field. "Oh. We picked up a little torque from the station's generators when we tripped out. Is that what you're after?"

"No, but it'll do." Fromm nodded. "Remember that. These big new platforms the Septs are building kick back." He brought back the original systems map. "Now, you're going to talk me through the first stage of our departure, aren't you?"

Steffi nodded, and began to take him through the series of steps that the Captain and her bridge crew would be running upstairs as they maneuvered the huge liner clear of the Noctis docking tree. Down here in the live training room things weren't as tense; just another session in the simulator, shadowing the bridge team. The training room was cramped, crammed with console emulators and with space for only a couple of people to crowd inside. In an emergency it could double as a replacement bridge—but it would have to be a truly desperate emergency to take out the flight deck, five levels down inside the hull.

"Okay, now she's pumping up the C-head ring. That's, um, five giga-Teslas? That's way more than she needs to maintain a steady one-gee field. Is she planning on buffering some really heavy shocks? Attitude control—we're steady. No thermal roll to speak of, not out here in Septagon B, so she's put just enough spin on the outer hull to hold us steady as we back out at five meters per second. That's going to take, uh, two minutes until we're clear far enough to begin a slow pitch up toward the departure corridor. Am I right?"

"So far so good." Max leaned back in his chair. "I hate these stations," he said conversationally. "It's not as if there's much other traffic—we've got nearly a thousand seconds to clear the approaches—but it's so damn crowded here it's like threading a needle with a mooring cable."

"One wrong nudge—"

"Yeah." The *Romanov* was a huge beast. Beehive shaped, it was three hundred meters in diameter at its fattest and nearly five hundred meters long. The enormously massive singularity lurking inside its drive kernel supplied it with power and let it twist spacetime into knots, but was absolutely no use for close-range maneuvering; and the hot thrusters it could use for altitude control would strip the skin off a hab if the Captain lit her up within a couple of kilometers. That left only the cold thrusters and gyrodynes for maintaining altitude during departure—but they had about as much effect as a team of ants trying to kick a dead whale down a beach. "One-sixty seconds to burner ignition, and we can crank up to departure speed, a hundred meters per second. Then just under an hour and a half to make it out to fifty kilometers and another blip on the burners to take us up to a thousand meters per second at half a gee. Another two hundred kilometers out, then we begin kernel spin-up. I haven't looked at the flight plan for this run, but if she does her usual, once the kernel is up and running the Captain will crank us up to twenty gees and hold for about twelve hours. And she won't mess around. That's why she ran up the bulkhead rings now, when she's got spare power to pump into them." He stretched his arms out overhead, almost touching the damage control board. "Seen one departure, seen 'em all. Until the next time."

"Right." Steffi pushed back her chair. "Do we have time for a coffee before the burn sequence?"

"I don't see why not."

Steffi stood up and squeezed past Max's chair, trailing a hand across his shoulder in passing. He pretended not to notice, but she caught the ghost of his smile reflected in the screens as she turned toward the door. Two or three weeks of stealing time together didn't make for a serious relationship in her estimate, but it beat sleeping alone on her first long cruise, and Max was more considerate than she'd expected. Not that she was incapable of coping. WhiteStar didn't employ child labor, and she'd joined up at thirty-two, with her first career under her: she'd known exactly what she was letting herself in for. If anyone had accused him of taking advantage of her, she'd have taken a pointy stick to them. But so far discretion had paid off, and Steffi had no complaints.

There was a vending machine near the facilities pod down the gray-painted crew corridor. She punched for two glasses of iced latte, thought about some biscuits, and decided against it. Bridge crew, even trainee bridge crew, dined with the upper-class passengers on a rota, and Max was up for dinner at the end of his shift in a couple of hours. It wouldn't do to spoil his appetite. She was about to head back to the auxiliary control center when she spotted a stranger in the corridor outside—probably a passenger, judging by his lack of ID. "Can I help you?" she asked, sizing him up. He was tall, blond, male, blandly handsome, and built like an army recruiting poster. *Not at all like Max,* a little voice in the back of her head said critically.

"Yah, yes. I was told the, ah, training bridge was on this level?" He had a strange accent, not hard to understand but slightly stilted. "I was told it was possible to visit it?"

"Yes, it is." She nodded. "But I'm afraid you'll have to make an appointment if you want to look around. It's in use throughout the voyage, and right now it's the backup control center—in case there's a problem with the main bridge. Are you wanting a tour?" He nodded. "In that case"—she steered him toward the nearest door back into passenger country—"can I suggest you take it up with your liaison officer after dinner? He or she will be able to take your details and arrange something for you tomorrow or the day after. I've got to get back to work now, so if you'll excuse me . . ."

She gently pushed him back toward the passenger section, waiting until he finished nodding and the door closed. Then she breathed a sigh of relief and ducked back through the closest door into wonderland. Max raised an eyebrow at her. "She's begun pushback," he said. "What kept you?"

"The passengers are wandering." She passed him an iced coffee. "I had to herd one out of the corridor just now."

"Happens every voyage. You lock a couple of thousand bored monkeys in a tin can, and you've got to expect one or two to go exploring. They'll stop poking around eventually, when they realize everything interesting is sealed off. Just remember to keep your cabin door locked whether you're in or out."

"Hah. I'll do that." She raised her glass. "Here's to a quiet life..."

"Wow!" Wednesday looked around the room, her eyes wide. *It's bigger than my bedroom back home. It's bigger than our entire apartment!* A pang of loss bit her. She shoved it aside hastily.

She stood in the middle of an ocean of deep-pile carpet the color of clotted cream and looked about. The room was so wide that the ceiling seemed low, even though it was out of reach. A couple of sofas and an occasional table huddled at one end as if they were lonely. One wall looked like raw, undressed stonework; there was a door in it, with a curved, pointy bit at the top, opening onto a boudoir like something out of a medieval fantasy, all rich wooden paneling and tapestries. A huge four-poster bed completed the impression, but the medievalism was only skin-deep. The next door along led to a bathroom with a tub almost as large as the bed recessed into the white-tiled floor.

"If you need anything, please call the purser's office," the steward told her. "Someone will be on hand to help you at all hours. Your trip itinerary should be able to tell you how all the suite utilities work, including the fabber in the closet over there." (The closet lurking behind another open gothic archway looked to be about the size of a small factory.) "Do you need anything else right now?" he asked.

"Uh, no." She looked around. "I mean, yeah, I have to go buy some odds and ends. But, uh, not right now."

"By your leave." He turned and left, smiling oddly, and the door to the corridor—no, the promenade deck, they called it—closed behind her.

"Wow!" she repeated. Then she glanced at the door. "Door, lock yourself." There was a discreet *clack* from the frame. "Wow!"

Wednesday ambled over to the nearest sofa and flopped down in it, then unfastened her boots. "Ouch." More than a day of wearing them had left her feet feeling like raw meat: she curled her toes in the carpet for almost a minute with her eyes closed, writhing slightly and panting. "Oh, that is so good!" After another minute, other senses began to intrude. "Hmm."

She walked toward the bathroom, leaving a trail of discarded clothing behind her. By the time she reached it she was naked. "Shower, shower, where are you?" she called. It turned out that the shower was in a separate cubicle from the toilet, the bathroom proper, and the— "A full-body hair remover?" She boggled slightly. What would you want to remove all your hair for? Legs or armpits or pubes she could see, but eyebrows?

"Manicure and pedicure facilities are available on D deck," recited a recording, just grainy enough not to make her wonder if a real person was in the room with her. "A range of basic clothing is available from the apartment fab. Fitted and designer items are available from the tailors on F deck . See the panel beside the sink for additional makeover and service options."

"Urk." Wednesday backed toward the shower cubicle, pulled a face, and sniffed one armpit. "Eew!" *First things first. What did Herman say? You're a rich, idle, bored heiress: play the part.*

She showered thoroughly, staying under the spray nozzles until her skin felt as if it was going to come off. She washed her hair thoroughly, trying to get the grit and desperation of the past week off her body. The all-body depilator she gave a wide berth— the consequences of an accident with the controls could be too embarrassing for words—but the mirror wall by the sink had a full skin programmer that could talk to her chromatophores, so she spent an absorbing half hour reprogramming her makeup: night-dark eyeliner, blue lips, dead white skin, and glossy black hair. *If anyone asks, I'm in mourning,* she thought, and a sudden stab of agonizing guilt made it less than a lie.

She hatched from the bathroom an hour and a half later, naked as the day she was born. The lounge seemed enormous, cold, and empty. Worse, she couldn't imagine putting on her old clothes. So she wandered over to the closet and looked inside. "Is there a clothing menu for this thing?" she asked.

A lightbug led her to the fabber, a large boxy extrusion from the wall of a walk-in wardrobe she hadn't suspected. "Please select options. Materials and energy will be billed to your room service total."

"Oh." Five minutes scrolling through patterns convinced her of one thing: whoever'd programmed the fab's design library hadn't done so with her in mind. Eventually she settled for some basic underwear, a pair of black trousers and a long-sleeved top that wasn't too offensive, and rubber-soled socks for her feet. The fab hummed and burped up a load of hot, fresh clothing a minute later, still smelling faintly of solvents. Wednesday pulled them on immediately. *Bet the shops are more expensive but have better stuff,* she thought cynically.

An hour spent poking around the shops on F deck convinced her that she was right. The names were unfamiliar, but the attitude of the staff—and the items in the displays—said it all. They were priced to satisfy exactly the sort of rich bitch Herman had suggested she play, but as far as Wednesday was concerned they were a dead loss: the target audience was too old, even if they were well preserved. The ultrafemme gowns and dresses had icky semiotics, the shops for people from cultures with sumptuary laws and dress codes were too weird, the everyday stuff was too formal—*What would I want to do with that, wear it to a business meeting?* she thought, fingering one exquisitely tailored jacket—and there was nothing flaky or uplevel to catch her imagination. No fun.

In the end, she bought a lacy white trouser-skirt combination to wear to dinner, and left it at that. The horrible truth was beginning to dawn on her: *I've got an enormous suite to myself, but nothing to do! And I'm here for a* week! *With no toys.* Wednesday didn't have anyone to share the voyage with unless she felt like pestering Frank, and she wasn't sure how he'd respond. He *looked* young, but it was hard to tell. *And he's got a job to do. And there's no news.* Not while the ship was engaged in a series of causality-violating jumps, lock-stitching space time to its drive kernel. *And the shops are crap.* She glanced across the diamond-walled atrium in growing disbelief. *And I bet the other Sybarite-class passengers are all boring assholes, diplomats, and rich old business queens and all.* Clearly, very few people her age traveled this way.

I'm already bored! And there are still three hours to go before dinner!

ғeeᴅɪɴɢ ᴛɪᴍe aᴛ the zoo," Max muttered darkly. "Wonder who they're feeding?"

"The social director, with any luck. Stuffed and basted." Steffi kept a straight face, staring right ahead as they headed into the dining room. "Stupid custom."

"Now, *now.*" Max nodded politely to a plumply padded dowager whose thirty-year physique belied the fact that her formal business suit was at least a century out of fashion. "Good evening, Mrs. Borozovski! How are you tonight?"

"I'm fine, Mr. Fromm!" She bobbed slightly, as if she'd

already been hitting the martinis. "And who's your little friend? A new squirt, or am I very mistaken?"

"Ahem. Allow me to introduce Junior Flight Lieutenant Stephanie Grace, our newest flight operations officer. If I may beg your pardon, it's considered bad form to refer to trainees as squirts, outside of the training academy; and in any case, Lieutenant Grace has graduate degrees in relativistic dynamics and engineering."

"Oh, I'm so sorry!" To her credit, the dowager flushed slightly.

"It's perfectly all right." Steffi forced a smile and breathed a sigh of relief when Max peeled off to steer Mrs. Borozovski toward a table. *No, I don't mind being patronized by rich drones one little bit, Mrs. Borozovski. Now, where's the table I'm supposed to ride herd on?*

It was a completely spurious ritual, from Steffi's viewpoint. All the business class and higher suites were fully self-catering. There was no damn *need* to have a central galley and serve up a restricted menu and waste the valuable time of human chefs, not to mention the line officers who were required to turn up wearing mess uniforms and act like dinner party hosts. On the other hand, as Commodore Martindale had put it back at staff college, the difference between a steerage passenger flying in cold sleep and a Sybarite-class passenger flying in a luxury apartment was about two thousand ecus per day of transit time—and the experience. Any peasant could afford to travel cold, but to balance the books and make for a healthy profit required cosseting the rich idiots and honeymooning couples, to which end any passenger line worthy of the name devoted considerable ingenuity. Up to and including providing etiquette training for engineers, tailored dress uniforms for desk-pushers, and anything else that might help turn a boring voyage into a uniquely memorable experience for the upper crust. Which *especially* meant sparing no expense over the first night and subsequent weekly banquets. *At least they're not as bad as the house apes Sven puts up with,* she thought mordantly. *If I had his end of this job, I swear I'd go nuts...*

At least the honeymooning couples mostly stuck to ordering from room service or the food fabs in their rooms. Which left her sitting at the head of a table of twelve extremely lucrative passengers—think of it as twenty-four thousand ecus a day in value added to the bottom line—smiling, nodding politely, introducing them to one another, answering their inane questions, and passing the port.

Steffi made her way to her table, guided by a discreet pipper on the cuff of her brocade jacket. A handful of passengers had already arrived, but they knew enough to stand up as she arrived. "Please, be seated," she said, smiling easily as her chair slid out and retracted its arms for her. She nodded to the passengers, and one or two of them nodded back or even said "hello." Or something. She wasn't so sure about the sullen-looking girl in the deliberately slashed black lace top and hair that looked as if she'd stuck her fingers in a power socket, but the three hail-fellow-well-met types in the similar green shirts, two blond men and a straw-haired woman, all looked as if they were about to jump up and salute her. The fat probably-a-merchant-banker and her anorexic beanpole of a male companion just ignored her—probably offended that she wasn't at least a commander—and the withered old actuary from Turku didn't seem to notice her, but that was par for the course. *Senile old cretin,* Steffi thought, writing him off. Anyone that rich who wouldn't stump up the cash for a telomere reset and AGE purge when their hair was turning white was not worth paying attention to. The middle-aged lady cellist from Nippon looked friendly enough, but a bit confused—her translator wasn't keeping up with the conversation—and that just left a honeymooning couple who had predictably elected to call room service instead.

"I'm Junior Flight Lieutenant Steffi Grace, and, on behalf of WhiteStar Lines, I'd like to welcome you to our table for the first night banquet en route to New Dresden. If you'd like to examine the menu, I'm sure your stewards will be with you shortly. In the meantime, I'd like to particularly recommend the—" she glanced at her cuff—"Venusian Cabernet Sauvignon blanc to accompany the salmon entrées." Imported at vast expense from the diamond-domed vineyards of Ishtar Planitia, the better to stroke the egos of the twenty-four-thousand-ecu diners.

Things went all right through the entrées, and Steffi made sure to knock back her antidrunk cap with the first mouthful of wine. It *was* an okay vintage, if you could get past the fact that it was wine, and—stripped of the ability to get drunk on it—wine was just sour grape juice. "Can I ask where you're from?" she asked the square-jawed blonde as she filled her glass. "I've seen you around, I think, but we haven't spoken before."

"I am Mathilde, of clade Todt, division Sixt. These are my clade-mates Peter and Hans," said the woman, waving one beefy hand to take in the strapping young men to either side of her. *Are they young?* wondered Steffi: they looked awfully self-assured and well coordinated. Normally you didn't see that sort of instinctive grace in anyone who was less than sixty, not without martial arts practice. Most people eventually picked up that kind of economical motion if their bodies didn't nose-dive into senescence by middle age, before they had time to mature, but this looked like the product of hard training, if not anabolic steroids. "We are traveling to Newpeace, as a youth enlightenment and learning mission." She smiled superciliously. "That is, we are to learn about the other worlds that have discovered the benefits of ReMastery and spread harmony among them."

"Uh-huh. And what *is* it, to be ReMastered, if you don't mind my asking? Is it some sort of club?" Steffi prodded. They were, after all, paying her wages. Curiosity about her employers was a powerful instinct.

"It is everything," Mathilde said gushingly. She caught herself. "It is a way of life." Slightly shy and bashful now, as if she had let too much slip: "It is very fulfilling."

"Yes, but—" Steffi felt her forehead wrinkling with concentration. *Why do I feel as if I'm being looked down on?* she wondered. *Never mind.* "And you?" she asked the kid with the black hair. If she *was* a kid; she was about the same build as Steffi, after all.

"Oh, don't mind me, I'll just sit in this corner and drink myself into a new liver. I'm sure the trust fund will pay." The last sentence came out in a monotone as she caught Steffi's eye, and Steffi realized: *Something's wrong here.*

"We try to take our drinking easy, at least until after the meal," she said lightly. "What was your name again?"

"Wednesday," the girl—*Young woman? Dangerous drunk?*—said quietly. "That's what they call me. Victoria Strowger on your passenger list. That's what my ID calls me."

"Whichever you prefer," Steffi said warily.

The starters arrived, delicately poached small medallions of salmon served under a white sauce, and Steffi managed to get fat Fiona the merchant banker rolling on a paean to the merits of virtual-rate currency triangulation versus more indirect, causality-conserving means of converting funds between worlds separated by a gulf of light years. She was somewhat relieved to find that a lecture on the credit control implications of time travel was sufficient to hold the rapt if slightly incomprehending attention of the three youth leaders from clade Todt, whatever that was. Wednesday, meanwhile, plowed into her third glass of wine with a grim determination that reminded Steffi of some of the much older and more grizzled travelers she'd met—not actual alcoholics, but people possessed by a demon that badly wanted them to wake up with a hangover on the morrow, a demon that demanded an exorcism by the most painful terms available short of self-mutilation. Getting drunk this soon in a voyage, before the boredom began to bite, wasn't a healthy sign. And as for her dress sense, even though Steffi was no follower of style, she could see that Wednesday was relying on a talent for improvisation that must have been labeled "not needed on voyage."

The shit refrained from hitting the fan until dessert was served. Steffi had made the tactical mistake of asking Mathilde again just what being ReMastered could do for her—*Is it a religion? Or a political theory?* she'd been wondering ever since the *very fulfilling* crack—and Mathilde decided to deliver a lecture. "Being ReMastered would give you a new perspective on life," Mathilde explained earnestly to the entire table. Even Peter and Hans nodded appreciatively. "It is a way of life that ensures all our actions are directed toward the greatest good. We are not, however, slaves: there is none of the submissiveness of the decadent and degenerate Dar al-Islam. We are fresh and free and strong and joyfully bend our shoulders to the great work out of common cause, with the aim of building a bright future in which all humans will be free to maximize their potential, free of the shadow of the antihuman Eschaton, and free of the chains of superstitious unscientific thinking."

Wednesday, who until then had been rolling the stem of her empty wineglass between her fingers—Steffi had discreetly scaled back on the frequency of top-ups after her fourth—put her glass down on the table. She licked a fingertip, and began slowly rubbing it around the lip of the glass.

"The clades of the ReMastered are organized among divisions, and their members work together. We rear our children in the best way, with all the devotion and attention to detail that a creche can deliver, and we find useful and meaningful work for them as soon as they are old enough to need purpose and direction. We teach morality—not the morality of the weak, but the morality of the strong—and we raise them to be healthy; the best phenotypes go back into the pool to generate the next harvest, but we don't simply leave that to brute nature. As intelligent beings we are above random chance." *Whir, whir* went Wednesday's finger. "We want strong, healthy, intelligent workers, not degenerate secondhanders and drones—"

Mathilde stopped talking, apparently oblivious to the glassy-eyed and slightly horrified stares she was receiving from the merchant banker and the actuary, and glared at Wednesday. "Stop doing that," she snapped.

"Tell me what happens to the people you *don't need*," Wednesday said in a threatening monotone, "then I'll stop."

"We do not do anything—" Mathilde caught herself, took a deep breath, and looked down her nose at Wednesday. "Occasionally a planetary government petitions us for admission. Then we send advisers to help them work out how best to deal with their criminal elements and decadent factions. *Will* you stop doing that, child? It is disruptive. I would go further and say it was typical of your indolence if I didn't believe this was merely an aberration on your part." She smiled, baring even, gleaming teeth that gave the lie to her veiled jab.

Wednesday smiled right back and kept rubbing the rim of the glass. The Japanese lady cellist chose that moment to join in with her own fingertip, smiling and nodding at her in linguistically challenged camaraderie. Steffi glanced at Mathilde. If looks could kill, Wednesday would be a smoking hole in the bulkhead. "If you don't take over worlds," Wednesday said, slurring slightly, "how's it that people *want* to join you? 'Mean t'say, I've only heard a bit about the concentration camps, an' obviously he's gotta grudge, but you'd think the summary executions and forced labor'd make joining the ReMastered 'bout as popular as rabies." She bared her teeth at Steffi, in a flicker of amusement that vanished as fast as it had come. *Hum, hum, hum* went the fingertip.

"There are no concentration camps," Mathilde said icily. "Our enemies spread lies"—her look took in the whole length of the table, as if no one was above suspicion—"and obviously some fools fall for them." She lingered over Wednesday. "But repeating such slanders—"

"Wanna meet anin—an, uh, ex-inmate?" Wednesday cocked her head on one side. *She's drunk as a skunk,* Steffi realized with a cold feeling in her overfull stomach. *Damn, how'd she get so shit-faced? She's handling it well, but*—The last thing she needed was Mathilde going for Wednesday's throat over the cheeseboard. Not if she wanted to keep the other Syb-class passengers happy. "Got least one of 'em aboard this ship. Call *him* a liar, why don'tcha."

"I think that's quite enough." Steffi forced herself to smile. "Time to change the subject, if you don't mind," she added, with a warning glance at Wednesday. But the kid couldn't seem to take the hint, even when it was delivered by sledgehammer.

"I've had more than enough," Wednesday slurred, sitting up straight but staying focused on Mathilde. *They're like a pair of cats, squaring off,* Steffi realized, wondering if she was going to have to break up a fight. Except that Mathilde didn't look remotely drunk, and Wednesday looked as if she was too drunk to care that the ReMastered woman was built like the northern end of a southbound assault gunship, with muscles where most people had opinions. "I'm *sick* of this bullshit. Here we all are, sitting round"—she waved a hand vaguely at the rest of the dining room, then blinked in surprise—"sitting round the table when down in steerage refugee kids are, are..."

Steffi was out of her chair almost before she realized she'd come to a decision. Wednesday's back was tense as steel when she wrapped one arm around her shoulders. "Come on," she said gently. "Come with me. You're right, you don't need to be here. Leave everything to me, I'll get it sorted out. Stand up?" For a moment she was sure it wouldn't work, but a second later Wednesday pushed herself upright. She would have been swaying but for Steffi's supporting arm. "Come on, come with me. You're doing fine." She steered Wednesday round toward the nearest door, barely noticing the ReMastered woman's stone-hard glare drilling into her—or was it Wednesday? "Come on." To the gold braid on her left cuff: "Table six—someone cover for me, please. Taking a distressed guest back to her room."

They were barely past the doorway when Wednesday tried to break away. Steffi grabbed her. "No! 'M going to—" *Oh shit!* Steffi repositioned her grip and hustled Wednesday toward the potted palm she'd taken a tentative lurch toward. But once she was head-down over the plant pot Wednesday proved she was made of stern stuff, drawing deep gulping breaths and slowly getting her stomach under control.

"Table six. Is anyone there?" Steffi mumbled into her cuff. "I've got a situation here. Who's covering?"

A voice in her earbud: "'Lo, Steffi. I've asked Max to cover for you. Are you going to be long?"

Steffi looked at the young woman, leaning on the rim of the plant pot, and winced. "Think I'm going to miss the tail end."

"Okay, check. Banquet control over and out."

She straightened up in time to see Wednesday doing likewise, leaning against the wall with her eyes shut. "Come on. What's your room?" She prodded her guest list, still handily loaded in her cuff. "Let's get you back there."

Wednesday shambled along passively if somewhat disjointedly, like a puppet with too-loose strings. "Lying bitch," she mumbled quietly as Steffi rolled her into the nearest lift. "Lying. Through her teeth."

"You're not used to drinking this much, are you?" Steffi ventured. *Wow, you're going to have a mammoth hangover, antidrunk or not!*

"Not . . . not alcohol. Didn't wanna be there. But couldn't stay 'lone."

Heads she's maudlin, tails she's depressed. Want to bet she wants someone to talk to? Steffi punched up A deck and Wednesday's cylinder, and concentrated on keeping her upright as they passed through fluctuating tidal zones between the electrograv rings embedded in the hull. "Any reason why not?" she asked casually.

"Mom and Dad and Jerm—lying *bitch!*" It was almost a snarl. *I was right,* Steffi realized unhappily. *Got her away just in time.* "Couldn't stay 'lone," Wednesday added for emphasis.

"What happened?" Steffi asked quietly as the elevator slowed then began to move sideways.

"They're dead an' I'm not." The kid's face was a picture of misery. "*Fucking* ReMastered liar!"

"They're dead? Who, your family?"

Wednesday made a sound halfway between a sob and a snort. "Who'dya think?"

The elevator stopped moving. Doors sighed open onto a corridor, opposite a blandly anonymous stateroom door. Steffi blipped it with her control override and it swung open. Wednesday knew which way to stagger. For a moment Steffi considered leaving her—then sighed and followed her in. "Your parents are dead? Is that why you don't want to be alone?"

Wednesday turned to face her, cheeks streaked with tears. Weirdly, her heavy makeup didn't run. *Chromatophores, built into her skin?* "Been two days," she said, swaying. "Since they were murdered."

"Murdered—"

"By. By the. By—" Then her stomach caught up with her and Wednesday headed for the bathroom in something midway between a controlled fall and a sprint. Steffi waited outside, listening to her throw up, lost in thought. *Murdered? Well, well, how interesting . . .*

---

it was 0300 hours, day-shift cycle, shortly before the starship made its first jump from point A to point A´ across a couple of parsecs of flat space-time.

The comforter was a crumpled mass, spilled halfway across the floor. The ceiling was dialed down to shades of red and black, tunnels of warm dark light washing across the room.

Wednesday rubbed her forehead tiredly. The analgesics and rat's liver pills had taken care of most of the symptoms, and the liter or two of water she'd methodically chugged down had begun to combat the dehydration, but the rest of it—the shame and embarrassment and angst—wouldn't succumb so easily to chemical prophylaxis.

"I'm an ass," she muttered to herself, slouching to her feet. She headed back to the bathroom again, for the third time in an hour. "*Stupid.* And ugly, and a little bit dumb on the side." She looked at the bathtub speculatively. "Guess I could always drown myself. Or cut my wrists. Or something." *Let the fuckers win.* She blinked at the mirror-wall on the other side of the room. "I'm an embarrassment." The figure in the mirror stared right back, a dark-eyed tragic waif with a rat's nest of black hair and lips the color of a drowned woman's. Breasts and hips slim, waist slimmer, arms and legs *too long.* She stood up and stared at herself. Her mind wandered, seeking solace a few nights back. *What did Blow see in me?* she wondered. *No way to find out now. Should have asked him when I had the chance...* She was alone here, more isolated than she'd ever been. "I'm a waste of vacuum."

On her way back into the bedroom she spotted a blinking light on the writing desk. For want of anything better to do she wandered over. It was something to do with the blotter. "What's this?" she asked aloud: "Ship, what does this light mean?"

"You have voice mail," the ship replied soothingly. "Voice calls are spooled to mail while guests sleep unless an override is in force. Do you want to review your messages?"

Wednesday nodded, then snorted at her own idiocy. "Yeah. I guess."

Message received, thirty-six minutes ago. From: Frank Johnson. "Hi, Wednesday? Guess you're asleep. Should have checked the time—I keep weird hours. Listen, the story went out okay. Sorry I missed supper, but those social things don't work for me real well. Ping me if you feel like hitting one of the bars sometime. Bye."

"Huh. Ship, is Frank Johnson still awake?" she asked.

"Frank Johnson is awake and accepting calls," the liaison network replied.

"Oh, oh." Suddenly it mattered to her very much that someone else was awake and keeping crazy hours. "Voice call to Frank Johnson."

There was a brief pause, then a chime. "Hello?" He sounded surprised.

"Frank?"

"Hello, Wednesday. What's up?"

"Oh, nothing," she said tiredly. "Just, I couldn't sleep. Bad thoughts. You mentioned a bar. Is it, like, too late for you?"

A pause. "No, not too late. You want to meet up now?"

Her turn to pause. "Yeah. If you want."

"Well, we could meet at—"

"Can you come round here?" she asked impulsively. "I don't want to go out on my own."

"Uh-huh." He sounded amused. "Okay, I'll be round in about ten minutes."

She cut the call. "*Gods and pests!*" She looked around at the discarded clothes, suddenly realizing that she was naked and what it must look like. "Damn! damn!" She bounced to her feet and grabbed her leggings and top. She paused for a moment, then wrapped the sarong around her waist, dialed her jacket to a many-layered lacy thing, threw the other stuff in the closet for sorting out later, and ran back to the bathroom to dial the lights up. "My *hair!*" It was a mess. "Well, what the fuck. I'm not planning on dragging him into bed, am I?" She stuck her tongue out at the mirror, then went to work on the wet bar in the corner of the main room.

When he arrived Frank was carrying a bag. He put it down on the carpet as he looked around, bemused. "You said your friends were paying, but this is ridiculous," he rumbled.

"It is, isn't it?" She looked up at him, challenging.

He grinned, then stifled a yawn. "I guess so." He nudged the bag with his foot. "You said you didn't want to go out so I bought some stuff along just in case—" Suddenly he looked awkward.

"That's okay." She took his arm and dragged him over to the huge floppy sofa that filled one side of the main room. "What you got in there?"

He pulled out a bottle. "Sambuca. From Bolivar. And, let's see, a genuine single malt from Speyside. That's on Old Earth, you know. And here's a disgusting chocolate liqueur from some-where about which the less said the better. Got any glasses?"

"Yep." She walked over to the bar and came back with glasses and a jug of ice. She sat down cross-legged at the other side of the sofa and poured a glassful of chocolate liqueur for herself, pre-tending not to notice Frank's mock shudder. "You weren't at din-ner."

"Those fake formal feast clusterfucks don't do anything for me," he announced. "They're there to make the rich passengers think they're getting a valuable service—more valuable than trav-eling deadhead in steerage, anyway. I guess if you do business or are in shipping, you can make a lot of contacts that way, but in general the kind of people I'd like to talk to over a meal don't travel by liner." He looked at her sharply. "Enjoy yourself?"

She nearly took the question at face value, although his tone suggested irony. "I nearly threw up in a plant pot after making a fool of myself." She winced. "She asked for it, though."

"Who did?" Frank raised his glass: "Your health."

"Bottoms up. Poisonous toy bitch kept going on about how great being *ReMastered* was—" She stopped. Frank looked stricken. "Did I say something wrong?" she asked.

"Was she a blonde? Head half-shaved at one side to show off a tattoo?"

Wednesday stared at him through a haze of conflicting emo-tions. "Yes," she said. "Why?"

He put his glass down, rattling on the tabletop. "You could have been killed," he said shakily.

"What do you—" She leaned toward him. "You said they run Newpeace. Concentration camps, secret police shit. Do you think they're that dangerous here, though?"

"They're dangerous everywhere!" Frank straightened up and picked up his glass, took a hefty mouthful, and coughed for a while. "Never, *never,* push a ReMastered button. Please? Tell me you won't do it again?"

"I was drunk." Wednesday flushed. His concern was immedi-ate and clear, cutting through the fog of worry. "Hey, I'm not crazy."

"*Not crazy.*" He chuckled edgily. "Is that why you didn't want to go out on your own?"

"No. Yes." She peered at him, wondering why she trusted him. *Alone with a gorilla after midnight and* he *wonders if I'm crazy?* "I don't know. Should I?"

"You should always know why you do things," Frank said seriously. "Inviting strange men for a late-night drink, for example." He picked up the liqueur bottle. "Want a refill? Or should I fuck off now before we both end up with hangovers tomorrow?"

She pushed her glass toward him. "Stay," she said impulsively. "I feel safer while you're around. Couldn't sleep, anyway." A faint smile tugged at the corners of her mouth. "Do *you* think I'm crazy?"

as days passed the boredom subsided somewhat. She'd stayed in her room for the whole of the next day, playing with the ship's extensive games library, but most of the other online players were old hands who had forgotten more about strategy than the entire Magna tournament team. After a while she ventured out, first to see if there really wasn't anything she could find to wear, then to visit a public bar with Frank. Who introduced her to fresh zero-gee farmed seafood and single malts. Then she'd spent some time with Steffi, who had hastily introduced her to her old friend Sven the clown and made her excuses. Sven, it turned out, also knew Frank: it was a small world aboard ship.

"So what's the thing with the face paint about?" she asked Svengali, one late-shift afternoon.

The clown frowned thoughtfully. "Think caricature. Think parody. Think emphasis on nonverbal communications cues, okay? If this was a virtual, I'd be an avatar with a homunculus-shaped head and body, bright blue nose, and huge kawaii eyes. But it isn't, and I'm not a surgical basket case, so you have to settle for programmable grease. It's amazing what it can do to someone's perception of you—you'd be really surprised."

"Probably." Wednesday took a swig from her glass—something fluorescent green, with red bubbles in it, and about the same alcohol concentration as a strong beer—and pointed at his jacket. "But the double seam—"

"Not going to leave me *any* tricks, are you?" Svengali sighed.

"No," Wednesday agreed, and the clown pulled a ferocious face. "You're very good at this," she said, trying to be conciliatory. "Does it pay a lot?"

"It pays"—Svengali caught himself—"hey, that's enough about me. Why don't we talk about you, for a change?"

"Uh-huh, you don't get off the hook that easily." Wednesday grinned.

"Yeah, well, it gets hard when the audience is old enough to look behind the mirror. *Mutter*—"

"What?"

Svengali reached toward her head fast, then pulled his hand back to reveal a butterfly fluttering white-and-blue wings inside the cage of his fingers: "—hear me better, now? Or, oh dear, did I just disconnect your brain?" He stared at the butterfly thoughtfully, then blew on it, transforming it into a white mouse.

"Wow," said Wednesday sarcastically. "That was *really* convincing."

"Really? Hold out your hand."

Wednesday held out her hand, slightly reluctantly, and Svengali released the mouse. "Hey, it's real!" The mouse, terrified, demonstrated precisely how real it was with a highly accurate rendition of poor bladder control. "Ick. Is that—"

"Yes." Before she could drop it, Svengali picked it up by its tail and hid it in his cupped hands. When he opened them a moment later, a butterfly fluttered away.

"Wow!" Wednesday did a little double take, then frowned at her hand. "Uh. 'Scuse me."

"Take your time," Svengali said magnanimously, leaning back in his chair as she hastily stood up and vanished toward the nearest restroom. His smile widened. "Homing override on," he told the air in front of him. "Return to base." The butterfly/mouse 'bot was stowed carefully away in the small case in his pocket long before she returned.

"Are you going to tell me how you did that?"

"Nope."

"Lawyer!"

"Am not." Svengali crossed his arms stubbornly. "Now *you* tell *me* how you did *that*."

"What, this?" Her face slowly brightened from turquoise to sky-blue.

"Yeah, that's pretty good."

"Programmable cosmetic chromatophores." Her face faded back toward its normal color, except for a touch of ruby on her lips and midnight blue lining on her eyelids. "I had them installed when we moved to Magna."

"Uh-huh. Want to take a walk?" asked Svengali, seeing that her glass was nearly empty.

"Hmm." She stared at him, then grinned again. "Trying not to let me get too drunk?"

"It's my job to look after passengers, not line the sick-bay's pockets. We can come back for another drink later."

"Okay." She was on her feet. "Where to?"

"Oh, I don't know," he said carelessly. "Let's just walk. Have you explored the ship yet?"

Her grin widened. "That would be telling."

Gods, but she's sharp, he told himself. *If she's got the stomach for it, she might even make it in* my *field.* "You're right—this job doesn't pay nearly enough," he grumbled. "I'm supposed to keep you all amused, not be the amusement myself. They should have put an upper age limit on the clientele. Big kids, all of you." They were already out in the corridor, another high-class hotel passage with sound-deadening carpet, expensively carved wooden paneling, and indirect lights shining on brightly meaningless abstract art installations every few meters. "Nine days. I hate to think what you're like when you're bored."

"I can keep to myself." Wednesday pulled her hands back into the long and elaborately embroidered cuffs of her jacket. "I'm not a child. Well, not everywhere. Legal standards differ."

"Yes, yes, and if you'd been born in the New Republic you'd be married with three or four children by now, but that doesn't mean you'd be an autonomous adult. I'm not supposed to keep an eye on you, I'm supposed to keep you from getting bored. All part of the service. What do you do with yourself when you want some cheap amusement, may I ask, if that isn't an indelicate question?"

"Oh, lots of things," she said idly. Raising an eyebrow at him: "But I don't think you want to know all the details. Something tells me I'm not your type."

"Well whoop-de-do. How perceptive, sister." Svengali steered them down a side passage then through a door into a conference suite, then out the far side of the room—which doubled as an emergency airlock—and into another passage. "More competition for the boys." He pulled a comical face. "But seriously. What did you get up to at home when you were bored?"

"I used to be big on elevator surfing. Vacuum tunneling, too. I was into tai chi, but I sort of let it drop. And, oh, I read spy thrillers." She glanced around. "We're not in passenger country anymore, are we?"

There were no carpets or works of art, the doors were wider and of bare metal, and the ceiling was a flat, emissive glare. "Nope. This is one of the service passages." Svengali was disappointed at her lack of surprise, but he decided to continue anyway.

"They connect all the public spaces. This is a crew lift. They don't run on cables, they're little self-powered pressurized vehicles running in the tunnels, and they can change direction at will. You don't want to try surfing these cars—it's too dangerous. *That*"— he pointed at an unmarked narrow door about half a meter high, sized for a small dwarf—"is the service door into a passenger suite. They're automatically locked while the room's occupied, but the valet 'bots use them while you're out and about."

"'Bots? Like, android amahs?"

"Who do you think made your bed?" Svengali carried on down the passage. "Human spaces and human furniture are built for roughly human-shaped people. They could put something like an industrial fab in each room, or even make everything out of structured matter, but many people get nervous when they're too near smart stuff, and having mobile valet 'bots on trolleys is cheaper than providing one per room."

"Uh-huh. So you're telling me that everywhere in the ship is, like, connected to everywhere else? Using old-fashioned doors and passages and ducts?" She was so wide-eyed that he decided it could only be sarcasm.

"If you design so that it'll only work with smart-matter utilities, something dumb will happen. That's the fifteenth corollary of Murphy's Law, or something. This ship is *supposed* to be able to get home with just a human crew, you know. That's partly why people are willing to pay for it." A side door opened onto a spiral staircase, cobwebby steps of nearly translucent aerogel ascending and descending into a dim blue mist in each direction. "Up or down, m'lady?"

"Up, first."

"You realize we're only able to do this because I've got a badge," Svengali remarked, as they climbed. The kid had long legs and was in good shape. He had to push himself to keep ahead of her.

"I guessed." She snuffled something that might have been a laugh. "It's still cool. What are those guts for?"

He followed her finger to the peristaltic pipes in the recess that ran alongside the stairs. "Probably semisolid waste disposal. They can reconfigure this stairwell into a tunnel if there's a major gravity outage, you know."

"Isn't that unlikely?"

"Probably." He carried on climbing for a bit. "Doesn't it worry you to be climbing a staircase inside what is basically a skyscraper sitting on top of a stasis chamber containing a twenty billion-ton extremal black hole?"

"I assume"—she paused for breath—"that if anything went wrong with it, it would all be over too fast to worry about."

"Probably." He paused. "That's why most of the crew—not me, I'm with Entertainments and Diversions, I mean the black gang, engineering ops—are along. In case something goes wrong, and they have to improvise."

"Well, isn't *that* comforting to know."

More sarcasm from Wednesday. It ran off him like water off a duck's back. "Here we are."

"Where?" She gawked past his shoulder at the boringly ordinary-looking door.

"Here." He smirked. "The backstage entrance to the live action theater on C deck. Want to see a performance? Or maybe the theater bar?"

"Wow." She grinned. "Send in the clowns!"

With a flourish, Svengali passed her a red nose. Then they went inside.

preparing for ghosts and dogs _____

Rachel Mansour, commissioner, UN Standing Committee on Interstellar Disarmament (Investigative Branch), walked slowly down the intimidatingly wide steps in front of the building of the Ministry of Cosmic Harmony. Behind her, huge marble columns supported a massive mirror-finished geodesic hemisphere that loomed over the neighborhood like a giant cyborg turtle. A sea of people flooded around her across the Plaza of Public Affairs, office workers and bureaucrats going about their daily work between the offices in the ministry basements, and the scattered subdepartments and public malls at the other side of the open space. The Eastern Palace squatted to her right, a pink-and-white brick mansion that had been converted to a museum to the Hegemony and the people's revolution that had overturned it more than a century earlier, here in Sarajevo, capital of the planetary empire.

She felt light-headed, an effect of coming out into the chilly open air after her claustrophobic interview with the subminister in charge of security arrangements for foreign embassies. After twenty-six days aboard the *Gloriana,* everything from the unprocessed air to the color of daylight seemed peculiar. There was perhaps just a small amount of gravitational adjustment, too—and a head-spinning load of mild culture shock.

She marched down the steps and out onto the plaza. Vendors selling spiced cocoa drinks, stir-fried octopi, and bootlegged recordings of old public executions tried to attract her attention. She ignored them. *He didn't say no,* she thought, remembering the subminister frowning ear to ear behind his desk: he wasn't very happy. "You are telling me that our security is inadequate?" he'd challenged her.

"No, I'm telling you that three other diplomatic security corps failed, in series, and two of them were forewarned. Your people *might* be better, but I hope you'll forgive me for not taking it on trust."

"Go ahead with your scheme, then, if the Muscovites agree. We will of course deny all knowledge if it goes wrong."

It was a step up from what she'd have gotten a generation ago, but New Dresden wasn't *that* bad. They had learned the enlightened self-interest meme here, and picked up the idea of a loyal opposition. They even elected their government officials, these days, although in this city the Party maintained its hereditary veto. All told, New Dresden was more civilized than many places she could have ended up. Less so than some others—but so what? *As long as they follow their best interests. And don't go haring off into the darkness again, like they did seventy years ago.* Still, maybe it would be for the best if she kept Martin out of the frame. She'd have to text him via the embassy channel. She tugged her jacket tighter across her shoulders, trying to think her way into the mind of the bureaucratic herd in their dark, closely tailored uniforms. But she couldn't fool herself about the subminister's likely report to his bosses.

People didn't always follow their best interests. Human beings were distressingly bad at risk analysis, lousy with hidden motivations and neuroses, anything but the clean rational actors that economists or diplomats wanted so desperately to believe in, and diplomats had to go by capabilities, not intentions. In dealing with the Muscovite diplomats in residence the Party officials must feel as if they were handling a hungry and aroused venomous snake, one that could turn on them and bite at any moment. They'd tolerate George Cho playing his little shell game with Ambassador Morrow for precisely as long as it increased the likelihood of Morrow's issuing the recall code, and not a second longer.

Speaking of whom, the Ambassador—easily identifiable by the two bodyguards—was sitting at a table at the pavement restaurant. Rachel walked round to the kitchen side then marched up to the nearest bodyguard—who was focusing on the square, not on the waiters approaching from the restaurant entrance—and tapped him on the shoulder. "Rachel Mansour, to see the Honorable Elspeth Morrow."

The bodyguard jumped. "Whoa!"

Morrow looked up, her face colorless and her expression bored. "You're late. George Cho said I should talk to you. Strongly implied that I needed to talk to you. Who *are* you?"

Rachel pulled out a chair and sat down. "I work for the same people as George. Different department, though. Officially, I'm on protocol. Unofficially, I'll deny everything." She smiled faintly.

Morrow waved at the chair with poor grace. "Okay, spook. So, what does George want?"

Rachel leaned back, then glanced at the bodyguard. "You know about the, ah, problem that concerns us." She studied Morrow intently, seeing a slim woman, evidently in her early forties. Moscow hadn't been good at antiaging therapy, but she could easily have been twenty years older. She wore her chestnut hair shoulder-length, and her green eyes seemed haunted by... just haunted. There had to be hundreds of millions of ghosts already riding at her shoulder, and the knowledge that she could add to their ranks—*What must that do to her?* Rachel wondered. "Forgive me for asking, but did you know Maureen Davis, Simonette Black, or Maurice Pendelton well?" she asked.

Morrow nodded. "Maurice was an old friend," she said slowly. "I didn't know Black other than by repute. Maureen... we knew each other. But Maurice is the one I feel for." She leaned forward. "What do you know about this?" she asked quietly. "Why did George bring you? You're black ops, aren't you?"

Rachel raised a hand to summon a waiter. "I'm, um, working with George's team from the other side," she said quietly. "George works for a diplomatic solution. Me, it's my job to... well, George very urgently wants to ensure that if someone tries to kill you—which we think is a high probability in the next week or so—firstly, we want them to fail, and secondly, they should fail in such a way that we can find out who they are and why they're doing it, *and* roll up not only the point assassin but their entire network."

"You do assassinations yourself?" Elspeth stared at her as if she'd sprouted a second head. "I didn't know Earth did—"

"No!" Rachel gave a little self-deprecating laugh. "Quite the opposite." The waiter arrived. "I'll have the mango croquette and roast shoulder of pork, thanks. And a glass of, um, the traditional red bonnet viper tisane?" She spoke without looking up, but from the corner of her vision noticed the bodyguard shadowing the waiter with aggressive vigilance. She nodded at Morrow. "The UN, as you can imagine, would very much like to resolve the current impasse between the government of Moscow in Exile and New Dresden. If for no other reason than to avoid the horrible precedent it would create if your vengeance fleet completes its mission. We especially *don't* want to see a situation where a party or parties unknown butcher so many of the remaining Muscovite government-in-exile's senior ranks that the situation becomes irrevocable. We want to know who is trying to engineer this situation, and why."

Morrow nodded. "Well, so do I," she said calmly. "That's why I have bodyguards."

Rachel managed a faint smile. "With all due respect, I'm sure your bodyguard is perfectly adequate for dealing with run-of-the-mill problems. However, in all three cases to date the assassin succeeded in passing through a secured zone and making an unobstructed getaway. This tells us that we're not dealing with an ordinary lunatic—we're dealing with a formidable professional, or even a team. Ordinary guards don't cut it. If I was the killer, you would be dead by now. My briefcase could be loaded with a bomb, your bodyguard could be shot with his own weapon . . . do you see?"

Elspeth nodded reluctantly.

"I'm here to keep you alive," Rachel said quietly. "There's a— well, I can't go into our sources. But we think there's probably going to be an attempt on your life between six and ten days from now."

"Oh." Morrow shook her head. Oddly, she seemed to relax a trifle, as if the immediacy of the warning, the concreteness of the high jeopardy, gave her something to cling to. "What do you think you can do if this master assassin wants to kill me?"

The waiter arrived with Rachel's order on a tray. "Oh, I can think of half a dozen possibilities," Rachel said. She smiled tiredly. Then she peered at Elspeth's face closely until the ambassador blinked. "We'll have to run it past the ship's surgeon, but I think Plan A can be made to work."

"What? What have you got in mind?"

"Plan A is the shell game." Rachel put her glass down. "We're assuming that our unidentified but highly competent assassins are also well informed. If this is the case, they'll probably learn or guess that you've been warned before they set up the hit. So what George would like to do is play a shell game with them. Step zero is to send Dr. Baxter off-planet—somewhere where we're fairly certain there are no assassins. We'd like you to ensure that you've got as few public appearances and important meetings as possible during the window of opportunity.

"And then... well, I'm about your height, and the body mass difference can be finessed with padding and loose clothing. The real trick will be getting the face and hair and posture right. We're going to ensure that for your remaining public appearances you have a body double. Bait, in other words. *You* will be hiding in a locked room in a nuclear bunker with a closed-cycle air supply and half an assault division sitting on top of it—or as a guest on board a UN diplomatic yacht, sovereign territory of Earth, with a couple of cruisers from the New Dresden navy keeping an eye on it, if you prefer. It's up to you: they want to keep you alive, too, as long as those missiles are heading in this direction. But I'm going to hang my tail out where someone can try to grab it—not with a long gun, but up close and personal, so we can snatch them."

Elspeth looked at her with something like awe—or whatever the appropriate expression was for dealing with suicidal idiots. "How much do they pay you to do this job?" she asked. "I've heard some foolhardy things in my time, but that's about the craziest—" She shook her head.

"I don't do this for money," Rachel murmured. *Responsibility. Get it wrong, and nearly a billion people die.* She glanced at the square. "I was here about ten years ago. Did you ever take the time to go round the museums?"

"Oh, I've been round the Imperial Peace Museum and the People's Palace of the Judiciary," Elspeth replied. "Captured it all." She tapped a broad signet ring and a sapphire spot blinked on it. "These people have the most remarkable history—more history than a world ought to have, if you ask me." She fixed Rachel with a contemplative stare. "Did you know they've had more world wars than Old Earth?"

"I was vaguely aware of that," Rachel said drily, having crammed three thousand pages of local history on her first journey here, many years earlier. "How are the museums these days?"

"Big. Oh, this month there's a most extensive display of regional burial costumes, some sort of once-in-a-decade exhibition that's on now." Slowing even more, Elspeth continued thoughtfully: "There was a whole gallery explaining the sequence of conquests that enabled the Eastern Empire to defeat their enemies in the south and get a stranglehold on the remaining independent cornucopia-owning fabwerks. Fascinating stuff."

"Nothing on the mass graves, I take it," Rachel observed.

"No." Elspeth shook her head. "Nor the blank spots on the map of North Transylvania."

"Ah." Rachel nodded. "They haven't gotten around to talking about it yet?"

"Life extension, amnesia extension. It takes longer to admit to the crimes when the criminals are still taking an active role in government." Elspeth drained her glass, then looked away. "Why were you there?" she murmured.

"War crimes commission. I'd rather not talk about it, thanks." Rachel finished her drink. "I'd better get back to the embassy to start preparations." She noticed Elspeth's expression. "I'm sorry, but we've got to get under way as soon as possible. It's going to take time to work up to this. I think I'll skip the museums."

For a moment she felt agonizingly old: she felt every minute of her age, a length of time no human being could endure without learning to ignore it from moment to moment. She had made a habit of reinventing her life every thirty years, forcing herself to adopt new habits and attitudes and friends, but even so a common core of identity remained; a bright spark of rage against the sort of people who could do the sort of thing that had happened in North Transylvania, less than a century earlier. One of Rachel's most recent peculiarities was that she'd recently found that museums made her feel ill, physically nauseous, with their depictions of horrors and atrocities disguised as history—especially when they were horrors and atrocities that she had lived through. Or worse, their glib evasions and refusals to face the truth.

"I could—" Elspeth shook her head. "There's more to you than you're letting on."

Rachel smiled at her sourly. "Why, thank you very much." She sniffed. "I said my job was about bomb disposal. But maybe it'd be more accurate to say I'm in the business of abolishing history."

"Abolishing history?" The Ambassador frowned. "That sounds positively revisionist."

"I mean, abolishing the kinds of events they build places like the Imperial Peace Museum to remember." She glanced at Elspeth. "Your call?"

Ambassador Morrow stared at her through half-narrowed eyes. "I think your ambition is very laudable," she said slowly. "And I'd like to hear about your experiences here sometime." *But not right now. I don't want to lose my lunch,* Rachel projected cynically. "Meanwhile, why don't you work with Willem here to arrange a follow-on meeting, at our mutual convenience?"

"I'll do that." Rachel nodded. "Take care."

"I shall," said Morrow, standing up and holding her arms out for her coat. "You, too," she said impulsively, then her bodyguards and secretary followed her, the latter watching Rachel mistrustfully as his mistress walked away. They vanished into the crowd, and her main course arrived. Rachel ate it slowly, her thoughts elsewhere. *I wonder what Martin will think?*

"ʯou *can't* be serious!"

She'd rarely seen him so disturbed, and never by something she'd told him: "Why? What makes you think I'm joking?"

"I—" He was pacing, always a bad sign. "I don't." *Ah, a sign of realism.* "I just don't like it, for extremely large values of *don't* and *like*." He turned to face her, his back to the wall-screen of the promenade deck: with the almost flat horizon of the planet behind him, it looked as if he was walking on the atmosphere. "Please, Rachel. Please tell me this isn't as bad as it sounds?"

She took a deep breath. "Martin, if I wanted to kill myself, do you think I'd go about it this indirectly?"

"No, but I think your sense of responsibility"—he saw where he was going almost before she did, and swerved to avoid the abyss—"may lead you into working within operational constraints that you don't need to be bound by." He stopped and took a deep breath. "Phew. Don't mean to lecture you. It's your specialty, and so on." Then he looked at her, with worry in his eyes, and she felt herself beginning to melt: "But are you sure it's safe?"

"Don't you go quoting William Palmer's last words at me," she threw back at him. "Of course I'm not sure it's safe!" She folded her arms defensively. "It's as safe as I can make it, and for sure it's safer than letting some lunatic sign a death warrant for 800 million mostly innocent people. But it's not *safe*-safe. Now if you're through trying to mother me, will you listen while I talk you through the threat tree and tell me if you spot anything that everybody else has missed?"

"The threat tree—" Martin almost went cross-eyed trying to hold the topic in his head. "Rachel?"

"Oh shit!" She looked at him with mingled affection and exasperation. Two years of being married to him hadn't blunted the former, but she'd been a big girl with her own life before Martin—in his late sixties, despite looking like a midtwentysomething—had been even a twinkling in his mother's eye. And sometimes she felt like a cradle snatcher. He didn't yet have the chilly detachment that came from having a child die of avoidable old age, embraced by reason of either religious conviction or plain old-fashioned boredom with life. Maybe he never would, and she'd love him no less for it, but at times it made him a mite hard to live with. "Do you really think that I'd do something rash enough to cost me this?" She took two steps forward and buried her chin in the base of his neck, as his arms automatically wrapped around her.

"I *know* you would, Rache. I know about you and your quixotic campaigns to fix entire fucked-up planets. Remember?"

She whispered in his ear: "Only because you'd do the same."

"Yeah, but I was doing it strictly cash on delivery. And for the best possible reason." Because the nearest thing this crazy universe could provide to a deity had phoned him up one day and asked him how much he'd charge for sabotaging time machines before the lunatics who built them could switch them on and destroy the coherency of history, including the chain of events leading to the creation of the god in question. "*You* tend to do it when you get overenthusiastic."

"No, I tend to do it when I get *angry*," she replied, and goosed him. He yelped. "You don't like it when I get angry!"

"No, no, I like you fine." He gasped. She laughed: she couldn't help herself. A moment later Martin was chuckling, too, leaning on her shoulder for support.

After a while they sobered up. "I'm not going to let some crazy get close enough to kill me, Martin. I'm just going to wear the face and stand at the back of a room with a couple of tons of concealed security in front of me. I want them to *think* they've got a clean shot at me, not give them the real thing."

"I've seen too many harebrained schemes like this go wrong." She let go of him, took a step back to watch his face. "And it leaves me feeling like a spare wheel. Not"—he glanced over his shoulder—"that I'm anything else, here."

"Well, that's what you get for marrying into the diplomatic corps." She frowned. "But there's one thing you could do for me. I asked George, and he says it's okay. It's not dangerous—"

"Not dangerous?" He squinted suspiciously. "That'll be a first for something you cooked up."

"Shut up. Listen, George thought it would be a good idea if while I'm at the Muscovite embassy running this little honeypot scheme, you took a trip up the beanstalk and had a guided tour of the *Romanov* while she's in dock. Your usual employer built bits of her, and I can get you an intro with the Captain. I just want you to go take a look around, see if you smell anything fishy. We can make it official if you want."

"The last time you guys wanted me to go take an *unofficial* sniff around a ship I seem to recall we both got shanghaied into a six-month cruise to a war zone," he said drily.

"That's not the idea this time." She smiled, then turned away. Mixed memories: Martin had not enjoyed the experience much, and at the time neither had she, but if it hadn't happened, they wouldn't have met, wouldn't have married, wouldn't be together. It was too easy, after the event, to gloss over the dark, frightening aspects of a bad experience inextricably linked to something else that was very good indeed. "I'm not sure what, if anything, I expect you to find. Probably nothing, but if you can hit on the Captain for a full passenger manifest including stopovers, and ask around if anyone's been behaving oddly. I mean, if there's a passenger in first class who never shows up at dinner because the voices in his head tell him to stay in his cabin and polish the guns..."

"Check." He sighed. "It's a WhiteStar ship, isn't it?"

"Yes. Why, is that good or bad?"

"Commercial, *very* commercial. I hope you guys have got something on the bottom line to offer the Captain, or he's not going to be too keen on wasting time on someone like me."

"*She,* Captain Nazma Hussein. And she's not going to yelp too loudly. Why do you think George put you on the payroll? She doesn't need to know you're down as an unpaid intern; just turn up and wave your diplomatic passport at her and act polite but firm. If you get any shit, pass it on to George." She grinned. "It's about the only perk of the job."

"You're going to take care, aren't you?" He stared at her.

"You bet."

"Okay." He closed the gap between them, and she wrapped her arms around him. He leaned close to kiss her forehead. "Let's hope you can get this nailed down so we can go home soon."

"Oh, I'm sure we will." She held him tight. "And I'm not going to take any risks, Martin. I want to live long enough to see that child of ours decanted."

three days of frenetic preparation passed like quicksilver running down a rainy gutter, until:

"Four hours ago? First passengers should have hit the terminal when? Very good. Thanks, I'll be ready." Rachel flipped her phone shut and tried to get her racing pulse back under control. "It's started," she called through the open door.

"Come over here. I want to give this a last run-through," said Tranh.

Rachel walked across the hand-woven rug and paused in the open doorway. "What kind of way is that to talk to a foreign ambassador?" she asked, forcing herself to stand with her legs slightly apart, the way Elspeth did. Tranh was waiting in the Ambassador's bedroom with Gail and a worried-looking Jane, still busy setting up the mobile communications switch on Morrow's desk. Like Rachel, Gail was dressed for a formal diplomatic reception: unlike Rachel, she wore her own face along with the dark suit and gown of office of a dignitary.

Tranh peered at her intently. "Hair," he said.

"Let me look." Gail approached Rachel, holding a brush as if it were a handgun. "No, looks all right to me. Hmm." She reached out and adjusted a stray wisp. "How does it feel?"

Rachel grimaced. "Like wearing a rubber mask, how do you think it feels?"

"As long as you can wear it comfortably. No slipping?"

"No. Membrane pumps seem to be fine." The layered gunk was threaded with osmotic pumps, able to suck up sweat from down below and exude it through realistic-looking pores.

"Other stuff?"

"Fine." Rachel turned round slowly. "Can't bend over too easily. Wish the armor could sweat, too."

"Your gun's showing," Tranh said critically. "When you let the robe fall open—that's better." Rachel hitched it into place. "Hmm. Looks okay to me. Wire test." There were no wires, but an elaborate mix of military-grade intelligent comms to tie the ambush team together.

"Testing, testing."

Tranh held up a hand. "Tests out okay. *Can you hear me?*" She winced, and he hastily hit a slider on the communications panel. "That better?" She nodded.

Glued into a skin-tight mask, wearing somebody else's clothes over body armor and trying to conceal a handgun, Rachel felt anything except better. But at least Martin was out of the picture for the moment—on his way up the planetary beanstalk to poke around the liner docked in geosynchronous orbit. "Gail, remind me of the order of battle?"

"The order—oh." She cleared her throat. "It's 1730. Doors open, 1800. We're expecting Subminister for Cultural Affairs Ivan Hasek, the usual dozen or so cultural attachés, deputy ambassadors, sixteen assorted business dignitaries, including six locals anxious to resolve reparations lawsuits, three from Septagon, who're concerned about commodity futures in event of a rather unpleasant future shortage of Dresdeners to trade with them, and seven export agents for defunct Muscovite firms. There's Colonel Ghove of the Ministry of Education, Professor-Doctor Franck from the Ministry of Internal Enlightenment, the diva Rhona Geiss, who is apparently due to sing for us, about a billion journalists—four, actually—and a few dozen refugees who live here or are passing through and took up the invitation. Plus the caterers, a quartet of musicians, eight dancers, three entertainers, eleven waiters, a bunch of students on a cultural exchange trip, a video crew making a documentary about what happens to nations after their planet dies, and a partridge in a pear tree. I double-checked the list with Pritkin and the ambassador, and you've got a clear field—no existing acquaintances according to your service log."

"Delightful." Rachel winced. "Horizon is five hours off. Got any rat's liver pills for me?"

Gail produced a strip of tablets with a flourish and a small grin. "Have one on me."

"Uck." Rachel popped the first pill, resigning herself to an evening of sobriety. "Toilet?"

"Along the hall, door under the main stairs on the left. Cubicles all wired, of course."

"Guards?"

"Two on the front, two on the back, and two on each landing. They've been briefed. Safeword is—"

"'Ghosts.' I got it. And 'dogs' for an intruder."

"Right." Tranh stood up. "You happy?"

"As happy as..." Rachel gave it some thought: "...anyone would be in my shoes. How's Elspeth taking it?"

"I could phone her if you want?"

"No, I don't think so." Rachel could see it all in her mind's eye. A drably boring safe house on the other side of town, discreetly ringed by a prince's escort of secret policemen. Ambassador Morrow would be trying to relax, with George Cho to keep her company, along with a subminister from the Ministry of External Affairs and her secretary, whatshisname. There was growing tension over Earth's diplomatic corps muscling in on the mess: Earth was a third party with only a vague claim to involvement, thanks to the assassin's choice of transport. The only reason Dresdener spooks weren't handling this was the likely response of the Muscovite diplomatic corps if they dropped the ball. The ticking clock, the slowly rising tension as they waited for the call from the embassy. Anxiety: *What if they're right?* And uncertainty: *What if they're wrong?* And paranoia: *What if these people from Earth are behind it all?* It was enough to sour Rachel's stomach, not a good way to start a long and stressful evening.

She concentrated on her autonomic implants for a while. The Dresdener authorities had a serious bias against personal augmentation and the unregulated use of smart matter: Rachel's ability to override her thalamus, accelerate her reflexes, and see in the dark would go down like a lead balloon if they came to light. But they wouldn't, not unless someone came out of the darkness and tried to kill her. That was only too possible, now they were into the eighty-hour frame between the *Romanov*'s arrival and its clearance for departure from the beanstalk's orbital dock. And she had reason to be nervous. Someone had managed to infiltrate three diplomatic residences, one of them under a state of heightened security, carry out three kills, and get away clean. That implied very good intelligence, or inside help, or both. And if the inside help knew about the substitution . . .

"Time check," said Tranh. "The first guests should be"—he glanced at the switch—"*are* arriving now."

There was a discreet knock at the main door to the outer room. "I'll check it," said Gail, walking over. Rachel slid out of sight behind the inner door as Gail held a brief whispered conversation. "It's Chrystoff," she said, and Rachel relaxed slightly. Morrow's bodyguard was one of the few people on the whitelist—if *he* was an assassin, they'd lost before they even got started.

"Good," she said, walking back into the middle of the room. She caught the bodyguard's eye: "You happy with this?"

"No." He returned the inspection. "But, you're—it's uncanny." He looked tense. "It's not you that I'm worried about."

"Indeed." She nodded soberly. "I need to go downstairs and greet people. I really don't expect our hypothetical hitter to risk witnesses, so as long as I stay out of view of the outside we should be all right. The fun starts if any of the guests goes out of bounds or when the hitter departs from the script. Ready?"

Chrystoff froze for a moment, then gave a slight nod.

"Then let's get this show on the road."

With the ship docked and resupply under way, Steffi was annoyingly busy. In addition to spending some of her off-hours with Wednesday—the kid had problems and needed a shoulder to unload on, but it was remarkably draining to be in the firing line—she was filling in for Max and Evan, running errands between Bridge and Engineering, generally acting as understudy and gofer for the executive team, and minding the shop while her superiors were dealing with the port authorities. If it went on this way, she'd be lucky to get any time on the surface at all—and after three weeks of constant work she needed to get out of the ship for a while very badly indeed. If she didn't do her share on the surface, Svengali would have harsh words for her; of that, she was certain. Which was why Elena's call from the purser's office came as an unwelcome distraction.

"Lieutenant? We have a situation here. I'm on tube four, northside. Can you come up right away?"

Steffi glanced at the two engineering auxiliaries who were hooking up the ship's external service cables—power, so they could strip down the number two generator, and crypto, so they could dump the bulk mail spool. "I can give you five minutes. That's all. On my way. What's the situation?"

"I can't tell you until you get here."

"What do you mean, 'can't'?" Steffi was already moving toward the nearest crew lift capsule. *Got to sign off the cable hookup, then see Dr. Lewis gets her transport for the new surgery unit...*

"It's very irregular." Elena sounded apologetic. "I've got an override B-5."

"A—" Steffi blinked. "Okay, I'm on my way." She twitched her rings to a different setting, then told the lift to take her to the lock bay. "Max? Steffi here. I've got a problem. Do you know something about an override B-5 coming up?"

Max sounded distracted. "A B-5? No, I haven't heard anything. You can try to field it if it's within your remit. If it goes over your head, get back to me. I'm covering for Chi right now, so I've got my hands full."

"Uh, okay." Steffi shook her head. "B-5, isn't that a *diplomatic* exception?"

"Diplomatic, customs, police, whatever. If they've got a warrant for a passenger, it's the purser's office. If it's to do with shipboard ops, get back to me."

"Okay. Steffi out." The elevator slowed, then opened its doors on the passenger country side of docking tube four. This level of the tube—a pressurized cylinder the diameter of a subsonic trashhauler jet—was a wide corridor, ramping up at the far end into the arrivals processing hall of the station. At the ship end, various lock doors and high-capacity elevators opened off it. Just then, a trickle of passengers were idling on their way portside. Elena and a crewman from the purser's office were waiting by the barrier with a passenger—no, wait, he was on the wrong side, wasn't he?

"Hello, Elena. Sir." She smiled professionally. "How can I help you?" She sized him up rapidly: dark hair, nondescript, young-looking with the self-assurance that came with age, wearing sandals, utility kilt, and a shirt in a style that had been everywhere back home. Then he held up a small booklet. With a white cover.

"My name is Martin Springfield," he said diffidently, "and I'm attached to the UN special diplomatic mission currently in residence in Sarajevo." He smiled faintly. "*Nicky* didn't look like this last time I was aboard, I must say."

"*Nicky?* Excuse me?" Elena was trying to catch her eye, but too late.

"That's what we called her back in the yard. Must have been eight or nine years ago." Springfield nodded to himself, as if confirming something: "I'm sorry to have to pull this on you, but I'm here because Ambassador Cho needs some questions answered urgently. Is there somewhere private we can talk?"

"Private—" Steffi's eyes nearly crossed as she tried to reconcile conflicting instincts: *Get this annoying civilian out of the way so I can go back to work;* and *oh shit,* government *stuff! What do I have to do now?* "Um, yes, I suppose so." She cast a warning glance at Elena, who shrugged and looked helpless. "If you'd be so good as to step this way? Can I have a look at that, sir?"

"It's genuine," Elena volunteered. "Carte blanche. He's who he says he is. I already checked."

Steffi forced herself to smile again: "I'm sure you did, or you wouldn't have called me." She looked at Martin. "Follow me."

As if everything wasn't complicated enough, as she turned, a small clot of people were coming down the tube—a couple of staff entertainers, one or two business travelers, a handful of tired-looking recently thawed steerage customers with their shipping trunks, and Wednesday. Wednesday noticed her at the same time and couldn't leave well alone. "Uh, Lieutenant Grace? Are you busy? I just wanted to say, I'm sorry about the other day—"

"It's all right," Steffi said tiredly, wondering how she was going to talk her way out of this. "Are *you* all right? Going groundside, I see—do you have anything in mind? Some sightseeing?"

Wednesday brightened slightly. "I'm sightseeing, yeah." Then she was abruptly sober. "There's a memorial ceremony tomorrow at the, the embassy. In the capital. Anyone from Moscow who's in-system is invited. It landed in my mailbox this morning. Thought I ought to go. It's been five years, empire time."

"Well, you go," Steffi said hastily. "If you need to talk when you get back to the ship, feel free to call me—I'm just a bit snowed under right now." To her relief Wednesday nodded, then hurried off to catch up with the flock of day-trippers. *What did I let myself in for?* she wondered. After that devastating breakdown on the first night, she'd sat with Wednesday for a couple of hours while she poured out her grief. It had left Steffi wanting to strangle someone—starting with whoever had killed the kid's family, followed by the kid herself when she realized how much of a time sink Wednesday could be. But she'd filed a report with the stewards, disentangled herself carefully, and when she checked the next day Wednesday seemed to be fine. And she was spending a lot of time with the troll from B312. They were resilient at that age. She'd been made of rubber herself, back when her parents were splitting up; but she didn't remember collapsing on a total stranger's shoulder and spilling her soul, or trying to pick a fight over supper. Spoiled, like most rich kids, she figured. Wednesday had probably never had anything to worry about in her life.

Steffi reached the crew elevator and realized with a start that the man from the embassy was still with her. *What is he, the human glueball?* she wondered. "We can find a corner of the executive planning suite, or maybe a conference room. Or if it's okay with you, I can go check on a couple of jobs I'm meant to be supervising." *Let's get you out of my hair, huh?*

"If you can check those jobs in person, I'll just tag along and stay out of your way while you're doing it." Springfield leaned against the side of the lift car. He looked either tired or worried—or both. "But I'm afraid I'm going to be generating a lot of work for you. Ambassador Cho sent me to poke around here because I'm the nearest thing to a shipping specialist he's got. We have a bit of a needle and haystack problem, I'm afraid. Specifically, we have reason to think that one or more of the long-stay passengers have been using this vessel as a vehicle for serial naughtiness at the last few ports of call."

The elevator began to slow as it neared the power hookup bay. "Are we talking about smuggling, sir? Or barratry, or hijacking? Because if not, I don't see what this could possibly have to do with WhiteStar. It's been a remarkably peaceful voyage so far."

The doors hissed open, and Steffi stepped out. Yuri was leaning against the wall beside the big gray switchbox. "All hooked up, ma'am. Would you like the tour?"

Steffi nodded. It took her only a minute to confirm that Yuri and Jill—who had hurried off, needed elsewhere—had done a good job. "Okay, let's test it, turn it on, and sign it off." She waited while Yuri called down to the engine room and ran through the checklist before tripping in the circuit. The cabinet-sized switchbox hummed audibly as it came under load, nearly fifty megawatts of electricity surging into it through superconductor cables no fatter than Steffi's thumb. "Okay, here's my chop." She signed off on Yuri's pad, then sealed the cabinet.

"Let's go find a conference room," she told Martin. "If you still feel you need to check our records...?"

"It's not whether *I* feel any need, I'm afraid," he said quietly, then waited for the lift pod doors to close: "I don't expect you to have any trouble in flight. The person or people we're looking for are more likely to be causing trouble groundside."

"Trouble? What kind of trouble?"

Springfield looked grim. "I can't tell you. But it's bad enough to get a full-dress diplomatic mission out here to paper over the cracks. If you want confirmation, wire Victoria McEllwaine in Legal back at WhiteStar head office and ask her what you should do. Meanwhile, I need to go over your entire passenger manifest since the current cruise began. And your temporary staff, for that matter—anyone who's been here for less than six months. I may also need to gain access to staterooms. If you can't authorize a search, point me at someone who can. Finally, I need to make an inspection tour of your engineering spaces and check cargo consignments for certain destinations—any small to medium items that have been drawn out here by passengers, checked in from Earth, Turku, and Eiger's World."

"Is that all?" Steffi asked disbelievingly. He'd outlined enough work there to keep someone occupied for a week. With passenger churn approaching 40 percent per destination, they'd gone through six or seven thousand embarkations, not to mention the Entertainments staff: they'd shipped an entire chamber orchestra from Rosencrantz to Eiger, never mind the other irregular performers that Ents kept hiring and firing. "I'd better get you sorted out right away. If you don't mind, I'm going to boot you upstairs to my CO—I'm due off duty in two hours with shore leave tomorrow."

"Well, I won't keep you—but let's get started. I'm supposed to report back within twenty-four hours. *With* results. And then I may have to call on you to help me arrest someone."

Meanwhile, Frank was groundside and frustrated. "Can you explain why they won't see me? I made this appointment forty-three days ago; it's been cleared via the consulate in Tokyo. Is there some kind of problem?"

"Problem." The man on the small screen cleared his throat. "You could say that." He eyed Frank curiously. "I'm afraid we're in the middle of a staff training drill right now, and Minister Baxter isn't available. Also, all embassy engagements have been scaled back, and I can't find any mention of you in our workgroup diary. Would you like to make a fresh appointment for sometime next week?"

"My ship leaves the day after tomorrow," he said as calmly as he could manage. "So next week is right out. Would Minister Baxter be available for a phone interview instead? If security is a concern, there's no need for face-to-face contact."

"I'll just check." The screen blanked for a moment, then: "I'm sorry, sir, but the Minister isn't available at all until next Thursday. Can I help you make any alternative arrangements? For example, by long-range channel?"

"I'll have to check my budget," Frank admitted. "I have a limited bandwidth spend. Can I get back to you on that? Would you mind just double-checking that I'm not on your list anywhere? If the Minister's unavailable, would it be possible to arrange a chat with Ambassador Morrow instead?"

"I'm sorry, but the Ambassador's busy, too. As I said, sir, this is about the worst possible week you could have asked for an interview. If you leave things with me, I'll see what I can do, but I'm making no promises."

Frank put his temporary phone away and stood up tiredly. At times like this he felt as if he was walking blindfolded along a corridor pre-greased and strewn with banana skins by a cosmic jester. *Why now? Why did they have to lose the fucking thing now, of all times?* A quote from Baxter, or even Morrow, admitting that their colleagues were being stalked—that would be explosive. Only they weren't playing ball. The whole thing smelled like a discreet security lockdown: scheduled interviews canceled, public appearances held to carefully controlled zones with vetted guest lists, the bland stench of denial hovering over the rotting corpse of business as usual. Just like one of Mom's dinner parties when she'd been trying to break back into the charmed circle of political movers and fixers who'd dropped her the first time around, after her electoral defeat.

The air was still cool and slightly damp in the park, but the heated benches were dry enough to work on. Frank folded up his mobile office and stood up. The poplars were flowering, and he walked slowly under a ceiling of catkins, bouncing and shedding in the morning breeze. The path merged with two others at one of the bronze war memorials that were heartbreakingly common hereabouts. Frank paused for a minute to scan it with his glasses, capturing the moment forever. Almost a hundred years earlier, at this very spot, an enemy battalion had put up a spirited resistance to the forces of the All-Conquering. Their souls, large and warlike, had gone to Valhalla: the victors had raised the stele not out of magnanimity but with the more subtle intention of magnifying their own prowess. *Nobody likes to boast that they massacred a bunch of terrified, starving, ill-equipped conscripts,* Frank reminded himself. *It's easier to be a hero when your vanquished enemies are giants.* Something he'd have to bring up if he ever got close enough to interview the honorable Elspeth Morrow. "So how does it feel sentencing to death 140 million children, 90 million crumblies, and another 600-million-odd ordinary folks who were content to mind their own business and don't even know who you are?"

Farther along the path Frank passed a patrolling gardener 'bot. Judging from the smell, it was collecting and fermenting either slugs or waste from the citizens who walked their dogs at dawn. The trees were farther apart on this walk, with park benches between them and fields stretching away beyond. Each bench bore a weathered pewter plaque, stained almost gray by age: *In loving memory of Private Ivar Vincik, by his parents,* or *Gone forever but not forgotten, Artillery Sergeant Georg Legat.* The park wore its history as proudly as a row of medals: from the memorials to the fallen to the white charnel house built from the skulls and femurs of the enemy battalion, used by the groundskeepers to store their lawnmowers.

The trees came to an end, and the path began to descend toward a concrete underpass that slid beneath the road that separated park from town center. If you could call it a town center, these days. First there'd been a small rural village. Then there'd been a battle. Then there'd been another village, which grew into a town before the next battle flattened it. Then the town had been rebuilt and turned into a city, which had been bombed heavily and rebuilt again. Then the Mall that Ate Vondrak had turned into the Arcology that Absorbed Vondrak, all concrete towers and gleaming glassy Penrose-tiled roof, a groundscraper sprawled across the landscape like a sleeping giant. The place was heavily contaminated by history, war memorials marking off the worst pollution hot spots.

It was a quiet day, but there was still some traffic and a few people about at ground level even that early in the morning—a couple out for an early-morning run together, three kids on walksters, an old woman with a huge backpack, worn boots, and the wiry look of a hiker poring over an archaic moving map display. A convoy of local delivery vans hummed past on the road deck, nestling behind their long-haul tractor like a queue of ducklings. A seagull, surprisingly far inland, circled overhead, raucously claiming its territory.

"When's the next train to Potrobar?" he asked aloud.

"You have twenty-nine minutes. Options: Make a reservation. Display route to station. Rescan—"

"Reservation and route, please." The ubiquitous geocomputing network there was crude compared to the varied services on Earth, but it did the job, and did it without inserting animated advertorials, which was a blessing. A light path flickered into view in front of him, strobing toward one of the arcology entrances. Frank followed it across the ornamental cobblestones, past a gaggle of flocking unicyclists and a fountain containing a diuretic-afflicted Eros.

The train station was on level six, a glazed atrium with sliding doors along one side to give access to the passenger compartments. Frank was slouched in a seat, pecking at his keyboard in a desultory manner (trying to capture the atmosphere of a chrome-and-concrete station was like trying to turn a burned lump of charcoal back into a tree, he thought dispiritedly) when his phone bleeped for attention. "Yeah?" he asked, keeping to voice-only—too easy for someone to snatch his window/camera in this crowded place.

"Frank? It's me. I'm here. Where are you?"

"You're—" His eyes crossed with the unexpected mental effort of trying to figure it out, then he hit on the caller's geocache location. "Eh. What do you want, Wednesday?"

"I've, uh, I've only just got off the ship, but I was wondering, are you busy this evening?" It came out in a rush. "See, there's this wine-and-cheese reception thingy, and I've been invited to it, says I can bring a guest, and I haven't done one of these things before, but I have been *strongly advised* to go—"

Frank tried not to sigh. "I've just had an interview fall through. If I can't refill the slot, I guess I might be free, but probably not. Just what kind of do is it?"

"It's some kind of fifth-anniversary dead light get-together, a reunion for any Moscow citizens who're on Dresden. At the embassy, you know? My, uh, friends said you might be interested."

Frank sat bolt upright, barely noticing the other commuters on the platform, as they began to move toward the doors. "Wait, that's excellent!" he said excitedly. "I was wanting to get some local color. Maybe get some interview slots with ordinary people. When is it, you said—" The doors were opening as passengers disembarked: others moved to take their place.

"The Muscovite high consulate in Sarajevo. Tonight at—"

Frank started. The platform was emptying fast, and the train was waiting. "Whoa! Mail me? Got to catch a train. Bye." He hung up fast and trotted over to the doors, stepping aboard just as the warning beeper went off.

"Potrobar?" he muttered to himself, glancing around for an empty seat. "*Potrobar?* What the fuck am I going *there* for?" He sighed, and forced himself to sit down as the PA system gave a musical chime and the train lifted from the track bed and began to slide toward the tube entrance. "When's the next train from Potrobar to Sarajevo?" he asked plaintively.

ring ring. "hey, what took you so long? I've been waiting for *hours*! I'm going to be late—"

"You are not late. There will be another capsule in less than half an hour, Wednesday. Did you receive my message about the reception?"

"Yes." Wednesday sighed theatrically. "I'm on my way there. Will you tell me what this is all about?"

There was a momentary pause. "In due course."

Wednesday shook her head. "In other words, no." She bent down and buckled up her boots. They looked really fine with the white lacy shalwar trousers she'd bought for dinner and never worn. "So what's the point of me going there?"

"There is going to be trouble," said Herman, his voice a distant monotone. "The conspirators who are currently assassinating Muscovite diplomats—"

"*What?*"

"—Please do not interrupt. Did you think you were the only target?"

"But, but—"

"The chancelleries of a hundred worlds will be shaken by the exposure of this conspiracy, Wednesday. *If* the primary annealing state vector collapses to—excuse me. If the outcome I am betting against myself on comes to pass. I apologize, human languages are poor vehicles for describing temporal paradoxes."

"You're going to have to try harder if you want to impress. I'm just an airhead party animal, me."

"Just so." Pause. "Attend. Three ambassadors have been murdered. Their deaths coincide with the arrival of this ship in orbit around whichever planet they were on at the time. On this planet, there is an ambassador, and another senior government official. The reasons I brought you here are threefold. Firstly, I am interested in knowing who is killing these diplomats, and why, because I believe it will answer a very important question—who destroyed Moscow." There was another brief pause. "Backward chaining from the resolution of that situation, I must have sent a message to my earlier state vector—acting in my capacity as an ex-officio oracle and deity within the light cone—to pick you up at an early age. Your involvement was implicit in the development of this situation, although I don't yet fully understand why, and I believe the reason the faction of the assassins tried to kill you is connected. The information you stumbled across on Old Newfie was more important than I realized at the time. Unfortunately, unless I can arrange transport there for you, it may not be easy to retrieve it."

"You want to take me back *home*?" It came out as a squeak. Wednesday stood up hastily: "You didn't say anything about that! Isn't it dangerous? How will we get there—"

"That was the second reason," Herman continued implacably. "My third reason is this: I am a distributed intelligence service, linked by causal channels. I am highly dependent on state coherency that can only be maintained within the light cone— whenever the ship that is the focus of my attention makes an FTL transit, I lose contact. You are my reset switch. You are also my blind spot coverage. If I am inaccessible when critical events occur, you are sufficiently intelligent and resourceful that, if adequately informed, you can act as my proxy aboard ship. Now. Are you ready?"

"Ready for—" Wednesday took a deep breath. "What *am* I meant to be ready for?" she asked, her voice puzzled and slightly worried. "Is it going to be dangerous?" She pulled on her jacket (which she had dilated to an ankle-skimming coat, showy but thin and useless against the elements).

"Yes."

"Oh, how nice." Wednesday pulled a face. "Is there anything else?"

"Yes. You should be aware of several things. Firstly, there is another human agent of mine involved in this situation. His name is Martin Springfield. You can trust him implicitly if you meet him. He is acting as my unofficial liaison with another diplomatic element that is investigating the situation—more or less on the same side. Secondly, I owe you an apology."

"An—" Wednesday stopped dead. "What's that supposed to mean?" she asked suspiciously.

"I failed to prevent the destruction of your home world. I am worried, Wednesday. Preventing incidents like that is the purpose of my—this component's—existence. A failure to do so suggests a failure of my warning mechanisms. A failure of intelligence on my part suggests that the entities responsible for the destruction of Moscow are far more powerful than previously realized. Or are agencies of such an entity."

Wednesday leaned against the wall. "*What?* But you're the Eschaton!"

"Not quite. It is true that I am a component of the ensemble intelligence referred to as the Eschaton." Herman's voice had gone very flat, as if to emphasize the fact that any color in its tone was simply a modulation trick. "The Eschaton preserves global causality within a realm approximately a thousand parsecs in radius. It does so by recursively transmitting information back in time to itself, which is used to allow it to edit out temporal anomalies. Such temporal paradoxes are an inevitable side effect of permitting faster-than-light travel, or of operating an ensemble intelligence employing timelike logic mechanisms. I receive orders from deep time and execute them knowing that in doing so I ensure that the descendant state vector is going to exist long enough to issue those orders. If I do *not* receive such orders, then it may be that the events are not observable by me. Or my future state vector. This situation may occur if the Eschaton is disrupted or edited out of the future of this time-line. I am advising you, Wednesday, that I *should* have prevented the destruction of Moscow. That I failed to do so raises questions over my future survival."

"Oh fuck! You're telling me—"

"There appears to be a complex play in progress against me, executed by a party or parties unknown. I revise my previous estimate that the threat was emergent from the ReMastered. Their desire to destroy me is well understood, as are their capabilities, and countermeasures have been in place for some time. This threat emerges from a higher realm. The possibility of a hostile Eschaton-equivalent intelligence existing in the future of this light cone must now be considered. It is possible that a ReMastered faction is being manipulated by such an external entity. My ability to project ahead has therefore been called into question. Fallback logic modules employing neo-Bayesian reasoning suggest that when you return to the ship they will send a team of agents after you, but this is a purely speculative assumption. You must be on your guard at all times. Your job is to draw out the hostile proxies and expose them to me, starting at the embassy memorial ceremony. If you fail, the consequences could be far worse than the destruction of a single planet."

Click. "Oh shit." For a moment she thought she was going to be all right, but then her stomach twisted. She barely made it to the bathroom in time, holding back the dry heaves until she was over the toilet bowl. *Why me? How did I end up in this mess?* she asked the mirror, sniffing and trying to dry her eyes. *It's like some kind of curse!*

FifLy MinuLes laLer, it was a shaken but more composed Wednesday who climbed the two steps down from the space elevator capsule into a concrete-and-steel arrivals hall, presented her passport to the immigration official, and staggered blinking into the late-afternoon sunlight on New Dresden.

"Wow," she said softly.

Her rings vibrated for attention. She sighed. "Cancel block."

"Are you feeling less stressed?" asked Herman, as if nothing had happened.

"I think so."

"Good. Now please pay attention to where we are going. I am adding your destination to the public geotracking system. Follow the green dot."

"Green dot—okay." A green dot appeared on the floor, and Wednesday followed it passively, feeling drained and depressed. She'd almost psyched herself into looking forward to the reception, but Herman's news had unhinged her again, bringing her tenuous optimism crashing down. Maybe Frank would be able to cheer her up, but just then she wanted only to go back to her luxury suite and lock the door and get stinking drunk.

It took another three hours of boredom, dozing in the seats of a maglev capsule hurtling at thousands of kilometers per hour through an evacuated tunnel buried deep under oceans and continents, before she arrived in the capital. *Typical, why couldn't they build the beanstalk closer to the main city? Or move the city?* she sniffed to herself. Getting around on a planet seemed to take a very long time, for no obvious reason.

Sarajevo was old, with lots of stone buildings and steel-and-glass skyscrapers. It was badly air-conditioned, with strange eddying breezes and air currents and a really disorienting, upsetting blue-and-white fractal plasma image in place of a decent ceiling. It was also full of strange-looking people in weird clothes moving fast and doing incomprehensible things. She passed three women in fake peasant costume—New Dresden had never been backward enough to have a real peasantry—waving credit terminals. A bunch of people in rainbow-colored luminous plastic gowns roller-bladed past, surrounded by compact remotes buzzing around at ear level. Cars, silent and melted-looking, slunk through the streets. A fellow in grimy ripped technical mountaineering gear, bubble tent folded at his feet, seemed to be offering her an empty ceramic coffee cup. People in glowing glasses gesticulated at invisible interfaces; laser dots all over the place danced ahead of people who needed guidance. It wasn't like Septagon, it was like—

It's like home. If home had been bigger and brasher and more developed, she realized, tenuously making a connection to her memories of their last family visit to Grandma's house.

One thing pricked her attention: it was the lack of difference. She'd been worried at first about going down-well wearing a party costume she'd have been comfortable with back home. "Don't worry," Herman told her. "Moscow and Dresden are both McWorlds—the original colonists had similar backgrounds and aspirations. The culture will feel familiar to you. You can thank media diffusion for that; it will not be like the New Republic, or Turku, or even as different as Septagon." And indeed, it wasn't. Even the street signs looked the same.

"And we were nearly *at war* with these people?" she asked.

"The usual stupid reasons. Competitive trade advantage, immigration policy, political insecurity, cheap slow transport—cheap enough to facilitate trade, too expensive to facilitate federalization or the other adjustments human nations make to minimize the risk of war. The McWorlds all took something from the dominant terrestrial globalized culture with them when they were settled, but they have diverged since then—in some cases, radically. Do not make the mistake of assuming you can discuss politics or actions of the government safely here."

"As if I would." Wednesday followed her green dot round a

corner and up a spiraling ramp onto a road-spanning walkway, then into a roofed-over mall. "Where am I supposed to be meeting Frank?"

"He should be waiting for you. Along this road. There."

He was sitting on a bench in front of an abstract bronze sculpture, rattling away on his antique keyboard. Killing time. "Frank, are you okay?"

He looked up at her and pulled a face—a grimace that might have been intended as a smile but succeeded in doing nothing to reassure her. His eyes were red-rimmed and had bags under them, and his clothing looked as if he'd been living in it for a couple of days. "I, I think so." He shook his head. "Brr." He yawned widely. "Haven't slept for a long, uh . . ." He trailed off.

Party overload, she thought dispassionately. She reached out and took his hand, tugging. "Come on!"

Frank lurched to his feet and caught his balance. The keyboard concertinaed away into a pocket. He yawned again. "Are we in time?"

She blinked, checking her timepiece: "Sure!" she said brightly. "What have you been doing?"

"Not sleeping." Frank shook himself. "I'm a mess. Mind if I freshen up first?" He looked almost apologetic.

She grinned at him. "That looks like a public toilet over there."

"Okay. Two minutes."

He took nearer to a quarter of an hour, but when he returned he'd had a shower and run his outerwear through a fastcleaner. "Sorry 'bout that. Do I look better?"

"You look fine," she said diplomatically. "At least, you'll pass. Are you going to fall over on me?"

"Nope." He dry swallowed a capsule and shuddered slightly. "Not until we get back to the ship." He tapped the pocket with his keyboard in it. "Captured enough color for three features, interviewed four midlevel government officials and six random civilians, grabbed about four hours of full-motion. One *last* push and—" This time his smile looked less stressed.

"Okay, let's go." She took his hand again and led him along the street.

"You know where we're going? The embassy reception hall?"

"Never been there." She pointed at the floor. "Got a guide."

"Oh *good,* tell everyone where we're going," he muttered. "I just hope they don't mistake me for a vagrant."

"An, uh, what? What was that?"

"A vagrant?" He raised an eyebrow at her. "They don't have them where you come from? Lucky."

She checked the word in her lexicon. "I'll tell them you're my guest," she said, and patted his hand. Having Frank around made her feel safe, like walking through a strange town with a huge and ferocious guard dog—the biological kind—to protect her. Her spirits rose as they neared the embassy.

Embassies were traditionally the public representatives of a nation abroad. As such, they tended to be built with a swagger, gratuitously broad facades and conspicuously gilded flagpoles. The Muscovite embassy was typical of the breed, a big, classically styled limestone-and-marble heap squatting sullenly behind a row of poplar trees, a discreet virtual fence, and a lawn that appeared to have been trimmed with a micrometer gauge and nail scissors. But something about it wasn't quite right. It might have been the flag out front—set to half-mast ever since the dreadful day, years ago, when the diplomatic causal channel went dead— or something more subtle. There was a down-at-heel air to it, of retired gentry keeping up appearances but quietly living beyond their means.

And then there was the security cordon.

"I'm Wed—uh, Victoria Strowger," Wednesday chattered to the two armed cops as they examined her passport, "and this is Frank Johnson, my guest, and isn't this exciting?" She clapped her hands as they waved her through the archway of an explosive sniffer. "I can't believe I've been invited to a real embassy function! Wow, is that the Ambassador? No?"

"You don't have to lay it on quite that thick," Frank said tiredly, catching up with her a minute later. "They're not idiots. Pull a stunt like that at a *real* checkpoint, and they'll have you in an interrogation cell before your feet touch the ground."

"Huh?" She shook her head. "A real checkpoint? What was that about, then?"

"What it was about was telling everybody that there are guards about. There are all sorts of real defenses all around us, and barely out of view. Dogs, drones, all sorts of surveillance crap. Guess I was right—this stinks of a high-alert panic."

"Oh." She leaned closer to him as she glanced around. There was a large marquee dome behind one wing of the embassy, lights strung between trees—and a handful of adults, one or two of them in elaborate finery but most of them simply wearing office garb, wandering around clutching glasses of fizzy wine. "Are we in danger?" *From what Herman said—*

"I don't think so. At least, I hope not."

There were tables in the dome, attentive catering staff and bottles of wine and battalions of glasses waiting to be filled, a spread of canapés and hand rolls and other bite-sized snacks laid out for the guests. A clump of bored-looking visitors clutched their obligatory glass and disposable platter, and in one or two cases a sad-looking handheld flag. The first time Wednesday saw a flag she had to look away, unsure whether to laugh or cry. Patriotism had never been a huge Muscovite virtue, and to see the way the fat woman in the red pants held on to her flag as if it were a life preserver made Wednesday want to slap her and yell *Grow up! It's all over!* Except it also felt like...like watching Jerm, aged three, playing with the pewter pot containing Grandpa's ashes. Abuse of the dead, an infection of history. And now, *he* was gone. She looked away, sniffed, and tried to clear the haze in her eyes. She'd never much liked her kid brother anyway, but not having him around to dislike felt *wrong.*

A man and a woman wearing sober outfits that would have been at home in a law office were working the guest crowd in a low-key manner. Wednesday's turn came remarkably fast. "Hello, I'm pleased you could be here today," said the woman, fixing Wednesday with a professionally polished smile that was almost as tightly lacquered as her hair. "I'm Mary-Louise. I don't believe I've had the pleasure of meeting you before?"

"Hi, I'm Wednesday." She forced a tired smile. Crying earlier had dried out the skin around her eyes. "I'm just passing through, actually, on board the *Romanov.* Is this a regular event?"

"We host one like it every year to mark the anniversary. Is there one where you live, can I ask?"

"I don't think so," Wednesday said doubtfully. "Centris Magna, in Septagon. Quite a lot of us went there from Old New-fie—"

"Station eleven! Is that where you came from?"

"Yes."

"Oh, very good! I had a cousin there. Listen, here's Subminister Hasek, come to be very cultural with us tonight. We've got food, drink, a media presentation, and Rhona Geiss will be singing—but I've got to see to everyone else. Help yourself to everything, and if you need anything else, Mr. Tranh there will see to you." She vanished in a flurry of wide sleeves and coattails, leaving Wednesday to watch in bemusement as a corpulent old man the size of a brown bear shambled slowly into the dome, a gleaming, polished woman at either side. One of them reminded Wednesday of Steffi so much that she blinked, overtaken by an urge to say hello to the friendly ship's officer. When she looked again, the moment of recognition passed. A gaggle of teenagers gave ground to the threesome reluctantly as they walked in front of a circle of stewards setting up a table.

Wednesday accepted a glass of wine and cast around for Frank, but he'd wandered off somewhere while the greeters had been working her. *Expect trouble.* Sure, but what kind?

A row of glass doors had been shoved back from the room at one side of the embassy, and a couple of embassy staffers were arranging rows of chairs across the floor, then out onto the manicured lawn. The far wall of the reception room had become a screen, a blue-white-green disc eerily similar to the one Wednesday had seen from orbit as she boarded the orbit-to-surface elevator capsule. It floated in the middle of a sea of stars. *Home,* she thought, dully. She hadn't felt homesick for years, not really, and then it had been for Old Newfie rather than this abstraction of a place she'd been born on—but now she felt a certain dangerous nostalgia begin to bite, and an equal and opposite cynical impulse to sneer at the idea. *What has Moscow ever done for me?* she asked herself. Then memory stabbed at her: her parents, the look on Mayor Pocock's face as they'd hauled down the flag in the hub concourse before the evacuation . . . too many memories. Memories she couldn't escape.

Herman spoke in her earbud: "Most people come for the readings, remain for the singing of the national anthem, *then* leave and get steaming drunk. You might want to emulate them."

Twenty minutes and one glass of wine later, Wednesday found a corner seat at one end of the front row. The other visitors were filtering in slowly, nothing like as organized as a funeral party entering a chapel of rest. By all appearances a number of them were already leading her at the drinking.

As the room filled up, and some people spilled onto the overflow chairs on the lawn, Wednesday felt someone sit in the chair next to her. "Frank?" She glanced round.

"These are your people?" he said. Something in his expression made her wonder if he had internal ghosts of his own to struggle with. He seemed haunted by something.

"What is it?" she asked.

He shook his head. "Some other time." She turned round to face the front. A few stragglers were still filling the seats, but a door had opened to one side of the podium and a dignified-looking albeit slightly portly woman—possibly middle-aged, possibly a centenarian, it was difficult to tell—walked up to the stage.

With her chestnut hair tied back with a ribbon, her black embroidered coat buttoned at the waist and cut back above and below, and the diamond-studded chain of office draped across her shoulders, she was exactly what Wednesday had expected the Ambassador to be. She cleared her throat and the sound system caught and exploded her rasping breath across the lawn. "Welcome," she said. "Again, welcome. Today is the fifth anniversary, absolute time standard years, of the death, and exile, of our compatriots. I"—she paused, an unreadable expression on her face— "I know that, like you, I have difficulty understanding that event. We can't go home, now or ever. The door is shut, all options closed. There is no sense of closure: no body in a coffin, no assailant under arrest and charged with murder.

"But—" She took a deep breath: "*I shall try to be brief.* We are still here, however much we mourn our friends and relatives who were engulfed by the holocaust. *We* survive. We bear witness. We go on, and we will rebuild our lives, and we will remember them.

"Someone destroyed our homes. As an agent of the surviving caretaker government, I dedicate my life to this task: to bear witness, and to identify the guilty parties, whoever they are and wherever they may be sheltering. They will be held to account, and the accounting will be sufficient to deter anyone else who ever contemplates such monstrous acts in future."

She paused, head tilted slightly to one side as if she was listening to something—and, as she continued, Wednesday realized, *She* is *listening to something. Someone is reading her a speech and she's simply echoing it!* Startled, she almost missed the Ambassador's next words: "We will now pause for a minute in silent contemplation. Those of us who believe in the intervention of higher agencies may wish to pray; those of us who don't may take heart from the fact that we are not alone, and we will make sure that our friends and families did not die in vain."

Wednesday was disinclined to meditate on much of anything.

She looked around surreptitiously, examining fixtures and fittings. The ambassador's girth—*She's not fat, but she's carrying a lot of padding around the waist. And those boxes around the podium... and the guy at the back there, and that woman in the dark suit and business glasses...* Something smelled wrong. In fact, something smelled *killing zone,* a game Herman had taught her years before. How to spot an ambush. *This is just like a, a trap,* she realized. *But who—*

Wednesday turned back and was watching the Ambassador's eyes as it happened. They widened slightly as somebody a couple of rows behind Wednesday made a nervous noise. Then the Ambassador snapped into motion, sudden as a machine, arms coming up to protect her face as she ducked.

Then:

Why am I lying down? Wednesday wondered fuzzily. *Why?* She could see, but everything was blurry and her ears ached. *I feel sick.* She tried to moan and catch her breath and there was an acrid stink of burning. Abruptly she realized that her right hand was wet and sticky, and she was curled around something bony. Dampness. She tried to lever herself up with her left hand, and the air was full of dust, the lights were out, and thinly, in the distance through the ringing in her ears, she heard screams.

A flicker of light. A moment later, she was clearer. The podium—the woman wasn't there. The boxes to either side had exploded like air bags, blasting heavy shields into the air in front of the Ambassador as she ducked. But behind her, behind them... Wednesday sat up and glanced down, realized someone was screaming. There was blood on the back of her hand, blood on her sleeve, blood on the chairs. *A bomb,* she thought fuzzily. Then: *I ought to do something.* People were screaming. A hand and an arm lay in the middle of the aisle next to her, the elbow a grisly red mess. Frank was lying on the floor next to her. The back of his head looked as if it had been sprayed with red paint. As she recognized him, he moved, one arm flailing at the ground in a stunned reflex. The woman who had been seated behind him was still seated, but her head ended in a glutinous stump somewhere between her neck and her nose. *Bomb,* Wednesday realized again, confused but trying to hold on to the thought. More thoughts: *Herman warned me. Frank!*

She leaned over him in panic. "Frank! Talk to me!" He opened his mouth and tried to say something. She winced, unable to hear him. *Is he dying?* she wondered, feeling lost and anxious.

"Frank!" A dizzy laugh welled up as she tried to remember details from a first-aid course she'd taken years ago—*Is he breathing? Yes. Is he bleeding?* It was hard to tell; there was so much blood everywhere that she couldn't see if it was his. Frank mumbled something at her. He wasn't flailing around. In fact, he seemed to be trying to move. "Wait, you mustn't—" Frank sat up. He felt around the back of his head and winced, then peered at Wednesday owlishly.

"Dizzy," he said, and slowly toppled toward her.

Wednesday managed to brace herself with one arm as he fainted. *He must weigh over a hundred kilos,* she realized fuzzily. She looked round, searching for help, but the shout died in her throat. It hadn't been a big bomb—not much more than a grenade—but it had burst in the middle of the audience, ripping half a dozen bodies into bloody pulp, and splashing meat and bone and blood around like evil paint. A man with half his clothes blasted off his body and his upper torso painted red stumbled into the epicenter blindly, arms outstretched as if looking for someone. A woman, sitting in her chair like an incisor seated in a jaw between the empty red holes of pulled teeth, screamed and clutched her shredded arm. Nightmares merged at the edges, bleeding over into daylight, rawhead and bloodybones come out to play. Wednesday licked her lips, tasted bright metal dampness, and whimpered as her stomach tried to eject wine and half-digested canapés.

The next thing she knew, a man in black was standing over her, a gun at the ceiling—looking past her, talking urgently to a floating drone. She tried to shake her head. Something was crushing her. "—an you walk?" he said. "—your friend?"

"Mmf. Try." She pushed against Frank's deadweight, and Frank tensed and groaned. "Frank—" The guard was away, bending over another body and suddenly dropping to his knees, frantically pumping at a still chest.

"I'm, I'm—" He blinked, sleepily. "Wednesday?"

Sit up, she thought fuzzily. "Are you okay?"

"I think—" He paused. "My head." For a miracle, the weight on her shoulder slackened. "Are you hurt?" he asked her.

"I—" She leaned against him, now. "Not badly. I think."

"Can't stay here," he said faintly. "The bomb. Before the bomb. Saw you, Sven."

"Saw who?"

"Jim. Clown." He looked as if he was fading. Wednesday

leaned toward him. "Sven was here. Wearing a waiter's—" His eyelids fluttered.

"Make sense! What are you *saying?*" she hissed, driven by a sense of urgency she didn't understand. "What do you mean—" "Svengali. Back. Performer." His eyes opened. "Got to find Sven."

"Are you telling me you saw him—" Shock brought Wednesday into focus.

"Yes. Yes. Find him. He's..." Frank's eyes closed.

Wednesday waved at a passing guard: "Here!" A head turned. "My friend, concussion. Help?"

"Oh shit, another—" The guard waved one of her colleagues over. "Medic!"

Wednesday slid after Frank, torn between a pressing need to see that he was all right and a conviction that she should go look for the clown. Leaving Frank felt *wrong,* like letting go of her only lifeline to stability. Just an hour ago he'd seemed so solid he could anchor her to the universe, but now everything was in flux. She stumbled toward the side door, her head whirling, guts churning. Her right hand stung, a hot, aching pain. *Svengali?* She wondered: *what could he be doing here?* A short passage and another open door brought her weaving and stumbling onto the lawn at the back of the embassy building. Bright light glared down from overhead floods, starkly silhouetting a swarm of cops buzzing around the perimeter like disturbed hornets. *Sven?* she thought.

She stumbled around the side of the building. A woman blocked her way: "You can't come—"

"My friend!" She gasped, and pushed past. For some reason, no arms restrained her. Bodies were laid out on the grass under the harsh spotlights, some of them unmoving, others with people in paramedic orange frantically working over them. Other people stood or shambled around in a daze, prodded by a couple of enhanced police dogs that seemed to have a better idea of what was going on than any of the humans. Only a couple of minutes had passed, and the noise of sirens was still getting closer, audible over the ringing in her ears.

She found him squatting on the grass, wearing face cake and a red nose spattered with blood, holding his head in his hands. His costume was a clown's parody of a snobbish chef's outfit. "Sven?" She gasped.

He looked up, eyes red, a trickle of blood running from one nostril. "Wed-Wed—"

"We've got to go," she said, trying to think of anything else that wasn't inane. "We'll miss our, our..."

"You go, girl, I'll, I—" He shook his head, looking dizzy. "Help?"

Was he here to perform? she asked herself. Then: "You're hurt? Come on, on your feet. Back to the dining room. There's medical triage in there, first aid. Let's get you seen to and pick up Frank and catch a taxi. If we stay here, they'll ask questions till we miss the ship."

"Ship." His hands came down. He looked at her eyes cautiously, expression slightly puzzled. "Came here to, had to, set up? Frank? Hurt? Is he—"

"Deafened and shocked, I think." She shivered, feeling cold.

"But we can't just—"

"We can. Listen, you're one of my *two* guests, right? And we'll give them a statement but we've got to do that right now, our ship leaves tonight. If you're a guest, they won't grill you like a performer or staff. I hope."

Svengali tried to stand up, and Wednesday backed off to give him room. "Must. Just tell the, the medics—" He staggered, and somehow Wednesday caught his left arm and pulled it over her shoulder—and she was walking Svengali drunkenly around toward the front of the embassy as the first ambulance arrived on a whine of electric motors.

"i don't fucking *believe* this!"

Rachel had never, ever, seen George Cho lose his temper before. It was impressive, and would have been frightening if she hadn't had more important things to worry about than her boss flapping around like a headless chicken.

"They missed," she said with forced detachment. "Six dead and however many more injured, but they missed. The reactive armor deflected most of the shrapnel straight up, and I hit the floor in time." She clenched her hands together to keep them from shaking.

"Why weren't the grounds sealed off afterward? Why don't we know who—the cameras—"

"Did you think they would be amateurs?" she asked angrily, pacing past him to look out the window overseeing the lawn. The indoor lights had blown, along with most of the unshielded electronics in the embassy. The EMP pulse had been small, but was sufficient to do for most non-MilSpec equipment on-site. And someone had done a real number on the cameras with a brace of self-adhesive clown-face stickers. "Murderous clowns, but not amateurs."

The convoy of ambulances had taken most of the injured to various local clinics, which had activated their major incident plans immediately. Those vehicles that were left were parked, sirens silenced, not in any hurry to remove the bodies until the SOC team had finished mapping the mess left by the bomb and Forensics had taken their sample grams of flesh, and the polite men and women in their long black coats had asked their pointed questions of the catering staff—

"We set them up for a long gun," Rachel reminded him, shuddering slightly. Remembering the icy feeling in her guts as she'd walked out onstage wearing a bulletproof vest, knowing there was a reactive armor shield in front of her, and a crash cart with resuscitation and stabilization gear waiting behind the door, and an ambulance in back. Knowing that a sniper would have to shoot in through a fixed arc constrained by the windows and the podium at the back of the room, knowing the ballistic radar at the front of the killing zone *should* be able to blow the armor slabs into the path of a bullet-sized guided missile before it could reach her, knowing there were two anti-sniper teams waiting in the hedgerow out front—she'd still been unsure whether each breath would be her last. "They weren't stupid. Didn't bring a knife to a gunfight. Took an antipersonnel mine instead."

"And they got away with it again." George sat down heavily on the edge of the lacquered and jade-inlaid desk, head bowed. "We should have fucking *known*—"

"Tranh?" called Rachel.

"We leaked," the researcher said quietly. "We made it a honeypot, and we attracted the wasps, but probably only one of the passengers from the *Romanov* was involved, and we can't tell which one because they fried the surveillance records and probably exfiltrated among the wounded. For all we know the assassin is among the dead. Worse, if they're from an advanced infrastructure society like Septagon or somewhere with access to brain-mapping gear, the killer could have been any other guest or member of staff they managed to get five minutes alone with. And we couldn't prove a thing. It looks like the only thing left to do is bring down the hammer and stop the ship leaving. Detain everybody. Want me to get on line to Martin? Have him lock it down?"

"Don't do that yet," said Rachel.

"Yes, do it," said Cho. He took a deep breath. "We're going to have to arrest them," he told Rachel. "Even if it tips them off. They already know something—must suspect, surely, or else they wouldn't have declined the honeypot—"

"Not necessarily," Rachel said urgently. "Listen, if you hold the ship, we'll probably uncover an assassin—a *dead* one, if these people are as ruthless as we think. If we do that, what happens next? I'll tell you what happens next: there's a hiatus, then a different killer starts making the rounds, and this time we'll have broken the traffic analysis chain so we won't know where they are or where they're going next. We need to let them run—but we have to stay in front of them."

George stood up and paced across the room. "I can't take the risk. They've grown increasingly reckless, from selective assassination to indiscriminate bombing! What next, a briefcase nuke? Don't you think they're capable of that?"

"They—" Rachel stopped dead. "They almost certainly are," she admitted. "But don't you think that makes it all the more important that we keep track of them and try to take them alive, so we can find out who's behind it?"

"You want to go aboard the ship," said Tranh.

"I don't see any alternative." There was a horrible familiarity to the situation; to keep on top of a crisis moving at FTL speeds, you had to ride the bullet. "My recommendation is that we let the *Romanov* depart on schedule, but that I—and any other core team members you see fit to assign to me—should be on board as passengers, and you serve your bill of attainder on the Master and tell her that she's damn well going to do as I say in event of an emergency.

"Meanwhile, the rest of the team should proceed aboard the *Gloriana* to the next destination where there's a Muscovite embassy—I think that'll be Vienna? Or wherever—and set up the next trap. Leaving behind a diplomatic support group here to keep an eye on Morrow and Baxter, and anyone off the *Romanov* who's staying on." She swallowed. "While we're under way, I'll liaise with the ship's crew to try to identify anyone who's acting suspiciously. Before and after the events. Martin may have spotted something while we were busy down here, but I haven't had time to check yet. If we can get access to the onboard monitoring feeds, we might be able to wrap everything up before we arrive at the next port of call."

"You'll have no backup," said Cho. "If they panic and decide to bury the evidence—"

"I'll be right there to stop them," Rachel said firmly. She glanced out the window. "It won't be the first time. But if we do it, we have to do it right now. The *Romanov* is due to depart in less than five hours. I need to be on board with a sensible cover story and a full intrusion kit. A diplomatic bag, if possible, with full military cornucopia, just like the one we used last time." She pretended not to notice George's wince. "And I need to get out of this

fucking rubber mask, and call Martin to tell him to stay aboard the
Romanov, if you don't mind."

"If I—" George shook his head. "Tranh. How do you evaluate
Rachel's proposed course of action?"

"I'm afraid she's right," Tranh said stiffly. "But I—" he
paused. "Who do you need?"

"For a job like this?" Rachel shrugged. "*Nobody* is ready for
this. I submit that the best cover is no cover. If I go with Martin,
we should be overt—a couple of UN diplomats taking low-
priority transport between postings, to meet up with the rest of our
mission on Newpeace. No cover story at all, in other words—it
takes the least effort to set up and it also gives me a clear line of
authority back home, reason to talk to the Captain, that sort of
thing. I'll—" She looked worried. "First New Prague, then Newpeace. I heard that name before somewhere, didn't I? Something
bad, some atrocity."

"Newpeace." George made a curse of it. "Yes. You don't want
to go there without immunity. Even *with* immunity. I'm going to
have to send you the internal briefings on the place, Rachel. You
don't want to land there."

"Is it that bad?"

"It's a dictatorship run by the ReMastered," Tranh said grimly.
"Nasty little local ideology that seems to pop up like a poisonous
toadstool in patches. And that fits with a bit of intel our back-
office trawl pulled in. We've been grepping the public feeds for
any references to Moscow, and we got a high probability hit off of
a warblogger who's traveling on the *Romanov.* He's poking
around the Moscow business from the other end, making some
unsubstantiated but very paranoid suggestions about survivors—
not diplomats—being tracked down and murdered. What's *more*
interesting is that he's on board the *Romanov* and *ReMastered* was
one of the keyword hits that flagged his column in our trawl.
Nothing but innuendo so far, and he's got an axe to grind—I was
following up his history when things fell apart here—but they're a
local power, and they've been known to meddle in foreign affairs
before now."

"They're also ruthless enough that if they're involved in this
mess, I don't want you going anywhere near one of their worlds,
with or without diplomatic papers," George added. "Look, you've
got five hours until departure, and you're going to take at least
three to get up the beanstalk and into orbit. Get going. Get ready.

I'll get Gianni to open a credit line to the mission for you to use, and you, Tranh, you're going along as Rachel's backup. Make sure to brief her on who these ReMastered are, just in case. Rachel, Martin will travel with you. He knows the ship, so he's your technical adviser. We'll talk by channel once you're under way and damn the expense. Right now I've got this mess to clean up. So don't hang around." He extended a hand. After a moment, Rachel took it. "Good luck," he said. "I've got a feeling you're going to need it."

the horror never ended, but after a while you could learn to live with it, Rachel reflected. Or rather, you learned to live *between* it, in the intervals, the white space between the columns of news, the quiet, civilized times that made the job worthwhile. You learned to live in order to make the whitespace bigger, to *reduce* the news, to work toward the end of history, to make the universe safe for peace. And you knew it was a zero-sum game at best and eventually you'd lose, but you were on the right side so that didn't matter. Somebody had to do it. And then—

Scum. There was no other word for it. Fragmentation grenades in the audience at a nondenominational secular-friendly memorial ceremony spelled *scum*. The audience screaming, a child with her hand blown off, a woman with no head. The pale-faced girl in the front row, desperately leaning over her friend, his head bloodied by the—

"Is the payload ready?" she asked mildly.

"One moment." Pritkin unplugged his diagnostic probe. "Primed. Stick your finger in here. Shared secret time."

"Okay." Rachel extended a hand, wrapped her fingers around the probe and waited for it to bleep, signifying successful quantum key exchange. Pritkin stuck the probe back into the slot in the large traveler's trunk and waited for the light on its base to begin blinking red. Then he ejected it. "It's all yours. Armed and loaded." He straightened up and put the probe away.

"Which department is this one billed to?" Rachel asked. "After the last time . . ."

"Department of Collective Defense." Pritkin smiled grimly. "You may find its inventory tree a little alarming."

"Indeed." Rachel eyed the trunk appraisingly. "Full military fabworks?"

"Yup. This little cornucopia can, with a bit of guidance and your authority, generate an entire military-industrial complex. Try not to lose it."

"Once was an accident, twice would be careless. All right." She spoke to the trunk. "Do you recognize me?"

The trunk spoke back, in a flat monotone: "Authorized officer commanding. You have control."

"Hey, I like that. Trunk, follow me." She nodded to Pritkin. "See you at Newpeace."

Scum! she thought, her rage controlled for the time being, directed and channeled. *I'm coming for you. And when I find you, you'll be sorry . . .*

the express elevator up the beanstalk gave Rachel time to confront the horrors and try to shove them back into a corner of her mind. Tranh, she noted, was even more quiet and reserved than normal. The elevator car was almost two-thirds full, carrying a good number of crew members and tourists returning to the *Romanov* before it departed; also a sprinkling of quiet, worried-looking Dresdener citizens. While the R-bombs remained decades away, and the recall codes could still be issued, the panic hadn't set in. Only the most paranoid tinfoil-hat wearers would be thinking about emigrating already. But with a population of hundreds of millions, even the lunatic fringe was large enough to populate a medium-sized city, and some of the middle-aged men and small family groups wore the cautious, haunted expression of refugees. They'd probably be checking in to steerage, to sleep away the long jump sequence without spending precious savings. Rachel figured her assassin wouldn't be among them. He or she would want to be awake, to plan the next atrocity and keep a weather eye open for pursuers.

She tilted her seat back as far as it would go and waited for the oppressive shove of acceleration to go away. The car was only pulling two gees, but it was enough to make walking unfeasible and lifting a drinking cup uncomfortably difficult. The glowing blue space elevator cable zipped past beyond the transparent ceiling, an endless string with knots flickering by several times a second—the bulbous shells of the boost coils that coupled the car to its invisible magnetic corridor. *They're up there,* she reminded herself. *Along with a couple of thousand innocent passengers and crew.* Over six hundred people had come down from the *Romanov* while it was docked; nearly four hundred had returned to the ship. Of those, three hundred and fifty had been aboard the ship—and taken their leave on the surfaces of each planet it had visited, including the ones where Muscovite diplomats had been attacked. Only twenty or so of the passengers had been at the embassy reception, but that didn't mean anything. *If it is a bunch like the ReMastered, there won't be a causal link,* she decided. *They're not fools.* She'd spent the first hour of the journey skimming George's diplomatic backgrounder on known ReMastered black operations and was wondering how the hell she'd failed to hear about them before. *It's a big galaxy, but not that big when you get, what was Rosa's term, bampots like these running amok.* Working to a hunch was risky; it could blind you to who was really pulling your strings—but now she'd seen Tranh's dossier, Rachel had a gut-deep feeling that they were somehow involved. The whole thing had the stench of diplomatic black ops all over it, and these guys were clearly crazy and ruthless enough to be responsible. The only question was *why.*

"Why the fuck didn't you tell us this was a possibility?" she'd asked Tranh, halfway through reading—and then rereading in disbelief—the first page.

He'd shrugged apologetically, squirming under the acceleration load. "George said to keep it low-key. To avoid prejudicing the investigation."

"Prejudice, hah." Rachel had looked away.

Despite her violent aversion to museums, Rachel had an overdeveloped sense of historical contingency. Thanks to the arrival of cheap life-prolongation mods, her generation was one of the first to have lived through enough history to have a bellyful of it. She'd grown up in a throwback religious community that didn't accept any social development postdating the midtwentieth century, and spent her first few adult decades as a troubled but outwardly dutiful surrendered wife. Then she'd hit middle age and jumped the hedge to see the world, the flesh, and the devil for herself. Along the way she'd acquired a powerful conviction that history was a series of accidents—God was either absent or playing a very elaborate practical joke (the Eschaton didn't count, having explicitly denied that it was a deity)—and that the seeds of evil usually germinated in the footprints of people who knew how everybody else ought to behave and felt the need to tell them so. When she'd been born, there had still been people alive who remembered the Cold War, the gray behemoth of ideology slouching toward a nuclear destination. And the ReMastered rang some uneasy bells in the echoing library of her memory. She'd heard of things like this before. *Why hasn't anybody stepped on them yet?* she wondered.

As she considered the question there was a chime. The elevator car slowed, and, for a stomach-churning moment, spun upside down. Acceleration resumed, pressing down on her like a lead-weighted net. "We will arrive in reception bay three in approximately nineteen minutes," announced the cabin attendant. "Slowing to one gee two minutes before arrival, if you need to use the en suite facilities."

Tranh caught her eye. "You ready?" He grunted.

"Yes." Rachel didn't elaborate. Tranh was nervous, and he'd let her know. "Done reading." She tapped her secure notepad to demonstrate, and he attempted to nod—unwise and uncomfortable, judging from his grimace. Earlier, Rachel had tried holding the pad up, two-handed, and found it workable, except that her arms tried to go to sleep if she held the position for more than a couple of minutes. For a gadget that could fit in her wallet it felt remarkably like a lead brick. But there was something unhealthily compulsive about reading about the ReMastered. It was like scratching a fleabite until it bled: she didn't want to do it but found herself unable to stop.

Scum, she thought as she read the in-depth report on New-peace. *How did they get away with it? It's the most brilliant, horrible, thing I've seen in years.* It made the imperial megalomania and straitlaced frigidity of the New Republic seem cozy and forgivable by comparison. *Seminars on history's most onerous tyrannies—so they know which errors of* leniency *to avoid?*

The planet arrayed above her head was showing a visible disc, gibbous and misty, with a thin rind of atmosphere. *Are they out to conquer this world, too?* she wondered. The ReMastered showed every sign of being aggressively expansionist, convinced their ideology was the one true way. But logistical nightmares and the presence of STL bombers around almost every target world made interstellar power grabs unfeasibly risky. It was as if, during Earth's nineteenth century, every imperialist set on colonizing another land had been forced to resupply by wooden sailing ship across the breadth of the Pacific Ocean, while facing defenders armed with nuclear-tipped missiles.

"So they came from Tonto and executed a classic Maoist-Fischerite insurgency campaign, mediated by zombies with brain implants driven by causal channel from a nest in the same solar system," she noted beneath a harrowing account of the Peace Enforcement Agency's subversion. Arranging a terrorist insurgency to justify a state clampdown, then providing the tools and trained personnel for the panicking incumbents to deploy, before decapitating them in a coup and consolidating power. "Hmm." *And if they grab the levers of power cleanly, before anyone realizes that half their politicians are brain-scooped moppets, they can decommission the STL bombers before they become a threat. Which in turn means... Hey, have they actually invented a repeatable strategy for interstellar conquest? And if so, did they come from somewhere else, before Tonto? In which case...*

The whole ReMastered project, to destroy the Eschaton and replace it with another god, one with access to the uploaded memories of every human being who'd ever lived—and then to recreate humanity in the image of the new god they intended to serve—sounded so ridiculous on the face of it that it pleaded to be written off as a crackpot religion from the darkness beyond the terrestrial light cone. But something about it made Rachel's skin crawl. *I've heard of something like this before, somewhere else. But where?*

She was still trying to answer the question when there was a succession of chimes, the elevator capsule spun around once more, and the view was replaced with smooth metal walls inching past at a snail's pace. She had her safety harness unbuckled before the attendant managed to say, "Welcome to orbital transfer station three." By the time the doors were open, she was on her feet with her pad stowed in a pocket, ready to collect her luggage from the hold.

The station blurred past her, unnoticed: departure gates, an outgoing customs desk she cleared with an imperious wave of her diplomatic tags, bowing and scraping from functionaries, a luggage trolley to carry her heavy case. Then she reached a docking tunnel that was more like a shopping mall, all carpet and glassed-in side bays exhibiting the blandishments of a hundred luxury stores and hotels. The white-gloved officer from the purser's team at the desk took one look at her passport and priority pass, and tried to usher her through into a VIP lift. She had to make him wait until Tranh caught up.

"Where are we berthed?" she asked.

"Ah, if I can see your—ah, I see." The Junior Lieutenant blinked through the manifest. "Ma'am, sir, if you'd like to follow me, you're to be accommodated on Bravo deck, that's executive territory. I show a Queen-class suite reserved for each of you. If you'd just care to wait a moment while I find out if they're ready—this was a very-short-notice booking, I'm terribly sorry—ah, yes. This way. Please?"

"Is Martin Springfield about?" she asked anxiously.

"Springfield? I know of no—oh, him. Yes he is. He's in a meeting with Flying Officer Fromm. Do you want me to page him for you?"

"No, that's fine. We're traveling together. If you could message him my room details when he comes out of his meeting?"

More corridors, more lifts. Exquisite wood paneling, carved on distant worlds and imported at vast expense for the fitting-out of the liner. Gilded statuary in niches, hand-woven rugs on the floors of the first-class quarters. *So this is what Martin works on for a living?* she wondered. A door gaped wide and two white-uniformed stewards bowed as Rachel tiredly led her luggage inside. "That will be all for now, thanks," she said, dismissing them. As the door closed, she looked around. "Well, that's an improvement over the last time..."

Last time Rachel had traveled on a diplomatic passport she'd had a cramped berth in officer territory on a battlecruiser. This time she probably had more space to herself than the Admiral's suite. She locked the door, bent to unfasten her shoes, and stretched her feet in the thick pile carpet. "I ought to do this more often," she told the ceiling. Her eyes were threatening to close from exhaustion—she'd been on her feet and alert for danger most of the time since the debacle at the embassy, and it was four in the morning, by Sarajevo local time—but business came first. From her shoulder bag she removed a compact receiver and busied herself quartering the room until she was satisfied that the only wireless traffic she could pick up consisted of legitimate emanations from room service. She sighed and put the machine down, then raised her phone. "Voice mail for Martin, copy to Tranh," she said. "I'm going to crash out for four hours, then I'm going back on duty. Call me if there are any developments. If not, we'll meet up to discuss our strategy tomorrow after I have time to talk to the Captain. Martin, feel free to come round whenever you get out of your meeting. Over."

Finally, she checked the door. It was locked. *Good,* she thought. She walked over to the bed, set a wake-up alarm on her rings, and collapsed, not bothering to undress first. She was asleep almost as soon as her head hit the pillows, and the nightmares, when they came, were as bad as she'd feared.

lights, sirens, and night. A welter of impressions had closed around Wednesday, threatening to engulf her and cast her adrift on a sea of nightmare fodder. Svengali staggered alongside her, nursing an arm. A paramedic shone a torch in her face. She waved it aside. "He needs help!" she shouted, holding the clown upright. She sat beside him for an eternity while a paramedic strapped up his arm, ran a teraherz scanner across his skull to check for fractures—someone else was working on her bruised forehead, but it was hard to keep track of things.

An indeterminate time later she was standing up. "We need to get to the port," she was explaining in nightmare slow motion to a police officer who didn't seem to understand: "Our ship leaves in a couple of hours—"

She kept having to repeat herself. Why did she keep having to repeat herself? Nobody was listening. Lights, sirens. She was sitting down now, and the lights were flashing past and the sirens were overhead... *I'm in a police car,* she realized hazily. Sitting between Svengali and Frank. Frank had one arm around her shoulders, sheltering her. But this was wrong. They hadn't done anything wrong, had they? Were they under arrest? *Going to miss the flight—*

"Here you go." The door opened. Frank clambered out, then held Wednesday's arm, helping her out of the car. "We're holding the capsule for you—step this way." And it was true. She felt tears of relief prickling at her eyelids, trying to escape. Leaning on Frank. Svengali behind her, and two more carloads—the police were helping, shunting the off-worlders off-world. The full VIP treatment. *Why?* she wondered vaguely. Then a moment's thought brought it home: *Anything to look helpful to the diplomats...*

Wednesday began to function again sixty kilometers above the equator, as the maglev pod began to power up from subsonic cruise to full orbital ascent acceleration.

"How do you feel?" she asked Frank, her voice sounding distant and flat beneath the ringing in her ears.

"Like shit." He grimaced. His head was bandaged into something that resembled a translucent blue turtle shell and he looked woozy from the painkillers they'd planted on him. "Told me to go straight to sick-bay." He looked at her, concerned. "Did you just say something?"

"No," she said.

"You'll have to speak up. I'm having difficulty hearing."

"What happened to Sven?" she asked.

Svengali, who was sitting on Frank's far side, took it on himself to answer. "Someone tried to kill the Ambassador," he said slowly. "The Dresdener government shat a brick. I have no idea why they let us go—"

"No. It was you," Frank said flatly. "Because you're Muscovite. Aren't you?"

"Yes." Wednesday nodded uncertainly. "Whatever that means..."

"So." Frank nodded tiredly. "They assumed your guests were, too. As the embassy net was down and all they had to go on were passports issued by wherever the guests lived—you're traveling on Septagon ID, but you're not a citizen yet, right?"

"Oh." Wednesday shook her head slowly, her neck muscles complaining because of the unaccustomed gee load. "*Oh!* Who could it be?" she asked hesitantly. "I thought you said whoever was after me—" Her eyes narrowed.

"Who's after you?" Svengali asked, clearly puzzled.

"I was *sure.*" Frank looked frustrated. "The, the security alert. They canceled my interviews. In fact, that was the only public appearance the Ambassador put in while we were groundside. And did you notice the way she didn't go outside? Didn't even move outside of that podium with the reactive armor? But they left the windows and doors open. And there were cops everywhere on the grounds as soon as that bomb went off. Didn't she look padded—"

"The Ambassador was miming the speech," said Wednesday.

"What?" Svengali looked surprised. "What do you mean she was miming?"

"I saw her," Wednesday said. "I was right in the front row. It was the way she spoke—and she was wearing an earbud. From where I was sitting I could see it. Wearing body armor, too, I guess. You know what? I think they *expected* something to happen. Only not what did, if you follow me."

"An assassination attempt. The wrong assassination attempt." Frank sounded almost dreamy. "On the wrong target. Not you, Wednesday." He gave her arm a light squeeze. "A different assassin. One who didn't play ball. Sven, what were you doing down there?"

"I was hired to do a fucking floor show after dinner!" he

snapped tensely. "What do you think? This isn't a vacation for me, laughing boy."

"That's okay," said Frank. He closed his eyes and leaned back in his chair.

"Sorry," Svengali grumbled.

"This would be for the house you're planning on buying when you retire," prompted Wednesday, a cold sweat prickling in the small of her back.

"Yeah, that's it," Svengali agreed, sounding almost grateful.

"I hope you get there," she said in a small voice.

"I hope they find the fucking assholes who crashed the party," Frank said, sounding distantly angry. Wednesday stroked his knuckles, soothing him into silence, then leaned against his shoulder.

The rest of the trip back to orbit passed uneventfully.

several new passengers had joined the *Romanov* at New Dresden. One of them had taken an imperial suite with the nobs on A deck while the rest were accommodated variously in business- and tourist-class staterooms, but all of them had these things in common: they had booked rooms on the liner at short notice roughly a day after a private yacht, the *Heidegger*, had briefly called at Dresden station, and they were all traveling under false passports.

The luxury suite was not an extravagance, but a necessity. As was the way Lars swept it regularly for transmitters and the various species of insect that might creep into a room aboard a luxury liner that had been booked by an arms merchant from Hut Breasil. Portia wanted the cubic volume for conferencing and a base of operations, and the cover identity excused some of the rather more alarming contents of her personal luggage. Which was why Mathilde, answering the invitation to visit the imperial suite, was startled to find the door being held open for her by an armed bodyguard and the room's occupant seated on a chaise longue in front of an open crate of self-propelled gun launchers.

"U. Mathilde Todt. Come in." Hoechst inclined her head. "You look confused," she said.

"Ah. I was expecting—"

Hoechst beamed at her. "An austerity regime?" She rose. "Yes, well, cover identities must be maintained. And why would a rich arms dealer travel in cabbage class?"

Marx let the door close behind the woman. She stepped forward, as if sleepwalking. "It's been too long."

Hoechst nodded. "Consider yourself under direction again."
Mathilde rubbed her face. "You're my new control? Out here
in person?" A note of gratified surprise crept into her voice.
"Unlike U. Scott, I don't believe in letting things slide,"
Hoechst said drily. "I've been running around for the past two
months, tying ligatures around leaks. Now it's your turn. Tell me
how it's going."

"It's—" Mathilde licked her lips—"I've got everything in
place for both the scenarios I was given, the abduction or the other
one. Everything except the primary strike team. We've scoped out
all the critical points, and the necessary equipment is on board.
We had to suborn three baggage loaders and one bellboy to get it
in place, but it's done, and they swallowed the cover story—there
was no need to get technical with them." *Getting technical* was a
euphemism for sinking a tree of nanoelectrodes into their brain
stems and turning them into moppets—meat puppets. What it left
behind afterward wasn't much use for anything except uploading
and forwarding to the Propagators. "Peter is my number two in
charge of line ops, and Mark is ready with the astrogation side of
things. In fact, we're ready to go whenever you give the word."

"Good." Hoechst was no longer smiling. "Now tell me what's
gone wrong. I want to know *everything*."

"With the plan? Nothing's—"

"No, I mean *everything*. Every little thing that might have
drawn attention to you."

"Uh, well, um. We're not used to working undercover or in
feral conditions, and I think we made one or two mistakes in the
early days. Luckily our ops cover is just about perfect; because
they know we're ReMastered, they make allowances for our being
odd. It's astonishing how willing they are to believe that we're
harmless passengers. Nobody even questioned that we were a
youth leadership group! I thought it was absurd—"

Portia cleared her throat pointedly. Mathilde nearly jumped
out of her skin. "Let's get something straight." Hoechst's gaze
drilled into the young task group leader. "If you've done your job
right, you have nothing to fear. If you've made honest but noncrit-
ical mistakes, and admit them and help remedy the situation, you
have nothing to fear. What you should be afraid of is the consequences of *covering up*. Do I make myself clear? So cut the nervous chatter and tell me. What went wrong? What should I be
aware of?"

"Oh." Mathilde stared at her for a moment as if she'd sprouted a second head. Then her shoulders slumped very slightly. "Hans made a scene with one of the passengers on our first night aboard ship. We were all in one of the social areas—a bar, I believe they call them—when one of the ferals attempted to poison him with some sort of intoxicant. Nobody hurt, though. There is a small but vociferous group of passengers who appear to dislike us for some reason. But apart from that, not much has happened that I would classify as untoward. Hans I disciplined, and I consider the matter closed. The others—" She shrugged. "I cannot control what feral humans think of our program. I was uncertain I should even draw it to your attention..."

"I understand completely." Hoechst bent her head over the cargo case, inspecting the boxy black plastic contents within. "The, ah, excesses of some of our predecessors have cast ReMastery in a very poor light, I'm afraid, and our overall goal of extending its benefits to everyone can only make them more suspicious." She brooded for a moment. "I don't intend to aggravate the situation." She looked up, catching Mathilde's gaze: "There will be no reports of atrocities or excesses arising from this intervention. One way or another."

Mathilde smiled slowly.

wednesday ran through abandoned hab spaces in the high-gee rings of an ancient station. Doorways gaped like empty eye sockets to either side of her; the floor sucked at her heels like molasses, dragging her backward. Something unseen ran behind her, dogging her footsteps like a nightmare—the skitter of claws, the clack of boots. She knew it was sharpening knives for her, but she couldn't remember why—everything behind her was blank. Ahead of her was bad, too. Something hidden, something waiting. The pursuer was catching up, and when it caught her a fountain of red pulp splattered across her face. She was in the entrance to a toilet block on the admin deck, and there was a body and when she tugged at it, saying, "Come on, Dad," it looked round and it wasn't her father, blue-faced with asphyxia; it was Sven the clown, and he was *smiling.*

She came awake with a gasp. Her heart felt as if it was about to burst, and the sheets under her were cold and clammy with sweat. Her left arm was numb, trapped under her because she lay on her side and behind—

A grunting snuffle that might have been a snore. She shifted, and he rolled against her back, curled protectively around her. Wednesday closed her eyes and leaned back. *Remember,* she thought dreamily, and shuddered. She could still almost smell the hot metallic taste of blood on her lips, the fecal stink of ruptured intestines. She'd gone to her stateroom and scrubbed for half an hour in the shower, but still felt as if she was soiled by the visceral fallout. Then he'd called, from the sick-bay, checking out. She'd told him she wanted to see him, and he'd come to her. Opened the door and dragged him inside and down onto the floor like animals. His urgency was as strong as hers. She smiled, still sleepy, and shuffled her hips back toward him until she could feel his penis against the small of her back.

"Frank?" she said quietly.

Another mumbled snore. He moved against her in his sleep. He'd been very careful: aware of his physical bulk. Not what she'd expected, but what she'd needed. Afterward, they'd clung together as if they were drowning, and he'd cried. *Is this wise?* she wondered. And then: *Who cares?*

Sleeping, Frank surrounded her. The slow rumble of his breath and the huge bulk of his body made her feel safe, really safe, for the first time since the terrible night of the party. She knew it for a bitter illusion, but it was a good one, and comforting. *I hope he doesn't want to pretend this never happened,* she mused.

An indefinite time later, Wednesday carefully crawled out of bed to go to the bathroom. Almost as soon as she was upright, her earlobe vibrated like an angry bee. "Hello?" she said angrily, trying to subvocalize. "What kind of time do you call this?"

"Wednesday." It was her own voice, weird and hollow-sounding as usual when it came from outside her own head. "Can you hear me?"

"Yeah. Herman? It's middle of night shift here. I was trying to sleep."

"Your motion triggered a callback to alert me. The ship you are on has already undocked and is now accelerating toward its primary jump point. Once it jumps, the causal channel I am currently using will decohere, and you will be on your own. Normally the *Romanov*'s flight plan would take it via two hops to New Prague, but a number of new passengers joined the ship at Dresden station, and you can expect a diversion."

"A *diversion?*" Wednesday yawned, desperately wishing she was awake, or back in bed. She glanced through the door wistfully: Frank was a dark mountain range across the spine of the sleeping platform.

"The ReMastered group aboard your vessel has been exchanging coded communications with the office of an arms dealer from Hut Breasil. The arms dealer and their bodyguards are now aboard the *Romanov*. At the same time, the arms dealer has exchanged message traffic with the office of one Overdepartmentsecretary Blumlein on Newpeace, the de facto chairman of the Planetary Oversight Directorate and maximum leader of the Ministry of State Security. I lack informants on the ground, but I believe the arms dealer is a cover identity for a senior MOSS official who is taking personal control over the mop-up operation arising from their internal conflict over the incident at Moscow."

"Whoa—stop! What do you mean? What mop-up? MOSS? What internal conflict?" Wednesday clutched her head. "What's this got to do with me?" *I want to go back to bed!*

Herman kept his tone of voice even and slow, patient as ever. "I am developing a hypothesis about the destruction of your home, and the motivation behind the assassinations. Moscow system, and New Dresden, lie along the ReMastered race's axis of expansion. Newpeace and Tonto are merely their most recent conquests, and the closest to Earth. They lie close to both Moscow and New Dresden, and those worlds would be logical targets for subversion and conquest. However, the ReMastered are prone to internal rifts and departmental feuding. They can be manipulated by outside influences such as the Eschaton. It is possible that one such department within the Ministry of State Security on Newpeace was induced to exploit their growing influence over domestic political figures in Moscow to use them as a proxy agency in a side project, the development of a causality-violation weapon. Such devices are hazardous not only because the Eschaton intervenes to prevent their deployment later up the time line, but because they tend to be unstable—"

"Later up the *what?* Hey, I thought you *were* the Eschaton! What *is* this?"

"Can a T-helper lymphocyte in a capillary in your little finger claim to be you? Of course I am part of the Eschaton, but I cannot claim to *be* the Eschaton. The Eschaton acquires most of its power by being able to harness causality violation—time travel—for computational purposes. Working causality-violation devices in the hands of others—whether designed as weapons, or as time machines, or as computers—would threaten the stability of its time line. That is why agencies such as I exist—to monitor requests from the oracle to take action that will defend the Eschaton's causal integrity. In the case of Moscow, the most reasonable explanation is that the Muscovite government was experimenting with weapons of temporal disruption and blew their own star up by accident. But there was absolutely no rational explanation for why they might want to develop such weapons, left to their own devices. Which is why evidence of ReMastered infiltration would be most interesting. Especially in conjunction with the silence of the oracle."

Wednesday was silent for a minute. Then: "Are you telling me that some asshole in the military destroyed my world *by accident?* Or because the ReMastered asked them to?"

"Not exactly." A few seconds' silence. Wednesday's emotions churned, aghast and outraged. "When acquiring a new planet, the ReMastered do not walk in and take everything over at gunpoint. They infiltrate by inducing a crisis and being invited in to calm things down. Their main tool is their expertise in uploading and neural interfaces. While blackmail is often used for indirect leverage, they frequently work by abducting key midlevel officials— pithing them, copying their existing neural architecture, then installing an implant. Sometimes they leave the personality in place, just add an override switch—or they wipe everything and turn the body into a remote-control meat puppet. By using a causal channel to control the body, they can ensure that nobody will be able to tell that it's being run by a ReMastered agent unless it is subjected to a brain scan or forced to make an FTL transit. The ReMastered are patient; frequently they will arrive in a system, take fifty to a hundred low-to-mid-ranking officials, then wait twenty or thirty years until one or more of their moppets is promoted into a position of influence. It is a very slow and labor-intensive process, but far cheaper and safer than attempting an overt war of interstellar conquest."

"You mean they do this regularly?"

"Not often. They have fewer than twenty worlds, so far. My models do not predict that they will become a major threat for at least two centuries."

"Oh." Wednesday fell silent. "But none of the diplomats are puppets," she pointed out. "They'd have made FTL transfers to get to their embassies. So there's no evidence, is there?"

"There *is* evidence," Herman pointed out. "The ReMastered focus on you, and the items you found aboard Old Newfie before its evacuation, suggest that it was used as a point of entry for some years, and that the insurgency group operating in Moscow were careless. The ReMastered focus on assassinating Muscovite diplomats is itself suggestive, although I am not yet certain of their motives. The faction responsible appears to want to force the Muscovite diplomatic corps to send the irrevocable go code to the R-bombers, thus precipitating a political crisis on New Dresden with implications elsewhere. But it is difficult to be sure."

"But you—you"—Wednesday struggled for words—"You're part of the Eschaton. Can't you *stop* them? Don't you *want* to stop them?"

"Why do you think I am talking to you?" Her own voice, calm and sympathetic. "I cannot undo the destruction of Moscow because the accident did not trigger the Eschaton's temporal immune response. Higher agencies are investigating the possibility of a threat to the Eschaton itself. *I* am trying to prevent the ReMastered from achieving their goal of taking New Dresden, or whatever else they want to achieve. I'm also trying to stop them from acquiring the final technical reports from the weapons project on Moscow. And I'm trying to ensure that the diplomatic corps from Earth is alerted to the threat. This is a low-level response by the standards of the Eschaton. The ReMastered belief system requires the destruction of the Eschaton. They are nowhere near acquiring that capability, and have not yet triggered the Eschaton's primary defense reflexes, but if they do . . . you would not wish to live within a thousand light years."

"Oh." It came out sounding weak, and Wednesday hated herself for it. "And what about me? What am *I* going to do afterward? My family . . ." A huge sense of loss stopped her in her tracks. She glanced at the sleeping figure in the bed and the sense of loss subsided, but only a fraction.

"You are old enough to make up your own mind about your future. And I cannot accept responsibility for events that I was not forewarned about or involved in. But I will ensure that you do not lack money in the short term, while you sort your life out, if you survive the next few days."

"If?" Wednesday paced over toward the picture wall. "What do you mean, *if?*"

"The ReMastered group from MOSS is aboard this ship for a reason. Sometime after the next jump I expect them to do something drastic. It might be as crude as an attempt to snatch and puppetize you, but there are too many witnesses aboard this ship to whom you might have spoken. A more sensible approach would be to ensure that this ship never reaches its destination. You should prepare yourself. Learn the crew access spaces and the details I downloaded into your ring. One other thing: three diplomats from Earth's United Nations Organization have joined the ship. You can trust them implicitly. In particular, you can talk to Martin Springfield, who has worked for me in the past. He may be able to help protect you. And one other point. If you get the chance to reacquire the documentary evidence of ReMastered weapons tests in Moscow system, turn it over to the diplomats. That is the one thing you can do that will cause the most damage to the ReMastered."

"I'll bear it in mind." Her voice wavered. "But you said they're going to break the door down and kidnap me—what am I supposed to do about that?"

"Simple: don't be in your cabin when they come for you." Herman paused. "Too much time. I have downloaded some further design patterns into your rings. Keep your jacket by you at all times."

"My *jacket?*"

"Yes. You never know when you'll need it." Herman's tone was light. "Good luck, and goodbye. Oh, and if by some chance the *Romanov* ends up at New Prague, talk to Rachel before you decide to take a day trip to the surface. Otherwise, it might come as a shock..."

Click. The call ended. Wednesday cursed quietly for a moment, then noticed a change in the room. She glanced up.

"What was that about?" asked Frank, his expression grave. "Was someone picking an argument?"

She stared at him, her heart suddenly pounding and her mouth dry. "My invisible friend—" she began. "When do we jump?"

"Not for at least a day. Why don't you come here and tell me about it?" He moved to one side of the bed, making a space for her.

"But I—" She stopped, the sense of dread receding somewhat. "A day?" Long habit and ingrained distrust told her that mentioning Herman to anyone would only get her into trouble. Logic, and something else, told her that concealing him from Frank would be a mistake. "I'm not supposed to talk about it," she said. "And you'll think I'm crazy!"

"No." He looked at her thoughtfully. "I don't think you're crazy." His expression was open and surprisingly vulnerable—

which only made him harder for her to read. "Why don't you start at the beginning?"

She climbed into bed and leaned against him. He put an arm round her shoulders as she took a deep breath. "When I was ten I had an invisible friend," she admitted. "I only discovered he worked for the Eschaton after home blew up..."

Martin glanced up as Rachel opened the door to the cramped office cube, off to one side of the executive planning suite. His face was lined and weary. "You're all right?" he asked.

"Never been better." Rachel pulled a face, then yawned. "Damn, need a wake-up dose." She looked at the table, glanced at the young-looking Lieutenant sitting at the other side of it from Martin. "Introduce me?"

"Yeah. This is Junior Flight Lieutenant Stephanie Grace. Just back from ground leave. While she's been away I've been working with her boss, Flying Officer Max Fromm. Um, Steffi? This is my wife, Rachel Mansour. Rachel is a cultural attaché with—"

"Not *that* introduction." Rachel grinned humorlessly as she held up a warrant card. Her head, surrounded by the UN three-W logo on a background of stars. "Black Chamber. That's Colonel Mansour, Combined Defense Corps, on detached duty with the UN Standing Committee on Interstellar Disarmament. Purely for purposes of pulling rank where appropriate, you understand. I'd rather the passengers and crew outside your chain of command didn't learn of my presence just yet. Do we understand each other?"

The kid—no, she was probably well out of her teens, quite possibly already into her second or third career—looked worried. "May I ask what you think is going on? Because if it's anything that threatens the ship, the Captain needs to know as a matter of urgency."

"Hmm." Rachel paused. "Until six hours ago, I thought we were looking for a criminal—a serial killer—who was traveling aboard your ship and killing a different victim in every port." She stopped.

The Lieutenant winced, then met her eyes. "I hardly think that would normally warrant a Black Chamber investigation, would it, Colonel?"

"It does if the victims are all ambassadors from a planetary government in exile that has launched R-bombs on another planet," Rachel said quietly. "*That* stays under your hat, Lieutenant: our serial killer is trying to precipitate a war using weapons of mass destruction. I'll brief your Captain myself, but if word of it gets back to me through other channels—"

"Understood." Steffi looked worried. "Okay, so that's why your husband"— Her eyes flickered toward Martin—"has been dredging through our transit records for the past six months. But you said there was something else."

"Uh-huh." Rachel met her eyes. "It's a motive thing. I don't think it's a lone serial killer; I think we're up against a professional assassin, or a team of assassins, from an interstellar power. And they're intent on obscuring their tracks. Now they know we're onto them, they could do anything. I hope they won't do anything that threatens the ship, but I can't be sure." She shrugged uncomfortably.

Steffi looked alarmed. "Then I must insist you tell the Captain immediately. If there's any question that the, uh, killer might do something aboard her vessel, she's responsible for it. Master and commander and all that. And so far"— her gesture took in the mound of open windows and entity/relationship diagrams in the table-sized screen—"we're not getting very far. We have about two and a half thousand passengers, and seven hundred crew. We generate over three thousand personnel movements every time we berth, and frankly, the two of us are snowed under. If you've got something solid to tell the skipper, it'll make it easier for me to get you more help."

"Okay, then let's go see the Captain." Martin stood up. "Want me to come along?" he asked.

Rachel took a deep breath. "Think you can carry on without us for a while? I don't expect it'll take long to fill her in . . ."

"I'll keep at it." Martin shook his head. "I'm still working through the tourist-class passengers. I thought it was going to be simple, then Steffi here asked what if a passenger disembarked and checked out, did the job, then took passage under a different name in a different class? It's a real mess."

"Not totally," Steffi volunteered. "We have some biometrics on file. But we're not geared up for police-style trawls through our customer base, and pulling everyone's genome out for inspection would normally take an order from—" She glanced at the ceiling. "So shall we go visit the skipper?"

captain nazma hussein was not having a good day.

First departure had to be delayed six hours because of some stupid mess downside, delaying a couple of passengers who had diplomatic-grade clout—enough to hold the ship, even though each hour's delay cost thousands. Then there was a problem with mass balance in one of the four ullage tanks that ringed the lower hemisphere of the liner's hull, a flow instability suggesting that a stabilizer baffle had been damaged during the last docking maneuver. She'd managed to get away from the flight deck, leaving Victor in charge of the straightforward departure, only to find a queue headed by the deputy purser waiting in front of her desk for orders and/or ruffled-feather smoothing. And now this . . .

"Run that by me again," she said, doing her best to maintain the illusion of impassive alertness that always came hard after a twelve-hour shift. "Just what do you expect to happen aboard my ship?"

The diplomat looked as tired as she felt. "One or more of your passengers or short-term crew have been bumping off people at each planetside port of call," she explained again. "Now, I've been ordered to make sure it doesn't happen again. Which is all very well, but I've got reason to believe that the killer is acting under orders and may try to cover their tracks by any means at their disposal."

"Disposal?" Captain Hussein raised one sharply sculpted eyebrow. "Are you talking about a matter of killing witnesses or passengers? Or actions that might jeopardize the operational safety of my ship?"

The woman—Rachel something-or-other—shrugged. "I don't know," she said bluntly. "I'm sorry I can't reassure you, but I wouldn't put anything past these scum. I was downside yesterday, and we managed to abort their latest hit, but the trap misfired, mostly because they demonstrated a remarkable willingness to kill innocent bystanders. It looks as if they started out trying to keep a low profile, but they're willing to go to any lengths to achieve their goals, and I can't guarantee that they won't do something stupid."

"Wonderful." Nazma glanced sideways at her overflowing schedule screen. Numerous blocks winked red, irreconcilable critical path elements, overlapping dependencies that had been thrown out of balance by the late departure. "Do you know *who* you're looking for? What would you have me do when you find them?" She looked past the diplomat. The trainee kid was doing her best to melt into the wall, clearly hoping she wouldn't dump on her for being the bearer of bad tidings. *Tough, let her worry for a few minutes.* Nazma gave her a grade-three Hard Stare, then looked back at the spook. It hadn't been so many years that she had forgotten what the kid would be feeling, but it wouldn't hurt to make her ponder the responsibilities of a mistress and commander for a while. "I really hope you're not going to suggest anything like a change of destination."

"Ah, no." The woman, to her credit, looked abashed. *Bet that's* exactly *what you were about to suggest,* Nazma told herself. "And, um, the safety of your ship is paramount. My main concern is that we identify them so that they can be discreetly arrested when we arrive at the next port of call—or sooner, if there's any sign that they're a threat to anyone else." Nazma relaxed slightly. *So, you're not totally out of touch with reality, huh?* Then the diplomat spoiled it by continuing: "The trouble is, you generate so many personnel movements that we've got a pool of about 200 suspects, and only ten days to check them. That's the number who've been downside on all of the planets where an incident occurred—if we're looking for a team, alternating targets, the pool goes up to 460 or so. So I was wondering if we could borrow some more staff—say, from the purser's office—to help clear them." She forced a tense smile at Nazma.

Give me patience! Captain Hussein glanced back at her display. The red bars weren't getting any shorter, and every additional hour added to the critical path added sixteen thousand to her operating overhead. But the alternative... "Lieutenant Grace." She watched Steffi straighten her back attentively. "Please convey my compliments to Commander Lewis, and inform her that she's to provide you with any and all personnel and resources from her division that you deem necessary to requisition for, for Colonel—"

"Mansour," offered the woman.

"—Colonel Mansour's search. When you have a final suspect list I want to see it before any action is taken. File daily updates with Safety and Security, cc'd to my desk. I also want to know if you *don't* find a murderer aboard my ship, of course." She nodded at the spook. "Satisfied?"

Rachel looked surprised. "More than," she admitted. This time her smile was genuine. "Thank you!"

"Don't." Nazma waved it away. "I wouldn't be doing my job if

I didn't take murderers running around my ship seriously." She sniffed, nostrils flaring as if at the scent of skullduggery. "Just as long as you keep it low-key and don't frighten the passengers. Now, I trust you will excuse me, but I have a ship to run."

he looks like a gorilla, Martin thought apprehensively as he approached the warblogger across the half-empty lounge. The journalist was slouched in a sofa with a smile on his face, one arm around a pale-skinned young woman with a serious blackness habit—black hair, black boots, black leggings, black jacket—and a big baby blue dressing on her left temple. She was leaning against him in a manner that spelled more than casual affection. *Isn't that sweet,* Martin thought cynically. The blogger must have been about two meters tall, but was built so broadly he looked squat, and it wasn't flab. Close-cropped silver-speckled black hair, old-fashioned big horn-rimmed data glasses, and more black leather. The woman was talking to him quietly, occasionally leaning her chin on his shoulder. The gorilla was all ears, grunting agreement from time to time. They were so wrapped up in each other that they didn't seem to have noticed Martin watching them. *Here goes,* he thought, and walked over.

"Hi there," he said quietly. "Are you, um, Frank Johnson of the London *Times?*"

The gorilla glanced up at him sharply, one eyebrow rising. The young woman was also staring. Martin barely noticed her, fine-boned alarm and black nail paint. "Who's asking?" said the big guy.

Martin sat down opposite them, sprawling inelegantly in the sofa's overstuffed grip. "Name's Springfield. I'm with the UN diplomatic service." *That's odd,* he realized distantly. Both of them had tensed, focusing on him. *What's up?* "Are you Frank Johnson? Before I go any further—" He held up his diplomatic passport, and the big guy squinted at it dubiously.

"Yeah," he rumbled. "And this isn't a social call, is it?" He rubbed his left arm meditatively and winced slightly, and Martin put two and two together.

"Were you at the Muscovite embassy reception yesterday evening?" he asked. He glanced at the young woman. "Either of you?" She started, then leaned against the big guy, looking away, feigning boredom.

"I see a diplomatic passport," Frank said defensively. He

stared at Martin. "And I see some guy asking pointed questions, and I wonder whether the purser's office will confirm if the passport is genuine when I ask them? No offense, but what you're asking could be seen as a violation of journalistic privilege."

Martin leaned back and watched the man. He didn't *look* stupid: just big, thoughtful, and...*Huh. Got to start somewhere, right? And he's not top of the list by a long way.* "Could be," he said reflectively. "But I'm not asking for the random hell of it."

"Okay. So why don't you tell me what you want to know and why, and I'll tell you if I can answer?"

"Um." Martin's eyes narrowed. The woman was staring at him with clear fascination. "If you were at the Moscow embassy in Sarajevo, you probably saw rather a lot of bodies." The journalist winced. *A palpable hit.* "Maybe you weren't aware that the same thing also happened before. We have reason to believe that the responsible party"—he paused, watching the implication sink in—"was probably aboard this ship. Now, I can't compel you to talk to me. But if you know anything at all, and you don't tell me, you're helping whoever blew up all those people to get away with it." *Holed below the waterline:* the journalist was nodding slightly, unconscious agreement nibbling away at his resolute dedication to the cause of journalistic impartiality. "I'm trying to put together a picture of what happened that night to aid the investigation, and if you'd like to make a statement, that would be very helpful." He gave a small shrug. "I'm not a cop. It's just a case of drafting every warm body who can hold a recorder."

Frank leaned forward, frowning. "I'm going to check your passport, if you don't mind," he said. "Do you?" He held out a hand. Martin thought for a moment, then reluctantly handed the white-spined tablet over. Beside him the woman leaned over to look at it. Frank glanced at the passport then snapped his fingers for a privacy cone and said something muffled to the ship's passenger liaison network. After a moment he nodded and snapped his fingers again. "Okay," he said, and handed the passport back. "I'll talk to you."

Martin nodded, his initial apprehension subsiding. Frank was going to be reasonable—and having an experienced journalist's view of affairs would be good. He pulled out a small voice recorder and put it on the low table between them. "This is an auditing recorder, write-once. Martin Springfield interviewing—"

"Wait. Your name is *Martin* Springfield?" It was the young woman, sitting straight up and staring at him.

"Wednesday—" The big guy started.

"Yeah. I'm Martin Springfield. Why?"

The girl licked her lips. "Are you a friend of Herman?"

Martin blanked for a moment. *What the fuck?* A myriad of memories churned up all at once, a hollow voice whispering by dead of night over illicit smuggled causal channels. "I've worked for him," Martin heard himself admitting as his heart gave a lurch. "Where did you hear the name?"

"I do stuff for him, too." She licked her lips.

"Wednesday." Frank glared at Martin. "Shit. You don't want to go telling everyone about—"

"It's okay," said Martin. He raised his recorder. "Recorder. Command delete. Execute." He put it down. *What the fuck is going on here?* He had a hollow feeling in the pit of his stomach. This couldn't be a coincidence, and if Herman was involved, it meant the whole diplomatic ball of string had just gotten a lot knottier. "Ship, can you put a privacy cone around this table? Key override red koala greenback."

"Override acknowledged. Privacy cone in place." All the sounds from outside the magic circle became faint and muffled.

"What are you doing here?" Wednesday asked, tensing. Martin glanced from her to Frank and back. He frowned; their body language told its own story. "Back downside—" she swallowed. "Were they after me?"

"You?" Martin blinked. "What makes you think you were the target of a bombing?"

"It wouldn't be the first time," rumbled Frank. He looked at Martin warningly. "She's a refugee from Moscow, one of the survivors of the peripheral stations. She settled in Septagon, except someone murdered her family, apparently for something she'd taken, or left behind, or something. And they tried to follow her here."

Martin felt his face freeze, a sudden bolt of excitement stabbing through him. "Did *Herman* send you here?" he asked her directly.

"Yes." She crossed her arms defensively. "I'm beginning to think listening to him is a very bad idea."

You and me both, Martin agreed silently. "In my experience Herman never does anything at random. Did he tell you my name?" She nodded. "Well, then. It looks like Herman believes your problem and my problem are connected—and they're part of something that interests him." He looked at Frank. "This isn't news to you. Where do you come in?"

Frank scratched his head, his expression distant. "Y'know, that's a very good question. I'm roving diplomatic correspondent for the *Times*. This trip I was basically doing a tour of the trouble spots in the Moscow/Dresden crisis. She just walked up and dumped her story in my lap." He looked sideways at Wednesday.

She shuffled. "Herman told me to find you," she said slowly. "Said that if you broadcast what was going on, the people hunting me would probably lay off."

"Which is true, up to a point," Martin murmured, more to himself than to anyone else. "What else?" he demanded.

Wednesday took a deep breath. "I grew up on one of Moscow's outlying stations. Just before the evacuation, Herman had me go check something out. I found a, a body. In the Customs section. He'd been murdered. Herman had me hide some documents near there, stuff from the Captain's cabin of the evac ship. I got away with it; nobody noticed that bit." She shuddered, clearly unhappy about something. "Then, a couple of weeks ago, someone murdered my family and tried to kill me." She clung to Frank like a drowning woman to a life raft.

"I don't believe in coincidences," Martin said slowly, the sweat in the small of his back freezing. *Herman's involved in this.* A dead certainty, and frightening enough that his palms were clammy. Herman was the cover name that an agent—human or otherwise—of the Eschaton had used when it sent him on lucrative errands in the past. *So there's something really serious following her around. Wait till I tell Rachel! She'll shit a brick!* He caught Wednesday's gaze. "Listen, I'd like you to talk to my wife as soon as possible. She's—you probably saw her on stage. At the embassy." He swallowed. "She's the expert in dealing with murderous bampots. Between us we can make sure you're safe. Meanwhile, do you have any idea who's after you? Because if we could narrow it down or confirm it's the same bunch who're after the Muscovite diplomatic corps, it would make things much easier—"

"Sure I do." Wednesday nodded. "Herman told me last night. It's a faction of the ReMastered. There's a group of them aboard this ship, traveling to Newpeace. He reckons they're going to do something drastic after the first jump." She grimaced. "We were just trying to figure out what to do..."

clowning around _____

Franz was snared.

Some time ago he'd heard a story about wild animals—he wasn't sure what species—which, when snared, would chew a leg off to escape the hunter's trap. It was a comforting myth, but clearly false in his estimate: because when you got down to it, when your own hand was wedged in the steel jaws of a dilemma, you learned to make do with what you'd got.

Hoechst had come up from the depths of the Directorate like a ravening black widow, carrying away Erica and menacing him with the poisoned chalice of her acquisitive desire. His own survival was at stake: *I wasn't expecting that.* But he'd done as she told him, and she hadn't lied. She hadn't bitten his head off and nibbled daintily at the pulsing stump of his neck as she consummated her desire. Even though his trapped conscience hurt as violently as a physical limb. Her luggage included almost fifty grams of memory diamond, loaded with the souls and genomes of everyone in U. Scott's network who'd failed her purge. Each morning he awakened with his heart racing, panting with the knowledge that he was walking along the lip of a seething crater. Knowing that death at her hands would be a purely temporary experience, that he'd awaken with his love and uncounted billions more in the simulation spaces of the unborn god, did not make it easier to bear. For one thing, the unborn god had to be built—and that meant the destruction of the enemy. And for seconds...

Falling in love was like losing your religion. They were two sides of a coin that Franz and Erica had flipped some years ago, out among the feral humans. He was no longer sure what he believed. The idea of the unborn god picking over the bones of his human fallibility made his skin crawl. But this was foreshadowed: when the ReMastered finally destroyed the Eschaton and began their monumental task of reimplementation, the deity they'd build in their own image would hardly be a merciful and forgiving one. Perhaps it would be better to die the permanent death than to meet his share in the collective creation, down at the omega point at the end of time. But the more he contemplated it, the more he found that he couldn't quite bring himself to pick one horn of the dilemma—either to chew away the restraining grip of his conscience and flee alone, or to force the black widow to execute him out of sheer disgust.

Which was why, on the evening of the first full day in flight, one hour before the first jump, he was kneeling on the floor of Portia's Sybarite-class stateroom next to Marx, helping him load ammunition into a brace of handheld recoilless gun launchers while Samow and Mathilde armed their little bags of tricks. *We're really going to do this,* he thought disbelievingly, as he stared at a squat cartridge. *She's really going to do it.*

The idea was disorienting. Franz had thought, in his more optimistic—unrealistic—moments that maybe he and Erica could manage the trick: that perhaps they could flee the iron determination of the ReMastered race, escape from history, run and hide and find a distant world, live and work and indulge in the strange perversion called love, die forever and molder to humus, never to rise beneath the baleful gaze of the omniscient end child. But escape was a cruel illusion, like freedom, or love. A cruel illusion intended to temper the steel of the ReMastered.

He snapped the round into the box magazine before him, then picked up another and loaded it on top. It was the size of his thumb, nose gleaming with sensors and tail pocked with the tiny vents of solid-fuel rocket motors. *One shot, one kill.* Every time he pushed another BLAM into the magazine he felt something inside him clench up, thinking of Jamil plunging the propagation bush into the back of Erica's head, turning her into so much more reliable meat to place on the altar of the unborn god for judgment. *Kill them all, god will know his own* meeting *god is dead: we must become the new gods.*

"This one's full," he said, and passed it to Marx.

"That's enough for this set." Marx carefully set aside one of the handguns and a linked bundle of magazines. "Okay, next one. Hurry up, we've only got an hour to get this sorted."

"I'm hurrying." Franz's hands flew. "Nobody's told me what I'm assigned to do during the action."

"Maybe that's because she hasn't decided if she wants you alive for it."

Franz tried not to react in any way before Marx's harsh assessment. It was all too possible that it was a test, and any sign of weakness might determine the outcome. "I obey and I labor for the unborn," he said mildly, working on the ammunition case. "Hmm. The power charge on this one is low. How old is this box?" The big guided antipersonnel rounds needed a trickle charge of power while they were on the shelf—the biggest drawback of smart weapons was the maintenance load.

"It's in date. Anyway, we'll be using them soon enough."

I could defect, he told himself. *All I'd have to do is tell the Captain what's happening*—Except he didn't know who else might be involved. All he knew about was Portia's team, and Mathilde's group. There might be others. *Restart. If I defect*— Erica would be dead forever, or doomed to resurrection beneath the hostile scrutiny of an angry god. Even if he could get his hands on the package of souls Portia was carrying for the Propagators, he had no easy way of instantiating Erica's mind, let alone growing her a new body. That was privileged technology within the Directorate, ruthlessly controlled by the Propagators for their own purposes, and expensive and rare outside it. *And if Hoechst is telling the truth*—there were worse things to be than a DepSec's serf. Much worse.

"Ah, Franz." A warm voice, behind him. He forced himself to focus on what his hands were doing—pick, load, pick, load. *She doesn't mean anything,* he thought. "Come with me. I've got a little job for you."

He found himself standing up almost without willing it, like a sleepwalker. "I'm ready."

"Hah! So I see." Hoechst beckoned toward one of the side doors opening off her suite. "Over here."

He followed her over and she opened the door of what he'd taken for a closet. Spot on: it was indeed a closet. With a chair in it, straps dangling from the armrests and front legs.

"What's this?" he asked, heart thudding.

"Got a little job for you." Hoechst smiled. "I've been studying this love phenomenon, and it has some interesting applications." Her smile slipped. "It's a pity we can't just work our way through the passengers until we have the girl, then puppetize her and force her to comply." She shook her head. "But whoever's behind her almost certainly took precautions. So we'll have to do this the old-fashioned way."

"The old—" Franz stopped. "What do you mean?"

Hoechst pulled out a tablet and tapped it. A video loop started cycling, just a couple of seconds showing its target waving at someone off-screen. "Him." She pointed at the face. "I'm giving you Marx and Luna. While everyone else is executing Plan Able, you will go to his cabin and bring him here. Undamaged, to the extent possible. I want a bargaining chip."

"Hmm." Franz shrugged. "Wouldn't it be easier simply to force her?"

"This *is* force, of a kind." Hoechst grinned at him. "Don't you recognize it?" The grin vanished. "She has a history of evading capture, Franz. Kerguelen was not entirely negligent: he was up against experience. I've been reading U. Scott's field files, predigested raw transcripts, not the pap he was content with. She won't dodge *me*."

"Ah," Franz said faintly. "So what do you want me to do with him?"

"Just snatch him and bring him here while I'm dealing with the rest of the ship. If he cooperates, he and the girl can both be allowed to live—that's the truth, not a convenient fiction. Although they and the rest of the passengers will be sent for ReMastering when we arrive at Newpeace."

"Got it." Franz frowned. *She's going to ReMaster everyone on the entire ship? Is she planning on making it disappear?* "Do you want anything else?"

"Yes." Hoechst leaned close, until he could feel her breath on his cheek. "This is job number one for you. I've got another lined up after we dock with station eleven. It's going to be fun!" She patted him on the back. "Cheer up. Only another three weeks to go, and we'll be home again. Then, if you're good, maybe we can see about giving you back your toy."

steffi stifled a yawn as she lowered herself into the chair at the head of the table in the dining room. An overlong shift spent poring over personnel movements with Rachel had left her bleary-eyed and wanting to throttle some of the more willfully persistent tourists. Having to follow that by stealing ten minutes to freshen up, then sitting at the head of a dining table for three or four hours of stroking the oversized egos of the more stupid upper-class passengers, was the kind of icing she didn't need on her cake. *But it's better than being on the outside of the investigation,* she told herself. And maybe she'd get some quality time with Max afterward; he was sitting up on the high table at the other side of the room, lofty but affable, everybody's favorite picture of a senior officer. He'd need to blow off steam, too.

"Mind if I join you?" She looked round. It was Martin, the diplomatic spook's right hand.

"By all means." She managed a wan smile, keeping up appearances. Down the table, the middle-aged Nipponese woman smiled back at her, evidently mistaking its target, triggering an exchange of polite nods. By which time Martin was sitting to her left and idly scrolling through the menu. She looked around the table. It was half-empty. The troublesome kid was evidently eating in her room. So, come to think of it, were those creepy cultural exchange students from Tonto. *Fucking stupid cover,* she thought. *A blind idiot could see there's more to them than that.* No such luck with the bankers, though.

"How's your day been?" she asked quietly as the stewards collected the empty soup bowls. "I haven't seen your wife in here—is she working?"

"Probably." Martin winced and pinched the bridge of his nose. "She's looking for someone, and she tends to overdo it when she's got her teeth into something. I tell her to take some time off, it'll make her more effective, but...I've spent all day interviewing tourists. It's giving me a headache."

"Did any of them have anything useful to say?" she asked.

"Not for the most part, no."

Liar, she thought, tensing. *What are you concealing?*

The lighting strips lining the arched sculpture niches along the walls flickered, distracting her.

"'Scuse me." Steffi raised her left hand and twisted her interface rings urgently, hunting the command channel. The lights aboard a starship never flickered without a reason—especially not aboard a luxury liner with multiple redundant power circuits. Steffi hadn't felt any vibration, but that didn't mean anything. The ship's curved-space generators were powerful enough to buffer a steady thirty gees of acceleration, and absorb the jolt of any impact unless it was large enough to cause a major structural failure. "Bridge comm, Grace here. Bridge—" She frowned. "That's odd." She glanced across the room at Max. He was standing up, turning to step down off the raised platform of the high table. He caught her eye, jerked his chin toward the main entrance, then strode toward it. Across the room she saw stewards discreetly breaking off their tasks, disappearing in the direction of their emergency stations.

She caught up with Max a couple of meters down the hall. "Bridge isn't answering."

"I know." He opened an unmarked side door. "Nearest emergency locker is—ah, here." Yanking the yellow-and-black handle forward, he pulled out the crash drawer and handed her an emergency bag—rebreather hood, gloves, multitool, first-aid 'bots. "No callback." He looked thoughtful. "One moment—"

"Already there." Steffi had her tablet fully unfolded; she pasted it against the wall and tried to bring up the ship's damage-control schematics. "Shit, why is it so *slow?* She stabbed at a local diagnostic pane. "There's no bandwidth! Shipnet is down."

"We've got lights, air, and gravity." He looked thoughtful. "What's out is data. Listen, it may just be a major network crash. Relativistics weren't due to start jump spool-up for half an hour yet, so we're probably okay if we sit tight. You're not trained for this, so I want you to go back to the dining room and keep a lid on the passengers. Relay any orders you hear and keep your ears open and try to stay out of trouble until you're needed. Meanwhile, I'm going to get some stewards together and go find out what's happening. Bridge first, engineering control if the bridge is out... Your story for the passengers is that everything is under control, line crew is investigating and there'll be an announcement in due course. Think you can handle it?"

"I'll do my best."

Steffi headed for the passenger corridor, sparing a glance behind her as he waved a hand at a crewman who'd appeared from one of the service spaces: "Hey, you! Over here, I've got a job for you right now..."

Everything seemed to be under control in the dining room. Steffi did a quick survey. The passengers were still wrapped up in conversation, not yet having noticed anything unusual. *Small mercies...* For a moment she considered leaving them in ignorance, but as soon as someone tried to check mail or call a friend they'd realize something was up.

She took a step up onto the platform supporting the high table. "Excuse me, ladies and gentlemen, may I have your attention, please?"

Curious eyes turned toward her. "As some of you may have noticed, we've experienced a minor technical anomaly in the past few minutes. I'd like to assure you that the engineering crew are working on it, and there is no danger—"

The lights flickered for a moment, then went out. One or two stifled screams rose from the corners of the room—then the lights came back on. And with them a stranger's voice, amplified, over the passenger liaison circuit, its tone calm and collected: "We regret to inform you that there has been a minor problem with the propulsion and engineering control center. There is no cause for alarm. Everything is under control, and we will be diverting to a nearby port rather than proceeding directly to New Prague. WhiteStar Line will announce a compensation package for your inconvenience in due course. In the meantime, we would appreciate it if you would return to your cabins and stay there until further notice. When the passenger liaison network is back up, please do not hesitate to use it to contact one of our team. We're here to help you."

rachel was looking for Wednesday in the mostly-deserted D deck lounges when the gadget went off under the bridge. The bridge was on E deck. It was separated from D deck by two pressure bulkheads, a structural truss, and an electrograv ring designed to even out tidal surges, so the immediate blast effect was lost on her.

Martin had called her a couple of hours earlier, full visual via an office cam. "It checks out and it stinks like a month-dead cheese," he insisted. "She's a Moscow survivor, someone's been trying to abduct or kill her, she was at the embassy reception when you were—oh, and there's something else."

His cheek twitched. He was about as agitated as she'd ever seen him get. "What else?" she demanded, annoyed with herself for going after such a transparent hook.

"She's got a friend called Herman, and he's why she's here." Martin shut up. She stared at him through the magic mirror in her visual field.

"You're kidding."

"Nope. *Frank* didn't know any more—but I mean, hit me with the clue bat, right?"

"Oh shit." She'd had to lean against the wall. "Did she pass anything else on to you?" She'd gone dizzy for a moment, as things dropped into place. *Herman* was the cover name an agent of the Eschaton had used to contact Martin, paying him to run obscure errands—errands that had emergent side effects that shook the chancelleries of a dozen worlds. *Herman* was only really interested in human beings when they tried to build time machines, violate causality, experiment with forbidden weapons. *Moscow* had died when, entirely without warning, its star had exploded. Which just *didn't happen,* not to G-type dwarf stars in the middle of the main sequence of their life cycles.

"Yes. Maybe it's a coincidence, and then again maybe there's a large pig on final approach to the main docking bay—see the reaction control clusters on each flank? Herman said it was something to do with the ReMastered group aboard this ship and that they're going to pull something after the first jump. Tonight, in other words. Rachel, I am *not* happy. This—"

"Stop. Let's not go there right now." She shook her head. "I need to find the girl before whoever's looking for her catches up with us. Send me her details?"

"Sure." Martin shuffled the rings on his left hand, and her tablet bleeped, then threw up a picture—young-looking physio, dark hair built up in an outrageous swirl, eye shadow like midnight. "Hard to miss. You'll probably find her with Frank the journalist; they seem to be personally involved. Oh, she's as young as she looks, too, so go easy on her."

Rachel frowned pensively. "Don't worry about me, worry about her. You go and have a word with the Captain—tell her we're expecting some kind of trouble from a group of passengers. If necessary, tell her exactly who—but don't tell her where the warning came from. There might be a leak in the crew. Besides which, if we overreact, we might not have a chance to learn anything . . ."

"Happy hunting." He'd smiled at her until she cut the call. And that was why she came to be prowling past nine-tenths empty lounges and casually eyeballing the few passengers who were out in public, chatting, drinking, or schmoozing in the overstuffed furniture that seemed to be a WhiteStar trademark. Wednesday seemed to have vanished, along with her new boyfriend, and neither of them were carrying their locater badges. *Damn these privacy freaks, anyway!* Nowhere did she see a skinny girl with spiky hair and a serious luminosity deficiency, or a journalist built like a silverback gorilla.

Two hours after she'd begun, Rachel had combed decks G through D, making a pass around each circle corridor and checking every single public room, and she was getting frustrated. *Where on earth can she have gotten to?* she asked herself. Leaving a message on Wednesday's voice mail didn't seem to have gotten anywhere. It was getting to the point where she had half a mind to raise things with Steffi, see if the crew couldn't do the job more efficiently: if only she could eliminate all the crew from the suspects list—

The luminous ceiling tiles flickered briefly, and the world filled with multicolored static. A vast silence went off inside her head. Rachel felt herself falling and tried to raise her arms to protect herself. *Vertigo!* She hit the deck bruisingly hard and rolled sideways, her vision flickering. The static was slow to clear, leaving a line of bleeding ghost trails across her retinas. Rachel caught her breath, dizzy with fright, then realized that it wasn't her eyesight: her intraocular displays had crashed and were rebooting. "Shit!" She glanced around. The skinny guy sitting in the leather sofa next to the upright piano in the Gold Lounge was frowning, rolling his rings around his fingers as if puzzled by something. *Rings*—Rachel twisted her own master ring, spun through diagnostic menus until she came to the critical one. *EMP burst,* said her event log. Kilovolts and microamps per meter: someone had just dumped a huge electromagnetic pulse through the walls. There was a faint tang of ozone in the air. The fast fuses in her MilSpec implants had saved them, but the other passengers—

"Oh *shit!*" She picked herself up and lurched drunkenly into the corridor. "Get me Martin." *Service unavailable.* "Hell and damnation." *No surprise there. Why no sirens?* She glanced around hastily, looking for an emergency locker—they'd be tastefully concealed aboard a liner, but they'd still be there—*Why no partitions?* The fail-safe doors ought to be descending if something bad had happened. A chilly claw of fear tugged at her. "Shit, time to get moving..."

The small boy in one corner of the lounge was walking toward her. "Hey, ma'am? My gamescape just flaked on me—"

She cast the kid a sickly smile. "Not now," she said, then did a double take: "Why don't you go to your room and tell your folks about it? They'll be able to help you." *EMP / crashed implants and amusements / assassin traveling incognito / teen from Moscow being hunted / Eschaton involved / war crimes* —she had a nagging sense that a shoe had just dropped *hard,* an enormous boot with a heel stuffed with plutonium or weaponized anthrax or gray goo or something equally apocalyptic, and she'd misinterpreted it as the sound of one hand clapping. *Something like that.* She broke into a trot, heading for the next radial. *Got to find the damage-control point,* she told herself, *find out what's going on—*

She dodged a couple of confused passengers who seemed to be looking for someone. She spotted an anonymous gray side door into crew country and tried to open it. It refused to recognize her until she got tired of waiting and twisted the black-and-yellow emergency handle: from beyond it she could hear distant, muted sirens. The auxiliary lighting circuit had tripped, and the walls shed a lurid shadowless glow. "Send to Martin, off-line by best emergency mesh routing," she subvocalized to her personal assist, mumbling at her rings. "Martin, if you get this message, we're in deep shit. Something—" she turned a corner, followed signs for the G deck ops center—"big is going down, and I think we're sitting on the target." The ops center door was open ahead, a couple of crew just visible in the gloom inside doing something. One of them glanced at her, then stepped forward. "I think—"

She stopped dead, eyes wide, as the public address system came on: "We regret to inform you that there has been a minor problem with the propulsion and engineering control center..."

The man blocking the doorway was pointing an autonomous rifle at her. Rachel froze as it tracked her, snuffling slightly, its barrel pointing right at her face. "Who are you and what are you doing here?" he demanded.

"I, uh—" She stopped, heart hammering. "I was looking for a steward?" she asked, her voice rising in an involuntary squeak. She began to take a step back, then froze as the man tensed. He had blond hair, brown eyes, and pale skin: he was built with the sparse, muscular grace of a dancer or martial artist—*or special forces,* she realized. Even a cursory glance told her she wouldn't stand a chance if he decided to shoot her; the gun was some kind of smart shotgun/grenade launcher hybrid, probably able to fire around corners and see through walls. "My rings stopped working—What's this about help?" she asked, doing her best to look confused. It wasn't hard.

"There has been a minor accident," the goon said, sounding very calm but clipping his words: "Return to your cabin. Everything is under control." He stopped and stared at her coolly.

"Uh, yeah, under control, I can see that," Rachel muttered, backing away from him. He made no move to follow her, but simply stood in the doorway watching as she turned and walked back toward passenger country. Her skin crawled as if she could feel the gun watching the small of her back, eager to discharge. When she was far enough away she gave in to the impulse to run—he'd probably expect no less of a frightened passenger. Just as long as he didn't realize how good her night vision was. Good enough to have seen the woman slumped over the workstation in the gloom behind him. Good enough to have seen the other woman working on her back with something that looked disturbingly like a mobile neurosurgery toolkit.

Under control. "Shit," she mumbled, fumbling with the door and noticing for the first time that her hands were shaking. *Bad guys in G deck damage-control center, infoweapons in passenger country, what* else *do I need?* The door banged shut behind her. She shook her head. *Hijackers—*

She turned toward the central atrium, meaning to take the old-fashioned staircase back up to her room in search of Martin. She took a single step forward, and the dark-haired girl ran into her.

the air in the flight deck stank of blood, ozone, and feces. The desks and equipment racks around the room looked as if someone had run them through a scrap metal press; anything that wasn't bolted down had fallen over and shattered, hard, including the bridge officers unlucky enough to be in the room when the gadget had gone off. Bodies bent at strange angles lay beneath broken chairs or lay splayed across the floor, leaking.

Portia wrinkled her nose in distaste. "This really *won't* do," she insisted. "I want this mess cleared up as soon as we've got the surveillance net locked down. I want it to look like we've been in charge all along, not as if we just butchered the flight crew."

"Boss." Jamil nodded. He glanced at the front wall-screen, which had ripped away from the bulkhead and slumped into a thin sheet across the floor. "What about operational capacity?"

"That's a lower priority. We've got the auxiliary bridge, we'll run things from there for now." She pulled a face. "On second thoughts, before you tidy up get someone to reclaim anything they can get out of these." She stared at an officer who lay on the floor, her neck twisted and skull flattened. "Obviously, I don't expect total uploads."

"Thirty gees for a hundred milliseconds is about the same as falling off a fifteen-story building," Marx volunteered.

"So she didn't have a head for heights." Hoechst's cheek twitched. "Get going."

"Yes, boss." He hurried off to find someone with a neural spike.

As he left, Portia's phone rang. She raised the archaic rubbery box to her head. "Control, sitrep. Ah...yes, that's good. Is he all right? Fully programmed? Excellent, get him in front of a screen as soon as you get into the liaison router, we need to reassure the passengers there's a real officer in charge...What's the structural load-out like? How high did the surge...all right. Right. Good, I'm glad you told me. Yes, tell Maria to detain any other members of the crew who reach D-con on decks G through C...Yes, that's what I meant. I want any line officers who survived identified and segregated immediately. Stash them in the C deck D-con center for now and report back when you've got them all accounted for. Be discreet, but in event of resistance shoot first: the unborn god will know his own...Yeah, you, too. Over." She turned and nodded to Franz. "Right. Now it's your turn. I take it the girl isn't in her cabin?"

Franz straightened up. "She's missing. Her tag says she's there, but it looks like she fooled it deliberately and her own implants aren't compatible with these damn Earth-standard systems. One of the ship's junior officers was searching for her—I think she's gone to ground." He delivered his little speech with an impassive face, although his stomach tensed in anticipation of Hoechst's wrath.

"That's all right," she said mildly, taking him by surprise. "What did I tell you to expect earlier? Just keep an eye open for her. Mathilde's crew is configuring the passenger access points to work as a mesh field for celldar, and she'll have the entire ship under surveillance in a few hours. Now, what about the other one?"

"Taken, as per your orders. He'd returned to his room for some reason. Marx took him down with no problems, and we've got him stashed in the closet."

"Good. When the kid surfaces you can let her know we've got him, and what will happen to him if she doesn't cooperate." She looked pensive. "In the meantime, I want you to go and pay off the clown. Right away."

"The clown," Franz repeated. *The clown?* That was okay by him. No ethical dilemmas there, nothing to lose sleep over...

"Yes." She nodded. A muscle in her left cheek jumped. "Bring me the head of Svengali the clown."

"I don't have a spike—"

"*No* reclaim," she said firmly. She gave a delicate shudder of distaste. "There are some things that even the unborn god should be protected from."

"But that's final! If you kill him without reclaiming his soul—"

"Franz." She stared at him coldly.

"Boss."

She tilted her head to one side. "Sometimes I think you're too soft for this job," she said thoughtfully. "Are you?"

"Boss! No." He took a deep breath. "I have been slow to adjust to your management style. I *will* adapt." *That's right, gnaw your own leg off.*

She nodded slightly. "See that you do."

"Yes."

He knew when he was being dismissed. *Bring me the head of Sven the clown.* Well, if that was what she wanted, he'd do it. But the thought of killing the guy and not offering him the last rite was...tasteless? No, worse than that. Taste was a value judgment. This was final, a total extinction. The boss had said: *There are some things the unborn god should be protected from.* Meaning, memories that must never be mapped and archived for posterity lest the machineries of heaven expose the machinations of mortals who might arrive on the unborn god's doorstep exposed to criticism. Shit stank, and the unborn god must be born pure, once the abominably abhuman Eschaton was destroyed.

Franz paused just outside the bridge door and took a deep breath of pure filtered air that didn't stink of carnage. Samow's localized EMP bomb had blipped a massive current surge through the facilities deck below the bridge, accessed via a storage locker. It had overloaded the superconducting electrograv ring under the bridge, temporarily exposing everything above it—as far as the next deck and the next ring—to the bone-splintering drag of the ship's full thirty gees of acceleration for a fraction of a second. Meanwhile, Jamil and one of the trusted strike team goons had taken the training room, slaved to the bridge systems and doubling as an emergency bridge during the run-up to the ship's first jump. The officer on duty hadn't understood quite what was happening at first; Kurt had pithed and puppetized him, and that was their biometric token sorted.

Now they were about three light years off course, crunching

on the second jump of the series of four that the nav team had knocked together for them aboard the *Heidegger.* It was a calculated risk, taking over a liner under way, but so far it had worked well. The window of opportunity for the passengers and crew to do something about them was closing rapidly, and when Mathilde finished installing the ubiquitous surveillance software on the ship's passenger liaison network it would be locked down tighter than a supermax prison.

Portia's planning had placed a platoon of special forces troops aboard the liner even before she arrived with her team of spooks and specialists. All they really needed was to take a bridge room, the drive engineering spaces, a couple of damage-control centers, and central life support. Once they could track everybody's movements through walls and floors, and remotely lock the doors or cut off the air supply if they didn't like what they were seeing, the ship would be theirs. Which left Franz facing a dilemma.

There was no way Hoechst was going to let him run away. In fact, she'd probably kill him or send him for reimplementation as soon as look at him, once the *Romanov* arrived at Newpeace. It was stupid to expect her to grow a new body for Erica: that was a privilege even Director-level officials were rarely granted. If he could steal the memory diamond containing her reclaimed state vector and genetic map, then find some way to reach a polity where downloading and cloning weren't instruments of state under control of the technotheocracy, he might be able to do something . . . but how likely was that? *She's dead, and I'm fucked,* he told himself coldly. *All I can hope for is to try to convince Portia I'm a willing servant—*

He made his way along the radial corridor, empty of all human traffic (Jordaan's messing with the access permissions had locked almost all the crew out of the service tunnels for the duration of the takeover) and caught a crew elevator up to A deck and Hoechst's command suite. When the door opened for him, one of Mathilde's troops shoved a gun at him. "What do you want?"

"Got a job to do for the boss." He stepped inside and the door slid shut behind him. "Is Mathilde here?"

"No." The guard lowered his gun, went back to his position next to the door. "What do you need?"

"I need to use the ubiq tap as soon as everything's installed. That, and I'd like to draw a sidearm and a neural spike. Boss wants a loose end tied off."

"Uh-huh." The soldier sounded vaguely amused. "Ferris will sort you out."

The main room was a mess. Someone had been digging into the floor, opening up crawl spaces and installing a loom of cables that ran to a compact signal-processing mainframe squatting on the remains of what had once been a very expensive dressing table. Three or four techs were hunched over various connectors or blinking and gesturing at the air, shepherding their mobile code around the ship's passenger liaison net. Another soldier was busy with a ruggedized communications console, very low-tech but entirely independent of the shipboard systems. She looked up as Franz came in. "What do you want?"

"Crewman"— he consulted his implant—"4365, Svengali Q., no last name, occupation, entertainments specialist, subtype juvenile. I need to know where he is. And I need to draw a gun."

"Crewman 4365," she drawled, "is currently locked in—" she frowned. "No. He's down on H deck, radial four, orange ring, in the second-class dining area doing..." Her brow wrinkled. "What's a 'birthday party'?"

"Never mind. Is he scheduled there for much longer?"

"Yes, but there are other passengers—"

"That's all right." Franz glanced around. "Now, about a handgun."

"Over there. Boss's bedroom, there's a crate by the sleeping platform. Uh-oh, incoming call." She was back at her console without a second glance.

Portia's bedroom was a mess. Discarded equipment cases were scattered across the floor, the remains of a half-eaten meal cooling on the pillows. Franz found the crate and rummaged in it until he found a carton that contained a machine pistol and a couple of factory-packed magazines loaded with BLAMs. He held the gun to his forehead for long enough for its tiny brain to handshake with his implants, and upload its recent ballistic performance record and a simple aiming network. Franz didn't much like carrying a gun; while he knew how to use one, having to do so in his line of work would usually mean that his cover was blown and his job, if not his life, was over. He rummaged further, and despite Portia's injunction, he took a neural spike. You never knew...

He was about to leave the room when he noticed something else. There was a pile of dirty clothing heaped on an open suitcase next to the bed. It looked like stuff the boss had been wearing earlier. He paused, momentarily curious. *Would she?* he wondered. *Is it worth a look?* Well yes, it was...probably. He glanced at the half-open door. There was nobody in sight. He knelt and ran his hands around the inside of the case, then the lid. He felt a lump in one side pocket. Cursing himself for his optimism, he unzipped the pouch and pulled out a small box. Then he stopped cursing. "Wow," he breathed. He flipped the box open, then hastily closed it again, stood up, and shoved it into one hip pocket, then headed back into the reception room, his pulse pounding with guilty intent.

The box had contained a gemstone the size of his thumb, sitting atop a ceramic block studded with optical ports—the reader/writer head. It was memory diamond, atoms arranged in a lattice of alternating carbon 12 and carbon 13 nuclei: the preferred data storage format for the unborn god's chosen few. Dense and durable, twelve grams was enough to store a thousand neural maps and their associated genome data. This was Hoechst's soul repository, where the upload data from anyone she terminated in the course of service would be stored until they could be archived by the Propagators, against the day when the unborn god would be assembled and draw upon the frozen imprints. Such careless concealment in a piece of nondescript luggage had to be deliberate; probably she'd decided the ship's strong room was too obvious a target. It was a symbol of her authority, of her power of life after death over those who served her. He could expect no mercy if she found him in possession of it. But if he could dig a single stored mind out of it and put it back, he'd be fine. And that was exactly the prospect that had his hands sweating and his heart pounding with pity and fear...and hope.

Nobody paid any attention as he slipped back into the dayroom. "I'm going down to drop in on my target," he told the comms specialist. "Got a field phone?"

"Sure." She tossed him a ruggedized handset. "Turns back into a pumpkin next jump. Bring it back for a reset." *Must be a causal channel,* he realized. The untappable instant quantum devices were the tool of choice for communications security—at least between FTL hops.

"Check." He slipped it into his pocket. "See you around."

there was an uproar in the dining room. Steffi stood up. "Please!" she shouted. "Please calm down! The situation's under control—"

Predictably, it didn't work. But she had to try: "Listen! Please sit down. Lieutenant Commander Fromm is investigating this problem. I assure you nothing serious is wrong, but if you would just *sit down* and give us time to sort things out—"

"I'd give up, if I were you," Martin said quietly. Half the passengers were flocking toward the exits, evidently in a hurry to return to their rooms. The rest were milling around like a herd of frightened sheep, unsure whose lead to follow. "They're not going to listen. What the hell *is* happening, anyway?"

"I don't—" Steffi caught herself. *Shit! Play dumb, idiot!* "Max is looking into it. At best, some idiot's played a prank with the liaison network. At worst?" She shrugged.

"Who made the announcement?" Martin asked.

"I don't know." *But I can guess.* She frowned. "And no *way* would the skipper divert from our course—for one thing, New Prague is about the closest port of call on our route! For another—" She shrugged. "It doesn't add up."

"I'm not going to say the word," Martin said slowly, "but I think something has gone very wrong. Something to do with the investigation."

Steffi's guts turned to ice. Confirmation of her own worst fears: it was a stitch-up. "I couldn't possibly comment. I should be heading to my duty station—" She forced herself to pause for a couple of seconds. "What would you do if this was your call?"

"It's either a genuine accident, in which case damage control is on top of it or we'd be dead already, or—well, you put it together; the net's down, a stranger is announcing some weird accident and telling passengers to go to their rooms, and we've got a couple of killers loose on board. Frankly, I'd send everyone to their cabins. They're self-contained with emergency oxygen supplies and fabs for basic food, it's where they want to go, they can hole up, and if it *is* a hijacking, it'll give the hijackers a headache. Meanwhile we can find out what's going on and either try to help out or find somewhere to hole up." The ghost of a smile tugged at his lips, then fell away. "Seriously. Get them out of here. Dispersal is good."

"Shit!" She stood up and raised her voice again: "*If* you'd all go straight to your cabins and stay out of the corridors until somebody tells you it's all right, that would help us immensely."

Almost at once the crush at the exits redoubled as first-class passengers streamed away from their seats. Within a minute the dining room was almost empty. "Right. Now what?" She asked, edgily. If Max was all right, he should have sent a runner by now. So he wasn't, and the shit had presumably hit the fan. Twitching her rings didn't seem to help; she was still locked out of the network.

"Now we go somewhere unexpected. Uh, your rings still not working?" She nodded. "Right, switch off everything."

"But—"

"Just *do* it." Martin reached into a pocket and pulled out a battered-looking leather-bound hardback book. "PA, global peripheral shutdown. Go to voice-only." He shook his head, wincing slightly. "I know it feels weird, but—"

Steffi shrugged uncomfortably, then blinked her way through a series of menus until she found the hard power-down option on her personal area network. "Are you sure about it?"

"Sure? Who's sure of anything? But if someone's taking over the ship, they're going to view nailing down line officers—even trainees—as a priority. Way I'd plan it, first your comms would go down, then people would simply vanish one by one." Steffi blinked and nodded, then sent the final command and watched the clock projected in her visual field wink out. Martin stood up. "Come on." They followed the last diners out into the main radial heading for the central concourse, but before they'd passed the nearest crossway Martin paused at a side door. "Can you open this?"

"Sure." Steffi grasped the handle and twisted. Sensors in the handle recognized her handprint and gave way. "Not much here but some stores and—"

"First thing to do is to cover up that uniform." Martin was already through the door. "Got to get you looking like a steward or a passenger. Don't think they'll be looking for me or Rachel yet." He pushed open the next door, onto a dizzying spiral of steps broken every six meters by another pressure door. "Come on, long climb ahead."

Steffi tensed, wondering if she was going to have to break his neck there and then. "Why do you—"

"Because you're a line officer, why else? If we're being hijacked, you know how to fly this damn thing; at least you're in the chain of command. I know enough about the drive layout on this tub to spin up the kernel, but if we get control back, we're going to need you to authenticate us to the flight systems and log me in as flight engineer. If I'm wrong, we'll hear about it as soon as the PLN comes back up. So start climbing!"

Steffi relaxed. "Okay, I'm climbing, I'm climbing."

"You—" Rachel swayed on her feet. The girl shook her head violently, looking spooked, and muttered something inaudible. Then she glanced over her shoulder. "Are you Victoria Strowger?"

Wednesday's head whipped round. "Who wants to know?"

Her shoulders set, she was clearly on the defensive. "Calm down," said Rachel. "I'm Martin's partner. Listen, the ReMastered are going to be all over us in a couple of minutes if we don't get the hell out of the public spaces. All I want is to ask you a couple of questions. Can we take this up in my suite?"

Wednesday stared at her, eyes narrowing in calculation. "Okay. What's going on?"

Rachel took a deep breath. "I think the ship's being hijacked. Do you know where Frank is?"

"I—no." Wednesday looked shaken. "He was going to go back to his room to fetch something, he said."

"Oh dear." Rachel tried to keep a straight face; the kid looked really worried at her tone of voice. "Are you coming? We can look him up later."

"But I need to find him!" There was an edgy note of panic in her voice.

"Believe me, right now he's either completely safe, or he's already a prisoner, and they'll be using him as bait for you."

"Fuck!" Wednesday looked alarmed.

"Come *on*," coaxed Rachel. "Do you want them to find both of you?" A sick sense of dread dogged her: if Martin was right,

Wednesday and Frank were romantically entangled. She cringed at the memory of how *she'd* once felt, knowing Martin had been taken. "Listen, we'll find him later—get to safety first, though, or we won't be able to. Switch your rings off right now, unless you want to be found. I know you're not on the shipboard net, but if they're still emitting, the bad guys may know how to ping them." Rachel turned toward the main stairwell. It was filling up with people, chattering hordes of passengers coming out to see what was going on, or heading back to their rooms; a handful of harried-looking stewards scurried hither and yon, or tried to answer questions for which they didn't have any answers.

"You know what's going on, don't you?" Rachel concentrated on the stairs, trying to ignore her shaking muscles and the urge to shiver whenever she thought back to what she'd seen in the D-con room. Six flights to go. "What *is* going on?"

"Shut up and climb." *Five* flights to go. "Shit!" They were nearing D deck, and the crowd was thinner—there were fewer staterooms—and there was the first sign of trouble, a man standing in the middle of the landing and blocking the next flight of stairs. His face was half-obscured by a pair of bulky low-tech imaging goggles, like something out of the dawn of the infowar age; but the large-caliber gun he held looked lethally functional.

"You. Stop. Who are you and where are you going?"

Rachel stopped. She could feel Wednesday a step behind her, shivering—about to break and run, if she didn't do something fast. "I'm Rachel Mansour, this is my daughter Anita. We were just going back to our suite. It's on B deck. What's going on?" She stared at the gun apprehensively, trying to look as if she was surprised to see it. *Ooh, isn't it big!* She steeled herself, prepping her military implants for the inevitable. If he checked the manifest and realized—

"I'm with the shipboard security detail. We've got reason to believe there's a dangerous criminal loose aboard ship." He stared at them as if memorizing their faces. "When you get to your rooms, stay there until you hear an announcement that it's safe to leave." He stepped to one side and waved them on. Rachel took a deep breath and sidled past him, glancing over her shoulder to make sure Wednesday was still there.

After a moment's hesitation the young woman followed her. She had the wit to keep quiet until they were round the next spiral in the staircase. "Shipboard security my ass. What the fuck was *that* about?"

"Network's down," murmured Rachel. "They've probably got a list of names, but they don't know who I am, and I lied about who you are. It'll last about five milliseconds once they get the ship's systems working for them, but we're in the clear for now."

"Yeah, but who's Anita?"

Rachel paused between steps to catch her breath for a moment. *Three flights to go.* "Anita's been dead for thirty years," she said shortly.

"Oh—I didn't know."

"Leave it." Rachel resumed climbing. She could feel it in her calves, and she could hear Wednesday breathing hard. "You get used to letting go and moving on. After a while. Not all of them die."

"She was, your daughter?"

"Ask me some other time." *Two flights to go. Save your breath.* She slowed as they came up to the next landing, emergency pressure doors poised like guillotine blades overhead, waiting to cut the spiraling diamond-walled staircase into segments. But there was no checkpoint. *They don't have enough people,* she thought hopefully. *We might get away with this.*

"My suite. Can't go. Back?"

"No." *One more flight.* "Not far now." They paused at the top of the next flight. Wednesday was panting hard. Rachel leaned against the wall, feeling the hot iron ache in her calves and a burning in her lungs. Even militarized muscles didn't enjoy climbing fifty vertical meters of stairs without a break. "Okay, this way."

Rachel palmed the door open and waved Wednesday inside. The kid glanced at her for a moment, her expression troubled. "Is this—"

"Talk inside." She nodded, and Rachel followed her in. "Sit down. Got some stuff to do."

"Stuff?"

Rachel was already leaning over her trunk. "I want—hmm." She raised the lid and stuck her finger in the authentication slot, then rapidly scrolled through items on the built-in hard screen. She glanced at Wednesday. "Come over here. I need to know what size clothing you take."

"Clothing? Earth measurements? Or Sept—"

"Just stand up. Your name's Anita and you don't exist, but you're down on the passenger list. So we'll just have to make sure you don't look like Victoria Strowger when they get the passenger liaison net back up again, all right?"

"What's going *on*?"

Rachel straightened up as the trunk began to whine, holding a small scanner. "I was hoping *you* could tell *me*. That jacket's programmable, isn't it? You've made them panic, and they're springing a trap. Can it do any colors other than black? Prematurely, I hope. Quick, they could be calling any minute. Why don't you tell me how you got in this mess—"

ᴛʜᴇʀᴇ ᴡᴀꜱ ɴᴏ knock on the door. It swung open, and two figures leapt inside. But then one of them kicked it shut—and by the time Rachel finished turning around Martin was leaning against the door, his eyes half-shut, breathing deeply.

"Martin—" She glanced sideways as she stood up, knees wobbly with relief. "I was beginning to think they'd grabbed you." They met in the vestibule and she hugged him, then looked past his shoulder at the other arrival. "Aha! Glad you could make it. Martin, which plan were you thinking of using?"

"Plan B," said Martin. "We've got that spare ID you put on the manifest."

"Uh-oh." Rachel let go of him, turned, and stared at the bathroom door. "We may have a problem."

The bathroom door opened. "Is this what you wanted?" Wednesday asked plaintively. Rachel blinked at her. In the space of ten minutes her hair had turned blond and curly, the stark black eyeliner had vanished, and the black leather jacket with the spiky shoulders had been replaced by a pink dress with layered puffball underskirts. "My ass looks *huge* in this. I feel like a real idiot!" She noticed Steffi. "Oh, hi there. This isn't about the other night, is it?"

Steffi sat down hard on the end of the bed. "Just *what* are you doing here?" she demanded, a hard edge in her voice.

"Um." Rachel fixed Martin with a steely gaze. "We seem to have a slight problem. Can't really have two Anitas running around, can we?"

"No—" Martin rubbed his forehead tiredly. "Shit! What a mess. One false set of ident tags, and two people to hide. Looks like we've got a problem, folks."

"Can I just wear a flowerpot on my head and pretend I'm a tree? I know the idea is to look different, but this is just plain embarrassing."

"Somehow I don't think that would fool them for long." Martin scratched his chin. "Steffi?"

"Let me think." She leaned her chin on one fist. "I feel so useless right now. I should really be trying to link up with the bridge crew or D-com—"

"Your attention, please. This is your acting Captain speaking." Everyone looked up instinctively at the voice emanating from the emergency comm panel beside the door. "There has been an accident on the bridge. Captain Hussein has been incapacitated. In her absence I, Lieutenant Commander Fromm, am in charge of this vessel. For your safety and comfort you should remain in your rooms until further notice. Passenger liaison facilities will be re-enabled shortly, and if you need anything, your needs will be attended to. In view of the crisis, I have asked for volunteer help. We are lucky to be carrying a group from Tonto, and I have enlisted these people to provide assistance in this critical period. Please comply with any instructions they issue. I will make further announcements when the situation is fully under control."

"Uh-oh," said Wednesday.

"He's gone crazy!" Steffi exploded. "The skipper would never do that, she'd—" Her eyes were wide. "It's a hijacking, isn't it? But why is Max cooperating?"

"I hate to break it to you," Martin said gently, "but that wasn't Lieutenant Commander Fromm you were listening to. It was his voicebox, but not him talking."

"What do you mean?" Steffi stared at him, trying to figure out how much he might know.

"The ReMastered have made something of a specialty out of brain mapping and digitization," said Rachel, her tone dispassionate. "They can save minds to off-line storage and reincarnate them later—at great expense—by building a new body. But mostly they use the technique to turn living bodies into puppets. Zombies, zimboes with the illusion of self-awareness, whatever." She clenched her hands together. "That's how they take planets. They acquire some key government officers, destabilize the place by exploiting local political tensions, declare a state of emergency—using their puppets—and move in."

Steffi's face was white. *Shit! I have to warn Sven! We've got to get out of here!* "Max went to the flight deck to find out what was going on! I let him—"

"Don't blame yourself. They've got the bridge, drive engineering control, damage control, sentries on the main stairs, and passengers under lock and key in their rooms. This was a well-planned operation." Rachel glanced at Wednesday. "Bet you they're turning over your suite right now. And yours," she added, looking back at Steffi. "They made a big mistake, missing you."

"But I, I—" Steffi stopped. She looked horrified.

"It'll take them time to check on us in here," Martin said slowly, thinking aloud. "When they do, we want you well hidden. You're probably the senior line officer on the ship. We'll need you around for your pass codes and retinal print if we're to stand a chance of taking back control." He glanced at the cupboard. "Once we arrive where they're diverting us to. *If* we get there without them tagging us in a search. Ever heard of a priest's hole?"

"A what?" Steffi looked dazed. "What are you talking about? I'm just a trainee flight officer! I don't have clearance—"

Martin walked over to the trunk containing the military fabricator. "You'll be the ranking line officer on the ship once this is over," he told her. "Rache, can you clear everything out of the walk-in? I'm going to need some basic tools, some supports, and a load of paneling to fit. Plus any special toys you can have the fab turn out in less than half an hour that won't show up as weapons on a teraherz scan. Bet you they're working on a ubiquitous surveillance mesh already. Need clothing for you, me, and the kid; it's in the deception and evasion library. Steffi, have you got a rebreather mask? We'll need a couple of buckets, some cushions, something to cover one of the buckets with—"

"Rebreather mask?"

"We've got maybe an hour," Martin said impatiently. He pointed at Wednesday. "You're going to be Anita. *You*—" he pointed at Steffi—"are going to be Anne—Anne Frank. Rachel, run the kid through the Anita background while I get our stowaway stowed. Steffi? You and I are going to build a false back to the wardrobe, and I'm going to wall you in until we get wherever we're going. The name of this phase of the game is hide-and-seek, and the goal is to stay out of custody for now. Once we know which way the wind's blowing we'll see about taking back the ship."

"If you can hear me, blink twice."

Blink blink.

"That's good. You're Frank, aren't you? Blink once for yes."

Blink.

"All right. Now listen carefully. You are in big trouble. You have been kidnapped. The people who are holding you have no intention of releasing you. I'm one of them, but I'm different. In a moment, I'm going to give you back control of your vocal cords so you can talk. They're only going to leave me alone with you for a couple of minutes, and we may not be able to talk again, so it's important that you don't scream or give me any trouble. Otherwise, we're both as good as dead. If you understand, blink once."

Blink.

"Okay...say hello?"

"He—hell—ack."

"Take your time, your throat's probably a bit sore. Here, try to swallow some of this...better?"

"Who'urr ooh?"

"I'm one of your kidnappers. But I'm not entirely happy about it. You're here because you're important to someone we're interested in. A girl called Wednesday. You know her?" *Pause.* "Come on, *I'm* not the one who wants to get at the contents of her head." *Pause.* "All right. Let me explain.

"Wednesday knows...something. I'm not sure what. She's somewhere aboard this ship, don't know where, and the other—kidnappers—are trying to find her before we arrive where we're going. When we get there, they're going to use you as a hostage to try to make her tell us everything she knows. Trouble is, once she gives them the—the information, her usefulness will be at an end. Yours, too. You're both witnesses.

"Now, two or three things could happen. They might just shoot you, but I don't rate that as very likely. More probably, you'll end up in a reprocessing camp. Or they'll just pith you and turn you into a meat puppet. None of these options are very good for you, are they?"

"No fucking way." Pause. "What do *you* want?"

"I happen not to agree with the others. But if they find out what I really think, they'll kill me—I'm a traitor. So I need to find a way out that, uh, doesn't give them what they want. So they don't get the, the immigration records. Or the go codes. Or the weapon test reports. In fact, I want them to go out the airlock. And I want to vanish, see? I don't want them to find me, ever again. And I figured you could help me do that. They don't know I'm here, talking to you. Between us we can fool them. They've hijacked this ship, but they haven't done the job properly. If you help me, we can regain control and turn everything over to the surviving ship's officers, and I can disappear and you'll be free."

"What about Wednesday?"

"Her, too."

Pause. "So what do you want me to do?"

"For starters, you can look after this diamond for me."

the clown died with a grin on his face and a warm gun in his hand.

Franz had tracked him down to H deck, where the comms sergeant had said he was working on a "birthday party." Gun in pocket, Franz walked down the stairwell to give himself time to think about how to do the job. It wasn't as if hits were his specialty; on the contrary, you only did wetwork in Septagon if your cover evaporated and you needed to clear out fast. Sparrowfart surveillance was deliberately absent there, but as soon as the body count began rising it would come down like a suffocating cloud. Franz shuddered slightly, thinking about the risks Hoechst's team had run, and checked the schematics in his inner eye one more time. Radial four, orange ring, second-class dining area—there were four entrances, two accessible from passenger country. *Not good,* he decided. Even with the ship under the thumb of the ReMastered, a chase and shoot-out could result in a real mess. It wasn't a good idea to underestimate the clown. He was a slippery customer.

At D deck Franz hit the checkpoint. Strasser stared at him coldly as he came down the stairs. "What do you want?" he demanded.

"Check with control," Franz grunted. "Are you free yet?"

"What for?"

"Got a job. Loose end to take care of. I need to cover three exits—"

"Wait." Strasser raised his bulky phone. "Maria? Yeah, it's me. Look, I've got U. Bergman here. He says he's running an errand and he needs backup. Am I—oh. Yes, all right, I'll do that." He pocketed the phone and frowned. "What do you want me to do?"

Franz told him.

"Okay. I think that'll work." Strasser looked thoughtful. "We're spread thin. Can we get this out of the way fast?"

"Yes, but I'll need two more pairs of hands. Who do you suggest?"

"We can collect Colette and Byrne on the way down. I'll

send them round the back while I cover the red ring entrance. I'll message you when we're in position. Sure you want to do it this way?"

Franz took a deep breath. "I don't want to alarm him. If we scare him, he'll lash out, and there's no way of knowing what he's carrying. Remember, this guy has carried out more hits than we've had hot meals."

"I doubt it. I'll make sure we're in position in not less than six minutes and not more than fifteen. If he leaves, you want us to abort to Plan B and take him in his berth. That right?"

"Right." Franz headed for the stairwell. "Get Colette and Byrne in the loop, and I'll brief them on the way there."

Eight minutes later Franz was walking through the orange ring corridor, past smoothly curving walls and doors opening onto recreational facilities, public bathrooms, corridors leading to shared dormitories. Second class was sparsely furnished, thin carpet barely damping out the noise of footsteps, none of the hand-carved paneling and sculpture that featured in first and Sybarite.

"Coming up on the entrance now," Franz murmured. "I'll blip when I'm ready." He rang off and held his phone loosely in his left hand. There was a racket coming from up ahead, round the curve, high-pitched voices *shouting. What's going on, some kind of riot?* he wondered as he headed for the door.

Turning the corner he witnessed a scene he'd never imagined. It *was* a riot, but none of the rioters were much taller than waist height, and they all seemed to be enjoying themselves hugely: either that or they were souls in torment, judging by the shrieking and squalling. It vaguely resembled a creche from back home, but no conditioner would have tolerated this sort of indiscipline for an instant. About thirty small children were racing around the room, some of them naked, others wearing elaborate costumes. The lights were flashing through different color combinations, and the walls were flicking up one fantasy scene after another—flaming grottoes, desert sands, rain forests. A gaggle of silvery balloons buzzed overhead, ducking almost within fingertip reach, then dodging aside as fast as overloaded motors could shift them. The music was deafening, some kind of rhythmic pounding bass line with voices singing a nonsense refrain.

Franz ducked down and caught the nearest rioter by the hand. "What's going on?" he demanded. The little girl stared at him wide-eyed, then pulled her hand away and ran off. "Shit," he muttered. Then a little savage in a loincloth spotted him and ambled over, shyly, one hand behind his back. "Hello."

"Hello!" *Whack.* "Heeheehee—"

Franz managed to restrain himself from shooting the kid—it might alert the target. "Fuck!" His head hurt. What had the boy used? A club? He shook his head again.

"Hello. Who are you?"

"I'm—" He paused. The girl leaning over him looked taller— no, that wasn't it. She looked *older,* in some indefinable way. She was no bigger than the other children, but there was something assured and poised about her despite the seven-year-old body, all elbows and knees. "I'm Franz. Who are you?"

"I'm Jennifer," the girl said casually. "This is Barnabas's birthday party, you know. You shouldn't just come barging in here. People will talk. They'll get the wrong idea."

"Well." Franz thought for a moment. "I came here to talk, so that's not a problem. Is Sven the clown about?"

"Yes." She smirked at him unhelpfully.

"Are you going to tell me where he is?"

"No." He stood up, ready to loom over her, but she didn't show any sign of intimidation. "I really don't think you've got his best interests in mind."

Best interests in mind? What the hell kind of infant is this? "Isn't he going to be a better judge of that than you?"

To his surprise, she acted as if she was seriously considering the idea. "Possibly," she admitted. "If you stay right there, I'll ask him." *Pause.* "Hey, Sven! What you say?"

"I say," said a voice right behind Franz's ear, "he's right. Don't move, what-what?" Franz froze, feeling a hard prod in the small of his back. "That's right. Sound screen *on.* Jen, if you'd be so good as to keep the party running? I'm going to take a little walk with my friend here. Friend, when I stop talking you're going to turn around slowly and start walking. Or I'll have to shoot your balls off. I'm told it hurts."

Franz turned round slowly. The clown barely came up to his chin. His face was a bizarre plastic mask: gigantic grinning lips, bulbous nose, green spikes of hair. He wore a pink tutu, elaborate mountaineering boots, and held something resembling a makeup compact in his right hand as if it was a gun.

"What's that?" he asked.

"Start walking." The clown nodded toward the door.

"If I do that, you'll die," Franz said calmly.

"I will, will I? Then so shall you." The face behind the plastic grin wasn't smiling, and the makeup compact wasn't wavering. It was probably some kind of low-caliber pistol. "Who sent you?"

"Your client." Franz leaned back against the wall and laced his fingers together in front of him to stop his hands shaking.

"*My* client. Can you describe this mysterious client?"

"You were approached on Earth by a man who identified himself as Gordon Black. He contacted you in the usual way and offered you a fee of twenty thousand per target plus expenses and soft money, installments payable with each successive hit, zero for a miss. Black was about my height, dark hair, his cover was an export agent from—"

"Stop. All right. What do you *want?* Seeking me out like this, I assume the deal's off, what-what?"

"That's right." Franz tried to make himself relax, pretend this was just another informer and cat's-paw like the idiots he'd had to deal with on Magna. It wasn't easy with a bunch of raucous children running around outside their cone of silence and a gun pointing at his guts. He knew Svengali's record; U. Scott hadn't stinted on the expenses when it came to covering his own trail of errors. "The business in Sarajevo with the trap suggests that the arrangement has no future. Someone's identified the sequence."

"Yes, well, this wouldn't have happened if you'd taken my original advice about changing ships at Turku," Svengali said waspishly. "Traffic analysis is always a problem. Like attempts to sever connections and evade obligations on the part of employers. Did you think I worked alone?"

"No," Franz said evenly, "but my boss may take some convincing. 'Bring me the head of Svengali the clown,' she said. I think you'll agree that's pretty fucking stupid on the face of it, which is why I decided to interpret her orders creatively and have a little chat with you first. Then maybe you can carry your head in to see her while it's still attached to your body."

"Hmm." Svengali looked thoughtful, insofar as Franz could see any expression at all under the layers of pseudoflesh. "Yes, well I think I'll take you up on the offer, and thank you for making it. The sooner this is sorted out, the better."

"I'm glad you agree." Franz straightened up. "We walk out of here together after I signal my backup. I take it your backup is aboard the ship?"

"Believe whatever you want." Svengali shrugged. "Send your signal, pretty boy."

"Sure." Franz held up his mobile and squeezed the speed button. *Idiot,* he thought disgustedly. Svengali had screwed up, making the fatal assumption that having a friend aboard to keep watch would be sufficient unto the day. It hadn't occurred to him that they might be unable to deliver any damning evidence for rather a long time if the entire ship disappeared. Or that the ReMastered might not want a professional assassin running around while they were trying to sort everything out. Then he gestured at the door. "After you?"

"You first."

"All right." Franz walked through the door back into the corridor. "Who was the kid?" he asked curiously.

"Who, Jen? Oh, she's just a Lolita from childcare. Helping out with the party."

"Party? What ideology are they?" Franz added, sounding puzzled.

"Not ideology, birthday. Don't you have any idea—"

One moment the clown was two paces behind Franz, the small box held loosely in his right hand. The next instant he was flattened against the wall and bringing the gun up to bear on Franz, his lips pulled back with a rictus of hate. Then he twitched violently, a shudder rippling all the way through him from head to toes. He collapsed like a discarded glove puppet.

Franz turned round slowly. "Took your time," he said.

"Not really. I had to get into position without alerting him." Strasser bent over the clown and put his weapon away. "Come and help me move this before it bleeds out and makes a mess on the carpet."

Franz joined him. Together they lifted the body. Whatever Strasser had shot him with had turned Svengali's eyes ruby red from burst blood vessels. He felt like a warm sack of meat.

"Let's get him into one of the lifts," Franz volunteered. "The boss wants to see his head. I reckon we ought to oblige her."

MARTIN WAS STILL piling the contents of the walk-in closet up against the newly fitted partition when the passenger liaison net came back up. It made its presence known in several ways—with a flood of ultrawideband radiation, a loud chime, and a human voice broadcast throughout the ship.

"Your attention, please. Passenger liaison is now fully reconstructed and accepting requests. I am Lieutenant Commander

Max Fromm, acting Captain. I would like to apologize for the loss of service. Two hours ago, a technical glitch in our drive control circuit exposed the occupants of the flight deck and other engineering spaces to a temporary overgee load. A number of the crew have been incapacitated. As the senior line officer, I have moved control to the auxiliary bridge, and we are diverting to the nearest station with repair facilities. We will arrive there in thirty-two hours and will probably be able to proceed on our scheduled voyage approximately two days later.

"I regret to inform you that it is believed that this incident may not have been accidental. It has been reported that our passenger manifest includes a pair of individuals belonging to a terrorist group identified with revanchist Muscovite nationalism. Crew and deputies drawn from the ReMastered youth leadership cadre aboard this vessel are combing the ship as I speak, and we expect to have the killers in custody shortly. In the meantime, the privacy blocks provided by WhiteStar for your comfort are being temporarily suspended to facilitate the search.

"Please stay in your cabins if at all possible. Please enable your communications nodes at all times. Before leaving your cabins, please contact passenger liaison and let us know why. I will announce the all clear in due course, but your cooperation would be appreciated while the emergency is in effect."

"Corpsefuckers!" Wednesday stood up and paced over to the main door, like a restless cat. "What do they—"

"Anita," Rachel said warningly.

Wednesday sighed. "Yes, Mom?"

Martin finished shoving the big diplomatic fab trunk up against the panels and turned round. *She's got the exasperated adolescent bit down perfectly,* he noted approvingly. And she'd managed to change her appearance completely. Her hair was a mass of blond ringlets and she'd switched from black leather and tight leggings to a femme dress that rustled when she moved. The bows in her hair made her look about five years younger, but the pout was the same, and with the work Rachel had done on her cheeks and fingerprints—*let's just hope they crashed the liaison system hard enough that they don't pay too much attention to the biometric tags,* he thought grimly. *Because—*

"Sit down, girl. You're making me dizzy."

"Aw, Mom!" She pulled a face.

Rachel pulled a face right back. "We need to look like a family," she'd pointed out half an hour earlier, while Martin was walling Steffi and a three-day supply of consumables into the priest's hole. "There's a chunk of familial backbiting, and a chunk of consistency, and we want you to look as unlike the Victoria Strowger they're hunting for as possible. Wednesday wears black and is extremely spiky. So you're going to wear pink, and be fluffy and frilly. At least for a while."

"Three fucking *days?*" Wednesday complained.

"They've crashed the liaison network," Rachel pointed out, "and crashed it hard. That's the only edge we've got, because when they bring it up again they'll be able to configure it as cell-dar—every ultrawideband node in the ship's corridors and state-rooms will be acting as a teraherz radar transmitter. With the right software loaded into the nodes they'll be able to see right through your clothing, in the dark, and track you wherever you go to within millimeters. We have to act as if we're under surveillance the whole time once the net comes back up, because if they're remotely competent—and they must be if they've just hijacked a liner with complete surprise—it'll give them total control over the ship and total surveillance over everybody they can see."

"Except someone hidden at the back of a closet inside a Fara-day cage," Martin murmured as he slotted another panel into place, still stinking of hot plastic and metal from the military fab-ricator's output hopper.

"Yes, Mom." Wednesday paced back to the armchair and dropped into it in a sea of lace. "Do you think they'll—"

The door chimed—then opened without pause. "Excuse us, sir and ladies." Three crewmen walked in without waiting, wearing the uniforms and peaked caps of the purser's office. The man in the lead had a neatly trimmed beard and dead eyes. "I am Lieu-tenant Commander Fromm and I apologize for the lack of warn-ing. Are you Rachel Mansour? And Martin Springfield?" He spoke like an automaton, voice almost devoid of inflection, and Martin noted a bruise near the hairline on his left temple, almost concealed by his cap.

"And our daughter Anita," Rachel added smoothly. Wednes-day frowned and looked away from the men, scuffing the carpet with her boot soles.

"Anita Mansour-Springfield?"

Fromm looked momentarily blank, but one of the men behind him checked a tablet: "That's what it says here, sir."

"Oh." Fromm still looked vacant. "Do you know of a Victoria Strowger?" he said stiffly.

"Who?" Rachel looked politely puzzled. "Is that the terrorist you're looking for?"

"Terr-or-ist." Fromm nodded stiffly. "If you see her, report to us immediately. Please." His eyes looked red, almost bloodshot. Martin peered at him intently. *He isn't blinking!* he realized. "I must revalidate your diplomatic credentials. Please. Your passports."

"Martin?" Rachel looked at him. "Would you fetch Commander Fromm our papers, please?" She remained seated on the chaise longue at the side of the dayroom, a picture of languor.

"All right." He walked over to the closet, throwing the doors wide, and retrieved the passports from the briefcase on top of the fab without turning on the closet light. *Let them get a glimpse of a cluttered closet with no room for anyone to hide...* "We should like you to withdraw surveillance from this suite," he added, as he handed the passports over. "And as soon as she's up to it, I'd like you to convey my best wishes for a speedy recovery and a happy code red to Captain Hussein. I'd like to see her when she's got time, if possible."

"I am sure Captain Hussein will see you," Fromm said slowly, and passed the passports to one of the other two officers for a check.

Captain Nazma Hussein is almost certainly dead, Martin realized, the cold hand of fear tickling his guts. *And you should know what a diplomatic code red means.* He forced a smile. "Are the papers in order?"

"Yes," the man behind Fromm said curtly. "We can go now."

Fromm turned round without a word and marched out the door. The two other men followed him. The one who'd checked their papers paused in the doorway. "If you hear anything, please call us," he said curtly. "We're from the ReMastered race, and we're here to help you."

The door clicked shut. Wednesday was on her feet almost immediately. "You fuckmonsters! I'm going to rip your heads off and shit down your necks! I—"

"*Anita!*" Rachel was on her feet, too. She grabbed Wednesday's shoulders swiftly and held her. "Stay calm."

Martin walked in front of her and held up an archaic paper notepad and a tiny stub of pencil. TERAHERZ CELLDAR SIGNAL IN HERE, he scribbled twitchily in small letters. REZ ONE CM. SOUND TOO. CANT READ XPRESSNS, CAN C GESTRS, SOLID OBJECTS IN POCKETS, GUNS.

"What's—" Wednesday gasped, then leaned her head against Rachel's shoulder. Rachel embraced her. She sobbed, the sound muffled. Rachel stroked the back of her neck slowly. CAPTAIN DEAD. FROMM REMASTERED ZOMBI.

"I'm not sure I believe this," Rachel said quietly. "It's awful, isn't it?"

Wednesday nodded wordlessly, tears flowing.

"Looks like they lost the liaison network completely," Martin observed, looking away. *What set that off?* he wondered. *Her family?* He wanted to be able to speak freely, to tell her that the scum who'd done it weren't going to get away, but he also wondered how true any such reassurance would be. "On the bright side, they revalidated our passports." *Including the one in the name of Anita, with Wednesday's face and biometric tags pasted in.* "Liaison," he said, raising his voice, "what's this station we're putting into for repairs?"

The liaison network took a moment to reply. Its voice was slightly flatter than it had been the day before. "Our repair destination is portal station eleven, Old Newfoundland. This station is not approved for passenger egress. Do you require further assistance?"

"That will be all," Martin said, his voice hollow.

"Old Newfie?" Wednesday asked incredulously, raising her tear-streaked face from Rachel's shoulder. "Did you hear that? We're going to *Old Newfie!*"

thirty–two hours:

They stayed in their suite as instructed, forcing small talk and chitchat to convey the impression of familial claustrophobia. Wednesday milked her role for all it was worth—her adolescent histrionics had a sharp edge of bitterness that made Martin fantasize about strangling her after a while, or at least breaking character sufficiently to give her a good tongue-lashing. But that wasn't on the cards. His book-sized personal assist, loaded with nonstandard signal-processing software, showed him some curious patterns in the ambient broadband signals, worryingly tagged sequential pulse trains.

"I'm bored," Wednesday said fractiously. "Can't I go out?"

"You heard what the officer said, dear," Rachel responded for about the fourth time, face set in a mask of unduly tried patience. "We're diverting somewhere for repairs, and they want to keep the common spaces clear for access." Wednesday scribbled furiously on Martin's paper notepad: OLD NEWF LIFE/SUPP DOWN HEAVY RAD. Rachel blinked. "Why don't you just watch another of those antique movies or something?"

WORRIED ABOUT FRANK.

Martin glanced up from his PA. "Nothing to gain by worrying, Anita," he murmured: "They've got everything under control, and there's nothing we can do to help."

"Don't want to watch a movie."

"Sometimes all you can do is try and wait it out," Rachel said philosophically. "When events are out of your control, trying to force them your way is counterproductive."

"That sounds like bullshit to me, Mom." Wednesday's eyes narrowed.

"Really?" Rachel looked only half-amused. "Let me give you an example, then, a story about my, uh, friend the bomb disposal specialist. She was called out of a meeting one day because the local police had been called in to deal with a troublesome artist..."

Wednesday sighed theatrically, then settled down to listen attentively. She seemed almost amused, as if she thought Rachel was spinning these stories out of whole cloth, making them up on the spur of the moment. *If only you knew,* thought Martin. Still, she was putting on a good act, especially under the stressful circumstances. He'd known more than a few mature adults who'd have gone to pieces under the pressure of knowing that the ship had been taken by hijackers, and they were the target of the operation. If only...

He shut down his PA's netlink and scribbled a note on it, leaving it where she'd spot it when Rachel finished. WHY OLD NEWF? "Anyway, here's the point: If my friend had tried to rush the crazy, she'd have triggered the bomb's defense perimeter. Instead she just waited for him to open up a loophole. He did it himself, really. That's what I mean by waiting, not forcing. You keep looking at the door. Was there something you were thinking of doing out there?"

"Oh, I just need to stretch my legs," she said disingenuously. It wasn't as if she hadn't been pacing up and down the floor every half hour as it was. "Maybe go look at the bridge, if they'll let me in, or see things. I think I left some of my stuff somewhere and I ought to get it back." She caught his eye and he nodded minutely.

LEFT STUFF OLD NEWF? "What did you lose?"

"Oh, it was my shoulder bag, you know the leather one with the badge on it? And some paper I was scribbling on. I think it was somewhere near the, um, purser's office. And there was a book in it."

"We'll see about getting it back later," Rachel said, glancing up from her tablet. "Are you sure you didn't leave it in the closet?" she asked.

"Quite sure, Mom," Wednesday said tightly. b-block toilet by police station—GOVMNT BACKUP DISK.

Martin managed not to jump out of his skin. "It was quite expensive, as I recall." He raised an eyebrow.

"One of a kind." Wednesday blinked furiously. "I want it back before someone else finds it," she said, forcing a tone of spoiled pique.

Trying to figure it out, whatever it was that Wednesday had stashed near the police station in Old Newfie, was infuriating, but he didn't dare say so openly while they might be under surveillance. The combination of ultrawideband transceivers, reprogrammed liaison network nodes, and speech recognition software had turned the entire ship into a panopticon prison—one where mentioning the wrong words could get a passenger into a world of pain. Martin's head hurt just thinking about it, and he had an idea from her tense, clipped answers to any questions he asked her that Rachel felt the same way.

They made it through a sleepless night (Wednesday staked out the smaller room off to one side of the suite for herself) and a deeply boring breakfast served up by the suite's fab. Everything tasted faintly of plasticizers, and sometime during the night the suite had switched over to its independent air supply and life support—a move that deeply unsettled Martin.

Wednesday was monopolizing the bathroom, trying to coax something more than a thin shower out of the auxiliary water-purification system, when a faint tremor rattled the floor, and the liaison system dinged for attention. Martin looked up instinctively. "Your attention please. We will be arriving at our emergency repair stop in just over one hour's time. Due to technical circumstances beyond our control, we would appreciate it if all passengers would assemble in the designated evacuation areas prior to docking. This is a precautionary measure, and you will be allowed to return to your cabins after arrival. Please be ready to move in fifteen minutes' time."

The bathroom door popped open, emitting a trickle of steam and a bedraggled-looking Wednesday: "What's that about?" she asked anxiously.

"Probably nothing." Rachel stared at her and blinked rapidly, a code they were evolving for added emphasis—or negation. "I think they just want us where they can keep an eye on us."

"Oh, so it's nearly over," Wednesday said heavily. "Do you think we should do it?"

"I think we all ought to play our parts, Anita," Rachel emphasized. "Might be a good idea to get dressed, too. They might want us to go groundside"—*blink blink*—"and we ought to be prepared."

"Oh goody." Wednesday pulled a face. "It'll be freezing! I'll wear my coat and trousers." And she vanished back into the bathroom.

"Think she'll be all right?" Martin asked.

Rachel slowly nodded. "She's bearing up well so far." She scribbled hastily on her notepad: COMM CENTER? CAUSAL CHANNELS? R-BOMBS?

"Well, we ought to go and see what they want, shouldn't we?" he asked. "Let me just get my shoes on."

"*Y'know, it's funny.* For years I've had this recurring dream, nightmare, what the fuck. I'd be going about my life just like normal, when suddenly they'd *be* there. In the background, just—running things. Business as usual, same as it ever is. And I'd shit myself and go to the port and buy a ticket to, like, anywhere else. And I'd get on the ship and they'd be there, too, and all the crew would be *them.* And then I'd get to wherever the ship was going, and it would be the same. And they'd be all around me and they'd, they'd . . ."

Frank's subvocalized monologue wavered. It was all he could do just then; after the ReMastered guy with the creepy eyes had told him what he wanted he'd put the block back. His throat and the back of his mouth felt anesthetized, his tongue huge and limp. They'd used much cruder restraints on his arms and legs, and his hands felt cold and hurt from poor circulation. If he hadn't seen worse, been through worse, back in the camps, he'd have been paralyzed with terror. But as things stood, what he felt most strongly was a terrible resignation and a sense of regret.

Wednesday, I should have got you off the ship as fast as possible. Can you forgive me? He kept circling back to the mistakes he'd made, the assumption of mediocrity on the part of her pursuers. Even after the bomb at the embassy reception, he'd told himself she ought to be safe aboard a liner under a neutral flag. And—he'd wanted to stay with her. He liked her; she was a breath of fresh air blown into a life that had lately been one damn editorial rant after another. When she'd asked him to drop in and jumped his bones as soon as he shut the door he could have said

"no" gracefully—if he'd wanted to. Instead, they'd given each
other something to think about, and inadvertently signed each others' death warrants.

ReMastered.

Frank was under no illusions about what it meant, an unfamiliar voice announcing an emergency on board, then his stateroom
door crashing open, a gun buzzing and clicking in his face. They'd
stuck him with a needleful of cold darkness, and he'd woken up in
this stultifying cubicle, trussed to a chair and aching, unable to
speak. *That* moment of panic had been terrible, though it had
passed: he'd thought his heart was going to give out. Then the
crazy one had come with a diamond the size of a quail's egg,
forced him to dry-swallow a king's ransom in memories and pain.

What are her chances? he wondered, trying to think about
something other than his own predicament—which, at a guess,
would end with a friendly smile and the wrong end of a cortical
spike as their anxiously meticulous executioners raped away his
free will and sense of self—by focusing on Wednesday. *If she's
with Martin or his partner, they might try to conceal her. Or she
could hide out somewhere. She's good at hiding.* She'd hidden a
lot from him; he'd only really figured out how lonely she was late
in the game, when she'd burrowed her chin into the base of his
neck and sobbed silently for ten minutes. (He'd felt like a shit,
fearing he'd misread her mind and manipulated her into bed—
until she'd taken his cock in her hand and whispered in his ear that
she was crying at her own foolishness for waiting so long. And
who, in the end, was he to deny her anything she wanted?)

The regret he felt was not for himself; he'd already outlived
his allotted time years ago, when the ReMastered spat him out like
a squeezed pip to drift through the cosmos and begin another life
elsewhere. He wasn't afraid for himself, he realized distantly,
because he'd been here already—it wasn't a surprise, just a long-
deferred horror. But he felt a simmering anger and bitterness that
Wednesday was going to go through that, too, sooner or later, the
night of darkness in an improvised condemned cell that would
only end when the executioner switched on the lights and laid out
her tools.

hoechst stood at the back of the auxiliary bridge behind
Jamil and Friedrich, watching as the husks of the two puppetized
bridge officers maneuvered the *Romanov* in toward the darkened,

slowly precessing space station. Similar events would be unfolding in the engine control room above the drive kernel containment, where Mathilde was personally directing the engineering crew who had been selected for the privilege of serving the ReMastered. But the engineering spaces didn't have anything like the view that filled the front wall of the cramped secondary flight deck—the gigantic stacked wagon wheels of Old Newfie spinning in stately splendor before the wounded eye socket of eternity, a red-rimmed hollow gouged from the interstellar void by the explosion of Moscow Prime six years ago.

"Impressive, isn't it?" she asked Franz.

"Yes, boss." He stood beside her, hands clasped behind his back to conceal his nervousness.

"They did it to themselves." She shook her head slowly, almost disbelievingly. "With barely any prompting from U. Scott."

"How hot is it out there?" Franz asked nervously.

"Not too bad." Friedrich leaned past one of the zombies to examine a console display. "Looks to be about ten centiGrays per hour—you'd get sick in an hour or two if you went out there in a suit, but it's well within tolerances for the ship's shielding. And the station is probably all right, too, for short stays."

One of the puppets murmured something to the other, who leaned sideways and began working his way through a stack of thruster-control settings. Jamil had edited their parameters so that they thought they were alone on the bridge. They were completely focused on the docking maneuver.

"It's the most beautiful thing I've ever seen," Portia murmured, staring at the sheets of violet and red smoke that circled the shock ring of the star's death. "And the most ugly." Her hands tightened on the back of the command pilot's seat. With a visible effort she tore her concentration back to the job at hand, and glanced at Franz. "Is the hostage ready? How about you? Are you clear on what you've got to do?"

"Yes, boss." Franz nodded, trying not to show any sign of emotion. She smiled at him, a superficially friendly expression that set his teeth on edge. Part of him wanted to punch her in the face, to kick and bite and rip with his own hands until she stopped moving. Another part of him wanted to cast himself at her feet and plead for forgiveness. "We confine the passengers in the evacuation stations and dump the corridors to vacuum. Then I make the girl present herself and bring her to you and the others on the station. Um, may I ask how we're evacuating?"

"You may." Portia stared at the screen pensively as the puppets muttered to each other, scheduled a course adjustment to nudge the multimegaton mass of the liner closer toward the docking tree at the hub of the enormous station. Methane tanks drifted huge and bulbous at the other end of the spindle, rimed with a carbon monoxide frost deposited by the passing shock wave that had swept over the station years before.

"Boss?" Franz asked nervously.

"The *Heidegger* will be arriving in a day and a half. We simply remove the puppets and disable the liner's flight-control network before we leave. There's enough food aboard—with the resources on the station—to keep them alive for a couple of months, by which time we'll be able to send a cleanup team big enough to process them all. If they don't cooperate, the cleanup team can use the station for target practice: nobody will find out for decades. Once they're processed we can ship them off to one of the core worlds on the *Romanov* for reprocessing. This is as good a place to store them as any, don't you think?"

"But the records! If anyone finds them—"

"Relax, they won't. Nobody's been back here in years. The station's too uneconomical to recommission without a destination in mind, and too far off the track to be worth retrieving for scrap. All we have to do is retrieve the stolen records, send out the signals via the station manager's TALIGENT channel, and configure the *Romanov* as a prison hulk for a couple of months."

"What if they—" Franz stopped.

"You were thinking about the missing bridge officer, weren't you?" Hoechst prodded. "Don't bother. She's a trainee, and she's clearly not up to taking back the ship on her own, wherever she's hiding out. We'll leave you a guard detachment after the *Heidegger* gets here, just to make sure they don't try anything silly." She smiled, broadly. "If you can turn your mind to thinking up creative ways to booby-trap the flight deck after we've docked, that would be a good thing."

Franz glanced at the screen and resisted the urge to rub his palms on his trousers. "You want me to stay behind, with the prisoners?" He asked.

"Not only that: I want you to oversee their processing." She stared at him, inspecting his face with minute interest. "If you do well, I'll take it as a sign that you are worth persisting with. I was impressed by the way you handled the clown, Franz. Keep me satisfied and it will be worth your while. Great rewards come to my willing supporters." Her smile faded, a sign that she was thinking dark thoughts. "Now I think it's time you winkled out the girl."

the evacuation assembly point for B deck was near the rim. A radial corridor ran out from it to an emergency airlock that breached the ship's inner hull. Worried passengers converged on it, some of them carrying bags stuffed with their essentials, others empty-handed. A few scattered stewards, harried and just as worried as the passengers, urged them along. Wednesday trailed after Rachel, holding back just a little. "What do you think they're doing, Mom?" she asked. *Mom? Who do you think you're kidding?* she asked herself ironically. Every time she used the word she felt a tiny stab of betrayal, although it was unfair to Rachel; the woman from Earth had done far more for her than she'd had any reason to expect.

"I'm not sure." Rachel looked worried. "It's possible there's some trouble with the ship's systems, since the incident that injured the bridge crew—" *blink, blink.*

Wednesday nodded and pulled a face, sighed theatrically. *Am I looking bored yet?* She glanced around. There weren't that many passengers: they were mostly first-class travelers, rich business travelers and minor aristocracy from those worlds that had such. *Where's Frank?* she wondered, searching frantically while trying not to be obvious about it. *If I got him into this . . . !*

"Excuse me? Where are we going?" a worried-looking man asked Rachel, plucking at her arm. "You see, nobody's told us any—"

"Don't worry." Rachel managed a forced smile. "We're just going to the evacuation station. It's only a precaution, doesn't mean they're going to evacuate us."

"Oh good." Still looking worried, he scampered ahead, leaving them in an island of quiet.

"Nervous?" Martin asked quietly, making Wednesday jump.

"Nervous?" She glared at him angrily. "If they've hurt—" They rounded the curve of the corridor and passed the red-painted crash doors recessed into the wall and blocking access to the airlock tube. The evacuation station was a circular open space about eight meters across, as crowded and nervous as a diplomatic cocktail party where the Ambassador had just announced his resignation. There was standing room only, and a couple of stressed-looking stewards holding their arms across the entrance to the evacuation airlock just in case some of the more skittish passengers decided to rush it for some reason.

"May I have your attention please?" A tall, blond man with hollows under his eyes called from one side of the room. "Would you mind clearing the inner pressure doors, please? That's right, if you could move into the room, we can get this over with cleanly."

Oh, shit! Wednesday tensed and ran her right thumb up the frogging she'd had her pressure-smart jacket grow. She'd dialed it into a turquoise tailcoat; it felt stiff and heavy, and simultaneously thin and vulnerable—stretched to cover more than its pressure limit, it'd be useless in an emergency depressurization. The whole idea of walking into an airlock when the bad guys had taken the ship struck her as the height of idiocy, even wearing her lacy white shalwar trousers over pressure leggings and boots—

But people behind her were pushing forward, and the doors back onto the corridor were dropping slowly down, sealing off her route back to the cabins. "What's—" she began, but Martin gripped her hand.

"Wait," he said tensely.

"We have an announcement to make," the blond man called. "If I can have *silence,* please—that's better." He smiled thinly. "We're about fifteen minutes from docking with the repair station. When we do so, you may be asked to evacuate onto the port ring in good order. We won't know for sure if that will be necessary, or if you can return to your rooms, until after we dock. If you have to evacuate, try to do so in an orderly way—no pushing, give everybody room to move, keep walking once you hit the dockside until you reach the designated assembly area. Remember, this isn't a critical pressure evacuation. There's no risk that you'll end up breathing vacuum, and you don't need to run."

He looked around the room. There was a brief mutter of comment, but no dissent. "And now for another matter," he announced. "I've got a special message for Victoria Strowger, who I *believe* is in this room somewhere." Wednesday jerked involuntarily, feeling Martin's fingers dig into her wrist. "Your friend Frank is down on F deck. He sends his regards. As a rule we're trying to keep everyone together at their designated evacuation stations, but if you want to see your friend again, you can step forward now, and

I'll take you there." His smile widened. "This is your only chance, I'm afraid. Once we dock it'll be too late."

Wednesday glanced between Rachel and Martin frantically. She wanted to scream: *What do I do* now? Martin looked puzzled, but dawning horror was writ large on Rachel's face. The man at the front was still talking, something about evacuation procedures. It was so slickly done, the message, that she half doubted she'd heard it.

"*Go*," Rachel mouthed at her. A quick scribble on her paper pad: U GOT VALUE — PLAY 4 TIME.

"But—" Wednesday looked back at Martin, who was now clearly worried. *They've got Frank,* she thought frantically. *They've got Frank!* She'd been afraid, walking in there, that it was a trap, but she hadn't realized just what kind it would be.

Rachel was still scribbling. OLD NF == UR HOME GRND. Realization dawned: Wednesday nodded, feeling sick in the pit of her stomach. "Okay," she said, and before she could change her mind she began to shove through the crowd of bodies toward the front of the room, where the blackmailer was waiting for her.

"So who the fuck are you?" Wednesday asked belligerently. "And what do you want?"

The woman in charge of the hijackers smiled indulgently. "You can call me Portia, my dear. And all I want is a little talk."

Wednesday sized her up suspiciously. The blond guy stood behind her blocking the doorway, and there were a couple of guards—one of them manning a comms console, the other watching her from behind the leader—but they'd made no move to search her or apply restraints or anything. This Portia woman wasn't what she'd expected, either. She wasn't angry, or evil-tempered, or anything. Nor was she wearing one-piece overalls with built-in pressure seals like the others. In fact, she seemed friendly and slightly indulgent. *I'd be indulgent, too, if everything was going my way,* Wednesday warned herself. "What do you want?" she demanded. "And where's Frank?"

"Your friend isn't here." Portia sniffed. "He's in a suite on B deck that hasn't, ah, been evacuated." She flashed Wednesday a grin, baring perfect teeth at her. "Would you like to talk to him? Just to prove that he's all right? My offer was genuine, by the way, when I said you could see him again. In fact, I'll go further; if you cooperate fully with me, then once our business is over you can have him back, intact."

"You're a liar. Why should you?" Wednesday regretted the words almost before they were out of her mouth: *Stupid, goading her when she holds all the cards!*

But Portia didn't take it amiss. "Over the years I've found that a reputation for keeping my word is a valuable tool—it makes negotiating much easier if everybody knows you're trustworthy. You, ah, *don't* know that yet—but if you want to talk to your friend...?"

"Ah—" Wednesday felt a sick tension in her gut. "Yeah. I'll talk to him." *Shit! If he's all right*—A second interior voice kicked in, icily cold—*They'll be watching you both for leverage. Make no mistake, she's not doing this just for you.*

"Get the prisoner on the secure terminal," Portia told the guard at the desk.

Wednesday moved to sit down in the offered chair. The camera's-eye view certainly showed her Frank. Her breath caught; they'd put him in a chair and taped his arms down, and he looked ill. His skin was sallow and dry. He looked up at the camera, bleary-eyed, and started. "Wednesday, is that you?" he said, his voice rasping.

"It's me." She clasped her hands behind her back to keep from fidgeting. "Are you all right?"

He rolled his head sideways, as if trying to see something behind the camera. After a moment he replied, "No, I'm a bit tied up." He shook his head. "They got you, too. Was it me?"

"No," she lied, guessing what the truth would do to him. Behind the terminal she saw Portia make a little tight smile. *Bitch.*

Reality check. "What was the last thing I did the night before the, uh, accident?" she asked, hoping desperately that he'd get it wrong, that he was just a machinima avatar, and that she'd been caught but he remained at liberty.

"You made a phone call." He closed his eyes. "They kept my throat under block too long," he added. "Talking hurts."

"That's enough," said Portia. The comms specialist leaned over and killed the connection before Wednesday could protest. "Satisfied?" she asked.

"Huh." Wednesday scowled furiously. "So, you've got us." She shrugged. "What do you fucking *want?*"

The blond guy at the back of the room, the smiling black-mailer from the evacuation bay, cleared his throat. "Boss?"

"Tell her, Franz." Portia nodded agreeably, but Wednesday noticed that when she spoke to her soldiers her smile peeled away, exposing a frigid chill in her eyes.

"You misplaced something belonging to our, uh, predecessors," Franz said. He looked uneasy. "We know you hid it on the station. We want it back. When you return it to us, we have a couple of errands to run, then we'll be leaving." He raised an eyebrow. "Boss?"

"Here's the deal," Portia said easily. "You take us to the items you left behind. We'll bring your friend Frank along so you can see him, and those nosy diplomats you were hiding out with. No, we weren't taken in by that business with the passports. Do you think we're stupid? It was easier to leave you hiding out in their cabin; that way you immobilized yourselves, saving us the trouble. But I digress . . . if you give us what we want, we'll leave you on board the station when we go. Our own ship will be arriving here soon. We'll send a rescue and salvage expedition for the liner and everybody aboard it as soon as we're clear. Despite what you're thinking, we're not interested in killing people, wholesale or retail: there's been a change of management at the top, and our job is to clean up after them."

"Clean up?" Wednesday said skeptically. "Clean up *what*?"

Portia sighed. "My predecessor had some rather silly plans to, um, build himself an empire." She flashed Wednesday that grin again. "I'm not going to make any excuses. You wouldn't believe them anyway. To cut a long story short, he succeeded in taking over some key members of the strategic operations staff in the Moscow government. His ambitions were bigger than his common sense—he wanted to short-circuit a very long-term project of ours, of the whole of the ReMastered actually, by developing a device that's one of a class known collectively as causality-violation weapons. He also wanted to carve out an empire for himself, as maximum leader—an interstellar empire. It was quite the audacious plan, really. It's a very good thing for all of us that he was no good at the little detail work. *Unfortunately*"—she cleared her throat—"the weapons lab on Moscow apparently tried to test the gadget prematurely. Something went wrong, spectacularly wrong."

"You're trying to tell me it was an accident?" Wednesday demanded.

"No." Portia looked uncomfortable for a moment. "But the idiot responsible—the treacherous idiot, I stress—is, ah, dead. As a direct consequence of the event. In fact, it's my job to mop up after him, tidy up the loose ends, and so on. Which includes stopping the R-bombs—I suppose you know about them?—by sending the abort codes. Which were in the bag you took, taken from the station administrator's desk, along with a bunch of other records that are of no use to you but of considerable interest to me, insofar as they'll help me root out the last of his co-conspirators."

"Oh." Wednesday thought for a while. "So you want to clear everything up. Make it all better."

"Yes." Portia smiled brilliantly at her. "Would you like to help us? I stress that to do anything else would amount to complicity in genocide."

Wednesday straightened up. "I suppose so," she muttered with barely concealed ill grace. "If you promise this will put an end to it all, and nobody will get hurt?"

"You have my word." Portia nodded gravely. "Shall we do it?"

Behind her, the one called Franz opened the door.

darkness, stench, and a faint humming. Over the past two days, Steffi's world had closed in with nightmarish speed. Now it was a rectangle two meters long, two meters high, and one meter wide. She shared it with a plastic bucket full of excrement, a bag of dry food, and a large water bottle. Most of the time she kept the torch switched off to conserve power. She'd spent some time trying to read, and she'd done some isometric exercises—careful to ensure there was no risk of kicking the bucket over—and spent some more time sleeping fitfully. But the boredom was setting in, and when she'd heard the announcement through the wall of her cell telling them to prepare for evacuation it had come as a relief. If the hijackers were off-loading the passengers, it meant there wouldn't be anyone to get in her way when she did what had to be done.

A liner the size of the *Romanov* didn't vibrate, didn't hum, and didn't echo when docking on to a station. In fact, any sound or vibration would be a very bad sign indeed, shock waves overloading the antisound suppressors, jolts maxing out the electrogravitics, supports buckling and bulkheads crumpling. But the closet Steffi had helped Martin build her false wall into adjoined the corridor, and after the muffled sound of a slamming door she'd heard faint footsteps, then nothing. The silence went on for an eternity of minutes, like the loudest noise she'd ever heard.

I'm going to get you, she repeated to herself. *You've taken my ship, rounded up my fellow officers, and, and—* An echo of an earlier life intruded: *back-stabbing bastards.* She wondered about Max, in the privacy of her head: he wasn't likely to have avoided the hijackers, and they might think they could use him against her. If they even cared, if they knew who she was and what she could do. *Fat chance.* Steffi was grimly certain that nobody knew the truth about her—nobody but Sven, and if her partner and front man had talked, they'd have torn the ship apart to get their hands on her. Svengali knew things about Steffi—and she knew things about him—that would have gotten either of them a one-way trip into the judicial systems of a dozen planets if the other ever cut a deal. But Steffi trusted Svengali completely. They'd worked together for a decade, culminating in this insanely ambitious tour: wet-working their way across the galaxy, two political pest control operatives against an entire government-in-exile. The promised payoff would have been enough to see both of them into comfortable retirement, *if* the back-stabbing scumbags who were paying for the grand slam hadn't panicked and hijacked the ship instead. And now, with the plans wrecked and Svengali quite possibly out of action, Steffi was seeing red.

After an hour of careful planning, she turned the torch on and put her ear to the closet wall. Nothing. "Here goes," she mumbled to herself, picking up the box cutter Martin had left her. The tiles he'd had the fabricator spam out were rigid and hard to cut at first, stiffened by the fine copper wire mesh of the Faraday cage threading through them. She stabbed at one edge, then worked the blade through and began tugging it down from the top of her hideaway.

Grunting with effort, Steffi sawed a slit all the way down one side of the wall, then continued sideways at the bottom. Finally, she squatted and peeled the corner up toward her. Fumbling in the twilight she found her way out blocked by something solid. It brought it all home to her, and suddenly the stinking darkness seemed to close around her head like a fist. Gasping, she shoved as hard as she could, and the obstruction shifted.

A minute later she found the light switch in the closet. *Well, that's done it,* she told herself, heart pounding and stomach fluttering with nervous anticipation. *If they're out there—*

She opened the door. The suite was empty. "Huh." She took three steps forward, into the dayroom, reveling in her sudden freedom to move, taking in deep breaths of the clean air—suddenly recognizing for what it was the fetor she'd spent more than a day immersed in. Glancing around, she saw the desk. There was some kind of notepad on it, paper covered with writing in dumb pigment. Frowning, she picked it up and began to read by torchlight.

All passengers moving to evac stations. Arriving Old Newfie/station on Moscow system periphery half/hr. Help? May be evac'ing ship.

Not trust Lt. Cdr. Fromm. The ReMastered good at controlling people. Fromm is a puppet. PL is now a ubiq. surveillance net. Query officer bypass working?

Feel free to use the fabricator in the trunk. It makes good toys, and you've got blanket resource access permissions.

Steffi felt her knees go weak. The thing in the closet was a general purpose fabricator, a cornucopia machine? She forced herself to sit down for a moment and close her eyes. "Fuck!" she said softly. The possibilities were endless. Then she took a deep breath. **Query officer bypass working.** If the hijackers were still aboard and had turned the liaison network into a surveillance grid, they would already know about her. But if they *had* evacuated the ship, she might just have a chance, *especially* if they'd left the line crew authorization system in place.

Steffi thrust her left hand into her pocket and pulled out her control rings. Sliding them onto her fingers one by one she mouthed the subvocal commands to start up her interface. *If they're watching, they'll be here any moment,* she told herself. But nothing happened; the timer began to spiral in her visual field, and the twist of a ring told her that she had new mail, but there was no knock on the door.

Slowly, she felt the ghost of a grin rising to her face as she scrolled rapidly through the ship's status reports. In dock, evacuation systems tripped, drive systems tripped, bridge systems shut down, life support on homeostatic standby. "Thought you'd nailed down all the loose ends, did you? We'll see about that!" She turned back to the closet and leaned over the control panel of the fabricator. "Give me an index," she snapped at it. "Show me guns. All the guns you can make . . ."

old newfie's basic systems had continued to run while the radiation shock front swept over it. Humans might be gone, life support might be dead—algal ponds crashed, macroscopic plants killed, even the cockroaches fried by the kiloGray radiation pulse—but the multimegaton wheel continued to spin endlessly in the frigid void, waiting for an uncertain return.

Wednesday's breath steamed in the darkness of the docking hub. One of Portia's minions had rigged up floodlights around the boarding tube from the liner, and stark shadows cut across the gray floor toward the spin coupling zoner. Dim silhouettes drifted slowly round, rotating between the floor and cathedral-high ceiling over a period of minutes.

"Can you hurry it up a bit?" Portia told her phone. "We need to be able to see in here."

"Any moment. We're still looking for the main breaker board." Jamil and one of the other goons had headed off into the station to look for a backup power supply, wearing low-light goggles and rebreather masks in case they hit a gas trap. Getting the main reactors going would be difficult in the extreme—it would take weeks of painstaking work, checking out the reactor windings, then inching through the laborious task of bootstrapping a fusion cycle—but if they could find a backup fuel cell and light up the docking hub, they'd be able to rig a cable from the *Romanov* to the hub's switchboard, and provide power and heat and air circulation to the administrative sectors. Old Newfie had once supported thousands of inhabitants. With a source of power, it could support them again for weeks or months, even without reseeding the life support and air farms.

"So where did you hide the backup cartridge?" Franz asked Wednesday, deceptively casual.

Wednesday frowned. "Somewhere in the police station—it was years ago, you know?" She stared at him. Something about the blond guy didn't ring true. He looked excessively tense. "You'll need power for the lifts in order to reach it."

"This is no time for games," he said, glancing at Hoechst, who was listening to her comm. "You don't want to cross her."

"Don't I?" Wednesday glanced up at the axial cranes, skeletal gantries looming like lightning-struck trees out of the darkness high above. "I'd never have guessed."

Portia nodded and lowered her comm. "We have lights," she said, a note of satisfaction in her voice. Moments later, a loud *clack* echoed through the docking hub. The emergency floods came on overhead, casting a faint greenish glow across the floorscape. "We should have heat and fans in a few minutes," she added, sounding satisfied. A nod at one of her other minions, a woman with straight hair the color of straw. "Start moving the passengers aboard, Mathilde, I want the passengers off that ship in ten minutes."

"You're evacuating it?" Wednesday stared.

"Yes. We seem to be missing a Junior Flight Lieutenant. I don't want her getting any silly ideas about flying off while we're all aboard the station." Portia smiled thinly. "I'll admit that if she can hide from a ubiquitous celldar net and shoot her way past the guards who are waiting she might have a chance, but somehow I doubt it."

"Oh." Wednesday deflated. She felt her rings vibrate, saw a pop-up notice in her left eye: *new mail.* She tried to conceal her surprise. (*Mail? Here?*) "Why were you killing our ambassadors?" she asked impulsively.

"Was I?" Hoechst raised an eyebrow. "Why were you hiding out with a pair of spooks from Earth?"

"Spooks?" Wednesday shook her head in puzzlement. "They wanted to help, once you *hijacked* the *ship*—"

Portia looked amused. "*Everybody* wants to help," she said, raising her comm to her mouth. "You. Whoever I'm speaking to—Jordaan? Yes, it's me. The two diplomats from Earth. And that fucking busybody journalist. We're going to the station administrator's office by way of a little detour along the way. Round up the diplomats and the scribbler. Take a backup and meet us at the station admin office in half an hour. Send Zursch and Anders to the communications room with the key, and have them wait for me there. I'll be along after I've finished with the other errands. Understood? Right. See you there." She focused on Wednesday. "It's quite simple." She took a deep breath. "I'm here to tidy up a huge mess that was left by my predecessor. If I don't tidy it up, a lot of people are going to die, starting with your friends who I just mentioned, because if I fail to tidy up the mess successfully, *I* will die, and a lot of my *people* will die, and killing your friends will be the easiest way of conveying to you—and them—just how angry that makes me. I don't really want to die, and I'd much rather not have to kill anybody—which is why I'm telling you this, to make sure you know it isn't a fucking game." She leaned toward Wednesday, her face drawn: "Have you got the picture yet?"

Wednesday recoiled. "I, uh . . ." She swallowed. "Yes."

"Good." Something seemed to go out of Hoechst, leaving her empty and tired. "Everybody thinks they're doing the right thing, kid. All the time. It's about the only rule that explains how fucked-up this universe is." A wan smile crept across her face. "*Nobody* is a villain in their own head, are they? We all *know* we're doing the right thing, which is why we're in this mess. So why don't you show me where this police post is, and we'll dig our way out of it together?"

"Uh, I, uh . . ." She was shaking, Wednesday realized distantly. Shaking with rage. *You fuckmonster, you killed my parents! And you want me to cooperate?* But it was an impotent fury: confronted with someone like Portia, there wasn't anything she could see that would make things better, no sign of any way out that didn't involve doing what the ReMastered wanted. Which was why they were the ReMastered, of course. *Not villains in their own heads.* "This way." *You have mail* blinked in her visual field as she walked across the frost-sparkling metal of the dock toward the empty shadows of the lift shafts. Almost instinctively, she twitched her fingers to accept.

> Hello, Wednesday. This is Herman. If you are reading this message, you are back on the Old Newfie communications net—which was not shut down when the station was evacuated. Please reply.

"Are you all right?" asked the one called Franz, reaching for her elbow as she stumbled.

"Just a slip. Icy," she muttered. She thrust her hands into her pocket to conceal her finger-twitched response.

I'm here. Where are you? *Send.*

The reply arrived as they waited while Jamil went over one of the lift motors with a circuit tester. It was icy cold in the station: breath clouded the air, sparkling in the twilight overspill from the lights.

'I' am where I always was. My causal channel is still linked into the station network. The station's other comms channels are still operational, including the diplomatic channel U. Hoechst intends to use to send the "stop" code to the Muscovite R-bombs. Hoechst acquired one of the "stop" codes from her predecessor, U. Scott. There is another code key in the station administrator's safe in the central control office. Svengali and his partner successfully panicked the surviving Muscovite diplomatic corps. My highest-probability scenario is that Hoechst's objective is to take control of the Muscovite R-bombs under cover of decommissioning them, then to use her own-ership of the R-bombs to convince both the Muscovite ambassadors and the Dresdener authorities that the R-bombs are committed to an irrevocable attack. This will lay the foundations for a ReMastered takeover of Dresden. The current junta members will flee, providing promotion avenues for ReMastered proxies and generating public disorder in anticipation of an attack that will never arrive.

The lift motors creaked and hummed, and lights flickered on inside the car. "Seems to be working," said Jamil, poking at the exposed control panel. "It's got a separate flywheel power supply that I'm spinning up right now. Everybody in. What floor are we looking for?" he asked Wednesday.

"Fourth," she mumbled.

Expect no mercy from the ReMastered. They will honor any promises they make to the letter, but semantic ambiguities will render them worthless.

Important note: U. Franz Bergman is a malcontent. Prior to Hoechst's arrival in Septagon he and his partner were preparing to defect. Hoechst's hold on him is his partner's upload data. An offer of medical reincarnation coupled with the upload record may constitute leverage in his case.

Your old implant conforms to Moscow open systems specifications and is therefore able to receive this message. Unfortunately, owing to a protocol mismatch, I cannot contact other people directly. Please copy and forward this message to: Martin Springfield, Rachel Mansour, Frank Johnson, by way of your Septagon-compliant interface.

The lift squealed to a halt. Wednesday shook herself. "Where now?" Portia demanded.

"Where?" The doors opened onto darkness. The air was freezing cold, musty, and held a residual fetor, the stench of long-dead things that had mummified in place.

"Can I have some light?"

Behind her, a torch flared into brightness, sweeping long shadows into the corners of the curving passage. Wednesday stepped out of the lift car cautiously, her breath steaming in the freezing air. "This way."

Trying to re-create the path she'd taken all those years ago came hard. She walked slowly, fingers twitching furiously as she copied and forwarded the message from Herman. No telling when it would arrive, but the mesh networks and routing algorithms used by implants in the developed worlds would spool the mail until she got within personal network range of someone who could handshake with them—maybe even one of the ReMastered, if they'd had their systems upgraded for work out in the feral worlds.

Frozen carpet creaked beneath her feet. Her pulse sped, and she glanced behind her, half-expecting to hear the clicking clatter of claws. Portia, Jamil, and Franz—an unlikely triptych of scheming evil—kept her moving on. They were near the toilet. "Here," she said, her voice small.

"You're not going to—" Franz stopped.

"What is it?" Portia demanded.

"There's a body in there. I think." Wednesday swallowed.

"Jamil. Check it out." Jamil pushed past, taking his torch. Portia produced a smaller one, not much more than a glow stick really. A minute of banging about, then he called, "She's right. I see a—hmm. Freeze-dried, I guess."

"Explain." Portia thrust her face at Wednesday.

"He, I, I—" Wednesday shuddered convulsively. "Like the paper said. I left it two decks down, three segments over," she added.

"Jamil, we're going," Portia called. "You'd better not be wasting our time," she told Wednesday grimly.

Wednesday led them back to the lift, which groaned and whined as it lowered them two more floors into the guts of the station. The gravity was higher there, but still not as harsh as she recalled; probably there'd been some momentum transfer between the different counterrotating sections, even superconducting magnetic bearings are unable to prevent atmospheric turbulence from bleeding off energy over time. *You have new mail,* Wednesday read, as the lift slowed. "Come on," Jamil said, pushing her forward. "Let's get this over with."

Message received. We understand. Get word out via hub comms? Any means necessary.—Martin

The gaping door and the darkness within loomed out of the darkness. The seed of a plan popped into Wednesday's head, unbidden. "I think I hid it in one of the cupboards. Can you give me a torch?" she asked.

"Here." Portia passed her the light wand.

"Let's see if I remember where..." Wednesday ducked into the room, her heart hammering and her hands damp. She'd only get one chance to do this.

Turning, she flashed the torch around overturned desks, open cupboards. *There.* She bent down and picked up a cartridge, crammed it into one pocket—scooped up a second and a third, then straightened up. "Wrong cupboard," she called. Where *had* she left it? She looked around, saw a flash of something the color of dried blood—leather. *Ah!* She pulled on it, and the bag slid into view. "Got it," she said, stepping back out into the corridor.

"Give it here." Portia held out her hand.

"Can't you wait until we get back to the hub?" Wednesday stared at her, bravado rising. The leather wallet with the diplomatic seal of the Moscow government on it and the bulge where she'd stashed the data cartridge hung from one hand.

"*Now!*" Portia insisted.

"You promised." Wednesday tightened her grip on the wallet and stared Portia in the eyes. "Going to break your word?"

"No." Hoechst blinked, then relaxed. "No, I'm not." She

looked like a woman awakening from a turbulent dream. "You want to hold it until you see your friends, you go right ahead. I assume it *is* the right wallet? And the data cartridge you took?"

"Yes," Wednesday said defensively, tightening her grip on it. The three riot cartridges she'd stolen felt huge in her hip pocket, certain to be visible. And while only Jamil had a gun slung in full sight, she had an edgy feeling that all the others were armed. They'd be carrying pistols, if nothing else. What was the old joke? *Never bring a taser to an artillery duel.*

"Then let's go visit the control center." Portia smiled. "Of course, if you're wasting my time, you'll have made me kill one of your friends, but you wouldn't do that, would you?"

"never bring a taser to an artillery duel," muttered Steffi, glancing between the compact machine pistol (with full terminal guidance for its fin-stabilized bullets, not to mention a teraherz radar sight to allow the user to make aimed shots through thin walls) and the solid-state multispectral laser cannon (with self-stabilizing turret platform and a quantum-nucleonic generator backpack that could boil a liter of water in under ten seconds). Regretfully, she picked the machine pistol, the laser's backpack being too unwieldy for the tight confines of a starship. But there was nothing stopping her from adding some other, less cumbersome toys, was there? After all, none of the spectators at her special one-woman military fashion show would be writing reviews afterward.

After half an hour, Steffi decided she was as ready as she'd ever be. The console by the door said that there was full pressure outside. *Negligent of them,* she thought as she pointed her gun through the door and scanned the corridor. It looked clear, ghostly gray in the synthetic colors displayed by her eye-patch gunsight. *Right, here goes.*

She moved toward the nearest intersection corridor with crew country, darting forward, then pausing to scan rooms to either side. *Need a DC center console,* she decided. The oppressive silence was a reminder of the constant menace around her. If the hijackers wanted to lock down a ship, they could have depressurized it: that they hadn't meant that they'd be back. Before then, she had to eliminate any guards they'd left behind, erase her presence from their surveillance system, and regain control.

Where are *they?* she asked herself, nerves on edge as she came close to the core staircase and lift utility ducts on this deck. *They're not stupid; they'll have left a guard. They've got the surveillance net, so they must know I'm moving around up here. So where's the ambush going to be?* Smart guards wouldn't risk losing her in a maze of passages and staterooms she knew better than they did. They'd simply lock the staircase doors between pressure zones, and nail her as soon as she conveniently locked herself in a narrow moving box.

Got it. Steffi ducked sideways into a narrow crew corridor and found herself facing the blank doors of a lift shaft. Readying herself, she hit the call button and crouched beside the doors, gun raised to scan. There were two possibilities. Either the lift car would contain an unpleasant surprise, or it would be empty—in which case, they'd be waiting for her wherever she arrived.

The gun showed her an empty cube before the doors opened. She moved instantly, jamming her key ring onto the emergency override pad on the control panel. Steffi clicked her tongue in concentration as she commanded the lift car to lower to motor maintenance position and open the doors. There was space on top of the pressurized car, a platform a meter and a half wide and a meter high, ridged with cables and motor controllers leading to the prime movers at each corner of the box. She scrambled aboard, then hit the button for the training bridge deck. What happened next would depend on how many guards they'd left behind for her. If there were enough to monitor the ship surveillance network as well as lay an ambush for her, she'd already lost, but she was gambling that her cover was still intact. As long as Svengali hadn't talked, she stood a chance, because only a paranoid would take the same precautions over a Junior Flight Lieutenant that they'd need to neutralize a professional assassin . . .

The lift seemed to take forever to climb down the shaft. Steffi crouched in the middle of the roof, curling herself around her gun. Her eye patch showed her a gray rectangle, ghost shadows unfolding below it—the empty body of the lift, descending into a tube of darkness too far away for the surface-piercing gunsights to see. Four decks, three, two—the lift slowed. Steffi changed her angle, aiming past the side of the lift where the doors opened, out into the corridor.

Three targets, range five meters, group shots, gun to automatic. The machine pistol stuttered unevenly and the recoil pushed at her wrists, jets of hot gas belching from the reaction-control ducts around the barrel to center it on each target for precisely four shots. It was all over in a second. Steffi twitched around, hunting movement. Nothing: just three indistinct lumps of gray against a background of rectangles.

She hit the DOWN button again, then opened the doors and glanced incuriously at the bodies. Her forehead wrinkled. There was blood everywhere, leaking from two strength-through-joy types she recognized from the dinner table, and from—"Max?" she said aloud, then she caught herself with a quiet snarl of fury. *The motherfucking clown who planned* this *is going to pay, with interest.* She checked her gun readouts: nothing was moving, up and down the corridor.

She pushed through a crew-side doorway, oriented herself on a narrow corridor, and headed for the emergency room. Instinct stopped her just short of the corner, dropping to one knee with gun raised. *Company?* she wondered, motionless, trying to scan a comprehensible picture through the corner wall with tiny flicks of her fingertips. *Yes? No?* There was something there, and it moved—

They fired simultaneously. Steffi sensed, and heard, the bullet zip past her head as her own gun went into spasm, squirting the remaining contents of its magazine through the wall in a surge of penetrator rounds. There was a damp sound from just around the corner, then a loud thud. Steffi reloaded mechanically, then made a final check and stepped out into the corridor in front of the emergency bridge, stepping over the body of the guard.

"Bridge systems. Speak to me," she commanded. "Are you listening?"

"Authenticating—welcome, Lieutenant Grace." The bridge door slid open to reveal empty chairs, an air of deceptive normality.

"Conversational interface, please." Steffi slid the door shut, then dropped into the pilot's chair and turned it to face the door, her gun at the ready. "Identify all other personnel aboard ship, their locations and identities. If anyone moves toward this deck, let me know. Next, display on screen two all-system upgrades to passenger liaison network since previous departure. List whereabouts of all passengers traveling from and native to Tonto and Newpeace." The walls began to fill up with information. "Dump specifics to my stash." Steffi smiled happily. "Are all officers authenticated by retinal scan? Good. Who authorized the last PLN reload? Good. Now stand by to record a new job sequence."

Wednesday had walked over to the desk at the front of the evacuation assembly point as if she didn't have a care in the world. Rachel watched with growing misgivings as she spoke quietly to the fair-haired guy and they left together through the side exit into crew country. Martin leaned close. "I hope she'll be all right."

Half an hour later it was their turn. The passengers were growing more restive, talking among themselves in a quiet buzz of nervous anticipation, when a woman ducked through the door. "Rachel Mansour? Martin Springfield? Please come forward!"

She gripped Martin's hand, squeezing out a message in a private code rusty from disuse: *"Rumbled."*

"Ack. Go?"

"Yes." She pulled him forward, pushing between a yakking family group and a self-important fellow in the robe of an Umbrian merchant banker. "You want to talk?"she asked, staring at the woman.

"No, I want you both to come with me," she said casually. "Someone else wants to talk to you."

"Then we'll be happy to comply," Rachel said, forcing a smile. *All this, and not even a briefing beforehand?* For a moment she wished she was back in the claustrophobic tenement off the Place du Molard, waiting for the bomb squad. She tried not to notice Martin, whose nervousness was transparently obvious. "Where do you want us to go?"

"Follow me." The woman opened the side door and motioned them through. She had a friend waiting on the other side, a big guy who held his gun openly and watched them with incurious eyes. "This way."

She led them up a short staircase and out into a wide cargo tunnel. The air became increasingly chilly as they walked along it. Rachel shivered. She wasn't dressed for an excursion into a freezer hold. "Where are we?"

"Keep it for the boss."

"If you say so." Rachel tried to keep her voice light, as if this was a mystery excursion managed by the crew to keep bored passengers amused. They turned a corner onto a wider docking tunnel, then up a ramp that led into a vast twilight space. Floods glittered high above as the gravity did an alarmingly abrupt fade, dropping to less than a tenth of normal in the space of a few meters. *We're outside the ship,* she squeezed. Martin nodded. Not for the first time she wished she dared use her implants to text him, but the risk of interception in the absence of a secured quantum channel was too great. *If only I knew how complete their surveillance capability was,* she told herself. *If.* She shivered violently and watched her breath steam before her face. "Far to go?"

The blond woman motioned her toward a doorway at the far side of the docking hub. Warm light shone from it. "Shit, it's cold out here," Martin muttered. They hurried forward without any urging on the part of their guards.

"Stop." The one with the gun held up a hand as they neared the door. "Mathilde?"

"Yah." The blond woman produced a bulky comm and spoke into it. "Mathilde here. The two—diplomats. Outside control. I'm sending them in." She turned and glared at Rachel and Martin, waving at the door. "That way."

"Where else?" Rachel looked around as she entered the room. It was brightly lit, and a whine from overhead suggested that a local aircon unit was fighting a losing battle against the chill. The man with the gun was behind them, and for a sickening moment as she saw the largely empty room, she wondered if he was meant to kill them and leave their bodies there. Then a door slid open in the wall opposite.

"Go in." Gun-boy waved them forward. "It's a lift."

"Okay, I'm going, I'm going." Rachel stepped forward. Martin followed her, with Gun-boy trailing to the rear. The doors closed and the lift began to move, sinking toward the high-gee levels of the station. It squealed as it went, long-idle wheels protesting as they clawed along toothed rails that had chilled below normal operating temperatures. They descended in silence, Rachel leaning against Martin in the far corner of the cargo lift from the guard. The guard kept his weapon on them the whole time, seemingly immune to distraction.

The lift juddered to a halt, and its door slid open on a well-lit corridor. There were more fans, humming and grating at overload. The chill was less extreme, and when the guard waved them toward an open door at the other end of the passage, Rachel couldn't see her breath. "Where are we?" she asked.

"Waiting for the boss. Go right in." Gun-boy looked bored and annoyed, but not inclined toward immediate violence. Rachel tensed, then nodded and went right in. There was a sign on the open door she read as she passed it: director's suite. *Well, what a surprise,* she thought tiredly, mentally kicking herself for not having seen this coming. Then her implant twitched. She had to suppress a start as she blinked, rapidly: *new mail* here, *of all places? How...*

She read it quickly, almost trancing out—almost missing the deep pile carpet, the withered brown trees in their pots to either side of the big wood-topped desk, and the door leading into the inner office. Then *more* mail came in—this time, a reply from Martin. She glanced at him sharply, then turned round to stare at Gun-boy. The goon leaned against the wall just inside the doorway. "Who is this boss of yours?" she asked. "Do we have to wait long?"

"You wait until she gets here." The fan in the office rattled slightly, pumping tepid air in to dilute the chill. A thin layer of dust covered the desk, the visitor's chairs, an empty watercooler.

"Mind if I sit down?" asked Martin.

"Be my guest." Gun-boy raised an ironic eyebrow, and Martin sat down hastily before he changed his mind. Rachel stepped sideways in front of him, and he slipped an arm protectively around her waist, under the hem of her jacket.

"Can you tell us anything?" Rachel asked quietly as Martin slipped something into her waistband. "Like what this is all about?"

"No."

"Okay." Rachel sighed. "If that's how you want it." She sat down on the chair to Martin's right and leaned against him, putting her left arm behind his shoulder. *So they're not monitoring the station protocols for traffic yet,* she thought, hungry for hope. *If they were, that mail from Wednesday would have set them off.* She let her arm drop behind Martin's back, then twisted her wrist round and fumbled with the object in her waistband until it went up her sleeve to mate with its companion.

Click. She felt, rather than heard, the noise. The gadget made handshake with her implants, and a countdown timer appeared in her vision: the number of seconds it would take for the gel-phase fuel cell to power up and the gadget to begin assembling itself. She'd seldom felt so naked in her life. If they'd extended the surface-piercing radar surveillance network from the ship into this room seven shades of alarm would be going off right now, and Gun-boy would put a bullet through her face long before the gadget was ready. Otherwise—

A creaking whine from the corridor announced the arrival of

another lift car. A few seconds later Mathilde appeared, this time leading Frank. Frank was in a bad way, his skin ashen and his hands taped together in front of him. He looked around, eyes unreadable, wearing the same clothes he'd been in when Martin had interviewed him. They were the worse for wear. "Sit," Mathilde told him, pointing to the chair next to Rachel. She produced a box cutter: "Hold out your hands. We've got the girl. Piss us off, and you'll never see her again."

Frank cleared his throat. "I understand," he grunted, rubbing his wrists. He glared at her resentfully. "What now?"

"You wait." Mathilde took a step back to stand beside Gun-boy.

"Lining up all your targets, huh?"

She cast Martin a very ugly look. "Wait for the boss. She won't be long now."

"You're Frank, aren't you? What happened?" Rachel whispered to him.

Frank grunted, and rubbed at his wrists again. "Got me early. In my room. You're his partner?" He jerked his chin at Martin. "Thought I was the only one at first. Where are we?"

"Old Newfie. Wednesday's station. Listen, we hid her but they—had you. She went with them."

"Shit!" He met her eyes with an expression of terrible resignation. "You know what this means."

Rachel gave a slight nod in the direction of the guards. "Don't say it."

"You can say anything you like," Mathilde called, grinning maliciously at him. "We have complete freedom of speech—anything you want to say we will listen to."

"Fuck you!" Frank glared at her.

"Shut up." Gun-boy pointed his machine pistol at Frank. For a tense moment Rachel was sure he would say something. The seconds stretched out into an infinitely long moment as Frank and the guard stared—then Frank slumped back in his chair.

"'Sokay. I can let go." Frank glanced at her and yawned, his jaw muscles crackling. "I'm used to it—was used to it." He rubbed his hands together, making small circling movements. Rachel tried not to show any sign of having noticed his frantic control gestures. *Someone's got a backlog of e-mail,* she guessed, *or itchy fingers.*

They sat in silence for a couple of minutes, then a buzzing noise from along the corridor announced the imminent arrival of yet another self-propelled lift car. Rachel looked round automatically.

The doors opened. Many footsteps, moving toward the office in the curious broken rhythm of fractional gee. First in was a skinny, edgy-looking man; then a woman of a certain age, her eyes cold and her expression satisfied. Then Wednesday, walking in front of a guy with long hair in a ponytail, holding a boxy urban combat weapon. Her expression was ugly when she saw Frank looking like a morning-after wreck.

"Rachel Mansour, from the UN, I presume?" The woman walked behind the station manager's desk, turned the chair round, and sat down in it. "I'm very pleased to meet you." She smiled as she reached into an outer pocket and placed a compact pistol on the desk in front of her, its barrel pointed at Rachel. "I see you've already met our young runaway. That will make things much simpler. Just one more person to come, then I think we'll begin."

they'd untaped his hands; leaning back, ignoring the guard, Frank had twitched his rings, switching his optic implants and ear pickups to record promiscuously. There was no point missing anything, even his own execution.

BING. He'd jumped a little when the mail flag came up; something from Wednesday. But the guard hadn't noticed. None of them noticed. Just typical ReMastered foot soldiers, obedient and lethal. He read the message and felt his palms go damp. He was glad he was sitting down. *So now Wednesday's invisible friend is sending me e-mail? But he's got to use her as a relay because she's the only one of us with a setup compatible with this station? Shit.*

Frank reflected bleakly on the need for bandwidth. *If there's some way to get that report out, wherever we are... we can't all just vanish, can we?* But the truth was anything but reassuring. Liners *did* vanish from time to time, and if this was the hijacking it appeared to be—bearing all the slick signs of ReMastered covert ops, the sly subversion of emergency reflexes—then there was no way word would ever get out.

BING. More mail from Wednesday had arrived, broadcast to him and Rachel and Martin—what? Some sort of code attachment, a new interface protocol for his implant to talk to the station's ether. He tried to keep his face impassive as he mentally crossed his fingers and loaded the untrusted executable.

Then the newcomers arrived. Frank stared at them, his world narrowed suddenly to a single panicky choice, a flashback going back decades. He took it all in, Wednesday sullen between two guards, the woman in front holding the leather satchel, smiling at him. He remembered the bright sunlight on the rooftop of the Demosthenes Hotel, the acrid smell of propane stoves and dog shit wafting on the breeze across downtown Samara. Alice turning toward the parapet with a camera drone in her hands. The woman, again. Blond destruction on the day it rained bullets, the day when everything changed.

Frank blinked up at her. "Oh holy shitting fucking Christ, it's *you*—"

"Increasing my little piggie count, this time." Her smile broadened, turning ugly at the edges. "We really must stop bumping into each other like this, mustn't we?"

"Shit, shit, shit—" Frank felt nauseous. The hot smell of Alice's blood was in his nose; the roar and screams of the crowd as the bullets began spattering into them. "You were in Samara. On Newpeace. Who *are* you?" He barely noticed Wednesday's jolt of surprise from the other side of the room as he focused in on the woman's face.

"I'm U. Portia Hoechst, DepartmentSecretariat of Division Four of the Department of External Environmental Control, planetary dominion of Newpeace. The 'U' is short for ubermensch, or ubermadchen, take your pick." Her smile was as wide as a shark's gape. "At this point in the proceedings I'm supposed to gloatingly tell you my evil plans before I kill you. Then, if you believe the movies, a steel-jawed hero is supposed to erupt through the walls and teach me the error of my ways with extreme prejudice."

She snorted. "Except there aren't any steel-jawed heroes within sixteen light years of this station." A hint of mirth in her eyes. "Not even that Third Lieutenant you've got squirreled away, at least not once the guards are through with her." Frank felt his nails digging into the palms of his hands; his vision went gray and pixelated for a few seconds, and his heart pounded before he realized that it was the firmware patch from Wednesday loading on his implant's virtual machine, combined with a raw, primal rage.

"Why are you telling us this?" Rachel asked quietly.

"Because I like a fucking audience!" Hoechst sat up. "And it's going to be over soon, anyway." She stopped smiling. "Oh, about the 'let me tell you everything before I kill you' bit: I'm not going to kill you. You might wish I *had*, but I'm not. As soon as I've got this station on auxiliary internal power and disabled external communications, all the passengers and crew are coming aboard. It won't be much fun, but you'll be able to last for the couple of months it takes for a rescue ship to reach you. Even you, Frank." A flicker of a smile. "No reeducation camps here. You're getting the VIP treatment."

Frank stayed quiet, his guts tense. *Fuck, we're still on the net!* he realized. The station's causal channels were still working. This packet from Herman, whoever he was, was a protocol converter— with gathering disbelief Frank realized that he wasn't cut off anymore. He could send mail. Or even pipe his raw recording feed straight to Eric, back home, there to do whatever he could with the posthumous spool. *Take it like you give it, you fuckers!* he thought triumphantly. His hands folded together against the cold, nobody saw him twisting his rings, setting up the narrowcast stream to his inbox on Earth. *I am a camera!*

sᴛeffi ᴡaᴛched ᴛhe rerun of Svengali's execution in grainy monochrome, tracking it through the labyrinthine maze of the surveillance system take spooled by the ship's memory as the bridge systems hummed around her, rewinding the vessel's software model of itself back to the state it had been in before the ReMastered lobotomized it.

She'd thought she was angry when the double-crossing clients ran amok, angry when she'd spent long hours crouched in a dark closet space with the soft-shoe shuffle of guards outside the door. But she hadn't been angry at all. Not in comparison to her current state of mind. Livid with rage just barely began to describe it.

She'd worked with Sven for just short of a decade. In many ways they'd been closer than a married couple—herself the pretty face up front and visible, and he the fixer in the background, oiling the gears and reeling in the contracts. He'd found her when she was a teen punk, heading for rehab or a one-way trip to the exile colonies, seen through the rust and grime to the hard metal beneath, and polished it to a brilliant shine. In the early years she'd adored him, back before she matured enough to see him as he really was—theirs hadn't been a sexual relationship (beyond an early exploratory fumbling), but it was a partnership based on need, and mutual respect, and blood. And now, just as they'd been on the edge of their greatest coup—

"I'm going to find you, and you're going to wish you'd committed suicide first," she told the face frozen to the screen. "And then—" her eyebrows furrowed—"I'm going to..." *Going to do what?*

Steffi leaned back her chair and closed her eyes, forcing the tight ball of rage back into the recesses of her skull, out of the way until it was needed. *Where do I stand?* She had the key to their bank accounts, if she needed it. And she had a couple of other keys, picked up here or there. She'd been in an office in Turku and a roadside rest stop on Eiger's World, and a house on Earth, too, all in the past six months. Sven had done his homework before taking on the job, explained the alarming consequences of success to her and the importance of finding the keys. There'd been no point rummaging by the roadside, but she had *two* of them in her pocket, now, keys to the gates of hell itself. That had to count for something, didn't it? And if the dim-witted UN diplomats didn't know who she was, then all that left was the ReMastered.

If I can take them out of the picture, I can become *Lieutenant Steffi Grace, and nobody will know any different,* she realized. *Or I can try for the third key, and access to a Muscovite diplomatic channel.* She began to smile, her lips pulling back from her teeth in an expression very close to a feral snarl. *See how they like it when I derail their plans.* She sat up and leaned toward the pilot console. "Bridge systems, get me the full station package on our current port. Display dockside schematics on window four. Do you have access to the loading bay external cameras? Do you have access to the station communications network? Good. Record new job sequence, activation key *rosebud.*"

"ˈɥoʊˈrɛ ɡoʊɪŋ ˈto maroon us," Wednesday said flatly. She took a stride toward the desk, but a tense motion with a gun barrel stopped her sharply. She turned to stare at Frank, wringing her hands together. Frank raised an eyebrow at her. *What can I do about it?* he thought, his stomach turning over. *Why couldn't you have stayed hidden?*

"I'm not going to leave you alone for long." Hoechst shrugged. "My own ship's heading for home with a message too secret to trust to certain, shall we say, monitored channels. While it's gone I need to take the *Romanov* on a little errand. I'm mopping up after my predecessor—one U. Vannevar Scott—who got a little bit too big for his boots." That flickering smile. Almost without willing it Frank found himself staring at Wednesday. She looked as scared as he felt, her face drained and pale, but resolute, the condemned facing the scaffold. He forced himself to look back at Hoechst. The blinking status display in his left eye told its own story: every word that hit his ears was stripped down to its constituent bits, entangled with a qubit interface somewhere in the magical weirdness of a causal channel, the other end of which would pipe the data into Eric's inbox. *Let's see how topical we can make this news, shall we,* he thought at Hoechst, feeling the fear slowly turn to a warm glow of triumphant accomplishment. *J'accuse!*

"Scott decided to carve out his own little Directorate," Hoechst continued, oblivious to the true size of her potential audience. "First, he needed a lever. That lever was going to be a bucolic backwater called Moscow. He got funding and clearance to operate on Moscow by offering the Directorate a new way of developing weapons forbidden by the Enemy—you call it the Eschaton—like temporal ablators. Moscow was going to be his weapons proving ground, a backwater nobody would expect to be going after causality-violation devices. *Actually* he wanted to be dictator of a whole bunch of planets, and Moscow was going to be his tool of conquest—also his insurance against the wrath of the High Directorate. But he got sloppy. He puppetized half the Muscovite military high command—an administrative backwater on that planet, nobody paid much attention to them—and thoroughly subverted the interstellar deterrent group. But then he decided to accelerate the weapons test program he'd promised the Directorate and use them himself instead of the original clumsy R-bomb plan."

Wednesday stared at her. "You're telling me the nova was a fucked-up weapons test?"

"Well, sure. In fact, it was an *unauthorized* fuck up." Hoechst looked pensive. She reached into her jacket pocket and pulled out a small key, placing it very carefully in the middle of the desk in front of her. "We all make mistakes. In Scott's case, it was his last; he'd gotten sloppy, and the—my boss—cleared me to take him down and rectify the situation. That was before we drained him and discovered certain unpleasant facts about his treason. *That cartridge*"—she held out a hand toward Wednesday—"is one of the loose ends. Immigration records of Scott's agents moving in and out of Moscow. And details of the weapons project and the test schedule. Nothing we want to leave lying around. It's a *severe* political embarrassment."

"There's more, isn't there?" Frank asked, fascinated.

"Well, no shit!" Hoechst looked at him curiously, as if wondering why he was so interested in the abstract issues, rather than the proximate fate of his own skin. "There's a flight of four R-bombs coming." She frowned. "The cover story is that they're aimed at New Dresden. And that's what the Muscovite diplomats think."

"What did he—"

"Shut the fuck up!" Hoechst frowned. She tapped one finger on the key. "They're supposed to be running on New Dresden. That's the official target ops plan that was on file, isn't it? That's what the Muscovite diplomats think. And they're next to invisible when they're under way. Except our fucking asshole Ubermensch Vannevar Scott was too cute by half. While he was puppetizing the Muscovite Defense Ministry, the *first* group he hit was the deterrence operations staff, including the flight crew of one of the bombers—the one that isn't responding to messages. He was planning his defection at least ten years before Moscow went bang: one of those fucking bombers is running on *Newpeace,* our new regional capital, which is about as distant from Moscow as New Dresden.

"Not many ReMastered know this," she added drily, "and my boss wants to keep it that way."

Frank sat up straight. "Are you telling us the business with New Dresden, the ambassadors—"

"*I* haven't been bumping off foreign diplomats." She shook her head vehemently. "That was Scott's plan. I told you he was sloppy, didn't I? When things went wrong, when Moscow Prime exploded, he took steps to sweep the dirt under the rug. He paid an extremely accomplished assassin, the one you called Svengali." For a moment she looked extremely tired. "Which is presumably what brought you aboard the *Romanov,*" she murmured in Rachel's direction. Rachel stared at her, face impassive. "Svengali won't be bothering us anymore, needless to say."

"You want me to believe that this was all *one man's* rogue operation?" Rachel asked, her voice low and controlled.

"Pretty much." For a moment Hoechst looked terribly old. "Don't underestimate him: U. Scott was one of the highest-ranking officials in, ah, External State Security. The foreign espionage service, in other words. And he was planning a coup. He was going to take Moscow and use the R-bombs to hold the entire Directorate at bay, and he was going to leverage his takeover of Moscow to destabilize New Dresden, via the trade war. He was already infiltrating the Dresden Foreign Ministry—without authorization. If he succeeded, he'd have had two planets, the beginnings of his own pocket interstellar empire." She looked at Frank, meeting his eyes. "I know what you think of us. Regardless of that, whatever you think of our ideology, we are not insane, and we are not suicidal. One of the goals of the ReMastered Directorate is to render interstellar warfare not merely unthinkable, but impossible. Scott had to go."

She sounds as if she's trying to convince herself, Frank realized with a sinking feeling. This was *not* what he'd wanted to hear from her. He'd expected venomously triumphant self-justification, perhaps, or a gloating confession. *Not this!* he thought despairingly. *If Eric decides to run this, it'll be about the best piece of pro-ReMastered press they could ask for!* The pot of gold at the end of Frank's starbow had just turned out to be a chamber pot full of shit—and despite what he'd said earlier about journalistic ethics being a crock, he couldn't see any obvious holes in her argument. Even releasing the prisoners in Hoechst's stolen memory diamond—expensive as such a process would be—would probably not reverse its effect by much.

She took a deep breath and continued her confession: "Luckily, Scott pushed too hard, and the wheels came off. There are a couple of thousand Ubers on Newpeace, not to mention the ordinary humans, who would perhaps be of some concern to you. We're spread terribly thin; if we have to evacuate that planet, we'd lose half a century's hard work. There's no way we could possibly convince all the Muscovite ambassadors to agree to cancel the R-bomb attack if they knew the truth. Doesn't that mean something to you?"

Frank nodded, dazed. He looked around, taking in other shocked expressions. The tension in the ReMastered soldiers. The twitchy look on the blond guy standing against the wall next to Wednesday said it all. She'd laid out the dictator's new suit in front of them, and it was threadbare: they were clearly shocked by Hoechst's revelations. The spook from the revolution on Newpeace all those years ago, the gray eminence at the center of a web of interstellar assassination and intrigue, turned out to be a fixer who was desperately trying to *save* a planet from the posthumous legacy of a genocidal megalomaniac—

"It takes two to send the cancel code. I've got one of them—right here." She tapped the key again. "There's a causal channel connected to the taligent offense control network: they abandoned it when they evacuated the station, but it wasn't disconnected. I had Zursch and Anders collect the station manager's key and take it there already. Hardware authentication, you see, all you need are the tokens. You don't disconnect causal channels without good reason; they're too expensive to set up in the first place.

"You have no idea how much it cost us to get our hands on this key—we had to extract it from the Ambassador to Newpeace. You don't need to concern yourselves with how. The station manager's was easier—silly fool actually left it in his office safe." She shrugged. "There's a diplomatic channel here, down in the communications center. One that's linked into the military TALIGENT network."

BING. New mail. *Not now,* Frank thought irritably, blinking it open before him. From: Wednesday. GOT 2 GO. SORRY. *Huh?* He glanced at her. "What—"

"You'll be wanting that cartridge, I suppose," Wednesday said, her expression sullen. "What happens to us then?"

"I destroy it in front of you." Hoechst nodded at Frank. "You're here to witness this." A flicker of a grin. "Same as last time, without the unpleasant aftereffects. Which were not of my choosing, I should add." Her gaze fell on Rachel next. "I then send the cancel codes to the R-bombs, using the station manager's console, and take the *Romanov* to go pick up the crews and destroy the evidence. *You* get to wait here in the cold and try to keep everybody on the station alive until the rescue ship from Tonto arrives. After that—" She shook her head. "Not my department."

"Diplomatic immunity," Rachel said in a voice as dry as bone.

"Are you going to get picky? If it means a couple of hundred million innocent people die as a result?" Hoechst stared at her through narrowed eyes. "Thought not."

"May I see the key?" Wednesday walked closer to the desk.

"Sure." Hoechst held it up, twirling it slowly between forefinger and thumb, evidently enjoying the gesture. "Now, Wednesday child, if you'd be so good as to hand me the cartridge—"

The lights flickered.

Hoechst froze. "Mathilde," she said thoughtfully, "it occurs to me that we haven't heard from Joanna, or Stepan and Roman for that matter. I want you to take every available body—not you, Franz, you're staying here—and deal with that missing Third Lieutenant. Then find out what happened to Joanna and her boys. Nothing good, I expect."

"Yes, boss." Mathilde headed for the door immediately, looking annoyed. She tagged Gun-boy on the way through. "C'mon, hunting time."

The lights flickered again. "What do you suppose she's doing?" asked Frank.

steffi whistled as she walked, hastily, toward the docking tunnel. A head-up clock counted down in front of her left eye: *eighty-two, eighty-one, eighty*... She broke into a trot as the count headed for the final minute.

Big passenger-carrying spaceships were not designed to undock from big, high-population space stations by accident, or indeed anything short of a carefully choreographed and scheduled departure, overseen by the port authorities and the ship's bridge crew. Fail-safe clamps pressurized by the atmosphere aboard both craft held the *Romanov*'s docking level against the hull of Old Newfie's lifesystem, thousands of tons of force that could only be released by a controlled depressurization of the clamp rings. But Old Newfie had been reconfigured for undocking without port command authority before the final evacuation, and Steffi had usurped control over the *Romanov*'s life circuit as final officer on board. She'd given the bridge system a program to execute it, and she didn't want to be around when the watchdog timer counted down to zero and set it off.

The main boarding ramp was in sight, a tunnel rising up to the loading deck of the station, huge station pressure doors visible to either side as looming shadows. Steffi ducked into a side door and trotted up the maintenance path alongside the main ramp, gray walls closing in bare centimeters to either side of her shoulders. *Forty-seven, forty-six*... And she was facing the emergency airlock, a domed door set in a solid bulkhead beside the main tunnel. She spun the manual override wheel and stepped into the rotating chamber, cranked it round—basic hand cranks were provided in case of a power failure—and tumbled out into the shadows alongside the big station doors.

Too close, she thought, pulling her night-vision goggles down. The twilit dock was a maze of shadows and eerily glowing heat patches. A huge slug trail of luminosity led away from the tunnel, toward a door leading to the main customs post—waste heat from the passengers whom the ReMastered had taken aboard the station, probably. But there was nobody in sight. *Careless,* Steffi thought, and she darted away from the airlock toward the towering wall of one of the station spokes, determined and ready to execute the second stage of her plan.

Something thumped her left arm exactly like a blow from a careless passerby, just as her threat indicator lit up and her eye patch outlined a door that had just opened. Steffi reacted instinctively, her little machine pistol chattering to itself. The bullet paths curved weirdly in the Coriolis force, spiraling toward the target as the rounds overcorrected for the changing centrifugal effect: another bullet whispered through the air where her head had been a fraction of a second earlier, then her attacker collapsed. Steffi ran as fast as she could for the tower, but something was wrong. She felt as if she weighed too much, and when she tried to reach for a reload her left arm flopped around, not working properly.

"Shit." She crouched in the doorway, heart pounding, panting for breath in the freezing air. *Now* the pain started, coming in waves that almost made her faint. Her left hand felt sticky. She put down her gun and fumbled, one-handed, for one of the gel trauma packs she'd had the cornucopia spit out for her. "It's only a flesh wound," she told herself through chattering teeth. "It's only—"

The gel pack went in and for a moment everything was gray and grainy. Then the pain didn't so much subside as begin to regularize, not driving her to the brink of unconsciousness, becoming possible to manage. Steffi leaned back against the wall and panted, then picked up her gun. *If I stay here, they'll see my heat trace,* she realized. *And besides...*

Two, one, zero: the countdown stopped. A noise like a million steam kettles boiling as one came from the vicinity of the docking doors. Steffi winced as her eardrums pulsed once, twice—then with a huge crashing boom the doors slammed down into the space the *Romanov's* tunnel had just pulled away from.

Got you, you bastards! she thought, although exhaustion and pain sapped the realization of all pleasure. *Now let's see how accurate that floor plan is.*

hoechst looked uncertain for a moment, as a faint vibration traveled through the deck. "The passengers are all in the customs hall," she said, glancing at Franz. "Why don't you go—"

Frank, distracted, glanced sideways at Wednesday. He sat up. "What are you—"

Wednesday pulled a plastic cylinder out of her pocket and held it toward Hoechst. "Share and enjoy." There was a note of anger in her voice, and something else, something like triumph that made Frank dive for the floor, covering his eyes as she tossed the cylinder at the desk—

There was a brilliant flash of blue and a loud bang.

Wednesday was already halfway to the door as a hot, damp wave pummeled across the top of Frank's head. It solidified almost instantly, aerogel foam congealing in a hazy fine mesh of fog with glass-sharp knife edges. Someone inside the fogbank was coughing and gargling. The remaining guard dived into it, desperately trying to batter and scoop his way through to Hoechst, choking in the misty sponge created by the riot bomb.

Frank rolled over on his back, taking in a confused kaleidoscope of impressions. *Someone* zipped past his face in a blur of motion. A buzzing rattle set his teeth on edge. Vague shadows at the limits of vision turned and fell. There was a scream, sharply cut off, a gurgling sound from the fogbank, a painfully loud bang from a riot gun discharging through a doorway, and more blue foam drifting into the room, blocking the door, congealing in sticky, spiky lumps.

He finished rolling, gasping for breath. *I'm still alive?* he wondered, dully. "Wednesday!" he called.

"Save it." That was Martin. A groaning sound came from the floor.

"You. Frank. Help me." That was Rachel's voice, panting, gasping. *What's wrong?* he wondered. He sat up, momentarily chagrined not to have seen the fight, expecting a soldier's gun in his face at any moment.

"We've *got* to get her out of there!" Rachel was half-inside the riot foam fogbank, hacking at it with a plastic-bladed knife she'd assembled from the stiffened lapels of her jacket by some kind of sartorial black magic. "Unless it's set to melt, she's going to suffocate!"

The remaining ReMastered guard lay on the floor, splayed out as if a compact tornado had zapped him with a UV optical taser. The edgy one, the traitor, sat very still, watching everything alertly. For some reason he seemed very calm. "You," Frank gasped. "Help."

"No." He cocked his head on one side, eyes bright, and very deliberately crossed his arms. "Let her choke."

"What? I don't understand—"

Frank bent over one of the guards, searching his belt for some kind of knife, anything to help Rachel with. Martin seemed stunned, shaking his head like a punch-drunk fighter. The semiconscious man at Frank's feet stirred. Frank did a double take and changed tasks, rolling the man over. "Anyone got some tape?"

"I have." The guy who'd given Frank the diamond sounded drained by the effort of talking. He stood up slowly, paused when Rachel looked round at him, then slowly knelt and pulled a roll of utility tape from one pocket. He yanked the guard's arms round and taped his wrists together behind his back, then repeated the job on his ankles and moved on. "I'd really be happier if you'd leave Portia to die," he added slowly, raising his voice and looking at Rachel as she panted, digging large lumps of bluish glassy foam loose from the mound. "She's killed more people than you've had hot meals."

"But if I leave her, what does that make *me?*" Rachel gasped between attacks.

"She's—" Frank stopped as Rachel straightened up, shaking her head. He looked past her; she'd dug as far as the edge of the desk, far enough to see that the blue-tinted foam was turning red.

"What the fuck do we do now?"

"We—" the blond guy stopped. "Portia lies," he said conversationally. "She lies instinctively. I don't know whether she was telling the truth or not, but that girl got away with, with the evidence. The smoking gun. I don't know what she thinks she's doing, but if she gets the evidence to the communications room where the secure hotline terminal to the R-bombers is located—or if *you* do—she could destroy a planet. She's got the key. Right now we've got a problem in the shape of about twelve other ReMastered soldiers, mostly standing guard over the passengers, but at least two of them will be on the *Romanov*'s emergency bridge. Unless Portia was right and that missing officer—" He stopped.

"What is it?" Frank leaned toward him: "Tell me, dammit!"

"Portia sent the other key to the comms room. Wednesday's on her way—she's not a fool, she's got something in mind—and Portia as good as told her that she'd ordered her family killed." For a moment the blond man looked as if someone had walked over his grave. "What's she going to do now?"

"Oh shit." Martin was struggling to his feet, lurching drunkenly. "We have to get to the comms room. Franz, can you talk your way past whoever's guarding it?"

"I can try." The blond guy—Franz—stared at him. "Can I rely on you to support my petition for diplomatic asylum if I do? And to help me obtain a body for one of the involuntary uploads in the memory diamond he's carrying?" He nodded at Frank.

"You want to—*okay,* yes. I think I can swing asylum for you.

You won't have to worry about the ReMastered on Earth. They won't be looking our way for a very long time to come." Rachel stood up, still panting, red-faced and looking as if she'd run a marathon. "Military boost," she said, managing to force a smile as Frank focused on her. "I just hope the comms center systems are shut down right now—"

"Involuntary?" Frank interrupted. "Would they be a suitable witness for, um, excesses committed by *her?*" He cracked his knuckles.

"I think so," Franz said, almost absentmindedly. "The comms center must still be running, no? For the evacuation." He examined the mound of blue foam that blocked the exit Wednesday had taken. "Telemetry during undocking, availability for ships coming to visit in the future—like the *Romanov*—that sort of thing."

"Do we know where it *is?*" Frank asked.

"As far as I know, our only expert on the layout of this station is currently running away from us carrying one of the two keys it will take to kill everyone on Newpeace." Franz carefully placed a hand on top of a foamy stalagmite and tugged, then winced: his palm was red when he pulled it away. "I suggest we try to figure out a way to go round."

"Mail her," Frank suggested to Rachel.

She paused, thoughtful. "Not yet. But she sideloaded us the local comms protocol stack—"

He twitched his rings. "Yeah, there's an online map. Follow the yellow brick road." He looked worried. "I hope she's all right."

the station's communication center was a broad, semi-circular space a couple of decks below the station manager's office. Two horseshoe-shaped desks provided a workspace for three chairs each; one-half of the wall was occupied by a systems diagram depicting the mesh of long-distance bandwidth bearers that constituted the Moscow system's intrasystem network of causal channels. "Intrasystem" was a bit of an understatement— Old Newfie and some of the other stations were actually light years outside the system's Oort cloud, and the network also showed those interstellar channels that reached out across the gulf of parsecs to neighboring worlds—and the control center was hardly the core of the comms system. Most of the real action took place in a sealed server room full of silent equipment racks on the floor below. But human management demanded a hierarchy of control, and from this nerve center commands could be issued to send flash messages across interstellar space, queries to the home world, even directives to the TALIGENT defense hotline network.

The flat wall opposite the curved systems map was a solid slab of diamond-reinforced glass, triple-glazed against the chilly vacuum. It looked out from one wall of a spoke, gazing toward infinity. The void wheeled around it outside, a baleful red-and-violet smoke ring covering half the sky.

The room had been left in good order when the station was evacuated. Dark as a desert night and chilly as a freezer, the dust had slowly settled in a thin layer across the workstations and procedure folders. Years passed as the smoke ring whirled larger, blowing toward the window. Then the humans returned. First came two soldiers, quiet and subdued in the face of the staring void: then a small death, remorseless and fast.

Lying outstretched in the duct above the room, looking down through the air recirculation grille, Wednesday explored her third and final cartridge by touch. It wasn't like the two riot foam grenades, and this was a headache: there was someone down there, and she looked vaguely familiar. It was hard to tell through the grille—

Fuckmonsters! Family killers. She remembered Jerm taunting her, Dad looking worried—he did a lot of that—Indica stern and slightly withdrawn from reality, her distant willowy mother. Love and rage, sorrow and a sense of loss. She looked down through the grille, saw the woman sitting back to back in the nearer horseshoe. *They're ReMastered.* She'd heard quite enough about them from Frank to know what they were about. Portia and her mocking grin. Wednesday's teeth ground with hatred, hot tears of rage prickling at the sides of her eyes. *Oh, you're going to regret this!*

She risked a peek of light from her rings, illuminating the scored casing on this cartridge. The activation button had a dial setting with numbers on it, and there was no half-open end. *Is it a banger?* she wondered. It seemed unlikely, on the face of it—grenades on a space station were a crazy idea—but you couldn't rule anything out. So she dialed her jacket to shrink-fit, pulled the hood over her face, and sealed it to the leggings she wore under her trousers. *E-mail:* Herman, what the fuck is this? *Attach image: Send.* Her fingers were trembling with cold. *Come on, reply...*

BING. This is a type-20 impact-fused grenade. Stun radius: five

meters. Lethal radius: two meters. EMP minimized, tissue ablation maximized. *Attachment: operations manual.* What are you doing with it?

E-mail: Herman, I'm going to make them pay for Mom, Dad, and Jerm. *Send.*

The woman looked up at her, and Wednesday froze. "You'd better come down right now," Steffi called up to her. The gun muzzle was a black emptiness, pointing right at her face. "No messing."

"Shit," Wednesday mumbled under her breath. Louder, "That you, Steffi?"

"Fuck. Hello, wunderkind." The gun muzzle didn't move. "I said come down here right now. That's an order."

"I'm coming." Something told her that the grenade wouldn't be much use. Wednesday bunched her legs up and kicked hard, twice. The grille fell away. Wednesday lowered herself feet-first through the hole, then dropped; in the low-gee environment it seemed to take forever to reach the floor. "What were you going to do if I didn't, shoot me?"

"Yes," said Steffi. Her eyes were hollow: she looked as if she hadn't slept for days. And her voice was curiously flat, lacking all sign of emotion.

Wednesday shrugged uneasily and held her hands out. "Look," she said, "I brought one of the keys along."

"A key." Steffi motioned her toward the unoccupied chair. "How useful," she murmured. "Do you know what it's a key to?"

"Yeah." Wednesday grinned angrily. "It's a key to the Moscow defense communications network."

BING. *Mail from Herman:* Wednesday, danger, listen to Rachel.

Huh. Her eyes tracked to the console they'd been nearest. There were a number of authentication key slots in it, and it was much more primitive-looking, even crude, than the others. "I think that's it."

"Good guess." Steffi kept the gun on her. "Put your key in the slot."

"Huh?"

"I said, put your key in the slot. Or I'll do it for you, over your dead body."

"Okay, okay, no need to get nasty." Wednesday leaned sideways and clicked the key she'd swiped from Hoechst's desk into the slot. She shivered. "'Scuse me," she said, and zipped her jacket up, then tugged the gloves over her hands. "Cold in here, isn't it?"

"What do you think the code keys do?" Steffi asked mildly.

"Huh? They tell the bombers to commit to an attack or to cancel it, of course." Wednesday shook her head. "We've just been through all this. The head ReMastered woman—" She stopped, fright and revulsion working on her together.

"Carry on," said Steffi. She sounded tired, and Wednesday stared at her, seeing for the first time the nasty smear of goop all over her left arm.

"They've been lying," Wednesday said flatly. "That's what this is all about. The R-bombs aren't all heading for New Dresden, some are heading for a ReMastered world. The ReMastered who took the ship were trying to stop that."

"How interesting." A flicker of pain crossed Steffi's face as she turned her left hand over and opened it to reveal two keys. "Take these and insert them into slots four and eight on the same console."

"What?" Wednesday stared at them in disbelief.

"Do it!" snapped Steffi. The gun barrel twitched at her impatiently.

"I'm doing it." Wednesday stood up and leaned over Steffi carefully, taking the first key, moving slowly so as not to alarm her. She slid it into one of the slots Steffi had named. A diode lit up next to it, and suddenly the screen board below the keys flickered on. "Holy shit!"

"You can say that again." A ghost of a smile flickered around Steffi's lips. "Do you like the ReMastered, Wednesday?"

"Fuck!" She turned her head away and spat at the ice-cold deck. "You know better than that."

BING. *Mail from Rachel: Wednesday, what's going on?*

"Well and good. Now do the same with the second key."

"Okay." Wednesday took the key and slid it into the remaining empty slot, her heart pounding with tension. She stared at it for a moment that dragged on. *This is it,* she thought. Suddenly possibilities seemed to open up around her, endless vistas of the possible. Horizons of power. She'd been powerless for so long it seemed almost like the natural state of existence. She turned round and glanced at Steffi, old and tired. The gun didn't seem too significant anymore. "Would you like to tell me what you're planning?" she asked.

"What do you think?" Steffi asked. "They killed Sven, kid. Sven was my partner." A flicker of fury crossed her face. "I'm not going to let them get away with that. Undocked the ship, to stop them escaping. Shot my way past the guards. Now they've got to come to me." She looked at the console, and her gaze lingered on the keys and their glowing authentication lights. "So sit down and shut up."

Wednesday sat, staring at Steffi. The gun didn't move away from her. Doubts began to gnaw at the edges of her certainty. *What does she want?* Wednesday wondered. *Three keys, that's enough to send an irrevocable go code, isn't it?*

"What are you going to do?" asked Wednesday.

"What does it look like?" Steffi put her gun down carefully on the desk beside her, next to something boxy. She picked it up.

"I don't know," Wednesday said cautiously. "What do you want?"

"Revenge. An audience." Steffi's cheek twitched. "Something puerile like that."

Wednesday shook her head. "I don't understand."

"Well, you can answer a question." Steffi held the box close to her and Wednesday saw that it was some kind of pocket data tablet, its surface glowing with virtual buttons. "How did you get here? Did *they* send you? Did she think giving me an extra key was a good idea?"

"I don't understand what you mean." Wednesday stared at her. "I ran away from them. The boss woman, Hurst or whatever she's called—she had me and Frank and the diplomats in the station mayor's office when something happened. She sent half her guards off to look for you and I, I—" She realized she was breathing too fast, but she couldn't stop. There were flashing lights at the corners of her vision. **BING.** *Mail from*—Wednesday killed her message interface. "She forced me to give her the papers. But it was in the police station, and last time I was there I ransacked the arms locker, so I grabbed a riot bomb and when she told me to give her the papers I grabbed the key and dropped a foam ball in front of her." She finished in a breathless gabble, watching Steffi's face.

"Oh, very good!" Steffi grinned humorlessly. "So you just happened to be running down here with a key to the defense network?"

"Yes," Wednesday said simply.

"And one of those bombers is running on one of *their*

worlds." Steffi shook her head. "Idiots!" she murmured. There was a musical chime from the console next to her. "Ah, about time." She raised her voice as she tapped a button. "Yes, who am I speaking to?"

"It's Rachel," said Wednesday.

"Steffi, is that you?" Rachel said simultaneously over the conference circuit.

"Yes, it's me." Steffi closed her eyes but kept her hand on the gadget.

"You got rid of the ship, didn't you? Why did you do that?"

"Oh, it won't go far. *They* were planning on using it: undocking was the easiest way to stop them. As it is, you've got bandwidth here—you can call for help and someone will come and pick you up. And the other passengers."

"She has keys," Wednesday called, motivated by an impulse halfway between guilt and malice. "They're in the console now."

"You little—" Steffi stopped, glared at her. "Yes, I've got three keys," she told the speakerphone. "They're all locked and loaded into the TALIGENT terminal." She relaxed slightly. "Are you listening?"

"Yes," Rachel said tensely.

"Good. Just so we understand each other."

"How's Wednesday?" asked Rachel.

Steffi nodded to her. "I'm fine," she called. "Just a bit, uh, confused. Are you calling on behalf of the corpsefucker?"

Rachel sounded weary. "She's dead, Wednesday. You can't breathe riot foam. You let her have it right in the face." For an instant Wednesday felt nothing but exultation. Then a moment later she wondered: *What's happening to me?*

"That's very good," Steffi said approvingly.

"She had it coming," Wednesday mumbled.

"Yes, I daresay she did," Rachel replied—clearly the open mike was very sensitive. "That's why I'm calling. It looks like we won. The ReMastered can't get to the ship, Hoechst is dead, half of them are missing, the rest are doing what U. Franz tells them—and he wants to defect. You've got the keys, *Frank* is right now filing an exclusive report that blows the lid off their operations in Moscow and New Dresden, and it's all over." She paused for a moment. "So why have you locked yourselves in?"

Wednesday glanced at Steffi in surprise.

"Because you're going to do exactly what I tell you to do," Steffi said, her tone deceptively casual. Her face was wan, but she hung on to the box in her right hand. "I've got perimeter surveillance systems on all surfaces in here. The taligent terminal is armed and on the same subnet as this tablet. Wednesday can tell you I'm not bluffing." She swallowed. "Fun things you can do with a tablet." Her hand tightened on it. "If I take my thumb *off* this screen, it'll send a message to the terminal. I think you can guess what it will say."

Wednesday stared at her. "It sends an irrevocable go code? How did you figure out how to do that?"

Steffi sighed. "How did I get the keys in the first place?" She shook her head. "You shouldn't have gone to that embassy reception, kid. You could have been hurt."

Rachel cleared her throat. "Hoechst was certain Svengali was the assassin. And she had his paymaster's records."

"What made you think Sven worked alone?" Steffi winked at Wednesday, a horribly knowing look that made her try to burrow into her chair to avoid it. She felt unclean.

"You set off that bomb—"

"No, that was someone else," Steffi said thoughtfully. "One of Hoechst's little surprises. I think she was trying to kill me. I just nailed a couple of others in the comfort of their own diplomatic residences. And relieved them of certain items from their personal safes, by way of insurance." She held up the tablet: "Which brings me to the subject at hand." She looked at Wednesday. "Can either of you give me a good reason *not* to transmit the irrevocable go code?"

Wednesday licked her lips. "They killed my parents and brother. They destroyed my home, in case you hadn't noticed. They did—*things*—to Frank. And you want me to tell you not to kill 'em all?"

Steffi looked amused. "Out of the mouths of babes," she called in the direction of the mike. "What's *your* offer, Rachel?"

"Let me get back to you in a minute." Rachel sounded very tense. "You're not helping, Wednesday: remember, only one of the R-bombs is heading for a ReMastered world. The rest are still running on New Dresden. Think about that before you open your mouth again."

"I'll give you five minutes to talk to your boss," said Steffi. "You might consider my pecuniary motives while you're at it." Then she flicked a switch on the console next to her and raised an eyebrow at Wednesday. "Do you *really* want me to kill everyone on two planets?" she asked.

"I'm not sure." Wednesday looked out of the picture window pensively. A huge whorl of violet-red gas, spokes of blue running radially through it, drifted across a black velvet backdrop iced with the unblinking pinpricks of a million stars. *Frank is alive,* she thought. *Hoechst is dead, though. Will they prosecute me? I could claim self-defense against hijackers.* The celestial smoke ring swung slowly past outside, a brilliant graveyard marker that would last a million years or more. *And* Frank *hates them, too.* But then she thought about New Dresden and the people she'd passed through like a ghost that had outlived the destruction of her planet. Jostling kids in a perfectly ordinary city. Blue skies and tall buildings. "I think I'm too insignificant to make that kind of decision," she said slowly. "I don't know who could." She shivered as a thought struck her. "I'm glad the murderer's dead. But to blame everyone behind them, their whole civilization..."

She stopped as she saw a shadow of a frown cross Steffi's face, and forced herself to shrug, miming disinterest. Suddenly her heart was pounding and her palms sweating. She slowly stood up and, when Steffi said nothing, walked toward one side of the window. As she did so, she waited for the solar nebula to vanish from the view, leaving nothing but a scattering of stars across the blackness. Then she twisted a control tab in one jacket pocket. It stiffened around her, waistband tightening and sealing against her pressure leggings under the lacy trousers. *Black against a black background,* she thought, taking deep breaths. She ran a hand through her hair and surreptitiously popped the seal that held her hood closed inside the collar of her jacket. Then she turned to face Steffi. "What do you want?" she asked as casually as she could manage.

Steffi chuckled, a deeply ugly sound. "I *want* about, oh, 50 million in bearer bonds, a yacht with independent jump capability, and some hostages to see me out of the immediate vicinity—oh, and that bitch's head on a trophy plaque. Along with the guy who killed Sven. *He* won't be coming back. What the hell did you think, kid? We were in this for the good of our souls?" She sat up. "You still listening in, Rachel?"

Martin replied. "She's trying to find someone to talk to on Earth," he said diffidently. "They've got to authenticate her before she can tell them what the situation is—"

"Bullshit!" Steffi snorted. "I'll give you one hour, no more. At the end of an hour, if you aren't making the right noises, you can kiss Dresden and Newpeace goodbye. If the answer's yes, I'll tell you who to deposit the bonds with and we can discuss the next step, namely transport. The TALIGENT terminal stays with me— it's a causal channel, you know it'll decohere at the first jump, but until then you'll know where I am." She looked thoughtful. "As a first step, though, you can bring me Hoechst's head, and the head of the scumbag who killed Sven. *Not* attached to their bodies. I know that doesn't sound like your idea of fun, but I want to be sure they're dead."

Wednesday stared at her in disgust. *Is this what it comes down to?* she wondered. *Is this what you get if you stop worrying you might be a monster?* She glanced behind her at the window, nervously. *I thought I knew you.* Then over at the side of the room. *Comms, reactivate,* she told her implant.

BING. *Wednesday, please respond?* It was Rachel.

I'm listening. Who is Steffi, really?

The reply took a few seconds to come. Wednesday leaned against the wall beside the window, experimenting with the fabric texturing controls at the back of her jacket, seeing just how sticky she could make it go without losing its structural integrity. There was some setting called "gecko's feet" that seemed pretty strong...

Near as I can tell, she's an alias for Miranda Katachurian. Citizen, Novy Kurdistan, last seen eleven years ago with a criminal record as long as your arm. Wanted for questioning in connection with armed robbery charges, then vanished.

"Steffi," Wednesday asked hesitantly, "what did you do it for?"

BING. *Wednesday? Are you all right? Do you need help? Frank.*

"For?" Steffi looked puzzled for a moment. Then her expression cleared. "We did it for the money, kid."

L8R: LUV U, she replied to Frank, then glanced at Rachel's last message as she answered Steffi.

"And you're, uh, going to send the irrevocable go code to the R-bombers if you don't get what you want?"

Steffi grinned. "You're learning." Wednesday nodded, hastily composing a final reply.

"And doesn't it strike you that there's something *wrong* about that?"

"Why should it?" Steffi stared at her. "The universe doesn't owe me a living, and you can't eat ideals, kid. It's time you grew up and got over your history."

Case closed, sent Wednesday. "I guess you're right," she said, leaning back against the wall as hard as she could and dialing the stickiness up to max. Then she brought up her right hand and threw underhand at Steffi. "Here, catch!" With her left hand she yanked hard on her collar, pulling the hood up and over her head and triggering the jacket's blowout reflex. Then she waited to die.

The noise was so loud that it felt like a punch in the stomach and a slap on the ears, leaving her head ringing. A fraction of a second later there was a second noise, a gigantic *whoosh,* like a dinosaur sneezing. Leviathan tried to tear her from the wall with his tentacles; she could feel her arms and legs flailing in the tornado gale. Something hit her so hard she tried to scream, sending a white-hot nail of pain up her right ankle. Her ears hurt with a deep dull ache that made her want to stick knife blades into them to scratch out the source of the pain. Then the noise began to die away as the station's pressure baffles slammed shut around the rupture, her helmet seal secured itself and inflated in a blast of canned air from the jacket vesicles, and her vision began to clear.

Wednesday gasped and tried to move, then remembered to unglue the back of her jacket. The room was a mess. There was no sign of Steffi, or the two chairs at the console, or half the racks that had cluttered the place up. An explosion of snow: they'd kept essential manuals on hard copy, and the blast and subsequent decompression had shredded and strewn the bound papers everywhere. But the window—

Wednesday looked out past shattered glass knives, out at a gulf of 40 trillion kilometers of memories and cold. Eyelids of unblinking red and green stared back at her from around an iron pupil, the graveyard of a shattered star. With an effort of will she tore her gaze away and walked carefully across the wreckage until she found the TALIGENT terminal, lying on its side, still held to the deck by a rat's nest of cables. She bent over and carefully pulled the keys out. Then she walked over to the window and deliberately threw one of them out into the abyss. The others she pocketed— after all, the diplomats from Earth would be needing them.

As the last key disappeared, a mail window from Rachel popped up. Urgent! Wednesday, please respond! Are you hurt? Do you need help?

Wednesday ignored it and went in search of the emergency airlock kit instead. She didn't have time to answer mail: it would probably take her most of her remaining oxygen supply to get the airlock set up so she could safely re-enter the land of the living beyond the pressure bulkhead. She had to prioritize, just like Herman had shown her all those years ago, alone in the cold darkness beyond the stars.

Her friends would be waiting for her on the other side of the wall: Martin who'd helped her to hide, and Rachel who'd shown her what to do without knowing it, and Frank, who meant more to her than she was sure was sensible. They would still be there when she'd worked out what she meant to do. And they'd be there to help her when she said goodbye to home for the final time and turned her back on the iron sunrise.

Home. It was getting to be a strange place, as alien as a hotel room on a distant planet. Rachel walked into the hall and dropped her shoulder bag, blinking tiredly: it was still three in the morning by the shipboard time of the *Gloriana* even though it was two in the afternoon there in Geneva, and the cumulative effects of switching from the hundred-kilosecond diplomatic clock back to a terrestrial time zone was going to give her bad jet lag.

Behind her, Martin yawned hugely. "How's it look?" he asked.

"It's all there." She ran a finger along the sideboard tiredly. Something buzzed in the next room, a household dust precipitator in need of a new filter or a robot scavenger with a damaged knee. "Place hasn't burned down while we've been away." She stared with distaste at the bulletin board on the wall, flashing red with notices of overdue bills. "Really got to get a proper housing agent who understands three-month trips at short notice. Last time I was away this long they sent the polis round to break down the door in case I'd died or something."

"You're not dead." Martin yawned again and let the front door swing shut. "I'm not dead. I just feel that way . . ."

Three months away from home had built up an enormous backlog of maintenance tasks, and Rachel couldn't face them just then. "Listen. I'm going to have a shower, then go to bed," she said. "You want to stay up and order some food in, be my guest. Or check the bills. But it can wait until tomorrow. Right?"

"You have a point." Martin shrugged and leaned the big suitcase against the wall next to a hideously ugly wooden statue of the prophet Yusuf Smith that Rachel had picked up in a casbah somewhere in Morocco a few years earlier. "I was going to message Wednesday, see how she and Frank are doing, but—bed first."

"Yeah." Rachel stumbled up the steps to the mezzanine, dropping her sandals and clothes as she went, and gratefully registered that the house automatics had changed the sheets and freshened the comforter. "Home sweet home, safe at last." After weeks of tension and the paranoid days at the mercy of the ReMastered, it seemed almost too good to be true.

she returned to consciousness slowly, half-aware of a pounding headache and a nauseated stomach, in conjunction with sore leg muscles and crumpled bedding and a thick, warm sense of exhaustion that pervaded her body as if she'd been drugged. *Someday they'll develop a drug for jet lag that really works,* she thought fuzzily before another thought intruded. Where was Martin?

"Ow!" she moaned, opening her eyes.

Martin was sitting up in bed watching her, concerned. "You awake? I've been checking the mail, and we've got a problem."

"Shit!" Rachel came to full consciousness in an instant, exhausted but painfully aware that she'd screwed up. "What is it?"

"Something about a meeting you're meant to be in later today. Like, in an hour's time. I nearly missed it—it's directed to the household, flagged as low priority. What could it be?"

"Shit! It's a stitch-up. Who is it?"

Martin blinked at the screen on the wardrobe door. "Something to do with the Entertainments and Culture Pecuniary Oversight Committee?" he asked, looking puzzled.

"Double shit!" A horrible sense of *déjà vu* gripped her as she tried to sit up. "What time is it?"

"It's two in the afternoon." Martin yawned. "Let me forward it to you."

Rachel read fast. "Departmental audit," she said tersely. "I'm going to have to get into headquarters, in a hurry."

Martin blinked. "I thought you'd taken care of that nonsense."

"Me? I've been away. Thought you might have noticed." She frowned. "Leaving the fox in charge of the henhouse, it would seem. I wonder if my sources have found anything out about her..."

Bleary-eyed and tired, she spawned a couple of search agents to filter her mail—both the public accounts and a couple of carefully anonymized private ones.

"Looks like the asshole in Ents is acting up. Since I missed some kind of audit investigation six weeks ago, she managed to file a default reprimand against me. She's gotten wind I'm back in town and is moving to file criminal malfeasance charges, embezzling or misuse of funds, or something equally spurious. She's running a board of inquiry right now. If I don't get there—"

"I'll call you a pod." Martin was already out of bed. "Any idea what she's got against you?"

"I don't know—" Rachel froze. The search had stopped, highlighting something new and alarming. "Oops! Head office are pissed."

"Head office?"

"Black Chamber, not Entertainments and Culture. They don't want her digging." Rachel began to smile. "'Stop her,' they say. They don't say how."

"Take care," said Martin, a flicker of concern on his face. "You don't want to overreact."

"Overreact?" She raised an eyebrow. "The bitch tried to get me slung out on my ass, she tried to obstruct a UXB operation, and she's trying to file criminal charges against me, and I'm overreacting?" She paused over the arms locker at the back of the closet. "No, *that* would be overreacting. Don't want to get blood in the carpet."

He stared at her. "Did I just hear what I think I heard? You're going to take her down?"

"Yeah. Although I don't think I'll need to use violence. That would be unsubtle, and I swore off unsubtle, oh, about thirty seconds ago." Rachel peeled a transdermal patch onto the inside of her left elbow. Her gaze turned to the open case by the bedroom door, full of items she'd acquired over the course of the cruise on the *Romanov*. Gradually she began to smile. "I've got to make a couple of calls. This should be fun..."

The UN headquarters campus hadn't changed visibly in Rachel's absence—the same neoclassical glass-and-steel skyscraper, looming over old Geneva's stone arteries and quaint domes, the same big statues of founders Otto von Bismarck and Tim Berners-Lee sitting out front in the plaza. Rachel headed into the lobby, looking around tensely. There was a civil cop standing by the ornate reception throne, talking to the human greeter there. Rachel nodded in their direction then moved on toward the antique elevator bank, feeling reassured. *I wonder how George is doing?* she asked herself as the doors slid open. *Handling the aftermath of the New Moscow cleanup. Big headache, that.*

The dossier on Madam Chairman that had been sitting in her mailbox—as per her back-channel requests, pulling in favors while she was away—was rather interesting, albeit increasingly worrying when she thought about the implications. Rising star, come out of nowhere, promoted rapidly, rivals recanting or resigning in disgrace or meeting with disaster: it was all a bit carnivorous for the normally laid-back UN, and to have a desk monster like that aiming squarely at her raised all sorts of nasty questions. Especially when you started asking where she'd gotten the money to buy that big house on the lakeshore . . .

The dossier wasn't the only thing Rachel found in her inbox when she ran a search. Formal notice of a disciplinary tribunal, filed that morning with a hearing scheduled for early afternoon, was not exactly the sort of thing she expected to find mixed in with the bills—not when it could have been sent direct to her phone and flagged as a priority item. She paused outside the committee room, composing her face in a careful smile, then opened the door.

"—Has shown no sign of compliance with the designated administrative orders in spite of disciplinary notices delivered four months, three months, and most recently two days ago—" The speaker paused. "Yes?"

Rachel smiled. "Hello, Gilda." Madam Chairwoman sat up straight and stared at her. Two yes-men to either side, and a secretary-recorder, and some gray-faced executive from accounts who'd been invited to witness all followed suit. "Sorry I'm late, but if you wanted to get my attention, you really ought to have mailed me direct rather than disguising the summons as a laundry bill."

"Hello, *Rachel.*" Madam Chairman smiled coldly. "We were just discussing your negligent attitude to departmental procedures. So good of you to furnish us with a further example."

"Really?" Rachel shut the door carefully, then turned back to face the room.

"You're Mansour, eh?" began the accountant. "We've been hearing about you for weeks." He tapped his tablet portentously. "Nothing good. What have you got to say?"

"Me? Oh, not much." Rachel grinned. "But *she's* got a lot of explaining to do."

"I don't think so." Madam Chairman was tight-lipped with irritation. "We were just discussing your suspension pending a full investigation of your accounting irregularities—"

Rachel opened her hand. "Accounting irregularities cut both ways," she said casually.

"I—" Madam Chairman stopped dead. "Is this some sort of joke?" she demanded.

Rachel shook her head. "No joke," she said easily. She glanced at the yes-men. "You really don't want to get involved in this. It's going to be messy."

"I'm not sure I understand." Gray-face glanced between her and Madam Chairman. "What are you talking about?"

Rachel pointed a finger at him and polled her phone. "Ah, Dr. Pullman. My apologies. I take it she didn't tell you who I work for?"

"Who you—" Gray-face, Pullman, looked confused for a moment. "What do you mean?"

"I'm Black Chamber. On the books via Ents purely for diplomatic cover and petty cash, which raises the question of why Gilda here thinks it's her job to go sniffing around my work assignments as if she's responsible for them."

"Ah." Pullman nodded thoughtfully. *Good poker face,* Rachel thought. Then he crossed his arms defensively. "That's interesting."

The yes-men were beginning to shuffle uneasily. "Look, I really don't think this is germane to the matter of your time-keeping," one of them began.

"Oh, but it is," Rachel said smoothly. She pointed at Madam Chairman. "Because you're not supposed to be digging into Black Chamber discretionary funding arrangements. I'm afraid I'm going to have to have you arrested."

"What?" Madam Chairman looked tense. "You can't do that! You aren't attached to any recognized security service!"

"Oh, but I am." Rachel's smile widened. She raised one hand and checked her phone. "By the way, do you know something? You shouldn't have tried digging so obviously. That wasn't very clever, Gilda. It made people question your bona fides. You're not the only person who can pick holes in an expense account, and I'm sure your colleagues will be very interested to know where you got the money to buy that big dacha outside Sevastopol. It's funny where the trail leads. Not that there's any expectation of exclusivity of service in your employment contract, Gilda, but we really don't expect you to be diverting contingency funds intended for the Black Chamber into your own pocket."

"What *is* this nonsense?" Gilda demanded. She lurched to her feet, clearly upset. "You're trying to distract attention from your own misdeeds! This is transparent blackmail—"

Rachel twisted one of her rings. The door behind her opened, and the cop from the lobby came in. "That's her," Rachel said, pointing at Madam Chairman. "She's all yours."

"You can't!" Gilda backed toward the window. "You've got no grounds!"

"Yes I have." The cop flipped her visor up and stared at her tiredly. "Ye'll be Gilda Morgenstern? I'm Inspector Rosa Mac-Dougal. On February 4 of this year you was in a meeting with Rachel Mansour, here. You tried to stop her leaving, didn't you? Aye, that wisnae so canny, was it? Her on her way to a UXB call-out an' all, did it not occur to ye that it's a statutory offense to obstruct a bomb disposal officer in the course of her duties? Or d'ye deny it was you what did that?"

Yes-man number two was looking at his boss in veiled horror. "Gilda, was it really—"

"Take her in and book her," said Rachel, shaking her head. "I'll deal with the other stuff later." She looked at the auditor, Pullman. "You don't want to get involved in this."

"Bitch!" Madam Chairman walked around the conference table, all rustling silk and hissing vitriol. "I had you—"

"Now stop right there," Inspector MacDougal warned.

Rachel glanced at the inspector, barely registering the angry bureaucrat raising a hand, the protests from the yes-man to her left, as she blinked at an unexpected thought. *Lining her pockets diverting Black Chamber funds, gathering intel about our field activities, big dacha near Sevastopol, works in Ents and Culture—* Something wasn't right here, and there was more to it than simple embezzlement.

She tensed as Madam Chairman pointed a shaking finger at her. "Fraud!" She snapped. "I know your kind! Leeching funds from the diplomatic corps to prop up your corrupt schemes, then claiming you're a defender of the public interest. You're just another blood-sucking pawn of the Eschaton! And I can prove—"

Oh shit, Rachel thought, and she went *quick,* reached out through air like molasses to grab Rosa's shoulder and tug her sharply away from the bureaucrat, vision graying at the edges as her implants kicked in. *I know where I've heard that line before, and recently—*

"Hey!" Inspector MacDougal protested as she stumbled backward. On the other side of the table Pullman was beginning to rise, a startled expression on his face as Gilda, her face contorted with rage, raised her other hand, an irridescent metallic bulb protruding between her fingers. She lunged toward Rachel, holding the device at arm's length.

Off-balance, Rachel tried to turn away, but even with boosted reflexes there was a limit to what she could achieve without leverage. She scrabbled for the table edge on her way down toward the floor, feet unable to gain traction as she watched Madam Chairman, Gilda, a bureaucrat possessed, thrust the ReMastered implement toward her.

The first shot surprised Rachel almost as much as her attacker. Gilda jerked backward, eyes widening in confusion as a spray of red erupted behind her. Another shot, and Rachel hit the floor, rebounded in time to see MacDougal's sidearm pointed at the woman. *This is so bad,* Rachel realized with a gut-deep stab of horror as time snapped back into focus, and she thumped painfully against the table legs. *If they're here . . .*

"Oh dear," said Pullman, his face ashen. "Was that really necessary?"

"Yes," MacDougal huffed emphatically. She lowered her gun. "You. There's a monitor on this room, isn't there? I'm taking the log. I want it forwarded to LJ control immediately under seal of evidence." She glanced down at her gun's muzzle recorder, breathing deeply. "Along with the take from this thing."

"You killed her!" Minion Number One sat bolt upright, an expression of horror stealing over him. "She won't be able to—" He stopped.

"Upload them all, the unborn god will know its own," Rachel said grimly, pulling herself to her feet. "Did you ever hear her say that?"

"No—" Minion Number One was staring at Minion Number Two, who hadn't moved since Gilda stood up. A fine thread of drool descended from the side of the man's mouth. "What's wrong? What have you done to Alex?"

"Aye, what's going on?" Rosa demanded. "What *is* that thing?" She gestured at the neural spike, which had rolled half under the table. Rachel glanced at it, then looked at the inspector. The cop was putting a good face on things, but her hands were shaky and her posture tense.

"Some of the shit I work with followed me home." She laced her fingers together and began dialing her rings hastily. She frowned at Rosa, then glanced around the other committee members. "We're all in this together. Let's just hope that she was an isolated case."

"An isolated case of *what?*" asked MacDougal.

"You'll want to check her genetic profile against a murder, Maureen Davis, diplomatic corps, about six months ago." Rachel realized she was breathing heavily. "Also anyone who's visitied her house in the past year. Colleagues, friends, whoever. Her type uses proxies."

"And what type would those be?" Rosa stared at her through narrowed eyes.

"ReMastered." Rachel twisted her rings. "George? Okay, message." She waited for the voice mail intro to finish. "I have a suspect in the murder of Maureen Davis, Muscovite embassy." She paused. "They're here. A cell. Infiltrating us." A frown wrinkled her forehead. "Probably the rogue faction, but I'm not sure." She glanced at MacDougal. "Can you find out if she ever attended a function with a woman name of Steffi Grace, aka Miranda Katachurian? In the past year or so?"

"You're saying this is related to a murder case?" asked Mac-Dougal, as the door opened for Building Security, and a buzzing swarm of concern erupted into the room.

"More than one," Rachel said grimly. "And they're still happening." *What's going to become of us?* she wondered dully and, just for a moment, longed for the clear-cut certainties of a madman with a home brew nuclear device. But something told her that this one wouldn't go away at the sting of a police wasp: indeed, it was only just beginning.

And outside the office—still hundreds of light years away—the Iron Sunrise continued to expand in its silent and deadly splendor, bearing down upon an Earth shrouded in comforting darkness.

About the Author

CHARLES STROSS is a full-time writer who was born in Leeds, England, in 1964. He studied in London and Bradford, gaining degrees in pharmacy and computer science, and has worked in a variety of jobs, including pharmacist, technical author, software engineer, and freelance journalist. Visit his website at www. antipope.org/charlie/index.html.